Eliza Fowler Haywood

**The Invisible Spy**

Eliza Fowler Haywood

**The Invisible Spy**

ISBN/EAN: 9783337295691

Printed in Europe, USA, Canada, Australia, Japan

Cover: Foto ©Andreas Hilbeck / pixelio.de

More available books at **www.hansebooks.com**

THE

# INVISIBLE SPY.

## BY EXPLORABILIS.

N TWO VOLUMES.

LONDON:
Printed for HARRISON and Co. N° 18, Paternoſter Row.
M DCC LXXXVIII,

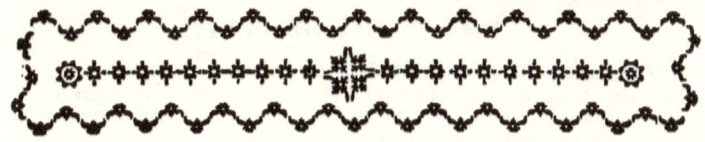

THE

# INVISIBLE SPY.

VOLUME THE FIRST.

BOOK I.

## CHAP. I.

## INTRODUCTION.

### TO THE PUBLICK.

 Have obferved that when a new book beginsto make a noife in the world, every one is defirous of becoming acquainted with the author; and this impatience increafes, the more he endeavours to conceal himfelf. I expect to hear an hundred different names infcribed to the Invifible, fome of which I fhould, perhaps, be proud of, others as much afhamed to own. Some will doubtlefs take me for a philofoper, others for a fool; with fome I fhall pafs for a man of pleafure, with others for a ftoick; fome will look upon me as a courtier, others as a patriot: but whether I am any one of thefe, or whether I am even a man or a woman, they will find it, after all their conjectures, as difficult to difcover as the longitude.

I think it therefore a duty incumbent on my good-nature to put an early ftop to fuch fruitlefs inquifitions; and alfo at the fame time to fatisfy, in fome meafure, the curiofity of the publick, by giving an account of the means by which I attained the gift of invifibility I poffefs.

Know then, gentle reader, that in the former part of my life it was my good fortune to do a fignal fervice to a cer-

tain venerable perfon fince dead: he was defcended from the ancient Magi of the Chaldeans, inherited their wifdom, and was well verfed in all the myftick fecrets of their art. Befides his gratitude for the good offices I had done him, he feemed to have found fomething in my humour and manner of behaviour that extremely pleafed him; he would often have me with him, and entertained me with difcourfes on things of which otherwife I fhould have had no idea.

But it was not long that I enjoyed this benefit. He fent for me one day, to let me know he was much indifpofed, and defired I would come immediately to him: I went, and found him, not as I expected, in bed, but fitting in an eafy chair. After the firft falutations were over, and I had placed myfelf pretty near him—' My good friend,' faid he, taking hold of my hand, ' I feel that I ' muft fhortly quit this bufy world; the ' filver cord is loofened, the golden howl ' is broken, every thing within me haf- ' tens to a fpeedy diffolution; and I was ' willing to fee you once more before I ' fet out on my journey to that land of ' fhades; as Hamlet truly fays—

" That undifcover'd country, from whofe
" bourn
" No traveller returns."

' As the remembrance of you,' continued he, ' will certainly accompany ' me beyond the grave, I would wifh, ' methinks, to hold fome place in your

A 2　　　　' while

‘ while you remain on earth, to the end
‘ that I may not be quite a ſtranger to
‘ you when we meet in eternity. I have
‘ no land, nor tenements, nor gold, nor
‘ ſilver, to bequeath, yet am not deſtitute
‘ of ſomething which may be equally
‘ worthy your acceptance.’

Then, after a little pauſe—‘ Take
‘ this,’ added he, giving me a key; ‘ it
‘ will admit you into a cloſet which no
‘ one but myſelf has ever entered. I call
‘ it my cabinet of curioſities, and I be-
‘ lieve you will find ſuch things there as
‘ will deſerve that name: chuſe from
‘ among them any one that moſt ſuits
‘ your fancy, and accept it as a token
‘ of my love.’

He ſaid no more, but rung his bell for
a ſervant, who, by his orders, conducted
me by a narrow winding ſtair-caſe to the
top of the houſe, and left me at a little
door, which I opened with the key that
had b..en given me, and found myſelf
in a ſmall ſquare room, built after the
manner of a turret. All the furniture
was an old wicker chair, with a piece of
blanket thrown careleſsly over it, I ſuppoſe to defend the ſage from the air when
he ſat there to ſtudy: near it was placed
a table, not leſs antiquated, with two
globes, a ſtandiſh with ſome paper, and
ſeveral books in manuſcript, but wrote
in characters too unintelligible for me to
comprehend any part of what they contained. Juſt in the middle of the cieling
hung a pretty large chryſtal ball, filled
with a ſhining yellowiſh powder, and this
inſcription paſted on it—

THE ILLUSIVE POWDER.

A ſmall quantity of this powder,
blown through the quill of a porcupine
when the Moon is in Aries, raiſes
ſplendid viſions in the people’s eyes; and,
if applied when the ſame planet is in Can-
cer, ſpreads univerſal terror and diſmay.

I eaſily perceived that this was one of
the curioſities my friend had mentioned,
and a great one indeed it was; but, as
I had neither intereſt nor inclination to
impoſe upon my fellow-creatures, I
judged it fitter for the poſſeſſion of ſome
one or other of the mighty rulers of the
earth.

I then turned towards the walls, which
were all hung round with teleſcopes,
horoſcopes, microſcopes, taliſmans, mul-
tipliers, magnifiers of all degrees and

ſizes, loadſtones cut in various forms,
and great numbers of mathematical in-
ſtruments; but theſe, as I was altogether
ignorant of their uſes, I paſſed ſlightly
over, till I came to a hand-bell, which
having the appearance of no other than
ſuch as I had ordinarily ſeen at a lady’s
tea-table, I ſhould have taken no notice
of, but for a label prefixed to it, on
which I found theſe words—

THE SYMPATHETICK BELL,

The leaſt tinkle of which not only
ſets all the bells of the whole country,
be it of ever ſo large extent, in motion,
without the help of men to pluck the
ropes, but alſo makes them play whatever changes the party is pleaſed to no-
minate.

Though I thought art could produce
no greater wonder than this bell, yet I
felt no ſtrong deſire of becoming maſter
of it; but proceeded to examine what
farther rarities this extraordinary cabinet
would preſent. The next I took notice
of was a phial, not much unlike thoſe
which are commonly ſold in the ſhops
with French Hungary-water: it had this
inſcription—

SALTS OF MEDITATION,

Which, held cloſe to the noſtrils for
the ſpace of three ſeconds and a half, cor-
rects all vague and wandering thoughts,
fixes the mind, and enables it to ponder
juſtly on any ſubject that requires deliberation.

This beneficial ſecret I alſo rejected,
through a mere point of conſcience, as
thinking it would be a much better ſer-
vice to mankind if in the poſſeſſion of the
divines, lawyers, politicians, or phyſicians; eſpecially the two laſt mentioned,
as it might prevent the one from engaging in any enterprize they have not abilities or courage to go through with; and
the other from falling into thoſe groſs
miſtakes they are frequently guilty of in
relation to the caſe of the diſeaſed.

The next, and indeed the firſt thing
that raiſed in me any covetous emotions,
was the apparatus of a belt, but ſeemed
no more than a collection of atoms gathered together in that form, and playing in the ſun-beams. I could not perſuade myſelf it was a real ſubſtance, till
I took

I took it down, and then found it fo light, that if I fhut my eyes I knew not that I had any thing in my hand. The label annexed to it had thefe words—

### THE BELT OF INVISIBILITY,

Which, faftened round the body, next the fkin, no fooner becomes warm, than it renders the party invifible to all human eyes.

A little farther, on the fame fide of the wall, was placed a tablet, or pocket-book; which, on examining, I found was compofed of a clear glafly fubftance, firm, yet thin as the bubbles which we fometimes fee rife on the furface of the waters: it was malleable, and doubled in many foldings, fo that, when fhut, it feemed very fmall; but, when extended, was more long and broad than any fheet I ever faw of imperial pap.r. It's ufes were decyphered in the following infcription—

### THE WONDERFUL TABLET,

Which, in whatever place it is fpread open, receives the impreflion of every word that is fpoken, in as diftinct a manner as if engraved; and can no way be expunged but by the breath of a virgin, of fo pure an innocence as not to have even thought on the difference of fexes. After fuch a one, if fuch a one is to be found, has blown pretty hard upon it for the fpace of feven feconds and three quarters, fhe muft wipe it gently with the firft down under the left wing of an unfledged fwan, plucked when the Moon is in three degrees of Virgo: this done, the Tablet will be entirely free from all former memorandums, and fit to take a new impreflion.

*Note*, That the virgin muft exceed twelve years of age.

I was very much divided between thefe two: the Belt of Invifibility put a thoufand rambles into my head, which promifed difcoveries highly flattering to the inquifitivenefs of my humour; but then the Tablet, recording every thing I fhould hear fpoken. which I confefs my memory is too defective to retain, filled me with the moft ardent defire of becoming mafter of fo ineftimable a treafure. In fine, I wanted both; fo encroaching is

the temper of mankind, that the grant of one favour generally paves the way for foliciting a fecond.

While I was in this dilemma, a ftratagem occurred, which I hefitated not to put in practice, and found it anfwer to my wifhes. I took both the Belt and Tablet in my hand; and having carefully locked the door of the cabinet, returned to the adept: he faw the Belt, which being long, hung over my wrift; but not perceiving I had the Tablet— 'The choice you have made,' faid he with a fmile, ' confirms the truth of ' what I always believed, that curiofity ' is the moft prevailing paffion of the ' human mind.'

' However juft that pofition may be,' replied I, ' that propenfity is not ftrong ' enough in me, to make me able to de- ' cide between the wonderful Tablet, ' and the no lefs wonderful Belt: they ' appear to me of fuch equal eftimation, ' that whenever I would fix on the one, ' the benefits of the other rife up in op- ' pofition to my choice; and I know not ' which of the two I fhould receive with ' moft pleafure, or leave with the leaft ' regret. I have therefore brought both ' down to you, and intreat you will de- ' termine for me.'

I foon perceived he underftood my meaning perfectly well; for, after a little paufe—' When I made you the offer,' faid he, ' of whatever you liked beft ' among my collection of curiofities, I ' intended not that your acceptance of ' one thing fhould render you unhappy ' through the want of another: take, ' then, I befeech you, both the Belt and ' the Tablet; you fhall leave neither of ' them behind you; nor do I wonder ' you fhould defire to unite them; they ' are, in a manner, concomitant; and ' the fatisfaction that either of them ' would be able to procure, would be ' incompleat without the affiftance of the ' other.'

Thus was I put in poffeffion of a treafure, which I thought the more valuable, as I was pretty certain no other perfon, in this kingdom at leaft, enjoyed the like. After making proper acknowledgments to the obliging donor, I took my leave, and returned home with a heart overflowing with delight.

I was not long before I made trial of my Belt, and found the effects as the label had defcribed. I alfo opened my Tablet, fpoke, and faw my words immediately

mediately imprinted on it. I then procured some swans-down, according to direction, and entreated several young ladies to breathe upon it, one after another: but though I dare answer for their virtue, the favour they did me was in vain; the impression remained still indelible.

Indeed, when I began to confider maturely on the conditions preferibed in the label of the Tablet, I was fenfible that it was not enough for a virgin to be perfectly innocent; she must alfo be equally ignorant, to be qualified for the performance of the talk required: and not to have once thought on the difference of fexes, feemed a thing fcarce possible, after fix or feven years of age at moft; and would have been as great a prodigy as either of thofe which had been beftowed upon me by the adept.

What would I not have given for fuch a one as Doranda in Shakefpeare's Inchanted Ifland! but fuch a hope being vain, I was extremely puzzled, and knew not what to do. At laft, however, a lucky thought got me over the difficulty; it was this: I prevailed, for a fmall fum of money, with a very poor widow, who had feveral children, to let me have a girl of about three years old, to bring up and educate as I judged proper. I then committed my little purchafe to the care of an elderly woman, whofe diferetion I had experienced. I communicated to her the whole of my defign, and infurufted her how to proceed in order to render it effectual.

The little creature was kept in an upper room, which had no window in it but a fky-light in the roof of the houfe; fo could be witnefs of nothing that paffed below. Her diet was thin, and very fparing. She was not permitted to fleep above half the time generally allowed for repofe; and fo no living thing but the old woman, who lay with her, gave her food, and did all that was neceffary about her.

I frequently vifited them in my invifibility, and was highly pleafed and diverted with the diligence of my good old woman. She not only obeyed my order with the utmoft punctuality, but did many things of her own accord, which, though very requifite, I had not thought of. To prevent her young charge from falling into any of thofe diftempers which the want of exercife

fometimes occafions, fhe contrived to make a fwing for her acrofs the room; taught her to play at battledore and fhuttlecock; to tofs the ball, and catch it at the rebound; and fuch like childifh gambols, which both delighted her mind, and kept her limbs in a continual motion.

This conduct, and this regimen, conftantly obferved, maintained my virgin's purity inviolate; as I did not fail to make an effay in a few days after fhe entered into her thirteenth year, and the fuccefs of my endeavours made me not regret the pains I had been at for fuch a length of time.

Now it runs in my head that fome people will not credit one word of all this; for as there are many who believe too much, there are yet many more who will believe nothing at all but what their own fhallow reafon enables them to comprehend. Well, then, let them judge as they think fit; let them puzzle their wife noddles till they ache; I fhall fit fnug in my invifibility, while they lofe half the pleafure, and, it may be, all the improvement, of my lucubrations.

But thofe who refolve to purfue me through the following pages with an ingenuous candour, I flatter myfelf will lofe nothing by the chace. They will find me in various places, though not in fo many as perhaps they may expect. They would in vain feek me at court balls, city feafts, the halls of juftice, or meetings for elections; nor do I much haunt the opera or playhoufes. In fine, I avoid all crowds, all mixed affemblies, except the mafquerade and Venetian balls. I am a member of the eftablifhed church; but, as I am not afhamed of appearing at divine worfhip, never put on my Invifible Belt when I go there. I revere regal authority, but feldom vifit the cabinets of princes; becaufe they are generally fo filled with a thick fog, that the chryftalline texture of my Tablets could not receive what was faid there fo as to be read diftinctly: nor do I much care to venture myfelf among their minifters of ftate, or any of their under working tools; the floors of their rooms, in which their cabals are held, are compofed of fuch flippery materials, that at the leaft *faux pas* might endanger my invifibility, if not my neck. I fhould be more frequently with the military gentlemen,

tlemen, but that they are to apt to draw their swords without occasion, that while they think they are fencing in the air, they might chance to cut my belt asunder. And what a figure I should make, when one half of me was discovered, and the other was concealed! I will not mention the consequence such a sight might produce in some of them.

But it would be of little importance to the publick to be told where I am not, unless they also know where I am. Have patience, then, good people, and you shall be satisfied.

Sometimes I step in at one or other of those gaming-houses which are above law, by being under the protection of the great; but I seldom stay long in any of them, as I can see nothing there but what I have seen an hundred times before in those lesser assemblies of the same kind that have been so justly put down by authority.

Sometimes I peep into the closet of an antiquarian, where I find matter enough to excite both my pity and contempt. What greater instance can we have of the depravity of human nature, than in a rich curmudgeon, who, while he grumbles to allow his family necessary food, chearfully unties his bags, and pours out fifty, or, it may be, an hundred guineas, for the purchase of a bit of old copper; only because a fellow of more wit than honesty tells him it was found under the ruins of an ancient wall, where it had been buried ever since the time of Julius Cæsar, or Severus?

Sometimes, too, I amuse myself with turning over the collection of a virtuoso; where I am always filled with the utmost astonishment, at finding sums sufficient to endow an hospital lavished in the purchase of wings of butterflies, the shells of fishes, dried reptiles, the paw of some exotick animal, and such like baubles, neither pleasing in their prospect nor useful in their natures.

Sometimes I make one at the levee of a rich heir, just arrived from his travels to the possession of an overgrown estate; where I cannot help trembling for the future fate of the poor youth, on seeing him besieged with a crowd of marriage-brokers, pleasure-brokers, exchange-brokers, lawyers, gamesters, French taylors, Dresden milliners, petitioning harlots, congratulating poets; in fine,

with sharpers, flatterers, and sycophants, of every kind.

Sometimes I mingle in the route of a woman of quality; see who wins, who loses, at play; and in what manner ladies are frequently obliged to pay their debts of honour.

When I have nothing better to employ my time, I loiter away some hours in St. James's Park, Kensington Gardens; or at Vauxhall, Ranelagh, and Mary-le-bon; and am often witness of some scenes exciting present mirth and future reflection.

But my chief delight is in the drawing-room of some celebrated toasts, whence I often steal into their bed-chambers.—But don't be frighted, ladies; I never carry my inspections farther than the *ruelle*.

These are some few particulars of the tour I have made. To give the whole detail would be too tedious. I shall therefore only say that, wherever I am found, I shall always be found a lover of morality; and no enemy to religion, or any of it's worthy professors, of what sect or denomination soever.

And now, reader, having let thee into the secret of my history, as far as it is convenient for me to reveal, I shall leave thee to enjoy the advantage of those discoveries my invisibility enabled me to make.

## CHAP. II.

CONTAINS SOME PREMISES VERY NECESSARY TO BE OBSERVED BY EVERY READER; AND ALSO AN ACCOUNT OF THE AUTHOR'S FIRST INVISIBLE VISIT.

IT was in the beginning of that season of the year which affords most food for an enquiring mind, that I had got all things in order to sally forth on my invisible progressions. The august representatives of the whole body of the people were just ready to assemble; the expounders of the Law were hurrying to Westminster Hall, and those of the Gospel to pay their compliments at St. James's. The ships of war were mostly moored; and their gallant commanders had quitted the rough, athletick toil, for the soft charms of ease and luxury. The land-heroes, who, having no employment

ployment for their fwords, had paffed
their days in rural fports, now hunted
after a different fort of game, at the theatres and mafquerades. Frequent con-
fultations were held at the toilets of the
ladies, on ways and means to outfhine
each other in the circle. Former amours
were now revived, and even new ones
every day commenced. Madam Intelligence, with her thoufand and ten
thoufand emiffaries, all loaded with reports, fome true, fome falfe, flew fwiftly
through each quarter of this great metropolis; and had every pore of every
human body been an ear, they all might
have been fully gratified.

Befides the gratification of a darling
paffion, I had another, and much more
juftifiable reafon, for the value I fet
upon the legacy of my departed friend;
which is this: I have it in my power to
pluck off the mafk of hypocrify from the
fceming faint; to expofe vice and folly
in all their various modes and attitudes;
to ftrip a bad action of all the fpecious
pretences made to conceal or palliate it,
and fhew it in it's native uglinefs. At
the fame time, I have alfo the means to
refcue injured innocence from the cruel
attacks begun by envy and fcandal, and
propagated by prejudice and ill-nature.
In fine, I am enabled, by this precious
gift, to fet both things and perfons in
their proper colours; and not in fuch as,
either through malice or partial favour,
they are frequently made to appear.

I fhould be forry, however, if any
thing I have faid fhould give the reader
occafion to imagine I am going to prefent him with a book of fcandal: no;
the fecrets of families, and characters of
perfons, fhall be always facred with me.
I fhall give no man the opportunity of
indulging a malicious pleafure of laughing at his neighbour's faults. My aim,
in this work, is not to ridicule, but re-
form. I would touch the hearts, not
call a blufh upon the face. And, as
few people have errors fo peculiar to
themfelves, as there are not many guilty
of the like, if the offender keeps his own
counfel, he may very well pafs undif-
tinguifhed among the crowd of others
equally culpable.

Verramond is juftly accounted one of
the moft accomplifhed gentlemen of the
prefent age. The gracefulnefs of his
perfon, the engaging manner of his converfation, his fine addrefs, and uncommon capacity, make his company de-

fired by all the young and gay part
of the world; as his great learning,
and perfect knowledge of men and things,
render him the oracle of the more grave
and ferious. I had frequently the honour of meeting him at feveral places
where I vifited, and found nothing in
him which could in the leaft contradict
thofe high ideas fame had given me of
him.

It was therefore natural for me to take
the advantage of my gift of invifibility,
in order to view this great perfon in his
moft retired moments; I mean, when
he was alone, and divefted of all thofe
modes and ceremonies which often difguife the real man, and fhew him to the
publick far different from what he is.

Accordingly, the firft vifit I made in
my Belt was at his houfe. I flipped in
as foon as I faw the door opened, went
up ftairs, and paffed through feveral
rooms, till I came to that where he was
fitting. I found him with a book in
his hand, on which he feemed very intent. I doubted not but it was a treatife
of philofophy, or fome other piece of
learning or wit, fuitable to the capacity
of fo great a genius: but how much
was I furprized, when, looking over
his fhoulder, I perceived it was Hoyle's
Method of Playing the Game of Whift!
He appeared more than ordinarily taken
up with one page, for he read it over
three or four times; then ftarted up from
his chair, and throwing the book from
him in a rage—'Curfe on this ftuff!'
cried he; 'it is good for nothing but to
'teach a man how to undo himfelf
'with more art.' After walking for
fome minutes backwards and forwards
in the room with a difordered motion,
he flung himfelf into his chair, and fell
into a profound reverie; in which I
know not how long he might have continued, if he had not been rouzed from
it by the approach of a perfon who I
prefently found was his fteward.

The bufinefs on which this man came
into the room was no way pleafing to
Verramond; but becaufe I would avoid
the troublefome repetitions of 'faid he,'
and 'replied he,' and 'refumed the
'other,' and fuch-like introductions to
every fpeech, I fhall prefent all thofe
dialogues which are proper to be communicated to the publick, in the fame
manner as in the printed copies of theatrical performances.

*Steward.* My lord, the feveral tradefmen

men whom your lordſhip ordered to come this morning are below, and wait your lordſhip's commands.

*Verramond.* I have no commands for them at all; ſo ſend them away.

*Steward.* Shall I bid them attend your lordſhip to-morrow?

*Verramond.* Aye, to-morrow ſix months, if you will; for I ſhall ſcarce have any buſineſs with them before.

*Steward.* My lord, I told them they ſhould all be paid off this morning. What excuſe can I make to them for ſuch a diſappointment?

*Verramond.* E'en what you will.. If you can invent nothing better, you may tell them that you lyed when you made that promiſe in my name.

*Steward.* Your lordſhip knows it was by your own order I made that promiſe; and that you ſent me into the city yeſterday for money, which I doubted not but was to make good what I had told them. If your lordſhip pleaſes to conſider, it is now a long time ſince they brought in their bills, and they have had a great deal of patience.

*Verramond.* Rot their patience! Do you think to make a merit to me of their patience? Go, I ſay; ſend them away, and let me hear no more of them.

The tone in which Verramond uttered theſe words was ſo auſtere, that the honeſt domeſtick had not courage to reply, but left the room immediately; probably to receive no ſofter treatment below, from thoſe he was compelled to diſappoint, than he had juſt met with above, for attempting to intercede in their behalf.

Lord Macro was preſently after introduced. The late ſullenneſs of Verramond ſeemed now entirely diſſipated. Whatever was in his heart, his countenance wore only ſmiles; and he ran to receive him with open arms, and all the teſtimonies of the moſt perfect ſatisfaction: and yet, as I ſoon found by the diſcourſe they had together, this very Macro, the night before, had won of him at play fifteen hundred pounds, which was the ſum he had ſet apart for the payment of his creditors. Their converſation turning wholly upon gaming, a ſubject neither entertaining nor improving, I ſhall give my readers no more than a bare ſpecimen of it.

*Lord Macro.* My dear Verramond, I could not be eaſy till I ſaw you this morning: I thought you left the company ſomewhat abruptly laſt night, and was afraid your ill luck had given you ſome chagrin.

*Verramond.* Not in the leaſt, my dear Macro. I never think any thing loſt that a friend gains. But I remembered that I had ſome letters to write; otherwiſe ſhould have ſtaid and truſted Fortune with a brace or two of hundreds farther.

*Lord Macro.* As it is an honour to get the better of your lordſhip in any thing, ſo it will be no diſgrace to be overcome by a perſon of ſuch ſuperior abilities; therefore, I am ready to give you your revenge when you think fit.

*Verramond.* Nay, as for that, Macro, it muſt be confeſſed you know the game better than I.

Here followed a long ſucceſſion of mutual compliments on each other's ſkill in play; of which growing heartily tired, I was beginning to think of leaving the place; and ſhould have done ſo, if the appearance of the ſteward a ſecond time had not made me expect ſome change in the ſcene. His errand, and the ſucceſs it met with, will not, perhaps, appear ſo extraordinary to thoſe acquainted with the modiſh way of thinking, as it then did to me.

*Steward.* Farmer Hobſon is below, my lord. The poor man has rode hard all night, on purpoſe to reach town this morning, and lay his miſerable condition before your lordſhip.

*Verramond.* Piſh! what have I to do with his condition?

*Steward.* He ſays, my lord, that his crop proved ſo bad laſt year, that he had ſcarce wherewith to ſtock the ground; that Mr. Hardmeat, your lordſhip's ſteward in the country, is very ſenſible of his misfortunes; yet, though there are but five quarters due, threatens to turn him out of the farm next week. He therefore humbly hopes your lordſhip will take compaſſion on him, as he has ſix ſmall children, and his wife now lying in of the ſeventh.

*Verramond.* What buſineſs have ſuch fellows to get children? Does he expect my rent ſhall go for the maintenance of his brats?

*Steward.* He begs your lordſhip to B consider

confider that, for hefe eleven years he has rented the farm, he has always paid your lordfhip honeftly; and does not doubt, through Providence, but to do fo ftill, if your lordfhip is pleafed to have patience till next harveft is over, and not ruin him at once.

*Verramond.* Let me hear no more of this ftuff! I leave all to Mr. Hardmeat: he knows what he has to do; and I fhall give myfelf no trouble about it.

The fteward, with whofe good-nature I was infinitely charmed, had his mouth open to urge fomething farther in behalf of the diftreffed farmer, but was prevented by a fervant that inftant coming in, and prefenting a letter to Verramond; who then bid him go down, and tell the unhappy fupplicant he might return home, for there was no anfwer to be given to his complaint.

Verramond would not open the letter he had juft received till he knew who fent it; but, on his footman's informing him it came from Mr. Gamble, he haftily broke the feal, and found the contents as follows—

' MY EVER-HONOURED LORD,

' I Happened to be engaged laft night ' at a houfe where the conftable, ' with his poffe, made a forcible en- ' trance, demolifhed our tables, put ' moft of the company to flight, and ' feized the reft. I was unluckily one ' of the laft clafs; and committed to ' durance vile, as Hudibras fays, as ' your lordfhip will perceive by the ' date hereof.

' A perfon here has undertaken, for a ' fee of five guineas, to procure my im- ' mediate difcharge; and I do not ' doubt, by the method he propofes, but ' he is able to do it. I am not, how- ' ever, at prefent, mafter of as many ' fhillings: nor can any way raife the ' money he demands; having been ' obliged, the day before this accident ' befel me, to leave my watch, linen, ' and beft apparel, at Mr. Grub's, in ' truft for a fmall fum required of me ' by the parifh-officers, on account of a ' baftard child, which a wench of the ' town has done me the honour to fwear ' I am the father of.

' All my hopes, therefore, of get- ' ting out of limbo, are in your lord- ' fhip's generofity; which if you vouch- ' fafe to grant me this one more proof

' of, I fhall, if poffible, be more than ' ever, with the moft profound duty, ' dear patron, your devoted vaffal,

' RICHARD GAMBLE.

' BRIDEWELL.

' P. S. I had forgot to acquaint ' your lordfhip, that I fhall have need ' of more than the above-mentioned ' fum, for difcharging the fees of this ' curfed hole; without the payment ' of which I cannot be releafed.'

Verramond hefitated not a moment to comply with this requeft, nor even whether he fhould exceed what was defired of him: he drew out his purfe, put ten guineas into the footman's hands, and ordered him to run directly to Bridewell. ' Carry that money to ' Mr. Gamble, with his compliments; ' and let him know he fhould be glad ' to fee him, as foon as he has recovered ' his liberty.'

Who will fay now that Verramond is not liberal? But, alas! how ill-placed an act of benevolence was this? Was it not rather caprice than true charity, which induced him to beftow this money to fave a common fharper from the punifhment he juftly merited; yet, at the fame time, refufe to an honeft, induftrious tenant, a fmall refpite of payment, though to preferve him and his poor family from deftruction? But Gamble was a neceffary perfon at a gaming-table; he was of importance to his pleafure that way: and the farmer being only regarded for the rent he paid, when deficient in that, muft be thrown out like a piece of ufelefs lumber, and his place occupied by fome one who promifed to be of greater utility.

Yet do I not think fuch a conduct is always to be afcribed to the fault of nature. Verramond has certainly the feeds of virtue and honour in his foul; but they are fuffocated and choaked up by his immoderate love of play. Strange is it, that a man, capable of thinking fo juftly, will not be at the pains of thinking at all, but fuffer himfelf to be fwayed, by a darling propenfity, to actions which, if he once reflected upon, he would be fo far from perpetrating, that he would defpife the very temptation of being guilty of!

CHAP.

### CHAP. III.

PRESENTS THE READER WITH SOME PASSAGES WHICH CANNOT FAIL OF ENTERTAINING THOSE NOT INTERESTED IN THEM, AND MAY BE OF SERVICE TO THOSE WHO ARE.

AMONG the numerous troops of British toasts, there are few who shine with more distinguished lustre, in all publick places, than the beautiful Marcella. Besides an exact symmetry of features, a most delicate complexion, and a fine-turned shape, there is something peculiarly enchanting in her air and mien. I never see her, without being reminded of the celebrated description Milton gives of Eve in her state of innocence—

‘ Grace was in all her steps, heav'n in her
          ‘ eye,
‘ In ev'ry gesture dignity and love.’

She was married very young to Celadon; and though neither of their hearts had been consulted in the match, yet they had the reputation of living well together. They behaved to each other with the greatest complaisance in publick; and if any cause of discontent ever happened between them, both had the discretion to keep it extremely private. I could not, therefore, expect to make any extraordinary discoveries in this family. The door, however, happening to be open one day as I passed by, I stepped in without any previous design; and, now I did so, was rather excited by curiosity of seeing some fine pictures, which I had been told were in the house, than of prying into the behaviour of the owners.

But it frequently falls out, that what we least seek we most easily find; and those things we imagine farthest from us, are in effect the nearest. In passing through the several rooms in this house, I saw Marcella writing in her closet; and never was I so much amazed as now, to find so fair a form harbour a mind capable of dictating these lines—

‘ TO FILLAMOUR.

‘ DEAREST OF YOUR SEX,
‘ THANKS to the powers of love
          ‘ and liberty, that hated bar to
‘ all my happiness is removed for a

‘ short time! Celadon is gone upon a
‘ party of pleasure, and this night is
‘ entirely my own. If, therefore, no
‘ more agreeable engagement detains
‘ you, come here between the hours of
‘ twelve and one. I shall take care to
‘ send all the family to bed, except the
‘ faithful Rachel; who shall attend to
‘ admit you, on your giving a gentle
‘ rap against the shutter of the parlour-
‘ window next the door. Let me know
‘ by the bearer whether I may expect
‘ you; though it is a blessing I scarce
‘ doubt of, if any of that affection be
‘ sincere, as you have often vowed to
‘ the believing and passionate

‘ MARCELLA.’

Having sealed this billet, she called her chambermaid, and ordered her to send it, as directed, by a trusty porter; then threw herself upon a couch, took the novel of Sylvia and Philander, read a little in it, sighed, and seemed all dissolved in the most tender languishment; when her emissary returned, and brought this answer to her summons—

‘ TO THE CHARMING MARCELLA.

‘ DEAR ANGEL,
‘ I Am at present surrounded with a
          ‘ great deal of company, and have
‘ no opportunity to thank as I would
‘ the kindness of yours. I can only
‘ say, that nothing shall keep me from
‘ flying to my adorable Marcella at the
‘ appointed hour: till then, adieu. Be
‘ assured that I am always, with the
‘ utmost ardency, your devoted vassal,

‘ FILLAMOUR.’

The fair libertine now expressed the highest satisfaction, and immediately fell into discourse with her confidante, Rachel, concerning the manner in which this nocturnal guest should be concealed, and how neither his entrance n. r his exit be discovered, or even suspecte', by any of the family.

I had no curiosity to know any thing farther of this affair, so took the first opportunity of leaving the house; extremely troubled in my mind that a woman, whose beauty had so much attracted my respect, should prove herself so unworthy of it by her conduct.

‘ With

' With what boldnefs,' faid I within myfelf, ' does the lovely wanton run ' headlong to her ruin; fearlefs of ' guilt, and of the punifhment which, ' one time or other, muft be the un- ' failing confequence !

" As if that faultlefs form could act no
    " crime,
" But Heaven, on looking on it, muft for-
    " give !"

I went home, and got my Tablets cleared from the impure contents of the above-recited epiftles. I wifhed, in- deed, to think no more of this tranfac- tion; and, to fecond my endeavours that way, towards evening fallied out again, equipped in my Invifible Belt, like a true knight-errant, in fearch of fuch adventures as chance fhould pre- fent me with.

I went to the houfe of an elderly lady, with whom I formerly had been ac- quainted. She was at that time looked upon as a pattern of piety and prudence: fathers, hufbands, brothers, all who had any concern for the virtue and re- putation of the female part of their fa- mily, recommended her example for their imitation; but, at laft, after a long feries of the moft laudable and becoming actions, fhe at once degenerated into the very reverfe of what fhe had been; fell into all the fafhionable follies of the times, at an age when others are begin- ning to grow weary of them, and com- menced a coquette at fifty-five.

I had been told fuch things, in rela- tion to her conduct, as feemed to me too unaccountable to be believed; and was extremely forry to find, in the vifit I now made her, all thofe reports con- firmed by the teftimony of my own fenfes.

This lady, whom I fhall diftinguifh by the name of Lamia, fets an high value upon herf lf for her great fkill at picquet. She challenged Grizelda, another anti- quated belle, who alfo pretends to be an adept in that fcience, to play with her for an hundred guineas the firft four games in fix. The other loved money; and, not doubting fhe fhould come off conqueror, readily embraced the pro- pofal; and the night agreed upon be- tween them for the decifion of this event, happened to be that in which I went. Grizelda came to the door juft as I did; fo I flipped in behind, and fol- lowed her up ftairs; where fhe was re- ceived by Lamia with the greateft po-

litenefs and fhew of affection. The card-table was called for, and the la- dies fat oppofite to each other. I placed myfelf at the end of the table, that, be- ing between them, I might have the better opportunity of obferving what both did. They were now very feri- ous, and attentive to the bufinefs they were upon: played, or rather cheated, each other with great caution; for I foon perceived that it was in this latter part of the art of gaming that the excel- lence of either chiefly confifted.

For a time, each was fo taken up with her own *petites fourberies*, as not to have leifure to obferve thofe practifed by her adverfary. At laft, however, Lamia having re-taken in a card fhe had laid out, Grizelda perceived it, and ac- cufed her of the change. Rage and dif- dain, on finding herfelf detected, made the cheeks of the other glow with a deeper fcarlet than the carmine had given them; and her eyes, even in de- fpight of age, fparkle with fires which love and youth had never power to fill them with. The other was no lefs en- flamed.—But their refentment will beft be fhewn in the expreffions made ufe of by themfelves.

*Lamia.* I am furprized you can fufpect me guilty of fo mean a thing as cheating at cards. Sure you cannot think I va- lue the trifle we are playing for! What is an hundred guineas to me? I re- gard an hundred no more than a pinch of fnuff.

*Grizelda.* Madam, I value an hun- dred guineas as little as yourfelf; but I hate to be impofed upon.

*Lamia.* What do you mean, Ma- dam? Do you fay I have impofed upon you?

*Grizelda.* I fay you would have done it, Madam, if my eyes had not been quicker than your hands.

*Lamia.* Madam, I fcorn your words! and if you were not in my houfe, fhould tell you that you lyed.

*Grizelda.* And if it were not in re- fpect to your age, Madam, I fhould tell you that you were a bafe woman, and had invited me hither only to cheat me of my money.

*Lamia.* My age!—good lack, my age!—I leave the world to judge which of us two looks the oldeft. I beg, Ma- dam, you will not deceive yourfelf. It is not your long falfe locks, hanging dangling on each fide your face, that hide the wrinkles of it.

*Grizelda.*

INVISIBLES

R. Smirke del.                    Sherlott sculp.

Plate II.                Published as the Act directs by Harrison & Co. Aug.t 1. 1788.

*Grizelda.* I wear no plumpers, Madam! Do you not remember, when one of yours dropped out of your mouth at Lady Betty's drawing-room, how all the company were frighted at you, and cried out you had loft half your face?

I ftarted on hearing this reproach of Grizelda, being, at that time, utterly unacquainted with the meaning of it ; but, as it is highly probable that a great many of my readers may be as ignorant in this point as myfelf then was, I fhall explain it, by giving a direction of the ufe and preparation of plumpers, as I have fince received it from the waiting-maid of a woman of condition.

A SURE WAY TO HELP LANK CHEEKS.

TAKE a piece of the fineft, cleaneft fponge you can get. Cut out of it two fmall bolfters, and place them between your cheeks and teeth, if you have any; if not, the gums will ferve to keep them up. On taking them out of your mouth, going to bed, throw them into a tea-cup of rofe or orange-flower water, and let them foak all night : this will not only cleanfe them from whatever impurites they may have happened to have received, but will alfo give a delectable flavour to the breath.—*Probatum eft.*

Thefe ladies purfued their mutual altercations for a confiderable time, in a fashion which the intelligent reader may eafily conceive by the fample I have given. I fhall therefore only fay that, after having charged each other with all the vices and foibles that either of them could think of, they at laft quarrelled themfelves into a reconciliation, begged each other's pardon, and went to play a fecond time: then fell out again; and provocations on both fides being renewed, and reproaches ftill growing more piquant, Lamia tore the cards, and threw them into the fire. Grizelda called for her chair, and left the houfe in a great fury. I gladly followed her out, being heartily fick of what I had feen between thefe fair, or rather unfair antagonifts; but had no opportunity of getting away before, as the door had never once been opened.

It was now near two hours paft midnight; and I found more fatisfaction in the thoughts of going to my repofe, than in

thofe difcoveries my invifibility had entertained me with. I was making all the fpeed I could to my apartment for that purpofe, but fate decreed it otherwife, and had contrived an accident which renewed all my former curiofity. In my way home I paffed through the ftreet where Marcella lived; and the fight of her houfe bringing frefh into my mind what the morning had prefented, I could not keep myfelf from ftopping fhort, to make reflections on the conduct of that fair fallen angel. ' She is doubt-' lefs by this time in the arms of her ' beloved Fillamour,' faid I to myfelf; ' and, while revelling in the pleafures of ' a loofe inclination, forfeits all fenfe of ' honour, duty, fame, and even what ' is owing to the merit of thofe charms ' nature has endowed her with; and ' oh! ftrange paradox of a vicious flame! ' renders herfelf cheap and contemptible ' in the eyes of the very man whofe ' efteem fhe moft wifhes to preferve!'

How long I fhould have remained in this reverie I know not, but I was roufed from it by the fudden appearance of Celadon, who, with a light carried before him, came haftily down the ftreet, and knocked at his own door. To fee him return at a time when I knew he was fo little expected, made me not doubt but that he had received fome information of the injury done him, and came in order to detect and revenge himfelf on the guilty pair. I trembled for poor Marcella; but what grounds I had to do fo, as well as the event of this night's tranfaction, muft be left to the next chapter.

## CHAP. IV.

CONCLUDES AN ADVENTURE OF A VERY SINGULAR NATURE IN IT'S CONSEQUENCES.

THE anxiety I was under to know what would become of poor Marcella, immediately determined me to follow her hufband into the houfe. A manfervant not having obeyed his lady's commands in going to bed, having fomething or other wherewith to employ himfelf in his own room, on hearing fomebody at the door, looked through the window, and perceiving it was his mafter, flew down ftairs, and gave him entrance on the firft knock.

Rachel,

Rachel, who had been posted centinel in a back-parlour, in order to watch the break of day, and conduct Fillamour out of the house before any of the family were stirring, now came running out on hearing the street-door opened; but, scarce could an apparition have spread a greater terror through her whole frame than did the sight of Celadon at this juncture.

*Rachel.* Lord, Sir, who could have thought your honour would have come home to-night?

*Celadon.* I did not design it, indeed; but, is it so strange a thing that a man should change his mind?

In speaking this he was passing on, but she threw herself between him and the foot of the stairs, and catching fast hold of the sleeve of his coat, prevented him from going up, with these words:

*Rachel.* Oh, dear Sir! I beg you will not disturb my lady; she is gone to bed very much discomposed: pray be so good as to step into the parlour; there is a good fire, and I will go and see if she is awake, and tell her you are here.

*Celadon.* My wife ill! What is the matter with her?

*Rachel.* I do not know, Sir, but she was seized with a sort of a—— I can't tell the name of it, indeed not I; but I believe it was something like a fit; and so, Sir, she went to bed; but I will go and let her know you are come.

*Celadon.* No, no, she may be asleep, and it would be a pity to wake her; therefore I'll take your advice, Mrs. Rachel, and sit a little in the parlour.—Tom, do you go to bed, I shall not want any thing to night.

The fellow did as he was commanded; and I could easily perceive, by Rachel's countenance, that she was upon the wing to be gone too, impatient, I suppose, to apprize Marcella of what had happened, and assist her in contriving some means for concealing her gallant: but whatever her thoughts were, Celadon had that moment got something in his head which effectually prevented any schemes she might otherwise have laid for securing the honour of her lady. Tom was no sooner gone than Celadon took hold of both her hands, and drew her gently into the parlour, with these words—

*Celadon.* Come, Mrs. Rachel, if I am so complaisant to my wife's disorder as to refrain going to bed to her, I think I may very well be allowed the pleasure of your company, by way of consolation.

*Rachel.* Oh, dear Sir! what pleasure can you find in the company of such a one as I?

*Celadon.* As much as I can wish. Come, sit down; nay, you shall sit by me; now we are alone, there is no occasion for all this distance between us. I have a great deal to say to you; nothing, sure, was ever so lucky as my coming home to-night! I like you, I love you, and have longed, almost ever since you came into the family, for an opportunity to tell you so.

*Rachel.* Lord, Sir, how strangely you talk to one! I wish your honour would let me go up stairs, to see how my lady does.

*Celadon.* No, indeed, I shall not suffer you to run away, and leave me alone here; if my wife wants any thing she will ring her bell. Come, none of this coyness; let me tell you, child, too much reserve in private with a man who loves you, and has it in his power to make your fortune, is as unbecoming as too much familiarity would be in publick. You may depend upon it, whatever favours you bestow on me shall be returned with others no less agreeable to yourself. I know very well how a person of my station ought to behave towards one of you in these cases, and shall act accordingly.

Rachel made no reply to all this, but hung down her head, and looked extremely silly. Celadon, interpreting her silence as a half consent to his desires, began now to add kisses and embraces to his solicitations: the warmth with which he pressed her, soon wrought the effect it was intended for; though I easily perceived the most prevailing argument he made use of was taking out his purse, and pouring twenty guineas into her lap. The transport which sparkled in the eyes of this mercenary creature, on beholding the glittering bait, put me immediately in mind of what Mr. Dryden makes Jupiter say in his play of Amphytrion—

' When I made
' This gold, I made a greater god than Jove,
' And gave my own omnipotence away.'

But it is little to be wondered at that a girl, such as this Rachel, should fall prostrate before that reigning idol of the world

world, who has for it's votaries not only men of the greatest parts and abilities, but also too many among those who make the highest professions of honour, probity, and virtue; nay, I am sorry to say, of religion: daily experience, however, and a very small observation of the corruption of the present age, evinces this melancholy truth.

So finding a scene was likely to ensue, which it was not agreeable to my inclination, or any way proper that I should be witness of, I withdrew into an adjacent parlour, where solitude, darkness, and the profound silence of every thing about me, contributed to promote the most solemn meditations. I reflected on the extreme folly, as well as wickedness, of giving way to an inordinate gratification of the senses, and the certain danger, and almost certain infamy, which attends the doing so. On this occasion several passages and accidents relating to many of my acquaintance occurred fresh to my mind; and when I remembered how some, who had been endowed by Heaven and Fortune with every requisite, excepting virtue, to compleat their happiness, yet by the want of that alone had exposed themselves to a condition the most abject and contemptible to which a reasonable being can possibly be reduced, I could not forbear crying out with the inimitable Cowley—

‘ All this world's noise appears to me
‘ But as a dull, ill-acted comedy.’

While I was thus ruminating, and wondering within myself what would be the consequence of this night's transaction, I perceived through the crevices of the window-shutters, that the day began to break, and presently after heard a certain rustling upon the stairs: it was occasioned by Marcella and Fillamour, who, on finding Rachel did not come up as they expected, and the light was pretty far advancing, were creeping softly down. The noise Marcella made in unfastening the chain that went across the street-door, waked Celadon and Rachel, who it seems had both fallen asleep: the former, on hearing the noise, was running out of the parlour, to see what was the matter; but Rachel prevented him, by saying, she was sure it was only one of the footmen, who went out more early than ordinary to the stable. This excuse

might have solved all, if Marcella herself had not unluckily been her own betrayer. That lady, incensed beyond measure, pushed open the door of the room where Rachel was ordered to attend, beginning to upbraid before she saw her.

*Marcella.* So, minx, you have served me finely; it is almost broad day. I have knocked the heel of my shoe almost off, for I would not ring for fear of alarming the family. I suppose you have been asleep: this it is to place any dependance on servants.

Celadon, on hearing his wife's voice before she entered, had stepped behind a screen, either suspecting something of the truth, or because he was unwilling to be surprized with Rachel at that hour; and Rachel, doubly confounded between her lady's reproaches and the knowledge who was witness of them, that she was utterly unable to speak one word for some time, but shook her head, winked, and pointed to the screen, thinking, by those significant gestures, to prevent Marcella from saying any thing farther; till finding she was again opening her mouth, she recovered herself enough to cry out—

*Rachel.* Lord, Madam, do not stand talking here; you will certainly get cold, and make yourself worse; consider you are half naked; pray go to bed again.

*Marcella.* What does the wench mean? but I suppose you have been at the ratifia bottle, and stupified yourself, according to custom. Well, 'tis your own loss; for I dare swear Fillamour would have given you no less a present than five guineas for your diligence, if you had come up as you ought to have done: 'tis now quite light in the street, and a thousand to one but some of the neighbours may have seen him go out.

*Celadon coming forward.* So, Madam, I find you have been diverting yourself, and Fillamour is the man to whom I am obliged for giving you consolation in my absence.

That person must know very little of nature, who does not easily conceive what Marcella felt in so shocking a juncture; surprize, shame, and vexation for having thus foolishly exposed her guilt, quite overwhelmed her heart; she gave a great shriek, and sunk, half-fainting, into a chair. Rachel ran to her assistance, and at the same time willing to retrieve,

retrieve, if poffible, told Celadon that he muft not take any notice of her lady's words; that fhe went very ill to bed; that fhe was delirious, and knew not what fhe faid. This, however, had no effect upon him; he was too well convinced of the injury that had been done him, and loaded his tranfgreffing wife with every invective that a hufband, in his circumftances, could invent.

But certainly it is impoffible for any woman to behave with greater courage and refolution than Marcella now did; fhe prefently regained her fenfes, and after having made Rachel leave the room, a moment's reflection ferved her to reply to the reproaches made her by her hufband, in thefe terms—

*Marcella.* Well, Sir, I confefs appearances are againft me, nor do I wonder at, nor will refent the afperity of your treatment. Though guilty of no real crime, my vanity has led me into a folly which merits all you have faid to me. I have not, in fact, difhonoured either myfelf or you, and my behaviour this night has only mortified the pride and arrogance of a man who would have rivalled you in my efteem and affection.

*Celadon.* Excellent, i'faith—beyond imagination. I have been told, indeed, that a woman need but look down upon her apron-ftring to find an excufe for the moft enormous crime fhe can be guilty of; but this of yours is fuch a one, as cannot fail of giving a good deal of diverfion in a court of judicature; though I fcarce think it will fave either Fillamour's eftate from the penalty the law inflicts on an attempt to baftardize an honourable family, or his throat from the juftice of my fword.

The boldnefs of Marcella was not to be awed by thefe menaces; fhe found fhe had too much underftanding to be impofed upon by the fhallow artifice fhe had made ufe of; that he now heartily difpifed her, and that fhe had no longer any meafures to preferve with him: therefore, collecting all the courage fhe was miftrefs of, fhe threw her eyes upon him with a contempt equal to that which he looked upon her, and made him this reply—

*Marcella.* 'Tis mighty well, Sir; you are at your liberty to make ufe of all the weapons in your power for revenge; but I would have you to remember, that whether Fillamour cuts your throat, or

you cut his, and are hanged for it, the matter will be of little importance to me; and as for a court of judicature, I believe you will find it very difficult to make good any accufations you may exhibit againft me there: no one ever faw me in bed with Fillamour, much lefs can prove any criminal converfation between us, fo that the ridicule would turn wholly upon yourfelf; and perhaps provoke me, as I have had no child by you, to bring in a bill of impotency, in which cafe I fhould have all my fortune returned; a thing your prefent circumftances would not very well bear, as fome part of your eftate is already mortgaged.

To all this Celadon was able to make no other reply, than that he ftood amazed at her audacity; that he found fhe was abandoned to all fenfe of fhame; that fhe was a monfter of impudence, and fuch like: at which fhe feemed not in the leaft moved, but proceeded to reafon with him in the fame determined fafhion fhe had begun.

*Marcella.* Look you, Celadon, all the fury you can be poffeffed of will remedy nothing: let us argue like rational creatures; whatever opinion we may have of each other, the only way to preferve either of our characters, is to live well together in the eyes of the world. I tell you that I am innocent, and it is for your eafe and intereft, as well as mine, that you fhould believe I am fo; which if you do, I faithfully promife to regulate my conduct in fuch a nfanner as to bring no difreputation on myfelf, or difhonour to you; but if you fly into extremes, you will oblige me to do the fame; and, what but our mutual infamy and deftruction can be the end of fuch a conteft? I leave you to confider on what I have faid, and wait your cooler moments for an anfwer.

With thefe words fhe went haftily out of the room. Celadon offered not to detain her, but continued walking backwards and forwards, uttering, by feveral difordered geftures, the inward agitations of his mind. After fome moments paffed in the filent expreffion of his rage, he called to the fervants, moft of whom were now ftirring, to get a bed prepared for him in another chamber; but I am of opinion, that when he retired thither, it was lefs to fleep than to reflect how it would beft become him to behave under the

the fhocking circumftance he was now involved in.

Finding no farther difcoveries were likely to be made at this time, I left the houfe on the firft opening of the ftreet-door, and returned home; where, fatigued as I was for want of reft, the aftonifhment I was in at the behaviour of Marcella would not fuffer the leaft flumber to clofe my eyes.

For fome days I was extremely impatient to know the refult of this affair; but, hearing no talk of it about town, began to conclude that the wife's arguments had prevailed, and the hufband had fubmitted his refentment to his convenience. I foon found I was not deceived in my conjectures, for in lefs than a week I faw Celadon and Marcella taking the air together in their own coach, with the fame appearance of ferenity in both their countenances, as if nothing of the adventure I have been relating had ever happened.

## CHAP. V.

SHEWS, THAT THOUGH A REMISSNESS OF CARE IN THE BRINGING UP OF CHILDREN, CAN SCARCE FAIL OF BEING ATTENDED WITH VERY BAD CONSEQUENCES; YET, THAT AN OVER EXACT CIRCUMSPECTION IN MINUTE THINGS, MAY SOMETIMES PROVE EQUALLY PERNICIOUS TO THEIR FUTURE WELFARE.

VARIOUS were the reports concerning Alinda, both while fhe was alive, and after her deceafe; but all the world could fay with any certainty, either of her affairs or conduct, might be comprized in the following articles.

That fhe was the only child of a very eminent and wealthy merchant in the city, who, on the death of his wife, left off bufinefs, and having purchafed an eftate of near a thoufand pounds a year in the country, retired thither to pafs the remainder of his days, taking Alinda with him, at that time about ten years of age.

That through fome peculiarities in his temper, fhe was educated in a very odd fafhion, fecluded from all converfation with the neighbouring gentry, and fcarce

fuffered to fpeak to any one out of their own family.

That after his death, which happened in her feventeenth year, fhe returned, with the confent of her guardians, to London, lived in a manner fuitable to her fortune, and had many advantageous offers of marriage, all which fhe rejected without giving any reafon for doing fo.

That at one and twenty fhe fell into a wafting diforder, wh ch was judged to proceed rather from fome inward grief preying upon her fpirits, than from any diftemper of the body; it baffled, however, all the fkill of the phyficians, and fhe expired after a tedious languifhment of near three years, leaving the poffeffion of her eftate to a nephew of her father's, who was the next of kin.

All thefe things, I fay, were publick; but as to the motive which made her avoid liftening to any propofals for changing her condition, or the caufe of that melancholy which brought on her death, every one fpoke of them as they thought proper, and according as the difpofitions of their own hearts inclined them to judge.

Few, however, were charitable enough to put the beft conftruction on her conduct; fome faid fhe was a man-hater; others, that loving the fex too well, fhe could not think of entering into a ftate which muft confine her to one alone. Thofe who entertained the moft favourable opinion, imagined fhe had unhappily engaged her heart where there was no poffibility of a return: this laft conjecture feemed indeed moft probable, and gained ground after fhe fell into that heavy languor which excluded her from all thofe pleafures fhe had been accuftomed to partake, and at length deprived her of life; but all this, to make ufe of the vulgar adage, was fpeaking without book; my gift of invifibility gave me alone the means of penetrating into the myftery.

As I had been acquainted with her, and vifited her while fhe continued to fee company, I frequently fent, or called to enquire after her health. One day when I did fo, a fervant belonging to her kinfman and heir at law came to the door at the fame time, and we both received for anfwer, that fhe expired the night before.

The fellow ran directly to inform his mafter,

C

master, to whom these tidings would probably be not unwelcome; and I went home, cla med on my Belt of Invisibility, and returned in a short time to the house of Alinda. The reader will perhaps wonder for what reason, and it is not fit I should keep him in ignorance.

There was a clergyman lived in the house with her, and performed the office of a chaplain; he was a person of whom her father having conceived a high opinion, had taken into his family, an I set over her in the manner of a preceptor, and he had ever since continued with her. I had several times dined with him at her table, and perceived he professed an extraordinary sanctity, and the extremest regard for the welfare of his fair patroness; and this it was that made me desirous of seeing in what manner he would behave upon her death.

I expected to have found him either in his own chamber, bewailing the early fate of so beneficent a friend, or sitting by her corpse religiously moralizing on the shadowy happiness of this transitory world; but, after seeking him in vain in these and several other rooms, at last I discovered him in a closet, where I knew she reposited her things of greatest value; he was busily employed in rummaging her bureau, from the little cell of which I saw him convey, as near as I could guess, between two and three hundred pieces of gold, and several bank-bills to a much greater amount; he then pulled out a drawer which contained her jewels; he first took up one, then another, surveyed them with a greedy eye, but laid them down again, and shut the drawer; but, after a moment's pause, opened it a second time, and took out a ring set round with large brilliants. ' I may keep this,' cried he; ' it will scarce be missed, or, if it be, I can pretend she made me a present of it in her life-time, and nobody will suspect the contrary.' Here he gave over his search, locked the bureau, put the key into his pocket, and went into his own room.

It would be hard for me to determine, whether astonishment or indignation was most predominant in me at this sight; I wished never to have beheld it, or that I had been at liberty to pluck the sacred robe from off the back of that vile prophaner of his order. I was going away with a mind more troubled than I can well express, when one of Alinda's maids came running into the room with a sealed packet in her hand, and delivered it to this disciple of Judas Iscariot, telling him at the same time, that it had been found under her mistress's pillow just after her death, but that she had forgot in the hurry to b ing it to him before.

He replied, with an affected indifference, that it was very well; that he would look over the papers, and take care that whatever injunctions they contained should be fulfilled; and with these words dismissed her.

The superscription on the cover of this packet was to a lady with whom Alinda had been extremely intimate, but had not seen for a considerable time, she being excluded, as well as the rest of her acquaintance, after she fell into that deep melancholy which ended her days. The priest immediately broke the seal, and found a little letter to the above-mentioned lady, the contents whereof were as follow—

' DEAR MADAM,

' THAT I have not seen you so long has not been owing to want of friendship, but to a resolution of depriving myself of every thing that was agreeable to me in life; and that I do not now, in these last moments of my life, ask to see you, is only because I would not tax your pity with the fight of so sad an object. I am blasted, my dear friend, withered in my bloom, and scarce the shadow of what I was. The inclosed memoirs will inform you of the cruel cause, which I intreat you will publish to the world after my decease; the shocking tale may perhaps be a serviceable warning to some parents as well as children. I have given my cousin ****** orders concerning some things I would have done; among the number of which is, that he will present you with my hoop diamond ring. I beg you will accept and wear it in remembrance of your dying friend,

' ALINDA.'

He started, bent his brows, turned pale and red by turns, and seemed in great confusion while looking over this little epistle; but all his emotions were very much increased on examining the papers that accompanied it: still as he read, he tore the leaves asunder and threw them on the fire, which happening not

not to burn very fiercely, I was quick enough to snatch from the intended devastation, and convey into my pocket, while he was taken up with the remaining pages, and thought himself secure by the time of his misdeeds being extinct in all devouring flames.

He had but just finished, when a servant came running into the room, and told him that Mr. ***** was below; and having been informed that Alinda's keys had been delivered to him, demanded to speak with him immediately. On this, the artful hypocrite composed his countenance, drew every feature into the attitude of solemn sadness, and holding a white handkerchief to his eyes, went down to act the part he thought would best become him before the kinsman of Alinda.

I followed close at his heels into the parlour, where Mr. ***** and two other persons waited for him. He began, with well-dissembled grief, to expatiate on the loss the world had in so excellent a lady as Alinda; and failed not, in his harangue, artfully to intermix some praises on himself, for the good principles his precepts had ingrafted on her mind.

Mr. ***** seemed to take very little notice of all he said on this occasion, and prevented him from going so far as perhaps he otherwise would have done, by telling him, in a very grave and reserved tone, that he was in great haste at present; that he came thither only to give the necessary orders concerning his cousin's funeral; and that till the melancholy ceremony was over, he should put a friend in possession of the house, and whatever effects it contained, therefore expected the keys of every thing should be immediately delivered.

To this the parson replied, that he had got them into his hands with no other view than to secure them for him, who had the undoubted right to all which his dear benefactress had been mistress of: ' For indeed,' continued he, ' I ap-
' prehended some foul play might have
' been attempted, as at the hour of her
' decease she had none but servants about
' her, some of whom had been too lately
' taken into the family to have given
' any great proofs of their integrity.'

After this they went through every room, examining what was to be found; all which scrutiny, as yet, afforded the heir no reason for complaint. On opening the above-mentioned bureau, and

looking over Alinda's jewels, he missed not the ring he had been defrauded of; but when the other private drawers presented him so little of what he expected, he could not forbear discovering some suspicion, as it must be owned he had sufficient cause; for the person who had been before-hand with him in the search, had left no more than eight guineas and one six and thirty piece in specie, with three or four bills of an inconsiderable value.

' I am surprized,' said Mr. *****,
' that a woman of my cousin's fortune
' should leave herself so bare of cash;
' and cannot imagine by what means
' she dissipated so large a yearly income.'
—' Alas, Sir!' replied the pretended zealot, with his hands and eyes lifted up to heaven, ' it ought not to appear strange
' to you, that a lady of your excellent
' kinswoman's charitable and benevolent
' disposition should refuse nothing in her
' power, when the cries of distress, and
' the moans of affliction, called for her
' assistance. If you would know in what
' manner she disposed of her money, en-
' quire of hospitals, the prisons, and the
' necessitous petitioners that every day
' received their sustenance from her
' bounty, and you will find an easy ac-
' count of her expences in her large and
' numerous donations.'

Mr. ***** only answered sullenly, that he should be better able to judge how he ought to think of the affair after he had spoke to her steward. On which the other, clapping his hand upon his breast, was beginning to make many asseverations, that till that moment he never knew what sum or sums the lady had by her when she died, or had ever looked, nor even entertained a thought of looking into any place where it might be supposed she kept her money. I staid not, however, to hear what effect his hypocrisy produced, but went home, being impatient to see the contents of Alinda's manuscript.

## CHAP. VI.

WILL FULLY SATISFY THE CURI-
OSITY THE FORMER MAY HAVE
EXCITED.

THE haste I made in snatching the following papers from the flames, happily preserved them so entirely from the deftruction to which they had been deftined, that though the edges were in many places much fcorched, yet not a fingle word throughout the whole was any way damaged; and the reader may depend on having the ftory as perfect as if he faw it in the heroine's own hand.

MEMOIRS OF THE UNFORTUNATE ALINDA, WROTE BY HERSELF, AND FAITHFULLY TRANSCRIBED FROM THE ORIGINAL COPY.

' I Am fenfible that many people have
' been very bufy with my fame while
' living; nor do I expect to be treated
' with lefs feverity after I am dead: I
' cannot, however, think of an eternal
' feparation from this world, without
' leaving fomething behind me which
' may ferve to clear up thofe paffages in
' my conduct which, by their being
' myfterious, have given room for cen-
' fure; and I do not this with any view
' of foftening the afperity of the ill-
' natured for the errors I have been
' guilty of, or of exciting compaffion
' in the more generous and gentle for
' my misfortunes, but merely to the end
' that, if I am condemned, I may be
' condemned for real, not imaginary,
' facts.
' Sorry am I to accufe a father who
' tenderly loved me: yet certain it is,
' that his over anxiety for my welfare
' has been the primary fource of every
' woe my heart has laboured under;
' and that, by his miftaken endeavours
' to make me great and happy, I have
' been rendered the moft miferable of
' created beings.
' The fortune I was born to he pof-
' feffed of, and fome natural endow-
' ments his affection fancied in me,
' made him flatter himfelf with the hopes
' of feeing me one day blaze forth in all
' the pomp of quality; nor could he
' endure the thoughts of marrying me
' to any man beneath the rank of right
' honourable: and for fear any partial
' inclination of my own fhould difap-
' point thefe high-raifed expectations,
' he kept me from the converfation of
' every one whom he thought capable of
' attracting a heart unbiaffed by inte-
' reft and unambitious of grandeur.
' Soon after my mother's death, he
' quitted bufinefs, and retired to an

' eftate he had fome time before pur-
' chafed in the country. When we
' removed, I was too young to have any
' tafte for the pleafures of the town,
' and regretted only the want of thofe
' play-fellows I had left behind: in-
' deed, I wonder that I was not quite
' moped. I was fuffered to go to no
' fchool, though there was a great one
' very near us; never ftirred beyond the
' precincts of our garden-walls; went
' not to church, becaufe there it would
' have been impoffible for me not to fee
' and be feen. No company vifited us;
' for my father deprived himfelf of the
' pleafure of converfing with any of the
' neighbouring gentry, for fear that, as
' I grew up, I might take a liking to
' fome one or other of their fons, none
' of whom he thought a match good
' enough for me, as they were not dig-
' nified with titles. I had learned writ-
' ing and dancing, but was far from
' being perfect in either; and my fa-
' ther, being unwilling I fhould be
' without thefe accomplifhments, took
' the pains himfelf to fet me copies to
' improve me in the one; and at length
' provided a mafter, too old and too
' ugly to give him any apprehenfions,
' to inftruct me in the other. Befides
' thefe two avocations, I had no amufe-
' ment except reading; which, as I
' much delighted in, my father con-
' ftantly fupplied me with fuch books
' as he thought proper for my fex and
' age.
' Excepting fome treatifes of divi-
' nity, the fubjects of my entertainment
' afforded little improvement to my un-
' derftanding, they confifting only in
' romances, and fome very old plays;
' fo that the ideas they infpired me with
' were as antiquated as the habits worn
' in the days of Queen Elizabeth; and
' I was utterly ignorant of the modes,
' manners, and cuftoms, of the age I
' lived in.
' In this ftupid and difpiriting
' fituation did I pafs full nineteen
' months; about the expiration of
' which time, my father happened into
' company with a perfon who wears the
' facred appearance of an ecclefiaftick,
' but is in reality one of thofe men-
' tioned in Holy Writ by the name of
' wolves in fheeps cloathing. His out-
' ward behaviour feems directed by the
' minifters of grace and goodnefs, while
            ' in

' in his treacherous heart a thoufand
' fiends lie in wait to bring ruin and de-
' ftruction on the credulous liftener to
' his wiles.—But, before I proceed [in
' my unhappy ftory, it is fit I fhould
' give a more particular character of the
' wretch who has fo great a fhare in it.
' Firft, for his extraction.—His fa-
' ther was a Frenchman, fervant to a
' perfon of diftinction in Normandy:
' but having more ambition than ho-
' nefty, found means to rob his mafter
' of a confiderable fum, and came over
' to England, where he fet up for a
' gentleman, and a moft zealous Pro-
' teftant; told a long plaufible ftory of
' the great hardfhips he had fuftained
' on the fcore of religion, and found
' here the fame pity and encouragement
' as many others had done who fly here
' for an afylum on the fame pretences.
' Soon after his arrival, he married
' a Dutchwoman, by whom he had a
' fon who inherits all his fa her's vir-
' tues, and is the perfon whofe ftory is
' fo unhappily interwoven with my
' own.
' Young Le Bris (for that is the name
' of this worthy family) difcovered in
' his youth fome indications of a good
' capacity for learning; infomuch that
' a certain lord, taking a great fancy to
' him, fent him to Weftminfter School,
' and afterwards to the univerfity, in
' order to qualify him for the pulpit;
' affuring him, that he fhould not be
' without a benefice as foon as he fhould
' be fit to receive it.
' But he had fcarce compleated his ftu-
' dies for that purpofe, when all his
' prefent fupport and future expect-
' ations vanifhed, on the fudden death
' of his noble patron; which was fol-
' lowed, in a few months after, by that
' of his father; fo that he was left en-
' tirely deftitute, his mother not being
' able to afford him the leaft affiftance.
' After many long and fruitlefs foli-
' citations for a living, he was glad to
' accept of a fmall curacy in one of the
' remoteft counties in England, where
' he refided feveral years; but was at
' laft turned out on account of neglect
' of duty, and other mifbehaviour. He
' then came back to London, and gave
' out printed bills for teaching French
' and Latin at very low rates; but find-
' ing little encouragement that way,
' turned Fleet parfon, and earned a pre-

' carious fuftenance by clandeftine mar-
' riages.
' It was in thefe wretched circum-
' ftances that my father met with him,
' being in town on fome bufinefs; and
' being told by fome one, who it is
' likely knew no more of him than
' what he was pleafed to fay of himfelf,
' that he was a very worthy, though
' diftreffed clergyman, made him the
' offer of a handfome falary to come
' into his family by way of chaplain;
' and withal, to inftruct me in the
' French language, and whatever elfe
' was fit for me to learn, or he was ca-
' pable of teaching. He readily em-
' braced the propofal; and, on my fa-
' ther's return, came down wi h him.
' My father prefented him to me as a
' kind of tutor or preceptor; told me I
' muft fubmit myfelf to his directions;
' be attentive to all he faid to me; and,
' in every thing, treat him with the
' greateft refpect and reverence: "For,"
' added he, " it is by the leffons he is
" capable of giving you, that you alone
" can make any fhining figure in the
" ftation wherein I hope to fee you
" placed."
' It will, perhaps, afford fome matter
' of furprize, that my father, who had
' hitherto preferved fuch an extreme cau-
' tion in preventing my having the leaft
' converfation with any man, fhould
' now fo ftrenuoufly recommend this
' perfon to me : but it muft be confi-
' dered, that he was no lefs than fix or
' feven and forty years of age; that,
' though not deformed, he was far from
' handfome; and, befides, had a certain
' aufterity in his manners which could
' not be very agreeable to youth.
' It was, indeed, fome time before I
' could be contented with the dominion
' given him over me; but my obedience to
' my father obliging me to behave to-
' wards him with efteem, cuftom at laft
' converted that complaifance, which was
' at firft no more than feigned, into fin-
' cere. A kind of affection, by degrees,
' mingled itfelf with the reverence I was
' bid to pay him; I was never fo happy
' as in the hours fet apart for receiving
' his inftructions; and the thoughts of
' the benefits that might be fuppofed to
' accrue from them, afforded lefs plea-
' fure than the praifes I was always cer-
' tain he would beftow on my docility.
' In fine, I not only loved the teacher
' for

'for the precept's fake, but, as the poet
'fays—

	"I lov'd the precepts for the teacher's
	"fake."

'Nor is it to be wondered at that I
'tafted more fatisfaction in his fociety
'than I had ever known before. I
'wanted not ideas, though hitherto I
'had nothing to improve them. I had
'been allowed to converfe with none
'but the fervants; who cou'd only di-
'vert me with idle tales of thieves, appa-
'ritions, and haunted houfes. My tu-
'tor, after having finifhed his graver
'leffons, would frequently entertain me
'with fome extraordinary incident or
'other, either taken from hiftory or ro-
'mance; but whether real or fictitious,
'I had fenfe enough to know were
'fuch as enlarged my underftanding as
'well as charmed my ears.
'It is certain, indeed, that he fpared
'no pains to infinuate himfelf into my
'good graces; and no lefs certain alfo,
'that the ungrateful defign he had in
'doing fo fucceeded, to the utter de-
'ftruction of the whole happinefs of my
'future life, and, at laft, of my life it-
'felf, as wi'l appear by thefe memoirs;
'which, while I am writing, I know
'not whether I fhall have ftrength to
'finifh.
'I fhall therefore reduce my unhappy
'fiory into as fhort a compafs as I can.
'In fpite of the little amiablenefs in my
'tutor had in his perfon, in fpite of the
'vaft difparity of years between us, I
'conceived the moft tender affection for
'him. Alas! I was then too young,
'too innocent, to know what was
'meant by the word Love, any farther
'than that love which we naturally bear
'to a father, brother, or fome other
'near relation; and thought not what
'I felt for him was any more, or would
'be attended with any other confe-
'quences; and as I apprehended no
'fhame or danger in the kindnefs I had
'for him, endeavoured not to put a ftop
'to the growth of it, nor even to con-
'ceal it.
'But Le Bris faw much better into
'my heart than I did myfelf; and dread-
'ing left my father fhould be alarmed
'at the too open fondnefs of my beha-
'viour to him, began to treat me with
'lefs familiarity, and exerted the ma-

'fter much more than he had done.
'This change both furprized and grieved
'me: I bore it, however, for two whole
'days, without feeming to take any no-
'tice of it; but on the third, being alone
'with him in his clofet, where I con-
'ftantly went every morning to receive
'my leffons—" What is the matter
"with you, my dear tutor?" faid I; "I
"hope I have done nothing to offend
"you? I am fure I would not wil-
"lingly be guilty of deferving that you
"fhould frown upon me."—"No,
"my precious charge," replied he, af-
'ter a paufe, "it is not in your na-
"ture to give offence; but I would not
"incur your father's difpleafure either
"towards you or me. Men are apt to
"be jealous of the affections of their
"children; and I am fometimes afraid
"that he fhould think you love me al-
"moft as well as you do him."—"In-
"deed I do fo—quite as well," cried I
'eagerly. "But why fhould he be an-
"gry at that, when he bid me ufe you
"with the fame love and refpect as I
"did himfelf?"
	"People, on fome occafions," an-
'fwered he, "will be difpleafed at a
"too exact performance of their own
"commands; and if my worthy patron,
"your father, fhould happen to be of
"this opinion, the confequence would
"infallibly be an eternal feparation be-
"tween us; he would drive me from
"his houfe, and I fhould never fee my
"pretty charge again."
	"If you think fo," returned I,
"though I have all kind of diffimula-
"tion, I will make him believe I am
"weary of learning of you, and that I
"cannot abide you."—"Dear, pretty
'angel!" cried he, tenderly taking me
'in his arms, "there is no need of go-
"ing to fuch extremes; I would only
"have you behave with more diftance
"towards me than you have done of
"late: and it will not be amifs if you
"fometimes complain that I fet you too
"hard leffons; becaufe, if you fhould
"feem to learn too faft, he may begin
"to think there will foon be no occafion
"for a tutor."—"Well," faid I, "I
"will do every thing you bid me; for
"indeed it would almoft break my heart
"to part with you." Here he kiffed
'off the tears that fell from my eyes in
'fpeaking thefe laft words, and I re-
'turned all his endearments with the
	'fame

' fame affection as the fondeſt child
' would do thoſe of the moſt indulgent
' parent.
' It will perhaps ſeem a little ſtrange,
' that a girl turned of thirteen, as I
' then was, ſhould think, or act in the
' manner I did; but the way in which I
' had been brought up, left me in the
' fame ignorance and innocence as
' others of ſix or ſeven years old.
' I obeyed his inſtructions with ſo
' much exactneſs, that my father was
' far from ſuſpecting either my folly, or
' the baſeneſs of the perſon he had ſet
' over me. The reſt of the family were
' no more quick-ſighted; nor could it
' be expected they ſhould be ſo. Our
' houſe-keeper, though a very good, was
' a ſilly old woman, and knew nothing
' beyond the œconomy of thoſe affairs
' committed to her charge. The maid
' who waited on me was her daughter,
' and had been bred to think every man
' who wore the habit of a parſon was
' to be worſhipped; and the other ſer-
' vants were too ſeldom with us to have
' any opportuninity of making diſco-
' veries.
' I arrived at my fourteenth year.
' My father kept my birth-day ſo far,
' as to order ſomething better than ordi-
' nary for dinner, and drank my health
' ſeveral times at table. Among other
' diſcourſe concerning me, he ſaid to
' Le Bris—" Well, doctor, your pupil
" will now begin to think herſelf a wo-
" man, and I muſt find a huſband for
" her who will be able to reward the
" care you have taken of her with a
" good fat benefice." To which the
' fawning hypocrite replied, that the
' pleaſure of ſeeing his worthy patron's
' daughter happy would be to him the
' beſt benefice he could obtain.
' Nothing farther paſſed, at this time,
' on the ſame ſubject; but the next morn-
' ing, when I was alone with my tutor
' in his cloſet—" Do you remember,
" my dear Miſs," cried he, with a very
' melancholy air, " what your father
" ſaid yeſterday? You will be mar-
" ried ſoon, and I ſhall loſe you for
" ever!"—" Do not talk ſo," replied I
' haſtily; " I do not want to be mar-
" ried: but if my father ſhould compel
" me to it, all the huſbands in the world
" ſhould not make me forget you; no,
" you ſhall always live with me; I
". would not part from you to be a
" dutcheſs."—" Nor would I part

" from you," ſaid he, taking me in his
' arms, " for an archbiſhoprick. And
" to be plain," continued he, " I have
" received letters ſince I have been here,
" with the offers of ſeveral great livings;
" but I have refuſed them all, rather
" than quit my dear pupil."—' Have
" you, indeed?" returned I, hanging
' fondly on him; " Oh how kind you
" have been! I ſhould be the moſt un-
" grateful creature upon earth, if I did
" not love you dearly for it."—" But
" will you always keep me with you?"
' cried he. " As long as I live," an-
' ſwered I. " Will you ſwear it?" re-
' joined he. " Yes," anſwered I; "a
" thouſand and a thouſand times over,
" if you deſire it."
' The wretch did not fail to take me
' at my word: I bound myſelf, by the
' moſt ſolemn imprecations that words
' could form, that, when I became miſ-
' treſs of my actions, he ſhould always
' live with me. After this, the hours
' we paſſed together were employed more
' in improving the fooliſh affection I had
' for him, than in any leſſons for im-
' proving my underſtanding. My fa-
' ther imputed the ſlow progreſs I made
' in my ſtudies not to any want of abi-
' lities in my teacher, but to my own
' neglect, and often chid me for it;
' which I bore patiently, as I believed it
' the ſureſt means of keeping my dear
' tutor with me. This he took ſo kindly,
' that he told me one day, he flattered
' himſelf I loved him almoſt as well as
' I did my father. " I hope it is no
" ſin," cried I childiſhly, " if I love
" you quite as well."—" Far from it,"
' anſwered he: " you are only his
" daughter by nature, but you are mine
" by affection; you are the child of my
" ſoul, and therefore ought to love
" me better."—" I am glad of that,"
' rejoined I; "for indeed I do love you
" a great deal better—I am ſure I do."
' It will ſcarce be doubted but that he
' now beſtowed upon me thoſe endear-
' ments I had declared myſelf ſo well ſa-
' tisfied with; and ſome minutes after,
' as I had turned to a looking glaſs to
' adjuſt ſome diſorder in my head-dreſs,
' he pulled me to him, and making me
' ſit upon his knee—" You are very
" pretty, my dear," ſaid he; " and
" have no defect in your ſhape, but be-
" ing a little too flat before." With
' theſe words, he thruſt one of his hands
' within my ſtays; telling me, that
' handling

' handling my breasts would make
' them grow, and I should then be a
' perfect beauty.

' Not conscious of any guilt, I was
' ignorant of shame; and thinking every
' thing he did was right, made not the
' least resistance; but suffered him, by
' degrees, to proceed to liberties, which
' had I known the meaning of, I should
' have stabbed him for attempting; but,
' as I have somewhere read—

" By no example warn'd how to beware,
" My very innocence became my snare."

' It will perhaps be supposed, that the
' perfidious man did not stop here, but
' proceeded yet farther, to the utter
' completion of my dishonour; but I
' shall do him the justice to say, that
' he never offered any such thing; though
' I have good reasons to believe he was
' prevented only by his fear of the con-
' sequences that might have attended it,
' to the ruin of a design which promised
' him more satisfaction than the enjoy-
' ment of my person.

' In the ridiculous way I have been
' describing did we continue till I was
' in my seventeenth year; about which
' time, my father being obliged to go
' to London on a law affair, he left the
' sole management of the family, as
' well as of myself, to his favourite
' chaplain, till he should return, which
' he expected to do in two months.

' He had not been gone full three
' weeks before a stranger came to our
' house on a visit to my tutor : he re-
' ceived him with great marks of civi-
' lity; and told me afterwards that he
' was the land-steward of a nobleman,
' who had sent him on purpose to court
' his acceptance of a benefice worth near
' eight hundred pounds per annum.
' As I suspected not the truth of this,
' I was terribly frightened; and cried
' out—" Then you will leave me at
" last!"—" It would be with an ex-
" treme reluctance I should do so,"
' replied he; " but what can I do? If
" I should hereafter be exposed to any
" misfortunes, how would the world
" blame me for having refused such an
" offer?"—" What misfortunes," said
' I, " have you to fear? I shall always
" have enough to support my dear
" tutor."

" My dear child," resumed he, " you
" forget that, when once you are mar-

" ried, there will be nothing in your
" power; all will he your husband's,
" who may take it into his head to turn
" me out of doors directly."—" No
" such matter," replied I hastily; " for
" I will make him promise and swear
" beforehand to keep you always in the
" family."—" Few men," said he,
" pay any regard, after they become
" husbands, to the promises and vows
" they made when they were lovers.
" In fine, my little angel," continued
' he, taking me tenderly in his arms,
" there is but one way to secure our
" lasting happiness, to which if you
" agree, I will immediately refuse the
" great offer now made me, with all my
" future hopes of rising in the church,
" and devote myself eternally to you."
' These last words I thought so highly
' obliging to me, that I hung about his
' neck, kissed his cheek, and cried I
' would do every thing he would have
' me. He then told me that a writing
' should be drawn up between us, by
' which we should mutually bind our-
' selves, under the penalty of the half
' of what either should be possessed of,
' never to separate.

' On my ready compliance with this
' proposal, he ventured to make a se-
' cond, even more impudent than the
' first. After seeming to consider a lit-
' tle within himself—" I have been
" thinking," said he, " that if the per-
" son you shall marry should happen
" to be of a cross, perverse nature,
" though for his own sake he will not
" drive me from his house, yet he may
" use me so ill as to compel me to go out
" of it of my own accord : suppose,
" therefore, you should bind yourself
" by the writing I have mentioned,
" and under the same penalty, never to
" marry any man without my con-
" sent?"

" Bless me!" cried I, a little sur-
' prized, " how can I do this? You
" know I must obey my father."—
" Heaven forbid you should do other-
" wise!" rejoined the artful hypocrite;
" you may be sure I shall never oppose
" either his will, or your own inclina-
" tion, in the choice of a husband :
" what I speak of is only a thing of
" form, which, when shewn to your
" husband, will oblige him to treat me
" with gratitude and respect."
' I was entirely satisfied with this;
' and replied, I would do what he de-
                                        ' sired

' fired as foon as he pleafed : on which—
" It happens luckily," faid he, " that
" the gentleman who came here on the
" bufinefs I told you of was bred to
" the law; I will let him know as
" much as is neceffary of our affair,
" and get him to draw up a proper in-
" ftrument." In fpeaking thefe words,
' he left me, and went in fearch of his
' friend, who at that time was walking
' in the garden, waiting, no doubt, his
' coming.

' I had little time allowed me to re-
' flect on what I was about to do. Le
' Bris immediately returned, bringing
' the lawyer with him ; the latter of
' whom defired to receive inftructions
' from my own mouth for what he was
' to write ; and accordingly I re eated
' the fenfe of the obligation I was to lay
' myfelf under, leaving it o him to put
' it in fuch words as he fhould find
' proper. If I had been miftrefs of the
' leaft fhare of common reafon, I muft
' have feen that all this fcheme was a
' thing previoufly concerted between
' thefe two villains ; for the lawyer im-
' mediately pulled out of his pocket a
' large parchment, with feals fixed to
' it, and every thing requifite to make
' the inftrument firm and valid : but I
' was infatuated ; all my little under-
' ftanding was fubjected to the will of
' this wicked tutor ; I gave an implicit
' faith to all he faid, and paid an im-
' plicit obedience to all his dictates.

' The lawyer took his leave next day,
' and nothing material happened till
' within a week of the time my father
' was expected home ; when, inftead of
' himfelf, came the melancholy account
' that he had been feized with an apo-
' plectick fit, and, though he recovered
' from it, expired within two hours
' after. He had made his will about
' a year before, by which he left me fole
' heir of every thing he was in poffeffion
' of, except a few legacies ; and in cafe
' his demife fhould happen before I
' was married, or of age appointed
' two gentlemen for his executors and
' my guardians. They both wrote to
' me, as did alfo my coufin *****, ac-
' quainting me that it was neceffary I
' fhould come to London directly on
' this occafion, and each inviting me
' to their refpective houfes ; which, as
' they lived in different parts of the
' town, I was at liberty to chufe which
' I liked beft.

' My tutor, however, diffuaded me
' from accepting any of their offers ;
' and told me he would write to a friend
' in London to provide a ready-fur-
' nifhed houfe for my reception, till
' things were fettled, and I fhould re-
' folve whether I would refide in town
' or country. Accordingly he did fo ;
' and when we came within ten miles
' of London, we were met on the road by
' the lawyer, who, as I have fince difco-
' vered, was his chief agent in every
' thing. He conducted us to a houfe
' in Jermyn Street, which was indeed
' very neat and commodious.

' It was late when we arrived ; but
' I did not fail to fend the next morn-
' ing to my two guardians and coufin
' *****, who all came to fee me the
' fame day, and expreffed themfelves in
' very affectionate terms. I prefented
' my tutor to them, as a perfon for
' whom my father had a high efteem ;
' on which they treated him with that
' refpect they fuppofed him to deferve.

' I now entered into a fcene of life al-
' together new to me. Several diftant
' relations, whom I knew only by their
' names, and many other gentlemen
' and ladies who had been acquainted
' with my mother, came to pay their
' refpects to me. All my mornings
' were taken up with meffages and
' compliments ; and all my afternoons
' with receiving and returning vifits.
' How ftrange was the tranfition ! From
' being confined to the narrow precincts
' of a lone country manfion, I had now
' the whole metropolis to range in ;
' inftead of the grave leffons of two old
' men, my ears were now conftantly
' filled with the flattering praifes of ad-
' dreffing beaus ; inftead of having no-
' thing to amufe my hours, new di-
' verfions, new entertainments, crouded
' upon each moment ; and I was in-
' ceffantly hurried from one pleafure to
' another, till my head grew giddy with
' the whirl of promifcuous pleafure .

' As I was young, not ugly, and
' looked upon as a rich heirefs, pro-
' pofals of marriage were every day
' made to me; all which I communi-
' cated to my tutor: but though many
' of them were much to my avantage,
' he always found fome reafon or
' other for refufing his confent ; and I
' accordingly rejected them to the fur-
' prize of all who knew me, and to the great
' diffatisfaction of my beft friends.

D  ' He

' He was not, however, half-pleased
' with the gay manner in which I lived;
' and, as soon as the affairs relating to
' my estate were settled, would fain have
' prevailed upon me to return into the
' country : but I had too high a relish
' for the diversions of the town to pay
' that regard to his advice I had for-
' merly done; and, instead of comply-
' ing with it, quitted the house I was
' in, hired another upon lease, and fur-
' nished it in the most elegant manner I
' could. He grew very grave on my
' behaviour; but as I kept firm to both
' the engagements I had made with him,
' he had no pretence to complain of my
' actions in other matters.

' For a time, indeed, my head was
' not the least turned towards marriage :
' I thought no farther of the men than
' to be vain and delighted with their
' flatteries. Happy would it have been
' for me had I continued always in this
' mind ! But my ill fate too soon, alas !
' presented me with an object which
' convinced me that all the joys of pub-
' lick admiration are nothing, when
' compared to one soft hour with the
' youth we love, and by whom we think
' we are beloved.

' I believe there is little need for me
' to say that this object, so enchanting
' to my senses, was the young, the hand-
' some, the accomplished Amasis. The
' world, to whom he made no secret of
' the passion he professed for me, was also
' witness in what manner I received it :
' we appeared together in all publick
' places; I treated him in all companies
' with a deference which shewed the
' esteem I had for him. My friends
' approved my choice; and the union
' between us was looked upon as a
' thing so absolutely determined, that
' many believed the ceremony was al-
' ready over, when, to their great sur-
' prize, they saw at once that we were
' utterly broke off; and, in a very short
' time after, the ungrateful Amasis be-
' come the husband of another.

' My tutor, on perceiving me inclined
' to favour Amasis more than I had
' ever done any of those who had hi-
' therto addressed me, began to rail at
' him, and tell me a thousand ridiculous
' stories he pretended to have heard in
' relation to his conduct. I still retained
' too much reverence for this wicked
' man to contradict what he said, but
' not enough to enable me to conquer

' my new passion : I loved Amasis,
' and continued to give him daily proofs
' of it. This so incensed him, that he
' told me, one day, that he wondered I
' would encourage the courtship of a
' man whom I must never expect to
' marry. " Why not, Sir ?" answered
' I : " neither his birth nor fortune are
" inferior to mine."—" Suppose them
" so," rejoined he, " the most material
" thing is wanting, which is my con-
" sent."—" When I gave you that
" power over me," said I, " you pro-
" mised never to thwart my inclina-
" tion." — " I did so," replied he ;
" but, to be plain with you, I then ex-
" pected all your inclination would be
" in favour of myself."—" Yourself !"
' cried I, more surprized than words
' can describe. " Yes, Alinda," re-
' sumed he ; " methinks the thing
" should not appear so odd to you. Call
" back to your remembrance the fami-
" liarities that have passed between us,
" and then justify, if you can, to virtue
" or to modesty, the least desire of giv-
" ing yourself to any other man."

' Rage, astonishment, and shame, for
' the folly I had been guilty of, so over-
' whelmed my heart at this reproach,
' that I had not power to speak one
' word; but stood looking on him with
' a countenance which, I believe, suf-
' ficiently expressed all those passions,
' while he went on in these terms—

" How often," continued he, " have
" you hung about my neck whole hours
" together, and, by the warm st fond-
" ness, tempted me to take every free-
" dom with you but the last ; which, if
" I had not been possessed of more ho-
" nour than you now shew of con-
" stancy, I also should have seized, and
" left you nothing to bestow upon a
" rival ?"

' The storm which had been gather-
' ing in my breast all the time he had
' been speaking, now burst out with,
' the extremest violence : I raved, and
' loaded him with epithets not very be-
' coming in me to make use of, yet not
' worse than he deserved. He heard me
' with a sullen silence ; but when I
' mentioned the cruelty and baseness of
' upbraiding me with the folli s of my
' childish innocence, he told me with a
' sneer, that he would advise me not to
' put that among my catalogue of com-
' plaints : " For," said he, " the world
" will scarce believe, that a lady of
" fourteen,

" fourteen, fifteen, and sixteen, had the
" same inclinations in toying with a
" gentleman as a baby has with it's
" nurse."

' I would have replied, that the man-
' ner in which I was educated kept me
' in the same ignorance as a baby; but
' something within rose in my throat,
' stopping the passage of my breath, and
' I sunk fainting in the chair where I
' was fitting. Whether he was really
' moved with this fight, or only affected
' to be so, I know not; but he ran to
' me, used proper means to bring me to
' myself, and, on my recovery, I found
' myself pressed very tenderly within his
' arms. His touch was now grown
' odious to me; I struggled to get loose.
" Be not thus unkind," cried he, hold-
" ing me still faster; " you once took
" pleasure in my embraces, you have
" confessed you did. Oh! then, recall
" those soft ideas, and we shall both be
" happy!"

" No!" answered I, breaking forcibly
' from him; " what then was the effect
" of too much innocence, would be
" now a guilt for which I should detest
" myself as much as I do you!"—" I
" still love you," said he. " Prove it,
" then," cried I fiercely, " by giving
" me up that writing which your arti-
" fices ensnared me to sign, and cease
" to oppose my marriage with Amasis."
—" No, Madam," replied he, " if you
" persist in the resolution of marrying
" Amasis, half your estate would be a
" small confolation to me for the loss of
" you; and you cannot sure imagine
" me to be weak enough to resign my
" claim to the one, after being deprived
" of the other!"

' I had not patience to continue this
' discourse, but retired to my chamber;
' where, throwing myself upon the bed,
' I vented some part of the anguish of
' my mind in a flood of tears: after
' which, finding some little ease, I began
' to reflect, that tormenting myself in
' this manner would avail nothing;
' and that I ought rather to try if any
' possible means could be found for ex-
' tricating me from the labyrinth I was
' entangled in.

' Accordingly I arose, muffled my-
' self up as well as I could to prevent
' being known, took a hackney-coach,
' and went to the chambers of an emi-
' nent lawyer. I related to him all the
' circumstances of my unhappy case,

' concealing only the names of the per-
' sons concerned in it. He listened at-
' tentively to what I said; and when I
' had done, asked me of what age I was
' when I entered into that engagement
' I now wanted to be freed from; which
' question I answering with sincerity, he
' shook his head, and told me that he
' was sorry to assure me I could have no
' relief from law; and that the best,
' and, indeed, the only method I could
' take, was to endeavour to compromise
' the affair with the gentleman.

' I returned home very disconsolate,
' and was above a week without being
' able to resolve on any thing; but my
' impatience to be united to the man I
' loved, and at the same time eased of
' the presence of the man I hated, at
' last determined me to follow the law-
' yer's advice. I sent for my wicked
' tutor into my chamber; talked to him
' in more obliging terms than I had
' done since the first discovery of his de-
' signs upon me; but represented to
' him the absurdity of thinking of mar-
' rying me himself; and concluded with
' telling him, that if he would cancel
' the engagement between us, I would
' make him a gratuity of a thousand
' pounds, and also be ready to do him
' any other service in my power.

' He rejected this proposal with the
' greatest contempt. " You are cer-
" tainly mad, Alinda," said he, " or
" take me to be so! A thousand pounds
" would be a fine equivalent, indeed,
" for the half of your estate, jewels,
" rich furniture, plate, and whatever
" else you are in possession of; to all
" which your marriage will give me an
" undoubted claim, and I accordingly
" shall seize."—" Suppose I never
" marry?" cried I. " Be it so," an-
" swered he; " I must still continue to
" live with you; and what you offer for
" my quitting you does not amount to
" five years purchase of my salary and
" board as your chaplain."

' These words making me imagine
' his chief objection was to the smallness
' of the sum, I told him I would double,
' nay, even treble it, for the pure use of
' my liberty; but he told me it would
' be in vain for me to tempt him with
' any offers of that kind; that no con-
' fideration whatever should prevail with
' him to depart from the agreement be-
' tween us; and he would always hold
' me to my bargain.

' The

' T'e determined air with which he
' spoke this, made me think it best not
' to urge him any farther at that time.
' The next day, however, and several
' succeeding ones, I failed not to renew
' the discourse; but though I made use
' of every argument my reason could
' supply me with; though I wept,
' prayed, raved, by turns cajoled and
' threatened; all I could say, all I could
' do, was ineffectual; and the more
' I laboured to bring him to compli-
' ance, the more stubborn his obstinacy
' grew.

' To make any one sensible what it
' was I suffered in this cruel dilemma,
' they must also be made sensible to
' what an infinite degree I loved the
' man whom it was now impossible for
' me to be happy with; and both these
' are inexpressible: I shall therefore
' only say, that I was very near being
' totally deprived of that little share of
' reason Heaven had bestowed upon
' me.

' Amasis, to whom I had confessed
' the tenderness I had for him, was all
' this while continually soliciting me to
' complete our union. One day, when
' he was more than ordinarily pressing on
' this occasion, and my heart being very
' full, I cried out, almost without know-
' ing what I said—' Oh, Amasis! you
" know not what you ask, when you
" ask me to marry you!" This excla-
' mation surprized him: but having be-
' gun, I now went on—" You expect,"
' said I, " an estate of twelve hundred
" pounds a year; but I will not deceive
" you, you find me worth only the half
" of what you have been made to
" hope."—" When I made my ad-
" dresses to the lovely Alinda," an-
' swered he, " I had no eye to the for-
" tune she might bring me. But where-
" fore this fruitless trial of my love? Your
" guardians have shewn me the writings
" of your estate; and I know to a single
" hundred what you are possessed of."
—" Suppose," rejoined I, " that I
" should have previously disposed of the
" one half of what otherwise our mar-
" riage would have given you?"—" I
" will suppose no such thing," replied
' he; " it cannot be!"—" It both can,
" and is," said I, bursting into tears;
" I have unwarily entered into an en-
" gagement, by which I forfeit the
" moiety of all I am mistress of, even

" to my very jewels, if ever I marry
" any man, except on certain condi-
" tions; which condition, I am now
" well assured, I never can obtain."
" Death!" cried he, starting up in a
' fury, " What condition?—When!—
" Where!—To whom!—On what ac-
" count was this engagement made!"
' Shame would not let me answer to
' these interrogatories, and I remained
' in a kind of stupid silence. " If by
" any artifices," pursued he, " you
" have been seduced to sign a compact
" of this wild nature, unfold the whole
" of the affair, and depend, that either
" the laws, or this avenging arm, shall
" do you justice." I now repented
' that I had so rashly divulged any part
' of this fatal secret; not but I should
' have been glad to have seen my wicked
' tutor punished; but I knew that, on
' the least attempt made for my redress,
' he would infallibly expose the follies
' I had been guilty of in regard to him;
' and, when compared with the loss of
' Amasis, my fortune, or even my life
' itself, seemed a less terrible misfor-
' tune: for this reason, therefore, I
' refused the entreaties of a beloved
' lover, and screened the villainy of a
' wretch whom my soul abhorred. In
' fine, I would reveal no more than I
' had done. Amasis left me in a very
' ill humour; and the next morning I
' received a billet from him, containing
' these stabbing lines—

" TO MISS ALINDA *****,

" MADAM,

" I Have been considering on the
" amazing account you gave me
" last night; and as you refuse to dis-
" cover either the person with whom
" you made this engagement, or the
" motives which induced you to it, can
" look on it as no other than a contract
" with some gentleman once happy in
" your affections. A second hand
" passion neither suits with the delicacy
" of my humour, nor to encroach upon
" the rights of another with my ho-
" nour: I shall therefore desist trou-
" bling you with any future visits, but
" shall be always glad to hear of your
" welfare, which I despair of doing
" till you prevail upon yourself to be
" just to your first vows. Sacrifice the
" affection

" affection you have for me to the
" obligations you are under to my
" rival. I yield to his prior title all the
" late glorious hopes I had conceived;
" and with you more happy with him,
" than it is now in your power to make
" your humble fervant,

" AMASIS."

' Here ended all my hopes of happi-
' nefs; all the foft ideas of love and
' marriage vanifhed for ever from my
' breaft, and were fucceeded by others
' of the moft dreadful nature. For fe-
' veral weeks I abandoned myfelf to
' grief and to defpair, but pride at length
' got the better of thefe paffions; and,
' to conceal the real fituation of my
' heart from the enquiring world, I all
' at once affected to be madly gay, and
' ran into fuch extravagancies, as,
' without being criminal in fact, juftly
' drew upon me the fevereft cenfures.
' But nature will not bear a perpetual
' violence. Grief and defpair were the
' ftrongeft paffions in me. In the midft
' of dancing, tears were ready to ftart
' from my eyes, and I fighs from my bo-
' fom, which, when I endeavoured to
' fupprefs, recoiled upon my heart, and
' fhook my frame with the m ft terrible
' revultions. The marriage of Amafis
' feconded the blow our parting had
' given: I could no longer diffemble
' what I felt, no longer appear the
' giddy, thoughtlefs libertine, but flew
' from one extreme to the other. I now
' would fee no company, fhut myfelf
' up in my chamber, denied accefs to
' my beft friends, and never went
' abroad. I fuffered not Le Bris to
' come into my prefence; and, I believe,
' perceiving me fo refolu e, he would
' have accepted of a fum of money to
' have quitted my houfe entirely: but
' I had now done with the world, had
' loft in Amafis all I valued in it, and
' would not give the monfter, whom I
' juftly looked upon as the fource of all
' my misfortunes, any more than I was
' compelled to do, his bare board and
' falary.
' Behold, by thefe memoirs, the be-
' ginning and progrefs of all my mife-
' ries! The end is near at hand; Death
' is already bufy at my heart, and
' allows no time to apologize for the
' errors of my conduct. Pity is all my
' afhes can expect!'

## CHAP. VII.

CONTAINS A VERY BRIEF ACCOUNT
OF SOME PASSAGES SUBSEQUENT
TO THE FOREGOING STORY,
WITH THE AUTHOR'S REMARKS
UPON THE WHOLE.

AS I know very well that folidity
has but a fmall fhare in the com-
pofition of the lady whom Alinda h d
intended to entruft with the publication
of her memoirs, I thought the fureft
way of having the will of the deceafed
performed, was not to trouble a perfon
of her character with the perufal of
them, but to take the opportunity of
my invifibility fhip to prefent them to the
world myfelf, which I accordingly
have done.

And now, as I doubt not but the
reader will be glad of being informed
farther concerning Le Bris, I fhall relate fuch particulars as have come to my
knowled e.

It muft be concluded, that this unworthy preceptor, in looking over the
papers of Alinda, had either not obferved, or afterwards forgot, that the
ring he had juft taken from among her
o her jewels, was the very fame mentioned in her letter to her friend, otherwife he would certainly have had cunning enough to have replaced it where
he found it.

Mr. *****, foon recollecting what
his coufin had faid to him in regard of
this little legacy, and miffing it from
her other trinkets, made a ftrict enquiry what was become of it. Le Bris,
having had her keys in his poffeffion,
was one of the firft interrogated; and,
on being fo, boldly replied, that fuch
a ring had been beftowed upon him by
Alinda. ' How can that be,' cried
the other; ' when, but three days be-
' fore her death, fhe bequeathed it to a
' lady of her acquaintance, and infifted
' on my promife of delivering it to her?'
—' She muft then be delirious,' faid
the parfon: ' but, however that might
' be, Heaven forbid I fhould detain
' what is even fufpected to be the right
' of another!' and, with thefe words,
prefented the ring to Mr. *****, who
received it from him without the leaft
ceremony.

This affair, notwithftanding the hy-
pocritical manner in which the ring was
returned,

returned, gave Mr. ***** oom to ima gine there had been fom foul play in relation to A inda's effects. The stew- ard proved by his books, that he had paid into her hands, a week before her death, two hundred and fifty po n s in fpecie, and more than twice that fum in Bank bills, being arrears he had re- ceived from the tenants. It feemed n likely to them that fhe could have dif- pofed of the money, much els have had any occafion to change the b lls in fo fhort a time; orders were therefore fent to the Bank to ftop the payment of f ch numbers till further notice: but the pre- caution came too late; the perfon who had fecreted them ha been already there, and converted all his paper into cafh.

The heir, however, was confident that he had been defrauded: he con- fulted council upon it, who all advifed him to have recourfe to equity. Whe- ther Le Bris had any hint given him of what was intended to be done againft him, or whether his own guilty con- fcience made him only apprehend it, is uncertain: but he had not courage to ftand the teft of examination; he fled the kingdom; after having thrown afide that robe which, had he been known for what he truly was, would long before have been ftripped from his facrilegious fhoulders.

But Providence would not permit him to enjoy his ill-got fpoils, nor a life he had devoted to fuch wicked purpofes. Defigning to turn trader at Jamaica, he embarked for that place; but the veffel being overtaken by a ftorm, was loft almoft in fight of fhore; and he, with many other, perhaps lefs guilty perfons, perifhed in the wreck. This laft piece of intelligence I received from his mo- ther; whom, though he had fupported during the life of Alinda, to prevent be- ing expofed by her clamours, he now left pennylefs, deftitute, and ftarving, in an extreme old age.

Thus did the vengeance of Heaven at laft overtake the wretch who, be- fides his other impieties, had been guilty of the moft cruel ingratitude and breach of truft, in impofing upon the fimplicity of a young creature com- mitted to his care, and utterly deftroy- ing all the views of his generous patron and benefactor.

As for the unfortunate Alinda, though it i certain her conduct cannot be wholly juftified, yet, according to my pinion, it o ght not to be wholly condemned. It would be pffing too f vere a judgment, to impute the fond- n fs the expref d for her wicked tutor to a wa ton inclination. If we confider the various arts of her feducer, the com- mands laid on her by her father to love and obey him s himfelf, the manner in which fhe was brought up, the per- fect ignorance fhe was kept in of the cuftoms of the world, and how other young ladies behaved; we fhall find t at thefe are all of them very ftrong pleas in her defence, and not forbear pitying the miftakes of fuch artlefs innocence.

I wifh as much could be alle ged in her behalf on the fcore of her beha- viour after breaking off with Amafis. The exceffes into which fhe ran, in order to conceal the difquiets of her mind for the lofs of that favourite lover. too evi- dently fhew that fhe facrifi ed two of the moft valuable characteriticks of woman- hood her prudence and her modefty, to one of the very worft—her pride.

Nor can I offer any th ng in vindica- ti n of the laft ftages of her life. If con- vinced of her error in being perpetually amongft promifcuous company, it was flying to an almoft as inexcufable ex- treme, to fhut herfelf up from her belt friends, and avoid the fociety of thofe whofe converfation might have diffi- pated her chagrin, and, at the fame time, improved her underftanding. To do this, feems to me, I muft confefs, to have more the favour of defpair, than of vir- tue or true fortitude.

There was, doubtlefs, a certain giddy propenfity in her nature, which wanted to be corrected by reafon, example, pre- cept, authority, and the rudiments of a good education; all which fhe was de- nied: and it muft therefore be acknow- ledged, that both her faults and misfor- tunes were entirely owing to the caprice and credulity of her father, and the bafe defigns of the perfon appointed to be her governor and inftructor.

# END OF THE FIRST BOOK.

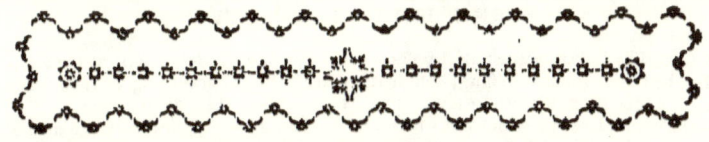

THE

# INVISIBLE SPY.

## BOOK II.

### CHAP. I.

THE AUTHOR, BY THE HELP OF
HIS INVISIBILITY, HAS DISCO-
VERED SUCH A CONTRAST IN
THE BEHAVIOUR OF TWO MAR-
RIED COUPLE OF DISTINCTION,
AS HE THINKS WOULD BE THE
UTMOST INJUSTICE TO THE PUB-
LICK TO CONCEAL.

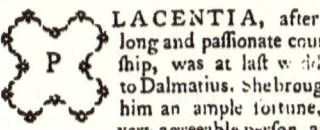LACENTIA, after a
long and paffionate court-
fhip, was at laft wedded
to Dalmatius. She brought
him an ample fortune, a
very agreeable perfon, and
an unblemifhed character. She had
ftudied the duties of a wife before fhe
became fo, and afterwards practifed
them in the ftricteft manner. Whenever
fhe found him gay, fhe heightened his
good humour by her own fprightlinefs;
and when fullen and perverfe, as was too
often the cafe, fhe endeavoured to diffi-
pate his chagrin, either by playing on
her fpinnet, or telling him fome diverting ftory. Without feeming to confult
his palate, fhe always took care to put
fuch difhes into his bill of fare as fhe
had perceived he fed upon with moft fatisfaction. Whatever company fuited
his tafte, were fure to be often invited by
her, and entertained with the greateft
marks of efteem and complaifance.

Her whole thoughts, indeed, were taken
up with obliging and making him happy: fhe had no will, no inclination of
her own; both were entirely regulated
by his: and, to add to all this, fhe was
an excellent œconomift, underftood the
management of a family perfectly well,
and knew how to make a grand appearance with lefs expence than fome others
are at who are accounted contemptibly
parfimonious.

What would fome hufbands give to
be bleffed with fo virtuous, fo tender, fo
endearing a companion! Dalmatius,
inftead of placing this jewel next his
heart, hung it carelefsly upon his fleeve;
either not knowing, or not regarding,
the true value of it.

During the courfe of feveral invifible
vifitations I made at their houfe, never
did I fee him treat her in any degree
proportionable to her merit. When in
his beft humours, he returned the ca-
reffes fhe gave him only with a cold indifference; but when any thing abroad
had happened to thwart his view, either
of pleafure or ambition, no man could
behave with more churlifhnefs at home.
But the manner in which this couple behaved to each other will beft appear from
their own words, which I fhall give a
fhort fpecimen of on two different occafions.

They were to go out together one
day, to call on fome friends who were
to accompany them on a party of pleafure,

fure. The landau waited at the door. He had juſt finiſhed dreſſing, and ſent up to know if his wife was ready. The meſſa_e could be ſcarce del'vered before ſhe came flying into the room, on which the following did gue enſued—

Placentia. I hope I have not made y_u wait for me?

Dalmatius. Not at all. It warts ſome min.tes of our appointment; but I know you women are generally ſo long equipping yourſelves, that I was willing to haſten you.

Placentia. I ſhould know but li tle of the value of time, if I waſted much of it in dreſſing. But i ray, my dear, how do you like me to-day?

Dalmatius. Like you! that's an odd queſtion. Why, as well as ever I did.

Placentia. I ſhould be miſerable if I did not thi k you did. But I mean, how do you like my cloaths? you ſ.e I am all in new.

Dalmatius. Are you indeed? I ſhould have ſeen nothing of it, if you had not told me: I never mind what women have on.

Placentia. Then I am diſappointed, my dear; for I aſſure you I conſulted your fancy more than my own in the choice I made of this ſilk; as i have heard you ſay an hundred times, I believe, that you thought blue and ſilver the moſt agreeable mixture that could be.

Dalmatius. So it is; but it may not happen to become every body: however, I muſt do you the juſtice to ſay, you look well enough in it, and I believe every body will think ſo.

Placentia. If you think ſo, my dear, it is all I wiſh.

In ſpeaking this, ſhe took hold of his hand, and kiſſed it with the greateſt warmth of affeXion. He returned the favour with a ſlight ſalute upon her cheek; then looking on his watch, ſaid he believed it was time to go, and went down ſtairs, ſhe following.

The truth of the affair is this. Dalmatius is not only vain and inſolent in his nature, but a'ſo amorous and inconſtant to an exceſs. Th gh he no longer had any eyes for the charms of his fair wife, his heart was but too ſuſceptible to thoſe of other women. Miranda for ſome time engroſſed all his devoirs; nor could her being married to the moſt intimate of his friends reſtrain him from making his unlawful addreſſes to her;

nor the vow ſhe had taken at the altar, deter her from gratifying an inclination he had found the way to inſpire.

The huſband of this lady is a man of ſo much indolerce, and ſo l ttle delicacy, that he never g ves himſelf the leaſt concern about what pleaſures his wife may indulge herſelf in, provided ſhe offers no interrupti n to thoſe he takes him elf. There are ſome, indeed, who ſay, that on their marriage they mutually agreed to allow e ich other a perfect latitude in this point; but, be that as it may, Miranda ſeems under no apprehenſions of her conduct being cal ed in queſtion by him.

Her amo.r with Dalmatius ſoon became ſo notorious, that it was in the mouth of every one. Placentia herſelf was the laſt that gave credit t it; that excell nt lady would not ſuffer her he rt to entertain ill thoughts of the man ſhe was bo nd to love, nor could any thing but the teſtimony of her own eyes have convinced her of the guilty truth.

Miranda came to viſit her one day when ſhe happened to be abroad; but Dalmatius being at home, the preſence of his wife was li tle wanted. She ſoon returned, however; and being told that Miranda was above, ran haſtily up to receive her; but not finding her in the room where company were uſually introduced, yet thinking ſhe heard the murmur of voices very near, ſhe ſtepped towards the place whence it ſeemed to proceed, and peeping through the keyhole of an adjacent chamber, ſaw her huſband and the lady in a poſture ſuch as could leave her no doubt of their criminal converſation.

The ſudden ſhock at firſt transfixed her feet; but preſently recovering herſelf, ſhe retired from the guilty ſcene, and went into her own chamber; where finding her woman at work, ſhe ordered her to go immediately down, and forbid the ſervants to take any notice of her being come home. ' I hear,' ſaid ſhe, ' that Miranda is below, and I am ' not very well, and would not ſee any ' company at this time.'

The woman being withdrawn, to do as ſhe was commanded, Placentia threw herſelf into an eaſy chair, and fell into a profound reverie. I was preſent all this while, but my Belt of Inviſibility did not enable me to penetrate into her thoughts; till ſeeming as if determined on ſomething ſhe had been debating
within

within herself, she rose suddenly from her seat, and burst into these words—' No, ' he shall never know I think him false, ' much less that I have detected him. ' Reproaches would avail me nothing, ' and might harden him in his crime. ' I am his wife; we must always live ' together, or be subject to the ridicule ' of a laughing and censorious world. ' Prudence, therefore, as well as duty, ' commands me to conceal the shameful ' discovery I have made; and rather en- ' deavour, by added tenderness, if pos- ' sible, to reclaim him, and oblige him ' to see I am at least as worthy of his af- ' fection as Miranda.'

I left her in this resolution, and found that for several days she strictly adhered to it; excepting only, that she could not so far dissemble her uneasiness as to be able to receive Miranda in the manner she had formerly done: she there- fore desisted from making her any far- ther invitations to her house, and always excused herself from accepting any sent to her by that lady.

This was enough, however, to give the lovers some apprehensions that she suspected their intrigue; but Miranda was of too vain and gay a temper to feel any inquietude on this score; and the ungraceful Dalmatius, finding himself treated by his wife with the same love and complaisance as ever, gave himself not the trouble either to examine, or be under the least concern, whether such a behaviour proceeded from her ignorance of his fault, or her discretion in over- looking it.

But the sweetest disposition may be embittered by continual provocations. Placentia, finding that all the efforts she made for regaining the affections of her husband were ineffectual, began by degrees to grow more remiss in her cares of pleasing; not that she ever departed from the essential duties of a wife, the only ceased the practice of those which, as the case stood between them, might justly be called works of supereroga- tion.

Being to have a great route at her house, just as she was going to send cards to invite the company, Dalmatius came into the room; and having looked over the catalogue of names, on finding Miranda's not there, began with an un- usual haughtiness to interrogate her on that occasion; and she now, for the first time, replied to what he said with as

much indifference as she had formerly done with submission.

*Dalmatius.* How happens it, Ma- dam, that Miranda is left out among the number of your guests?

*Placentia.* I had forgot her.

*Dalmatius.* It is well, then, that I reminded you : but methinks a lady of her rank and character in the world might well have deserved a place in your remembrance.

*Placentia.* It may be so; but one cannot invite every body.

*Dalmatius.* When any body is in- vited to our house, especially on these occasions, it would be the utmost ab- surdity to leave Miranda out; therefore I insist upon her coming, for your own sake.

*Placentia.* Oh, Sir, you need not give yourself any trouble on that score; I am certainly a judge how to behave to my own acquaintance: but if you are so desirous of having Miranda here to- morrow, the best way is for you to send a card as from yourself; I doubt not but the invitation will be full as agreeable, and as readily complied with.

*Dalmatius.* You talk in an odd manner, Madam! And, now I think on it, I met Miranda the other day in the Park, and she complained to me of a strange change in you towards her; that you have never returned the last visit she made you; have scarce spoke to her in any publick assembly, and seemed to shun her presence as much as possible. Pray what is the meaning of all this?

*Placentia.* That, Sir, is a question which perhaps neither you nor she would thank me for answering directly.

*Dalmatius.* I understand you, Ma- dam, however. You have got notions in your head not becoming in you to in- dulge, nor worthy any endeavours of mine to expel. I would only have you be wiser; and confider, that of all do- mestick animals a jealous wife is the most contemptible.

He flung out of the room with these words, and all the tokens of disdain and indignation in his countenance; leaving Placentia in a confusion not easy to be described. I could perceive, however, by the gestures of that unhappy lady, that she repented having gone so far; yet knowing herself the only injured, could not yield either to recede from her resolution on the account of Miranda, or make use of any attempts to soften

E                                         so

fo ill-founded a refentment in her hufband.

It is now faid that his amour with
Miranda is on the decline; that a new
face has utterly eclipfed all the charms
he lately found in hers; and that Placentia has at leaft this confolation under
her misfortune, to find that no one
beauty has the power long to retain the
heart fhe has loft: fo juft are the poet's
words—

‘ When fix'd to one, love fafe at anchor
‘ ride.;
‘ And dares the fury of the winds and
‘ tides;
‘ But lofing once that hold, to the wide
‘ ocean borne,
‘ It drives at will, to ev'ry wave a fcorn.'

Marriage, though a facred inftitution,
though ordained by Heaven to beftow
the fupremeft felicity we mortals are capable of enjoying, becomes the fevereft
curfe, when fouls ill fuited to each other
are joined in it's indiffoluble bonds; and
it too often happens, that thofe who by
nature and education are qualified to
give and receive the greateft happinefs,
are rendered the moft miferable, through
the perverfenefs of a bad-tempered partner.

Montelion has been twice married.
He has experienced both all the content-
ments, and all the inquietudes, of that
ftate, with women of humours as widely
different as light and darknefs; I had
almoft faid, as heaven from hell. His
firft lady, as fhe was excelled by none in
exterior perfections, fo fhe was equalled
but by very few in the more valuable
endowments of the mind. His life,
while in poffeffion of this treafure, was
one continued fcene of harmony and
love. But foon, alas! the blissful pro
fpect vanifhed; the fair, the virtuous, the
tender Erminia, died! and, to add to
the misfortune of her difconfolate hufband, left no pledge behind her of their
mutual affection.

Though in that feafon of life when
amorous flames are at their higheft bent,
thofe of Montelion feemed all buried in
the grave of his dear Erminia. He remained for feveral years the lonely oc-
cupier of a widowed bed. At laft,
however, the ardent defire of having an
heir for his eftate got fomewhat the better of his melancholy, and determined
him on a fecond venture.

In the choice he made, he confulted
neither fortune nor beauty: the one, indeed, he wanted not; and as for the
other, fince his Erminia's death all women were equal to him, and he regarded
the lovely and unlovely with the fame
indifference. He therefore married Ferocia, merely becaufe fhe was one of
the daughters of a fruitful family, and
likely to anfwer the only end which induced him once more to become a hufband.

Every body was aftonifhed at thefe
nuptials, and much more fo on the
knowledge of Ferocia's behaviour afterwards. But I fhall prefent my reader
with the character of this lady, as it
was given by an impartial hand in a letter to a friend.

‘ Ferocia, now the wife of Montelion,
‘ is a woman plain in her perfon, weak
‘ in her underftanding, capricious and
‘ fantaftick in her humour, unpolifhed
‘ in her manners; and, what is worfe
‘ than all, infufferably vain and info-
‘ lent on her new dignity, without one
‘ grain of true love or gratitude for the
‘ man who has raifed her to it.'

My gift of invifibility affifted me in
proving the truth of the above in all it's
parts. Farther I will not pretend to
fay; for though it is a vulgar adage,
that ‘ Where there is no modefty there
‘ is little fign of honefty,' and I have
heard fevere cenfures paffed upon her
virtue, yet I never could make any difcoveries to her prejudice on that fcore;
and am apt to believe that the rampant
airs fhe gives herfelf among the men,
are in reality, more owing to a fuddenly
than an amorous difpofition.

Montelion feems to fee her behaviour
in the fame light I do; yet, for the fake
of his own honour, cannot but wifh fhe
would act with more referve. They
had not been married above three
months, when he was feized with a fit
of the gout, which confined him to his
apartment. Ferocia came in, covered
over with jewels, and blazing like a
ftar; and, without expreffing any concern for his indifpofition, told him that
fhe was going to Lady Primwell's route;
on which enfued the following dialogue
between them—

*Montelion.* I flattered myfelf, Madam, with having the happinefs of your
company at home this evening, as I am
not in a condition to ftir out.

*Ferocia.* Oh heavens! I fhould make
the

the worft nurfe in the world! What good would my ftaying do you?

*Montelion.* A great deal, Madam; and I hope I need fay no more to engage you not to leave me.

*Ferocia.* Indeed, my lord, I muft go; I have given my promife.

*Montelion.* You will be eafily excufed. Nobody will expect a wife on a party of pleafure, when they know her hufband is confined by pain. Come, my dear, you muft not think that ftaying at home one night is an act of too much complaifance to a man who would refufe nothing for your fatisfaction.

In fpeaking this, he drew her gently towards him, and gave her two or three very tender kiffes; but, in doing fo, a little fnuff he had between his thumb and finger happened to fcatter on her glove; on which fhe ftarted from him, and returned his kind expreffions in thefe terms—

*Ferocia.* Pifh! How filly this is! You have fpoiled my gloves with your nafty fnuff. Here, John! William! run one of you to my dreffing-room, and bid Faddle bring me a pair of gloves in a minute.

*Montelion.* Don't put yourfelf into a paffion, my dear; but fit down, and refolve to oblige me. I'll call for cards, and we'll have a game at picquet.

She made no reply; but hung down her he·d, and ftood counting the fticks of her fan till Faddle came into the room.

*Ferocia.* Where are the gloves?

*Faddle.* Madam, I thought the fellow was miftaken, when he bid me bring gloves; as your ladyfhip had juft now a clean pair.

*Montelion.* Aye, Mrs. Faddle, there is no occafion. Rather get your lady's night-drefs ready; for fhe has changed her mind, and does not go abroad.

*Ferocia.* Indeed I both muft and will, my lord. Do you imagine, that becaufe you are fick, I muft mortify myfelf, and be mewed up with you till I am fick too? No, no; I am not weak enough to comply with fo unreafonable a requeft; therefore adieu. I fhall fierce fee you till late; and hope then to find your lordfhip better.

She waited not for any reply he might have made, but flounce! out of the room, followed by her woman. Montelion foon after heard the footman called to

attend her ladyfhip, and the chariot drive from the door. How would fome hufbands have refented fuch ufage! yet Montelion bore it, without any fhew of impatience, from one endowed with no charms to excite either love or refpect. His tamenefs, however, is not owing to any meannefs of fpirit in him, but rather to his good fenfe. He does not care to have his domeftick affairs become the talk of the town, nor to come to an open rupture with the woman he has made his wife; and having in vain effayed all the means that prudence and good-nature could fuggeft to bring her to a more reafonable way of thinking, he has at laft given over the attempt; feems not to regard whatever fhe does, but endeavours to lofe the thoughts of his private difquiets in the toils of publick bufinefs.

## CHAP. II.

RELATES A STRANGE INSTANCE OF BIGOTRY AND ENTHUSIASM IN A PARENT.

NOTHING is fo defirable as religion, nothing fo truly amiable as piety. What bleffings does it not diffufe to all who are within the reach of it's influence? From it all other virtues are derived, and by it alone we are enabled to act with vigour. Yet how often have we feen this heavenly quality perverted into it's very oppofite; and, from the fpirit of meeknefs, benevolence, mercy, charity, and univerfal love, become the fpirit of pride, contention, envy, hatred, and perfecution! Like the archangel, who ftanding neareft to the throne of glory, precipitated himfelf into the loweft hell.

Bigotry and fuperftition are the fureft engines which the fubtle enemy of mankind makes ufe of for our deftruction, All other crimes carry their ftings with them; confcience reproaches us for doing amifs, and we fall not again into the like without extreme remorfe and fhame: but the man poffeffed of this holy frenzy of the mind glories in his perfeverance, becaufe he looks upon it as the higheft virtue.

A gentleman, whom I fhall diftinguifh by the name of Flaminio, had attained to the age of fifty, without having been known to be guilty of any one

E 2　　　　thing

thing which could call in queftion either his honour, good-nature, or good fenfe. He had lived careffed by his friends, refpected by his acquaintance, and almoft adored by his tenants and dependants. He had one fon, and one daughter; and having loft his wife in bringing the latter into the world, he never ventured on a fecond, but laid out all his cares on the education of thefe two.

Adario, for fo I fhall call the fon, having finifhed his ftudies to the fatisfaction of all thofe who had the charge of inftructing him, in order to compleat the fine gentleman, was fent to make the tour of Europe, under the care of a difcreet and experienced governor. Ifabinda, the daughter, remained at home with her father; and being extremely beautiful, and miftrefs of every accomplifhment befitting her fex and rank, attracted the love and admiration of as many as had opportunity to be witnefs of her perfections.

Being fuch as I have defcribed it may eafily be fuppofed that, in a town like this, there were not few who declared themfelves her lovers. Lyfimor was among the number of thofe who had the leaft to fear, and the moft to hope for, in his addreffes to her. He had an agreeable perfon, was defcended of a good family, and was heir to an eftate adequate to his birth. He had been fellow-ftudent with Adario; and though, being fome years older, he had left the univerfity before him, they had always kept up a correfpondence. He was introduced to the acquaintance of the fifter by the intimacy he had with the brother; who failed not, before he went abroad, to recommend his friend's pretenfions to her in the ftrongeft terms.

He it was, indeed, who alone had the power of pleafing her. Her young heart prefently diftinguifhed him from all his rivals; but her modefty and difcretion would not permit her to give him any marks of a peculiar regard, till authorized to do fo by the perfon fhe had always been taught to confider as the fole difpofer of her fate.

Lyfimor, who had alfo been bred in the moft ftrict obedience, made not his court to Ifabinda without having firft communicated the paffion he had for her to his father, and received his approbation. The two old gentlemen had afterwards an interview on this occafion; and Flaminio, being perfectly fatisfied

with the propofals made by the other, readily gave his confent, on condition his daughter, whofe inclinations he faid he would never go about to force, fhould have no objection to the match.

The fame evening, as they were fitting together at fupper, Flaminio related to his daughter all that had paffed between him and the father of Lyfimor; and added, that he looked upon him as a very deferving young fellow; that his birth and fortune were unexceptionable; and that, if fhe had no averfion to his perfon, he fhould be heartily glad of an alliance with him.

Ifabinda blufhed like the fun juft peeping from a cloud, on hearing her father fpeak in this manner; and could fcarce recover herfelf from the glad furprize enough to tell him that, fince he was pleafed with fuch a union, fhe fhould be all obedience to his will. She faid no more; but the foft confufion fhe was in, and the joy which fhe could not reftrain from fparkling in her eyes, fufficiently teftified how much her inclinations correfponded with her duty. 'Well, 'then,' refumed he, 'from this time 'forward receive Lyfimor as the perfon 'by Heaven and me ordained to be 'your hufband.'

I leave it to my fair readers to conceive what delightful images muft fill the mind of Ifabinda, after this fanction to an affection which hitherto fhe had not dared to indulge, yet had it not in her power to fubdue. For my own part, though I was prefent during all the converfation fhe had with her father on this head, I left the houfe when fhe retired to her chamber; which fhe did more early than ordinary that night; I guefs, to have an opportunity of giving a loofe to the tranfports of her mind.

As for Lyfimor, the joy he felt on being acquainted with what his father had done for him, was very much allayed by the perfect ignorance he was in of having made any impreffion on the heart of his charming miftrefs. He went to vifit her the next day, hoping, yet trembling, for the event: but foon the lovely maid put an end to his fufpence, by affuring him, that for his fake alone fhe could refolve, without reluctance, on changing her condition.

Not only the lovers themfelves, but both their parents alfo, feemed equally impatient for the confummation of thefe nuptials. A fhort day was appointed for

for the celebration; the articles of settlement and jointure were drawing up; new habits, new coaches, new equipages, all necessary preparations were carrying on with the utmost expedition: when, lo! a sudden and unexpected storm bore down at once the pleasing prospect of their hopes; for ever dashed their expected joys, and spread a lasting scene of desolation and despair! How vainly, alas! do we depend on mortal happiness! The gaudy bubble fleets before us like the wind, eludes our grasp, and mocks the idle chace, as Sir Robert Howard justly expresses it—

> ' Short is th' uncertain reign and pomp of
>     ' mortal pride.
> ' New turns and changes ev'ry day
> ' Are of inconstant Chance the constant
>     ' arts.
> ' Soon she gives, soon takes away:
> ' She comes, embraces, nauseates you, and
>     ' parts.'

Flaminio, from being the most chearful, good-natured man, that could be of his age, became all at once transformed into the most sullen, gloomy, and discontented. From expressing the utmost eagerness for his daughter's wedding, he now appeared wholly negligent of every thing relating to it. When the father of Lysimor, and the lawyer employed to draw the marriage-writings, went to his house, he ordered his servants to say he was from home; made several tradesmen carry back the things he had bespoke for the solemnity; and, in fine, put an entire stop to all he had been so solicitous in forwarding.

The father of Lysimor began to think himself affronted by this proceeding, and both the lovers were amazed and troubled beyond description at it: but though the young gentleman came once or twice every day to visit his dear mistress, Flaminio so carefully avoided his presence, that he could get no opportunity of complaining to him; and Isabinda was too much terrified by the unusual austerity of his looks, to have the courage to open her lips to him on this score.

She was one afternoon alone in the fore-parlour, waiting the approach of Lysimor; when her father, who was in a back room, called her to him. She immediately obeyed; and, on her entrance, was accosted by him in this manner—

Flaminio. Well, Isabinda, I suppose you expect Lysimor here presently?

Isabinda. Yes, Sir. It is even the hour when he generally visits me.

Flaminio. His company may be spared at his time. I have something to say to you, and would not be interrupted. I have therefore given orders to the servants to tell him, when he comes, that you are gone abroad.

Isabinda. He will scarce believe that, because I promised to take a walk with him in the Mall after tea; but if you require my attendance, I will dismiss him the moment he comes.

Flaminio. No, it shall be as I have said. If you marry him, you will have opportunities enough to see each other; and if you do not, it will be best for you not to have settled your affections upon him.

Isabinda. Sir, I should never have entertained the least thoughts of marrying either him or any other man, without having first received your commands to do so.

Flaminio. However that may be, events we think most near are often the farthest from being accomplished; and, for that reason, a young maid ought never to dispose of her heart till it is accompanied by her hand.

Isabinda. I hope, Sir, that Lysimor has done nothing to forfeit the goodwill you once had for him.

Flaminio. No, no; I have nothing to say against the young gentleman: and should still approve of him for a son-in-law, but—

Isabinda. But what! I beseech you, Sir, keep me not on a rack more cruel than death!

Flaminio. I am sorry to see you so much concerned on his account; I hoped to have found you more indifferent: but, since your inclinations are so deeply engaged, wish from my soul there was a possibility for your union.

Isabinda. Ah, Sir, what prevents it!

Flaminio. A father's everlasting happiness or misery.

These words, the emphasis with which he uttered them, and the horror that appeared in his countenance, frighted the poor young lady almost into fits. She started trembled; and, not able to comprehend the meaning of what she heard, she

the most terrible ideas came into her mind; which made her rather dread than wish an explanation.

She stood pale as a ghost, and motionless a a statue; while her father, greatly agitated, walked backwards and forwards in the room with irregular and disordered steps. Both remained speechless for some time. At last—'I cannot as yet,' said he, ' bring myself to ' relieve the suspence I see you in; but ' will do it soon. Retire, therefore, my ' dear Isabinda, to your chamber,' continued he, with a deep sigh; ' and ' invoke the Almighty Dispenser of ' blessings to give you that composure ' of mind, which can alone enable you ' to support chearfully whatever fate ' he is pleased to ordain for you.'

She went to her chamber, as commanded; but whether to pray or weep, I will not pretend to inform my readers. I remained with Flaminio while he staid below, which was not long; then followed him up to his closet, where he shut himself in, plucking the door so hastily after him, I had not time to enter; but peeping through the key hole, I saw he had thrown himself prostrate on the floor, with his hands and eyes lifted up to heaven, seeming very earnest in devotion. I left him in this posture, and returned home, much surprized at what I had seen and heard.

Impatient, however, to get some farther light into an affair which at present appeared so mysterious to me, I went the next morning to Flaminio's house. I entered Isabinda's chamber with a servant who was carrying in a dish of chocolate. That unhappy lady was sitting leaning her elbow on a table, and her head upon her hand; her eyes red with the late-fallen tears, and all symptoms of despair and grief about her. But nothing being to be learnt here, I went in search of Flaminio, whom I found in his dressing-room. He was in a musing posture, but had a countenance much more serene than the day before. I had not been many minutes with him, before he rung his bell for a footman, whom he ordered to fetch Isabinda to him. She presently came; and I was witness of the following extraordinary dialogue—

*Flaminio.* Sit down, my child. I was to blame to leave you in the perplexity I did last night, but it was occasioned only by my too great tender-

ness. I could not easily resolve to tell you a thing which I feared would make you wish I had loved you less.

*Isabinda.* Sir, I have always looked upon your paternal affection to me as the greatest blessing of my life.

*Flaminio.* I believe you have; and I had never any cause to think you did not return that affection with an adequate proportion of filial love and duty.

*Isabinda.* I flatter myself, Sir, that no one of my actions has ever shewn the contrary.

*Flaminio.* None, indeed, my dearest child. I ought not, therefore, to have doubted of your ready compliance in a thing on which my soul's eternal peace depends. Tell me, my Isabinda, would you not willingly forego a trifling satisfaction to ensure your father's happiness both here and hereafter?

*Isabinda.* I should else, Sir, be unworthy of the goodness you have shewn me.

*Flaminio.* Well, then, my dearest Isabinda, I will no longer hesitate to make thee the confidante of a secret which hitherto has never escaped my own bosom. It is a story will very much surprize thee: but see thou mark me well, and be attentive to every particular.

*Isabinda.* You may be certain, Sir, I will be so.

*Flaminio.* Know, then, that going into the country to take possession of that estate which you have heard devolved on me by the death of my uncle, I fell into the acquaintance of a young lady in the neighbourhood, called Harriot. She was handsome. I had a heart entirely free; and I became, as I then thought, violently in love with her. But marriage being a thing of too serious a nature to be agreeable to my inclinations at that time, the addresses I made to her were extremely private. Such as they were, however, they succeeded but too well; and, on my promising to make her my wife, obtained all the gratification my passion could require.

Having finished the business which had brought me thither, I set out soon after on my return to London. Harriot took leave of me without much regret; being to follow in a few days with her father and the whole family, the winter season coming on. On her arrival, she sent me immediate notice; and I provided a

proper

proper place for our private interviews, which were not feldom, my amorous defires being yet unfatia.ed.

Perhaps her yo·th, beauty, and the extreme tendernefs fhe had for me, might have engaged me for a much longer time, had rot the charms of your dear mother rendered all thofe of the whole fex befides contemptible in my eyes. I adored her from the firft moment I beheld her. The flame fhe infpired me with was widely different from what I had ever felt before : marr age was no more a bughear to me; on the contrary, I languifhed ·o be linked in thofe bonds with a perfon of fuch diftinguifhed merit, and the means of attaining that felicity engroffed all my thoughts.

I now made a thoufand excufes to avoid meeting poor Harriot; and when her repeated folicitations drew me fometimes to her, my behaviour was fo cool, fo changed from what it was, that fhe could not but fee into the caufe; fhe grew jealous, inquifitive, and foon difcovered my honourable attachment.

Te rs, reproaches, and complaints, now furnifhed me with a pretence to quarrel. I told her I would fee her no more: and indeed fhe put it out of my power to break my word; for in three days after we had parted in this manner, fhe died; not without fome fufpicion of poifon, as I have heard it whifpered: but whether fhe had recourfe, in reality, to any fuch defperate method to rid her of a life fhe was grown weary of, or whether grief alone did the work of fate, I know not; but am too certain, however that might be, my ingratitude was the cruel caufe; though fhe was too generous ever to declare it; and not one of all her numerous kindred or acquaintance had the leaft intimation of the intercourfe between us.

The fhock I felt on the firft intelligence of this fad cataftrophe is inconceivable, and would doubtlefs have made a lafting impreffion on ne, if the progrefs I every day made in my courtfhip to the object of my virtuous affection, the gaining her confent to be mine, our marriage, and the hurry of pleafures attending that folemnity, had not too much taken up my heart to leave room for any other fenfations than thofe of joy and tranfport.

Events once obliterated from the mind by others of greater confequence to our happinefs, feldom or never recur

to it again. A long fucceffion of years paffed over without any remembrance of the unfortunate Harriot; and it is but very lately that the thoughts of her have begun to trouble my repofe.

But Heaven would not fuffer me to be always dead to a juft fenfibility of the crime I had been guilty of. Not many nights ago—whether fleeping or awake I cannot pret·nd to be pofitive— I faw, at leaft I thought I faw, that injured woman ftand by my bed-fide : I heard her, too, with a voice hollo v, yet fonorous as an echo, bid me repent, and atone for my paft tranfgreffion. 'How ' fhall I atone?' cried I. ' Devote to ' Heaven the deareft thing you have on ' earth,' replied the phantom, and in that inftant vanifhed from my fight.

It is not poffible for me to exprefs, much lefs for you to conceive, the horrors I fuftained after this amazing dream or apparition, I know not which to call it : but am fince convinced it was no other than my guardian angel, who, under the form of Harriot, inftructed me how to atone for my crim ; and fhould I neglect or difobey his admonition, it wou d more than double my tranfgreffion, and fink my foul down 'o the loweft hell. ' Devote to Heaven the deareft ' thing thou haft on earth,' the vifion faid. Now what have I on earth that is truly dear to me exc·pt your br the, and yourfelf? I have examined well my heart, and find that of the two you fit neareft there : it is you, therefore, my Ifabinda, that is ordained to be the facrifice; and, like faithful Abraham, I muft fubmit to lay my darling on the altar.

*Ifabinda.* Oh, Sir, you will not kill me!

*Flaminio.* Kill thee, my child! rather would I fuffer this flefh of mine to be torn with burning pincers, every limb diflocated, my breaft laid open, and my panting heart expofed to publick view, than hurt the fmalleft part of thy dear precious frame! No, I mean to prefent thee a living facrifice on the altar of piety; to confecrate the e to the fe vice of Heaven; and to make thee, while on ea th, a companion for the faints above. In fine, my Ifabinda, you muft be a nun.

*Ifabinda.* A nun! Oh heavens!

This poor young lady feemed no lefs terrified with the word Nun than fhe had been with that of Sacrifice: but all I can fay is, not all th. obedience Ifabinda had hitherto been practifed in, nor

**all**

all her father's authority, nor the arguments he urged, could either reconcile her to the way of life he enjoined, or oblige her to submit to it with any degree of will ngness; and her tears and entreaties being equally in vain to make him recede from the resolution he had taken, he dismiss'd her from his presence; telling her, in a very angry tone, that he had now done with persuasions, and should ake measures to bring her to her duty more becoming his character as a father.

## CHAP. III.

THE AUTHOR FINDS HIMSELF, THOUGH WITH AN INFINITE DEAL OF DIFFICULTY OBLIGED TO MAKE A DISCOVERY OF SOME PART OF THE UNHAPPY CONSE- QUENCES WHICH IMMEDIATELY ATTENDED THE CRUEL RESOLU- TION FLAMINIO HAD TAKEN IN REGARD TO HIS DAUGHTER.

I Had never yet attempted to see how Lysimor brooked the late delays that had been given to his intended nuptials, so now took it into my head to go. A servant, who was carrying out a wig-box, gave me an opportunity of slipping into the house. I found the old gentleman with a letter in his hand, which seemed to excite in him very great emotions; but as he had just finished the perusal as I entered the room, and was putting it into his pocket, I could not possibly know any thing of the contents. I was not, however, long unsatisfied. Lysimor was returned from a morning walk he had been taking, and entered a few moments after. He appeared in little better humour than his father; and, when he had paid the usual salutation, spoke in this manner—

*Lysimor.* Certainly, Sir, something very extraordinary must have happened to occasion this sudden change both in Flaminio and his daughter. I have been to enquire of her health this morning, after being disappointed of seeing her last night, and have a second time been denied access.

*Father.* I could have told you that, if I had known you had been there. I have just received a letter from Flaminio. See what the old coxcomb writes.

With these words he drew the letter

he had been reading from his pocket, and threw it on a table. Lysimor snatched it up with the greatest eagerness, and found the contents as follow—

‘ SIR,

‘ AN over-ruling fate deprives me of ‘ the honour of your alliance, ‘ and dispos s of my daughter in a dif- ‘ fe ent manner from what I once in- ‘ tended. I must therefore intreat your ‘ son will make no future visits at my ‘ house, nor take any steps to traverse ‘ those desig s which I am obliged to ‘ pursue in relation to Isabinda. As ‘ for yourself, Sir, I hope you'll impute ‘ this alteration in my conduct to what ‘ it really is, an unavoidable necessity; ‘ and not to want of respect in him, who ‘ in all things else would readily sub- ‘ scribe himself, Sir, your most obedient ‘ servant,

‘ FLAMINIO.’

Surprize and resentment now seemed to strive which should be most predo- minant in the countenance of Lysimor. He stamped, bit his lips, paused a while, then spoke.

*Lysimor.* This must be madness. No man in his senses could possibly act thus. What! after expressing the highest satisfaction in the intended union be- tween our families, after the warmest professions of respect to you, Sir, and of love to me, to affront both in so gross a manner, without the least cause given on our part; 'tis unaccountable, 'tis monstrous! But I cannot think Isa- binda shares in her father's phrenzy.

*Father.* Whatever she does, it be- hoves you not to think of her at all. Sooner would I have my family extinct, and my name perish to eternity, than have a branch of that stem grafted on a tree of mine; and I should be sorry to find you mean-spirited enough to retain a wish that way.

What reply Lysimor would have made I know not, for the old gentleman was called hastily out of the parlour to one who waited for him in another room. Lysimor, when alone, fell into a deep musing, in which he sighed and frowned alternately, and seemed divided between love and resentment. But whatever his thoughts were, he had no opportunity of indulging them. A servant presented him with a letter, which he said was brought

brought by a porter, who defired it might be given into his own hands, and waited for an anfwer. Lyfimor no fooner faw the characters on the fuperfcription, than the late palenefs in his cheeks was converted into the moft lively red. He broke the feal with trembling impatience, and found it contained thefe lines—

' DEAR SIR,

' MY father, in an unaccountable caprice, tears me from your arms, ' and is refolute to make me a nun, or ' rather a martyr of me. Prayers and ' tears are ineffectual to move him from ' his purpofe; I have tried both in vain; ' and it is by flight alone I can avoid a ' fate more dreadful to me than all I ' can fuffer by abandoning his protec-' t'on. If you have compaffion, I muft ' not now fay love, affift me in my ' efcape. I have made no intimacies, ' have no confidents on whom I dare ' rely in this d ftracting exigence, and ' there remain no four and twenty hours ' between me and the impoffibility of ' averting the doom that threatens me. ' I am at prefe t a clofe prifoner in my ' chamb r; and to morrow, early in the ' morning, am to take coach for Do-' ver, thence to embark for Dunkirk, ' under the care of a perfon whofe vi-' gilance I cannot hope to elude, and ' who is not to quit my fight one ' moment, till I am, beyond redemp-' tion, lodged within the walls of a con-' vent. A girl lately taken into the ' houfe, pitying my diftrefs, has pro-' mifed to get this conveyed to you, and ' alfo to greafe the hinges of the ftreet-' door, that I may go out with lefs ' noife when the family are all in bed, ' which I believe will be pretty early, as ' my father is too much out of humour ' to fee any company. If you will take ' upon you the trouble to wait for me ' at the end of our ftreet, next the ' fquare, between the hours of twelve ' and one, and conduct me to fome place ' where I may be fecreted till the fearch ' which doubtlefs will be made after me ' is over, I fhall endeavour to earn a ' fubfiftence by fuch ways as I am ca-' pable of, and fortune fhall prefent. ' If you ever truly loved me, you will ' not think this requeft too prefuming, ' but rather be forry for the fad acci-' dent that compels me to make it. I ' beg a line, in anfwer to this, may in-

' form me what I have to depend upon ' from your good nature, and what ' hope remains for the forlorn and moft ' wretched

' ISABINDA.'

The lover appeared extremely touched with this melancholy epiftle; and when he had finifhed, threw his arms acrofs his breaft, and cried out—' Poor Ifa-' binda! What dæmon has taken pof-' feffion of her father's brain!—B t I ' fhould be even yet more cruel to refufe ' the affiftance fhe im lores. No, love, ' honour, and generofity, forbid it! ' Whatever fhall be the confequence, I ' muft, I will defend her from the fate ' fhe dreads.' He then called his footman, and bid him order the perfon who brought this letter to wait for an anfwer at fome diftance from the houfe, left his father fhould happen to fee him, and be inquifitive from whom, and on what bufinefs he came. Having given thefe inftructions, he ran haftily into his chamber, where I followed, and faw him fit down to his bureau, and write in thefe terms—

' TO ISABINDA.

' MY FOR EVER DEAR ISABINDA,

' WHATEVER are my fufferings ' in this unexpected turn of our ' affairs, I cannot be wholly unhappy ' while I know you have had no part in ' the inflicting them. Why do you un-' kindly make that a requeft, which you ' ought to be convinced you might ' command from my affection? I have ' devoted myfelf entirely to your fer-' vice; and no change of circum-' ftances can ever make me withdraw a ' heart attracted by fo much beauty, and ' confirmed in it's choice by fo much ' merit. Yes, my charming Ifabinda, ' I am unalterably yours; and you may ' depend upon my love and honour for ' every thing you either do, or fhall ' hereafter ftand in need of. I fhall ' employ this day in procuring a proper ' place for your reception; and fha I an-' ticipate the hours you mention to ' watch for your enlargement, which I ' pray Heaven to facilitate, and bring ' you fafe to the arms of, my dear Ifa-' binda, your faithful and moft con-' ftant

' LYSIMOR.'

F He

He had but juſt diſpatched this, when his father came into the room; and, with a voice and air vaſtly different from what he had a few minutes before aſſumed, ſpoke to him in theſe terms—

*Father.* I believe, ſon, I nave interrupted your dreſſing: but no matter; I bring you news to conſole you for the loſs of your late miſtreſs. My old friend, Mr. Countwell, the banker, has been with me. His fair charge, Emilia, comes to town next week; and he has offered, for a ſmall premium, to make up a match between you. He aſſures me ſhe is a m ſt lovely young creature, is entirely independent of any one, and has twenty thouſand pounds in her pocket, which is more than double the fortune you would have had with the daughter of that fool Flaminio.

*Lyſimor.* I am greatly indebted to your goodneſs, Sir, and to the conſideration Mr. Countwell has of me; but, Sir, you know I have long loved Iſabinda, and you muſt give my heart ſome time to wean itſelf from it's former attachment.

*Father.* Pſhaw! one woman, like one nail, will drive out the thoughts of another. Your heart muſt be ſtrangely ſtupified, if it does not dance to the muſick of twenty thouſand pounds. Remember, ſon, the eſtate you are to enjoy at my deceaſe does not amount to quite ſixteen hundred pounds per annum; and that I have been obliged to mortgage ſome part of it, to diſcharge the debts your extravagant elder brother contracted before he died. Emilia's fortune will retrieve all. Well, the breaking off your match with Iſabinda is the moſt lucky thing that could have happened.

*Lyſimor.* But, Sir, we cannot be ſure the young lady will approve my ſuit.

*Father.* Mr. Countwell will manage that. He is a ſhrewd man, he knows what he does, and will undertake nothing without performing it. You have only to ſay a few fine things to Emilia, which you know well enough how to do, when once you get Iſabinda out of your head.

*Lyſimor.* Sir, I ſhall uſe my beſt endeavours to obey you in every thing.

*Father.* That is well ſaid. I want no obedience but what is for your own intereſt, and will leave you to reflect how many charms there are in twenty thouſand pounds, and then you will fall in love with the fortune, whether ever you do ſo with the lady or not.

This converſation being ended, I recollected that I had ſome affairs of my own to diſpatch, and began to think of retiring, but was prevented by Lyſimor; who walking in a continued and very haſty motion about the room, obliged me to keep cloſe in the corner where I had placed myſelf, and not venture to ſtir, leſt he ſhould ruſh againſt me. At firſt I was a little vexed at this confinement, but afterwards rejoiced heartily at it, as it gave me an opportunity of making a diſcovery, which otherwiſe, perhaps, I ſhould have found much more difficult to attain.

Lyſimor, after ruminating for a conſiderable time, rung the bell for his footman; who, on his entrance, received for his firſt command to ſhut the door: that done, he made no ſcruple to inform the fellow, who I ſoon found was in all his ſecrets, of the concern he was in for Iſabinda; the promiſe he had given of taking her under his protection; and the vexation he was in to find a proper lodging for her, ſo that his father might not ſuſpect he had any hand in her eſcape, nor her own be able to diſcover where ſhe was concealed.

To this the man, after a pretty long pauſe, replied, that he had a ſiſter who was a widow, and lived in a very remote and obſcure part of the town; that her houſe was clean, though ſmall; that her family conſiſted only of herſelf, an infant ſucking at her breaſt, and a country girl who did the buſineſs of a ſervant: and added, that if the lady could content herſelf with ſo mean an abode, he was certain ſhe might remain there concealed as long as ſhe ſhould think fit.

Lyſimor ſeemed overjoyed at this propoſal, and bid him go directly to his ſiſter, apprize her of the affair as far as it was neceſſary, and give her a ſtrict charge to prepare every thing in as decent a manner as ſhe could for the reception of her fair gueſt. The fellow went to execute his commiſſion, and I ſlid ſoftly round the room till I got to the door, and followed him, but not to the place where he was going; for having already found, by the diſcourſe he had with his maſter, the name and ſituation of the ſtreet, I had no buſineſs to take ſo long a walk, till ſomething more material excited my curioſity.

Lyſimor himſelf, however, was not
more

more punctual to the time appointed by Isabinda, than I was to know the issue of this adventure. It wanted some minutes of twelve when I arrived at the corner of the square, and had but just posted myself under a lamp, when I saw Lysimor come muffled up in his cloak, and attended by his servant. We had not waited above a quarter of an hour, before we saw Isabinda steal out of her father s house. with a bundle under her arm almost as big as herself. Lysimor, perceiving how she was loaded, made his man hasten to ease her of it; after which she rather flew than ran into the arms of her deliverer, for so she called him; adding—' Oh, can you pardon the trouble ' I have given you!' To which he replied—' Call not that a trouble which ' I shall always look upon as the greatest ' happiness of my life.' I could hear distinctly little more of what they said to each other, the footman being between us. They walked very fast through the square, and down a street which turned from it, where a hackney-coach waited to receive 'hem; and, as soon as they were entered, drove away with all imaginable speed. I had neither the will nor the power to pursue them, so returned home, to reflect at leisure on the passages I had been witness of.

## CHAP. IV.

CONTAINS SOME MORE INTEREST-
ING PARTICULARS OF THIS AD-
VENTURE; AND SHEWS THAT
PEOPLE, BY FLYING FROM ONE
THING WHICH THEY THINK
WOULD BE A MISFORTUNE, OF-
TEN RUN INTO OTHERS OF A NA-
TURE MORE TO BE DREADED.

MUCH as I had condemned Flaminio for his bigotted superstition, I could not wholly absolve Isabinda for the step she had taken. I wondered not that she was fearful of being forced into a state of life which few ladies of her years would chuse, but I wondered that she was not also fearful of putting herself into the power of a man who loved her, and whom she passionately loved. She must certainly either not have considered the dangers to which she might be exposed, or have depended too much on the strength of her own virtue. Besides, she could not

be so ignorant as not to know that no woman can be made a nun, any more than she can be made a wife, against her will; and a less share of courage than she shewed in this midnight elopement, would have enabled her, on her entrance within the walls of the convent, to declare she had neither call nor inclination to receive the veil; on which neither the abbess, nor the bishop of the diocese, could have consented to her admission into holy orders. It is true, that her father might have confined her there a pensioner as long as he thought fit; but as this would not have answered his end in devoting her to the service of the church, by way of propitiation for his offences, there is no doubt to be made but that he would shortly have recalled her home; and perhaps, too, been convinced of his folly in attempting a thing so absurd in itself, as well as cruel to his daughter.

I am sensible, that many of my fair young readers will be apt to quarrel with me for my animadversions on Isabinda's conduct in this point, and cry out, if they were in her place they would do the same. It is very likely, indeed, that they would do so; and full as likely that they would meet with something to make them heartily repent of their inadvertency. There are others again, who will say, that they can have no compassion for whatever misfortunes may befal a girl who thus rashly throws herself under the protection of a man not akin to her : but I believe the number of those who are so hard-hearted will be very few; except some professed prudes, who exclaim violently against the least misconduct in publick, yet make no scruple of giving themselves the greatest loose in private.

But to return to the melancholy detail I am now upon. Having little to do with my time the next morning, I went to the house where I knew Isabinda was placed for shelter from her father's power. I gained an easy access, the door being open, as is generally the custom in mean houses. On my going up stairs, I found the unhappy beauty sitting in a very pensive posture, leaning her head against the corner of a cupboard, which I suppose served her for a larder; for I saw a small slice of butter and the remains of a halfpenny roll lying. Frequent sighs issued from her breast, and some tears fell. Strange indeed would it have been, if a young lady, bred up in all the delicacies of life, could have worn a chearful countenance in such a change of situation; though, as the fellow had told his master, the room, and all the furniture it contained, was extremely clean, and shewed the housewifery of the owner, yet nothing could have more the face of poverty.

She seemed buried, as it were, in a profound contemplation; when the sound of somebody coming up the stairs made her raise her head a little, probably guessing from whom it proceeded. Lysimor presently appeared; and on sight of him, a dawn of joy oversspread her face. He ran to her, embraced her, and said the most tender things, intermixed with some expressions of concern, that the necessity of her being concealed left him not the power of providing a place for her more suitable to her merit and his affection. She could not now restrain her tears from flowing, which occasioned the following discourse.

*Isabinda.* Ah, Lysimor, I beg you will not talk to me in this manner; but rather use all your rhetorick to assist my weak endeavours to suit my humour to my condition! To be easy, I must forget what I have been, and wish to be no more than what I am.

*Lysimor.* You never can be other than the most charming and most worthy of your sex.

*Isabinda.* Alas! I have no longer any pretence to compliments like these: I have now, as the poet says,—

‘ No name, no family to call my own;
‘ But am an outcast, and a vagabond.’

As such I must hereafter live: and, that I may lose all remembrance of my former state, I have brought away my jewels and best apparel, for no other end than to dispose of them, and purchase others more conformable to my future circumstances.

*Lysimor.* Torture not thus a heart to which you are dearer than the vital blood that gives it motion! Can you believe I would suffer you to part with any of those appendages to your birth and rank? No, I would rather add to them. Do you not know that my whole fortune is at your devotion?

*Isabinda.* I must not, Sir, accept it.

*Lysimor.* Why not accept? too scrupulous Isabinda! But if you are above receiving the tribute of a lover, command whatever you may have occasion for on the score of a brother. My dear Alasio, I know, will readily discharge the obligation.

*Isabinda.* I am sure he will; and on that condition, if Providence presents no other way for my support, will not refuse your generous offer.

*Lysimor.* Think then no more of submitting to any thing unworthy of your character. I flatter myself our misfortunes are not of long continuance; that your father will repent him of his cruel resolution, and mine forget the affront offered to his family, and we may yet be happy.

*Isabinda.* I dare not entertain a hope so distant.

*Lysimor.* You know not how prophetick my passion may prove. In the mean time, I should be glad, methinks, to be made acquainted with the motive that has caused this sudden revolution in our fate.

*Isabinda.* Though I am loth to expose the secrets, I might say the follies, of a father, yet I cannot refuse you.

Perceiving now that she was preparing herself to make a detail of those particulars I had heard before, and in a preceding chapter have communicated to the reader, I would not stay to hear a second repetition, but came away, and left the lovers together for that time. From thence I went to the house of Flaminio; where I found, as I expected, every thing in distraction: messengers running backwards and forwards; some returning from their fruitless search of Isabinda, others going to places where they had not before been sent; and the old gentleman himself so overcome with rage and grief, that he was scarce capable of giving the necessary orders for what he most desired.

Some other adventures, which I shall hereafter publish, then falling in my way, I had no leisure to make a second visit to Isabinda for the space of near three weeks. But how shall I express my concern for that unfortunate young lady, when, on my going thither, I found her in the manner I did, and that all the apprehensions I had been in on her account had but too solid a foundation! When wild desire presides over the heart of man, what is his boasted honour? what

what his virtue? what his regard for the happiness and reputation of the wo man he pretends to love?—all shadowy nothings, vain ideas, which, I ke the Sybil's words wrote on the leaves of trees, are blown off and scattered through the air with every gust of passion. But to proceed.

No obstruction being in my way, I passed directly up to Isabinda's chamber; but finding the door fast locked, began to imagine she was ei her removed, or had ventured out to take the air; and was going down again, when I was prevented by the murmuring sound of persons talking within. I then put my ear close to the key-hole, and easily knew the voices to be those of Lysimor and Isabinda; on which I resolved to wait till the door should be opened, and in about three or four minutes after the woman of the house came up with two dishes of chocolate and some biscuits on a plate. She had the key in her pocket, and immediately g ve entrance to me as well as herself. It was now more than past mid-day, yet Isabinda had not left her bed. Lysimor was sitting on the side of it, as lately risen; having both his feet on a chair, without either shoes or slippers. I was a little surprized at seeing h m in this posture; till the chocolate being served, he said to the woman—

*Lysimor.* Has Jeffery prepared my boots as I directed last night?

*Woman.* Yes, an please your ho. nour. He has so besplashed them, and made the horses heels so dirty, that one would swear they had come a journey of twenty miles this morning.

*Lysimor.* That's right. It would have been ridiculous, after telling my father that I was gone a hunting, to have come home as clean as out of a lady's bedchamber. But go, and bid Jeffery bring the boots.

Lysimor spoke this with a very gay air, but Isabinda hung down her head; and, on the fellow's coming in, hid her face behind the curtain, nor uttered a syllable while he was in the room, which was no longer than to equip his master for departure. Lysimor was no sooner ready, and his servant withdrawn, than he approached the bed, and began to take his leave of Isabinda, with a very tender embrace, accompanied with some soft words. She made no other reply, for a considerable time, than returning

his caresses; but at last broke out into these expressions—

*Isabinda.* Ah, Lysimor, should you forget your vows, despise the conquest you have gained, and leave me to lament my easy faith, how miserable, how abandoned beyond the power of words to express, would be the condition of your Isabinda!

*Lysimor.* Unkind and causeless apprehension! My dearest love, let not the thoughts of such impossibilities disturb you. Could I be ungrateful, after being made happy in this proof of your affection, I must be lost to all sense of honour, unworthy of the name of man, and even to breathe vital air.

*Isabinda.* Well, then, I must, I will believe you; nor repent what I have done. But tell me, when will you come again?

*Lysimor.* To-morrow, if I can; if not, you may depend on seeing me next day. Be assured, that every hour will seem an age to me till I see you. Farewell, thou softest loveliest of thy sex!

He went; but, as I then fancied, with more the air of triumph than of real tenderness or respect in his deportment. Isabinda then called for the woman of the house to assist her in rising; and I left the place, with a heart full of forebodings for her future fate: indeed I truly pitied the ruined maid; and wished she never might have occasion to cry out, with Monimia in the tragedy—

'————How often has he sworn
' Nature should change, the sun and stars
   ' grow dark,
' Ere he would falsify his vows to me?
' Make haste confusion, then—sun, lose thy
   ' light,
' And stars drop down with sorrow to the
   ' earth,
' For he is false—
' False as the winds, the water, or the
   ' weather;
' Cruel as tigers o'er their trembling prey!
' I feel him in my breast! he tears my
   ' heart!
' And at each sigh he drinks the gushing
   ' blood!'

My curiosity having received this painful satisfaction, I imagined not that any farther discoveries, at least that would be material enough to compensate for the trouble I should take, could be made in relation to these lovers; and therefore thought of returning no more, either to
the

the apartment of Isabinda, or to the house of Lysimor. I should, indeed, have endeavoured to lose all memory of this unhappy transaction, if the talk of the town had not continually reminded me of it. Every one was full of Isabinda's flight. Few, if any, besides myself, were acquainted with the motive of it; and none knew to what place she was retired: and the perfect ignorance people were in on both these scores, occasioned various conjectures, and rendered the wonder much more lasting than otherwise it would have been.

But this was not all. Flaminio, pierced through with grief and indignation on not being able to find his daughter, and perhaps, too, with some mixture of remorse for the cause he had given her to leave him, fell into a violent fever, of which he died, after languishing some days. By his last testament he bequeathed to his daughter, if ever she should be found, the sum of three thousand pounds; in order, as he caused it to be expressed in the writing, to keep her above the contempt of the world; and likewise, for the smallness of the portion, to keep her in perpetual remembrance of the false step she had taken.

Soon after this, I received certain intelligence, that Lysimor was making his publick addresses to a fine young lady with a very large fortune. I doubted not but this was that same Emilia whom I had heard his father so strongly recommend, and was fired with the utmost impatience to see how poor Isabinda would behave on both these events. Accordingly, I went once more to the house where she had been concealed; but, to my great disappointment, found she was gone from thence; nor could all my search, joined with the assistance of my Invisible Belt, enable me, for some time, to discover to what part of the town or country she was removed.

## CHAP.. V.

COMPLEATS THE CATASTROPHE OF THIS TRULY TRAGICAL ADVENTURE.

ADARIO had proceeded on his travels no farther than Paris, when the account of his father's death obliged

him to return to England with all possible expedition. Soon after his coming, I made an unseen visit at his house, where I found him, not like most young heirs, exulting in being the entire master of himself and fortune, and contriving in what kind of luxuries he should dispose of both, but full of the most sincere and unaffected sorrow. He was, indeed, one of those few sons who look on the possession of an estate as no equivalent for the loss of a good parent, such as Flaminio ever had been to both his children, till that fatal caprice, which drove his daughter from his protection, had brought on her undoing, his own death, and was the source of other calamities of a yet more dreadful nature, as will presently appear.

The story of Isabinda's elopement, and the uncertainty what fate had since attended her, was a matter of great affliction to this young gentleman. He loved his sister with a very tender affection, and had hoped to have seen her, by this time, married to Lysimor: but as his esteem for that friend was no way lessened by the match being broke off; and besides, expecting to be better informed by him of the particulars of that affair, than he could be by any other person, he was impatient to see him, and I found had sent him that morning notice of his arrival; for a letter, in answer to his message, was delivered to him while I was there, the contents whereof were these—

' TO ADARIO.

' SIR,

' I Congratulate you on your safe return to England, and should gladly have paid my compliments to you in person, if that honour had not been prohibited by an authority which I must not presume to contend with. My father, resenting the affront given by yours, which you cannot but have been informed of, has forbid me, under the penalty of his eternal displeasure, to converse with any of your family. He was at home when your servant came, and heard the message you sent delivered to me; on which he repeated his former injunction, and exacted a solemn oath of my obedience to it. You will therefore pardon my not waiting on you, and believe, that
' the

'the difcontinuance of our acquaintance
'will always be extremely regretted by
'him who is, with all due refpect, Sir,
'your moft obedient fervant,

'LYSIMOR.'

'Alas!' cried Adario, throwing the
letter from him as foon as he had read
it, 'how cold, how diftant, is the air of
'this letter! how different from thofe I
'have been accuftomed to receive from
'Lyfimor! I find that, by one un-
'lucky accident, I have at once loft a fa-
'ther, a fifter, and a friend.'
I thought I had now entirely done
with this family; for, as Ifabinda was
not to be found, I expected nothing of
confequence could be learned either at
the houfe of Lyfimor or Adario, fo intended to make no more vifits to thofe
gentlemen. Chance, however, about
five months afterwards, changed my
refolution, and threw fomething in my
way which no diligence of my own could
ever have attained. As I was going
one morning on my invifible progreffion,
I happened to pafs by the houfe of Adario. He was at the door, and about to
ftep into a hackney-coach which waited
for him; when a fellow, who had the
appearance of a groom, came running
towards him, almoft breathlefs with the
hafte he had made, and cried out—'Oh,
'Sir, I have joyful news for you! I
'beg your honour will turn back to
'hear it.' Thefe words revived my
former curiofity; and finding Adario
complied with his fervant's requeft, I
followed them into the parlour, and was
witnefs of the enfuing difcourfe.
. *Groom.* Oh, Sir, I have feen my
young lady!
*Adario.* What young lady? Not
my fifter!
*Groom.* Yes, indeed, Sir! As I
was going to fetch the horfe your honour fent me for, I faw Madam Ifabinda looking through the window of a
houfe at the corner of a little lane juft
by Iflington.
*Adario.*. Are you fure it was fhe?
*Groom.* As fure as I am alive, Sir!
Though, poor lady, fhe is very much
altered; very thin, and pale.
*Adario.* I fancy you are miftaken.
If my fifter were fo near London, fhe
would certainly either have fent or come,
to claim the legacy left her by my father, which I fuppofe fhe has need enough

of by this time. I am refolved to be convinced, notwithstanding. Do you think
fhe lodges there?
*Groom.* Yes, Sir; for fhe was all
undreffed, and looked as if fhe was juft
out of bed.
*Adario.* And can you know the
houfe again?
*Groom.* O yes, Sir; I took particular notice of it.
*Adario.* Well, then, I will only fend
an excufe to the gentleman I was to
meet this morning, and go directly.
You fhall get upon the coach-box, and
order the fellow where to drive; but let
him ftop fhort of the houfe, that my
fifter, if it be fhe, may not be apprized
of my coming before fhe fees me.
While Adario was calling one of his
footmen to fend on the meffage he had
mentioned, I ran to the end of the ftreet,
went into a narrow dark paffage, and
plucked off my Belt; then having recovered the appearance of what I am, a
real fubftance, I popped into an empty
coach that had juft fet down a fare, and
bid the driver to follow wherever that
went which was ftanding at Adario's
door. Both the coaches drove with fuch
fpeed, that we foon reached the end of
our little journey. I quitted my vehicle the moment I faw the other preparing to ftop; but though I made all
imaginable hafte to put on my Belt, I
could fcarce have regained my invifibility time enough to have entered with
Adario, if he had not met with an ob-
ftruction in his paffage from the woman
of the houfe, who at firft denied fhe had
any lady lodged with her; then faid, fhe
had none of the name he enquired for:
on which he replied with fome heat, that
the lady might have reafons for concealing her real name. 'But tell her,'
cried he, 'that mine is Adario; that I
'am her brother, and muft needs fee
'her.' On this fhe feemed fomewhat
more compliable, and faid fhe would go
and acquaint the lady. Accordingly
fhe went up ftairs; but Adario was too
impatient to wait her return, and followed her directly: I was but one ftep
behind him; and we were both in the
room before fhe could deliver any part
of her meffage.
Ifabinda was adjufting fomething about
her drefs before a looking-glafs; but happening to turn her head juft as Adario
was within the door, fhrieked out—'Oh
'heavens, my brother!' and with thefe
words

words fell back in her chair. The woman went to fetch fome water. Adario ran to fupport the fainting fair; but
happening to caft his eyes upon the table, faw a letter lying there, the fuperfcription of which was in Ifabinda's
hand, and addreffed to Lyfimor. Emotions more ftrong than pity, at this time,
made him quit his' fifter to examine the
c' tents of this furprizing billet, which
were thefe—

‘ MY DEAR, DEAR LYSIMOR!

‘ FOR fuch you are, and ever muft
‘ be, to my fond floating heart;
‘ though I have too much caufe to fear
‘ the tender epithet is now no longer
‘ pleafing to you. Ah, Lyfimor, how
‘ fad is the reverfe of my condition!
‘ From feeing you twice or thrice every
‘ week, I now fee you not once a month;
‘ and even then how cold is your be-
‘ haviour! how fhort your vifits! How
‘ cruel is this to one who neither can,
‘ nor wifhes, to enjoy any converfation
‘ but yours! For pity's fake, if not
‘ for love, render my life more eafy, at
‘ leaft for the prefent, whatever you do
‘ hereafter. The infant I carry within
‘ me fympathizes in it's mother's an-
‘ guifh, and continually upbraids you
‘ with convulfive heavings. Even if
‘ your vows of everlafting conftancy
‘ fhould be forgot, let fome confider-
‘ ation of the unborn innocent, the
‘ pledge of our once mutual loves,
‘ oblige you to treat with lefs indif-
‘ ference it's unhappy mother,

        ‘ The ruined ISABINDA.

‘ P. S. I can no longer bear your
‘ abfence, elfe would not have
‘ troubled you with this com-
‘ plaint.’

What a letter was this to fall into a
brother's hands! Never did I fee a man
in fuch diftraction. ‘ Villain! villain
‘ Lyfimor!—Wretched Ifabinda!' cried
he out. Then turning towards her—
‘ But there needed not this proof in thy
‘ own hand,' added he; ‘ thy fhame is
‘ but too vifible.' Ifabinda, who by
the affiftance of the woman was now recovered from her fwoon, but not enough
to hear what her brother faid, threw
herfelf at his feet, and, with ftreaming
eyes, addreffed him in thefe terms—

Ifabinda. Oh, Sir! can you forgive
my concealing myfelf from you ?
Adario. Would to God that there
were equal reafon to forgive the caufe !
Ifabinda at this inftant turning up her
eyes, beheld her letter in his hand, and
cried out, with the greateft vehemence—
‘ I am now undone, indeed! irrecovera-
‘ bly loft to all hope of pardon or pity!
‘ —my fhame expofed to him from
‘ whom, of all the world, it fhould have
‘ been moft hid!'
Adario. Rife, fifter, and ceafe thefe
unavailing exclamations. Your fhame
will receive no addition by my knowledge of it; rather, perhaps, be reme-
died. But tell, and tell me truly, has
Lyfimor ever promifed marriage to
you?
Ifabinda. A thoufand and a thoufand times, and bound himfelf to the
performance by the moft folemn imprecations.
Adario. Then he is doubly a villain!
and, if you believe him, you are doubly
deceived. He courts another woman.
Ifabinda. Indeed, of late, I have fufpected this, and often accufed him of it,
and he as often has forfworn it.
Adario. Mere words of courfe! But
fay, have you no teftimony, under his
own hand, of the promife he made you,
either by letter or by formal obligation?
Ifabinda. None, none, alas!
On this Adario bit his lips, walked
two or three times about the room, then
paufed, and feemed as if debating within
himfelf in what manner he fhould behave: at laft fat down; and taking the
ftill weeping Ifabinda by the hand, endeavoured to affuage her grief.
Adario. Come, Ifabinda, dry your
tears. Love and credulity have feduced
your innocence. Great has been your
fault; but yet I cannot forget you are
my fifter, and that you have no friend
but me on whom you can depend for
confolation. What is paft cannot be
recalled, but it may be redreffed. Be
affured you fhall one way or other have
juftice.
Ifabinda. Ah, Sir, I befeech you
proceed not to extremities! If by my
crime you fhould be involved in any
danger or perplexities, it would fink
me quite.
Adario. I hope there will be no occafion. Lyfimor was once a man of honour, and may yet return to his firft
principles.

principles. On this you may rely, that I shall do nothing rashly, nor inconsistent with your interest and reputation.

After this, they fell into some discourse concerning the strange resolution Flaminio had taken of sending her to a monastery; the particulars of which the reader being already acquainted with, I shall pass over in silence. When Adario took his leave, he did it with a great deal of affection: but I was much divided in my thoughts, whether I should stay with Isabinda, or follow Adario home; the latter seemed most flattering to my curiosity, as, by many tokens, I perceived he had something in his head which he was impatient to put in execution. I was not deceived in my conjectures: Adario was no sooner in his own house, than he flew to his bureau; and, without taking any time for deliberation, wrote this epistle to Lysimor—

' SIR,

' CONSCIOUS guilt, without those
' commands you seem so zealous
' in observing, might well make you
' avoid the presence of a person you
' have so greatly injured. When I re-
' commended you to my sister, it was in
' order to become her protector, not her
' undoer. How cruelly you have abused
' this confidence, let your own heart re-
' mind you! But I have some hope,
' how much soever appearances at pre-
' sent are to the contrary, you still in-
' tend to do justice to your promises to
' Isabinda, and the claim she has to
' your affection. I need not tell you,
' that you can repair the misfortune you
' have brought upon her no otherwise
' than by an honourable marriage: I
' am ready to fulfil the agreement made
' between our fathers on that score,
' and give my sister the sum of eight
' thousand pounds, as was then stipu-
' lated. If you comply with this pro-
' posal, I shall be glad to see you at her
' lodgings, there to settle every thing:
' if not, shall expect you will meet me
' in another place; and give me the sa-
' tisfaction which every gentleman has
' a right to demand when he finds him-
' self ill used. I attend your determi-
' nation; and am, &c.

' ADARIO.'

He sent this by one of his servants, with a charge to give it into Lysimor's own

hands, and wait his answer. After which, being told dinner was ready, he went down, and placed himself at the table, though I believe with very little appetite; for his countenance had upon it all the marks of the greatest inward disturbance, which was not at all lessened when his man returned with this from Lysimor—

' SIR,

' SINCE I find you are so well ac-
' quainted with a secret which,
' for the lady's sake, I could wish had
' been inviolably kept, I think my-
' self obliged to deal sincerely with you
' on the occasion. You may be af-
' sured I can behave to no woman,
' much less your sister, otherwise than
' becomes a man of honour: but mar-
' riage is a thing quite out of the ques-
' tion, as I am certain my father never
' would consent to it. If any promises
' on that account ever escaped my lips,
' I remember nothing of them, and
' could make them with no other view
' than to give her modesty an excuse for
' yielding. I am sorry, however, for
' what has happened: but you cannot
' be insensible of the frailties of flesh
' and blood; and must know, as well
' as I, that when two young people,
' who like each other, are much alone
' together, such accidents will natu-
' rally occur. The resentment you
' threaten, on my non-compliance with
' your proposal, appears therefore to me
' a little unreasonable; I shall, notwith-
' standing, be ready to give you the
' satisfaction you desire, at any time or
' place you shall appoint. Yours, &c.
' LYSIMOR.'

All the blood now seemed to have forsook the heart of Adario to rush into his face: his lips trembled, his very eyeballs started with excess of passion. He hesitated not a moment what he should do; but, in this tempest of his mind, wrote as follows to Lysimor—

' SIR,

' I Want words to return the insolence
' and ingratitude of your reply;
' but have a sword at your service,
' which I expect you will try the metal
' of to-morrow morning about seven,
' in the field behind Montague House.
' As the dispute between us will ad-
' mit

G

‘ mit of no witneſſes, pray come
‘ alone to

‘ ADARIO.’

Though I knew my own dinner
waited for me, I could not prevail on
myſelf to go home, till Adario had diſpatched this billet to Lyſimor, and the
ſervant who carried it was come back
from that gentleman with a ſmall ſlip of
paper tied up, containing only theſe
words—

‘ SIR,

‘ YOU may depend that I ſhall not
‘   fail to meet you as deſired.

‘ LYSIMOR.’

I now quitted the houſe of Adario;
but, after having related the pains I
had already taken, I believe nobody will
ſuppoſe I negiected going the next
morning to the field, to ſee the iſſue of
this combat. I found Adario was there
firſt; but though he waited only a very
few minutes for Lyſimor, his impatience made him not forbear ſaluting
him in this manner.

*Adario.* I began to think, Lyſimor,
that the ſhame of having done a baſe
action would not ſuffer you to defend
it.

*Lyſimor.* Sir, whatever I dare do, I
always dare defend.

*Adario.* Then, Sir, this is no time
for words.

*Lyſimor.* I am ready for you, Sir.

Here ceaſed all farther ſpeech between
them, and on the part of Lyſimor for
ever. On the ſecond puſh, Adario
ran him quite through the body; he fell
that inſtant, and expired with only a
ſingle groan. His ſucceſsful antagoniſt
approached the body; and finding life
was totally extinguiſhed, gave a ſigh or
two to the memory of a man he once
had called his friend, then made the beſt
of his way home, in order to provide for
his own ſecurity, which the likelihood
there was of the challenge he had ſent to
the deceaſed being found rendered
highly neceſſary.

The meaſures he took, indeed, were
very prudent. He ſent immediately to
hire a poſt-chaiſe, which was to wait
for him in a ſtreet he mentioned, at ſome
diſtance from that in which he lived;
carried no baggage with him, but ordered a ſervant to follow him with it to
Calais; ſtaid no longer at his own houſe
han to write two ſhort letters; the one

to a gentleman who had been one of the
executors of his father’s will, which being only on family affairs, need not be
here inſerted ; the other was to his ſiſter
Iſabinda, and contained theſe lines—

‘ SISTER,

‘ FAILING to repair your wrongs
‘   by the way I hoped, I have re-
‘ venged them by the death of your ſe-
‘ ducer; for which I am obliged this
‘ moment to leave my native country,
‘ perhaps for ever. I have done what
‘ the honour of our family exiſted from
‘ me. It belongs to you to regulate
‘ your future conduct, ſo as to atone,
‘ in ſome meaſure, for the errors of the
‘ paſt. To enable you to do this, you
‘ ought to keep in eternal remembrance,
‘ that the follies of your fatal paſſion
‘ have not only brought the object of it
‘ to an untimely grave, but alſo drove
‘ from all the ſocial joys of life, into
‘ an irkſome baniſhment in a foreign
‘ land, him who might have been hap-
‘ py, if he had not been your brother,

‘ ADARIO.’

Thinking, perhaps, he had been
ſomewhat too ſevere in the above, he
added this poſtſcript, by way of cor-
dial—

‘ P. S. I ſhall conſtantly write to
‘ Mr. D——n : he will be able to
‘ inform you how to direct for me.
‘ You may be aſſured I ſhall re-
‘ ceive with pleaſure any letters
‘ that bring me an account of your
‘ welfare ; and, in ſpite of all that
‘ has happened, do you every ſer-
‘ vice in my power.’

After having ſent this by the groom
who had firſt diſcovered the place of her
abode, and given ſome neceſſary inſtructions to his other ſervants, he hurried away to meet the poſt-chaiſe, and I
ſaw him no more. As I had truly pitied Iſabinda, I could not forbear going
to ſee in what manner ſhe ſupported this
laſt dreadful accident. On my entrance, ſhe was in bed, and ſurrounded
by women and phyſicians. I gathered
from their diſcourſe, that the ſurprize
and grief ſhe had been in had cauſed an
abortion, accompanied with fits of a
very dangerous nature. On my next
viſit, however, I found her youth, and
the ſtrength of her conſtitution, had got
the better of her diſeaſe ; but though the
pains

pains of her body were removed, those of her mind still remained: she was extremely melancholy, had a thorough contempt for the world; and the thoughts of a monastery were now so far from being shocking to her, that she resolved to fly to one, as the only asylum from censure and from care. Accordingly, as I was afterwards informed, she went, on the re-establishment of her health, to Paris, and entered herself into the society of Benedictine Nuns; where I doubt not but she often sees her brother through the grate, as he still continues to reside in that city.

I have now finished all the account I am able to give of this melancholy transaction; in which the justice of Providence seems to me to be distinguishe! in somewhat of a peculiar manner; and may serve as a warning to our gay, amorous sparks, not to become the seducers of unwary innocence; especially if they will be at the trouble of reflecting, how the perfidy and ingratitude of Flaminio to the believing Harriet was afterwards retorted on his own darling daughter.

CHAP. VI.

GIVES THE ACCOUNT OF AN OCCURRENCE NO LESS REMARKABLE THAN ENTERTAINING; AND SHEWS, THAT THERE IS SCARCE ANY DIFFICULTY SO GREAT, BUT IT MAY BE GOT OVER BY THE HELP OF A READY INVENTION, IF PROPERLY EXERTED.

TO make some atonement for my last melancholy recital, to those of my readers who may not care to have their heads filled with subjects of too serious a nature, I shall now present them with one more likely to put in motion the risible muscles of the face, than to extort the falling of unwilling tears.

A gentleman, whom I shall call Conrade, had lived to the age of sixty without ever testifying the least inclination to marriage. He had been a man of pleasure in his youth; and probably the too great success he then found among the fair, had deterred him from entering into an honourable engagement with any of the sex: but there is no accounting for change of sentiment in this point; an accident sometimes puts that into our heads which before we never thought

of, or perhaps had an aversion to, as it fell out in the case of the gentleman I am speaking of. A long friendship had subsisted between him and Murcio; a gentleman who, though not so far advanced in years, had made a better use of his time; had been married, and was the father of three fine daughters, two of whom had always lived with him; but the youngest, after the death of his wife, was taken from him, and brought up under the care of an aunt in the country. The eldest of these ladies being now about to be disposed of in marriage, Conrade received and accepted an invitation to the wedding. Melanthe, sister to the bride, was a fine sparkling girl of nineteen; but whether it were that she appeared in reality more lovely than usual, or that the mirth and pleasantries common at such solemnities rekindled the long-smothered embers of amorous desire in the breast of Conrade, so it was, that he, who had been in the company of this young lady without ever taking any notice of her charms, all at once became extremely smitten with them; insomuch, that he resolved to acquaint her father with his new passion, and ask his consent to make his addresses to her; which he did not at all despair of obtaining on the terms he intended to propose.

Murc o had a pretty country-house at a village about ten or twelve miles up the river; where he constantly went every Saturday, and staid till Monday or Tuesday, and sometimes longer. It was while he was in this retirement, that Conrade chose to communicate to him the business he had in his head: accordingly he went thither, and found him entirely alone; Melanthe having been prevented from going, as she was accustomed to do, by a violent fit of the tooth-ache. This our old lover looked upon as a good omen, being desirous to engage the father in favour of his passion before he made any declaration to the daughter. He began with saying, that he now repented having lived so long a batchelor; that having a very large estate, he should be glad of an heir to enjoy it; that if he could prevail on a young lady whom he liked to marry him, he would endeavour to atone for the want of youth by all the indulgences in the power of a fond husband: and having thus prepared the way, told him, that if he thought proper to bestow

stow Melanthe upon him, he would defire no other fortune than her perfon ; yet would fettle a dowry upon her fuperior to what might be expected if fhe brought him ten thoufand pounds.

It is not to be imagined with what greedinefs Murcio fwallowed this propofal : he did not even affect to hefitate, or make the leaft demur at accepting it; on the contrary, he replied, that nothing could afford him a greater fatisfaction than fuch an alliance, and that he doubted not but Melanthe would receive the honour he intended her as a woman who knew her own intereft and happinefs. Both parties being equally tranfported, every thing was immediately agreed upon between them; but Murcio not being able to affure himfelf that his daughter would fo readily comply as he had made the lover hope fhe would; and fearing that, if fhe fhould give the old gentleman a rebuff on his firft onfet, it might difcourage him from making a fecond, and perhaps overturn the whole affair, refolved not to hazard the lofs of fo advantageous a match by leaving it to her own choice, but fent a fpecial meffenger to her with a letter, the contents whereof are thefe—

' DEAR CHILD,

' MY worthy friend Conrade has
' taken a great liking to you,
' and will make you his wife on fuch
' terms as would but little prove the
' paternal affection I have for you to re-
' ject. Be not you lefs thankful to
' Heaven for fo unhoped a blefling than
' I am; nor, on any foolifh pretences,
' either flight, or feem to flight, the
' good prefented to you. If you con-
' fider the vaft advantages of this
' match, a difparity of years can be no
' objection. I fay thus much, becaufe
' I would convince your reafon, not en-
' force your action; for I fhould be
' forry to find myfelf obliged to make
' ufe of the authority I have over you
' in a thing which you ought, and I
' hope will, receive with the fame fatis-
' faction I propofe it. Know, however,
' that I have already agreed on every
' thing for your marriage; that your
' future hufband is now here, and we
' fhall both be in town either to-mor-
' row or the enfuing day. I fend this
' on purpofe to prepare you to behave
' towards him in a proper manner,
' and as it is the abfolute command

' of him who is your affectionate fa-
' ther,

' MURCIO.'

I ftood behind Melanthe's chair while fhe was reading this epiftle, and never did I fee a poor young creature in fuch agitations. Scarce had fhe come to the end of the firft period, before fhe cried out—' His wife! his wife! What ' terms can the old creature propofe '. to compenfate for the odious title ' of wife to fuch a wretch!' Then going a little farther—' Juftly, indeed,' faid fhe, ' does my father fufpect my ' obedience in this point ; death itfelf ' would not be fo dreadful to me as ' compliance.' The more fhe proceeded, the higher her diftraction grew. ' What! fix my doom at once!' raved fhe out; ' at once refolve to cut me off ' from all the joys of life, and condemn ' me to everlafting mifery ! Is this a ' parent's love ! Oh, 'tis moft cruel, ' moft unnatural!' I know not to what extravagances fhe might have been hurried, by the fudden rufh of grief and defpair, if tears now had not afforded their relief; but though they a little foftened the afperity of her paffion, they had not the power to fubdue it: her tongue, indeed, ceafed from exclaiming againft her fate; but the agonies of her countenance difcovered how much fhe inwardly regretted it. While fhe was in this diftrefsful and pity-moving fituation, the gay, the lively Florimel, came in. This young lady was the moft beloved and intimate companion that Melanthe had; fhe faw her almoft every day, and always entered without ceremony. She feemed a little furprized, at firft fight, to find her thus; but immediately recovering herfelf, approached her with her accuftomed fprightlinefs.

*Florimel.* Heyday, Melanthe! what, in the name of wonder, makes you in this pickle? Is your favourite fquirrel dead? or has any accident happened to your laft new petit-en-l'air? or what other misfortune has befallen you ?

*Melanthe.* O Florimel, what would I not give to be in thy condition!

*Florimel.* My condition! Why, what do you find to envy in my condition ?

*Melanthe.* To have no father to controul your actions by an unreafonable exertion of his authority.

*Florimel.* Why, truly, as you fay, thefe old dads are troublefom- enough fometimes;

sometimes; yet, for all that, I should be heartily glad mine were alive again. But pray, what has yours done to make you wish yourself an orphan?

*Melanthe.* Read that, and see if I have not cause.

In speaking these words, she pointed to her father's letter, which lay open on the table. Florimel took it up, and read it, as desired. On examining the contents, she could not help looking a little grave; but having finished, resumed the discourse with her former vivacity.

*Florimel.* As sure as I am alive, both these old gentlemen are crackbrained; the one in thinking of you for a wife, and the other in consenting to give you such a husband.

*Melanthe.* One would, indeed, imagine they were not in their senses.

*Florimel.* For my part, I am so astonished, that I can scarce believe I am awake. But what will you do?

*Melanthe.* Nothing.

*Florimel.* 'Nothing can come of 'nothing,' as King Lear says in the play. I am less surprized, however, at your stupidity in so perplexing a dilemma, than I am at the folly of those who have involved you in it. Bless me! what can either your lover or father propose to themselves by such a disproportionate alliance, but horns on the one side, and disgrace to his family on the other?

*Melanthe.* No, Florimel, it shall never come to that; I will rather starve or beg.

*Florimel.* Look'ye, my dear, neither starving nor begging, as I take it, will agree with your constitution; something else must be thought on.

*Melanthe.* What else?

*Florimel.* Do you think, that when your father com s to know what an implacable aversion you have to this match, he will not be prevailed upon to recal the promise he has made to Conrade?

*Melanthe.* Impossible! I know his temper too well to flatter myself with such a hope. You might as well think to blow St. Paul's from it's foundation with a single breath, as move him to recede from any thing he has once resolved.

*Florimel.* Well, then, suppose some way could be contrived to make Conrade himself fly off? I have a project in my head that promises fair for it, if you will agree to join in the execution.

It is this: you must admit a spruce young gallant to lie with you all night; Conrade must be informed of the amour, in such a manner as to make him convinced of the truth of it; and the deuce is in him, if afterwards he insists on marrying you.

*Melanthe.* Fie, Florimel! How can you be so cruel as to rally my misfortunes?

*Florimel.* No, I protest I am as serious as a judge upon a criminal cause; and would have you make the experiment.

*Melanthe.* What, wouldst thou have me turn prostitute to avoid marriage!

*Florimel.* No such matter. I will engage that the gallant I mean shall lie as harmless by your side as an infant.

*Melanthe.* Pr'ythee do not torture me with such riddles.

*Florimel.* I shall presently explain them. The gallant I am speaking of, and who is to be your bedfellow, is no other than my own individual self. I shall put on a suit of my brother's cloaths; and do not doubt but that, when I am dressed and equipped in all my accoutrements, I shall be a figure handsome enough to make an old man jealous.

*Melanthe.* Sure never was so wild a scheme! But yet I cannot conceive how it is to be conducted, or which way it can answer the end you propose by it.

*Florimel.* Lord, you are strangely dull! or affect to be so; but I will shew you what I shall write to Conrade, and that may help to enlighten your understanding.

This witty lady waited not to hear what reply her friend would make, but ran to a desk, and immediately wrote the following lines—

' TO HUGH CONRADE, ESQ.

' SIR

' EVER since I heard of your intended marriage with Melanthe, ' I have been divided in my thoughts, ' whether the treachery of betraying a ' secret entrusted to me, or, by concealing it, expose a gentleman of your ' character to the worst of mischiefs, ' would be the most dishonourable action. The latter consideration has at ' last prevailed; and I think it my duty ' to inform you, that the lady you are ' about to make your wife has neither ' least nor honour to bestow upon you;

‘ both are already difpofed of to a per-
‘ fon fhe thinks more agreeable to her
‘ years. Not content with the many
‘ private affignations fhe has with him
‘ abroad, fhe frequently makes pre-
‘ tences, when her father goes into the
‘ country, to be left at home; where
‘ her chambermaid, who is in the fe-
‘ cret, admits this happy lover at mid-
‘ night, and lets him out early in the
‘ morning, before the other fervants of
‘ the houfe are ftirring. Murcio be-
‘ ing gone to *****, I am well affured
‘ it will be in your power to convince
‘ yourfelf of the certainty of this intel-
‘ ligence, by fending any one on whom
‘ you can depend to watch about the
‘ door, either for the entrance or exit of
‘ the favourite gallant. Act as you
‘ pleafe, however. I have difcharged
‘ the dictates of confcience in giving you
‘ this timely warning; and am,
                ‘ Your namelefs fervant.’

This fhe gave Melanthe to read; and,
as foon as fhe had done, was going to afk
her how fhe approved of the contrivance;
when the other prevented her, by crying
out—

*Melanthe.* Oh the wicked, lying letter! Dear Florimel, if this fhould be
fent, and Conrade fhould fhew it to my
father, I believe he would kill me.

*Florimel.* 'Tis poffible he may not
fhew it; but if he does, you have only
to prepare yourfelf for a little fcolding
and fwearing. The worft he can do is
to turn you out of doors; and then, to
ufe your own words, it can be but
ftarving or begging.

*Melanthe.* Oh, but my reputation,
Florimel!

*Florimel.* A fiddle of your reputation! Would you hazard nothing to
avoid being tacked, till death do you
part, to fuch a lump of decayed mer-
tality as Conrade? Befides, when the
affair is all over, and you are once got
free from this curfed engagement, it
will be eafy, by unravelling the plot,
to clear your reputation, and reconcile
you to your father into the bargain.

*Melanthe.* Oh, Florimel, if I was
fure of that!

*Florimel.* Truft to Fortune. I will
lay my life that, if you behave according to my directions, every thing will
go right.

*Melanthe.* Well, then, tell me what
I am to do.

*Florimel.* In the firft place, when
your father comes home, you muft
feem to be as well pleafed with the
match as he would have you be; and
pretend that you are mightily in love
with Conrade's eftate, whatever you are
with the man. Then, as for the old
wretch himfelf, you have nothing to do
but to fimper and look filly when he
makes his addreffes, and tell him that
you are all obedience to your father's
will.

*Melanthe.* This is a hard tafk, and
I am a very ill diffembler; I will try,
however, what I can do. But, Florimel, there is one thing that neither you
nor I, as yet, have thought upon: fuppofe Conrade fhould take it into his head
to watch the door himfelf, and draw
upon you in his paffion?

*Florimel.* What if he does? I fhall
have a fword as well as h..

*Melanthe.* But not underftand fo
well how to ufe it?

*Florimel.* I don't know that. But
if I can't fight as well, I am fure
I can run much better; fo pray do
not be under any concern on my account.

Thefe fair friends parted not till the
night was pretty far advanced; all which
time was taken up with fettling fome
farther particulars in relation to their
defign. Molly, the waiting-maid, was
called in; and, after a vow of fecrecy,
entrufted with the whole affair. She
feemed a good fmart girl, highly proper
for the bufinefs fhe was to be employed
in, and readily promifed her affiftance.
As I was very near as impatient as
themfelves for the fuccefs of this whim-
fical enterprize, I went every day to
Murcio's houfe, and found that Melanthe acted the part fhe had been taught
by Florimel fo as to give the utmoft fatisfaction both to her father and lover;
who now talked of nothing but to have
the wedding folemnized as foon as the
neceffary preparations for it could be
made.

Saturday being arrived, I made it my
bufinefs to enquire whether Murcio was
gone to his country-feat; and finding he
was, and that Melanthe ftaid at home,
concluded this was the day on which
the firft wheel of the machine was to be
put in motion; therefore hurried away
to the houfe of Conrade, where I
luckily came time enough to fee him receive the letter from Florimel. The
wrinkles

wrinkles of his face were greatly agitated while he was reading this epistle. At first his eyelids extended themselves; and his brows were elated with surprize, then were contracted into a frown of anger. Sometimes a sneer of contempt and unbelief lengthened the furrows round his withered lips. But the attitude of longest duration, was a pensive hanging down of his head, accompanied with counting the hairs upon his little finger; out of which at last he started, and cried to himself—' Many ' reasons may be urged both for and ' against my giving credit to this story; ' but whether built upon truth or malice, I have no need to be at the pains ' of considering: the author has pointed ' out the means of being convinced, ' and I will take his counsel.'

As I could not be certain that he would continue in this resolution, and much less so, that if he did, what the event of it would be, I went by break of day the next morning, and posted myself over-against Murcio's house. In a few minutes after Conrade came, wrapped in a cloak; but stood more aloof, yet near enough to see every thing that passed. We had not waited above a quarter of an hour, before the door we watched was softly opened, and a well-dressed beau rushed out. Conrade advanced as fast as his gout would let him; in order, I suppose, to see the face of this invader of his hoped-for happiness: but the pretended gallant was too nimble for his pursuit; but dropped a piece of paper, as if by accident fitted out with his handkerchief. Conrade immediately snatched it up, and found it was a billet. The superscription seemed to have been torn off, but the contents were these—

' DEAREST OF YOUR SEX,

' MY father is gone into the country,
' and I have made an excuse to
' he left behind. Come at the usual
' hour, and Molly will admit you to
' the arms of
' Yours.'

I easily perceived that this was a second plot of the young ladies to corroborate the first; and it had all the effect they could wish; and was also productive of something else, which neither of them at that time imagined, as will appear in the succeeding chapter.

## C H A P. VII.

IS A CONTINUANCE OF THIS MERRY HISTORY, WHICH PRESENTS SOMETHING AS LITTLE EXPECTED BY THE READER AS IT WAS BY THE PARTIES CONCERNED IN IT.

IT is not to be doubted but that Conrade, after having received this double confirmation of Melanthe's transgression, gave over all intentions of becoming her husband; yet, by what I could gather from his looks, and some expressions he let fall, the manner in which he should quit his pretentions was the occasion of a very great conflict in his mind. He was a good-natured man, and loth to accuse this young lady to her father; yet, to break off a match so far advanced, and which he had so earnestly solicited, without assigning any cause for the change of his resolution, he thought would not only make him appear ridiculous, but also put a final period to all conversation between him and his old friend; and he probably continued undetermined in this matter, till he found himself obliged to talk upon it to Murcio himself, who had appointed to come to town the next day in order to sign the marriage writings. That gentleman was at home; and having expected him some hours before he came, began, in a pleasant manner, to reproach his tardiness; to which Conrade replied, very gravely—' I am indeed, Sir, some- ' what beyond my time, yet I believe, ' soon enough for the business which ' now brings me.' Murcio seemed much surprized on hearing him speak in this manner; and poor Melanthe, who was present, well knowing that this alteration in her lover's behaviour was the effect of the plot concerted between her and Florimel, trembled for the event, and was no less shocked at the thoughts how much her innocence suffered in his opinion.

It is uncertain what return Murcio would have made, for the other prevented him from speaking, by adding, to what he had said before, that he had something of a very extraordinary nature, and which required no witnesses, to communicate to him. On which he made a sign to Melanthe

to

to leave the room; and she was no sooner withdrawn, than Conrade proceeded, though not without a good deal of hesitation, to declare himself in these terms—

*Conrade.* Dear Murcio, we have long been friends; and I should be heartily sorry that what I have to say should occasion a rupture between us. For my own part, there is no man living for whom I shall always preserve a greater esteem than for yourself.

*Murcio.* I cannot think, Sir, that you have any thing in your mind which should give me reason to regard you less.

*Conrade.* Reason is too frequently misled by passion. I know it by experience, and shall be glad to find yours is more strong; though, I confess, I have been to blame, and am sorry things have gone so far: but, Sir, I have considered that it is now too late in life for me to think of marriage, especially with so young a lady as Melanthe.

*Murcio.* This is an odd turn, indeed! Methinks, Sir, you should have considered this before you made any proposals of that sort, either to me or my daughter. A treaty of marriage, Sir, when concluded on and consented to by both parties, is a thing of too much consequence to be broke off by either, without putting the most gross affront upon the other.

*Conrade.* Not, Sir, when it can be proved that the consummation would be equally inconvenient for both.

*Murcio* As how for both? My daughter has never made the least objection.

*Conrade.* It may be so. Yet I am well assured she neither does, nor ever can, regard me with that affection which alone could make either me or herself happy in being united.

*Murcio.* A mere whim! a caprice of your own, founded only on the disparity of years! and I am amazed you should think of flying off from your engagement on so shallow a pretence.

*Conrade.* Perhaps I may have others. Suppose I know she loves another?

*Murcio.* Sir, I will suppose no such thing. She love another! No, Sir, she has been bred up in principles too virtuous, and is too modest, to place her affections on any one, till my commands, and the authority of the church, made it her duty to do so: and I must tell you, Sir, it is base in you to add to

the ill usage you are about to give her, by traducing her reputation.

*Conrade.* I scorn the unmanly thought. Be assured I have proofs of what I say.

*Murcio.* Produce them, then.

*Conrade.* I will, since I find the justification of my own honour depends upon it. There, Sir; read that, and be convinced.

In speaking this, he gave Murcio the letter that had been sent by Florimel; which the other, after having carelessly perused, threw from him; and looking on Conrade with the utmost scorn, said to him—

*Murcio.* A notable proof, indeed! There are few people without some enemies: but this is a piece of scandal too gross, too stupid, and the invention too ill concerted, to pass even on the most weak and credulous mind; and seems rather a poor, low contrivance, of your own, to evade fulfilling an engagement you have taken it into your head to repent of.

*Conrade.* You are free in your expressions, Sir; but I believe it will presently be my turn to retort that contempt you so unjustly treat me with. Do you know the hand-writing of your daughter?

*Murcio.* Yes, certainly I do.

*Conrade.* Then judge of the contents of this, and take shame to yourself for the injurious treatment you have given me.

The reader will easily imagine that it was Melanthe's little billet he now put into his hands; but no one can conceive, much less am I able to describe, the rage, the horror, the distraction, that shook the whole frame of this astonished parent, on finding himself no longer able to refuse giving credit to so terrible a misfortune. 'Death and furies!' cried he. 'Infamous, abandoned wretch!' Then, after loading her with all the foulest names that language could afford, he turned to Conrade—' Pardon 'me, dear Conrade,' said he. ' Had ' an angel told me what you did, with- ' out this cursed testimony, I should ' not have believed the story. But you ' shall have ample satisfaction: I'll turn ' this scandal to my family, this de- ' ceiver both of you and me, out of ' my doors this moment; never own ' her, never see her more, but leave her ' to the miseries she merits!' He was running out of the room; and it is probable,

bable, in the firſt emotions of his paſſion, would have done as he had threatened, if Conrade had not withheld him;
and partly by force, and partly by per-
ſuaſion, made him ſit down, while he
reaſoned with him in this manner—

*Conrade.* Dear Murcio, compoſe
yourſelf; and be not raſhly guilty of
a thing you hereafter may repent of.
Conſider that the errors of one branch
of a family reflect diſhonour on the
whole. You have other daughters
who, though pure as innocence itſelf,
yet, being of the ſame blood, may be
ſuſpected liable to the ſame faults; for
their ſakes, therefore, rather ſmother
than expoſe the crime of this fair offender.

*Murcio.* What! would you then
have me to forgive, encourage, and ſuffer her to continue in this ſhameful
proſtitution under my own roof!

*Conrade.* No; but I would have you
remember that ſhe is ſtill your child;
and that it is your duty, as a father,
to uſe your utmoſt efforts to retrieve her
from perdition, not ſink her deeper into it.

*Murcio.* As how retrieve her! Is
ſhe not already loſt, irrecoverably loſt,
to reputation as well as virtue!

*Conrade.* Not ſo, I hope. All yet
may be well, if her ſeducer can be prevailed upon to repair the injury he has
done her by an honourable marriage.

*Murcio.* A vain expectation!

*Conrade.* 'Tis worth attempting, at
leaſt. But firſt you muſt oblige her to
diſcover the name of this too happy
man; for you ſee that, either by deſign
or accident, the direction to him is torn
off the letter.

*Murcio.* I proteſt, in the diſtraction
of my thoughts, I had forgot that cir-
cumſtance; and alſo to aſk you by what
means this infamous ſcrawl came into
your poſſeſſion.

On this Conrade related to him all
the particulars he had obſerved while he
had been watching his rival's coming
out of the houſe; and when he had
done, in order to encourage Murcio to
take the advice he had juſt given him,
added this deſcription of the ſuppoſed
gallant—

*Conrade.* I was very much vexed
that I had not an opportunity of ſeeing
his face; but his back being towards
me, I could only take notice of his dreſs
and air; and do aſſure you he has all
the appearance of a man of faſhion, and

ſuch a one as to whom you could not
reaſonably have refuſed your daughter,
even if this accident had never happened.

*Murcio.* Oh, what a curſe it is to
have a diſobedient child!

He appeared in the moſt bitter anguiſh of mind while uttering theſe laſt
words; but having recovered himſelf a
little, took pen, ink, and paper, and
wrote the following lines to Melanthe—

' Thou Scandal to my Blood and Name!

'T HAT you ſtill live to receive
' this, thank the gentleman whom
' you would have wronged by intending
' to carry pollution to his bed. He has
' obtained a reprieve for you on this
' condition, that you declare the name
' and quality of your undoer, to the end
' that I may take ſuch meaſures as I
' ſhall judge proper, to oblige him to do
' juſtice to the honour of a family of
' which you are the only blemiſh.
' Think not to deny your crime; I have
' the infamous witneſs of it under your
' own hand: but be plain and open in
' your confeſſion, if you hope ever to
' obtain mercy, either from Heaven or
' your offended father,

' MURCIO.'

After having ſhewed this to Conrade,
he called for the waiting-maid, and bid
her give that letter to her miſtreſs, and
bring him an immediate anſwer. I
followed, and ſaw with what agonies
poor Melanthe read this cruel mandate.
Between the fears of what her father's
indignation might inflict upon her, and
the ſhame of appearing guilty of a crime
her ſoul diſdained, ſhe was ſo much
overwhelmed, that for ſome minutes ſhe
had not power to ſpeak; and when ſhe
did, it was only to utter this exclamation—

*Melanthe.* What will become of me!
Oh this vile plot of Florimel's!

*Molly.* Lord, Madam, do not put
yourſelf into this flurry! You know
your father's temper well enough, and
could not expect he would be leſs ſevere.
But it will be all over; and you muſt reſolve to bear it for a while.

*Melanthe.* I cannot, will not bear
it! I will go down this inſtant, diſcloſe
all, and clear my innocence.

*Molly.* Sure, Madam, you would not
be ſo mad! What, would you undo
all, and be forced to marry Conrade at
laſt?

H *Melanthe.*

_Melanthe._ Was there ever fo terrible a dilemma! What anfwer can I give?

_Molly._ Dear Madam, fay any thing. Tell him you are in love with—— Say any thing but the truth.

_Melanthe._ How filly am I to afk advice of fuch a giddy creature! — With this fhe turned herfelf towards a table whereon ftood a ftandifh, fat down, paufed a while, then began to write; but had fcarce finifhed two lines, before fhe left off, tore the paper, mufed again, and then began afrefh. The fecond effay met with the fame fate as the former, and fo did feveral fucceeding ones; till at laft fhe threw the pen out of her hand, ftarted up, and faid—

_Melanthe._ 'Tis in vain to attempt it. I cannot write.

_Molly._ Why then, Madam, fay nothing: e'en let him think as he pleafes, at prefent. If you will but pluck up a fpirit, we fhall do well enough. He will not kill you, for his own fake; and as for any thing elfe, you muft content yourfelf to fubmit to it. Nothing can be fo bad as marrying Conrade. I will go to Florimel prefently: if I am fo lucky as to find her at home, 'tis ten to one but fhe puts fomething into our heads.

_Melanthe._ Do fo. I wifh fhe were here.

While they were fpeaking, Murcio called very loud at the bottom of the ftairs for Molly to come down; on which fhe faid—' Do you hear, Madam? But 'I muft face the ftorm, for fear it fhould 'come hither, and terrify you worfe. I 'wifh you had as much courage as I 'have.'

She faid no more, but ran haftily down into the parlour; where I, with no lefs fpeed, attended her footfteps, quite impatient to hear how the pert baggage would behave.

_Murcio._ What is the reafon, minx, that I have no anfwer to the letter you carried up?

_Molly._ Lord, Sir, there was fome. what or other in that letter that has frighted my poor lady almoft out of her wits. She does nothing but cry and wring her hands. It would make your heart ache to fee her. She write an anfwer! No indeed, fhe is not in a condition to give an anfwer.

_Murcio._ If fhe can't, you muft, huffey! Who was that fellow you let out of my houfe yefterday morning?

_Molly._ I, Sir! I let out no fellow, not I.

_Murcio._ 'Tis falfe: my friend here, happening to pafs through the ftreet at that time, faw him come out.

_Molly._ Why then, Sir, your friend is no better than a pickthank for bringing you fuch idle ftories; and I am not afraid to tell him fo to his face.

_Murcio._ Was there ever fuch impudence!

_Conrade._ Come, come, Mrs. Molly, you had better confefs the truth; it will be for the good of your lady, and yourfelf too.

_Molly._ Sir, I fhall not tell a lye for the matter: I let out no fellow. There was a fine gentleman, indeed, that fat up all night playing at cards with my lady, that I let out; but no fellow, I affure you.

_Murcio._ Well; and pray, Mrs. Brazenface, what is the name of this fine gentleman?

_Molly._ Lord, Sir! do you think I know the names of all the gentlemen that come to vifit my lady? Indeed, I am not fo impertinent as to afk.

_Murcio._ No equivocation. Tell me this moment, or I fhall be your death!

_Molly._ Blefs me, Sir! how can you fright a body for nothing? But, if you would be my death twenty times over, I can fay no more than I have done.

_Conrade._ Dear Murcio, this girl is not worth the paffion you are in. I hope the young lady herfelf will fatisfy you, when once fhe confiders how much it is her intereft to do fo.

_Murcio._ Not while fhe has fuch a hardened wretch to encourage her obftinacy.—Huffey, pack up your trumpery, and get out of my houfe directly, or I fhall provide a place for you in Bridewell.

_Molly._ Oh, dear Sir! I fhall not give you that trouble; there are places enough to be had without your providing.

After fhe had left the room, and Murcio had vented his paffion in two or three hearty curfes, he turned to Conrade, and, with a tone of voice which expreffed the deepeft trouble of mind, uttered thefe words—' You fee, my 'dear friend, that both miftrefs and 'maid are alike incorrigible. What 'now remains for me to do, either to 'preferve my family from difgrace, or 'this degenerate girl from everlafting 'ruin?' The other, who doubtlefs condemned dcmned Melanthe more in his heart than he would let her father know he did, could find nothing to fay in her defence; but that he hoped, when the firſt confuſion of this diſcovery was a little over, ſhe would be brought to reaſon; and therefore intreated he would allow her ſome time to recolleƈt herſelf. As the converſation now began to conſiſt only of railings on the one ſide, and perſuaſions to moderation on the other, I eaſily perceived that nothing of importance would be the reſult; ſo reſolved to leave the two old gentlemen together, and accordingly took the firſt opportunity to get out of the houſe.

## CHAP. VIII.

PRESENTS SOMETHING WHICH, IF THE AUTHOR'S HOPES DO NOT DECEIVE HIM, WILL AFFORD AN EQUAL SHARE OF SATISFACTION AS SURPRIZE.

BEING very anxious for the ſituation of poor Melanthe, I fully deſigned to make another viſit to Murcio's houſe early the next morning; and accordingly got to Murcio's door juſt as Conrade had alighted from his coach, and was ſtepping in; ſo I had an eaſy acceſs, and followed him up into the dining-room, where Murcio was then ſitting, and expreſſed the ſatisfaƈtion he took in ſeeing him in words to this effeƈt—

*Murcio.* My dear friend, I am glad you are come to give me your opinion in a thing I am about to do. My ungracious daughter has given me no anſwer, made me no ſubmiſſions. I cannot keep her in my houſe; and if I turn her out of it, am in danger of having my whole family ſcandalized by her behaviour: I am therefore reſolved to ſend her to Cornwall, where I have a near kinſman.

*Conrade.* I flatter myſelf, Sir, that the intelligence I bring will ſave you that trouble, and the young lady ſo long a journey. I have diſcovered her favourite lover.

*Murcio.* Is it poſſible! For Heaven's ſake, who—what is he!

*Conrade.* One you little ſuſpeƈt, though I have ſeen him often here. It is Dorimon.

*Murcio.* Dorimon! Yes, ſince his re-

turn from his travels, he viſits here ſometimes. His ſiſter Florimel and Melanthe were brought up together at the boarding-ſchool; and, ſince they left it, have ſcarcely been two days aſunder. But I cannot think Dorimon has been her ſeducer: ſhe is neither above his hopes, nor below his expeƈtations. If he had any inclinations towards her, I know of nothing ſhould hinder him from making his honourable addreſſes. But what grounds have you for ſuch a ſuppoſition? ...

*Conrade.* You ſhall hear. You know I told you that I did not ſee his face; but, as I followed him a good part of the ſtreet, I took notice of his habit, which indeed had ſomewhat particular in it, and would have attraƈted my obſervation, had I ſeen it on any other perſon. It was a dark olive-coloured French barragon, laced with a very rich Point d'Eſpagne down the ſeams; he had alſo a fine flaxen wig, with a bag and a ſolitaire of an uncommon dimenſion. I then took him either for a foreigner, or one lately come from abroad. In the ſame dreſs, and as exaƈtly as I ſaw him then, did I ſee him, within this half hour, at the chocolate-houſe. I cannot, indeed, ſwear to the man, but I think may ſafely to the cloaths, eſpecially as I heard him ſay, on ſome gentlemen's praiſing the ſuit, and telling him they believed there was not ſuch another in England, that he was pretty ſure there was not; for he had beſpoke it at Paris, according to his own taſte, and it had not been come over long enough for any one to take a pattern by it.

*Murcio.* I muſt own there is a ſtrong probability in what you ſay; but yet, without a certa'nty, know not what meaſures I can purſue.

*Conrade.* If you will take my advice, ſend for him: I heard him ſay he ſhould dine at home, ſo is ſcarcely gone out. Give ſome diſtant hints, at firſt, concerning a marriage with your daughter; and, according to the anſwers he makes, you will be inſtruƈted how to proceed.

*Murcio.* It ſhall be ſo. I will not let him ſee I have any ſuſpicion of my daughter's fault; and, whether there be any thing between them or not, a propoſal of the nature you mention cannot ſeem ſtrange to him, as our families have always lived together in a perfeƈt harmony and good underſtanding.

He had no ſooner ſaid this, than he

H 2 called

called a fervant, and fent him with his compliments to. Dorimon, to let him know he defired to fpeak with him immediately, if not otherwife engaged. After this, the two friends had fome farther difcourfe concerning what fteps the father of Melanthe fhould take in this affair; when the fellow who had been fent on the above meffage returned, and told his mafter that Dorimon faid he would not fail doing himfelf the honour of obeying his commands in a few minutes : on which Conrade took his leave; and Murcio fat down, endeavouring to frame his temper and countenance fo as to be fuitable to the bufinefs he had in hand.

Dorimon appeared in a fhort time; and, the firft compliments being paft, Murcio began to open what he had to fay, by telling him that he had a great regard for his family; that he was a fine young gentleman; and that, being now five and twenty, he much wondered that he had not heard of his addreffing fome lady on the fcore of marriage. To which Dorimon replied, that marriage was a thing he had not as yet much thought upon; and that, having a fifter who took care of his houfe, a wife was the lefs neceffary to him. Murcio then demanded if he found any averfion in himfelf to changing his condition in favour of a woman of equal birth and fortune, and who would approve of his pretenfions. Dorimon feemed a little furprized at thefe interrogatories; but anfwered in the negative, with this provifo, that the perfon of the lady were equally agreeable. Murcio, thinking this reply a proper cue for explaining himfelf, did fo in the following manner—

*Murcio.* What think you, then, of my daughter Melanthe?

*Dorimon.* As of an angel, Sir, above my hopes.

*Murcio.* No fine fpeeches, Dorimon; deal fincerely with me. Do you like her well enough to marry her?

*Dorimon.* Yes, Sir, upon my foul! and fhould blefs the hand that gave her to me.

*Murcio.* Sir, I take you at your word; and give you mine that you fhall have her, and fix thoufand pounds, if you think that a fufficient dower.

*Dorimon.* I do, Sir; and, though Melanthe is a fufficient fortune of herfelf, fhall accept your offer, and make a fettlement accordingly.

*Murcio.* Then there remains no moft than to get the marriage-articles drawn which, if you pleafe, fhall be to-morrow morning.

*Dorimon.* It cannot be too foon. But, Sir, may I not have leave to fee her, to throw myfelf at her feet, and be affured fhe will not regret the happinefs you beftow upon me?

*Murcio.* Oh, Sir, you have nothing to apprehend on that account; for, to be plain with you, I defigned her for another. She rejected the propofal, for which fhe has been under fome difgrace : but, as I have fince difcovered, her difobedience was occafioned by the affection fhe has for you, I was the more eafily induced to pardon it. She does not yet know that I confent to gratify her inclinations : but you fhall have the pleafure of telling her yourfelf.

He then went to the door, and ordered a fervant to bid Melanthe come down : after which he turned back, and faid to Dorimon—' My daughter will wait on ' you prefently. I know you will ex- ' cufe my leaving you together : I have ' bufinefs calls me abroad; but expect ' to fee you to-morrow morning, and ' fhall have a lawyer here.' He laid no more; but went haftily away, to avoid feeing his daughter. He had not left the room above half a minute, before Melanthe entered, but with a confufion impoffible to be expreffed. She had expected no other, on being called down, than to meet fome terrible effects of her father's difpleafure. Her eyes, red with tears, were now caft down upon the floor, as fhe advanced with flow and trembling fteps ; nor faw fhe who was there, till Dorimon fprung forward, and took her by the hand with thefe words—

*Dorimon.* Charming Melanthe, how am I tranfported at the goodnefs of your father ! How incapable of expreffing my gratitude for the permiffion he has juft now given me of telling you how much, how truly I adore you !

*Melanthe.* Blefs me, Dorimon, what is the meaning of all this ! Where is my father ?

*Dorimon.* Gone, to give me the happy opportunity of endeavouring to infpire you with fentiments in favour of my paffion, and conformable to his will.

*Melanthe.* Your paffion, and his will ! Certainly, Dorimon, you muft either be mad, or I not in my fenfes! For Heaven's fake, explain this myftery !

He

He was going to reply, when his sister Florimel came tripping in. That young lady having been informed by Molly of all that had passed at Murcio's house, was extremely impatient to know how her fair friend behaved afterwards on that occasion. Melanthe no sooner saw her, than she flew into her arms, and cried—

*Melanthe.* My dear, dear Florimel, what would I not have given to have seen you last night!

*Florimel.* I was no less eager to be with you. But I find things have quite changed their face. I met your father at the door as I entered; the old gentleman seems to be in quite good humour, desired me to walk up, and told me I should find you and my brother together.

*Dorimon.* Aye, my dear sister, we are together; and, I hope, shall soon be joined to separate no more.

*Florimel.* Separate no more! As how?

*Dorimon.* By the indissoluble ties of marriage. Murcio, the generous Murcio, has bestowed her on me. To-morrow the articles are to be drawn, and there will then be nothing wanting but my angel's consent for the consummation of my bliss.

*Florimel.* And was this the business on which he sent for you in such haste?

*Dorimon.* The same.

Here Florimel burst into so violent a fit of laughter, as rendered her unable to speak for some time. In vain Dorimon asked several times over the cause of this extravagant mirth; and it was but by degrees she recovered herself enough to make this reply—

*Florimel.* I have found out the riddle! It was I, brother, that have made this match. Yes, with the assistance of that suit of cloaths you have on. Then addressing herself to Melanthe, proceeded thus—' You must know, ' my dear, that it was Conrade himself ' that watched me coming out of your ' house. I saw him stand perdu under ' Sir Thomas ******'s porch. He has ' certainly seen my brother in these ' cloaths; and, mistaking him for me, ' has passed him upon your father for ' your supposed gallant.' Dorimon now as much confounded, in his turn, as the two ladies had been in theirs; till his sister, having first obtained Melanthe's leave, related to him the whole

history of their contrivance to break the match with Conrade. This repetition occasioned some pleasantry between the brother and sister; but Melanthe was too much ashamed to bear any great part in it. Her new lover observing her seriousness, spoke in this manner—

*Dorimon.* I have got nothing, Florimel, by the account you have given, but the mortification of that vanity Murcio had inspired me with; and dare not now flatter myself that Melanthe will so readily, as I once hoped, acquiesce in the agreement made between us.

*Florimel.* If she does not, all will come out; and if so, Murcio will certainly return to his first engagement to give her to Conrade. What say you, Melanthe; have you aversion enough for my brother to run so great a risque?

This demand made Melanthe blush excessively. She paused, and hung down her head; but at last made this return—' So sudden a change in my for- ' tune might well excuse me from ' giving a direct answer to such a ques- ' tion. Of this, however, you may be ' assured, that I have not courage to ' disobey my father a second time, and ' that I love the sister too well to have ' any aversion to the brother.'

On this Dorimon kissed her hand with a great deal of warmth, and said many tender and passionate things to her; which, as the reader will easily conceive, I think it needless to repeat; and shall only add that, between the brother and the sister, Melanthe was at last prevailed upon to confess, that it would be without the least reluctance she should obey her father in the choice he had now made for her. Though there was now little cause to apprehend any disappointment in these nuptials, yet I resolved to see the thing fully concluded on; accordingly I went the next morning to Murcio's house, where I found him very busy with his lawyer. Dorimon came in soon after; and the writings were presently filled up, signed, sealed, and duly executed, by both parties: and the lawyer had no sooner left the room, than Murcio spoke to Dorimon in these terms—

*Murcio.* Well, Dorimon, I think there is nothing now wanting for the making you my son, except the ceremony of the church; and I don't care how soon that also was performed. I

do

do not love to fee affairs of this nature kept long in hand. Befides, you mult know, that on my daughter's refufing to marry the perfon I firlt propofed to her, I fwore in my paffion that I would never fee her face again till fhe was a wife.

*Dorimon.* You may be affured, Sir, I fhall think every moment an age; and I do not doubt but the knowledge of the vow you have made will very much expedite my wifhes.

*Murcio.* I am going directly to my little country-feat, and fhall leave you to confult with her about the day; but will write to the rector of ****, who is my kinfman, and defire he will perform the office: when that is over, would have you both come down to *****, where you may depend upon meeting with a fatherly reception.

Nothing farther, of any confequence, was faid by either of them. Murcio took coach for the country, and Dorimon went to the apartment of his miftrefs; where ftrenuoufly preffing her for the fpeedy confummation of his happinefs, her father's pretended vow ferved as an excufe for her compliance, and fhe confented that the wedding fhould be the next Sunday after. No accident retarded the fulfilling this agreement, and they were married on the day appointed; after which they fet out, accompanied by Florimel, for *****, to receive the bleffing Murcio had promifed to beftow upon them. As no one of the company had any reafon to be difcontented at what had happened, it is not to be doubted but the goddefs of chearfulnefs accompanied them in their little journey: I fay journey, becaufe the fifter of Dorimon having an averfion to the water, they went in a landau, in complaifance to her; but the fubject of their converfation is not in my power to relate, as I had no opportunity of being witnefs of it.

## CHAP. IX.

CONTAINS A SUCCINCT ACCOUNT OF SOME FARTHER PARTICULARS, IN SOME MEASURE RELATIVE TO THE FOREGOING ADVENTURE.

HAVING married my two newmade lovers, the reader will poffibly imagine, that the laft act of the

play is ended, and that I fhould now drop the curtain, to prepare for fome frefh fubject of entertainment; but he mult wait awhile; I have not yet done with any of my characters: and befides, as there are many things which feem to require a farther explanation, I cannot think of parting with my favourite Florimel, without giving her thofe juft praifes which her wit and good-humour may juftly claim. It is not unlikely, indeed, but that there may be fome overfcrupulous ladies in the world, who will be fo far from approving her character of this charming girl, that they will highly contemn her for affuming the air and habit of a man, though for never fo fhort a fpace of time; and even rail at Melanthe, for confenting to put in execution the ftratagem fhe had conceived for her deliverance from an evil fo juftly dreaded by her. Such as thefe will certainly think I have faid enough, if not too much, on the occafion, and perhaps throw afide the book, and cry they will read no farther. Well, be it fo; the lots will be entirely their own: I am pretty confident neither my reputation, nor the profits of my publifher, will fuffer by their ill-nature in this point. It is for the entertainment of the gay, the witty, and truly virtuous—who, by the way, are never cenforious—that thefe lucubrations are chiefly intended; and if I am fo fortunate as to pleafe them, fhould give myfelf no great pain what may be faid of me by thofe of the abovementioned clafs. In defiance, therefore, of thefe fair, or rather unfair criticks, I fhall proceed in what I have farther to relate concerning the principal fubjects of this narrative.

On their arrival at *****, they were received by Murcio with a fhew of the greateft fatisfaction; yet I, who took care to be there before them, in order to be witnefs of what fhould pafs at this firft interview, could eafily perceive that he embraced his fon-in-law with more cordiality and lefs conftraint than he did his daughter. The remembrance of her fuppofed fault doubtlefs rendered him unable to treat her with his accuftomed tendernefs: he fcarce touched her cheek in faluting her; and when he gave her his bleffing, added—' Pray Heaven ' your future conduct may deferve it!' It could not be otherwife, but that all the company muft comprehend the full meaning of thefe words: but poor Melanthe

lanthe was so much affected by them, that she burst into a flood of tears; and throwing herself a second time at her father's feet, addressed him in these pathetick terms—

*Melanthe.* Oh, Sir, I beg, I beseech you, by all the love you once had for me, to forgive the only act of disobedience I was ever guilty of; pardon but the aversion I had to the match you first proposed to me, and you will easily absolve the rest.

*Dorimon.* Yes, Sir, my dear, my charming wife, is as innocent of every thing that can deserve your blame, as I am from even the most distant wish of violating her purity, or dishonouring your family.

*Florimel.* Aye, aye, it is poor me that am alone in fault; but, since the mischief I have done has been productive of so much good, I scarce doubt of being excused by a gentleman of so much good sense as Murcio. I have delivered your daughter, Sir, by my contrivance, from the horrors of a forced marriage; I have procured a wife for my brother, with whom, if he is not the most happy, I am certain he deserves to be the most miserable, of all mankind; and I have got you a son-in-law, who I hope will merit that honour by his future behaviour.

Murcio, who could not form even the most distant guess at the meaning of all this, looked sometimes on the one, and sometimes on the other, with all the tokens of the utmost amazement, without being able to speak one syllable; which gave Florimel the opportunity of unravelling the whole mystery of the affair, as she had before promised Melanthe to take upon herself to do. In spite of the little resentment Murcio at first conceived for the trick that had been put upon him, he could not forbear smiling at the invention of the contriver; and the wit and spirit with which that young lady talked to him upon it, very much contributed to bring him into good humour : but that which entirely reconciled him to the wedded pair was, the consideration that Dorimon was wholly ignorant of the plot till after the marriage was concluded; and the assurance Melanthe gave him, that she was far from any intention to deceive him, but had flattered herself with the hope that Conrade would have

broke the engagement without mentioning to him the reasons he had for doing so. Though to have married his daughter to Conrade would have saved him six thousand pounds, yet the many ill consequences which would probably have attended so disproportionate a match, now occurring to his mind, which before he had not thought upon, made him not only contented, but rejoiced, that this change of hands had happened; and he could not forbear kissing and hugging Florimel for being the chief author of it.

Every one now endeavouring to outvie the other in giving testimonies of his good-humour, among the many gay and gallant things said by Dorimon on this occasion, he protested to keep his French cloaths as long as he lived, for a perpetual memento of the good they had done for him, and never wear them but on the anniversary of that happy day which gave his dear Melanthe to his arms. On falling afterwards into some discourse concerning the oddness of the accident which had brought about a marriage so little thought of by either of the parties, yet so agreeable to both, as well as to their friends, Murcio expressed himself in this manner—

*Murcio.* I cannot help thinking that there is something peculiarly remarkable in this transaction, and looks as if the hand of Heaven had directed the accomplishment.

*Florimel.* I dare almost engage my own life for the mutual happiness of theirs. Their humours are so exactly suited to each other, that neither of them are fit for any body else; and, now I consider on it, am amazed that, in the long acquaintance they had together, this business never came into either of their heads till chance put it there.

*Dorimon.* Nay, sister, I am now convinced, by the transport and the pleasing flutter at my heart, on the offer Murcio made of his daughter, that I was then passionately in love with her, though without knowing it.

*Melanthe.* And if you had been as indifferent to me, as I then thought you were, I should not certainly have been so soon and so easily persuaded to be yours.

*Murcio.* Well, all things have happened for the best; and there is nothing now wanting to compleat my satisfaction,

tion, but the clearing up Melanthe's innocence to Conrade. I should be glad he were here.

The word was scarce out of his mouth, when a servant came into the room, and informed him, that the person he had mentioned was below; on which he ordered he should be immediately introduced. The old gentleman, who had heard nothing of what had happened, nor seen Murcio since the conversation with him, repeated in a former chapter, had been impatient to know the success of his proposal to Dorimon; and finding he did not return to town as usual, made him this visit at *****, in order to gratify his curiosity. He had not advanced above half way into the room, when Murcio presented the bride and bridegroom to him; and told him he had been just wishing for him to congratulate the nuptials. Conrade endeavoured to compose himself enough to salute them with the accustomed forms; but as he had not in his heart believed that Dorimon would be prevailed upon to marry Melanthe, though he had advised her father to make the experiment, was so much surprized on finding the affair concluded, that he could not forbear testifying it in his looks, as well as by crying out—

*Conrade.* What, married!

*Florimel.* Yes, Sir, they are married: the indissoluble knot is tied; for which all due thanks be given to your fortunate mistake.

*Conrade.* My mistake, Madam! Pardon me, if I do not comprehend your meaning.

*Dorimon.* I believe you do not, Sir: yet it is to your mistaking another for me, that I am indebted for being put in possession of a happiness which otherwise I must have solicited for a long series of time, and perhaps at last never have obtained. I do assure you, Sir, I never presumed to entertain one wish to the dishonour of Melanthe; and was sleeping in my own bed when you imagined my just risen from her arms.

*Murcio* He tell you nothing but the truth. He is innocent, so is Melanthe. But here stands her gallant; here is the author of this enigma.

In concluding these words, which he had uttered with the most cheerful air, he patted Florimel upon her cheek, and gently pushed her towards Conrade: but that gentleman was now in such a

consternation, that he scarce knew where he was, much less had the power of distinguishing the sense of any thing he either saw or heard; till Florimel related to him, in her sprightly fashion, every particular of that stratagem which had occasioned the breaking off the intended match between him and Melanthe. Murcio also, and Dorimon, averring the truth of what she said, he began at last to see clearly into the whole affair; after which Melanthe, with a great deal of modesty and sweetness, addressed herself to him in these terms—

*Melanthe.* I hope, Sir, you will pardon the deception put upon you, as I was constrained to pursue so extraordinary a method, to avoid a thing which, in the end, must have been no less disagreeable to you than to myself. I shall always acknowledge my obligation to the generous offer your affection made: but love, Sir, is not in our power; if it were, my gratitude to you, the consideration of my own interest, and the duty owing to my father, would certainly have inspired me with it.

*Conrade.* Say no more, sweet lady. I am ashamed of my past folly; and only wish you would exert all the influence you have over your witty she-gallant, not to expose this story in print. I should be sorry, methinks, to see myself in a novel or play.

*Florimel.* No, no, Sir; you need be under no apprehensions on that score. I would not, for my own sake, have the world know I put on breeches; lest my husband, when I get one, should be afraid I would attempt to wear them afterwards.

This reply of Florimel's set the whole company into a fit of laughter, and would doubtless have been the occasion of many pleasant repartees, if the butler had not that instant given them a summons to the next room, where was a table elegantly spread with every thing suitable to the season. But, as I could not partake of any of the delicacies I saw before me, I thought it best to leave the house; so accordingly I slipped out, plucked off my belt, went into a boat and ordered the waterman to row as fast as possible to London; where being arrived, I contented myself with such fare as my own homely board afforded. Not many weeks had this adventure elapsed, before I heard that Florimel was married to a young

gentleman

gentleman whom for feveral years fhe had loved, and by whom fhe was equally beloved. My infatiate curiofity, on this information, led me to enquire into the hidden caufe which had fo long delayed the completion of their mutual wifhes; and, by ways and means too tedious to be here inferted, I at laft difcovered it to be fuch as attracted my higheft efteem and admiration.

Dorimon had been a little extravagant in his equipage and way of living while on his travels. Her whole fortune lay in his hands; and if called out, which in all probability would have been the cafe if fhe had married, he muft have been obliged to mortgage fome part of his eftate for the payment. It was therefore to fave her brother from fo great an inconvenience, that this generous young lady had been deaf to all the folicitations of a beloved lover, and the foft pleadings of her own heart, till Melanthe's fortune coming into the family, removed the only impediment to her wifhes. Thus, by the moft unfeen, undreamt-of means, does Providence difpofe every thing for the advantage of it's favourites. Florimel, by her wit, and contrivance to ferve her fair friend, without propofing the leaft intereft to herfelf, or even imagining fhe could have any, not only brought about her brother's happinefs, but met her own reward, in the accomplifhment of her felicity. Thefe two families live together in the moft perfect harmony; and Murcio, who is little lefs fond of Florimel than of his own daughter, paffes moft of his time among them. Conrade alfo is extremely intimate with both; infomuch that it is thought he will, at his deceafe, divide a good part of his large fortune between them.

END OF THE SECOND BOOK.

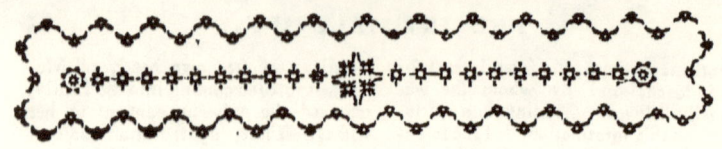

THE

# INVISIBLE SPY.

## BOOK III.

### CHAP. I.

IS A KIND OF WARNING-BELL TO
THE PUBLICK, AND GIVES A ME-
LANCHOLY, THOUGH TOO COM-
MON PROOF, THAT A PERSON IN
ENDEAVOURING, BY UNJUST OR
IMPRUDENT MEASURES, TO A-
VOID FALLING INTO AN IMA-
GINARY MISFORTUNE, IS FRE-
QUENTLY LIABLE TO BRING
ON EFFECTUALLY WHAT MIGHT
OTHERWISE NEVER HAVE HAP-
PENED.

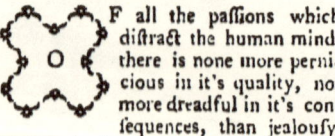F all the paſſions which
diſtract the human mind,
there is none more perni-
cious in it's quality, nor
more dreadful in it's conſequences, than jealouſy.
It is looked upon, indeed, as the moſt
certain proof of a ſtrong and violent affection; yet it is ſuch a proof as no one
would wiſh to experience, as it infallibly involves the beloved object in a
variety of diſquiets, whether innocent
or guilty: nor is the perſon poſſeſſed of
this raging fury leſs wretched; ſo juſt
are theſe words of Mr. Dryden—

' O jealouſy ! thou raging ill,
' Why haſt thou found a place in lover's
'   hearts ?
' Afflicting what thou canſt not kill,
' And poiſoning Love himſelf with his own
'   darts.'

And as the inimitable Shakeſpeare
yet more emphatically, in my opinion,
expreſſes it—

' O what damn'd minutes tells he o'er,
' Who doats, yet doubts; ſuſpects, yet ſtrong-
'   ly loves !'

But as jealouſy frequently takes poſſeſſion of the ſoul by almoſt imperceptible
degrees, the following little narrative
may ſerve as an antidote againſt it's poi-
ſon; and warn every one, married perſons eſpecially, not to give way to it's
firſt attacks, leſt it ſhould be in time,
wholly ſubdued by it.

Cleora had from her very infancy been
promiſed in marriage to the ſon of a
neighbouring gentleman, about three
years older than herſelf. An inclination for her intended huſband grew up
with her years; nor was his affection leſs
tender for her, whom he expected would
one day be his wife: but when the innocent

nocent pair became ripe for the con-.
summation of their mutual wishes, an
unhappy dispute happened between their
parents, which entirely broke off the
match at once, and they were forbid to
see each other any more. As I was not
at that time acquainted with either of
the lovers, I cannot pretend to describe
what their young hearts sustained in this
cruel separation: it was doubtless very
grievous to them both at first; but absence, and variety of amusements, provided for them by their respective parents, in order to dissipate their chagrin,
by degrees wrought the desired effects..
Leander, for so he was called, grew one
of the gayest men about the town; and.
Cleora was so far weaned from the remembrance of him, that she obeyed her
father without reluctance in receiving
the addresses of Aristus; who, after the
necessary forms of courtship, became her
husband.

Few nuptials gave a greater promise
of felicity. The births, the fortunes,
of the wedded pair, were equal; their
ages perfectly agreeable: she was not
quite nineteen, and he no more than five
and twenty; she was a very lovely woman he a most graceful man. He had
adored her to so romantick a height,
that it was thought, if he had not obtained her, a dagger or a bowl of poison
must have been his fate. She treated
him with all the tenderness that could
be expected from a virtuous woman by
a reasonable man. They were, in the
first months of their marriage, the envy
and admiration of as many as knew
them. But, alas! how uncertain is the
date of human happiness! When Heaven
is not pleased to bestow on us a contented
mind; I mean, when we do not ask that
blessing, and endeavour to acquire it; in
vain indulgent Fortune lavishes her
whole stock of bounties on us; we re-
pine amidst our plenty, enjoy nothing
we possess, and are wretches because we
will be so.

The bridal house, so lately the theatre
of joy and pleasure, soon became the cell
of gloomy sullenness and black despair.
The eyes of the beautiful Cleora were
frequently seen red with weeping: she
ceased to appear at any publick place,
and received very little company at
home; while on the brow of the once
chearful, gay Aristus, now loured a
heavy melancholy, and all the indications of a deep inward grief. Every

one saw the change, but none could
presently discern the cause: it could not,.
however, long be kept a secret; the servants who waited immediately on their
persons were the first who discovered it;
these reported it to the others, and they
failed not to whisper it to as many as
they were acquainted with—that their
master was prodigiously jealous of his
lady.

The first tokens he gave of this
frenzy, as I have been since informed,
was to debar Cleora from going to the
opera, the play, the masquerade, and all
routs and assemblies; all which places
she had been accustomed to frequent.
She obeyed him, notwithstanding, without murmuring or repining; and told
him, with a great deal of sweetness,
that if those diversions were infinitely
dearer to her than ever they had been,
she would readily sacrifice all the pleasure she took in them to that of testifying her love and duty to him. Not
contented with this, he proceeded farther, and forbade her to make any
visits without him, except to his mother, who lived but in the next street;
and then to let him know, that he might
meet her there, and bring her home.
Hard as this injunction seemed to her,
she complied with it; being resolved, if
possible, to chace from his mind all
those ideas she found he had conceived
in prejudice of her discretion, and convince him that she regarded nothing so
much as his satisfaction.

What more could woman do, or man
expect? yet all was not enough to make
this jealous husband easy. Whenever
they were abroad together, if any gentleman happened to be in company, the
least gallant thing said to her, or complaisance returned to it by her, immediately set the worm within his brain a
madding, and made him, on their coming home, reproach her in terms very
unbecoming in him to use of, and
and difficult for her to bear with patience: yet, nevertheless, he still loved
her, loved her to an excess; but, as the
poet says—

' No signs of love in jealous men remain,
' But that which sick men have of life,
' their pain.'

This behaviour of Aristus engrossed
much of the conversation of the town,
and various were the conjectures passed

upon it. Some highly blamed him; others were apt to imagine there had really been some imprudences on the part of Cleora; and not a few there were among her own sex, who, hating her for those very perfections which ought to have excited their esteem, scrupled not to pronounce her guilty of every thing she could be suspected of.

Much was this lady to be pitied. Deprived of all those pleasures to which her youth had been accustomed, ill-treated by her husband, censured by her acquaintance, and secluded from the society of those who might have found means of diverting, if not wholly dissipating her melancholy. To add to her misfortunes, she had no friend near her to whom she might complain. Her father, being a widower, had broke up house-keeping soon after her marriage, and was retired, with an intent to pass the remainder of his days with her elder sister, who was settled in a far distant county; so that the only person from whom she received any consolation was Miss Lucia, the sister of Ariftus, a young lady of great good-nature, and who believing her truly innocent, used her utmost endeavours to put all chimeras to her prejudice out of her brother's head,

The discourses which continually filled my ears about this family, and the different opinions the world had of the manner of their living together, made me resolve to have recourse to my Invisibility, in order to discover which was in the right. Accordingly, I went one day, equipped as usual, with my Belt and Tablet, to make a visit at their house. Ariftus was abroad; but I found Cleora, sitting in a very pensive posture, in her dressing-room. I had not been there above two minutes, before her footman came in, and presented her with a letter, which he told her was left for her by a porter, who said it required no answer, and was gone.

I must confess that, on hearing this, I was guilty of great injustice to Cleora, and began to be apprehensive that her husband's suspicions were founded on too solid reasons; but I was soon ashamed of my rash judgment, when, slipping behind her chair, and looking over her shoulder as she read, I perceived the letter was from Miss Lucia, and contained these lines—

'DEAR SISTER,

'WORDS cannot express how greatly I am troubled, on finding myself obliged to send this, instead of waiting on you in person. Be assured I love and value your conversation as I ought; and shall no less suffer in being deprived of it, Heaven knows for how long a time, than you will do in the knowledge of the cause. Some idle stories, of which, I dare believe, my brother's unhappy caprice has been the sole occasion, have reached the ears of my mamma, and made her think it improper for me to be seen with you, while the world continues to judge of you in the manner it does at present. She heard of your message to me, and strictly forbade me to obey the summons. You know too well, my dear Cleora, what duty is owing from a child to a parent, and also how much my father's will has left me in her power, to resent the painful proof I now give of my obedience to her. I wish, for my own sake, as well as yours, that she, my brother, and every one that knows us, were as well convinced as myself of your perfect innocence; but, till that happy time arrives, must content myself with the memory of the many happy hours we have passed together, and the hopes of many more yet to come, when once the horrid cloud which now separates us is removed. Farewell! That Heaven may send you comfort under your present affliction, and speedily relieve you from it, shall be the constant prayers of her who is, with the greatest sincerity, your most affectionate sister,

'LUCIA.'

Scarce had she gone through half this epistle, before her countenance betrayed the effect it produced. Disdain, rage, grief, seemed now to have united all their force to raise a tempest in her mind; which immediately broke forth in these and the like exclamations—'Deprived of my poor Lucia, too, and on so shocking a pretence! Good Heaven! for what unknown crime of mine, or of my ancestors, am I linked into such a family! Mother and son alike unjust, ungrateful, base, tyrannick! Have I renounced all the gay amusements of life, submitted my temper to the

'.the will of an imperious husband, and
' made it my whole study to oblige him,
' to meet at last with this ungenerous,
' this barbarous return! My virtue su-
' spected, my reputation traduced, and
' my conversation shunned as a dis-
' grace! Oh, 'tis too much—too much
' for human patience to sustain!'

Many other expressions of the same
nature did her pafsion vent; till, at last,
recollecting the request Lucia had made
in the postscript of her letter, she snatched
it haftily from off her toilet, and thrust
it into the fire; saying, at the same time,
' Poor Lucia, however, must not suffer
' for her friendship to me.'

Aristus being returned home, was that
instant coming up stairs ; which being
opposite to the room where Cleora was,
and the door open, he had an opportunity of seeing this last action, though
not of hearing the words which accompanied it. He flew like lightning to
the chimney, in order to save the paper,
not doubting but it contained something
that might add fresh fuel to his jealoufy; but, nimble as he was, the flames
were yet more quick, and left not the
least part of what he so much wanted
unconfumed. This difappointment,
joined with what he had seen Cleora do,
so much inflamed him, that looking on
her with eyes sparkling with indignation, he saluted her with this reproach—

*Aristus.* I perceive, Madam, you
will be still too cunning for me. Had I
come a moment sooner, I might, perhaps, have difcovered enough in that paper, to have filenced all your future
boaftings of virtue and fidelity.

*Cleora.* Oh, Sir, you need be under
no apprehenfions on that fcore. The
continuance of your bafe fufpicions deferve not that I should be at any pains to
undeceive you.

*Aristus.* No, 'twould be in vain:
too well I know you. Nor can you,
dare you, now attempt to juftify yourfelf, after the glaring proof I have received of your infidelity.

*Cleora.* What proof?

*Aristus.* That paper, perfidious woman!—that paper, whose ashes, could
they speak, would rife up in judgment
against you.

*Cleora.* This is madness, or fome
new pretext to ufe me ill. Pray, what
can the moft injurious of your imagina-

tions fuggeft on the burning of a bit of
paper?

*Aristus.* Did I not obferve your
countenance while throwing the lewd
fcrawl into the fire? Did not your
gloating eyes purfue it as you would the
fellow from whom it came? Were not
all the marks of guilt and confufion on
your cheeks on my approach? But this
is not all : I was told below that you
had juft received a letter by a porter.
Anfwer to that, thou hypocrite! Does
it become a married woman, of your
rank and circumftances, to receive letters, brought by fuch meffengers?

*Cleora.* A married woman! fay rather a married wretch! for fuch are all
who have hufbands like Aristus.

*Aristus.* Still you evade the queftion;
but, if you would not deferve to be the
wretch you call yourfelf, be once fincere,
and tell me from which of your pretended admirers that letter came.

*Cleora.* From none.

*Aristus.* Perhaps, then, fome female agents, fome fly promoters of your
amorous intrigues. But no equivoca-
tions : explain the whole, or, by Heaven, my fword——

*Cleora.* Do! kill me! it is the only
act of kindnefs you can fhew, and all I
now wifh to receive from you.

*Aristus.* So daring in your crimes,
abandoned creature! But get out of
my fight this moment, left I be indeed
provoked to do a deed I might hereafter
repent of.

*Cleora.* Monfter!—But to quit your
prefence is a command I shall always be
ready to obey.

It was with an unfpeakable haughti-
nefs that Cleora uttered thefe words as
she flung out of the room. I am apt to
believe, by the amazement Aristus now
appeared in, that this was the firft time
she had ever teftified any great marks of
refentment for his ill treatments of her.
He ftood for fome moments in a profound reverie; and, when he came out
of it, lifted up his hands and eyes to heaven, faying—' Good God! nothing
' but the moft perfect innocence, or the
' moft confummate guilt, could infpire
' a woman with fo much boldnefs.
' I know not what to think.' Then
folding his arms, again feemed loft in
meditation; which having indulged a
while, the fubject of it burft out in thefe
words—' If the were innocent, where-
' fore

' fore fhould fhe conceal from me the
' contents of that curfed letter? No,
' 'tis too plain fhe is guilty. In vain
' would my fond heart, that ftill doats
' on her, find excufes for her behaviour.
' Yet it would be fome eafe to be con-
' vinced: but it is impoffible; fhe has
' too much art. How true, O Dryden,
' are thy words—

" Fa'fe women to new joys unfeen can
" move;
  • There are no prints left in the paths of
" love.
" All other goods by publick marks are
" known;
" But this, we moft defire to keep, has
" none."

After this, he walked feveral times
backwards and forwards in the room,
then ran haftily down ftairs, as I imagined, in fearch of Cleora; but finding
he did not, and went out of the houfe, I
alfo left it too, having an engagement of
my own that evening.


CHAP. II.

IN WHICH THE READER IS RE-
QUESTED TO EXPECT NO MORE
THAN A CONTINUATION OF THE
SAME NARRATIVE BEGUN IN THE
PRECEDING CHAPTER.


THE diftrefs in which I left Cleora,
and the knowledge I now had of
her innocence very much affected me;
and I muft either have changed my nature, or have loft that happy gift of Invifibility which enabled me to difcover
almoft every thing, not to have flown the
next morning to the houfe of Ariftus, in
order to inform myfelf what effects the
converfation of the preceding night had
produced. I truly; pitied the unhappy pair:
for though Ariftus was unjuft and cruel
in his fufpicions, yet I plainly faw he fuffered no lefs in his own mind than what
he inflicted on his much-injured wife;
efpecially when I reflected that he was not
guilty through a want of affection for
her but a too violent excefs of it; as
is obferved by one of our beft Englifh
poets—

' The greater care the higher paffion fhews,
' We hold that deareft we moft fear to
' lofe.'

Indeed I foon found, how much more
than I could even have imagined this offending hufband deferved my commi-
feration. He was abroad, and Cleora
not yet rifen from her bed, when I made
my vifit; which, as near as I can remember, was fomewhat paft eleven
o'clock. Refolved, however, not to'
lofe my labour entirely, I had recourfe
for intelligence to the tatlers of the
kitchen; whom, according to my wifh,
I found bufy in difcourfe on the very
point I wanted. Some took the part of
their mafter, fome of their lady: and,
upon the whole, I found, that a fecond
quarrel having enfued after Ariftus came
home, Cleora had refufed either to fup
or fleep with him, but lay in a bed fhe
had ordered to be prepared for her in
another room; on which he went not to
his own, but had continued the whole
night walking about the houfe, and
behaved like a man totally deprived of
reafon; and that, when morning came,
he went out.

On a fudden, hearing the footman fay
that his mafter knocked at the ftreet-
door, I followed as faft as I could; being more curious to fee how Ariftus
would behave, than to hear what would
be the iffue of the conteft between the
fervants. Accordingly I got clofe in
the corner of an arch while he paffed by,
and could fee nothing in his countenance of that ferocity the fervants had
been defcribing; on the contrary, a
perfect compofure feemed to me to fit
upon all his features, and left not the
leaft traces of diffatisfaction. I attended him to the chamber which
Cleora had made choice of for her repofe, if it were poffible for her to take
any, the preceding night. He knocked
gently at the door; but finding it not
readily opened, retired, and went into
the dining-room; where he called a fervant, and bid him feek his wife's waiting-maid, and order her to come immediately to him. The young woman
prefently appeared; though, I eafily
difcerned, not without fome tremor of
the nerves; expecting, perhaps, to participate in the effects of her mafter's difpleafure: her countenance, however,
grew more affured, when he fpoke in
the moft courteous accents, faying—
    *Ariftus.* Is your lady awake yet,
Mrs. Betty?
    *Waiting-maid.* Yes, Sir.
    *Ariftus.* Then let her know I am
ready

ready for breakfaft; and afk if fhe will have the tea ferved where fhe is, or in her own dreffing-room, as ufual.

She faid no more; and, after making a low curtfey, went out of the room, very much furprized at this fudden turn; as indeed was I, after what I had feen and heard; nor was able to determine, as yet, whether the extraordinary complaifance he fhewed was real or affected. I was foon convinced, however, when the maid returned with this anfwer to his meffage—

*Waiting-maid.* Sir, my lady defires to be excufed. She has got a violent head-ache, and begs not to be difturbed.

*Ariftus.* Tell her I bring her news that will make her well. No—hold— I will go myfelf.

With thefe laft words he flew to the chamber; and, pufhing open the door, which was now unlocked, found his wife fitting in a very melancholy and dejected pofture. She ftarted up at fight of him; and, without giving him leave to fpeak, accofted him in thefe terms—

*Cleora.* 'Tis hard that no part of a houfe, of which I am flattered with the name of miftrefs, can protect me from the infults of a man who certainly married me with no other view than to make me miferable.

*Ariftus.* Oh, fay not fo! I will foon convince you to the contrary; nor fhall you ever more have caufe to fly the prefence of Ariftus. I own I have been to blame; have faid and done a thoufand things that I am afhamed to think of. But why, my dear Cleora, did you raife my paffion to that guilty height? Why conceal from me the author and contents of the letter which gave me fo much pain?

*Cleora.* It would be eafy for me to juftify my refufal.

*Ariftus.* I know it would, my angel; full well I know it would; but I am now let into the fecret, without your being guilty of a breach of friendfhip to oblige me.

*Cleora.* What is it you mean, Ariftus?

*Ariftus.* I have been this morning at my mother's; where, fpeaking of our unhappy quarrel, and the motive of it, my fifter immediately changed countenance; and, after vindicating your conduct with the utmoft vehemence, and as

feverely condemning mine, confeffed that it was herfelf that had fent that letter to you by a porter, and had defired you to burn it as foon as read.

*Cleora.* Dear Lucia! Oh that the brother had the fifter's temper!

*Ariftus.* Brother and fifter are equally devoted to you. If Lucia were Ariftus, fhe would do as Ariftus does; and if Ariftus were Lucia, he would act like Lucia. The difference of fexes makes all the difference in our fentiments or behaviour. Her's is a tender friendfhip, mine a raging love; which, while happy in your poffeffion, trembles at even the moft diftant poffibility of ever being lefs fo.

*Cleora.* Can it be love that fufpects my virtue?

*Ariftus.* By Heaven! my cooler moments have never fet you down as capable of wronging me, or of difhonouring yourfelf; but when paffion rages in the foul, reafon has little government over our thoughts or words. I know I have been much to blame; but, O Cleora! forgive a fault occafioned only by an excefs of fondnefs. So dear I prize you, that I envy the very air that breathes upon your lips; and wifh to grow for ever there, and keep out all intruders.

*Cleora.* But do you confider how wretched this caufelefs jealoufy has made me?

*Ariftus.* Yes, and could tear out my heart for having ever harboured the leaft unjuft fufpicion of you; yet have I fuffered torments much greater than was in my power to inflict. Could you be fenfible of the agonies I felt during this laft whole cruel night, you muft, you would forgive and pity me.

*Cleora.* Mine have not been lefs; yet could I forget all, had my reputation been untouched by your ill-ufage. You now know the purport of your fifter's letter; and can you think it poffible for me to fupport, with patience, the being looked upon by your kindred as a difgrace to the family I am come among?

*Ariftus.* Think not fo, my dear Cleora. My fifter was always affured of your innocence, and a ftrenuous vindicator of every thing you did. My mother never thought worfe than that fome little inadvertencies in your conduct had wrought me up to the follies I have been guilty of, which fhe has juft now feverely

verely chid me for. They will both wait on you this afternoon, and give you all the proofs in their power of the fincere refpect and tendernefs they have for you.

*Cleora.* Well, Ariftus, if I could be certain that this was the laft trial you would make of my good-nature, I might, perhaps, endeavour to think no more on what is paft.

*Ariftus.* If ever I fall back into my former errors, defpife me, hate me, think me the worft of men. No, be af-fured I am too much afhamed of what I have been, ever to be the like again; and, as a proof of the perfect confidence I now have in you, henceforward keep what company you pleafe. I fhall pre-fcribe no rules for your conduct; I fhall leave all to yourfelf, and be fatisfied that all you do is right.

*Cleora.* I fhall take the lefs liberty for your granting me fo much. But, if you fhould relapfe, remember what a certain celebrated author of our fex fays on this occafion—

‘ We women to ourfelves this juftice owe,
‘ That thofe who think us falfe, fhould
      ‘ find us fo.’

She fpoke this with fo enchanting a fmile, that Arifus, though not yet quite fure that what he did would be agree-able, could not forbear catching her in his arms, and holding her for fome time locked in the moft ftrict embrace; then letting her loofe, and looking on her with the extremeft tendernefs, cried—

*Arifus.* Do you then forgive me?

*Cleora.* I do.

With thefe words, fhe threw her fnowy arms about his neck, and put her face clofe to his, returning all the en-dearments he had juft before given her; after which, that is, as foon as the tranfport he was in would give him leave to fpeak, he faid—

*Arifus.* My for ever adored Cleora, depend upon it, that the whole ftudy of my life fhall be to requite this goodnefs.

*Cleora.* Treat me but as my actions deferve; I afk no more. But come, let us go to breakfaft.

With this they went arm in arm into the next room, where Mrs. Betty and the tea-equipage waited their approach. I now left this once more happy pair to enjoy the fweets of their reconciliation; and, as I doubted not but the contrition

of Arifus would be as lafting, as by many indications I had reafon to think it was fincere, expected not that any future events, worthy the attention of an Invi-fible Spy, would happen to call me to their houfe again. But, unhappily for the perfons concerned in it, a very few days after convinced me how little I was endowed with the fpirit of prophecy; and alfo, that when once the fatal fire of jealoufy has got poffeffion of the mind, though it may lie dormant for a while, yet the leaft wafting of a feather, or even a fhadow, is fufficient to give it mo-tion, and kindle the fmothered embers into a blaze.

I was loitering one morning in the Park. The air was ferene, and not cold, the time of the year confidered; for it was then November. Few peo-ple being there, I had an opportunity of indulging contemplation with the won-ders of nature; which, even in the moft barren feafon, affords matter to attract our admiration; and was almoft loft in thought, when I was fuddenly rouzed from it by the appearance of Cleora; who, in a rich, genteel difhabille, came tripping down the walk; and, after looking two or three times round her, feated herfelf on a bench juft oppofite to St. James's Houfe. My furprize to find a lady of her rank alone in that place ftopped my farther progrefs, and en-gaged me to draw near her, in order to obferve whether chance, or any parti-cular motive, had brought her hither. In lefs time than the taking a pinch of fnuff would laft, Arifus came as from the palace: he faw his wife at a diftance; croffed over, and came to her, faying—

*Arifus.* What, are you here, my dear, and alone?

*Cleora.* You fee I am; but I did not expect to be picked up by a gentleman this morning. We are well met, how-ever; and, if you have no bufinefs that requires hafte, fhould be glad you would give me your company while I ftay, which will not be long.

*Arifus.* With all my heart. I was only going to the coffee-houfe. And, in return for my complaifance, you fhall tell me by what accident I find you here thus unguarded.

*Cleora.* Can one be unguarded where there are fo many foldiers? But, you muft know, I have been among the fhops at Charing Crofs, and made a great many purchafes. I chufe to walk
**over**

the Park. I had William with me; but, as I knew the centry would not suffer him to pass through with the things, I sent him home the other way. When I came hither, I found the air so extremely pleasant, that I was tempted to sit down and enjoy a little of it; especially as I found nobody here that I thought would take notice of me. And now you have the whole history of my morning's transactions.

*Ariflus.* A very concise one. But suppose, my dear, you had met with any of the Bucks, the Bloods, or the Buffs, how would you have escaped their attacks?

*Cleora.* Why, I would have set my arms a-kimbo, and looked as fierce as they. Those sort of squires are never bold but to the fearful.

Finding, by their talking together in this gay manner, that they continued in perfect good-humour with each other, I thought I had no business to be an eves-dropper any longer, and was going to quit the place where I had stood; when, just as I had taken it into my head to do so, two gentlemen came down the walk; one of whom, in passing by the bench, stopped short, looked earnestly at Cleora, started, made a low bow, and then went on. She returned the salute, but with a confusion impossible to be expressed. She blushed; she trembled through every joint; her fan fell out of her hand; and she was ready to sink herself upon the seat. A less observing husband than Aristus must have taken notice of this sudden change; but the alarm it gave his jealous heart, was such as compelled him to be speechless for some moments. Cleora in vain endeavoured to recompose herself; all the efforts she made to suppress or to conceal her agitations, rendered them but the more violent, and consequently the more visible. Aristus, at last, broke silence with these words—

*Ariflus.* You seem disordered, Madam. The sight of these gentlemen has had a strange effect upon you.

*Cleora.* I was a little surprized at the sight of one of them. But that is not all: I am not well.

*Ariflus.* I see you are not, either in mind or body. My coming was unlucky. Had I been absent, you would doubtless have retained your former gaiety. But this is no place to expatiate on the cause of your disorder: I

will get one of the soldiers to call a chair; 'tis fit you should go home.

He waited not to hear what answer she would make, but rose hastily up, and spoke to one who was not upon duty. The fellow ran to do as he was desired, and presently returned with a chair. While he was gone, Cleora had recovered herself enough to say to Aristus— ' I perceive you are beginning to enter- ' tain sentiments to my disadvantage; ' but have patience till we get home, ' and I shall easily make this matter ' clear.' As he was putting her into the chair, she added—' You will fol- ' low presently.' To which he replied—' I shall not be long after you; ' though I believe your own medita- ' tions, at this time, will be more ' agreeable to you than the company of ' a husband.'

I perceived very plainly, by the countenance of Aristus, that a storm was gathering in his breast, which I doubted not would break forth in thunder. I could not help also being of opinion, that there were some appearances, on the part of Cleora, not much to her advantage. I thought, however, that the best way to form a true judgment of the accidents of that morning, were to see them when they were together; so forbore following either of them, and restrained my impatience till near the hour in which they usually dined, as being the most likely time to find Aristus at home. On my coming to their house, I found the door open, and a footman, in a laced livery, sitting on a bench in the hall, as waiting for an answer to some message he brought. I went directly up to the dining-room; no person being there, I passed on to Cleora's apartment, and found her writing at her bureau. A letter lay open before her, containing these lines—

' TO CLEORA.

' MADAM,

' I Heard not of your marriage till some
' weeks after it was consummated;
' and when I did, the hurry of my af-
' fairs, being then just going to Paris,
' prevented my congratulating you upon
' it. I returned to England but three
' days since; and the first enquiry I
' made, was concerning your health
' and place of abode: but the answers
' I received to these interrogatories were

K
' mingled

' mingled with fome other informa-
' tions, which make me not quite fare
' that a vifit from me might not give
' offence to that happy gentleman who
' is now your hufband. I would not
' therefore take the liberty of waiting
' on you till I had firft received your per-
' miffion. It is a bleffing I ardently
' long for; but, whether proper for you
' to grant or not, beg you will believe
' that I am, with an efteem too juftly
' grounded for change of circumftances
' to alter, Madam, your moft faithfully
' devoted, and moft humble fervant,
                              ' LEANDER.'

The anfwer given by Cleora to the
above billet was as follows—

' SIR,

' THAT I ftill retain a place in your
            ' remembrance, demands my
' grateful acknowledgments; and am
' forry to tell you, that it is at this dif-
' tance only I can pay my thanks. It
' is eafy for me to guefs of what nature
' the informations you mention have
' been, and think myfelf obliged fo far
' to confirm the truth of them, as to
' let you know the favour you intended
' me is wholly improper for me to re-
' ceive; and to defire you will attempt
' no future correfpondence of any kind
' with her who is no longer miftrefs of
' her actions, but who muft always
' preferve in her heart the beft wifhes
' for your welfare.

                              ' CLEORA.'

Having fealed this, fhe called her
maid Betty, and bid her deliver it to
the man who waited for it; then took
up Leander's letter, and read it two or
three times over to herfelf, with very
difturbed emotions; after which, fhe
rofe haftily from the pofture fhe had
been in, whether with a defign to burn,
or lay it carefully up, I cannot pretend
to fay, for her hufband that inftant
flew into the room, and fnatched it out
of her hand. She fhrieked; and, in
my opinion, very imprudently endeavoured to wreft it from him. His ftature, as well as ftrength, being much
fuperior to hers, he held it at arm's
length, and read the contents, in fpite of
all her weak efforts to hinder it; which
done, he clapped it into his pocket,
ftamped, bit his lips, meafured the room
with wild unequal paces, ftill as he

turned darting revengeful glances at the
trembling Cleora. Thefe, and other
fuch like frantick geftures, introduced
the following dialogue between them—

Cleora. What is there in that letter
can have moved you thus?

Ariftus. Was it not fent by him
whofe fight this morning threw you
into fuch diforder?

Cleora. I was a little furprized at
the fudden appearance of a perfon I had
not feen for a long time; but know not
that the diforder I was in proceeded
from that caufe.

Ariftus. He knew it did, and I fuppofe fent you this by way of confolation.

Cleora. You put an odd interpreta-
tion on his words, as well as on my
looks. Is this, Ariftus, the effect of all
thofe promifes you fo lately made?

Ariftus. When I made thofe promifes, I was fo weak as to believe there
was a poffibility of your being faithful:
but am now convinced of what you are;
know that you are the moft vile of women, and I the moft accurfed of men!

Cleora. You make yourfelf indeed the
one, by your unjuft fufpicions; but no
action of mine fhall ever prove I am the
other.

Ariftus. Death and furies! Did I
not meet the villain's fervant with a
letter from you in his hand!

Cleora. Suppofe you did. I wrote
to forbid his coming hither.

Ariftus. Yes, and no doubt to appoint a place more convenient.

Cleora. 'Tis falfe; nor would the
man whom your fufpicions wrong me
with, harbour a thought to the prejudice
either of my virtue or my reputation.
No, if you had half his honour, or
his love, I fhould not be the wretch I
am.

Ariftus. Then you confefs he loves
you?

Cleora. He loved me once; and
though Heaven thought fit to break off
our intended union, I believe ftill pre-
ferves an efteem for me.

Ariftus. As you for him. Hell and
vengeance! Dare you avow this to my
face! Have I then only the leavings,
the refufe, of a beloved rival! Audacious ftrumpet!

In fpeaking this, he ftruck her fo violent a blow over the face, that the blood
gufhed from her nofe and mouth; on
which fhe cried out—' Villain! there
                              ' wanted

'wanted but this to prove the basenefs 'of thy abject soul! But think not the 'name of wife shall make me tamely 'bear such usage; no, if the laws of 'England should refuse me justice, I 'will fly to the remotest corner of the 'earth, and seek refuge among the less 'barbarous Hottentots, rather than live 'beneath the roof with such a mon-'ster!'

How Aristus would have behaved on this is uncertain; a servant that moment entered the room, and told him that a gentleman, who it seems he had sent for that morning upon business, was now come to wait upon him. Whatever was in the mind of this distracted husband, he had no farther opportunity of shewing it at present; and only giving a furious look at Cleora, and muttering some inarticulate curses between his teeth as he went out, left her to ruminate on what was past. She no sooner found herself alone, than she rung the bell for her maid, who appeared quite frighted on seeing her lady in such a condition. The girl's exclamations made her turn to the looking-glass; and the injury that had been done her, it is probable, gave strength to her resentment, and she resolved to put in immediate execution what she had threatened Aristus with doing.

Betty had lived with her before her marriage, and was no stranger to the love that had been between her and Leander. The enraged fair-one, therefore, scrupled not to make her the confidant of the motive of this last quarrel with her husband, and the intention she had of quitting him for ever; then, after considering a little in what manner she should manage this affair, gave the following orders—' I would have you take a 'hackney-coach for expedition sake, 'and go to Mrs. Clip's the tirewoman: 'I know she lets lodgings. If she has 'any apartment ready, hire it directly; 'but if her house happens to be full, do 'not return without procuring one for 'me in some other; for I am determined 'to go this very day, and shall think 'every moment an age till I am out of 'this detested place.'

While the maid was gone, Cleora set about packing up her cloaths and jewels; which she did with such adroit-ness and dispatch, that in less than an hour every thing belonging to her was ready to be sent away. In a little

more than that time Betty returned, and told her that Mrs. Clip's first floor being let, she had agreed for the par-lours, which she said were very hand-some, and she believed her ladyship would approve of, at least till a better apartment could be provided. Cleora was satisfied; another coach was called to carry her, and the maid followed in the other with the luggage. Aristus was all this time abroad: he went out with the gentleman who had called on him, and his absence very much faci-litated the execution of his wife's design; for, had he been at home, 'tis certain that either his love or anger, or perhaps a mixture of both, would have attempt-ed to detain her. But what effects the steps she had taken produced, both on the one and the other, must be left to the succeeding chapter.

## CHAP. III.

IN WHICH THE CONSEQUENCES OF CLEORA'S ELOPEMENT ARE FUL-LY SHEWN, AND AN END PUT TO THAT SUSPENSE WHICH THE FORMER PAGES MAY HAVE EX-CITED IN THE MIND OF EVE-RY INTERESTED AND CURIOUS READER.

I Staid some hours at the house of Aristus, expecting to be witness of something extraordinary in his beha-viour, when he should be told of the de-parture of his wife; but he returning not in all that time, I grew weary of the tedious attendance, and quitted my post in order to go home; for as to Cle-ora, I had no thoughts of visiting her in her new apartment till next morning. It not being late, however, I took it into my head to call at a great coffee-house in my way, and lucky was it for the gratification of my curiosity that I did so. I found Aristus there; he was sitting at a table, in one corner of the room, some distance from the other company, with paper and a standish before him. I advanced with all the speed I could towards him, and saw him write the following billet to Leander—

'SIR.

'YOU are a villain, and have en-'deavoured to wrong me in a 'point too tender to be forgiven. I 'need

K 2

' need only tell you that I am the huf-
' band cf Cleora, to inform you both
' of what I mean, and what fort of fa-
' tisfaction my honour demands from
' you, which I expect you will give me
' to-morrow morning at feven, in the
' Artillery Ground, Tothill Fields.
' The bearer has orders to wait your
' anfwer to
                        ' ARISTUS.'

This he fent by a porter to the
Braund's Head in Bond Street; at
which houfe, as I afterwards difcovered,
he had, with a good deal of pains, got
intelligence that Leander conftantly fupped every night. I waited behind
Ariftus, with an impatience, perhaps,
not inferior to his own, to fee what reply Leander would make to the above,
till the porter returned from him with
thefe lines—

' SIR,
' THOUGH your telling me that
'     you are the hufband of Cleora,
' cannot make me in the leaft fenfible
' how I deferve the name of villain,
' yet I can eafily guefs at the fatisfac-
' tion you require, and fhall not fail to
' meet you at the hour and place ap-
' pointed, in hopes of being better in-
' formed for what imaginary caufe you
' treat in this manner a perfon who nei-
' ther knows, or ever had any defign
' to injure you.
                        ' LEANDER.'

Ariftus, after having read this, ftaid
no longer than to drink one difh of coffee. As I perceived he turned that way
which led to his own houfe, I could
not forbear accompanying him thither;
and I believe, by what I have to relate,
the reader will think I had no reafon to
repent the pains I took. He was no
fooner entered, than he afked haftily for
his wife, doubtlefs with an intention to
renew his reproaches, and give a vent
to fome part of the fury he was poffeffed
of: but never certainly did aftonifhment
work a more ftrange effect. On being
told fhe was gone, and the manner in
which fhe went, the fudden fhock at
once deprived him both of fpeech and
motion; his face grew pale as afhes;
his eyes were fixed in a ftupid ftare;
and had he been buried for three days,
fcarce could he have appeared more the
ghoft of what he was the moment be-

fore. His deadened faculties by degrees
reviving, the firft ufe he made of them
was to call up all the fervants; afking
firft one, and then another, why fhe
was fuffered to depart, why they did
not ftop her. To which they anfwered,
that having no order from him, they
durft not prefume fo far; and befides,
they knew nothing of her going till
they faw the coaches at the door, and
the portmanteaus carried out.
He next demanded to what place fhe
had directed herfelf to be carried; but
both Cleora and her maid having taken
the precaution to give no order to the
coachman till they were got fome diftance from the houfe, no one of them
was able to give him any information;
on which he fent them out of the room,
not without fome curfes on their indolence in not following the coaches: then,
thinking himfelf alone, began to give a
loofe to the dictates of his defpair and
rage in thefe expreffions—' Then fhe is
' loft, for ever loft to me! for if fhe
' fhould return, my honour, after this,
' would not permit me to receive her.
' Why did I ever marry! What de-
' mon tempted me to become the huf-
' band of a woman whom I knew all
' mankind muft love as well as I!
' Curfe on my fond paffion! curfe on
' her fatal charms! Oh the deceiver!
' the vile hypocrite! There is no longer
' any room for doubt; her flight has
' proved her guilt. Revenge is now
' my fole relief; fhe for the prefent has
' efcaped my reach, but I will ftab her
' image in Leander's heart. Oh that it
' were morning!'
While uttering the latter part of this
exclamation, he flew about the room as
if totally bereft of reafon; till his fpirits, at length exhaufted by the violence
of his rage, funk into the contrary extreme, that of dejection; he folded his
arms, fighed, and, with tears burfling
from his eyes, cried out—' Oh Cleora,
' Cleora! lovely, perfidious wanton, to
' what haft thou reduced me!' He
then threw himfelf down on a fettee,
with groans like thofe which iffue from
the breafts of men dying in their full vigour; whence, after having lain fome
time, he ftarted up, faying—' I will
' think no more! To hear of my dif-
' tractions would but foothe her pride.'
He feemed now a little more compofed, and called for fomething to eat;
but, on it's being brought, could not put
                                    one

●ne morfel into his mouth; fo rofe from table, and went up to his own chamber; where I did not think fit to purfue him, as having already feen enough to make me know the prefent difpofition of his mind. It was my full intention, however, to go in the morning to the Artillery Ground, to be fpectator of the combat between him and Leander; but was difappointed, by fleeping beyond the time they were to meet. This a little vexed me; but I confoled myfelf with the thoughts of being able to hear the event, by calling fome part of the day at the houfe of Ariftus, for I knew not where Leander lived. But my concern for Cleora carrying me firft to her lodgings, there I got all the intelligence I wanted. I found that lady, as I believe, juft rifen from her bed, for fhe was in a loofe entire defhabille. She feemed very penfive, and had the marks of her jealous hufband's refentment ftill flagrant on her lovely face. Betty was not with her when I came in, but entered immediately after, and furprized her with thefe words—

*Betty.* Oh, Madam, I have the ftrangeft thing to tell you!—Who does your ladyfhip think I have feen?

*Cleora.* Nay, I know not. Who, pray?

*Betty.* The very footman that brought your ladyfhip the letter yefterday, and put my mafter into fuch a rage. I was never fo confounded in my whole life.

*Cleora.* Confounded, for what?—Where did you fee him?

*Betty.* In the kitchen, Madam. When I went down, juft now, to put on the tea-kettle for breakfaft, who fhould I fee there but him talking to Mrs. Clip! His mafter lodges here in the apartment above.

*Cleora.* Good Heaven! Was there ever fo unfortunate an accident! To come to lodge in the fame houfe with the man whom at prefent it moft behoves me to avoid! Do you think he knows you?

*Betty.* O yes, Madam. Your ladyfhip may remember it was I that took the letter from him, and carried down your anfwer. I warrant he knows me again; but if he did not, I find Mrs. Clip has been babbling to him about your ladyfhip, for I heard her mention your name as I was upon the ftairs.

*Cleora.* Sure I was infatuated not to forbid that woman telling any body I was here. But I muft remove immediately: it would be my utter ruin if my hufband, or any of his friends, fhould hear I had lain in this houfe but only one night.

*Betty.* Very true, indeed, Madam; and as foon as your ladyfhip has had your breakfaft, I will go out and get another lodging.

*Cleora.* Don't talk of breakfafting, I will have you go this inftant; I am diftracted to think where I am.

*Betty.* Dear Madam, I beg you will not put yourfelf into fuch a hurry of fpirits. It feems Leander is gone abroad; and thefe gay gentlemen, when once they go out, feldom return all day. I will engage your ladyfhip fhall be removed before he knows any thing of your being here.

*Cleora.* You talk like a fool. As he went out fo early, he is the more likely to come home to drefs; therefore get away. I would not have him fee me here for all the world.

Betty, finding her lady fo refolute, made no farther delays, but went into the next room, and huddled on her capuchin and gloves; which done, fhe returned, and afked what part of the town would be moft agreeable to her; to which Cleora replied, that all fituations were alike to her, but fhould chufe fome one or other of the ftreets that turned out of the Strand, as fhe muft be private for a while, and had feweft acquaintance that way; and then bid her fend Mrs. Clip to her. The maid went out, and Mrs. Clip entered the room prefently after. Cleora told her the circumftances of her affairs laid her under a neceffity of removing from her houfe, and intreated fhe would not make mention of her having been there to any one who might enquire for her. The other expreffed a good deal of concern for lofing fo good a lodger, and affured her of obferving fecrecy in the point fhe defired.

While they were talking, a loud knocking at the door made Mrs. Clip run to the parlour window; and feeing who it was, cried out—' Blefs me, 'tis ' Leander! His cloaths are all bloody, ' and his arm in a fcarf! He has been ' fighting, that's certain! I thought ' there was fome fuch thing in hand, by ' his going out fo early this morning. ' I beg

' I beg your ladyſhip's pardon; I muſt
' run and ſee if he wants any thing I
' can do for him.'

Cleora was too much confounded at
the name of Leander, and the condition
ſhe heard he was in, to offer to detain
her; and, after ſhe was gone, fell into a
profound reverie, which held her for
half an hour; and perhaps might have
done ſo longer, if ſhe had not been
ſrouzed from it by a gentle knock at the
parlour-door: but how greatly was ſhe
ſurprized when, on her calling to the
perſon to come in, ſhe ſaw Leander enter! ſhe ſtarted, trembled, and, with a
faultering voice, ſpoke thus to him—

*Cleora.* Oh, Sir, a viſit from you is
wholly improper at this time!

*Leander.* I hope not ſo, Madam;
ſince I would not have ſo far intruded,
but to acquaint you with ſomething
which it may be convenient for you to
know. I have ſeen your huſband this
morning.

*Cleora.* Oh my foreboding heart! I
dread to aſk the conſequence of ſuch a
meeting!

*Leander.* You need not, Madam.
Ariſtus is unhurt, and I bear only one
ſlight token of his intent to take my
life.

*Cleora.* Then you have fought?

*Leander.* It was with the utmoſt regret I drew my ſword againſt the huſband of Cleora. But be pleaſed, Madam, to peruſe this billet; and you will
ſee the neceſſity that compelled me to it.

With theſe words he preſented to her
the challenge he had received the night
before from Ariſtus; which, as ſoon
as ſhe had looked over, ſhe returned to
him again, ſaying—

*Cleora.* Unjuſt Ariſtus! But I
thank Heaven nothing worſe has enſued.

*Leander.* Heaven, Madam, has indeed alone the praiſe; ſince it was not to
any ſuperior ſkill of mine, or to any
generoſity in my antagoniſt, that I am
indebted for my preſervation, but to a
kind of miracle.

*Cleora.* As how? Pray, Sir, inform me.

*Leander.* I know not, Madam,
whether I can make you ſenſible how
the thing happened, as your ſex are ignorant of the terms made uſe of in the
deſcription of ſuch rencounters; but I
will do my beſt. When firſt we met, I
would have endeavoured to reaſon him

out of a miſtake ſo injurious to you and
his own peace of mind, as well as to
myſelf; but he refuſed to liſten to any
arguments I had prepared, and flew upon
me with the rage of an incenſed lion.
By the manner of his fighting, I eaſily
perceived he came with a reſolution
either to kill or be killed; ſo, as I was
deſirous of avoiding both the one and
the other, I only ſtood upon my defence, and parried the puſhes he made;
though, in aiming at my breaſt, he ſeveral times expoſed his own. The moderation I obſerved but enraging him the
more, he attempted to cloſe with me;
and in that action I received a wound in
my right-arm, a little above the bend,
which hindered me from making any
uſe of that wriſt, I ſhifted my ſword
into the other hand; ſaying to him, at
the ſame time—' You ſee, Sir, I am
' diſabled; we muſt leave the deciſion
' of this affair till ſome other time.'—
' No,' cried he, ' I am not ſo weak as
' to loſe the advantage I have gained.'
On this I retreated ſome paces; and then
redoubling his attacks, the aukward op-
poſition I could now make would not
have protected me one moment longer,
if, in the very criſis of my fate, when
the point of his weapon was juſt ready
to transfix me to the earth, we had not
fortunately been ſeparated. Some people, whoſe windows had a proſpect of
the Artillery Ground, ſaw the firſt of
our engagement; and making all the
haſte they could to prevent the threatened
miſchief, arrived in the inſtant I have
mentioned, beat down the ſword of A-
riſtus, and placed themſelves before me
as a ſhield.

*Cleora.* Pray, Sir, what then did
Ariſtus do?

*Leander.* Walked ſullenly away,
purſued by the reproaches of my deli-
verers till he was out of hearing; and
it was with much ado that I prevailed
with them to offer him no farther in-
ſults. But, Madam, while I am giving you the hiſtory of my ill-treatment,
I fear it is in your power to preſent me
with a more ſhocking detail of the cauſe
that brought you hither.

*Cleora.* It is ſuch a one, indeed, as,
if the world be not as unjuſt as Ariſtus,
will eaſily abſolve me for the reſolution
I have taken of never living with him
more. But it would happen very unlucky for my reputation, ſhould it be
known I have ſeen you even this once; I
therefore

therefore intreat that, after I go hence, you will not think of making me any future vifits.

*Leander.* Though it is hard to fuffer for the faults of another, yet, Madam, he affured I fhall never defire any thing that may give Ariftus a pretence for his ill-treatment. I flatter myfelf, however, that the remembrance of our former tendernefs is not fo totally obliterated, but that friendfhip may fubfift between us: you may, at leaft, permit me to write to you fometimes.

*Cleora.* I know not whether even that would not be too much.

*Leander.* Neither virtue, nor duty to the beft of hufbands, could fet down as a fault the favour I requeft; and, to prevent all mifinterpretations of our innocent correfpondence, I fhall take fuch precautions as will keep it a fecret from all the world.

*Cleora.* Well, Sir, I cannot refufe this proof of your compaffion for me, and think I ought not to deprive myfelf of any innocent confolation under my prefent affliction ; you may therefore be affured, that I fhall receive and anfwer your letters, with all the fatisfaction a woman in my circumftances can or ought to feel.

He was going to make fome reply, when Betty returned from her errand. She was a little furprized at feeing him there; and faid nothing till her lady, impatient to know the fuccefs of what fhe had been about, fpoke thus to her—

*Cleora.* Well, Betty, have you done the bufinefs I fent you on ?

*Betty.* Yes, Madam. Pleafe to ftep into the next room, and I will give you an account.

*Cleora.* No, you may tell me here. I dare truft this gentleman's difcretion.

The maid then informed her that fhe had agreed for lodgings at the houfe of a great taylor, whom fhe named, in Norfolk Street. On this Cleora defired Leander to retire; faying fhe muft get herfelf ready, for fhe was determined to depart immediately. He offered not to oppofe her defign; but though the leave they took of each other now was accompanied with the greatest respect on his fide, and referve on her's, I could eafily perceive that this interview had rekindled in both their hearts thofe flames affection they before had felt.

After he had left the room, Cleora's things not having been unpacked, there needed little preparation for her going. She fent for Mrs. Clip, and made her a handfome prefent for the trouble fhe had given her houfe; but finding her a tattling woman, acquainted her not with that to which fhe was removing. I faw both the miftrefs and maid, with all their luggage, depart in the fame manner they had come; but did not accompany them to their new habitation, as I could not promife myfelf with finding any thing there as yet worthy my enquiry. The difcourfe of the town afterwards informed me, that Cleora had employed a lawyer, and was foliciting either to have her whole fortune returned, or an annual allowance to the amount of the intereft of it. Ariftus was at firft refractory to all propofals of this nature; but all his friends, and his mother in particular, joining their perfuafions, he at laft was prevailed on to fign articles of a final feparation; by which it was agreed, that fhe fhould have a penfion of three hundred pounds a year during his life; and, in cafe he died before her, her whole fortune reftored.

I frequently called upon Cleora, and found that, during this negociation with her hufband, fhe kept her refolution of not feeing Leander; but that affair was no fooner over, than he vifited her every day: the confequence of which may eafily be gueffed at, and was in a fhort time proved ; for they went to Paris together, and ftill continue to refide there. This laft action of Cleora's has doubtlefs given the world room to believe fhe had not been wronged by the fufpicions of Ariftus; but whoever is of this opinion does her a great deal of injuftice. The Invifible Spy is a witnefs for her, that her inclinations were virtuous, her difpofition grateful and fincere; and, had fhe been treated with that confidence a good wife ought to have been, no temptation would have had the power to have made her otherwife. Let all hufbands, therefore, beware how they provoke, by ill-ufage and diftruft, the fate they would avoid; and obferve this maxim of the poet's—

'  He that would keep the fair-one true and
'      kind,
'  By love muft clap a padlock on her
'      mind.'

CHAP.

# CHAP. IV.

PRESENTS A FULL VIEW OF THE
MUCH CELEBRATED SABINA, IN
AN IMPARTIAL DESCRIPTION OF
HER PERSON AND CHARACTER;
WITH SOME PARTICULARS IN RE-
LATION TO HER TWO AMOURS,
AND THE CONSEQUENCES WHICH
ATTENDED AN ASSIGNATION
WITH HER FAVOURITE YOUNG-
LY.

THAT children do not always behave in the same manner with
their parents, is not so much owing to
their being born with different propensities, as to their education, and the
company they may happen to fall into,
at an age when nature is most liable to
be swayed by example. We often see
the most virtuous couples unhappy in a
degenerate offspring, but we rarely see
good branches sprout from a vicious
stock. An evil disposition may be corrected by advice, by persuasion, by
example; and a good one perverted by
the same means: but when a person is so
unfortunate as to be descended from
base and wicked parents, is brought up
under them, is witness of all their actions, and has companions of the same
cast, it is scarce possible that such a one
can have a mind enriched with any noble or moral principles.

What other could the once-doating,
deceived Germanicus, expect in his
marriage with Sabina, than the vexations he has fatally experienced? Can
all the beauties of her person now make
atonement for the blemishes of her
mind? No; he rather curses than ad-
mires those charms that drew him in,
and wishes himself any thing, so he
were not a husband. Yet ask him why
he married, he will tell you he married
a woman of fortune, quality, and an
uncommon share of beauty. All this
is true; but a man not blinded by passion, would have examined by what
means the two former were obtained;
and, above all, what sort of disposition
was hid beneath the varnish of an outside loveliness. Was not her family
amongst the lowest rank, till one of them
raised himself to opulence by actions
which ought to have brought him to a
gibbet; and, instead of ennobling his

posterity, entailed on them perpetual infamy? Was she not trained up under a
mother whose bad conduct has been
equally notorious? Was she not, from
her most early years, soothed in every
vanity, pampered in every luxury, and
taught to think that appetites and passions were never given but to be indulged?

Could Germanicus be ignorant of
these glaring truths? If he were not,
yet rashly ventured on so unpromising a
union, who can pity the misfortunes,
the disquiets, the disgrace, it has involved him in? The many proofs she
gave of too warm an inclination before
marriage, as also several of the many
amours she had after she became a wife,
I shall pass over: the first that made any
great noise was that with Miramour,
perhaps owing to the manner of it's
commencement; which he thinking himself under no obligation to conceal, has
since made no secret of in all companies
whenever her name comes upon the
carpet.

This gentleman had a mistress, who,
on account of a certain haughtiness in
her temper and behaviour, he called
Roxana. He supported her in so genteel a manner, that, had her reputation
been equal to her appearance, she might
have been entitled to the best company.
Character, however, was the least thing
considered by Sabina in the choice of
her acquaintance. She accidentally met
with this lady at a milliner's, fell into
discourse with her, liked her, invited her
to her house, and there soon grew a great
intimacy between them. That Roxana
was kept by Miramour was no secret to
the town, nor did she attempt to make
any of it to Sabina; on the contrary,
she talked freely to her of their amorous
correspondence. But how dangerous is
it for one woman to boast too much of
the perfections of her lover, to another
no less sanguine in her constitution? Sabina, who had often seen Miramour
without taking any notice of him, now
became so fired with the rapturous description given of him by his mistress,
that she instantly became her rival, and
languished to experience in reality that
happiness which the other had given her
so high an idea of. As she never took
any thing of this nature into her head
without attempting to accomplish it,
and had no regard to decorum in the

manner

manner of her doing fo, fhe fent a billet to him by a porter, containing thefe lines—

' SIR,

' IF your attachment to the charms of
' your kept miftrefs makes you
' not look on the reft of womankind as
' infipid creatures, the invitation this
' brings you will not be unwelcome.
' A woman of quality, young, and in
' moft men's eyes handfome, has found
' fomething in you that excites in her
' the defire of a private interview, and
' to that end will call on you this even-
' ing about feven, at White's; till when
' muft remain, with a great deal of im-
' patience,

' Your INCOGNITA.'

The meffenger who carried this had ftrict orders not to tell from whom it came: curiofity, however—for it could be called no other paffion as yet—made Miramour punctual to the time, nor was Sabina lefs fo. He had not waited many minutes before fhe came. On his coming into the coach, he found her face entirely hid under her hood; which fhe told him, laughing, he muft not expect to fee, till they were in a place more proper for him to give her proof how agreeable it was to him. On this he ordered the coachman to drive to an adjacent tavern; where being fhewn into a private room, the lady foon threw off her difguife. He had not enough depended on the character fhe had given of herfelf, not to be furprized and tranfported on finding Sabina in the perfon of his incognita; and expreffed the fenfe he had of the honour fhe did, and the happinefs he hoped their meeting would beftow on him, in terms fo warm and fo paffionate, as infinitely charmed her. They paffed fome hours together to their mutual fatisfaction; nor parted without an appointment to fee each other the next day: but Sabina, not thinking it fafe to come often to fo publick a place as a tavern, undertook to provide a more proper fcene for the continuance of their intrigue.

As indolent as this lady is in moft other affairs, it muft be confeffed that no woman was ever more punctual, or more indefatigable, in every thing relating to love. On confulting with a female acquaintance, who had been often neceffary on fuch occafions, fhe was

advifed by her to hire a private lodging by the quarter, in fome obfcure nook of the town, to which fhe might retire whenever fhe had a mind, as it would be always ready, and neither herfelf nor the friends fhe fhould bring with her be taken any notice of. Sabina highly approving of what fhe faid, the project was put in immediate execution. The woman took upon herfelf the accomplifhment of what fhe had propofed, and eafily found a place every way fuitable for the bufinefs it was defigned. The chamber was neat, fpacious, and well furnifhed; there was a back-door to the houfe, through which any one might flip out in cafe of any danger of difcovery; and the landlady knew perfectly well the decorum fhe ought to obferve in regard to her guefts. The heroine of this adventure was very well pleafed with the accommodation procured for her; and having got this recefs, which, according to the French, fhe ufed to call her *petit maifon*, henceforward never met Miramour at any other place.

But there was one thing I forgot to mention in giving the character of this lady, which is the uncertainty of her temper. She is no lefs inconftant than fhe is amorous; and changes her lovers almoft as often as fhe does her cloaths, and never keeps either till they are worn out: a new friend, like a new fafhion, is always charming to her; but a very little time ferves to make her equally grow weary of both. She loved Miramour till fhe faw Youngly; but there was fomething in the perfon and converfation of this laft gentleman, that making reafon coincide with paffion, it is not to be wondered at that fhe gave him the preference; and a woman of a lefs mutable difpofition might have been eafily abfolved for transferring her affections to an object fo much more worthy than the late engroffer of her heart.

On her firft acquaintance with him, fhe made advances to him; which he is too much a man of pleafure to refift from any fine woman: he returned thofe of Sabina in a manner which made her think him as much devoted to her as fhe could wifh; and it was not long before fhe gave him an invitation to drink tea with her at her private apartment, where fhe told him they might laugh away an hour without interruption. He took the hint, and flew to the place of rendezvous; where it was not to be

L doubted

doubted but he found all the welcome he could wish or expect from the obliging fair. They had many interviews; but Youngly having by some accident heard of her intrigue with Miramour, he not only frequently reproached her with it, but also was far from feeling for her that affection in his heart, which otherwise her beauty might have inspired him with.

In the mean time Roxana, who from the commencement of Miramour's acquaintance with Sabina had seen him less often than she had been accustomed, and had also some other reasons to suspect a decrease of affection, began presently to imagine some new face had supplanted her. She complained to him of his unkindness, but he absolutely denied having given her any cause, and made a thousand excuses for his late behaviour: but this did not satisfy her, she was not to be deceived in matters of which she was so good a judge; and convinced that she had a rival, bent her whole thoughts on discovering the person. By an emissary whom she employed to watch Miramour wherever he went, she soon found out the place where he met the object of his new attachment; but as that lady was carried into the house in a chair, with the curtains close drawn, was still as far as ever from knowing the face that had undone her. Upon enquiry among the neighbours, she was informed that the house was noted for giving reception to people who liked each other more than they were willing the world should know; and this put a stratagem into her head, which was crowned with all the success she could wish or hope; not only for exploring what at present was a mystery to her, but also for being amply revenged on her fair rival.

The mistress of Miramour knew the town long before she knew him, and was not unacquainted with the customs of such houses. She went one morning to the governante of this; and, after saying she had been recommended by a person who knew her, told her she should be glad to have a chamber, to which she might sometimes come with a friend whom it was not convenient for her to see at home. The old gentlewoman replied, that her best room was rented by the quarter, by a lady who came often thither; and that the next, which was the only one she had to spare, she feared

would be too small. Roxana cried she did not regard how small it was, provided it was otherwise commodious. On this she shewed up to it; and finding it was divided from the other only by a thin wainscot partition, presently agreed for it; giving the old woman so good a premium in hand, that she was highly satisfied with her new incumbent.

Having accomplished so far of her design as to get possession of the very next room to that where her lover and his new mistress met, she began to consider, that to go thither alone might raise some suspicions in the woman of the house, and was a little at a loss what man she should take with her, and make pass for a gallant; as, whoever went, he must be made the confidante of the whole affair. At last she pitched upon the fellow she had employed as a spy upon Miramour. His appearance, indeed, was very mean; but that she thought might not be regarded: accordingly she went the next day, accompanied by her pretended gallant. They were there some time before the hour in which he had told her he had seen Miramour go in, in order to prepare things for a more perfect discovery. This was done by the young fellow's boring holes through the wainscot, in so dexterous a manner, that they could see all over the room without being seen themselves, though they stood close to the orifice. No one, however, came that night; and the impatient Roxana was obliged to return home as dissatisfied as ever.

The next day she repaired thither again, attended as before, and met with the same disappointment; but on the third was more successful. She had not been many minutes in the chamber, when a rustling of silks upon the stairs made her know somebody was coming up; on which she ran hastily, without making any noise, to one of the peepholes. But how great was her astonishment when she saw Sabina enter! Scarce could she refrain exclaiming aloud against the treachery of a woman who, after being made her confidante, had robbed her of the affections of her lover. But soon the current of her passion turned a different way; when, instead of Miramour, she saw Youngly push open the door, and throw himself into Sabina's arms; on which, withdrawing from her post—'You fool,' cried

cried she to her emiffary, ' to what a ' fruitlefs labour have you expofed me! ' It is not Miramour that I have all this ' while paid you for following. How ' could you be fo mope-eyed as to mif- ' take him!'—' Nay, Madam,' replied the fellow, ' I am fure I know Mr. Mi- ' ramour, and I will fwear that it was him ' I faw come into this houfe, and pre- ' fently after a lady in a chair, as I ' then told you.' Roxana knew not what to think of this, and faid no more; but liftening attentively to the con- verfation within, was prefently affured by it that her agent had neither deceived her, nor had been deceived himfelf, as will appear by the following dialogue—

*Sabina.* My dear, dear Youngly, I hope you will now believe that I love you above all the world.

*Youngly.* I know you love me enough to make me happy, and I ought to con- tent myfelf with the fhare I have in your affections.

*Sabina.* Do not talk of a fhare: by Heaven, you engrofs me all! my foul and all it's faculties are devoted to you.

*Youngly.* And yet the letter Mira- mour accidentally dropped in the Park, and I took up, flattered him with the fame affurances you now give me.

*Sabina.* As I unfortunately played the fool with him before I faw you, it was neceffary I fhould break with him by degrees.

*Youngly.* You had once, however, a real paffion for him.

*Sabina.* No, it was all in imagina- tion; I only fancied I loved him. You muft know, that filly, vain creature, his kept miftrefs, was always filling my ears with ftories of the violence of his af- fection for her; and it was more to fhew him the difference between fuch a wretch and a woman of quality, than any ex- traordinary liking I had to his perfon, that induced me to grant him the favours I did.

This was enough to let the liftening Roxana into the whole affair. It was with much ado fhe reftrained herfelf from flying into the next room, and re- turning the contempt thrown upon her by the laft words of Sabina; but juft as fhe was at the door, and ready to burft in on the unfufpecting pair, a fudden thought made her turn back. ' All I

' can fay to this perfidious woman,' cried fhe to herfelf, ' will avail me no- ' thing; the wrongs I have received de- ' mand a vengeance more compleat.' She then fat down again; and, calmly meditating on what fhe had to do, the fertility of her invention foon fupplied her with the means of repaying, with intereft, the double affront Sabina had given both to herfelf and Miramour, whom it is certain fhe loved with more fincerity than is commonly found among women of her profeffion. She ftaid till the lovers took their leaves of each other, and heard an appointment made between them to meet again on the enfuing Thurfday.

Having fully perfected in her mind the defign fhe foon after put in execu- tion, fhe called for the woman of the houfe, and faid to her—' Madam, I ' know not but fome gentlemen may ' pafs an hour or two with me here next ' Thurfday. They may poffibly come ' before me: but I defire you will give ' them admittance; and, to prevent mif- ' takes, as the furniture of the room is ' yellow, they fhall afk for the key of ' the yellow chamber.' The other re- plied, that fhe might depend on her punctuality in obferving her commands. After which Roxana went away; but what fhe meant by the orders fhe had given muft be left to the next chapter to explain.

## CHAP. V.

CONTAINS THE CATASTROPHE OF AN ADVENTURE, WHICH THE AU- THOR THINKS FIT TO DECLARE IS INSERTED IN THESE LUCU- BRATIONS LESS TO AMUSE HIS READER, THAN FOR THE SAKE OF SETTING IN A TRUE LIGHT THOSE FACTS WHICH SOME PEO- PLE HAVE ARTFULLY ENDEA- VOURED TO MISREPRESENT TO THE PUBLICK.

ROXANA being now fully fur- nifhed with materials for her re- venge on Sabina, without evpofing her beloved Miramour to the refentment of an injured hufband, wrote to the latter, the next morning, in words to this ef- fect—

' TO

' TO GERMANICUS.

' SIR,

' THIS brings you a very ungrateful ' piece of intelligence: but, in ' my opinion, whoever sees a person ' wronged, and conceals it, takes part ' in the offence; and, though innocent ' of the commencement of the crime, is ' accessary to the continuance of it. It ' would certainly be the utmost injustice, ' that you should be the last person to ' know what concerns yourself alone; ' and I therefore think it my duty to in- ' form you of what chance has disco- ' vered to me. Your wife, Sir, is false ' to your bed, and lavishes on Mr. ' Youngly all those favours which you ' have a right to engross. The guilty ' pair meet twice or thrice every week, ' at a lodging she rents by the quarter ' for that purpose. But to say your ' wife is guilty of so foul a crime, is do- ' ing nothing, without putting it in ' your power to prove her so: the thing, ' Sir, is easy, if you will follow my di- ' rections. The lovers have appointed ' to meet to-morrow, about seven, at ' their usual rendezvous; if you go at ' that time, or rather before it, to the ' third house on the left-hand in ***** ' Lane, on your asking for Mrs. *****, ' who is the keeper of this private bro- ' thel, and telling her you want the ' key of the yellow chamber, she will ' presently conduct you to a room ad- ' joining to that which is the scene of ' your wife's loose pleasures. There are ' holes already bored through the wains- ' cot, through which you may plainly ' discern all that passes. It is at your ' own option whether you will have any ' other witnesses of your wife's transf- ' gression than your own eyes and also ' how to behave towards her after de- ' tection. I have discharged the dic- ' tates of my conscience in giving you ' this information; and am, Sir,

' Your unknown Friend.'

' P. S. Be careful to drop no words ' that may give the woman of the ' house the least cause to suspect ' either who you are, or the motive ' of your coming.'

It is convenient I should now acquaint my reader, that all I have hitherto related of this story has come to my knowledge entirely by the report of the persons

chiefly concerned in it, and without the ' least assistance from my Belt of Invisi- bility. What yet remains to be told, I have the testimony of my own eyes and ears to avouch. The many odd ac- counts I have heard, from time to time, in relation to Sabina's conduct, made me resolve to go one day to the house of Germanicus, in order to satisfy my cu- riosity with seeing in what fashion this couple behaved to each other.

The lady was abroad when I came, and I found him up in his dining-room, diverting himself with playing on the flute; but soon after rouzed from that amusement by the above letter being de- livered to him by his man, saying it was brought by a fellow who the mo- ment he had put it into his hands va- nished like lightning from the door. The emotions with which he read it were very great, yet much less than might have been expected on such an occasion. He paused, then read again, examined every line with heedful eyes, and seemed extremely divided in his thoughts what credit he should give to the information: at last, said he to him- self—' If any one had formed this con- ' trivance, through a malicious design ' of ruining her reputation, or my peace ' of mind, they would certainly have ' taken other methods, and not, by ' pointing out the place, the hour, put ' it in my power to prove at once the ' falseness of the accusation.'

After this, he threw himself into an easy chair, leaned his head upon his hand, and in that posture continued musing for a considerable time; then seeming more resolved, started up and cried—' It is easy for me to make en- ' quiry if there be such a house, if kept ' by a woman of the name mentioned ' in the letter, and what character it ' bears. Yet, why should I do this?— ' No, it is better to follow the instruc- ' tions given me, and be at once af- ' sured. It shall be so. As Shake- ' speare makes Othello say—

" I'll see before I doubt; when I doubt,
    " prove:
" And on the proof there is no more but
    " this—
" Away at once with love or jealousy."

He had scarce done repeating these lines, when Sabina came in, singing an Italian air. Germanicus endeavoured

to

to recompose his countenance, but could not do it so well as not to make her take notice of the change, and ask if he were out of humour; to which he replied—

*Germanicus.* Out of humour, Madam? No, I have no cause; none in the world.

*Sabina.* I think not, indeed; but men will be peevish sometimes, cause or not cause.

*Germanicus.* I reserve all my gaiety for to-morrow, and would have you do so too. A kinsman of mine makes an entertainment, and has sent an invitation for us to be partakers of it.

*Sabina.* What, to-morrow?

*Germanicus.* Yes, my dear, to-morrow evening; so I desire you will not engage yourself elsewhere.

*Sabina.* Indeed I have engaged myself already to Lady Gape's assembly.

*Germanicus.* You have time enough, then, to send to excuse yourself from going.

*Sabina.* Indeed I shall not. I would not disappoint my dear Lady Gape for all the kinsmen in the world. But I would have you go: you may say I am not well, and then my absence cannot be taken amiss.

It was very plain to me, that Germanicus made this pretended invitation only as a trap to discover whether she had really any engagement on her hands that she would not be willing to break; and it is also as little to be doubted, but that her answers very much corroborated the contents of the epistle he had just received. He forced himself, however, to tell her, with a smile, that every thing should be as she would have it, and that he would no farther press her. Some company presently after coming in, I found there was nothing more to be learned at that time, so took the first opportunity of quitting the house; and went again, the next afternoon, in hopes of discovering something more.

On my arrival, the husband and wife were sitting together in the most seeming amicable manner. After some little time Germanicus rose up, and put on his hat and sword, in order, as he said, to go to his kinsman; on which Sabina, with a great deal of complaisance, said to him—

*Sabina.* You will not walk, sure, my dear! Have you ordered the horses to be put to?

*Germanicus.* No, my dear; I leave the coach for you.

*Sabina.* There is no occasion. I always chuse to go to these places in a chair.

*Germanicus.* That is as you please; but I shall walk, as I have three or four places to call at in my way to my cousin's; so farewel, my dear. I hope you will be as merry at the assembly, as I hope to be at the entertainment.

As I imagined Germanicus had something in his head more than I knew of, by his being so hasty to be gone, I followed him close at his heels, and found I had not been mistaken in my supposition. He went into a tavern, where two gentlemen, whom he had desired to meet him there, waited for him. The business he had with them, was to communicate the letter he had received from the unknown friend; and, after having considered a little on the matter, they agreed that they should all three go together; not only to prevent any indiscreet effects of his rage on the persons who wronged him, in case the affair should prove as the letter had represented, but also to be his witnesses, if he thought proper to bring it before a court of judicature. They staid till a little before seven; then went, according to the directions given by Roxana, and found every thing answered the description. They were shewn up into the yellow chamber; I still accompanied them; and made a fourth person, unfelt, as well as unseen, by any of them.

They had not been there above half an hour, before Sabina came into the next room; Youngly soon after joined her; and the much-injured husband, and his two friends, saw enough, from the peep-holes in the partition, to convince them of the truth of that information which had brought them thither. Difficult was it for Germanicus to restrain his fury on so shocking a spectacle; but his two friends reminding him that there was a much better way for him to shew his resentment, he was at length prevailed on to retire. They both went home with him, as did myself; resolving to see what farther events this night would produce. Sabina came not home till near two hours past midnight: but Germanicus had ordered that the door should not be opened; and, after her chairmen had knocked two or three times, he went himself to the parlour-window, and spoke to her in these terms—

*Germanicus.*

*Germanicus.* Pleafe, Madam, to return from whence you came, or wherever elfe you fhall think proper. My houfe fhall no longer be the fhelter of a proftitute.

*Sabina.* What, is the man mad! Sure you have been drinking bad wine to-night!

. *Germanicus.* No, Madam, the beft I ever drank in my life; it has opened my eyes, and fhewn me the viper I have fo long cherifhed in my bofom, and now throw off for ever. But I would not wifh you to ftay longer in the cold; you can have no entrance here; Mr. Youngly will doubtlefs afford you a part of his bed.

With thefe words he fhut the window; and Sabina, finding herfelf detected, and that her hufband was refolute, ordered her chair from the door; and after fome little confideration how to difpofe of herfelf, thought it beft to take her hufband's advice, and return to the place from whence fhe came, as it was

the only afylum to which fhe could have recourfe at fo unfeafonable an hour.

In the feveral vifits I afterwards made to Germanicus, I perceived he behaved with much more moderation than fome hufbands would have done. Philofophy had taught him to fupport with patience a misfortune which was irremediable; he contented himfelf with taking fuch revenge as the laws of England have provided in thefe cafes. Youngly was fummoned before a court of judicature, and a penalty inflicted on him for his offence; but it would have been larger, had it not been proved, by inconteftible evidences, that he had not been the firft who had feduced Sabina from her marriage-vows. As for the lady, fhe is now abandoned and defpifed by both her lovers; and if there be a poffibility that any thing can bring her to a juft fenfe of the faults fhe has been guilty of, it muft be the contempt fhe is treated with by all degrees of people.


END OF THE THIRD BOOK.

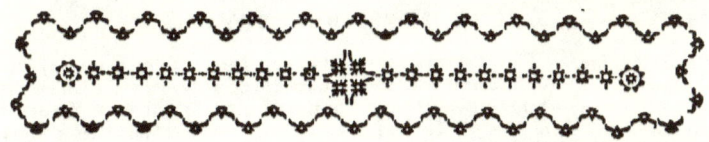

THE

# INVISIBLE SPY.

## BOOK IV.

### CHAP. I.

IN WHICH THE AUTHOR CONFESSES
HAVING BEEN GUILTY OF PETTY
LARCENY; BUT HOPES THAT
IT MERITS FORGIVENESS FROM
THOSE INTO WHOSE HANDS THIS
WORK MAY FALL, AS THE CHIEF
MOTIVE FOR COMMITTING IT
WAS TO OBLIGE THE PUBLICK.

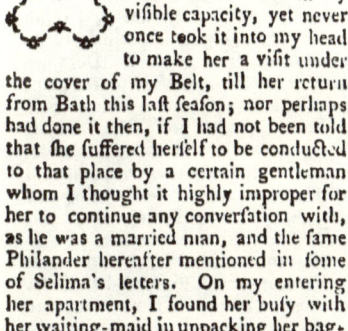Have been intimately ac-
quainted with Belinda for
a confiderable time in my
vifible capacity, yet never
once took it into my head
to make her a vifit under
the cover of my Belt, till her return
from Bath this laft feafon; nor perhaps
had done it then, if I had not been told
that fhe fuffered herfelf to be conducted
to that place by a certain gentleman
whom I thought it highly improper for
her to continue any converfation with,
as he was a married man, and the fame
Philander hereafter mentioned in fome
of Selima's letters. On my entering
her apartment, I found her bufy with
her waiting-maid in unpacking her baggage; which coming by the waggon, it
feems had arrived in town but the night

before. As I could promife myfelf but
little entertainment from the affortment
of ribbands, jewels, &c. I was thinking
to quit the place, and return at a more
fit feafon; when the maid, pulling out
a fattin bag full of papers, afked her
where fhe would have thofe writings
laid; on which Belinda turned her head
that way, and replied—' They are a
' heap of letters I received at Bath, of
' no manner of confequence. I have no
' room for fuch rubbifh; take and throw
' them all into the fire.'

The maid was juft going to do as fhe
was bid, but was ftopped by Belinda,
who fuddenly fcreamed out—' Hold!
' hold! I had forgot, that one day, in
' a hurry, I ftuffed two or three letters
' and poems of Philander's among them;
' and I would not have one line of that
' dear witty creature's deftroyed for all
' the world. Pour them all out of the
' bag, and look on the names fub-
' fcribed, that I may direct you how
' to feparate the wheat from the chaff.'
The maid then threw them all down
upon the carpet, and opened them one
by one; which done, Belinda added—
' You need fearch no farther; I have
' found all Philander's letters and
' poems in this drawer; fo cram toge-
' ther all you have there, and thruft them
' into

'into the fire.' This fentence was
punctually executed, according to the
beſt of the maid's belief; but the poor
girl knew not there was an Inviſible
Thief, who ſtood cloſe at her elbow,
and while ſhe turned her head another
way, had the dexterity to preſerve ſome
part of the condemned cargo, and ſlip
it into his pocket.

Selima at that time engroſſed great part
of the converſation in town. She was a
young woman of no fortune, and few
other endowments beſides her beauty,
of which, in the opinion of moſt people,
ſhe has an uncommon ſhare; though to
me there is a certain fierceneſs in her
eyes, and a boldneſs diffuſed through all
her features, which rob them of that
lovelineſs which they would otherwiſe
have. Such as ſhe is, however, ſhe
captivated the hearts of two perſons who
might have carried their addreſſes much
higher without danger of a refuſal: the
one is born to a title, and the other poſſeſſed of wealth which, whenever he
pleaſes, may procure him one; and neither of them can be thought deficient in
any of thoſe qualifications which conſti-
tute the fine gentleman. Yet Selima was
ſtill unmarried; both her lovers were
equally in ſuſpence, and nobody could tell
which, or whether either of them, would
be the happy man. It is not therefore
to be wondered at, that a perſon of my
humour ſhould be extremely deſirous of
being let into a ſecret which ſeemed ſo
impenetrable, even to thoſe who pretended to be moſt knowing in other
things; nor that I gladly embraced an
opportunity which bid ſo fair for the ſatisfaction of my curioſity, as the getting
her letters into my poſſeſſion, Belinda
having ſaid they contained the whole
hiſtory of this affair.

Behold now my theft! Belinda's
maid had no ſooner laid down the packet,
by her lady's orders, than I kept my
eye conſtantly fixed upon it, till a convenient moment offered for conveying it
from among the others, which I did with
great adroitneſs. After this I ſtaid no
longer with Belinda, not doubting but
I had now about me better materials for
my entertainment, than any I could expect to be furniſhed with in her apartment, at leaſt for the preſent.

The diſtance between Belinda's lodgings and my own ſeemed now to be twice
as long as uſual, though I believe I
meaſured much fewer paces than ever

I had done before, ſo great was my impatience to be at home, and examine the
treaſure I brought with me. To avoid
confuſion, I examined the dates of every
letter, and ſhall preſent them to my readers in the order they were ſent to her
while at Bath.

## LETTER I.

'DEAR BELINDA,

'I Received the favour of yours with
'a double ſatisfaction; firſt, as it
'brought me news of your ſafe arrival
'at that agreeable place, and that every
'thing in it anſwered your wiſhes and
'expectations; and ſecondly, as it aſ-
'ſures me of your friendſhip, by the
'kind concern you are pleaſed to ex-
'preſs for my welfare. As to my
'health, I have quite loſt that ugly cough
'which ſo much perſecuted me when
'you left London; but as to my affairs,
'they are ſtill in the ſame fluctuating
'and unſettled condition as ever. Do-
'rantes ſtill continues his addreſſes,
'Vanucius does the ſame. How happy
'might I be if I was loved but by one
'of them! but both equally purſuing
'me, impedes all the good fortune I
'might enjoy with either.

'You may remember how much my
'mamma was tranſported when Do-
'rantes firſt declared himſelf my lover.
'Vanucius, though not quite dropped,
'was then little regarded either by my-
'ſelf or her; but now the caſe is altered;
'ſhe charges me to treat both with an
'equal freedom; and, indeed, I think
'it would be highly impolitick to do
'otherwiſe. The truth is, Dorantes
'does not come ſo directly to the point
'as could be wiſhed: his courtſhip is
'paſſionate, tender, and full of fire; he
'ſwears I am the idol of his ſoul, that
'he could not live without me, and that
'all his hopes are centered in being one
'day happy in poſſeſſing me; yet,
'among all theſe fine ſpeeches, he ſel-
'dom mentions marriage; and when
'he does, it is in ſo ſlight and evaſive a
'manner, as to give me ſometimes cauſe
'to fear his deſigns are rather on my
'heart than hand. If this ſhould be
'his intention, and I were weak enough
'to have fixed my affection on him,
'how miſerable ſhould I be! But,
'thank Heaven, I have none of that
'ſoft folly in my compoſition by which
'I have

'I have seen so many of our sex misled;
'my ruling passions are interest and
'ambition; and I would not hesitate
'one moment to give myself to Vanu-
'cius, if the rank and title of Do-
'rantes did not tempt me to wait awhile
'the result of his pretensions.

' I was yesterday morning in the Mall
'with Vanucius: Dorantes was walk-
'ing there with some company; he
'changed colour, and seemed in some
'agitation on meeting us together.
'This I looked upon as a good sign;
'but in the afternoon, when he came to
'visit me, and I expected he would either
'have complained of my indifference to
'him, or reproached me for the publick
'encouragement I had given his rival;
'he did neither, but behaved the whole·
'time with all the calmness and insen-
'sibility of a Stoick. I must confess, I
'was never more disappointed in all
'my life, as I had frequently seen him
'kindle into jealousy on a less occasion;
'and could not help thinking that the
'violence of his passion was in a great
'measure abated, according to this
'maxim of Mr. Dryden—

'' Distrust in lovers is too warm a sun;
'' But yet 'tis night in love when that is
'' gone."

' On consulting with my mamma, I
'found she was of the same way of
'thinking; and it was agreed upon be-
'tween us, not to suffer ourselves to be
'trifled with any longer, but that the
'next time Vanucius made an offer of
'his hand, I should accept it. But,
'my dear Belinda, this morning has
'put a stop to the resolution of last
'night. I was scarce out of bed,
'when I received from Dorantes the
'most passionate billet that ever was dic-
'tated by the heart of man; occasioned,
'as he says, by dreaming he had me in
'his arms. If his love be half so im-
'patient to have me there as he pretends
'it is, he will certainly be now more
'pressing to make me his own than hi-
'therto he has been.

' My next, perhaps, may bring you
'the decision of my fate: mean time, I
'should be glad to hear what is doing
'at Bath, and what new conquests you
'have made there; for how much so-
'ever you may be envied by some of
'your acquaintance, be assured that
'every thing that contributes to your

'satisfaction, will always afford a se-
'cret pleasure to her who is, with the
'most perfect amity, &c.

' SELIMA.'

## LETTER II.

' DEAR BELINDA,

'I Am sorry to tell you, that the per-
'plexity of my own affairs has hin-
'dered me from being inquisitive enough
'into those of other people, for me to
'be able to send you the intelligence
'you request; but as I flatter myself,
'that what regards myself will be al-
'ways most interesting to you, I shall
'give you a brief detail of what has
'happened to me in relation to Dorantes,
'since his last kind letter mentioned in
'my former.

' He came the same evening. The
'discourse he entertained me with was
'of a piece with his epistle, all love and
'transport. He begged I would favour
'him with my company to the theatre
'in Drury Lane, where he had already
'sent a servant to keep places in the
'box; I consented, and went with him
'in his chariot. The play was Romeo
'and Juliet; he applied all the tender
'things spoke by the former of these
'lovers to his own passion, and pressed
'my hand with a vehemence of fond-
'ness, whenever he had an opportunity
'of doing so unperceived by the audi-
'ence.

' I saw him again next day. We
'were alone together in the dining-
'room; and my gown being a little
'more off my shoulder than ordinary,
'he laid his face upon my bare neck,
'crying—" Oh, I could dwell forever
"here!" On this I took courage to
'say to him—" Yet, Dorantes, when
"once I become your wife, these ar-
"dours will perhaps sink into a cold
"indifference."—" No, my angel!"
'returned he, " desire will rather in-
"crease by enjoyment of your person;
"the sweets contained in this dear
"frame are of too divine a nature ever
"to satiate." In speaking these words,
'he catched me suddenly in his arms,
'held me to his bosom, and joined his
'lips to mine with so newhat, I thought,
'of an unbecoming warmth. I strug-
'gled to get loose; and when I had
'done so, retired some paces from him,
'and said, with all the haughtiness I

M              ,' could

' could affume—" Forbear thefe liber-
" ties, Sir, till authorized by law to
" take them." He afked my pardon,
' apologized for what he had done by
' the violence of his paffion, and then
' fat down; but appeared more than or-
' dinarily penfive afterwards, fpoke lit-
' tle, and made his vifit much fhorter
' than ufual.

'On my acquainting my mamma with
' what had paffed between us, fhe did not
' at all like it, and went directly to her
' old friend, you know who I mean, to
' be advifed by him how to proceed in a
' circumftance at once fo intricate and
' critical. He told her, that my father
' ought to appear in this bufinefs; that
' it was his place, and his alone, to de-
' mand of Dorantes an explanation of
' his defigns in regard to the courtfhip
' he fo long had made to his daughter.
' My mamma had always been of his
' opinion; but knowing the indolence
' of my father's temper, had forbore
' mentioning it to him: however, fhe
' urged it to him, but all fhe could fay
' or offer has been ineffectual; his an-
' fwer was, that he did not know how
' to fpeak to a perfon of Dorantes's qua-
' lity on any fuch matter; that he would
' not interfere in it, and we might act
' as we thought proper ourfelves.

' This, you will own, is very vexa-
' tious; but there is no turning him out
' of his own way. Mamma is now re-
' folved, fince there is no other remedy,
' to take the tafk upon herfelf, as foon
' as Dorantes comes to town: he is at
' prefent gone on a hunting-match with
' fome gentlemen, but is expected to re-
' turn in two days at fartheft, and we
' fhall then fee the event. For my part,
' my fpirits are fo much fatigued and
' haraffed with this fufpence, that there
' is but one thing hinders me from put-
' ting an immediate end to it by mar-
' rying with Vanucius. The perfons
' of the men are equal to me; but, O
' Belinda! I am paffionately in love with
' the title of Dorantes! Would he were
' half as much fo with my perfon, he
' would not then delay one moment
' giving me the one in exchange for the
' other.

' The faithful Vanucius, whom I
' have flattered with the belief of not
' being indifferent to me, is every day
' foliciting me to fix a time to make him

' happy, while Dorantes feems to dally
' with my expectations; yet can I not
' refolve to reward the conftant fervices
' of the one, nor to renounce for ever
' the charming hope of rank, pre-
' cedence, the thoufand dear appen-
' dages of a woman of quality, which
' the other has it in his power to be-
' ftow on me. But I will trouble you
' no farther, than to affure you, that in
' whatever ftation my fate fhall place
' me, I fhall be ever, with the beft
' wifhes for your happinefs, &c.

' SELIMA.

' P. S. I am obliged to Philander
  ' for the part you tell me he takes
  ' in my concerns. Pray be fo
  ' good as to make my grateful
  ' acknowledgments acceptable to
  ' him.'

## LETTER III.

' DEAR BELINDA,

' I Would not let this poft efcape with-
  ' out writing. What I have now
' to fay to you, though greatly to the
' purpofe, muft be comprized in a few
' words. I am engaged to go this
' evening with Dorantes, and fome other
' company, on a party of pleafure, and
' am every moment expecting his lan-
' dau at the door, fo can but juft fnatch
' time to inform you, that my mamma
' has talked to him on the affair in
' queftion, and that his anfwers have
' been conformable to our utmoft wifhes.
' Yes, I am now convinced that all my
' apprehenfions were groundlefs, that
' he never meant to act otherwife than
' honourably with me: he has affured
' both her and myfelf, that every thing
' fhall foon be fettled for my future hap-
' pinefs. Rejoice with me, my dear
' creature! I have now a heart and
' head perfectly at eafe; and nothing
' to employ my thoughts, but how to
' behave becoming of the dignity to
' which, I flatter myfelf, a few days
' will raife me. Farewel. The author
' of my joys is already come; they call
' me to receive him; and I can add no
' more, than that I am, as ever, with un-
' feigned regard, &c.

' SELIMA.'

LETTER

## LETTER IV.

' DEAR BELINDA,

' LITTLE did I expect, and little
' is it in your power to imagine,
' what I have now to acquaint you with.
' So strange a reverse, so sudden, so
' shocking a revolution, sure never any
' woman but myself experienced! But
' I will keep you no longer in suspence:
' I have lost Dorantes, irrecoverably lost
' him! not through any misinanage-
' ment of my own, nor any want of af-
' fection in him, but through a previ-
' ous, much worse, and more irreme-
' diable accident. This is the sum of
' my misfortunes; I will now relate to
' you the particulars.

' He came to me the other day; and
' though the salutations he approached
' me with had their accustomed tender-
' nefs, yet I thought there was some-
' what in his countenance, and the
' whole air of his deportment, very dif-
' ferent from any thing I had ever seen
' in him before. He had not been in
' the room many minutes, before he told
' me that he had something of conse-
' quence to impart to me, and desired I
' would order myself to be denied to
' whoever should happen to come. I
' readily did as he desired; after which,
' he drew his chair close to me, sighed,
' and, looking me full in the face, sur-
' prized me with these words—" My
" dear Selima," said he, " I have de-
" ceived you; have you love enough for
" me to forgive it?"—" First let me
" know the nature of your offence," re-
' turned I. " 'Tis death to me to de-
" clare it," answered he; " yet can it
" be no longer hid. I have imposed
" upon you by a false pretence, pro-
" mised what is not in my power to per-
" form—I cannot marry you!"

' Judge, Belinda, of my confusion.
' But it is as impossible for you to con-
' ceive, as it is for me to describe, what
' I felt in that dreadful moment. Scarce
' could a thunderbolt have transfixed
' me more: I had no breath, no voice,
' but to echo part of his last words—
" Cannot marry! cannot marry!" cried
' I; and this I repeated several times
' over.

' He seemed all this time in very great
' agitations; and, after taking one of
' my hands, and tenderly pressing it to
' his lips—" Heaven knows," said he,

" how earnestly I desired the union I
" proposed! Gladly would I resign the
" one half of those years fate has al-
" lotted for my life, to have the other
" blessed with the possession of my Se-
" lima in the way she expects from me;
" but, alas! that hope is vain. The
" fatal secret is this: I am already mar-
" ried; my heedless and unwary youth
" was ensnared to give my hand to a
" creature who, though I never did,
" nor never will, live with as a wife,
" will not, on any consideration, be
" prevailed upon to resign the cursed
" claim she has to me as a husband.".

' Overwhelmed as I was with various
' passions, I at last assumed resolution
' enough to tell him that he had acted a
' most ungenerous and dishonourable
' part in making his addresses to me,
' knowing himself under so indissoluble
' an engagement to another. To which
' he replied, that at first he hoped to
' have got quit of his unfortunate tie;
' and that after he found all the offers
' he had made to that end were fruit-
' less, the passion he had for me would
' not suffer him to restrain himself from
' seeing me, conversing with me, and
' telling me how much he adored me.
' He then made a long harangue on the
' resistless power of my charms, and the
' violence of that flame they had in-
' spired him with; swore a thousand
' oaths, that the world had nothing in
' it but myself worth living for; and
' concluded with a proposal, that since
' he could not make me his wife, he
' would settle a thousand pounds a year
' upon me to be his mistress; and that it
' should be at my option either to live
' publickly with him as such, or to
' continue with my mamma, and re-
' ceive his visits in a private manner.

' This offer I rejected with more dis-
' dain than I had shewn to any of the
' like nature which had ever been made
' to me since my first being in the way
' of temptation; nor will you wonder
' that I did so. To be courted for
' a mistress by the very man who had so
' lately flattered me with the hopes of
' marriage, made me now look upon
' that as an affront, which, before my
' expectations had been raised to the
' height they had been, I might perhaps
' have taken as a proof of his affection.
' I ranted, stormed, concealed no part
' of the spite I was possessed of; but all
' I said seemed to make no great im-

M 2 ' pression

‘ preſſion on him; he bore it with a tem-
‘ per which I thought not at all con-
‘ ſiſtent with the violence of the paſ-
‘ ſion he had pretended; and, on his
‘ going away, calmly told me, that he
‘ would make the ſame propoſal he
‘ had done to me to no other woman
‘ in the world ; that it was no inconſi-
‘ derable one; and that, as he could do
‘ no more, he hoped my cooler moments
‘ would repreſent it as a thing worthy
‘ my attention.

‘ Indeed, my dear Belinda, I was
‘ half mad; and believe I gave myſelf
‘ ſome airs not any way becoming in
‘ me to a man of his quality. I met
‘ him in the Park this morning; but
‘ though he was alone, and I had only
‘ Flavia with me, he never offered to join
‘ us, but paſſed by with a ſlight bow. I
‘ ſuppoſe he reſents my behaviour; but
‘ it is no matter, ſince he is married.
‘ Vanucius is now my laſt reſource. If
‘ I could perſuade the man to purchaſe
‘ a title, he would be full as agreeable
‘ to me as Dorantes; but he is an un-
‘ ambitious creature, and I almoſt de-
‘ ſpair of it: I ſhall try, at leaſt, how
‘ far the love he has for me will pre-
‘ vail. My next will bring you news
‘ of what ſucceſs my endeavours will
‘ meet; till when I am, even in the
‘ midſt of my perplexity, &c.

‘ SELIMA.’


## LETTER V.

‘ DEAR BELINDA,

‘ IT is almoſt a ſin to diſturb the feli-
‘ city you enjoy with any melan-
‘ choly accounts : but freſh calamities
‘ will always occaſion freſh complaints;
‘ and while I am giving you a detail of
‘ my misfortunes, methinks I am eaſed
‘ of ſome part of the weight of them.
‘ You may ſay, indeed, that this is a
‘ ſelfiſh conſideration, and I cannot deny
‘ the accuſation; but have this to an-
‘ ſwer in my defence—“ However diſ-
“ agreeable the purport of my letters
“ are, they ſhew, at leaſt, the perfect
“ confidence I have in your friendſhip
“ and good-nature.”
‘ I am apt to think that, before I tell
‘ you, you will ſuſpect I am alſo de-
‘ ſerted by Vanucius; and though I
‘ cannot be poſitive that ſuch a conjec-
‘ ture would be entirely groundleſs, yet

‘ I have little reaſon to flatter myſelf
‘ with the contrary. I have neither ſeen
‘ nor heard from him for five whole
‘ days; and this morning he ſet out for
‘ Tunbridge, without taking any other
‘ leave of me, than ſending a ſlight ex-
‘ cuſe for not waiting on me before he
‘ went. But this is not all: a relation
‘ of his, who I know has always looked
‘ upon his courtſhip to me with an evil
‘ eye, and had, not long ago, ſo great a
‘ quarrel with him on the occaſion, that
‘ he was forbid his houſe, is now ſo far
‘ reinſtated in his good graces, as to be
‘ gone with him into the country; and
‘ I do not doubt but will take this op-
‘ portunity of filling his ears with a
‘ thouſand ſtories to my diſadvantage,
‘ as he has ever done ſince my firſt ac-
‘ quaintance with him.

‘ Thus, my dear Belinda, from hav-
‘ ing, as I thought, my choice of two
‘ of the beſt matches in town, I am
‘ likely to loſe all hopes of both, and
‘ alſo to fall into the contempt and ri-
‘ dicule of thoſe flirts who ſo lately en-
‘ vied my good fortune. This laſt cir-
‘ cumſtance is above all ſo truly morti-
‘ fying, that after it I know not whether
‘ I ſhall ever be able to ſhew my face
‘ in any publick aſſembly, but rather
‘ take the ſame pains to conceal myſelf,
‘ as I once did to be conſpicuous. But
‘ farewel. The more I reflect on theſe
‘ accidents, the leſs I am capable of re-
‘ ſtraining my paſſion enough to aſſure
‘ you, with how much ſincerity, &c.

‘ SELIMA.’


## LETTER VI.

‘ DEAR BELINDA,

‘ I Expected no leſs, from your known
‘ goodneſs, than the conſolatory
‘ ideas you endeavour to inſpire me
‘ with. You would fain perſuade me
‘ that I have no reaſon for deſpair; and
‘ that the ſame beauty which attracted
‘ the hearts of Dorantes and Vanucius,
‘ will alſo gain others of equal eſti-
‘ mation; but, alas! I have too much
‘ experience of myſelf, and of what the
‘ world thinks of me, to entertain ſo
‘ flattering a hope. You know very
‘ well, my dear, that on my firſt ſetting
‘ up for conqueſt, I ſhewed myſelf in
‘ all publick places, and expoſed to the
‘ view of all who ſaw me, almoſt every
‘ charm

‘ charm nature has beftowed upon me;
‘ yet never was addreffed, on the fcore
‘ of marriage, by any but thofe two
‘ whom I have now loft. Befides, I
‘ am now what they call blown upon:
‘ that admiration which my firft appear-
‘ ance excited, wears off by my being
‘ fo often feen; and I begin to be con-
‘ vinced, that it was more owing to the
‘ peculiarity of my drefs, and manner
‘ of behaviour, than to any real perfec-
‘ tions of my perfon, that I was fo much
‘ followed by a gaping multitude.

‘ You fee how I am humbled ; and,
‘ by what I have faid, may perhaps
‘ imagine that I have fo far done with
‘ the pride and vanities of the world, as
‘ to take up with a little mercer or wool-
‘ len-draper, if fuch a one fhould offer.
‘ But do not harbour fo defpicable an
‘ opinion of your friend : no, I will never
‘ fit behind a compter, or be the wife of
‘ one that does. But I need not make
‘ this declaration; as matters ftand, I
‘ am not likely to be the wife of any
‘ body : but ftill, with an inviolable
‘ refpect, &c.

‘ Selima.’

## LETTER VII.

‘ DEAREST BELINDA,

‘ NOW may all the gods of love and
‘ wit infpire my pen, to defcribe
‘ to you, as it deferves, the bleffed re-
‘ verfe in my condition fince the laft
‘ melancholy epiftle you received from
‘ me. I was then plunged in the loweft
‘ pit of defpair, and am now raifed to
‘ the higheft fummit of human feli-
‘ city. In a word, I am the contracted
‘ fpoufe of Dorantes; and, as foon as
‘ the preparations for our wedding can
‘ be got ready, I fhall be the declared
‘ ***** of *****. Methinks I fee
‘ the furprize I put you in. You will
‘ doubtlefs cry out—“ How can this be,
“ when Dorantes has already confeffed
“ himfelf the hufband of another?”
‘ It feems, indeed, a paradox; yet ftands
‘ in no need of fchool-learning to be
‘ explained, as you will prefently difco-
‘ ver.

‘ After the lofs of both my lovers, as
‘ I then imagined, I fcarce did any
‘ thing but lie upon the bed and weep
‘ for two whole days together. My
‘ father, inftead of faying any thing to

‘ confole my afflictions, added to them
‘ by his reproaches, He told me that
‘ he knew what it would come to; that
‘ dreffing myfelf up like a Bartholo-
‘ mew baby would never get me a huf-
‘ band; and fuch like ftuff, as you know
‘ his low way of expreffing himfelf :
‘ but, thank Heaven! the tables are
‘ now turned upon him; and if re-
‘ fpect for my mamma did not reftrain
‘ me, I fhould return his flouts with in-
‘ tereft.

‘ One afternoon, as I was fitting at
‘ the window, with the fafh up, mufing
‘ on my unhappy fate, I faw Dorantes’s
‘ chariot at the door. While his foot-
‘ man knocked, he looked out, and
‘ made me a very refpectful bow. I
‘ was amazed; but thought it would be
‘ too grofs an affront to a man of his
‘ quality to be denied to him, as he faw
‘ I was at home; nor had I time for
‘ fuch a thing, if I would have done it;
‘ for the maid, who opened the door,
‘ fhewed him directly up ftairs. On
‘ his entrance, I affumed one of thofe
‘ haughty airs, which vulgar, low-bred
‘ people, are apt to call impudent and
‘ faucy; and, with my head half turned
‘ another way, faid to him—“ I am fur-
“ prized to fee you here, Dorantes, af-
“ ter the converfation you entertained
“ me with at your laft vifit.”

“ Oh, Selima,” replied he, “ I came
“ not now to repeat the audacity I was
“ then guilty of, nor to offend your
“ ears with any future difcourfes of the
“ like nature, but to beg pardon for the
“ paft; and hope that what I have to of-
“ fer will make fome atonement.”—“ I
“ do not comprehend your meaning,”
‘ returned I; “ but, whatever it may
“ be, cannot think it becomes me to
“ continue any correfpondence with a
“ married man, who has pretended to
“ make his addreffes to me.”—“ I am
“ not married,” rejoined he eagerly;
“ and the trial I made of your virtue,
“ adds a double luftre to the beauty
“ that firft inflamed me, and I am
“ now much more your flave than
“ ever.”—“ Not married!” cried I ;
“ why then did you tell me fo ?”—
“ Pardon the innocent impofition I
“ practifed on you,” faid he, kiffing
‘ my hand: “ I was willing to fee in
“ what manner you would refent it;
“ your behaviour has anfwered to my
“ wifh, and I now offer you a hand
“ which

" which I never had one thought or
" wish to difpofe of to any other wo-
" man."
' Oh, Belinda, how did my heart
' flutter at thefe words ! As Semandra
' fays in the play—

" I took them all, and died upon the found:
" To the driv'n air my flying foul was
        " faften'd.
" Each charming fyllable he fpoke was
        " mine."

' The many paffionate and endearing
' things he faid to me would not come
' within the compafs of twenty letters:
' you muft therefore, till I have a better
' opportunity of relating the particu-
' lars, content yourfelf with a brief
' fummary of the whole, which is this ;
' that he is entirely at liberty to marry
' me, and he is refolved to do fo; that
' an agreement the fame night was made
' between us for that purpofe; and that
' mamma and her good friend, who
' luckily happened to be with her, were
' called in to be witneffes of it.
' Since every thing has been fettled
' thus happily for me, fome people have
' been impertinent enough to affure me,
' that to their own knowledge Dorantes
' was married feveral years ago, and
' that his wife is ftill alive; but this
' gives me no manner of concern. If
' there be any woman who has a claim
' of this nature on him, he has doubt-
' lefs found means to prevail on her
' to relinquifh it; fo I look upon it as
' none of my affair. He marries me in
' the face of the world; has promifed to
' prefent me at court ; and while I en-
' joy the title of ****** of ******,
' and the grandeur annexed to it, fhall
' not trouble myfelf with any whifpers
' that may go about the town in relation
' to the lawfulnefs or unlawfulnefs of
' my marriage.
' It is no inconfiderable addition to
' my contentment, to hear that you de-
' fign to return to town in a fhort time.
' I long to fee you, and to give you an
' airing in my own coach and fix, with
' three flaunting footmen on the back of
' it: we fhall cut a better figure, Belinda,
' than when we made our little excur-
' fions together in a mean, dirty hack.
' O, Fortune! Fortune! dear, propi-
' tious Fortune, how am I bound to
' praife thee ! But no more at prefent,

' than that I am, with the greateft good
' wifhes, &c.

                            ' SELIMA.

' P. S. I need not defire you to tell
' Philander what has happened; I
' know you will, and alfo that his
' regard for you will make him
' participate in the happinefs of
' your friend. Once more, adieu.'

Here end the letters of this celebrated
lady, who in a very little time after married Dorantes.

## CHAP. VI.

CONSISTS CHIEFLY OF SOME RE-
FLECTIONS OF THE AUTHOR'S
OWN ON FALSE TASTE, THE MIS-
TAKEN ROAD IN THE PURSUIT
OF FAME, AND THE FOLLY OF AN
ILL-DIRECTED EMULATION. TO
WHICH ARE ADDED, A FEW FAINT
SKETCHES TAKEN FROM THE
MOST AMIABLE ORIGINALS IN
MODERN LIFE.

THE celebrated Dr. Buffy tells us,
than when we fay a man has a fine
or true tafte, no more is meant by thofe
words, than that he has a found judgment, a clear head, and a nicely diftinguifhing capacity in judging of what
is really worthy and becoming, and
what is not fo; whether it be in the
choice of his amufements, his equipage,
his apparel, the furniture of his houfe,
the covering of his table, or whatever
elfe depends on the direction of the will
and fancy. Now, as every thing is beft
fhewn by it's oppofite, if the definition
given us by the French author of the
true tafte be juft, as I believe moft people will allow it is, to think and act
contrary to what he defcribes, is what
we call falfe tafte: but, in my opinion,
to think and do always what is wrong,
and at the fame time imagine that all we
think and do is right, is not of itfelf fufficient to take in the meaning of the
phrafe in it's full extent; there muft always
be added an affectation of being fingular,
over curious, over delicate, over elegant, fomewhat above the common le-
vel of mankind; in fine, the man of a
falfe tafte muft not be a fool of Heaven's
                                        making.

making, but his own. The late witty Earl of Rochester has presented us with a very picturesque character of the man of false taste, in the following lines—

' He was a fool through choice, not want
 ' of wit;
' His foppery, without the help of sense,
' Could ne'er have risen to such an excel-
 ' lence.
' Nature's a> lame in making a true fop
' As a phil 'fopher: the very top
' And dignity of fo'ly, we attain
' By studious search, and labour of the
 ' brain;
' By observation, counsel, and deep thought.
' God never made a coxcomb worth a groat:
' We owe that name to industry and arts ;
' An eminent fool must be a man of parts.'

A person may be endowed with great talents, yet, through a false taste in the manner of displaying them, be rendered ridiculous instead of respectable; and, while he aims at attracting universal ad-'miration, become the object of universal contempt. Hippias is profoundly learned, is well skilled in the most useful sciences, and endowed, both by nature and education, with every requisite to render him a worthy member of society; yet, by some unaccountable oddities of manners and behaviour, he makes himself hated where he might be loved, despised where he might be respected, and a mere cypher in a world where he might be a figure of the greatest consequence. He is not at all dissatisfied that every one knows and speaks of him as a man possessed of a very opulent fortune, yet affects to look down with scorn on all the pleasures, and even innocent amusements, it might afford him; and to such an excess does he carry this humour, that whatever is beyond the necessities of nature he treats as luxury and epicurisms; vainly imagining that the wearing of a threadbare coat, and a wig that the head it covers scarce remembers ever to have had a curl, entitles him to the character of a philosopher.

But this ostentatious humility, as I think it may be justly called, is not the most unpardonable error into which Hippias is led by his false taste: this serves only to make him ridiculous, but there is another which makes him hateful. The ambition he has of being reverenced as a Stoick, renders him deaf to the dictates of humanity, and wholly insensible of all social feeling for his fellow-

creatures. He partakes not in the joys or griefs of even those he calls his friends; nor would lift a finger, move a step, or speak a syllable, either to promote the one, or dissipate the other. The most distressful circumstance has not the power to touch his heart; and if any one knows him little enough to employ his assistance or advice in the extremest exigence, he replies, with a solemn and magisterial air, that he can say nothing to their complaints; that pity is a passion; and that, by the force of his reason, he has divested himself of all passions, of what kind soever. Thus does Hippias, by indulging one unhappy propensity, forfeit all the love and esteem the qualities he is possessed of would otherwise attract. The manner in which he is now looked upon gives me room to suspect that, whenever he makes his exit from this world, he will have an epitaph somewhat like what I read on a tomb-stone in a country church-yard—

' Here ******, stretch'd at his full length,
 ' is laid;
' Whom, living, no one lov'd, nor mourn'd
 ' when dead.'

Numberless are the instances might be given to prove the best capacities may be, and frequently are, perverted by false taste and misapplication. As one of our most eminent authors tells us, the love of fame is the universal passion; it is imprinted, in a more or less degree, on every human heart. Those who have great talents, are apt to think they can never render themselves sufficiently conspicuous; and those of weaker intellects, yet possessed of the same vanity, are sometimes so infatuated, as, rather than not to make a noise in the world, to do things which may incur a lampoon, since they cannot deserve a panegyrick. A private life, or, as they term it, a life of obscurity, is to some people the severest misfortune they can labour under: they will tell you, that they may as well be out of the world, as of no consequence in it; and few there are who will take the poet's word for a contrary passion—

' Th' unknown, untalk'd of man, is only
 ' blest;
' No anxious doubts his peaceful breast an-
 ' noy,
' From praise and censure equally remote;
 ' Nor

‘ Nor hope, nor fear, his happinefs de-
   ‘ ftroys,
‘ But fafe within himfelf, himfelf enjoys.’

There are alfo people who, having
no peculiarities of their own, affect
to imitate thofe they may fee in otheis;
efpecially if the perfon they copy after
be of a fuperior rank, or has the reputation of a wit. Thefe may properly enough be called fecond-hand
fools; for they generally take up the
follies juft when they are left off by the
perfons they would be thought exactly to
refemble: according to a vulgar adage—
‘ The fool will fometimes peep out of
\‘ the wifeft man.’ The leaft failing in
a perfon of diftinguifhed character is
prefently adopted by his inferiors, till it
becomes a fafhion. Emulation, however, when well-directed, is one of the
moft noble propenfities of the mind;
nothing can be more truly laudable than
an endeavour to fquare our actions by a
praife-worthy model: but I am forry to
fay, that this is not fo often the cafe as
every good man would wifh it were.

There are fome people fo unhappy,
as to take for a pattern all the bad they
can find, and neglect all the good; and
this, too, without defign, or any un-
toward inclination, but through mere
carelefinefs: and, provided they do fomething fuch a one or fuch a one does,
give not themfelves the trouble to examine whether what they imitate be a
beauty or a blemifh; or, indeed, whether it be either, or only a matter of indifference, and altogether unworthy of
regard. And, now I am upon this head,
I cannot forbear relating an example of
the fort I laft mentioned; which, though
it happened fome years ago, and is extremely trifling in itfelf, may ferve to
fhew how little care people fometimes
take in their choice of an object for imitation.

A young gentleman of my acquaintance, who paffed in the world for a
very pretty fellow, eitherwas, or affected
to be, becaufe it was the mode, a prodigious admirer of the late defervedly famous Sir Ifaac Newton. He had the
honour of being known to that truly
great man, frequently vifited him, and
had the opportunity of hearing many
things from him, which doubtlefs were
well worthy of being treafured in his memory; yet I could never find he took
particular notice of any thing but this I

am now going to repeat. Sir Ifaac had
him at his table one day, and happened
cafually to fay, that he thought nothing
fweeter than a bacon bone. My friend
immediately catched up the word, and
from that moment made it his own, and
on all occafions quoted it. If any one
afked him to eat with them, he would
reply—‘ Yes, if you have any bacon;
‘ for, as Sir Ifaac Newton fays, there is
‘ nothing fweeter than a bacon bone.’
In fine, he went to no place, mingled in
no converfation, without finding fome
means to introduce the fweetnefs of the
bacon bone; and repeated the above-
mentioned expreffion fo often, and fo
impertinently, that at laft he became the
jeft of all his companions, who, in deri-
fion, called him by no other name than
the Bacon Bone. Ridiculous as this
may appear, I can affure my reader,
that the gentleman I have been fpeaking
of does not ftand alone, but has many
parallels in my catalogue of obferva-
tions on a mifguided imitation, as I
could eafily prove; but my humour has
on a fudden changed it’s vein, and I begin to grow too ferious to recite any farther inftances of fo ludicrous a nature.
Degenerate as we mortals are faid to be,
yet even now there are not wanting
fome few illuftrious examples of both,
whom even an endeavour to copy after
would be fome merit in the attempter.

See where the noble Altamont ftands
forth a fhining pattern of exalted virtue! Dignity in his countenance; benevolence in his hand; the ftrricteft juftice, honour, and focial kindnefs, in his
heart. Near him you will always find
the chafte and fair Euphemia, his illuftrious confort; a numerous and beaute-
ous offspring with joyous fmiles play
round their feet; Juno and Hymen ho-
ver over their heads, and fhower continual bleffings on the happy pair. From
Altamont and Euphemia, ye hufbands,
fathers, learn the duties due to thofe
endearing names, and ceafe to imagine
that to fwerve from them is politenefs.

Learn you who languifh in a widowed bed, from Elifmonda learn to fupport the melancholy of your condition as
becomes you—Elifmonda, who though,
as Lee expreffes it, in all the full-grown
pride of glorious beauty, difdains all
overtures for a fecond marriage, fhuns
pomp and ceremony, nor haunts the
court nor publick walks; but in her
clofet ruminates what good is in her
pow**r**

power to do; who moft deferves, and who ftands moft in need of her relief; and all thofe cares fhe once employed to pleafe the beft of hufbands, are now taken up with acts of piety and foft compaffion.

Learn, ye fair ramblers after fhew and hurry, ye midnight gadders to mafquerades and balls, from lovely Amadea learn the timid modefty that beft befits and beft fecures the honour of a virgin ftate. She takes no pains to attract the eyes of the gaping multitude, and rather fhuns than covets popular admiration. She avoids being the firft in any new fafhion, and never runs into the extremes of it; goes to no routes, affemblies, or mafquerades; feldom indulges herfelf even with a play or opera; and, when fhe does, is always accompanied by fome grave relation, whofe prefence is a check on the impertinence of thofe whifflers who fkip from box to box, faying the fame thing to every fine woman they fee there. When fhe walks in the Park, fhe makes choice of thofe hours when the leaft company are there; and the only publick place you are fure to find her in, is at church.

The example of Dorilaus is a noble reprimand to thofe who fuffer themfelves to grow old in riots and debaucheries. Early he quitted the levities of youth; and as the filver fwan, emerging from the ftream, fhakes off the drops that hang upon it's wings, fo Dorilaus but dipped into the follies of the times, juft tafted the licentious pleafures of the town, then defpifed and threw them from him with abhorrence. Temptations of every kind have fince furrounded him, yet has he ftill remained unmoved; equally inflexible to the infinuations of luxury, and to the bribes of corruption. Steady in virtuous principles, the evil ones at length grew weary of their fruitlefs labour, and now fuffer him to enjoy a calm and undifturbed repofe, in the fociety of a few felect friends, who join with him in commiferating the infatuation of others.

If there were no cards nor dice in the world, Favonius would be looked upon as an almoft faultlefs being, and the voice of envy have nothing wherewith to caft a blemifh on his name. It cannot be denied, however, that Favonius has wit, honour, generofity, affability, and an unaffected fweetnefs of difpofition: qualifications which would greatly compenfate for his love of gaming, if it were not for two confiderations, which are thefe. Firft, That by indulging this unhappy propenfity, he lavifhes too much of that time which might be employed in the defence of the liberties of his country, and for the benefit of the commonwealth. Secondly, That his high character in the world makes many people ready, and even proud, to follow his example in this the fole error of which he can be accufed, while they neglect the leaft endeavour to imitate any one of the numerous virtues he is mafter of.

There are many others of both fexes ftill living, whofe characters would reflect honour on the imitators; and fome who, though the world has been fo unfortunate as to lofe, have left behind them fuch monuments of their virtues as never can be forgotten; their memory ftrikes a damp on guilt, and will be eternally venerated by all the wife and good. But this is a theme which, though perhaps little affecting to the greateft part of my readers, may yet be too melancholy to fome others, as well as to myfelf; I fhall therefore dwell no longer upon it, but return to a fubject more fuitable to the prefent difpofition of the times, which I am not fo ignorant as not to know an author ought always to confult, if he regards either his own reputation, or the intereft of his bookfeller.

## CHAP. VII.

GIVES A SUCCINCT RELATION OF TWO PRETTY EXTRAORDINARY ADVENTURES THAT PRESENTED THEMSELVES TO THE AUTHOR IN A MORNING RAMBLE.

A Clear and undifturbed fky, illuminated with a fmiling fun, and perfumed with a thoufand odours from the new-budding fpring, invited me to Hyde Park. I girded my invifible Belt about me, for the reafons I have already mentioned in a preceding chapter; and alfo put my Tablets in my pocket, though I had not the leaft expectation of meeting with any thing in that place which fhould give me occafion to make ufe of them. The fweet folemnity of this folitude afforded me infinitely more pleafure than ever I had found in a crouded Mall: it infpired me with the

N                           moft

moſt delightful ideas; which indulging, I wandered for I believe near two hours, without meeting with any one objeſt to interrupt my contemplations. How much longer I might have continued in in this agreeable reverie, I know not; for I was rouzed from it by the ſudden appearance of a gentleman at ſome diſtance from me, but who was advancing direſtly towards the path where I was. On his approach, I ſtepped a little on one ſide, to prevent his running againſt me. He walked backwards and forwards with ſome emotion, looked often on his watch, and diſcovered many ſigns of the utmoſt impatience. By the cockade in his hat, I doubted not of his being a military gentleman, and imagined that ſome diſpute of honour was that morning to be decided by the ſword; but I was ſoon convinced of my miſtake, the officer having more of Cupid than of Mars in his head.

I had not been many minutes, before a coach came up, and ſtopped very near the place where I ſtood. There were three women in it; one of whom, and much the richeſt dreſſed, I preſently knew to be the celebrated Lipathea: the others, as I afterwards found, were her woman and nurſe; this, it ſeems, being the firſt time of her coming abroad ſince her bringing into the world a ſon and heir, to the great joy of that honourable family, as the news writers expreſs it. On ſight of the coach, the young officer advanced briſkly towards it. Lipathea ſaw him at the ſame time; and, thruſting out her head, and half her body, with her accuſtomed loud laugh, called to him to come in. With theſe words, the door was immediately opened; the two women came out, and the officer jumped in: after which, the coachman was ordered to drive, as ſlow as he could, to the Walnut-tree Walk, and ſo round to the Ha-ha Wall, and back to the ſame place again.

I had no opportunity to follow them, ſo was obliged to content myſelf with hearing the diſcourſe that paſſed between the two women who were left behind. To this end I kept as cloſe to them as I could, with my Tablets in my hand; but the ſubjeſts they talked on were ſo trifling, that I did not think it worth while to ſpread them for the impreſſion of their words, till all at once the nurſe began to run into a long detail of the particulars ſhe knew, or could remember, that

had happened in the ſeveral families where ſhe had been; but the matters ſhe related being wholly inſignificant, and unworthy of record, I ſhut up my Tablets, and gave no farther ear to what ſhe ſaid. I quitted not the place, however, till the lovers returned from the tour they had been making. The coach ſtopped, and the captain was ſet down near the end of the ſame path where he had been taken up; and Lipathea beckoned her two attendants to come in, who by this time, I found, were heartily weary of their promenade.

The well-known charaſter of Lipathea, one would think, ſhould have hindered me from being much ſurprized at any thing ſhe did; yet could I not be an eye-witneſs of the glaring affront ſhe now put upon her huſband, and the modeſty of her ſex, without being ſeized with a conſternation impoſſible to be expreſſed. My meditations on this adventure had perhaps laſted till I came home, if they had not been interrupted by another which fell in my way, and afforded me, in it's conſequences, more matter for diverſion than the former. Beauty, or what is more than beauty, the power of attraſtion, is not confined to perſons of a high ſtation: Nature can exert herſelf as much in the cottage as the palace; and we ſometimes find more real graces under a plain, homely coif, than under a fine gauze cap ornamented with jewels; as the little incident I am about to rehearſe will abundantly evince.

As I was paſſing through St. James's Park, I met a young woman with a porringer in her hand, neatly covered with a large earthen ſaucer. She advanced with ſlow and cautious ſteps, leſt ſhe ſhould ſpill any part of what ſhe had brought. When ſhe drew near the Parade, a tall grenadier, who I found was her huſband, ſtepped forth from among his comrades, and received the meſs from her, as alſo a pewter ſpoon, which ſhe took out of her pocket, and gave to him at the ſame time. Though every thing about her was clean, yet the reader may eaſily ſuppoſe extremely mean : ſhe had a face, however, that ſtood in need of no advantages from dreſs to ſet it off. Never had I ſeen a finer pair of eyes, or a more ſoft and delicate complexion; and, to crown all the reſt of her perfeſtions, there appeared, not only in her countenance, but in every little motion and geſture, that which, in my opinion, is

the

the very foul of lovelinefs—a moft perfect innocence and fimplicity. I was not, however, the only admirer whom her charms had that morning attracted; a certain officer of diftinction, walking on the Parade with another gentleman, having feen her at fome diftance, quitted his companion, and came to the grenadier, accofting him in thefe terms—

*Officer.* So, grenadier, you are taking your morning's refrefhment. Is this pretty damfel your wife?

*Grenadier.* Yes, pleafe your honour.

*Officer.* She feems very young: you can't have been married long.

*Grenadier.* About three months, pleafe your honour.

*Officer.* I hope you ufe her well; I dare fay fhe deferves it.

*Grenadier.* I think fhe has no reafon to complain, Sir.—Have you, Peggy?

*Wife.* No, indeed.

*Officer.* I am glad of it. I would always have the women ufed well.

He faid no more, but turned upon his heel, and walked away with a carelefs air, as if nothing farther than what he had made fhew of was in his head; but I perceived he removed no farther than the end of the Canal, and kept an obfervant eye on thofe he had left behind. The grenadier having finifhed his little repaft, mingled with fome foldiers who were on the Parade, and his wife tripped out of the Park with much more hafte than fhe had come into it. The officer, who had never loft fight of her, followed, though for a while at fome diftance; and I kept very near him, refolving to fee what it was he aimed at, and what would be the iffue of his defigns, in cafe he had any of the nature I fufpected. She went through the Treafury; and when he faw fhe had entered there, he mended his pace; and coming up with her under the arched paffage, gave her a little flap on the fhoulder: fhe ftarted, and turned back; but, on feeing him, dropped a low curtfey, while he fpoke thus—

*Officer.* Well overtaken, pretty lafs. I wanted to fpeak with you: I fancy I have feen you fomewhere or other. Pray what countrywoman are you?

*Wife.* I was born in Lancafhire, fo pleafe your honour.

*Officer.* I thought fo; for I have heard fay all the Lancafhire girls are very handfome. And pray what brought you to London?

*Wife.* The hopes of getting into a good fervice, pleafe your honour; but not hearing of one prefently, and happening to get acquainted with my hufband in the mean time, I changed my condition.

*Officer.* You did well: there is nothing like being your own miftrefs. But you country folks are generally afraid of a red coat: how came you to venture on a foldier?

*Wife.* I don't know, Sir; it was my fate, I think.

*Officer.* Well, here is fomething to encourage you to love the army.

With thefe words he drew a fix-andthirty piece of gold out of his pocket, and made an offer of putting it into her hand; but fhe drew back, either afhamed or unwilling to accept it, and cried—'Oh, Sir, I have heard fay that women fhould never take money from the men!' To which he replied—'That is from your mean, dirty fellows; but it is ill-manners to refufe any thing given you by your fuperiors.' He now took hold of her hand; and a fecond effort obliging her to receive his prefent, fhe looked on it, turned it two or three times, and then faid—'Blefs me! what muft I do with this great piece of money?'

*Officer.* Oh, you will find a ufe for it; that pretty face of yours requires a thoufand things that the grenadier's pay will not enable him to purchafe for you. And, now I think on it, 'tis pity he fhould continue in that low ftation: I have it in my power to raife him, and I will do it; he fhall have a halbert forthwith. But I muft talk to you a little firft on that fcore. Where do you live? I will come and fee you.

*Wife.* Oh, dear Sir, we have not a place fit for your honour to come into.

*Officer.* No matter for that. I am not proud; and never fcruple to go to any place, how mean foever it be, where I can either do a pleafure to myfelf, or a fervice to my friends; therefore no excufes.

*Wife.* Your honour is very good. But I do not know how to tell you, for there is no fign near us. We lodge up one pair of ftairs, at a button-maker's, the next door but one to a chandler's fhop, in a little alley that turns out of King Street by a green ftall, and is no thoroughfare.

*Officer.*

*Officer.* I fhall never find it by this direction; you fhall fhew me where it is now.

*Wife.* Lord, Sir, what will the people in the ftreet fay, to fee me go cheek-by-jole with fuch a fine gentleman as your horour?

*Officer.* Well, then, you fhall walk before, and I will follow you.

*Wife.* But, Sir, my room is all dirty; I was juft going home to clean it, now I have carried my hufband his breakfaft.

*Officer.* I fhall not go in, nor vifit you, till after dark; to hinder, as you fay, the neighbours from ftaring at me. I will come this evening, about nine or ten o'clock. Your hufband is to be upon duty, but do you take care not to be out of the way; for it is abfolutely neceffary I fhould have fome difcourfe with you before I do any thing for him.

*Wife.* Lord, Sir, what bufinefs can your honour have with me that he muft not know!

*Officer.* You may tell him afterwards, if you will. But I won't detain you any longer; go home and pleafe yourfelf that your hufband fhall be a ferjeant to-morrow, and that I fhall raife him ftill higher, fo that he may come to be a captain at laft.

*Wife.* A captain!—Oh la! I fhould never have thought of fuch a thing!

*Officer.* It all depends upon yourfelf, and what I have to communicate to you; fo be fure be at home, and alone when I come.

*Wife.* Yes, pleafe your honour. I would not, for all the world, be fo rude as to difappoint you; though I am afhamed you fhould come into fuch a poor habitation as mine.

*Officer.* Never mind that, my pretty one; I fhall look on nothing in the place but yourfelf.

While he was fpeaking this, he caft his eyes about, and finding there was nobody in fight, gave her a kifs; after which fhe made a low curtfey, and turned away to go home, blufhing all the way fhe went like the fun through a gentle fhower in an April morning. He followed, as he faid he would, till he had feen her enter into her little dwelling; nor left the place, till he had taken fufficient notice of every thing, to be able to remember and know it again. I was now under a moft fenfible concern for this poor young creature, thus likely to be betrayed; not by any inclination to ill,

but merely through the fear of offending a perfon above her : quite ignorant of the fnares of the world, and untaught how to refift temptation, fhe was, alas! juft ready to fall into a real fault, by an endeavour to avoid an imaginary one. As Mr. Waller faid, though on a different occafion—

' Innocence and youth oft makes,
' In artlefs virgins fuch miftakes.'

Though I had not the leaft doubt but that the young wife of the grenadier would become a prey to the vicious inclination of her feducer, yet I had the curiofity to fee in what manner fhe would behave on the full difcovery of his defigns upon her. Accordingly, I went about nine o'clock to the little alley, and pofted myfelf on a bench at a door juft oppofite to the dwelling of the grenadier, refolving to go in with the officer when he fhould come. I had not waited above half an hour before he appeared : he was muffled up in his cloak; but, by the help of a fmall winking light from an adjacent fhop, I eafily knew him. He had taken too much notice of the houfe to be miftaken in it, and entered directly, the door being left open, as I fuppofe, for that purpofe. I followed clofe behind him; but never had my Invifibilityfhip been in fo much danger as it was now brought into by this adventure.

The grenadier, it feems, having been informed by his wife of every thing that had paffed between her and the officer, and more zealous in the defence of his honour than perhaps fome in a much higher ftation would have been, had prevailed, for fome pots of beer, on a brother grenadier to do duty for him that night, fo returned home before the hour appointed for his rival's approach; and havingarmed himfelf with a good oaken cudgel, ftood on the middle of the ftairs, ready to give a proper reception to that invader of his rights. My leader had not advanced above five or fix fteps of the ftairs, when he received a violent blow on the head; which, together with the furprize it gave him, made him reel back, and like to fall on the poor Invifible; but I haftily and prudently withdrew to the middle of the entry, and ftood aloof, to hear, at a more fafe diftance, what would be the end of this affair. The grenadier purfued his ftrokes; and the officer,

INVISIBLE SPY

Publish'd as the Act directs, by Harrison & Cᵒ July 1. 1788.

officer, being in no condition to defend
himself in that disadvantageous posture,
thought it best to make his escape; but
not having been accustomed to such steep
winding stairs fell down to the bottom. His antagonist, though better
acquainted with the passage, in attempting to follow him, had the same fate;
but being uppermost, soon recovered
himself; and catching hold of the officer by the collar as he was endeavouring to rise, forced him on his knees, and
continued buffeting him on the head and
face till he was covered all over with the
blood that gushed from his nose and
mouth, as I afterwards perceived.

The officer made several efforts to
draw his sword, and at length did so;
but the other finding what he was about,
immediately seized it by the hilt, wrested
it from him, snapped it asunder with his
foot, and threw it over his head. ' Rascal,
' will you murder me!' cried the officer.
' No,' replied the grenadier; ' I will only
' cool your courage, and make you re-
' member running after other men's
' wives.'—' Dog! do you know who I
' am?' demanded he. ' I only know you
'for a villain,' said the other, ' that
' would debauch my wife, and as such
' I'll use you.'—' Sirrah,' returned the
officer, ' I will make you pay dearly for
' this insolence! You know well
' enough that I am ******.'—' You
' lye!' rejoined the other, ' and deserve
' to be hanged for taking such a gen-
' 'leman's name in your mouth! ******
' would scorn to sneak into such a poor
' hut as this, to seduce any man's wife.'
The grenadier's hands were not idle all
this time; but the officer having at
length got upon his feet, they continued
wrestling together for some minutes, in
which combat the furious husband had
much the better; which put me in mind
of what Mr. Rowe says in Jane Shore—

' In spite of birth and dignity, a man
' Oppos'd against a man, is but a man.'

The officer now finding himself quite
disabled, and being still under the gripe
of his unrelenting enemy, called vehemently out for help; on which several
of the neighbours ran in with lighted
candles in their hands, and the entry was
presently full of men, women, and children; but never was such a spectacle as
this demolished beau. ' Bless me!
' what is the matter?' cried one; ' what

' is the matter?'—' Ask no questions.
' Here is half a crown for any one that
' will get me a chair immediately,' said
he; and the word was scarce out of his
mouth, before a cobler ran with all the
speed he could, to do as he desired. The
grenadier now affected the utmost surprize, and said—' All the world should
' never have made me believe it was your
' honour! I protest I took you for a
' rogue that wanted to come to bed to
' my wife while I was abroad, and
' thought I could not use such a one
' too ill.' The women, on hearing
this, guessed how the business was, and
looked at one another, and grinned: one
of them, however, was so charitable, as
to fetch a bowl of water, to wash the
blood off his face and garments. He made
use off what she brought, but gave no
other answer to what the grenadier had
said, than a look full of resentment and
confusion.

A chair being brought, he catched up
his hat and wig, which had fallen off in
the scuffle, went into it, leaving behind
him sufficient matter to employ the conversation of the whole alley for a considerable time. On hearing afterwards
the whole truth of the affair from the
grenadier and his wife, every one ap-
plauded the conduct of them both, and
laughed heartily at the disappointment
and correction of the lascivious officer.
For my own part, after I got home, the
satisfaction of finding myself safe from
the dangers into which my curiosity had
brought me, was succeeded by some
considerations on the passages I had
been witness of; and I could not help
being filled with the utmost astonishment,
that persons endowed with a liberal
education, and from whom much better
things might be expected, should, for the
sake of gratifying a foolish inclination,
the fleeting pleasure of a moment, not
only be guilty of the greatest injustice to
others, but also of the most abject de-
meaning of themselves.

## CHAP. VIII.

IS CALCULATED RATHER FOR AD-
MONITION THAN ENTERTAIN-
MENT, AND THEREFORE LIKELY
TO BE BUT LITTLE RELISHED.

HOW vainly do we boast the light
of reason, when we refuse to submit either our wills or actions to the
guidance

guidance of it's direction; when, through every stage of life, we suffer some darling passion to gain dominion over us, and utterly extinguish that glorious lamp we seem so proud of, and would be thought so eminently to possess above the rest of the creation! Prodigality is generally the vice of youth, and avarice of age: but though both these propensities proceed from a wrong turn of mind, and are diametrically opposite to found judgment, yet I think somewhat more be said in excuse of the one than of the other. The prodigal lavishes his stores in such things as do a pleasure to himself; and if he squanders away his patrimony in riotous living, and becomes miserable in the end, there are some who profit by his misfortunes; his money circulates, and the publick suffer nothing by his private ruin. The miser, on the contrary, not only denies himself all enjoyment of the goods of fortune, but also withholds them, as much as in his power, from every one else: he parts with nothing he can get into his clutches; amasses heaps of treasure; and smiles, with a wicked satisfaction, to see it lie rusting in his coffers, while numbers of his fellow-creatures are perishing for want of it.

Avarice, above all other passions, so takes up the soul, that it leaves not the least room for any of the nobler sensations. Love, friendship, pity, and even natural affection, are excluded thence. The covetous man regards only the gratification of that one sordid view; all his fears, his hopes, his cares, are centered there, and he seldom sticks at any thing to obtain it. Besides, what can be more absurd in itself, than for people to labour with all their might in heaping riches which they neither use, nor can assure themselves but that the next moment may dispossess them of? And it is remarkable, that the nearer they approach to the time when they can expect no other than to be snatched for ever from the idol they had worshipped, they grow the more eager to preserve it. The condition of those children who have the misfortune to be descended from parents of the humour I am speaking of, can never be too much commiserated, especially if they happen to be born with notions more just and elevated; an instance of which kind I am now going to relate.

A gentleman, whom I shall distin-

guish by the name of Avario, is sprung from a very ancient family in the west of England, has a large estate, and might have been beloved and respected by his neighbours, if the excessive parsimoniousness of his disposition did not make him do things which demean his rank, and even render him contemptible in the eyes both of his equals and inferiors. He was married, in his youth, to a lady of birth and fortune, but had no child for near twelve years; at the end of which time, however, she brought a son into the world; which, one would imagine, should have filled the father's heart with the highest satisfaction; but, instead of thanking Providence for sending him an heir of his own bowels for his estate, he only repined at the additional expence the new comer must necessarily occasion. His lady was sensibly afflicted at the little notice he took of the young Clyamon, for so the son of this unworthy father was called; but when she reproached him with his unkindness, he only gave her this churlish answer—That he saw no cause for any great rejoicing; for he supposed, as she had now began to teem, she should in a few years have more children than he should be able to maintain.

Clyamon, notwithstanding, grew a very fine boy; but would have had little to boast of from education, if his uncle by the mother's side, who was exceeding rich, and had no children, had not conceived a more than ordinary affection for him, and resolved to bestow on him all those advantages which were denied to him by the niggard disposition of his father. He told Avario, that if he would trust him with his son, he would breed him as his own, and take care he should want for none of those accomplishments which constitute the truly fine gentleman, in case he were capable of receiving them; 'Which,' added he, ' I do not at all doubt of, from ' the early promise of his childhood.' This offer was too agreeable to both the parents not to be readily accepted: the father rejoiced at being eased of an expence he could not foresee without regret: and the mother was highly pleased to think that her little darling would now receive a more polite education than she could hope the too great frugality of her husband would have allowed him.

Clyamon was about ten years of age when Sir Arthur Frankwill, for so this worthy

worthy uncle was called, took him under his protection, and carried him to a fine seat he had about twelve miles distant from Avario's. Doubly happy for him was now this change in his situation; for his mother dying soon after his removal, he would doubtless have been deprived of many indulgences he had hitherto enjoyed at home, but which were abundantly made up to him by the tender affection he was treated with by the good baronet. Sir Arthur, not approving of any of the schools in that part of the country, sent him to Eton, under the conduct of a faithful old servant; and in that place it was he received his first rudiments of learning. The improvements he made there were such as did honour to the masters, as well as to his own capacity. The accounts those gentlemen gave of him, in their letters to Sir Arthur, were confirmed by their pupil's behaviour whenever the times of breaking up gave him the liberty of going into the country. Both uncle and father were surprized on finding the swift progress he made in his learning; the one was charmed with the success of his endeavours, and the other quite transported that his son was in a fair way of being possessed of so many accomplishments without any cost to himself.

Having perfected himself in all he could be taught at Eton, he quitted the school, by his uncle's permission, and returned to the west; where, after having staid some time to make an acquaintance with the gentry, and take such diversions as the country afforded, his uncle thought proper he should finish his studies at one of the universities, and, for some reasons which he had within himself, made choice of Oxford. Clyamon accordingly went thither at the age of eighteen, and had the good fortune to have for his tutor a gentleman of deep learning, a keen discernment, and an unprejudiced judgment; who inspired him with such principles of justice and true honour as I believe he will never depart from. The admonitions of this worthy tutor, joined to a natural love of virtue in himself, entirely preserved him from running into any of those excesses too many of his age are guilty of: though nothing could be more gay and spirituous, yet every thing he said or did was governed by a certain decorum, without seeming to be so. He could be

chearful among the men of his acquaintance, without immorality or prophaneness; courtly among the ladies, without flattery or insincerity; respectful to his superiors, and maintain a proper distance to those below him without pride or ill-nature. In fine, his character and manners were such as made him highly esteemed by all the wife and good, and beloved even by those who would not be at the pains to imitate him.

After a stay of about three years at the university, he returned to Sir Arthur's; for that kind uncle and patron would needs have him continue to look upon his house as his chief home: nor did Avario at all oppose this motion, though he was now extremely proud of his son, went often to see him, and would always make him be present at every publick assembly or meeting in which he was himself a party. It is certain, indeed, never any young gentleman was more happy or contented in his mind than Clyamon at the time I am speaking of; he had but one wish beyond what he already possessed, and that remained no longer ungratified than while he forbore to mention it. He was as well acquainted, as books could make him, with most foreign parts, especially with those kingdoms and states which compose this quarter of the globe; but when he considered that the best description cannot but fall infinitely short of the prospect, he was very desirous of being an eye-witness of those things and places he had read of.

Sir Arthur highly approved of his nephew's inclination to travel; it seemed laudable to him, as he had himself often thought it was the only thing wanting to compleat his other accomplishments: and one day, as they were talking on that subject—' My dear Clyamon,' said he, ' the desire you have of seeing the ' world is truly praise worthy, and I ' think you cannot better employ two ' or three of those years which I hope ' Heaven has allotted for you, than in ' visiting the several courts of Europe: ' it will enlarge your ideas; and the ' difference of their manners and policies will, I doubt not, enable you to ' make such observations as may here- ' after be of service to your country. ' I think,' pursued he, ' there is no ne- ' cessity for putting you under the care ' of any person by way of governor; ' you are now arrived at years, and, I ' flatter

'flatter myfelf, at difcretion enough to be
'trufted by yourfelf: as to the reft, you
'may depend that I fhall fpare nothing
'to render the tour you make agreeable
'to you; and that, whatever remit-
'tances you fhall have occafion for,
'from time to time, fhall be punctually
'fent to you, on a letter of advice.'

This crowned all the other favours
Clyamon had received from his indulgent uncle; and, it is not to be doubted,
drew from him the moft grateful acknowledgments. It was neceffary,
however, Avario fhould be confulted:
the matter accordingly was propofed to
him; on which he teftified that he was
not void of natural affection, by the reluctance he expreffed for expofing to deferving a fon to the dangers of travel-
ling; but the arguments urged by Sir
Arthur, and the entreaties of Clyamon,
at length prevailed on him to confent.
Clyamon foon made it appear that it was
not to gratify a vain, unprofitable curiofity, but the laudable ambition of improving his mind, that had made him
fo defirous of going abroad. The letters he wrote to his father and uncle,
from France, Italy, Sweden, and feveral
parts of Germany, would have been very
well worth inferting in this work; but,
to the misfortune of the publick, I was
not then in poffeffion of my wonderful
Tablets; and though I heard them read
more than once, can remember little of
the particulars they contain. This worthy young gentleman had gleaned from
every field he paffed through whatever
he found capable of increafing the trea-
fures of his mind; and, in fomewhat
more than two years, returned to England, full fraught, though not bur-
thened, with underftanding, and an experience far above his years.

I might here entertain my reader with
the joy he was received with by his father and uncle, the compliments made
to him by the gentry in that part of the
country, and acclamations of the lower
fort of people; but I have no time to
wafte in fuch minute particulars, and
muft proceed to more material circumftances. Clyamon had no great relifh
for the country; he foon grew weary of
it's amufements: he loved company,
and had been accuftomed to a good deal,
both at Oxford, as well as while he was
on his travels; and, on account of the
great diftance between the gentlemen's
feats in that country, his uncle's love

of retirement, and his father's parfi-
mony, neither of their houfes were much
frequented. He wanted to come to
London; he had never been three whole
weeks together in it, and thought he
ought to be better acquainted with what
was done in the capital of the kingdom.
Sir Arthur was alfo willing he fhould
be known in a place where the accomplifhments he had given him might be
rendered more confpicuous; but as he
had more than performed the part of an
uncle, and fully difcharged him of the
promife he had made to Avario concerning his education, he thought it was
now high time for that gentleman to
take upon him the father, and make a
fettlement for his fon fufficient to enable
him to appear in the world according
to the eftate he was born to inherit.
This propofition was not altogether fo
pleafing to Avario as it ought to have
been; but as he could find nothing to
alledge againft the reafonablenefs of it,
he only evaded complying with it at
prefent by fome trifling excufe or other,
till Clyamon, unable to conceal his difcontent, Sir Arthur preffed more ftrenuoufly in his favour than he had done
before, and at length, though with much
difficulty, drew from that niggardly parent the fcanty fum of fifty guineas.
This was a light loading for the purfe
of a young gentleman bred in the manner Clyamon had been, and could not
be expected to hold out long in fo expenfive a town as London. Avario,
however, accompanied it with a promife
of letting him have more as foon as he
received money from his tenants, who,
he pretended, had been tardy in their
payments of late, and occafioned his
being very much out of cafh.

Clyamon could not keep himfelf from
being extreme'y fhocked at this treatment from a father who had been at no
expence for him fince he was ten years
old. Sir Arthur was no lefs chagrined,
though he concealed it from his nephew; and putting a Bank bill of fifty
pounds into his hand, faid to him—
'My dear Clyamon, I would not have
'you be difconcerted. You know your
'father's temper; but the more he
'hoards, the more will be your own at
'his deceafe. In the mean time, he
'affured I will not forfake you; I will
'continually urge him on your behalf,
'and alfo privately fupply you when-
'ever he is deficient: live therefore like
'yourfelf,

, yourself, and be entirely easy.' These comfortable words, from a mouth on which he knew he might depend, made Clyamon set out chearfully for London; but what happened to him after his arrival, must be the subject of another chapter.

## CHAP. IX.

### IS A CONTINUANCE OF WHAT THE FORMER BUT BEGAN.

THOUGH Clyamon never had an opportunity of making much acquaintance in this metropolis, and now arrived here at a season in which great part of the nobility and gentry retire to their country seats, yet was he soon known, and his conversation courted by those of the best rank who still remained in town. There were no operas indeed, no plays, no masquerades, to entertain him, but the gardens of Ranelagh, Vauxhall, and Mary-le-bon; or, to speak more properly, the gay company that frequent those places left him no want of any other amusement. The love of pleasure can never continue ungratified in a town like this; and it is not to be wondered at, if it sometimes got the better of all Clyamon's discretion; nor, if surrounded with temptations, that he could not always keep himself from giving way to passions which, in youth, and a sprightly disposition, are so natural, that they scarce deserve the name of faults. It is not my business to detain the reader's attention with an account of his gallantries with the fair-sex, if any of the particulars had come to my knowledge, which I freely confess they did not; I shall only say, that he had no amour which could call his honour in question, bring him into quarrels, or be productive of any other unhappy consequences.

The only mistake in conduct he had any great reason to repent of, he was led into more by the prevalence of example than inclination. He had never been in the least tainted with that epidemick vice the love of gaming, and rather wondered at the pleasure he saw it give others, than desired to be a partaker of it himself; yet did he inadvertently suffer himself one evening to engage in a party at that dangerous amusement, which he knew had proved so fa-

tal to many of the most opulent fortunes, and utterly unsuitable to a person in his present circumstances. The persons he played with were well experienced, and great proficients in their arts: they let him win at first some pieces; and this imaginary success luring him to go on, he became at length a loser of about seventy pounds; a trifling sum to a gentleman of his appearance, yet three times more than he at that time was master of.

He dissembled his chagrin as well as he was able, but confessed he had not that sum about him, and would send it the next morning: on which they told him his honour was a sufficient stake for ten times as much as he had lost, and would fain have prevailed with him to have played on; but he now saw the folly he had been guilty of, so pretending he had business, took leave of the company, carrying with him a humour very different from what he had brought, and from what he had ever been possessed of in his whole life before. Impossible is it to express, as he afterwards told me, how much he was disconcerted at this unlucky event: he knew it was expected he should promise to send the money next morning, and by what means he should acquit himself of that promise, and redeem his honour, puzzled him to a degree that made him almost distracted. He has often protested that he never closed his eyes in sleep during that whole night, but passed his restless hours in contriving how to extricate himself from the labyrinth into which he had so foolishly strayed. After much revolving in his mind, he at last bethought himself of borrowing the sum he wanted of a young gentleman with whom he was extremely intimate, and had a good fortune.

Pursuant to this resolution, he rose the next morning more early than he was accustomed, and went to his friend, who was not yet stirring; but on saying he had business of importance to impart to him, was easily admitted to his chamber. He told him, in few words, what had happened, the vexatious situation he was in, and the necessity he was under of borrowing a small sum, till he could receive a remittance from the country; to which the other replied—' Upon my ' soul, dear Clyamon, I should be glad ' to serve you on this occasion, but, ' faith, it is not in my power at present; ' it is not a week ago since I lost five

O ' hundred

' hundred pounds at that damned whift;
' and this, with fome other demands
' lately made upon me, have quite
' drained me of all my ready cafh. But
' I will tell you what I can do for you;
' I know a man who has often fupplied
' me, and feveral of my acquaintance,
' when they have had a bad run at play.
' He has always money by him, and
' will lend you what fum you pleafe on
' your advancing a premium. I will
' rife this minute, and go with you to
' him.'

Clyamon was highly pleafed at this offer; and, while the other was dref-fing, reflecting within himfelf how his affairs flood, and that the little prefents he had received from his father and uncle being now almoft exhaufted, he fhould foon have calls for more money than his gaming debt; thought it beft, fince he muft borrow, to bor-row as much as would fupply his ex-pences till his father fhould be prevailed upon to make him a fettlement, which he flattered himfelf would be in a fhort time. He communicated his intention to the gentleman, who approved it; and having got himfelf ready, they went to-gether to old Grub, for fo the ufurer was called. The wretch was juft com-ing out of his houfe when they came to it. On feeing them, he turned back, and conducted them into a little dirty parlour; but as the difcourfe that paffed between them was fomewhat extraordi-nary, I thought it worth writing down, as Clyamon fome time after repeated it to me word for word.

*Grub.* So, my young fquire!—'Tis a wonder to fee you out of your bed be-fore the fun has run three quarters of his courfe at leaft. I fuppofe you want a little of my affiftance; that brings you abroad thus early.

*Gentleman.* No, faith, Grub, not at prefent; but I have a friend here that does.

*Grub.* Your friend is welcome; I will ferve him if I can.—Pray, Sir, what can I do for you?

*Clyamon.* Sir, a prefent emergency lays me under a neceffity of raifing two hundred pounds immediately; if you have that fum by you, this gentleman will inform you who I am, and that I want neither the power nor the will to difcharge any obligation I fhall enter into on that fcore.

*Gentleman.* Aye, aye, Grub, his

note is as good as the Bank of Eng-land; you need not fear your money. His name is ****; he is an only fon, and heir to near two thoufand pounds a year.

*Grub.* The gentleman has an ho-neft face, indeed.

*Gentleman.* If you have any fcruple, Grub, I will join in the note with all my foul.

*Grub.* I believe there is no great oc-cafion; only in cafe of accidents a col-lateral fecurity may be neceffary.

*Gentleman.* Well, well, you fhall have it.

*Grub.* I fuppofe, Sir, you have ac-quainted the gentleman with the com-mon way of dealing in thefe affairs?

*Clyamon.* Sir, I am willing to allow you any intereft for your money that you can in reafon defire.

*Grub.* Sir, I am never out of reafon with any man. As to intereft, it is quite out of the queftion; I fhall take no more than what the law allows: but when we advance money upon a pinch, a cer-tain premium is expected.

*Clyamon.* Pleafe to name it.

*Grub.* Let me fee—you want two hundred pounds immediately, you fay. It is but a trifling fum, indeed; but too much for a poor man like me to lofe: we who lend money this way run a great rifque. Not that I doubt you, nor am unwilling to advance the money; but I think you can do no lefs than add an odd fifty in the note you make.

*Clyamon.* How, Sir! fifty pounds for the loan of two hundred, befides the in-tereft!

*Grub.* Lookye, Sir, I would not have you imagine I deal hardly with you. If you brought me a note on the beft tradefman in the city, payable one month after date, I do affure you that I would not difcount it a farthing lefs than twenty per cent. Confider, Sir, I may lie a great while out of my money. Difappointments fometimes happen; and when they do, I have not the heart to be fevere in point of time; I fcorn to dif-trefs a gentleman when I find he has it not in his power to pay, unlefs I hear he is going out of the kingdom, or to enter into the army; and then, indeed, it behoves me to take care of myfelf.

Clyamon, in favouring me with the recital of this dialogue, told me, that he had not prefence enough of mind to keep the fhock he felt at fo exorbitant a de-mand

mand from being vifible to the ufurer; who looking on him with no very pleafing afpect, faid to him—

*Grub.* I perceive you are diffatisfied, Sir; and if fo, I can keep my money, and you may try to fupply yourfelf at a cheaper rate elfewhere. For my part, I am at no lofs how to difpofe of the little I have: there are enow will be glad to receive it on the terms I offered you; and, it may be, not grumble to allow me a better advantage.

*Gentleman.* Nay—pfhaw—pr'ythee, Grub, don't be out of humour! My friend is not accuftomed to thefe things, and I had not time to inform him before we came.

*Grub.* Sir, I bear a confcience, and am above impofing on any one. I am afhamed to think of what is practifed at fome great coffee-houfes that fhall be namelefs; where, if a gentleman is necefitated to borrow ten pieces, he returns twenty for it the next morning, or, it may be, the fame night. No, no; fuch things are an abomination to me: I defire no more than a living profit; and whoever does not approve of my conditions, is at liberty to reject them; there is no harm done.

*Clyamon.* Not in the leaft, Sir: and as this is the firft time I ever had occafion to become a borrower, and was utterly ignorant of the methods I fhould take in fuch a fituation, I may deferve forgivenefs.

Thus was poor Clyamon compelled, by his impatience to difcharge his debt of honour, to acquiefce to the excufe made for him by his friend, and comply with the extortioner's demand. On which Grub was eafily brought into temper again; a note was prefently drawn for two hundred and fifty pounds; and being figned by both the gentlemen, the whole fum mentioned in it was delivered to Clyamon, who put two hundred pounds into his pocket, and returned the other fifty to Grub: ' This, ' Sir,' faid the old wary curmudgeon, ' I receive as a prefent from you, and ' thank you for it.' Clyamon alfo, in his turn, thanked him for the favour he had juft conferred upon him; after which they departed, feemingly with the moft perfect good-will towards each other: but it is a truth almoft unqueftionable, that the lender of this money had infinitely more fatisfaction in his mind than the borrower could poffibly have, Dear-

ly, indeed, did he pay for the means of difcharging an obligation which his inadvertency had brought him under: it was, however, of this fervice to him, that it made him deteft high gaming ever fince, and careful to avoid all company that might draw him into a fecond misfortune of the fame kind; as I remember to have formerly read in a very old, and now almoft exploded author—

' Wife is the man who, by one error taught,
' No more is in the fame temptation caught.'

There is a way of refraining from being guilty of indifcreet actions, without affecting to be over wife. Clyamon had this happy talent. He knew very well, that for a perfon of his years to fet up for a dictator, inftead of reforming his companions, would only incur their ridicule; and therefore contented himfelf with not making a party in the modifh vices and follies he was fpectator of, without feeming to condemn or be difpleafed at them. Confcious that, on his firft arrival in town, he had not taken all the care he fhould have done to regulate his way of living according to his prefent circumftances, he began to retrench his expences as much as poffibly he could, without letting the world fee he did fo, or finking too much beneath the character of a gentleman born to inherit the ample fortune he was. But in fpite of this fomewhat too late affumed œconomy, he foon found himfelf in a very great neceffity for a frefh fupply. He had been in London from the latter end of May to the beginning of October, and had received no remittances from the country fince he left it. All his uncle's remonftrances had not yet prevailed upon his father to make the propofed fettlement on him: the ufurer's loan was quite exhaufted; and he had, befides, other fmall debts to his tradefmen, fome of whom had already fent in their bills.

To add to thefe vexations, Grub vifited him almoft every day, complained he was out of cafh himfelf, and at length grew very importunate, and plainly told him, that he could lie no longer out of his money, and that if he did not fpeedily difcharge the note, he muft take proper meafures to force him to it. In this exigence, he wrote a very preffing letter to his father, intreating an order on his banker in London: but the obdurate

Avario only fent him an anfwer to this effect; that it was inconvenient for him to break into the fum in the hands of his banker; faid he muft wait awhile; that he fhould be in town himfelf the enfuing November, on the meeting of parliament, and that then he would do fomething for him: in the mean time bid him live fparingly, and fhun all places and company that might draw him into any un-neceffary expence.

Poor Clyamon had need enough for all that ftock of fpirits which nature had endued him with, to enable him to bear up amidft the perfecutions of his voracious creditors, and the unnatural behaviour of his father. He had now no other refource remaining, than an application to Sir Arthur; but very loth he was to be troublefome to that dear and beneficent uncle, to whom alone he was indebted for what he looked upon as infinitely more valuable than his being, his education; and was with much debate within himfelf, whether it were not better to endure the infults he was expofed to, rather than run the rifque of difpleafing a patron he had fo much caufe to love and reverence. But while he continued thus irrefolute in his mind, an accident happened which put a final end to all the contention in his thoughts on that fcore, by prefenting him with a misfortune, which was the more fevere, by it's being fudden and unapprehended.

The good Sir Arthur Frankwill died: Fate fnatched him from the world at once, without the leaft previous warning; and allowed no time for the making bequefts, either to his beloved Clyamon, or any other perfon, who elfe he might have thought worthy of a place in his remembrance; fo that leaving no will behind him, his whole eftate, together with all the perfonal effects he was pof-feffed of, devolved on a fon of his elder fifter, as being the firft of blood, and heir at law; a gentleman who had always looked upon Clyamon with too envious an eye to have any fincere friendfhip for him. The firft account of this misfortune was tranfmitted to Clyamon in a letter from the above-mentioned kinfman, and contained the following lines:—

' DEAR COUSIN,

' THIS comes to acquaint you with
' the lofs we both fuftain by the
' death of our dear uncle, who departed

' this life fix days ago. He was feized
' with an apopleEtick fit, out of which
' he never recovered, in fpite of all the
' endeavours that could be ufed. I did
' not fend to defire your company at
' the funeral, as it would have been a
' fuperfluous compliment to him, and
' a great fatigue and expence to your-
' felf in coming fo long a journey; but
' as I am fenfible of the affeEtion he had
' always for you, I inclofe a Bank bill
' of twenty pounds for mourning. I
' intend to difpofe of my uncle's houfe
' as foon as I can hear of a purchafer,
' and am now fending away all the fur-
' niture, fo can make no invitation to
' you to come hither; but fhall be glad
' if you pafs a few days with me at
' T——, on your return into the coun-
' try. So the hurry I am in at prefent,
' permits me to add no more, than that
' I am, &c.

' G. HAWKSMORE.'

It is certain, at this time, and indeed almoft at any other, there were few things could have happened more unfortunately for Clyamon than the death of his uncle; as he had not only loft in him an indulgent parent, a tender friend, and a kind protector, who had promifed never to forfake him, but alfo the only perfon in the world who had the moft influence over his father, and by whofe interceffion he hoped to have been foon relieved from the precarious fituation he was at prefent in. He had fcarce time enough to recover himfelf from the firft emotions of grief, on the above-mentioned melancholy account, when he received private intelligence that Grub intended to arreft him, and had even employed a fheriff's officer for that purpofe. He had no way to prevent this affront but by flying for refuge to the verge of the court; which he accordingly did, and took a lodging in Scotland Yard. Grub foon heard of his retreat; traced him to his afylum; and endeavoured, by all the means he could, to render it of no fervice to him: but Clyamon had laid his cafe before the board of green cloth, who had affured him of their proteEtion, till the arrival of his father fhould difcharge this troublefome affair.

The time was now near in which Avario was expeEted, and he ftaid not many days beyond it; but his prefence rather augmented, than put an end to
the

the diftrefs of Clyamon. That unnatural parent, on finding the condition
he was in, flew into the extremeft rage;
reproached his extravagancies, as he
called them, in the moft bitter terms;
fwore he would fee him fink under the
calamity to which he had reduced himfelf, rather than give a fingle guinea to
relieve him from it; and even curfed
the memory of the good Sir Arthur, for
having indulged him, as he faid, in notions fo contrary to what he ought to
have been infpired with. It was in
vain that Clyamon endeavoured to alleviate his fury; he would hearken to no
excufes, he foftened by no fubmiffions
he could make. One of the gentlemen
of the honourable board, at Clyamon's
requeft, urged the defence of that young
gentleman in the ftrongeft terms; but
Avario for many days continued deaf
to all remonftrances in his behalf, and
gave no other anfwer, than that, as his
fon had brought himfelf into this trouble by his folly, he muft endeavour to
get out of it by his wit. This cruel far-
cafin, when repeated to Clyamon, made
him almoft forget the duty of a fon; and,
as he confeffed to me, ready to burft into
exclamations which he would afterwards have reproached himfelf for having been guilty of uttering, or even
thinking of.

Grub, and fome other of his creditors, finding they could do no more to
him in the place where he was, took their
revenge in perfecuting him with un-
ceafing clamours; which threw him
fometimes into fuch fits of melancholy,
that if he had not been furnifhed with a
great ftock of morality and good fenfe,
would doubtlefs have pufhed him on
fome defperate method to end thofe mif-
fortunes which he faw no probability of
being removed from. Avario, in the
mean time, notwithftanding his churlifh
and fordid difpofition, was far from being eafy in his mind. The firft guft of
paffion being blown over, the merits of
Clyamon rofe in oppofition to the fault
he had been guilty of, and made it by
degrees feem lefs; he could not forbear
remembering that he was his fon, and
fuch a fon as every one who was a father wifhed his own might copy after.
In fine, nature and reafon joined their
forces, and pleaded ftrongly in behalf
of Clyamon, and almoft wrought him to
forgivenefs; but as often as he reflected
how much it would coft to pardon him,

and that he could not receive him into
favour without payment of his debts,
the thoughts of parting with his money
gave a fudden check to his paternal inclinations.

At length, however, fome hints which
Clyamon dropped in one of the many
petitionary letters he fent to him, making him apprehenfive that the moft
dreadful confequences might attend the
defpair of his offending fon, he became
determined to do fomething for him.
He fent a perfon to him with ten guineas
for his prefent fupport, and an offer of
making up his affairs, in cafe he could
prevail on his creditors to compound for
the one half of what was owing to them.
Clyamon accepted of his father's prefent, trifling as it was, with fubmiffion;
but could not forbear teftifying the utmoft difdain at propofing of a compo-
fition; for befides being certain that it
would never be complied with, the thing
itfelf appeared to him fo abject, that he
chofe to fuffer any thing rather than demean himfelf to mention it. This refufal put Avario into a fecond flame;
but he foon cooled again: and, after
fome little conflict within himfelf, the
neceffity there was of reftoring the liberty of an only fon, got the better of
his love of money. Loth, however, to
part with his darling pence as long as
there was a poffibility of keeping them,
he found out an expedient to protract
the doing a thing fo irkfome to him:
he communicated his intentions to Clyamon in a letter, which that young gentleman fhewing me afterwards, I found
contained words to this effect—

'  son,

' THOUGH I have been juftly irri-
'    tated againft you, firft by your
' extravagancies, and fince by your late
' obftinacy, yet I cannot forget I am
' your father, nor fuffer you to fink be-
' neath thofe misfortunes your folly
' and difobedience have brought you
' into. I have refolved to pay all your
' debts before I leave London; but as it
' is not convenient for me to do it
' fooner, would not have you venture
' out of the verge, for fear of bringing
' yourfelf into difgrace, and an addi-
' tional expence on me for your re-
' leafe. In the mean time, am content
' to allow you two guineas and a half
' per week, for the fubfiftence of your-
' felf and fervant. It is expected we
'                              fhall

‘ shall be diffolved about the middle of
‘ February, when writs will be iffued
‘ out for a new election; and I shall
‘ then set you clear in the world, and
‘ take you home with me; for I do not
‘ think it advifeable you should live in
‘ this luxurious town, till you are bet-
‘ ter acquainted with the true value of
‘ money than you feem to be at prefent.
‘ I hope, notwithftanding, that your
‘ future behaviour will atone for the er-
‘ rors of the paft, and I shall have no oc-
‘ cafion to repent the proof I now give
‘ you of being your affectionate father,

‘ AVARIO.’


The joy Clyamon would have felt, on
finding full fatisfaction would be given
to the demands of his impatient creditors, was very much abated by the
thoughts of being obliged to refide conftantly with his father in the country;
as the manner in which he knew he muft
live would be very difagreeable to his
humour, and widely different from what
he had been accuftomed to with his uncle. It alfo feemed a little hard to him,
that by delaying the difcharge of his
debts till his departure, he should be fecluded from all enjoyment of the pleafures of the town, even while he continued in it: but he faw into the policy
of his father in doing this; and, as there
was no remedy, endeavoured to be as
contented as poffible. In the anfwer he
gave to his father’s letter, he expreffed
himfelf in terms highly pleafing to him,
and brought on a perfect reconciliation,
as will prefently appear, on occafion of
an accident which happened foon after.


## CHAP. X.

CONCLUDES A NARRATIVE WHICH
HAS SOMEWHAT IN IT THAT
WILL, IN A MANNER, COMPEL
THOSE WHO SHALL BE MOST OF-
FENDED TO COUNTERFEIT AN
APPROBATION, FOR THE SAKE OF
THEIR OWN REPUTATION.

THOUGH the greateft intimacy
with Clyamon, and a long acquaintance with Avario, made me no
ftranger even to the minute particulars
of the tranfaction I am relating—I mean
as far as I could be informed by the
perfect confidence with which I was ho-

noured by both thefe gentlemen—yet, as
no fure dependance can be placed either
on what people fay of themfelves, or
the report given of them by others, I
should never have ventured to fpeak fo
pofitively in many things as I have done,
if the gift of Invifibility had not afforded
me an opportunity of accompanying
them when they thought themfelves entirely alone, and of beholding them in
thofe unguarded attitudes which are the
beft and only certain difcoverers of the
inward workings of the human mind.

It was my dear Belt could have alone
convinced me that, contrary to the general opinion of the world, it was not
ill-nature in Avario, or the ignorance
of what he ought to do, which had hindered him from being an affectionate
hufband, a tender father, a faithful
friend, and an indulgent mafter; but
merely his inordinate love of money,
and an unaccountable apprehenfion of
being reduced to the want of it, that
made him center his whole cares in his
bags, regardlefs of all the ties of blood
and nature, and rendered him almoft
incapable of practifing any focial virtue.

It was by this beneficial prefent that
I became affured Clyamon was much
more worthy than he took any pains to
appear; that in all ferious matters he
was fteady and unfhaken, and in his
pleafures decent and well-mannered; and
that, young as he was, he had fet up a
tribunal in his own heart, where reafon
prefiding as his fole judge, carefully
examined all his actions, and whatever
unruly paffion had got the ftart, ftopped
it in it’s career, and brought it back to
obedience.

Many interefting circumftances relating to this affair between father and
fon, are loft to the publick by my having been deprived for fome time of my
Chryftaline Tablets, which had been
ftolen from me, with feveral other things
of much lefs, though more feeming value, by an unfaithful fervant; but the
villain finding, I fuppofe, that he could
make nothing of the Tablets, and looking upon them only as a curiofity which
would pleafe nobody fo much as myfelf,
fealed them up, and caufed them to be
left for me at a coffee-houfe. My joy
at getting them again, made me forgive
the reft of the robbery, and feek no farther after the thief. I recovered my
purloined treafure juft about the time
that

that Clyamon was in the above-mentioned fituation; fo that what remains to be recited of this narrative, will be chiefly taken from the mouths of the perfons concerned in it. I was one morning in Clyamon's apartment, under the cover of my Belt, when a young gentleman of the name of Carelefs came to vifit him. After exchanging the *bon jour*, and fome other cuftomary falutations, Carelefs began the converfation between them in thefe terms—

*Carelefs.* Where do you think I was yefterday?

*Clyamon.* I am no conjuror.

*Carelefs.* Guefs.

*Clyamon.* It would be a needlefs trouble; pr'ythee fpare it me.

*Carelefs.* Why, faith, in the gallery of the Houfe of Commons.

*Clyamon.* The Houfe of Commons! It muft be a bufinefs of vaft importance fure, that could carry a fellow of thy gay, fprightly temper, into that grave, venerable place.

*Carelefs.* No, thank Heaven! bufinefs and I are perfect ftrangers to each other; but I had an hour or two upon my hands, and went thither merely to kill time: but was never more diverted in my whole life, than to fee how fome young members who had got their heads together, and were giggling over a copy of verfes infcribed to Fanny Murray, were put to filence in an inftant, and looked as filly as a fchool-boy under the lafh of correction, on the fpeaker's crying out, with an audible and aufterre voice—' To order, gentle-' men!—for fhame!—to order.'

*Clyamon.* Methinks, indeed, they might have found a more proper place and time for laughter. Was my father in the houfe, pray?

*Carelefs.* O yes; and I affure you the old gentleman made as wife a figure as any there: he faid nothing indeed, but fat as ferious as a judge upon a criminal caufe, leaning both his hands upon his gold-headed cane, and his chin upon his hands, and liftening with great attention to a very long, and, I fuppofe, learned harangue, of a leading member. —How do you defign to difpofe of yourfelf to-day?

*Clyamon.* I have not yet confidered.

*Carelefs.* 'Tis a glorious morning! —Are you for the Park? I come on purpofe to afk you.

*Clyamon.* With all my heart.

*Carelefs.* Come along, then. I dare fwear the Mall is half full by this time. Let us go, and laugh at the great vulgar and the fmall, as Cowley fays.

Juft as they were going out of the room, a letter was prefented to Clyamon from his father; which he turning back to read, I ftepped behind him, and found it contained thefe lines—

' DEAR CLY,

' I Have fomething to impart to you, ' which is of the utmoft confequence ' to my peace of mind, and your future ' happinefs: be careful, therefore, not ' to be out of the way to-morrow morn- ' ing, when I fhall call upon you as I ' go to the Houfe; for what I have to ' propofe cannot be fettled too foon. Be ' affured I am impatient to fee you make ' as good a figure in the world as I ' think you deferve; and that no more ' is required of you, than a juft fenfe ' of your duty to me, and a regard for ' what is your own intereft, to preferve ' me always your very indulgent and ' loving father,

' AVARIO.'

Clyamon was fo tranfported with the kindnefs of this epiftle, that he could not forbear fhewing it to Carelefs; who, knowing the temper of Avario, had no fooner looked over, than he faid—

*Carelefs.* I will lay my life upon it, that the old gentleman has found out fome rich widow or heirefs for you, with whofe fortune you may make a figure in the world, and fave his own till he can keep it no longer.

*Clyamon.* I hope not fo, for as yet I have no inclination to marry; and, whenever I do, fhall like to have a wife of my own chufing.

*Carelefs.* You muft be cautious, neverthelefs, not to venture a fecond *brulee* with him; for he feems to have fet his heart very much upon this bufinefs, whatever it is that he has now got into his head.

*Clyamon.* Deuce take you for putting it into mine! But I will think no more on it. If the thing fhould be as you imagine, I fhall have time enough to be uneafy after knowing it. But come, 'tis almoft two o'clock; let us away.

With thefe words they went to the Mall, and I returned home; where reflecting, as I always did after thefe excurfions, on what I had feen and heard,

I could

I could not help being of the same opinion with Mr. Careless, as touching the intentions of Avario; and feared that poor Clyamon, with all his merit, would be obliged to become a prey to some old well-jointured Jezebel, or rich dowdy who owed her virginity to her uglinefs. By what I have often freely confessed concerning the inquifitiveness of my disposition, the reader will easily suppose I felt no small impatience for the event of Avario's visit to his son; and indeed, I believe that young gentleman himself could scarce be more anxious. That I might lose nothing of what should pass between them, I took care to post myself very early in Clyamon's apartment; and it was well I did so, both for the satisfaction of my own curiosity, and the emolument of the publick, for Avario came in presently after me.

As they had not seen each other for some time, Clyamon threw himself on his knees, and in that posture thanked his father for the pardon he had vouchsafed to his offence, as well as for his kind promise he had given for the discharge of his debts. Avario seemed very much pleased with this submission, raised and embraced him with great affection; and, after they were seated, replied to what he had said in these terms—

*Avario.* It is a great deal of money, indeed, the folly you have been guilty of will cost me; but it is the first, and, I flatter myself, will be the last I shall have to complain of: so we will say no more of what is past. I came now to talk with you on a subject more agreeable to us both.

*Clyamon.* I have the greatest reason in the world, Sir, to hope every thing from your goodness.

*Avario.* Aye, Clyamon, you are my only son. You may be sure I have nothing so much at heart as your welfare, and I think I have now hit upon something that will make you as happy as you can wish to be. Your late uncle, Sir Arthur, was always teazing me on the score of a constant allowance for you out of my estate, to the end you may be in a manner independent, and I have at length resolved to do it.

*Clyamon.* Whatever you are pleased to grant, Sir, I shall take care to employ so as to give you no cause to repent your bounty.

*Avario.* But that is not all, Clya-

mon: what I shall do for you will put you in a way of making yourself a much greater man than you would be by what you will enjoy on my decease.

*Clyamon.* I am not ambitious, Sir; but shall readily embrace any laudable means of raising my fortune.

*Avario.* Why, that's well said; and what I have to propose is not only laudable, but honourable too. It is this; you shall be a member of the House of Commons.

*Clyamon.* Sir, I should be proud to serve my country in any capacity; but in this, fear my youth and inexperience will be very just objections.

*Avario.* Tut, tut! there are much younger than you in the House; and, though I say it, of much less understanding too. As to the forms that are to be observed there, I can instruct you in them; and as to the rest, you will easily come into it yourself; therefore no more of such idle scruples: an over modesty and diffidence of yourself is the worst quality a man that aims to rise in the world can be possessed of. I have considered on this matter in all it's circumstances, before I mentioned it to you; and, in order to qualify you for a member, have resolved to assign over to you five hundred pounds per annum of my estate.

*Clyamon.* That, Sir, is more than I could have presumed to ask.

*Avario.* I mean, the rents of so much shall be received in your name; as to the cash, I think it much safer in my own hands than yours; but you shall want nothing that is necessary: and when the business of parliament calls you to London, give you leave to draw upon me for what sum, or sums, you shall find occasion for, in reason.

*Clyamon.* This, Sir, is far from putting me out of a state of dependance.

*Avario.* You ought not to desire it. Your uncle talked foolishly, very foolishly, on this head; and if it had not been for the obligation I had to him on the score of your education, I should have told him so. A son ought always to be dependant on his father; and I think you have very great cause to be content in being so, as you have experienced the paternal affection I have for you, by my readiness to forgive your faults, and to discharge those debts your extravagancies had contracted.

*Clyamon.* Sir, I shall always retain a
grateful

grateful sense of all you have done for me. But pray, Sir, since it is your pleasure that I should be a candidate at the ensuing election, what place have you in your eye for me? I suppose for some borough.

*Avario.* No, no; for our own county.

*Clyamon.* Then, Sir, do you decline standing yourself?

*Avario.* Yes, Clyamon. I grow old, and am weary of the fatigue of coming up to London once every year. I find it very expensive, as well as troublesome; for though I board while I am here at a pretty cheap rate, with one that was formerly my servant, yet I know not how it is, money runs strangely away in this town. Besides, I do not think I have been well used: I have had the honour of representing the county of ***** in three successive parliaments, and have got nothing by it, but the honour; and though I have constantly voted on the side of the court, and whenever any debate of consequence was to come upon the carpet, have always previously attended the levee of the minister, to know his will and pleasure; all the recompence I have had, has been sometimes a shake of the hand, a gracious nod, a smile, and ' How does my ' good friend Avario ?'

*Clyamon.* You amaze me, Sir! I never imagined a gentleman had any other interest in his election than the pleasure of having an opportunity to serve his country.

*Avario.* Serve his country!—a fiddle on the country! It would be well worth a gentleman's while, indeed, to cajole, treat, and bribe, every little dirty fellow that has a vote to give; to spend so much time and money; and, it may be, drink himself half dead into the bargain, at his election; if it were not for the sake of serving himself, instead of the rabble who make choice of him for their representative. No, no, boy; if we had not honour, favour, and preferment, in view, our electors would be obliged to court us to accept their votes, not we to solicit them.

*Clyamon.* But, Sir, supposing this to be the case, how do you think it possible I should acquire any of those advantages which you say you have failed in the pursuit of yourself?

*Avario.* I'll tell you, Clyamon. I could only give my bare vote for or

against any question; I never had the gift of either speaking or writing: now I am pretty sure you can do both; and a pathetick speech, or a strong pamphlet, are prevailing arguments with the ministry; a man that can do these may have any thing, may make his own price. So, Cly, it will be your own fault, if in a sessions or two you are not above receiving any assistance from me.

*Clyamon.* Sir, I shall be always ready to exert the little talents I am master of to promote whatever I think is for the good of the commonwealth.

*Avario.* Tut! what have you to do with the commonwealth? You are not to set up for a judge of what is for it's good, or what is not so; your business is to please the minister, and to think every thing right he takes upon him to maintain.

*Clyamon.* But, Sir, how is this consistent with my conscience or my honour?

*Avario.* Idle, very idle. I do not like these notions, Clyamon; they may tempt you to an opposition. I shall be afraid you are a Jacobite.

*Clyamon.* Why, Sir, are all men of honour Jacobites?

*Avario.* No; but this romantick, unprofitable honour you talk of, is either Jacobitism, or something as bad—enthusiasm and bigotry. Is not the court the source of true honour? Do not all honours, dignities, and promotions, flow from thence? Therefore I say, whoever is against the court will never rise to honour, or any thing else that is valuable.

*Clyamon.* Sir, you may be perfectly assured, that I shall always do my best in support of every measure which tends to the real honour of his majesty, and the good of my country; and never oppose any which do not oppose the constitution.

*Avario.* But you must not examine too scrupulously into these things. You are to suppose that those who are entrusted with the management of publick affairs are better acquainted with the constitution than you can pretend to be; and must therefore take it for granted, that whatever they say or do is right.

*Clyamon.* But, Sir, does not this implicit faith in the judgment of others, and giving up my own entirely, favour somewhat of a slavish submission?

P                *Avario.*

*Avario.* No, it is only good policy, and looked upon as such by all who know the world. Indeed, if after your voting, speaking, and writing, they should take no notice of you, it would behove you to pluck up a spirit, and extort that respect to your resentment, which they were not grateful enough to pay to your complaisance. I shall then give you leave to oppose them in every thing, whether it be wrong or whether it be right.

*Clyamon.* But would not this changing sides, Sir, make me become contemptible to both parties?

*Avario.* Not at all; it is a thing too commonly practised to be wondered at, and has often had a very good effect, when nothing else would do. Publico, for example. It was a good while, indeed, before they bid up to his price; but they found it necessary at last, and he now enjoys the fruits of his labour.

*Clyamon.* Yes, Sir, I have heard of many others who have been bought off the same way; but whatever has been done in former administrations, I hope the present will attempt nothing that ought to be opposed.

*Avario.* No, no, you are not to suppose they will; unless, as I just now observed, they force you to it by neglecting to recompense your services.

*Clyamon.* According to this, Sir, it will be very difficult, if not altogether impossible, for the people to distinguish between those who would defend, and those who would betray and sacrifice, the liberties of their constituents.

*Avario.* If the people are betrayed and sacrificed, as you call it, they can blame nobody but themselves. Why do they take money for their votes? Why do they, like Esau, sell their birth-rights for a mess of pottage? When a gentleman buys a county, a borough, or a corporation, he has doubtless a right to make the most of it he can.

*Clyamon.* This, Sir, is punishing corruption with corruption.

*Avario.* Aye; is it not just it should be so? Lookye, Clyamon, you are a novice in these affairs as yet, but a little time will make them familiar to you. I do not doubt but I shall hear of your being elected by the great man; and when once you are elected, your business is done; you will have no farther occasion for my instructions or assistance

either. But I shall say no more at present on this head: you must think of preparing yourself to set out on your journey to *****, in a day or two.

*Clyamon.* What, Sir, before you go?

*Avario.* Yes, yes. We shall not be dissolved so soon as we expected. I do not believe I shall be able to get down these six weeks or two months. There have been some odd turns of late: but no matter; they are secrets, and must be kept so. But it is highly necessary you should begin to make your interest; you are already known to the greatest part of the gentry, and I am pretty sure they will be all for you to a man. You must cultivate an acquaintance with the freeholders, ride about among them, invite some of the most leading men home, treat them handsomely, and make little presents to their wives and daughters, of snuff-boxes, rings, necklaces, and such toys, to please their fancies. I will get a friend of mine to purchase a cargo of them for you to take down, and will write to my steward to furnish you with what money you shall have occasion for.

*Clyamon.* Do they know, Sir, that you intend to decline standing any more?

*Avario.* Not yet; but I shall write to night to inform them of it, and to urge all my friends in your behalf. I hear your cousin Hawkmore has taken it into his head to offer himself as a candidate; and though he is not beloved, on account of the bustle he made about turnpikes, yet the large estate he is now in possession of by the death of Sir Arthur, may give him an influence over some people. So there is no time to be lost: I would have you leave London on Monday next. I have given orders that all your creditors shall be paid their full demands this day, and I think you can have no other business of consequence to detain you here.

*Clyamon.* None at all, Sir.

*Avario.* Well then, what friends you have to take leave of, you may see this afternoon; and come and dine with me to-morrow. It is Sunday, and you know is a leisure day, and I shall be at home. Though I am a boarder, I believe you will be welcome; or it may be I shall add a dish to the table; therefore do not fail to come.

*Clyamon.* You may depend, Sir,
that

that this command is too agreeable to me not to be punctually obeyed.

The old gentleman then said no more; but, after giving his son a gracious nod, went out of the room, with a countenance which denoted the most perfect satisfaction of mind. Clyamon waited on him down stairs; and I intended to follow, as soon as his return should give me an opportunity of going down; but was retarded by Mr. Carelefs, who came in immediately after Avario was out of the house. This gentleman, who it seems has a sincere friendship for Clyamon, had been extremely impatient, and indeed more anxious than could have been expected from a person of his gay, thoughtless disposition, to know the event of the letter he had received from his father, had been come to the house some time, and waited in the parlour till the departure of Avario made it proper for him to appear. Almost the first salutation he gave to Clyamon contained an entreaty for the satisfaction of his curiosity in this point, which the other very readily complied with, in general terms; but had too much discretion to expose his father's mercenary views; or, by relating the design he had of making him a member of parliament, reveal the motives he had for doing so, or the instructions he had given him for his behaviour after he should be elected.

Mr. Carelefs, after having congratulated his friend on his being re-established in the good graces of his father, and the honour that was about to recede to him, said a great many pleasant and spirited things to him on the occasion of his being likely to become a member of that august and respectable assembly. But the particulars of this discourse, entertaining as it was, I am entirely unable to repeat, my Tablets being already crouded with the preceding dialogue; and all I can remember is, that the two gentlemen, after chatting away an hour, agreed to dine together that day, and to that end adjourned to a tavern in the neighbourhood, leaving me at liberty to retire to my own apartment. I was extremely pleased with finding, by what I had seen that day of Clyamon, that I had not been deceived in the high-raised expectations I had entertained of his good sense and probity; and also with perceiving that Avario, in spite of his sordid and avaricious disposition, could

not help allowing the merits of a son, whose sentiments and principles were; in almost every thing, so directly opposite to his own.

The evening of the next day this worthy young gentleman called upon me, as he returned from having passed the former part of it with his father. He was much less reserved with me than he had been with Mr. Carelefs, which convinced me he knew how to refrain unbosoming himself to those whose solidity he had cause to doubt, and took a pleasure in being entirely open to those on whom he could depend that his confidence would not be abused either by wantonness or neglect. He repeated to me the rules prescribed to him by his father for the regulation of his conduct in parliament, and expressed the little obligation he thought himself under to him on that score, in terms the most strong and pathetic. These are some of his words—' The love of my country,' said he, ' I look upon as the first and ' greatest moral duty of mankind; and I ' think I may venture to assure myself, ' that I shall never be tempted to re-' nounce it on the prospect of any ad-' vantage offered, in what shape so-' ever.'

I then told him, that I believed the bulk of the people owed the grievances they complained of, greatly to the luxury of their representatives; who, having impaired their estates in the modish excesses of the times, found themselves under a necessity of entering into measures which otherwise they would never have complied with. ' Perhaps, too,' added I, ' to gratify the ambition of a ' beloved wife, or prevent the clamour ' of a turbulent one, may be one rea-' son to which the infringement of pub-' lick liberty may be ascribed.' Clyamon listened with great attention to what I said; and joining in my opinion, replied, that his own observation of some late instances confirmed the truth of this argument. ' The first of these ' excitements,' continued he, ' I have ' already experienced the danger of ' through my inadvertency, and shall ' be wary to avoid the snare in which I ' have been once entangled; and, as for ' the other, if ever I marry, shall en-' deavour to get a wife as near as pos-' sible to the description given by the ' poet of his mistress—

P 2 ———' A maid

'————————A maid
' Who knows not courts, yet courts does far
'    outshine
' In every starry beauty of the mind;
' One who, array'd in native loveliness,
' And sweet simplicity, defpifes art;
' And has a foul too great to ftoop to
'    pride,
' With the mean ways by which it aims at
'    grandeur.'

With thefe difcourfes we paffed the time he ftaid. I have not feen him fince, but heard of his fafe arrival at *****. Whether he will be elected for that county, cannot be determined at the time of my writing this; fo can only fay, that if he is, I doubt not but his character will appear to much more advantage, than in the faint fketch I have here been able to give of it.

FND OF THE FIRST VOLUME.

THE

# INVISIBLE SPY.

## VOLUME THE SECOND.

### BOOK V.

**CHAP. I.**

THE AUTHOR'S INTRODUCTION TO
THIS VOLUME CONSISTS ONLY
OF AN APOLOGY FOR MAKING
NO INTRODUCTION AT ALL, AND
HIS REASONS FOR THAT OMIS-
SION.

INCE my setting about
this work, I have seen fe-
veral late treatifes that are
half taken up with intro-
ductory prefaces to the
publick. On a ferious
examination to what end thofe long difcourfes were penned, they feemed to me
to have been occafioned either by one
or the other of the following motives:
firft, that an author having contracted
with his bookfeller for a certain number of fheets, without having well confidered whether his head be ftored with
fubject matter to make good his engagement, finds himfelf under a neceffity of filling up the vacant pages by
faying fomething by way of an introduction, preface, or advertifement to the
reader; or, fecondly, that fearing the eyes
of the publick will not be fufficiently
open to the merit of his performance,
or, perhaps, not have the curiofity even
to look into it at all, he thinks proper to
befpeak their favour by a pompous pre-

lude, and founds his own praifes, like
a trumpet at the door of a puppet-
fhew.

Now I am too great a lover of liberty
ever to bind myfelf by any fuch flavifh
agreement. The firft of thefe incen-
tives is quite out of the queftion, and
cannot poffibly have any weight with
me; and as to the fecond, as a more perfect knowledge of myfelf than I perceive
fome others have will not permit me to
be over vain in any thing I do, fo the
indolence of my nature will not permit
me to be over anxious for the fuccefs.
Befides, not having the temptation of the
motives aforefaid, I have more adventures to relate than can be eafily crouded
into this volume; therefore have neither
time nor paper to fpare for an addrefs,
which would afford fo little fatisfaction
to myfelf in the writing, and perhaps
lefs to my reader in the perufing.

**CHAP. II.**

CONTAINS SUCH MATTER AS, IT IS
HIGHLY PROBABLE, WILL BE THE
LEAST PLEASING TO THOSE FOR
WHOSE SERVICE IT IS MOST IN-
TENDED.

THERE is, according to the wife
man's phrafe, a folly under the
fun, which, in my opinion, has as little

to be said for it as any of the many other of the present age; and that is, an insatiable inquisitiveness into future events; as if the foreknowledge of what is to come, would enable us either to alleviate or avert the decrees of Providence: yet are all ages, all degrees, of both sexes, tainted more or less with this epidemick frenzy. It cannot but afford the most astonishing, as well as melancholy reflections, in a thinking mind, to observe how many impostors, in and about this great town, are maintained by pretending to the art of divination, while the industrious followers of lawful occupations perish for want of due encouragement.

As I was one day on my Invisible Progressions, I accompanied a mingled crowd of people into a house situated in one of the most obscure parts of the city. At first I imagined that this was some private chapel, where persons resorted to pay their adorations to the Deity in a manner not authorized by the government; but was soon convinced of my mistake, when, instead of a pulpit and desk, I found the room we came into furnished only with globes and telescopes, and other implements of a soothsayer and astrologer. I had not patience to hear what idle predictions this oracle would spout forth, especially as I had no acquaintance with any of those who I saw came to consult him; so took my leave of the deceiver and the deceived, full of indignation against the one, and a pity, mingled with contempt, for the other: for what can be said in defence of the understanding of those people who waste their time and money in consulting those abject dealers in futurity! creatures who would make you believe they can read the most hidden decrees of fate in the grounds of coffee, tea, and chocolate! I had often heard much talk of these conjurors, but not till I was convinced by the testimony of my own sense, could ever be brought to believe, that persons endowed with a liberal education could descend so far as to listen to their inconsistent prate, much less give credit to what they uttered; but so strong is the desire of looking into the feeds of time, especially among the fair sex, that sometimes the most proud, as well as the most nice and delicate, will throw aside all consideration of what they are, or would be thought, and, for the sake of

being told their fortune, send for, caress, and associate themselves with, the very lowest and most dirty wretches in human nature.

Lysetta is descended from a very ancient and honourable house. She lived till considerably turned on the wrong side of thirty without discovering the least inclination for marriage, much less gave any room for the most censorious ever to suspect she encouraged any private gallantries; and the whole tenor of her conduct was such, as no one could imagine her capable of harbouring any notions beneath the dignity of her birth and character. A long acquaintance gave me the privilege of visiting her pretty frequently, and never was denied access. I was one day at her house when she had no other company than a young lady with whom she was extremely intimate. While we were drinking tea, her woman came running into the room, and with a significant tone of voice, said—'Madam, the woman you know of is below.'—'Tis very well,' replied Lysetta; 'shew her into my chamber, and bid her stay a little.' Then turning to her friend, they smiled on each other, nodded, winked, and seemed big with some secret between themselves.

I found, by all this, that my presence might very well be spared at this time; so turned down my cup, and took my leave. As I was going down stairs, I heard Lysetta order herself to be denied to whoever should come that evening; which convincing me of what I before had reason to imagine, that there was something more than ordinary in hand, I resolved, if possible, to fathom the mystery. Accordingly I went home, popped on my Invisible Belt, put my Tablets in my pocket, and returned with all speed. A lazy footman, lolling against a post, with the door wide open behind him, gave me an easy entrance into the house. I very well knew the situation of Lysetta's chamber, and went directly thither; but, to my great mortification, found the ladies had bolted themselves in; and all I could distinguish of what was doing, for some time, was only the hoarse bass of a loud laugh from Lysetta, and the squeaking treble of a shrill tee-hee from the other.

I stood centinel, however, at the top of the stair-case, and at last was happily relieved. Lysetta opened the door, and called

R. Smirke del.                                                    Walker, sculp.

INVISIBLE SPY

called to her woman to bring clean cups. Having now gained admittance, I soon perceived what they were about. A coffee-pot upon the table; the dregs of the liquor it had contained poured into a bason; several cups, with more figures on the inside than the outside, and the yet recent circles they had left on being whelmed down on a damask napkin spread on one corner of the table; presently informed me they were employed in the art and mystery of conjuration. The priestess of these farcical rites was a mean-habited, ill-looked woman; and, though not old, had her nose saddled with a pair of spectacles almost as big as the tops of the cups she pretended to inspect: she was placed between the two ladies, who seemed to treat her with the greatest marks of freedom and civility.

Lysetta, I found, had been so complaisant to her friend as to let her be first served: but it was now her own turn; and fresh cups being brought, and the coffee-oracle having judiciously poured the quantity of a tea-spoonful into each, the lady took it into her hand, threw out the liquor, whelmed it on the cloth, and turned it round three times. All being concluded, the prophetess took up the first with the most solemn air, looked stedfastly into it, then on Lysetta; and, after having repeated this several times, at last delivered her predictions in these terms—

*Fortune-teller.* I see a ring, Madam; your ladyship will be married.

*Lysetta.* 'Tis rather a mourning-ring; some of my kindred or friends, perhaps, may die.

*Fortune-teller.* I can say nothing to that, Madam, as yet: but I am positive here is a wedding-ring, a heart just by it; and a little farther there is a great house, with a high wall, and a pair of gates. Your ladyship will have some gentleman that has a fine seat in the country —it looks almost like a castle.

*Lysetta.* I know nothing of it. But what else do you see?

*Fortune-teller.* Here is a man, Madam, that seems to bring you money. Here are papers, too; I do not know but they may be bills.

*Lysetta.* Very likely; for I expect my banker here either to-day or tomorrow.

*Fortune-teller.* Then here is a bundle of something brought to your ladyship's head.

*Lysetta.* Oh, that is a new sack I have making. But is there nothing more?

*Fortune-teller.* Not in this cup, Madam: but I will look into the next.

*Lysetta.* Do; for you have told me nothing of any consequence.

*Fortune-teller.* There is a great deal here, Madam, I can perceive already. Here is a gentleman sitting in an easy chair, leaning his elbow upon the table, and seems to be in a deep study.

*Lysetta.* Pish! what's this to me?

*Fortune-teller.* Yes, Madam, it is a great deal to you; for here is your ladyship, and the very same gentleman on his knees before you. You turn your head away, and look a little scornful; but he has you by the hand. Bless me! here you are both together again; he is talking very earnestly to you. I never saw any thing so plain; your ladyship may see it yourself.

In speaking these last words, she held the cup to Lysetta, and with a pin pointed out the eyes, the nose, and mouth, of the pretended figure; but Lysetta pushed it from her, and said—

*Lysetta.* I could never see any thing in a cup in my life. But what sort of a man is he?

*Fortune-teller.* Pretty tall, Madam; well shaped; very genteel; has a fair complexion, and somewhat of a languishment in his eyes.

*Lysetta.* I cannot recollect that I know any man who answers this description.

*Fortune-teller.* I scarce think you do, Madam, at present; but your ladyship may take my word for it, that you will see and be courted by such a one; for here is a figure of three over his head: it must be either in three days, or three weeks, at farthest. Let me consider—— aye, the moon was at the full yesterday —this event must happen before she enters into her next quarter. But the next cup, it may be, will shew it more clearly.

With this she took up the third cup; and had no sooner looked into it, than she set it down again, clapped her hands together, and cried out—

*Fortune-teller.* Bless me! now I am positive your ladyship will very soon be married! Here is an altar, a book upon it, it, and a parſon; all as exact as if they were drawn by a pencil.

She then took up the cup again; and perceiving Lyſetta began to look a little more ſerious than ſhe had done, went on in this manner,—

*Fortune-teller.* Well, this is wonderful, indeed! Of all the cups I ever turned in my life, I never ſaw any thing like this! Here is your ladyſhip hand in hand with that ſaid gentleman who I told you was in the other. I would now ſwear that your ladyſhip will be a wife before any one imagines you have any thoughts that way.

*Lyſetta.* I have a very good opinion of your ſkill, yet am certain you are miſtaken in this prediction; for, to tell you the truth, I am reſolved never to marry.

*Fortune-teller.* Your ladyſhip may reſolve what you pleaſe; but if the ſtars reſolve the contrary, all your reſolutions will come to nothing. Madam, there is no reſiſting fate: this gentleman is ordained to be your huſband; and, how much ſoever you may ſet yourſelf againſt it, the decrees of deſtiny are inevitable, and you muſt ſubmit.

*Lyſetta.* Oh, Heavens! whether I will or not!

*Fortune-teller.* Undoubtedly, Madam. There is no withſtanding the ſuperior powers; and thoſe things which we think the fartheſt removed from us, are frequently the moſt near at hand; ſo that deſign what you will, reſolve what you will, it is all in vain; your ladyſhip is ordained to be a wife, and the gentleman I ſee in theſe cups muſt be your huſband.

*Lyſetta.* Well, if ſuch a thing ſhould come to paſs, ſhall I be happy?

*Fortune-teller.* There is nothing in the cup, Madam, that ſhews the contrary.

The cups having been all examined, the prophetess, after receiving a handſome gratuity for her trouble, took her leave, and left Lyſetta and her fair companion to ſeaſon between them ſores on the wonders of her art. But no Chryſaline Remembrancer being now quite full, it is not in my power to relate the particulars of their diſcourſe; and can only ſay, that they both ſeemed to give an implicit credit to every thing ſhe had pretended to reveal.

PRESENTS THE READER WITH A VERY FOOLISH ADVENTURE OF LYSETTA'S, TO WHICH ALL THAT WAS CONTAINED IN THE PRECEDING CHAPTER WAS ONLY A PRELUDE.

HAVING diſcovered this folly in Lyſetta, which before I could never have imagined, I began now to be cenſorious enough to ſuſpect ſhe might alſo be guilty of others, and therefore took it into my head to make her ſome Inviſible Viſits, at thoſe hours in which it was likely her behaviour was moſt unguarded. In order to ſatisfy my curioſity, I went one morning, and found her buſy in looking over ſome new pamphlets, juſt ſent her by her bookſeller. As I always thought the moſt certain way to form a true judgment of a woman's mind was in knowing what ſort of reading ſhe moſt delighted in, I was glad to perceive that this lady made choice of only ſuch books as ſhewed her neither a wanton nor a coquette, and returned all thoſe which, by their titles, diſcovered the leaſt tendency to prophaneneſs or obſcenity. After this, ſhe began to open the leaves of one of them; but before ſhe had gone through half the leaves it contained, was interrupted by her footman, who brought her a letter, and ſaid the perſon waited for an anſwer. I ſlipped behind her chair while ſhe broke the ſeal, and the contents were as follow—

'TO THE HONOURABLE LYSETTA.

'MAY IT PLEASE YOUR LADYSHIP,
'MADAM,

'I Hope your goodneſs will pardon the liberty a ſtranger takes in 'writing to you; but as I am not ſo 'fortunate to be acquainted with any 'perſon who can introduce me to your 'ladyſhip, I am obliged to become my 'own ſolicitor, and moſt humbly re'queſt you will allow me the privilege 'of waiting on you this afternoon, if no 'previous engagement intervenes be'tween me and my deſires, having 'ſomething to communicate of the ut'moſt 'moft moment to the peace of him who 'has the honour to be, with the moft 'profound refpect, your ladyfhip's fin- 'cerely devoted fervant,

'ORSAMES.'

Lyfetta feemed a good deal confound- ed on reading this little epiftle; and after paufing a while, argued with her- felf in this manner—' Good God! if 'this fhould be the man the fortune- 'teller told me of! fhe faid I fhould 'hear or fee fomething of him within 'three days, and this is but the fecond 'fince the prediction. If I was fure he 'was the perfon fhe mentioned, I think 'I ought not to give him leave to vifit 'me, at leaft not on his firft requefting 'it; yet I fhould be glad, methinks, to 'fee if he any way anfwers the defcrip- 'tion fhe gave of him: befides, if I 'fhould refufe him,' fome accident or 'another would bring us together; for 'it is certain, there is no fuch thing as 'difappointing fate. Why, therefore, 'fhould I keep myfelf in fufpence? No, 'I will fee him, and hear what he has 'to fay. It may be he may come upon 'fome other bufinefs than what I ima- 'gine, and then it would be vaftly filly 'in me to avoid him. Whoever he is, 'or whatever his defigns are, it can be 'of no prejudice to fee him once. He 'cannot run away with me, cannot have 'me againft my will.'

She then called her fervant, and bid him fay that fhe fhould be at home. The fellow ran down, but had fcarce time to deliver the meffage he was charged with, before fhe repented of it, as may be feen by this exclamation: ' Lord! 'what have I done! if he is really the 'perfon I take him to be, he muft think 'me ftrangely forward in fo eafily grant- ◄ 'ing him admittance.'

While fhe was fpeaking this, fhe ran to the ftair-cafe with an intent to retract what fhe had faid; but a fecond thought witholding her, fhe turned back into the room, and cried out—' What a fool 'I am! he does not know that I have 'confulted a fortune-teller, nor that I 'have any reafon to guefs at the bufi- 'nefs that brings him hither. Why, 'therefore, fhould I fhun him? What 'fhame can my feeing him reflect upon 'me? It will be time enough to forbid 'his vifits when he has declared him- 'felf my lover.'

How long fhe would have continued in that mind is uncertain. Two ladies came in that inftant to defire her com- pany with them to the Park, being a fine morning; to which fhe confenting, I left them, and went home, but with a full refolution to return in the afternoon, and fee what event the expected inter- view would produce. Accordingly I put on my Belt of Invifibility, and went to the houfe of Lyfetta. I faw a chair waiting, but the door was fhut, and I was obliged to ftay in the ftreet a confi- derable time, before it was opened for any perfon, either to go in or out. I got entrance at laft, and paffed direct- ly to the dining-room, where I found the perfon I was defirous of beholding. On my looking earneftly on him, I faw he had fo much the refemblance of the picture drawn for him by the fortune- teller, that I prefently perceived fhe muft be better acquainted with his features than the cups could make her, and that in reality fhe was a marriage-broker, under the difguife of a coffee-grounds calculator. He had placed himfelf very clofe to Lyfetta on a fettee, and muft have been making a declaration of love to her by the anfwer fhe gave juft as I came into the room.

*Lyfetta.* Sir, it does not become me to hearken to any profeffions of this na- ture, from a perfon, to whofe family, fortune, and character, I am fo entire a ftranger.

*Orfames.* It will be eafy for me, Madam, to give you full fatisfaction in all thefe particulars; but till I can do fo, I beg you will permit me, at leaft, to convince you of my paffion.

*Lyfetta.* Though, Sir, there is no room to doubt, either by your appearance or behaviour, that you are a gentle- man and a man of honour, yet I fhould be glad, methinks, to know fome one perfon with whom you are acquainted.

*Orfames.* Unfortunately for me, Ma- dam, there is not a foul in this town who can give any account of me. This, perhaps, you will think odd; but per- mit me to give a fhort fketch of my hiftory, and you will ceafe to wonder at it.

*Lyfetta.* Then, pray Sir, oblige me fo far.

*Orfames.* It is no boaft in me, Ma- dam, to affure your ladyfhip, that my family is among the number of the moft ancient in England, having been fettled here long before the Conqueft, and many

Q of

of them been bishops, judges, and privy-counsellors; but my father, taking some disgust at the measures in a late reign, resolved to quit his native country for ever; and to that end sold the seat of his ancestors, with a very considerable estate in Somersetshire, and carried the purchase-money, together with his whole family, to Philadelphia, where he had then a brother, reputed the most wealthy merchant in that place. It was there, Madam, I was born, and am the only surviving issue of my parents, and consequently the sole heir of their possessions, as also of my uncle's, he dying without leaving any child behind him. I fear I tire you, Madam.

*Lysetta.* No, Sir, I beg you will go on.

*Orsames.* From my very infancy there was somewhat in my nature which could not relish the manners of these Americans, though born among them. I had read a great deal, and heard much concerning England, and had always a passionate desire to come to it; but my father, even after my arriving at maturity, would never listen to any intreaties on that score. After his death, my uncle was no less averse to my removal; but on his demise, finding myself freed from all dependency, and entirely master of my own actions, I left all my effects to be disposed of by a person whose integrity I am well assured of, and taking with me only a thousand guineas, just for present use, embarked in the first ship that sailed for England, where I happily arrived about six weeks since.

*Lysetta.* But would it not have been better, Sir, that you had staid at Philadelphia till your affairs had been settled?

*Orsames.* Not at all, Madam; I have friends there that will manage for me as well as if I were there in person. Besides, an irresistible impulse hurried me to England. I could not then account for my impatience, but am now convinced it was my guardian angel called me to behold in reality that lovely face I have so often seen in dreams.

*Lysetta.* What! dream of me!

*Orsames.* Yes, Madam, though so many leagues distant, my spirit has been often with you, conversed with you, and avowed that flame my mortal part now feels.

*Lys'ta.* Is it possible!

*Orsames.* True, by Heaven!

*Lysetta.* And are you certain I am the same you saw in your sleep?

*Orsames.* I could not be deceived; the first moment my eyes were blest with your presence at the Chapel Royal, I forgot the solemnity of the place, and the pious business that had brought me thither.

*Lysetta.* 'Tis very wonderful; but 'tis time enough to talk of these things. As you have related to me the former part of your life, I should like to know in what manner you intend to regulate the future.

*Orsames.* That must be submitted to my charming directress; all my affairs, as well as my heart, must henceforth be at your disposal. I had thoughts, indeed, of purchasing a small estate, of about fifteen hundred or two thousand pounds a year; but whether I should put the remainder of my fortune into the publick funds, or lay it out on an employment at court, I had not yet determined.

*Lysetta.* Oh, by all means buy a place; the court is the only thing upon earth.

*Orsames.* Next to your company I believe it is; and since you approve the thought, shall infallibly pursue it.

*Lysetta.* Whoever you marry, Sir, will doubtless be of my opinion.

*Orsames.* Ah! do not wrong my faithful heart so much as to imagine it capable of being charmed by any other. No, if all my love, my services, my prayers, should fail to move the adorable Lysetta, I vow an eternal celibacy.

*Lysetta.* You men always talk thus when you would impose on the credulity of our sex; but, Sir, it is time alone that is the true touch-stone of sincerity.

*Orsames.* Madam, it is, and to that I shall trust the decision of my fate; therefore, I once more implore your permission to repeat my vows, and pay you the tribute which beauty like yours demands from love like mine.

*Lysetta.* I will not hear so much of love; but, as you are a stranger in town, and as yet have no acquaintance, I cannot be so ungenteel to refuse you the privilege of visiting me sometimes.

At these words, he threw himself upon his knees; and, catching hold of both her hands, pressed first the one and then the other to his lips, with the greatest appearance of transport; all which she suffered,

suffered, nor difcovered the leaft re-luctance. I know not how long he might have continued in this mute court-fhip, if the found of fomebody at the door had not obliged him fuddenly to rife. It was Lyfetta's fervant, who im-mediately entered, and prefented her with two letters, which had been juft left her by the poft. She looked on the fuper-fcriptions, then threw them carelefsly on the table, without fhewing any impa-tience to examine the contents; but her lover, either through politenefs, or be-caufe he had acted enough of his part for the firft time, thought proper to take his leave, faying, he would do himfelf the honour to wait on her the next day.

He was no fooner gone than fhe be-gan to give a loofe to thofe agitations his prefence and difcourfe had occafioned, and which fhe had not without great difficulty reftrained from being vifible. It was in thefe terms fhe expreffed her-felf, which, incoherent as they are, I fhall deliver them to my readers, juft as I found them the next morning engrav-ed on my Tablets. ' Well, this is the ' oddeft accident ; fure there was never ' any thing fo aftonifhing ! Let people ' fay what they will, there is a great ' deal in the throwing of a cup ; that ' woman is certainly the devil ; how ' exactly fhe defcribed this gentleman ! ' I have faid I would never marry, but ' if the ftars have ordained it otherwife, ' it is in vain to refift; and if his for-' tune be fuch as he pretends it is, I can ' fee no caufe for any one to blame me.'

Here fhe ftopped, and fell into a little reverie; but foon coming out of it, thus renewed her ejaculations: ' There is no-' thing in the perfon nor addrefs of this ' new lover but what is perfectly agree-' able ; and I believe I fhall like him ' well enough on a little more acquaint-' ance with him : he feems vaftly charm-' ed with me ; but one ought not to ' build on what the men fay on thefe ' occafions. There is fomething ftrange-' ly particular, indeed, in his dreaming ' of me without ever having feen me : ' in fine, the more I confider, the more ' I find the hand of fate is in this bufi-' nefs, and I muft fubmit.'

After this, fhe feemed fomewhat more compofed, and began to read the letters fhe had received. I alfo looked over them at the fame time; but found they were only from relations, of family af-fairs of no moment to the publick, or to the narrative I am reciting. When I came home, had thrown myfelf into an eafy-chair, and began to ruminate on the extraordinary fcene I had been wit-nefs of, I knew not whether the bafe defign, which I now plainly perceived had been concerted between the for-tune-teller and Or ames, or the weaknefs and infatuation of Lyfetta in giving credit to their romantick lyes, had the moft right to engrofs my amazement. But when I reflected more deeply on the various impofitions I daily faw practifed, my wonder ceafed, on account either of the fortune-teller or the fortune-hunter, and fixed itfelf entirely on the fimplicity of Lyfetta. It now feemed no ftrange to me, that the moft illiterate and abject wretches fhould be endowed with a na-tural ftore of cunning, which, backed by impudence, renders them capable of forming contrivances to deceive ; elfe how do we often fee pick pockets and houfe breakers circumvent the watch-fulnefs of the moft cautious ? But then, thofe fort of pilferers rob us when our heads are turned another way, or when we are fleeping in our beds; but in lif-tening to fortune-tellers, we are defraud-ed with our eyes open, and give, as it were, our own confent to the worft kind of theft, that of ftealing away our un-derftanding.

People guilty of this egregious folly, when detected in it, pretend they con-fult thofe ridiculous oracles for no other end than merely to divert themfelves, without believing, or even remembering one fyllable of the predictions delivered to them. This may, perhaps, at firft be true; but there are too many inftances which prove, that cuftom, by degrees, turns into earneft what might once be meant as a jeft. The reafon is this: thofe fubtle creatures frequently find means, either by emiffari s, or by in-finuating themfelves among fervants, to get into the fecrets of families, and one real fact ferving to make all they fay believed, gives them the power to work the perfon who depends upon them almoft to any point they aim at. The moft pernicious defigns have been carried on this way. Hufbands have been fet againft their wives, and wives againft their hufbands ; parents have been made to difregard their children, and children to forget all obedience to their parents ; the beft matches have been broke off, and the moft difpro ortionable ones made : in fine, there is no kind of mischief but what has happened when a fortune-teller has been bribed by some base person, who has an in'erest in bringing about such events. Therefore, as there is a strict law in force against these pretended dealers in futurity, I cannot help saying, that I regret it's not being executed with greater punctuality; since the more simple an evil appears, the more dangerous it proves in it's effects.

## CHAP. IV.

CONTAINS THE CATASTROPHE OF AN AFFAIR, WHICH THE REPETITION OF OUGHT NOT. TO GIVE OFFENCE TO ANY ONE, EXCEPT THE PERSON WHOSE RESENTMENT THE AUTHOR WILL NOT LOOK UPON AS A MISFORTUNE.

LYSETTA was so strongly persuaded in her mind, that it was her fate to marry Orsames, that she made not the least attempt to check the growing inclination she had for him, but rather thought it a virtue in her to encourage the most tender sentiments for a person ordained by Heaven to be her husband. I made several visits to her, both in my visible and invisible capacity, and seldom went without finding Orsames there, and every time more free and degagé than before. He made so swift a progress in his courtship, that in less than a month he became the major domo of her family, commanded all the servants, and behaved as if already their master. To add to all this, Lysetta suffered him to conduct her to all publick places, sat in the same box at the playhouse, and always dined and supped with her, whatever company were there: in a word, they were never asunder but in those hours when decency obliged them to be so.

So strange a revolution in the behaviour of Lysetta, made a great noise in the town; all her acquaintance were surprized; all her friends and kindred were much alarmed at it; especially as the person to whom she shewed these extraordinary favours was altogether unknown, nor could they get the least account of him. Those, who either through a long conversation or affinity of blood,

could take the privilege of discoursing with her on this head, did it in a very free manner; but the answers she gave to their interrogatories were far from being satisfactory. When she told them his history as he had related it, they treated it with contempt. Some said that he was an impostor; others, more modest, that they wished he was not so; to both which she returned, that whatever he were, she was certain it was her fate to marry him, and desired they would give themselves no pain on that occasion. As she was naturally of a haughty, obstinate disposition, it is highly probable, that the remonstrances they took the liberty of making to her, rather strengthened than abated her resolution of giving herself to him. I was at her house one day, under cover of my Invisible Belt, when I heard the following conversation between them—

*Orsames.* Condemn me not, my angel, for being sometimes melancholy even in your presence. Though you have promised to make me one day the happiest of mankind, and I look upon every word of that dear mouth as unfailing as an oracle, yet when I consider the length of time between me and the consummation of my wishes, the impatience of my passion will not permit me to be gay.

*Lysetta.* You men are always in such a hurry in every thing you do.

*Orsames.* Ah, Madam, 'tis a dreadful thing to have one's happiness depend on the uncertain winds and waves; it may be yet two months before my effects can arrive from Philadelphia.

*Lysetta.* And do you call that so long a time?

*Orsames.* A million of ages in the account of love, and even, according to common calculation, longer than human nature can sustain continual torments; eight whole weeks, six and fifty anxious days, and as many restless nights; upwards of thirteen hundred hours of tedious expectation; and minutes almost numberless, wasted in pain which might be passed in pleasure, if you would shorten the tremendous date.

*Lysetta.* What would you have me do?

*Orsames.* Ah! if you loved, you need not be told, but of yourself generously bring the blessed event nearer to my wishes.

*Lysetta.* You would not have me marry

marry till your affairs are fettled, and things can be done to our mutual fatisfaction.

*Orfames.* I underftand you, Madam; the articles of jointure and pin money, I know, are cuftomary in modifh marriages; but the paffion you have infpired me with is of too fublime a nature to ftoop to fuch mean forms. I afk not what your fortune is, but will fettle the whole of mine upon you; your lovely perfon is all the treafure I am ambitious of preferving; the reft fhall be at your difpofal.

*Lyfetta.* That is kind, indeed; but more than I defire or would accept of.

*Orfames.* Oh! that you had no other fortune than your beauty! then would the fincerity of my love be proved by endowing you with all that Heaven has made me mafter of. Alas! you know not how ardently, how faithfully I adore you.

*Lyfetta.* Yes, I am vain enough to think I have fome fhare in your affections.

*Orfames.* Some fhare! Oh! could you be fenfible of the thoufandth part of what I feel, pity, if not love, would compel you to eafe my throbbing heart of the fufpence it labours under, and you would give yourfelf to my burning, bleeding paffion.

*Lyfetta.* I have already faid I will be yours, and now again repeat it.

*Orfames.* But when, my angel!

In fpeaking thefe words he threw himfelf upon his knees before her, burft into a flood of well-diffembled tears, and grafped her *robe de chambre* with agonies which I cannot but fay had much the appearance of reality, while in thefe terms he profecuted his defign—

*Orfames.* I have till now fupported life but in the rapturous hope of being one day bleffed in your poffeffion: but even hope, by it's uncertainty, becomes at laft too weak an aid; and foon, very foon, my adorable Lyfetta, will you behold your faithful lover a cold breathlefs corpfe, unlefs the balm of your kindnefs recruits the vital lamp, and gives frefh vigour to my depreffed and breaking heart.

*Lyfetta.* I cannot bear to hear and fee you thus. Rife, Sir; this pofture does not become the man whom I intend to make my hufband.

· *Orfames.* No, by Heaven, I never will quit your feet without an affurance

of my happinefs. Say, then, oh fay! when fhall be the blifsful day that makes you mine!

*Lyfetta.* Since it muft be fo, even when you pleafe.—No, hold, I had forgot myfelf.

*Orfames.* Oh, Heavens, what now?

*Lyfetta.* I promifed a clergyman, my near kinfman, that if ever I married, he fhould perform the ceremony; he is at prefent out of town, but will return next Sunday, and on the Tuefday following it fhall not be my fault if we do not attend him at the altar.

*Orfames.* Extatick found! May I depend on the performance of this heavenly promife!

*Lyfetta.* You may, and be entirely eafy on that point; and take now my hand, as an earneft of my giving it you in a more folemn manner before a parfon; henceforward I fhall look upon myfelf as yours.

*Orfames.* Angel! goddefs! Thus then let me feal the covenant on thofe charming lips that have pronounced it.

*Lyfetta.* The covenant will not hold good in law without both parties interchangeably fign their affent.

She uttered thefe words with a moft pleafing fmile, and at the fame time threw her arms about his neck, and returned the paffionate falute fhe had received from him, adding this tender expreffion—' My dear, dear Orfames, I ' do not now blufh to confefs to you, ' that from the firft moment you de-' clared yourfelf my lover, my heart ' correfponded with your vows, and ' told me what would be the event.' He affected too much tranfport, on hearing her fpeak in this manner, to be able to make any other reply than kiffes and embraces, which, as fhe was far from repelling, or feeming the leaft offended at, I know not what advantages he might have taken, on finding her thus foftened by his artifices, if a fudden interruption had not, happily for her, broke off this dangerous entertainment. A footman came and told her that her aunt, lady Gravelove, was come to vifit her; on which fhe cried out with fome peevifhnefs—' Pifh! why did you not / fav I was from home?' Then turning fondly to Orfames, faid—

*Lyfetta.* Do you chufe to join company with my aunt? or fhall I fetch fome book to amufe you with till fhe is gone?

*Orfames.*

*Orfames.* No, my dearest love; this lady has always looked upon me with an unpleasing eye, especially of late, therefore will not offend her with my presence; neither are my spirits enough composed, in the excess of joy you have inspired me with, to read any thing with attention; so will take a little walk.

*Lysetta.* Do so; but I shall expect you back to supper: my aunt seldom stays longer than to drink tea, and I am sure I shall not prefs her at this time.

No more was said on either side; they embraced and parted; she went into the next room, and he down stairs, in order to go where his business or inclination called him. As I never believed this fellow was what he pretended, I had taken some pains to discover the truth of his circumstances, but without any success, till it now came into my mind to follow him after he had left Lysetta's house; which I did, resolving not to lose sight of him till he should return to her again.

He went directly to Drury Lane, walked very fast, and never stopped till he came to the entrance of a narrow passage between that place and Wild Street, where he stood still, and looked round him, I suppose, to see if any one was near who might know him; for day was not yet quite shut in: then passed a little farther, looked about him again, and finding the coast, as he thought, clear, none being in the alley but his Invisible Attendant, slipped hastily into a little dirty alehouse, where an old woman met him, and told him his friends were all above; on which he ran up stairs, and pushed open the door of a room, pretty spacious indeed, but had otherwise all the signs of beggary and wretchedness about it. Here we found five or six men tolerably well habited, but had something in their countenances which made me guess their occupation before they discovered it by their conversation; for they were no better than a gang of thieves and sharpers: they were sitting round a table with a great bowl of punch before them, when Orfames rushed in, and, with a gay air, accosted them in these terms:—

*Orfames.* Wish me joy, my lads; my hearts of steel, wish me joy; I have gained my point; all is over, all is over.

*First Man.* What, married!

*Orfames.* No, but as good as married; the wench and her twelve thousand pounds are as sure to me, as if I had the one in my arms, and the other in my pocket. Tuesday is the day, my buffs! But I must have more money, by G—d! I have not a single doit left.

*Second Man.* How! all the fifty pieces gone already!

*Orfames.* Ay, faith, and well laid out too; I shall return it with interest; you are all to share in the money, and the woman too. But come, how stands stock among you?

*Third Man.* Cursed low: though we have been all out to-day, we have not collected above thirty pieces, and four gold watches that must be knocked to pieces, and the cases melted down, or the makers names may betray us.

*Fourth Man.* The road grows worse and worse every day, I think.

*Orfames.* But did you get nothing from the ladies the fortune-teller told you were to take the air this morning on Barnes Common?

*Fifth Man.* I should have done; but, as the devil would have it, just as they were going to pull out their purses, three gentlemen, with fire-arms, came galloping towards us, and obliged me to make off without my booty.

*Orfames.* 'Twas damn'd unlucky!

*First Man.* One meets with a thousand disappointments; for my part, I am half sick of the business, and so I believe we are all.

*Second Man.* Ay, faith; for, what with feeing inn-keepers, coachmen, fortune-tellers, and other such necessary informers, we have the least part of the profit to ourselves.

*Third Man.* Ay, 'I wish, Orfames, you were once married, that you might set up a gaming-table under the sanction of your lady's name. Gaming is ten times a more profitable, as well as a safer way of thieving.

*Orfames.* You know it was my bargain, and you may depend upon my honour, that it shall be the first thing I will do.

*Fourth Man.* It will be a joyful day; for, since taxes have been so high, and trade so low, such numbers of shopkeepers are obliged to take the road, that we old practitioners can scarce get a living by it.

*Orfames.* Well, well, all this will be over

over in a fhort time: but you muft raife me fome cafh; I can eafily give you an account of the fifty pieces.

*Fifth Man.* No, no, it needs not; we know you would not fink upon us.

*Orfames.* I chufe, however, to do it. The firft article is five guineas to the fortune-teller, as an earneft of the hundred fhe is to receive after my marriage with Lyfetta. The fecond, is twenty pounds for a gold fnuff-box, which I pretended to have brought from Philadelphia, and prefented to her ladyfhip. The third, is about ten more, fpent in three feveral jaunts I made with her to Richmond, Windfor, and Greenwich. The remainder, you may believe, might well be fpent in donations to her fervants, board-wages to my own man, paying my lodgings at two guineas a week, chair-hire, and other neceffary expences.

*Firft Man.* You could do no lefs.

*Second Man.* Ay, ay, nothing of all this could have been fpared. But what fum do you demand at prefent?

*Orfames.* I believe twenty pieces will defray the whole charges of the wedding, which is all I want; afterwards, my boys, I fhall have enough for you all.

On this, every one turned out his pockets, and the fum was immediately made up, and laid upon the table; which Orfames put into his purfe: and then fome difcourfe enfued among this vicious company, which I chufe to pafs over in filence, as it would be no fit entertainment for the chafte ears of my fair readers. Orfames ftaid with them about two hours, and then took his leave in order to fup with Lyfetta, as fhe had defired he would. I accompanied him not thither, but went home to my own apartment, more full of confufion at the difcovery I had made than I am able to exprefs. Though I half defpifed Lyfetta for the follies I had feen her guilty of; yet, when I reflected on her birth, and the character fhe had maintained in the world, I could not bear the thoughts of her becoming the victim of the bafe defign concerted againft her; and her fortune, reputation, and eternal peace of mind, the prey of fuch a neft of villains.

My whole ftudy was now fully bent to fnatch this unfortunate lady from that gulph of perdition fhe was upon the brink of, and fo near plunging into. I was extremely divided in my thoughts what to do upon this occafion. To give her any hints concerning the dangers

to which fhe expofed herfelf and reputation, by encouraging the addreffes of a man whofe character fhe was fo little acquainted with, I knew would be in vain, as fhe had rejected all the warnings given her on that fcore, and refufed to liften to the admonitions of her beft friends and neareft kindred. I had it in my power, indeed, to inform her of much more than any of them could even guefs at: but then I could not relate the fcene I had been witnefs of, without difcovering, at the fame time, the fecret of my Invifible Belt; which was by no means proper for me to entruft her with.

To acquaint her by letter with what I knew concerning Orfames, and the villainous confpiracy which had been formed to ruin her, I feared would be to as little purpofe; and doubted not but fhe would look upon an anonymous intimation only as a piece of malice, and treat it with the contempt it might feem to merit. As this, however, was the only method I could take to fave her, with any convenience to myfelf, I refolved to purfue it; and accordingly wrote to her next morning a full account of all I had been witnefs of between Orfames and his wicked companions. I made this letter be left at her houfe before the time in which fhe ufually got out of bed, to the end fhe might have leifure to confider the contents, without being interrupted by any company coming in. As I was defirous of feeing in what manner fhe would receive this intelligence, I went, under cover of my Belt, and gained entrance juft as fhe had finifhed the perufal.

Her behaviour was fuch as I apprehended it would be. She tore the letter, ftormed, and cried out—' Was there ' ever fo much impudence! Sure the ' perfon who fent this infamous fcrawl ' muft have a very mean opinion of my ' underftanding, to think I could give ' the leaft credit to fuch a vile afper ' fion!—Orfames an impoftor! a com ' panion for thieves and vagabonds!— ' ridiculous!' And then again—' This ' muft certainly be a contrivance of fome ' of my wife kindred to break off the ' match. I could find in my heart to ' fend for Orfames, and marry him ' this inftant, to fhew how much I de ' fpife their little malice. But 'tis no ' matter, Tuefday will foon arrive, and ' that will put an end to all.'

I ftaid

I ſtaid a full hour, in the ſuppoſition that Orſames would make her a morning viſit; but finding, by ſome diſcourſe ſhe had with her maid, that ſhe did not expect him, and was making herſelf ready to go among the ſhops for things ſhe wanted, I quitted her apartment, much diſconcerted at the ill ſucceſs of what I had done. However, as I had little elſe to employ my time that day, I went again in the afternoon. Orſames was now there, and two ladies of Lyſetta's particular acquaintance. Whether ſhe had mentioned any thing to him of the letter, I cannot be certain; but am apt to think ſhe had not; for he appeared with an alertneſs which, by all I could diſcover, had nothing of conſtraint in it. Cards were called for; and they were juſt going to ſit down to whiſt, when word was brought to Lyſetta, that her couſin, Captain Platoon, was juſt arrived from Carliſle, and come to wait upon her; on which ſhe ordered him to be ſhewed up immediately. Orſames, who I perceived had turned pale as aſhes on hearing this gentleman's name, now roſe haſtily from his chair, and ſaid to Lyſetta—' I have juſt thought of ſome buſineſs ' I had to diſpatch—your ladyſhip muſt ' excuſe me—the affair that calls me is ' of conſequence—I cannot ſtay.'

She was going to make ſome reply, but the captain came that inſtant into the room. While he was paying his compliments to his couſin and the other ladies, Orſames had taken up his hat, and was endeavouring to ſlip out unperceived; but the quick-ſightedneſs of Lyſetta prevented him: ſhe ran to him, and catching hold of his ſleeve, ſaid— ' You ſhall not go; at leaſt till I have ' preſented you to my couſin.' Then turning to the captain, ſaid—' This is a ' gentleman, couſin, whoſe acquaint- ' ance, I believe, you will hereafter ' think yourſelf happy in.'

On this the captain advanced, with great politeneſs, to embrace the perſon his kinſwoman preſented to him; but had no ſooner fixed his eyes upon his face, than he ſtarted back with the utmoſt aſtoniſhment, and cried out to Lyſetta— ' What is the meaning of this, Ma- ' dam? Who would you introduce to ' me?' She was opening her mouth to make ſome anſwer; but Orſames, who was drawing as faſt as he could towards the door, hindered her from ſpeaking, by ſaying, with a heſitating voice—

' Madam, the gentleman does not ſeem ' to deſire any new acquaintance. I ' will wait on your ladyſhip another ' time.' In ſpeaking this, he got to the top of the ſtair-caſe; and, it is likely, would have made but one ſtep to the bottom, if the captain had not prevented him, by running to him, and catching faſt hold of him by the collar, dragged him back, ſaying, at the ſame time—' No, raſcal! you muſt not ' think to leave this place till you have ' confeſſed what devil gave you the im- ' pudence to introduce yourſelf into ſuch ' company, and on what villainous de- ' ſign you are thus diſguiſed in the ha- ' bit of a gentleman.' Then addreſſing himſelf to Lyſetta, who ſtood as mo- tionleſs as if transfixed with thunder, went on thus—' Madam, by what ' means ſoever this villain has impoſed ' on you, I do aſſure you, upon my ho- ' nour, that two months ago he was a ' private man in Captain Cutcomb's ' company, and drummed out of the ' regiment for pig-ſtealing, and other ' miſdemeanors; for ſome of which, in- ' deed, he ought to have been hanged.'

On theſe words Lyſetta ſcreamed out— ' Oh, Heavens!' and fell into a ſwoon. The captain ſeeing this, quitted his pri- ſoner, to run with the two ladies to her aſſiſtance; and Orſames took this op- portunity of making his eſcape. Proper means being applied, ſhe ſoon reco- vered; and the ſwelling paſſions which had occaſioned this diſorder, vented themſelves in tears. The captain ap- peared a little impatient to know how ſhe became acquainted with ſuch a wretch as Orſames; but ſhe told him ſhe was not then in a condition to inform him of the particulars; ſaid ſhe was very ill, and muſt lie down, and deſired to ſee him another time: on which he took his leave, as did the two ladies; who knowing Orſames had profeſſed himſelf her lover, and the encourage- ment ſhe had given him, I could per- ceive ſmiled within themſelves at the diſcovery. Thus was Lyſetta preſerved from ruin; and had no other puniſhment for her folly, than being laughed at by thoſe who were privy to the affair. As for Orſames, I have ſince met him about town, in a very ſhabby and tattered condition. The gang of villains, his aſſociates, I believe, are diſperſed; and one of them has made his exit at Ty- burn.

CHAP.

## CHAP. V.

TREATS ON VARIOUS MATTERS, SOME OF WHICH, THE AUTHOR DARES VENTURE TO ASSURE THE PUBLICK, WILL HEREAFTER BE FOUND NOT ONLY MORE ENTERTAINING, BUT ALSO OF MORE CONSEQUENCE, THAN AT PRESENT THEY APPEAR TO BE.

I Had been told that Lady Playfield's route was an assemblage of the most brilliant and polite persons of both sexes; and though I never had any great opinion of this sort of meetings, yet I was tempted to go thither, in order to be myself a witness how far the description that had been given me was consonant to truth. As I am an entire stranger to her ladyship, and did not care for the formality of being introduced by any one who went there, I chose to make this visit in my Invisible capacity. The great number of wax tapers, the sparkle of the ladies jewels, and the extraordinary beauty of some among them, was dazzling to my eyes at first entrance: but I soon found that I had the same fault to find with this, as I had done in all other mixed company I ever saw; a kind of hurry and confusion, which destroys that solid conversation that is so agreeable when only a few select friends are met together. It was near nine o'clock when I went thither, yet there were several who came in after me. Lady Playfield received all of them with her accustomed politeness; but, for a great while, there was nothing in the salutations, on either side, which engrossed my attention so far, as to make me spread my Tablets to retain it.

I was, indeed, quite indolent to every thing that was said, till the entrance of Lady Allmode gave a little spur to my curiosity. I had heard much talk of this lady, not only for her being extravagantly fond of every new fashion, but also for a certain peculiarity in her manner of conversation, which made her admired by people of a low education, and as much laughed at by those of a superior. I had been told that she had an utter aversion to plain English; and so thorough a contempt for what she called the vulgar way of speaking, that when

she talked, even on the most common things, she interlarded all she said with the hardest words she could pick out of the dictionary, and frequently coined new ones of her own, which never were, nor scarce ever will be, found in any vocabulary. Lady Playfield, I perceived, received her with a great deal of respect. I was then at some distance; but, on finding they were entering into conversation, drew more near, to have an opportunity of hearing, and improving myself, by a person of whom so extraordinary a description had been given me. After the first compliments were over, Lady Playfield addressed herself to her in these terms—

*Lady Playfield.* Though I am always happy when I see your ladyship, yet now I can scarce forbear complaining of your unkindness in coming without Miss Arabella. I hear she has been in town above a week.

*Lady Allmode.* I could not have been guilty of so enormous a solecism in good breeding, as not to have brought her to pay her duty to your ladyship, if there had been a possibility in nature to have done it.

*Lady Playfield.* I hope Miss is well, Madam.

*Lady Allmode.* Perfectly so, Madam, as to her health; but such a fight! such a figure!—a greater metamorphosis than any in Ovid.

*Lady Playfield.* What does your ladyship mean?

*Lady Allmode.* Oh, Madam, the remotest corner of the most desart of the three Arabias never produced such a creature; such a Tramontane, as the Italians elegantly phrase it. Well, there people who live a great way from London, are such absurdians, such awkwardnesses! Would your ladyship believe it? they sent the girl home in a cap that quite covered the drum of her ears.

*Lady Playfield.* That might be to prevent her catching cold in the coach.

*Lady Allmode.* Oh, Jupiter! how am I surprized to hear your ladyship talk in this manner!—But this is not all. The girl had several new suits of cloaths, when she left London, made in the genteelest taste; my country aunt taking it into her head, that either I had allowed too scanty a pattern, or that she had outgrown them, out of mere good-

R                          will

will and fimplicity, has lengthened all her petticoats to fuch a ridiculous fize, that they almoft come down to the buckles of her fhoes; I proteft one can fcarce fee whether fhe has any ancles.

On this a gentleman, who ftood pretty near, approached Lady Allmode; and, with a moft ironical tone, replied to what fhe had faid in thefe words—

*Gentleman.* Your ladyfhip muft ex-cufe the miftake your aunt has made. I fancy the fafhion of going half naked may not yet have reached fo far as Wales.

*Lady Allmode.* You certainly fpeak the rationalii of the thing, Sir. Few of thefe mountaineers regard any thing but loading their tables with provifions, feafting their tenants, paying their debts, ftanding up for the liberties of their country, and fuch like antiquated ob-folete cuftoms. For my part, all my faculties are immerged in a profoundity of aftonifhment, to think that my aunt could marry and fettle among fuch aliens to politenefs, fuch heathens to the laws of good-breeding and the drawing-room.

*Gentleman.* Perhaps, Madam, the cuftoms and manners you mention were in vogue at the time of your aunt's mar-riage?

*Lady Allmode.* I proteft, Sir, you have hit upon the folution of this enig-ma. It was, indeed, in the reign of Queen Anne that fhe married.

·I had feen enough of this fine lady, and did not chufe to have my Tablets crouded with any more of her unintel-ligible jargon; fo retired to another part of the room, where I faw three ladies got together, who feemed very earneft in difcourfe. But little was I like to be the better for my near approach; for being on the topick of fcandal, each was fo full, and fo highly delighted with the thoughts of it, that all fpeaking at the fame time, prevented me from hearing diftinctly what was faid by any of them; and all I could gather, at laft, was, that a certain lady of their acquaintance had been caught with her footman.

As I had been informed of the parti-culars of this ftory before, the foible of the tranfgreffing fair did not fo much engrofs my meditations, as the plea-fure thofe of her own fex feemed to take in expofing it; and I could not help faying to myfelf, with the poet—

'There is a luft in man, no charm can
    'tame,
'Of loudly publifhing his neighbour's fhame.
'On eagle's wings immortal fcandals fly;
'While virtuous actions are but born, and
    'die.'

But this was a place more proper to collect matter for reflection hereafter, than to indulge it at prefent; fo I paffed on among the gaming-tables, which were eleven in number, and none of them un-occupied. Here it was pleafant enough to obferve the various attitudes of thofe who played: and I think there is not a more fure way of judging people's difpo-fitions, than to fee them at this diver-fion. Some of thofe who fwept the ftakes, received the favours Fortune be-ftowed on them with an eafe and calm-nefs which fhewed they had not been over-anxious whether fhe fmiled or frowned; but there were many more, who fnatched up the glittering metal with a greedinefs which fufficiently de-monftrated that avarice was the chief ex-citement to what they did. As for the lofers, it gave me an infinite fatisfaction to fee the unconcerned behaviour of fome few among them; while others, again, filled me with a no lefs fenfible difquiet at their impatience. I was afhamed to find a gentleman of rank and fortune forget all politenefs, and fometimes even common decency, to thofe who had his money in their pockets; and forry in my heart to fee a lady bite her lips, wrinkle her forehead with unbecoming frowns, diftort every feature, and disfi-gure all the charms which nature had beftowed on her, for the lofs of what was not worth half that anxiety to pre-ferve. 'Good Heaven!' faid I to my-felf, 'if this be the effect of gaming, 'what madnefs is it to venture one's 'peace in that uncertain gulph!'

The beautiful Ifmena was this night among the number of the unfortunates, but not of the impatients. I ftood be-hind her chair, and faw her empty a well-filled purfe, and take out of it even the laft guinea with a fmile. She was, indeed, a young lady lately come to the poffeffion of a very large fortune, and could not want what fhe had thrown away: but the fame might alfo be faid of Clarinda, who played at the fame ta-ble with her, and had alfo loft a confi-derable fum to Sir Charles Fairlove, with whom thefe two ladies had been

engaged

engaged the whole evening at picquet.
But fee the difference! the latter of them
rofe from the table in a fury, tore her
fan, and cried—

*Clarinda.* Curfe the cards!—I will
play no more this night, that I am refolved; at leaft with Sir Charles.

*Ifmena.* Nay, Madam, we have no
reafon to be angry with Sir Charles,
for having done by us what we would
gladly have done by him. For my part,
though he has ftripped me of all I had
about me, I am as good friends with
him as ever.

*Sir Charles.* I hope fo, Madam; otherwife the good luck I have had at play
would prove the greateft misfortune of
my life.

*Clarinda.* The devil's in the cards
to-night, I think! I never loft at
picquet in my life before; and now I
have thrown away——I cannot juftly
fay how much, but I'll fee.

She then turned to the table, and
poured out of a purfe what was remaining in it; and having counted the fum,
went on in the fame heat as before.

*Clarinda.* Yes, by Heaven I thought
fo!—No lefs than fix and twenty pieces!

*Sir Charles.* I fhould be forry, Madam, to give you any difquiet on the
fcore of fuch a trifle; but I can do no more
than offer you a chance for regaining all
you have loft. If you pleafe, I will
ftake the whole againft five of yours.

*Clarinda.* I fhould lofe that too, I
fuppofe.

*Ifmena.* Venture it, however. If
you lofe it, I'll be your halves, and fend
you the money to-morrow morning.

*Clarinda.* Well, then, I will make
one more effay.

With thefe words, fhe fat down again.
They played; fhe was the winner; and
now appeared as gay and happy as fhe
had lately been difcontented. Sir Charles
fmiled, with fome difdain, at this reverfe in her humour; and, turning to
Ifmena, faid—

*Sir Charles.* Now, Madam, you muft
take up the winner.

*Ifmena.* She muft give me credit,
then, Sir. You both know I have no
ftake to lay down.

*Clarinda.* You muft excufe me for
that, Madam; it may turn my luck. Befides, one has no heart to play, when
one does not fee the money on the table.

*Sir Charles.* Well, then, beautiful
Ifmena, I will give you credit; or, if
you pleafe, will play upon the fquare,
my honour againft yours.

*Ifmena.* With all my heart, Sir
Charles.

The ill-nature, the ill-manners, and,
indeed, the ingratitude of Clarinda, in
refufing to give the credit of a ftake at
cards to a friend who had juft before offered to pay half the loffes fhe fhould
fuftain in playing with another, made
that young lady as difagreeable in my
eyes, as the fweetnefs of difpofition and
generofity of the fprightly Ifmena made
her charming to a much greater degree
than ever fhe had appeared to me before;
all lovely, as it muft be confeffed fhe is.
But, to proceed. Ifmena having accepted the challenge of Sir Charles, fhe
tried once more what chance would do
for her: chance was ftill againft her, and
Sir Charles again the conqueror. The
game being over, fhe faid, laughing—

*Ifmena.* Well, I may now fing—
' Fortune is my foe;' and content myfelf, for the remainder of the night,
with being an humble fpectator, fince I
am not in a condition to play myfelf.

*Sir Charles.* It will be your own
fault, then, Madam, if you are. I believe I have an hundred and fome odd
pieces about me, which are all at your
fervice.

*Ifmena.* I thank you, Sir Charles;
but I do not chufe to rifque fo much
at one fitting. I do not care, however,
if I become your debtor for twenty
pieces.

*Sir Charles.* You do me a pleafure, Madam, in accepting any part of
the offer I made you. There is the
trifle you mention: if you want more, I
beg you will command it.

*Ifmena.* No, Sir, I am determined
to play no farther than this. I am much
obliged to you for the favour, and will
return it to-morrow morning.

*Sir Charles.* There is no occafion,
Madam. I have bufinefs your way to-
morrow morning; and, if you permit
me that honour, will wait on you about
twelve.

*Ifmena.* You may depend, Sir, on
my being at home.

Clarinda, who had not opened her
mouth all this time, no fooner faw her
fair friend receive the money, than fhe
laid her hand on hers, and, with a gay
air,

R 2

air, faid to her—' Now, my dear, I am
' ready for you, if you pleafe; and
' willing to venture as much with you
' as you have borrowed of Sir Charles.'
To this Ifmena replied, with more ferioufnefs than fhe was wont to put on—' No,
' Madam, I have been very unlucky here,
' and am refolved to change hands; I
' fee Lady Longmore has given out at
' the whift table yonder, I'll go and take
' her place.'

With thefe words, fhe rofe haftily
from her feat, and did as fhe had faid.
Sir Charles followed her to the other
table, and ftood behind her chair till he
faw her win more than the fum he had
lent her. On the company's breaking
up, fhe looked round the room for Sir
Charles, in order, as I fuppofe, to return
the money to him; but if fhe had any
fuch defign, he had taken care to prevent it, by leaving the place before fhe
had done playing. This action of Sir
Charles, joined to fome amorous glances
I had perceived him to regard her with,
made me fufpect he had fome farther
view than mere complaifance in what he
had done; but as he was generally accounted a man of honour, and fhe had
an unblemifhed character, I fufpended
my judgment till I fhould fee the event
of the vifit fhe promifed to receive from
him the next morning.

After I had quitted this fcene of gay
confufion, as Mr. Addifon elegantly expreffes it, and had time to ruminate on
the tranfactions that evening had prefented me with; Sir Charles and Ifmena
ran very much in my head, but did not
fo totally engrofs my attention, as to
make me negligent to all others. I had
heard feveral of the affembly fay to each
other, that Mifs Allmode was a moft
beautiful young creature, and would certainly be the reigning toaft of the town,
if not fpoiled by the affectation of her
mother; and this diftinct defcription
gave me a curiofity both to fee the girl,
and in what manner her felf-fufficient
ladyfhip behaved towards her. Accordingly I laid down a plan for my progreffion the next morning, which was
this: to go to Lady Allmode's early, and
from thence to Ifmena at the time Sir
Charles had appointed. I then began
to remember that the night was far advanced, and went to bed, as it is probable
fome of my readers may find it neceffary
to do at this time.

## CHAP. VI.

CONTAINS SUCH THINGS AS ARE
NOT OFTEN TO BE MET WITH,
NEITHER IN THE ONE NOR THE
OTHER SEX; YET ARE, OR AT
LEAST OUGHT TO BE, EQUALLY
INTERESTING TO BOTH.

I Rofe next morning more early than
I had been accuftomed to do, in order to prepare for my two vifits; but,
in fpite of all the expedition I could
practife, I found myfelf obliged to poft-
pone either the one or the other till another day. So much time was elapfed,
firft in tranfcribing what I had feen at
Lady Playfield's, and then in getting the
dialogues engraved on my Tablets expunged, by the pure fingers of my yet
unpolluted virgin; that, when all was
ready, the clock wanted but few minutes of twelve. I hefitated not whether
I fhould go to Lady Allmode's or to Ifmena; for, being prepoffeffed in favour
of the latter, I went thither in a lucky
time. Sir Charles Fairlove was juft ftepping out of his chair: I followed him up
ftairs; and Ifmena received him with
great gaiety, accompanied with an equal
air of modefty. As foon as they were
feated, fhe faid to him—

*Ifmena.* Your money was very fortunate, Sir Charles: I did not lofe one
guinea after I became your borrower.

*Sir Charles.* Madam, I congratulate
myfelf for being fo happy to ferve you,
though on fo infignificant an occafion;
but fhould be better pleafed to have it in
my power to do fo in much greater
things.

*Ifmena.* I doubt not of your generofity; and, if ever I am reduced to the
fame exigence again, it is likely may
have recourfe to the fame hand. In the
mean time, Sir Charles, let me return
the favour you have already conferred
upon me.

*Sir Charles.* This trifle, Madam, is
neither worth your returning nor my receiving; nor fhould I have ever thought
on it, if I had not given you credit on an
infinitely more valuable account.

*Ifmena.* Credit! As how, Sir Charles?

*Sir Charles.* Yes, Madam, a debt I
am too impatient to wait long for the
payment of, and am come to claim.

*Ifmena.* You really well, Sir Charles;
but,

but, as I cannot comprehend the purport, am not prepared to give an answer.

*Sir Charles.* No, i'faith, Madam, you will find me extremely serious; sure you cannot be so strangely forgetful as not to recollect what you lost to me last night at play?

*Ismena.* I lost nothing but what I paid, Sir Charles.

*Sir Charles.* Nothing, Madam?

*Ismena.* No, upon my honour.

*Sir Charles.* You have named the very thing—your honour, Madam. When a lady ventures her honour at a gaming-table, and is so unlucky to lose, she must expect to pay the forfeit.

*Ismena.* What do you mean, Sir Charles?

*Sir Charles.* My meaning needs no explanation, Madam; you lost your honour to me, and I now demand the immediate possession of what I fairly won.

*Ismena.* Ridiculous!

*Sir Charles.* Madam, the contempt with which you treat my pretensions will not take away the validity of them. What was once your honour, is now no longer so, but mine, and at my disposal; and you would not, sure, go about to defraud me of the good that Fortune has bestowed upon me?

With these words, he threw his arms about her waist, with a freedom, which shewed he indeed looked upon her as his own: she seemed a little alarmed at this action, and, starting from him, endeavoured to repulse the temerity he was guilty of, by saying to him—

*Ismena.* Forbear; this fooling is offensive.

*Sir Charles.* Madam, this coyness is trifling; I am surprized you will oblige me to have recourse to force for what is so much my due, and I should set a higher value upon if chearfully resigned.

He then catched hold of her a second time, and made an offer to bear her into another room: the grasp he had taken of her, was not so strenuous, however, but that she easily disengaged herself; and, having done so, cried out with a voice and air full of the extremest disdain—

*Ismena.* Till this action, I scarce could think you were in earnest. Base, presuming man, how dare you entertain thoughts so unworthy of me!

*Sir Charles.* How dare you, Madam, hazard on the chance of a game at cards what seems so precious to you?

*Ismena.* Oh, despicable! to turn that

into a matter of seriousness which was only meant in jest!

*Sir Charles.* We men, Madam, take all the advantages we can, when we play with a fine woman; and you may be assured, I shall not easily be prevailed upon to relinquish those I have gained over you.

*Ismena.* The vain idea will little avail your vile purpose.

*Sir Charles.* You may be mistaken, Madam: the laws of Westminster Hall, indeed, will scarcely take any cognizance of an affair of this nature; but those laws by which the polite world are governed, I mean the laws of gaming, will infallibly give it on my side. That pride of yours will be humbled, when you see your stake of honour become the publick jest, and all that has passed between us the subject of a news-paper.

*Ismena.* I am confounded! You cannot certainly be the monster you appear!

*Sir Charles.* I would not wish you, Madam, to put me to the proof.

*Ismena.* Oh, Heavens! to what has one unguarded word exposed me!

She could not utter this exclamation without letting fall some tears, which I perceived had a great effect on Sir Charles, by the change it occasioned in his countenance: he affected, however, to take no notice of it, and resuming his former boldness, went on—

*Sir Charles.* You see, Madam, how it is; you are entirely in my power; and, if I cannot have my agreement, I will have my revenge, or at least an equivalent for both.

*Ismena.* What equivalent!

*Sir Charles.* You must redeem your forfeited honour by a sum of money.

*Ismena.* Name it, then.

*Sir Charles.* Let me consider, Madam—a woman's honour, as times now are, and beauty renders itself so cheap, will bear but a low price at the market; but, as you are well-born, well accomplished, are extremely handsome, and have more perfections than most of your sex can boast of, I think five hundred pounds is the least I can demand.

*Ismena.* You shall have it, Sir.

With this, she ran hastily to a little cabinet that stood in the room, and having taken from thence what she wanted, turned again to the table, saying—

*Ismena.* Those two Bank-bills, Sir, contain the sum you mentio; take them, and ease me of your presence.

*Sir Charles.* I must first examine, Madam,

Madam, if they are genuine: yes, they are right; and now, methinks, 'tis pity to rob you of so much money; five hundred pounds will purchase five hundred pretty trinkets, and I cannot receive it without feeling some concern.

*Ismena.* Oh, you need be under no concern on that score; were it five times the sum, I would gladly give it to be rid for ever, both of you and your impudent demand.

*Sir Charles.* Yet, in spite of all this severity, I shall willingly restore these bills on one condition.

*Ismena.* Sir, I shall make no conditions with you; therefore, be gone, and leave me.

*Sir Charles.* Not till you have heard me, Madam. The condition I would stipulate, is only this, that you will make a solemn promise never to play again, except for mere diversion, with some select friends, who you are certain will take no ungenerous advantage of you.

*Ismena.* There is little occasion for me to bind myself by a promise to avoid a thing which has already proved so mischievous: the insults I have received from you, will make me detest the sight of cards, and fly the society of all who pursue that dangerous amusement.

*Sir Charles.* It is enough; my ends are answered: and thus, on my knees, let me restore your bills, and with them, a heart which long has been devoted to you, and never harboured a wish to your dishonour.

Never had I known greater anxiety for any thing not relating to myself, or my particular friends, than I did for the issue of this conversation. I had been extremely scandalized at some part of Sir Charles's behaviour; yet, by many indications, could not set him down in my mind for the mercenary villain he affected to be; and was now as much rejoiced to see a likelihood of not having been deceived in my conjectures in his favour, as the reader will presently be convinced. Ismena, being too much amazed at this sudden turn to make an immediate reply, he went on thus, still kneeling—

*Sir Charles.* Oh, Ismena, forgive the seeming brutality I have been guilty of; I counterfeited the libertine, the villain, only to shew you there was a possibility for you to have met with such a one in reality; and assumed the most odious character, in order to render yours more

truly amiable. The tender passion you inspired me with, has made me keep a watchful eye over all your actions. I found you perfect in every thing except a too great readiness to follow the example of others in the destructive love of play. I know the dangers to which your sex are exposed by it, and that there were many snares spread for your innocence in particular; by this means, even last night, there were some in company who wanted but the same opportunity I had to behave as I have done, though with far different views. Oh! pardon, therefore, the only stratagem I could think of to clear your mind of a propensity which might in time have sullied all it's brightness.

*Ismena.* Rise, Sir Charles; the diversity, I might say, indeed, the perplexity of my thoughts, hindered me, till now, from observing the posture you were in. Pray be seated, Sir. If I may give credit to your words, I am infinitely obliged to you for the care you took of my reputation, when you saw it so totally neglected by myself.

*Sir Charles.* No, Madam, say not so; I dare believe you never have failed in a due regard for your reputation, and am certain that the breath of slander has never presumed to blast it; and I could not mean to reproach you for any thing that has been, but to warn you against what might be. An immoderate inclination for gaming in your sex, I take to be the same as an immoderate inclination to drinking is in ours: both are equally intoxicating and destructive to right reason; they make the brain grow giddy, incapable of reflection, or any other pursuit than the darling folly; and they run headlong on, enveloped in a mist of errors, where fortune, fame, and peace of mind, are sometimes irrecoverably lost.

*Ismena.* Oh, Sir Charles, you have opened my eyes to see what my inadvertency might one day have plunged me in.

*Sir Charles.* I know very well, Madam, you wanted only to be reminded of the danger, to enable you to avoid it. The manner in which I have done so, may have, perhaps, appeared too presuming; but I feared more gentle methods might not have had the effect.

*Ismena.* Make no apologies, Sir Charles; I am now convinced you meant me well, and I thank you for it.

*Sir Charles.* If you accept it as a proof of friendship, it may in time engage

gage you to believe, that a sincere and tender friendship in a person of my sex to one of yours, deserves a softer name, and call it love.

*Ismena.* We will not cavil about names; but must acknowledge, Sir Charles, by what motive soever you have been actuated, the benefit is mine.

*Sir Charles.* How bless'd am I in this confession! But, charming Ismena, may I not be permitted to wait on you sometimes, and have leave to hope the services I shall hereafter pay will not be rejected?

*Ismena.* I flatter myself with being able to regulate my future conduct, so as not to give you occasion to offer any of that frightful sort you have done this morning; and, if I should relapse into my former errors, could neither expect nor deserve you should take the same trouble for my reformation.

She spoke these words with so obliging a smile, that Sir Charles could not forbear testifying the transport he was in, by imprinting several passionate kisses on one of her hands; after which, looking on her with an equal mixture of tenderness and respect, he said—

*Sir Charles.* Incomparable Ismena! how impossible is it for me to express either what you deserve, or what I feel in a full sensibility of your perfections!

*Ismena.* I desire you will not go about to express either the one or the other. The only merit I can boast of is, in being so early convinced of my fault; and that I am so, is wholly owing to yourself. For I confess to you, Sir Charles, that though it is but lately I have begun to like play at all, yet, by conversing with those who seem to have no other way of passing their time, it grew by very swift degrees more pleasing to me; and I believe that it would, in time, have become so habitual to me, that I should have expected the hour of sitting down to cards as naturally as that of sitting down to dinner. But, in the mirror you have presented to me, I now see, that to indulge this amusement to an excess, is not only a folly below the dignity of a thinking mind, but also a kind of Scylla or Charybdis, formed by ourselves in the ocean of life, as if on purpose to wreck our fortunes, honour, reputation, and every thing that is dear.

*Sir Charles.* Oh, Madam! every word you speak on this occasion thrills me to the very soul; I am charmed, I am ravished to find in you such solid reason, such an amazing quickness of apprehension.

*Ismena.* You are relapsing into the panegyrick strain; but I will hear no more of it. You must give me leave to play the monitor in my turn; I have been your convert, and you must now be mine. Remember, Sir Charles, that to listen to the tongue of flattery, is no less pernicious than the folly you have taught me to be ashamed of.

*Sir Charles.* I grant it, Madam; but the just praises of real virtue cannot cause a blush either in the face of the giver or receiver.

*Ismena.* Well, I find you will have the better of the argument, whether the tenet you take upon you to maintain be right or wrong; therefore, to put an end to it, what think you of a turn or two in the Mall this morning?

*Sir Charles.* Madam, I shall be happy to attend you any where.

She then called for her capuchin and little muff; which being immediately brought, Sir Charles gave her his hand to lead her down stairs, and I retired to my apartment.

I had met with nothing a great while that gave me a more sensible satisfaction, than to find a lady, in all the pride of blooming youth, beautiful, gay, and surrounded with a crowd of flatterers, bear with so much chearfulness the conviction of her error, and testify so much gratitude to the person to whom she was indebted for her reformation. The rough method he had taken for this purpose, was so far from raising any resentment in her, after once knowing the motive, that she looked upon him as her best friend, esteemed, and loved him for it; conscious that it required no less than such a proceeding to rouze her from that thoughtlessness which alone had made her fall into an error, the danger of which she might otherwise have too late perceived.

I thought I had discovered something in these two accomplished persons, that seemed to me as if Heaven had ordained them for each other, and I soon found I had not been mistaken. They are now married with the highest approbation of all friends on both sides; and, in the opinion of as many as have the pleasure of of their acquaintance, bid fair to be one of the moſt happy pairs that ever entered into Hymen's bands.

## CHAP. VII.

THE AUTHOR HAS BEEN IN SOME DEBATE WITHIN HIMSELF, WHETHER HE SHOULD INSERT OR NOT, AS HE IS CONSCIOUS IT WILL BE LITTLE RELISHED BY THE FASHIONABLE GENTEEL PART OF HIS READERS.

THERE is ſomething very unaccountable in an over-curious diſpoſition; it makes us eager, impatient, anxious, indefatigable, in prying into things which promiſe us not the leaſt pleaſure in the diſcovery of when known. A reader who has not this propenſity in his nature, will doubtleſs think, by what I ſaid of Lady Allmode in the fifth chapter, that I had already ſeen enough of her behaviour to keep me from being deſirous of ſeeing more. But as every one is willing to find ſome excuſe or other, even for the ſillieſt things he can be guilty of, ſo I thought, that in being a ſpectator of Lady Allmode's conduct in her own family, and the manner in which ſhe trained up her daughter, ſomething might preſent itſelf to me that would more than compenſate for the time I ſhould expend in going to her houſe.

Accordingly I went, and gained an eaſy acceſs, the door happening to be open juſt as I reached it, to let out a footman in a gay livery, who had come to deliver ſome meſſage; but was a good deal bewildered on my entrance, as I had never been in the houſe before, and was entirely unacquainted with the ſituation of any of the rooms. The meaſure of time is always doubled when we wait for an event with impatience. I remained not long, however, in this dilemma: a ſervant running haſtily up the back ſtairs, with ſome drinking glaſſes on a ſilver waiter in his hand, I followed him into a room where a woman, by her appearance, I gueſſed was her ladyſhip's Abigail, received from him what he brought, and carried it into an inner chamber, the door of which ſhe ſhut after her, but not ſo ſuddenly as to prevent my entering with her.

Here I found Lady Allmode; but had ſhe appeared to me in any other place, ſhould never have known her for the ſame I had ſeen at Lady Playfield's route; ſo vaſt a difference is it in the power of art ſometimes to make. At the time of my coming in, ſhe was under the operation of having her eyebrows ſhaped with a ſmall pair of pincers, by one of thoſe perſons who go by the name of tyre-women; but, in my opinion, ought rather to be called facemenders, ſince their buſineſs is not ſo much to ornament the head as to rectify the defects of the features. The important work being over, Lady Allmode turned to a magnifier that ſtood upon her toilet, to ſee if all was right; and having looked into it, cried out haſtily—

*Lady.* Oh, Mrs. Prim, ſure your eyes are in eclipſe to-day! you have left no leſs than three exuberant hairs on my right brow, and I think arch'd it ſomewhat higher than the other.

*Mrs. Prim.* I beg pardon of your ladyſhip, but I will preſently remedy that error.

On this the artiſt employed her little inſtrument for a ſecond eſſay; after which Lady Allmode looked in the glaſs again, and ſaid—

*Lady.* It is very well now; but I look wretchedly to-day, and it is no wonder. What do you think, Mrs. Prim? That careleſs oat there put me to bed laſt night without my ſpermaceti maſk.

*Mrs. Prim.* That was a great omiſſion, indeed, Madam; but your ladyſhip muſt forgive it, Mrs. Pinup does not uſe to neglect theſe things.

*Pinup.* I am very ſorry for it, Mrs. Prim; but it was ſo late when her ladyſhip went to bed, and her ladyſhip was ſo ſleepy.

*Lady.* And your foolſhip ſo ſleepy too, I ſuppoſe. But that is not all, Mrs. Prim; the creature threw it into ſome corner or other where Veni got at it, and this morning it was found half devoured.

*Pinup.* Your ladyſhip knows I have almoſt cried my eyes out about it, and that I offered to beſpeak another, and pay for it out of my own pocket.

*Lady.* Pay for it, ideot!—But tell me, creature, what atonement can'ſt thou ever make for theſe depredations on my countenance? Here I ſhall loſe a whole day; for 'tis impoſſible I can think of appearing in publick.

*Mrs. Prim.*

*Mrs. Prim.* I dare anfwer for Mrs. Pinup, that fhe will never be guilty of the like fault again; therefore I beg your ladyfhip will forgive her.

*Lady.* Yes, yes, I have forgiven her, and I do forgive her; but fhe muft expect to be told of it fometimes: if fhe had lived with fome ladies, they would have turned her out of doors that inftant; *mais toujours les douceurs du cour* lay an embargo on my indignation.

*Pinup.* Your ladyfhip is all good-nefs.

*Lady.* Well, well, fay no more about it; I am forry I ftuck you; but take the Drefden fuit I had on yefterday, and let me fee you in it.

*Pinup.* I humbly thank your lady-fhip.

*Lady.* Say no more of it. Oh, *mon Dieu!* I begin to feel the effects of my difconcertion; every membrane through my whole frame has a pulfation in it; give me fomething to take this inftant, or I fhall faint. But as to the fpermaceti mafk, is it not poffible for you to get one ready for me before I fleep, elfe my face will be a perfect nutmeg-grater by to-morrow morning?

*Mrs. Prim.* Oh, your ladyfhip need be under no apprehenfion on that fcore, I always keep feveral; they want only fprinkling with a little orange-flower water, to take off the fcent; I will fend your ladyfhip one this afternoon. Has your ladyfhip any farther commands?

*Lady.* Yes, you may fend me a box of red for my cheeks; but do not let it be quite fo high-coloured as the laft.

*Mrs. Prim.* I fhall take care to mix it fo as to pleafe your ladyfhip.—In fpeaking this, fhe made her exit with abundance of low curtfies.

Pinup was returning to her lady's chamber, but met her juft coming out, in order to pafs into another room: on feeing her fhe faid to her—

*Lady.* I think this girl takes a long time in dreffing; go and fee if fhe is ready, and bid her come to me.

Finding now that there was fome pro-bability of my feeing the young lady, which had been, indeed, the chief mo-tive of my going thither, I attended Lady Allmode where fhe went, and placed myfelf in one corner of the room; where I did not wait above three or four mi-nutes before Pinup, who had gone im-mediately on her errand, returned lead-ing Mifs Allmode. She feemed to be

about fourteen years of age; her face was extremely pretty, and I believe na-ture had given her a fhape no lefs excel-lent, if it had not been d.formed by her ftay-maker. On her approach, Lady Allmode took her by the arm, turned her round feveral times, and examined her whole drefs from head to foot; after which, looking very well pleafed, fhe faid—

*Lady.* Ay, Mifs, now you look like what you are; I proteft, I fcarce knew you for my own child, in the obfolete condition you came from the country. Are you not highly delighted with your-felf?

*Mifs.* No, indeed, Madam; I think, fince 'tis the fafhion to have one's cloaths made in this manner, there ought to be as many chimnies in a room as there are chairs.

*Lady.* Sure, Mifs, you are not cold?

*Mifs.* It would be very ftrange, Ma-dam, if I were not, when my ftays are fo contrived that the air comes down to the very bottom of my back, and below the pit of my ftomach; and my petti-coats fo fhort, th t I am every minute fancying I have tucked them up in or-der to have my legs and feet wafhed; then as to my ears, I do declare I feel the wind blow from the one to the other, and pierces into my very brain.

*Lady.* O fye, Mifs; this being in the country has fpoiled you. Whatever is the fafhion is never either too cold or too hot.

*Mifs.* I muft beg your ladyfhip's pardon; for I am certain this fafhion is a great deal too much of both. The tightnefs of my fleeves, the load of flounces at my elbow, and the huge femi-circles, as heavy as panniers, hanging on each hip, make fome parts of me fweat, while all the reft are freezing.

*Lady.* Oh hideous! Frightful!—Sweat! What a word is there from the mouth of a fine young lady! Whenever you have occafion to complain of too much warmth, you fhould always fay, I perfpire. But I am furprized you fhould not be charmed with fo becoming a drefs.

*Mifs.* I feel uneafy, and quite un-comfortable, Madam.

*Lady.* A little ufe will reconcile you to it. Without vanity, Mifs, you are exceeding handfome; and now I have made you fit to appear in publick, the praifes that will be given you, and the

S                                    fine

fine things said to you, will raise such a gaieté du coeur, as will make you forget all that you call uncomfortable.

*Miss.* I should be glad, Madam, if any thing would do that.

*Lady.* You must learn to know yourself, Miss. Look in the glass; you have fine eyes, a very lovely mouth, a well-turned face, a delicate complexion, good hair; in fine, you are a compleat beauty. But what is beauty without the possessor understands how to manage it to advantage? A milk-maid may be a beauty, and no one take any notice of her. You must practise the art of displaying every charm, and rendering yourself conspicuous.

*Miss.* Indeed, Madam, I am quite ignorant of these things.

*Lady.* I perceive you are, Miss; but that is not your fault; my formal aunt has never given you any instructions in this point, I suppose: a few lessons, however, will soon put you in the way to make the most of what nature has bestowed upon you. In the first place, Miss, you must be sure to thrust out your chin as far as you are able; when you come into a room, always let your chin be the first thing seen of you, as if it were the harbinger of the rest of your person. Secondly, you must never keep your two hands together, in that stiff country manner you now do, for above the space of a moment; but throw sometimes the one and sometimes the other carelessly back, and lean it on your hip; but when you are speaking, be sure you employ both in gestures that may enforce attention to what you say. Then, as for your eyes, Miss, you must always keep them broad open, and be sure to have the last look of every one that takes notice of you.

*Miss.* Does your ladyship mean the men as well as the women?

*Lady.* Undoubtedly, the men to chuse. A polite woman, and who is fashionably genteel, is never ashamed of any thing she either sees or hears.

Her ladyship was going on with some farther directions concerning the management of the eyes, when she was interrupted by a footman, who came to acquaint her, that a person who called himself Monsieur Le Petit Solee had brought her ladyship a dozen pair of French shoes; on which she cried out in a kind of transport—'Oh, bring him up! bring him up this minute! I have been in-volved in the utmost distress; I have had nothing but odious English shoes upon my feet for a whole week past.'

As I was now heartily weary of my situation, and had no curiosity to see either Monsieur Le Petit Solee, or his French shoes, I took the opportunity of the door being open, and left this scene of folly and affectation, regretting the time I had thrown away in being there.

## CHAP. VIII.

WHEREIN THE POWER OF BEAUTY, WHEN ACCOMPANIED WITH VIRTUE, IS DISPLAYED, IN A VERY REMARKABLE, AS WELL AS AFFECTING OCCURRENCE.

VANITY, though placed rather among the follies than the vices of human nature, is yet sometimes productive of the very worst we can be guilty of; and the least mischief it does, when indulged to an excess, is to render the person possessed of it obstinate, proud, impatient of contradiction, deaf to reproof, full of imaginary merit, and apt to despise what is truly so in another. This weakness, to give it no worse a name, is generally ascribed to the softer sex; who being from their very childhood accustomed to flattery and praise, are too ready to believe they are in reality the angels and goddesses they are told they are: but, in my opinion, it is doing great injustice to the ladies, to say they are the only culpable; since we often find men who, without having the same excuse, are no less liable to fall into the same error.

Mutantius is one of the most graceful and most accomplished gentlemen of the present age. He has learning, wit, honour, generosity, and good-nature. In fine, he is such as might give him a just title to universal admiration, were he but a little less conscious of deserving it. To render his fine qualities yet more conspicuous, he had the advantages of being descended from a very ancient family, and in possession of an ample fortune. He had not long been arrived at age, before several considerable matches were proposed to him: all the men of his acquaintance, who had sisters or daughters, courted his alliance.' Whenever he appeared, the ladies put on their best

best looks; and not a few there were, who could not help betraying by their eyes the secret languishment of their hearts.

Having his choice of so many, was probably the cause that for a long time hindered him from attaching himself to any particular object. He was polite and gallant to all, but made a serious address to none. He would pay his morning devoirs to one, walk in the Mall with another, dine with a third, drink tea with a fourth, attend a fifth to the play, or some other publick entertainment: in a word, he divided his respects so equally between each, that no one had reason either to exult on the power of her own charms, or dread those of her competitors. The little deity of soft desires would not, however, suffer a man so formed for love to remain always among the number of insensibles. At length, a glance shot from Aristella's eyes was a dart that reached his very soul; all the different graces he had seen in other beauties, seemed now to him to be summed up in her.

Aristella was, indeed, very lovely, and had been well educated; but her father, by gaming and other extravagancies, had reduced his estate so low, that when divided between four daughters, which he left at his decease, the income was scarce sufficient to buy them cloaths according to their birth. Two of them, however, were married to tradesmen of good repute in the city; and a third to a gentleman of a small estate in the country. Aristella, who was the youngest, and the only one unprovided for, lived sometimes with one, and sometimes with another, of the sisters; and by this means, having few expences besides her dress, was enabled to appear in as genteel a manner as any woman of a moderate fortune could do.

It was at the house of one of her brother-in-law's, who was a linen-draper, and served Mutantius with hollands and cambricks, that he first beheld her. Happening to call there when the master was abroad, he was desired to walk into the parlour till his return. Aristella was at work with her sister when he came in; but the latter, knowing he was a good customer, threw aside what she was about, and received him with a great deal of politeness. Her husband not coming home so soon as he was expected, she made tea. Mutantius readily accepted the little regale she presented to him, as it gave him an opportunity of feasting his eyes on her fair sister. On their entering into conversation, the tongue of Aristella lost her nothing of what her eyes had gained; and as her beauty had in an instant captivated his heart, so her wit rivetted the chain, and made the conquest sure.

The tradesman at last returning, Mutantius, after having agreed for some things he wanted in the shop, and ordered them to be sent home, took an unwilling leave; but carried with him an idea, which had afterwards more influence than he at first imagined. Love, in it's beginnings, plays wantonly about the heart, tickling it with flattering images; but having once got full possession there, rules with tyrannick sway, and bears down all before it. Mutantius indulged the pleasing contemplation of Aristella's beauty till he was no longer able to live without seeing her, and for this purpose went again to the linen-draper's, pretending there were some things he had forgot to bespeak when he was there before. After having bought those things which the seeming want of had given him an excuse for going thither so soon again, and some previous discourse on ordinary matters, he told the draper that he should be glad to have his wife's advice concerning the trimming of some shirts which were then making for him. To this the other replied, that his wife would think herself honoured in doing him any service, but that she was at that time unfortunately abroad.

Mutantius was not sorry to hear she was out of the way; and resumed, briskly—'Well, then, I think it will be 'equal to me, if the young lady who 'was with her when I had the pleasure 'of drinking tea here, will do me that 'favour; she seemed, I thought, to 'have good-nature enough to grant 'such a request.'—'You mean my sis-'ter, Sir,' cried the draper. 'I think 'your wife called her so,' answered Mutantius. 'Yes, Sir,' rejoined the former; 'but she is gone down to Kent 'this morning.'—'I thought she had 'lived with you,' said Mutantius. 'Not 'constantly, Sir,' replied he; 'but she 'has left us now sooner than she would 'have done, on account of her sister's 'lying-in.'

It was easy for a man of so much wit,

and of so much design as Mutantius now had in his head, to get from the honest, unsuspecting draper, all he wanted to he informed of in relation to the circumstances of Aristella. As the inclinations of this gentleman, vehemently amorous as they were, had not at present the least tendency to marriage with the young beauty, concerning whose affairs he had been so inquisitive, he was far from being mortified on hearing she had no fortune, and was in a manner dependant upon her kindred; nor thought it less conducive to the interest of his passion that she was removed into the country, where he imagined he might find a more easy method of winning her to his desires than he could have done in town, under the eye of a sister who, by the little he had seen of her, he perceived to be a woman of great discretion. He lost no time; but the very next day, attended by one servant, posted down to Canterbury, within a quarter of a mile of which city Aristella at present resided.

Having no acquaintance in that part of the country, he took up his lodgings in one of the best inns; where pretending that it was mere curiosity to see that ancient city which had brought him thither several offered to accompany him to those places which most deserved the attention of a traveller. Among the number of these hospitable persons was the brother-in-law of Aristella. It is easy to suppose that Mutanius made use of all the arts he was master of to insinuate himself into the good graces of a person whose acquaintance was so necessary to his design: and, indeed, had not this accident happened, there seemed little probability of his accomplishing them; for Aristella kept so close in the house, that though he had been four days at Canterbury, and taken all imaginable pains to get a glimpse of her, he never yet had been so happy.

Mutantius had something in him no less engaging to the men, than enchanting to the women: he knows how to suit himself to the humour of every one he converses with; it was therefore not difficult for him to cultivate a friendship with a plain country gentleman, who, free from all guile, was equally free from all distrust. Beechly, for so he was called, had no other fault than loving his bottle too well; which Mutantius perceiving,

fell in with this foible, and thereby gained his whole heart.

These two gentlemen drinking together very late, Mutantius had plied the other so fast with glasses, that he became more than ordinarily intoxicated. Our lover obliged him to suffer himself to be attended home by his footman, and the next morning sent a polite message to enquire of his health. Beechly took this so kindly, that he came immediately after to the lodgings of Mutantius, to shew that he was well, and to desire he would do him the honour of dining with him that day. ' My wife,' said he, ' is in the straw: but she has a sister, who ' is at present with us; a good, smart, ' well behaved girl, and will receive you ' in the best manner she is able.'

It is not to be doubted, but that the heart of Mutantius fluttered with the most rapturous sensation, on hearing himself invited to a place where he was sure of enjoying the company of her he so much languished for, and had taken such pains to pursue. It is needless to say that he readily accepted so obliging a summons; nor that he prolonged the hour of complying with it. He was met by Beechly, at the gate, with all imaginable demonstrations of a sincere welcome, and conducted into the parlour; where Aristella, who soon after entered, was presented to him.

Whatever emotions Mutantius might feel in approaching to salute her, they were yet inferior to hers, in the first surprize of seeing him there. She had heard her brother Beechly talk of a fine gentleman lately come to Canterbury, and had had that morning received orders from him to prepare a handsome dinner for his entertainment; but as she had not heard him mention the name of his new friend, and had no curiosity to ask any thing concerning him, could little expect he was the same she had seen at her other sister's in London. She had, it seems, from the first interview with him, been possessed of sentiments in his favour; which, if not altogether so passionate as those she inspired him with, were yet no less soft and tender: but, conscious of the vast disparity between their fortunes, she had endeavoured to check the growth of an inclination which she thought could only be destructive of her peace. But on this second and unexpected meeting him again, the fled

wishes

wishes of her soul burst out afresh; a sudden flow of joy rushed over her heart; which, joined to the surprize she was in, spread a kind of will, though agreeable confusion, in her eyes and voice, while she made him those compliments which civility exacted from her to a stranger.

Mutantius, to whose penetrating eyes the change in her countenance was very visible, looked on it as a happy presage of the success of his designs, and the secret pleasure this imagination gave him, brightened all his air, and added new graces to every thing he said or did; so that Aristella became now quite lost in love and admiration. This day proved, indeed, extremely fortunate to Mutantius: dinner was no sooner over, than Beechly was called out to a person who waited to speak with him on some business in another room; the lover took this opportunity of declaring his passion to his mistress, and relating to her the pains he had taken to get a sight of her; and the answers she made, though very modest and discreet, were such as gave him no reason to despair. Beechly returning he broke off their conversation: he took Mutantius to shew him his garden; which, though not ornamented with statues, nor any exotick curiosities, were very pretty. Mutantius was lavish in his praises on every thing he saw; but, above all, his fancy seemed taken with a long grass walk, and a close arbour at the end of it. 'If I had such a walk as this in town,' said he, 'I should never trouble the Mall, Vauxhall, nor Ranelagh.'—'Since you cannot carry this with you,' replied Beechly, 'you shall be extremely welcome to make as much use of it as you think fit, while you stay in this part of the world.'

Mutantius thanked him; but said he was an early riser, and should chuse such a walk chiefly for the sake of meditation in a morning, and that to come at such hours might give too much trouble to the servants. 'I can easily remedy that difficulty, since you make it one,' answered the other. 'There is a door that opens behind the arbour into a little field, where I keep a cow: I seldom have occasion to make use of the key, and it is at your service; so you may come in as early or as late as you please, without disturbing any of my family, or being disturbed by them.'

The lover made a thousand acknowledgme ts to him for this favour, and received the key; which, in his mind, he looked upon as a sure passport to all the happiness he wished at present to enjoy.

He went the next morning, taking a hook in his hand, to prevent suspicion, in case he should be seen; though there was no great danger of that, as Beechly kept but two maids, and one man servant; who, it might be supposed, had too much business in a morning to ramble in the garden: but he might reasonably hope to meet with Aristella; who, having nothing to employ her time, might probably amuse some part of it in that agreeable place. It is likely, however, he might have been disappointed for many days together, if Fortune had not now befriended him, as she had hitherto done during the course of this adventure.

Aristella was there, indeed, before him, in the same walk, and very near the arbour through which he entered. She had come thither to gather cinquefoil for her sister, the nurse who attended her being apprehensive she would fall into a feverish disorder. It is likely she was little less surprized, on seeing him in that place, than she had been when introduced to him by her brother; but as I was not present, and have this part of the story from the report of others, can relate nothing of the particulars of their discourse; and only say, in general, that he spared no vows nor protestations to convince her of his passion; and that he prevailed on her to return to him again after having carried in the herbs. His entreaties, joined to her own secret inclinations, engaged her to see him the next day. This meeting was succeeded by another, that by a third, and so on for several mornings together, every one of them still more endearing him to her affections; but. in spite of the pleasure she took in his addresses, she could not keep herself from some doubt of the sincerity of his passion, whenever she reflected on the inequality of their fortunes. One day, expressing herself very emphatically on that occasion, he cried out—'Talk not of fortune; by Heaven, your heart is all I wish!' This he repeated so often, and so tenderly, that she at length confessed it was already his.

Having brought her to this point, he now thought proper to let her know the real

real aim of all his courtſhip: he began with telling her, that beauty ſuch as hers merited to be ſet off with all the advantages of dreſs and grandeur; that ſhe had waſted too much of her youth on a mean dependance on her kindred; and concluded with the offer of a large ſettlement; proteſting to her, at the ſame time, that he would never marry any other woman, and that ſhe ſhould live in every thing like his wife except the name.

If a dagger had pierced the gentle breaſt of Ariſtella, it could not have given her more pain than did this cruel declaration. For ſome moments ſhe was unable to make any reply, but burſt into a flood of tears, and diſcovered all the ſymptoms of the moſt violent grief. He endeavoured to calm this tempeſt in her mind by all the arts that love and wit could inſpire: but all was now in vain; a virtuous pride, by degrees, got the better of her ſorrows; and, ſtarting from him, ſhe cried out—' Deceitful ' and ungenerous man! think not that ' your baſe deſires ſhall triumph over the ' weakneſs I have confeſſed for you!— ' No, I will never ſee you more; nor ' henceforward think of you but with ' horror and deteſtation!'

In ſpeaking theſe words, ſhe flew out of the arbour. Rage gave wings to her feet; yet Mutantius would certainly have overtaken her, if the ſight of a man whom Beechly had employed to do ſome work in the garden had not made him turn back. He went to his lodgings much diſconcerted at this accident; but the knowledge he had of Ariſtella's affection for him, kept him from totally deſpairing. He repaired to the arbour next morning, but no Ariſtella appeared; he went again, but had no better ſucceſs. Reſolved to ſee her, if poſſible, he made a viſit at the houſe, and told Beechly, in a free manner, that he was come to take a ſecond dinner with him; to which he replied with a compliment ſuitable to the occaſion.

Mutantius was again diſappointed: Ariſtella, hearing he was there, ſent word to her brother that ſhe had a violent tooth-ache, and deſired he would excuſe her from coming down. This drove the lover almoſt to diſtraction: he went home, wrote to her, and made his footman go, as of his own accord, to chat with the ſervants, and loiter about the houſe till he ſhould ſee Ariſtella, and

deliver the letter to her. The fellow found means to execute his commiſſion; Ariſtella took the letter on his preſenting it to her, and went up into her chamber; but, after reflecting a little, would not truſt her own heart ſo far as to read this dangerous epiſtle: ſhe therefore put it under a cover; and, having ſealed and directed it, came down, and gave it to the man, ſaying—' There's my anſwer ' to your maſter's letter.'

Never had the vanity of Mutantius met with ſo ſevere a ſhock; yet could he not forbear revering the virtue he attempted to deſtroy. If before he loved, he now adored her; and the more he conſidered her perfections, the more he found her worthy to be his wife; yet, when he thought of marriage, the idea of that ſtate was irkſome to him. He knew that at preſent he was the idol of the fair, but ſhould ceaſe to be ſo if once he became a huſband. He could not bear to loſe his darling admiration, yet was equally unable to bear life without the enjoyment of Ariſtella. After ſome debate within himſelf, his paſſion, however, got the better of his vanity; and he reſolved to marry Ariſtella; but which way to let her know he meant to do ſo, ſeemed as great a difficulty as any he had paſſed through in attempting to ſeduce her: he was convinced ſhe would neither ſee him, nor receive a letter from him; yet, in ſpite of all this, Love, fertile in contrivances, put a ſtratagem into his head which had the deſired effect: it was this—

Beechly's new-born ſon had not been yet baptized, on account of the mother's having been more than ordinarily indiſpoſed during her lying-in. He offered to be one of the ſponſors, which the other gladly accepted. Ariſtella could not now avoid his preſence; but behaved with ſo much reſerve, ſcarce ever looking towards him, that a man leſs conſcious of his own merit might have been abaſhed. After ſome time, when moſt of the company were engaged in converſation, he found an opportunity to ſay to her—' Madam, I beſeech you will ' forgive the raſh propoſal I preſumed ' to make you; be aſſured I have hear- ' tily repented of it, and have now no ' deſigns upon you but what are truly ' honourable.' To which ſhe replied— ' Sir, I ſhall never believe a man means ' me well, who has once thought ſo ' poorly of me.'—' I only beg,' re- turned famed he, ' the liberty of entertaining ' you once more in private; and if what ' I have then to fay does not merit your ' pardon and favour, I fhall leave Can- ' terbury, and perhaps the world, for ' ever.' He could add no more at that time, Beechly calling him to pledge him in a bumber to the young Chriftian; but, before they parted, he found means to enforce what he had laft faid with fo moving an air, that fhe confented to fee him the next morning.

The confequence of this interview was a full forgivenefs of what was paft on the fide of Ariftella; and on that of Mutantius, a folemn vow of making her his wife the moment fhe confented to be fo: but added, that there were feme circumftances in his affairs which requir. d their marriage fhould be kept fecret for a time. To this laft article fhe made no direct anfwer, at prefent; but the next day, when they met again by appointment, fuffered herfelf to be overcome by his perfuafions, and promifed that every thing fhould be as he would have it. It was at laft agreed upon between them, that he fhould return to London in a few days; and that fhe fhould follow, as foon as her fifter's recovery permitted to take her leave with decency.

Both thefe lovers were now in a ftate of perfect contentment, and each of them obferved their promife with the utmoft punctuality: but what afterwards befel them, muft be the fubject of another chapter.

## C H A P. IX.

CONTAINS ONLY A CONTINUATION OF THE SAME NARRATIVE, BEGUN IN THE FOREGOING CHAPTER, AND WILL NOT BE CONCLUDED IN THIS.

MUTANTIUS being apprized, by a letter from Ariftella, of the day fhe fhould come to town, went in his own coach to Greenwich to meet her, and conducted her to a very handfome lodging, in one of the beft ftreets near Bloomfbury Square, where he had alfo provided fervants to attend her. She was at firft a little fcrupulous of putting herfelf under his protection, till the facred ceremony had been performed. He perceived the apprehenfions fhe was un-

der, and immediately relieved them, by renewing his proteftations that the next morning fhould make his perfon as inviolably hers as his heart had been from the firft moment he beheld her; and, at the fame time, fhewed her a ring and licence, which he had already prepared for that purpofe. He fupped with her that evening; but when it was over, very refpectfully retired, to leave her to that repofe he judged neceffary after the fatigue of the journey.

I come now to that part of the ftory which I had an opportunity of being both an eye and ear-witnefs of. I was acquainted with the gentlewoman of the houfe where Ariftella was placed, and happened to call there on fome bufinefs the very next morning after that young lady had been brought thither. My friend told me, among other difcourfe, that fhe had lett her lodgings at a very high rent; but was apprehenfive the perfon they were for was no better than a kept woman. On my afking what ground fhe had for fuch a fufpicion fhe replied, that fhe had lett them to a gentleman of fortune, called Mutantius, for the ufe of a lady whom he brought to take poffeffion of them the night before; and that he had hired fervants to wait upon her, who knew as little of the lady as fhe did. She farther added, that the lady was young and pretty; and that fhe could not help thinking it a little odd fuch a one fhould be under the care of fo gay a fpark as Mutantius.

As I was perfectly acquainted with the character of Mutantius, I was of opinion fhe was in the right; and advifed her to fay nothing till fhe faw farther into the matter, and not lofe fo beneficial a lodger on a bare conjecture. She approved of what I faid, and I took my leave, but not to go home. What fhe had told me filled me with a curiofity to difcover fomething more of this affair; fo went no farther than the firft blind alley I found, where I put on my Invifible Belt, and returned again juft as Mutantius knocked at the door. I entered with him, and followed him up ftairs. The fight of Ariftella convinced me that the good woman had not been miftaken in the defcription fhe gave me of her. The lovers ran into eachother's arms; and Mutantius, looking on her with the greateft tendernefs, fpoke thus—

*Mutantius.* Now, my deareft Ariftella,

stella, I am come to put a final end to all your doubts either of my love or honour.

*Ariftella.* I am pleased to think that the perfect confidence I have shewn in both gives me some sort of claim to the proof you are now about to give of them, since I must confess myself in every other respect so unworthy of you.

*Mutantius.* You are worthy of every thing. But, my dear, you forget that there is another teftimony that I expect from you of the regard you have for me.

*Ariftella.* Name it; that my ready compliance may convince you how happy I think myself in every opportunity of obliging you.

*Mutantius.* It is that you will be content that for some time our marriage may be kept a fecret.

*Ariftella.* You know I have promifed it.

*Mutantius.* Yes, in general terms: but you have fifters, who are very dear to you; and though I doubt not of their difcretion, I cannot think a fecret fafe when trufted in fo many hands. Will then your love for me enable you to endure their reproaches for your fuppofed difhonour, rather than reveal what is inconvenient for me to be made known?

*Ariftella.* The trial is a little fevere, but will not laft for ever.

*Mutantius.* No, my dear. A time will come when your innocence fhall be fully cleared, and, like the fun, fhine brighter after this fhort eclipfe; till then, may I depend that the name of wife and hufband fhall be known only between ourfelves?

*Ariftella.* You may.

*Mutantius.* Swear it, then.

*Ariftella.* By all that's facred.

*Mutantius.* Hold, my dear: I would have you firft underftand the full extent of the vow you are about to make. You fwear that no imaginary provocation on my fide, nor no unjuft contempt nor ill treatment you may meet with from the world, fhall ever extort from you a confeffion that you are my wife, till I myfelf fhall publickly acknowledge you to be fo.

*Ariftella.* All this I folemnly fwear; and invoke Heaven to blefs me as I fhall religiously obferve it.

*Mutantius.* Charming generous creature!—And, in return, to prevent all future apprehenfions in prejudice of my faith

or conftancy from rifing in your breaft; if it were poffible for me to take a bafe advantage of the obligation I have laid you under, and make my addreffes to another woman on the fcore of marriage, I here releafe you from your vow, and leave you at liberty to declare yourfelf my wife, affert your prior right, and proclaim me for a villain.

*Ariftella.* Heaven forbid it fhould ever come to that!

*Mutantius.* No, my Ariftella; there is no danger. I have already rejected greater offers than ever will be made to me again. To deal fincerely with you, there has been always in my nature an extreme repugnancy to the name of marriage; the name of hufband was irkfome to me: no woman but yourfelf had ever charms to reconcile me to it; but your beauty, fweetnefs, and unaffected modefty, have now informed my foul, and, by degrees, will make me as proud of Hymen's fetters as I fhould once have been afhamed of them.

*Ariftella.* It fhall be my whole ftudy to make them eafy to you.

*Mutantius.* I know it will. But, come, my love, a coach waits to carry us to church; that folemn fcene which fixes the everlafting happinefs or mifery of all who approach it in the manner we do.

On concluding thefe words, he took her by the hand, and led her down ftairs. I was clofe behind them when they went into the coach, which was ordered to drive to Clerkenwell. I prefently fuppofed he made choice of this place as there was the leaft danger of his being feen by any one who knew him. I followed on foot; but came time enough to fee Mutantius refign that liberty he had once fet fo high a value on as to refolve never to part with. The ceremony was performed by the curate of the parifh; and the clerk efficiated as father, to give away the bride. After all was over, Mutantius defired their marriage might be regiftered, and a certificate of it given to Ariftella; both which were accordingly done.

I now left the new-wedded pair to difpofe of themfelves as they thought fit, and returned to my apartment, in order to ruminate at leifure on an adventure which feemed to me to have in it many inconfiftencies. But the more I thought on this adventure, the more I was confounded; and the refult of all my meditations

tations was, that it muſt be left to time to unravel the myſtery: I kept, however, a watchful eye on the behaviour of Mutantius, but was little the wiſer for the pains I took, as I found he only lived in the ſame gay and gallant manner he he had always done in reſpect to the ladies.

But now, methinks, I hear the reader cry out with ſome impatience—' How ' did Ariſtella behave all this time? ' How could ſhe, the wife of this incon- ' ſtant man, ſupport the ſhare that others ' had in his affections?' It is, indeed, impoſſible for me to ſay in what manner ſhe would have reſented ſo provoking a cricumſtance, if known to her; but ſhe lived too retired for it to reach her ears: ſhe had, however, other troubles more than ſufficient for human fortitude to ſuſtain; but of what nature, muſt be left to the next chapter to explain.

## CHAP. X.

THE CATASTROPHE OF THIS AD-
VENTURE CANNOT FAIL OF EX-
CITING COMPASSION IN THE
BREASTS OF MY FAIR READERS,
AND ALSO AFFORD MATTER OF
SPECULATION TO THE OTHER
SEX.

THE purſuit of other adventures, which ſhall be inſerted in their proper places before the concluſion of this work, hindered me for a long time from going to ſee in what manner Ariſtella was treated by Mutantius; but at length, ſome uneaſy reflections on her account raiſed an impatience in me to know the certainty of her preſent ſtate. Accordingly I went one day to the houſe where ſhe was lodged; but, to my great ſurprize, found ſhe had made but a ſhort ſtay there, and had been removed a conſiderable time before my coming. On my aſking ſome queſtions of my friend concerning the reaſon of it, the good woman anſwered me in theſe or the like terms—' The affair was juſt as I ex- ' pected,' ſaid ſhe. ' I pity the poor ' young gentlewoman, indeed; ſhe has ' not the looks of ſuch a one; but I ' ſuppoſe ſhe has been decoyed by abun- ' dance of fair promiſes: I wonder, ' however, that Mutantius, knowing the ' character of my houſe, and that I always ' had people of the beſt faſhion lodge

' with me, ſhould offer to bring a kept- ' miſtreſs under my roof; but I was very ' free with him, and told him my mind ' plainly on the occaſion.'

' And pray what anſwer did he make,' cried I, with ſome impatience, ' when ' you called her a kept-miſtreſs?'— ' Very little to the purpoſe, truly,' reſumed ſhe; ' he only ſaid that ſhe was a ' gentlewoman, and a friend of his, and, ' as ſuch, expected that I ſhould treat ' her civilly. I told him, it was not in ' my nature to treat any body uncivilly, ' but that I would encourage no ſuch ' doings; and therefore deſired he would ' provide another lodging for her. On ' this, he flew into a paſſion, told me I ' was an ignorant, fooliſh woman, and ' the like; but I did not regard his ' bouncing; and, as he found I was re- ' ſolute, took his Madam away in a few ' days afterwards.'

The manner in which this woman ſpoke, made me extremely commiſerate the condition of Ariſtella, who, though a lawful wife, was obliged, through the caprice of Mutantius, and the vow ſhe had taken, to endure all the contumely due to a proſtitute. I would have given almoſt any thing but the ſecret of my Inviſible Belt and Tablets to have cleared Ariſtella's innocence in the fulleſt manner to this gentlewoman; but as there was no doing one without the other, I was compelled to content myſelf with getting out of her directions to the place where this much injured lady was removed, reſolving to take the firſt opportunity to ſee what atonement the behaviour of Mutantius made to her in private, for the injuſtice he did her reputation in publick.

I was ſo lucky as to find them together the firſt day I went; but the ſcene I was witneſs of, inſtead of diminiſhing, very much added to the concern I had carried with me. Ariſtella was ſitting very melancholy in one corner of the room, Mutantius in another, with all the marks of diſcontent and ill-humour in his countenance. By what followed, it appears that ſhe had been ſpeaking ſomewhat to him in relation to the diſcovery of their marriage. I doubt not, by what I ſaw of her behaviour, both before and afterwards, that ſhe expreſſed herſelf in very gentle terms on the occaſion; but the bare mention of ſuch a thing to a man of his preſent way of thinking, was of itſelf a ſufficient offence. I have already

T
ready

ready described the posture I found him in; but, just as I entered the room, he replied to what she had said, and that reply drew on a conversation which let me into the whole of both their sentiments.

*Mutantius.* I am sorry to find you have so little regard for me, and indeed so little prudence, as, whenever I am with you, to fall eternally upon a subject which you know is disagreeable to me.

*Aristella.* If you loved me half so well as you once pretended, it would not be so disagreeable; and you would, at least, acquaint me with the reasons which oblige me to live in the manner I do.

*Mutantius.* Perhaps it is not proper for me to reveal them.

*Aristella.* Oh, Mutantius! I know not what to think of my condition. Why did you marry me?

*Mutantius.* Because I then liked you better than any other woman, and if I do not still continue to do so, it is your own fault. I hate to be teazed; besides, the conditions of our marriage were that it should be kept a secret.

*Aristella.* Yes, for a time.

*Mutantius.* That time will not be shortened by your impatience.

*Aristella.* It may, for if it lasts much longer my heart must infallibly break.

*Mutantius.* Pish! women's hearts are not made of such brittle stuff; the head is in more danger, when swelled with pride and vanity.

*Aristella.* Indeed, Sir, I think it would at least become you to be a little more serious on the occasion.

*Mutantius.* With all my heart, Madam, as serious as you please; for 'faith I am not in a humour to be merry. Seriously, then, you seem to me to be one of the most ungrateful and most unreasonable women under the sun. Have I not taken you from a dependance on your sisters? Have you not now good lodgings, servants to wait on you, and an allowance sufficient to support you in a fashion beyond what you could ever have expected? yet all this is nothing in your account.

*Aristella.* Nothing, when balanced against a life of infamy: the very servants you upbraid me with, despise me while they serve me; the people of the house treat me but with an enforced civility; I pass my days as one who was an alien to the world, and had no business in it; never partake the joys of social conversation, never visit, nor am

visited, and scarce dare venture to breathe the open air, lest I should be seen by any who have known me, especially by my sisters, who, mean as you think of them, know how to set a just value upon reputation, and to scorn all riches without it.

*Mutantius.* A very fine catalogue of complaints, truly! Have you any more?

*Aristella.* Yes, one thing more, which, with what indifference soever you may now regard me, ought not, methinks, to escape your consideration. You know I am far advanced in my pregnancy; perhaps, too, of a son; and can you support the thoughts, that an infant, born the lawful heir of your estate and name, shall be saluted, on his first seeing the light, with the odious title of bastard?

*Mutantius.* What will he be the worse, unless you expect to have so wise a child as to know what is said of him as soon as he comes into the world?

*Aristella.* Oh, Mutantius! Mutantius! this is cruel dealing.

She said no more, but wept bitterly. Mutantius, who, it must be owned, has some good-nature, seemed much moved at seeing her thus; and having looked on her some moments with a great deal of tenderness, bid her come to him: she obeyed, but advanced with the most sorrowful and dejected air; he pulled her to him, made her sit upon his knee, and kissing away the tears, he spoke thus—

*Mutantius.* Come, my poor Aristella, do not be so foolish; you have no cause for weeping; you know yourself virtuous, and I know you are so, and have no need to be afflicted at the mistaken opinion others may have of you, especially as it is not to last always.

*Aristella.* If I were certain when this event would happen, even though it were much longer than I hope it will, I should wait with patience.

*Mutantius.* You must depend for that upon my love and honour; it is not in my power to assign the day and hour. To deal sincerely with you, I have been a railer at marriage, have refused offers of that nature as much above my expectations as I was above yours, and I cannot all at once submit to be pointed at for a husband, and hear people laugh and cry out, that I had thrown myself away: but of this, my dear, you may assure yourself, that I will endeavour to get rid of these scruples as soon as possible. In the mean time, I will give you as much of my company as can be
spared

spared from busness and other attachments which are not to be dispensed with. I came on purpose to devote this whole day to you, drive me not from you by your discontent; kiss me, and give me your promise that you will be entirely eas'.

She complied readily with the first part of this injunction, and said she would do her best to perform the other. But by what I had now seen of the behaviour and disposition of Mutantius, I found reason to believe it would be yet a great while before he would bring himself to make a declaration of his marriage; so resolved not to take the trouble of any farther inquisitions, but wait till common fame should give me intelligence of it. This event, however, happened much sooner than I expected; but was brought about by an accident which excited the extremest pity instead of congratulations. The unfortunate Aristella was not born to enjoy a happiness she so ardently had wished for, and so long been made to hope; death alone had the power to give what life in vain had waited for; and the same breath which told me Mutantius had acknowledged her for his wife, informed me also that she was no more.

Aristella, on her leaving the country, was charged with letters and some little presents from Mrs. Beechly to her two sisters in London; but being hindered from executing this commission in person, by the obligation Mutantius had laid her under, she sent what was entrusted to her care by a porter, accompanied with a little billet from herself; in which she told them, that an affair of the utmost consequence kept her at present from seeing them, but that she hoped to do so in a short time and would then acquaint them with the reasons for having absented herself, and begged they would entertain no unfavourable thoughts of her conduct in this point.

As she was circumstanced, it was not in her power to have acted otherwise: yet what satisfaction could such a letter give the two sisters? for a girl to banish herself from her kindred, without acquainting them with the motive, or the place to which she was retired, had a right to raise in them conjectures of the worst sort. They were distracted at the thoughts of her supposed ruin, and spared no pains to find her out, in order to bring her home, and snatch her from the shame they imagined she was involved in.

Fruitless was their search for a long time; but chance, at length, discovered not only where she lived, but also that she was supported by a gentleman, and looked upon as a kept mistress. Quite enraged, they went to the house where she was lodged, and the door happening to be open, flew up stairs without any ceremony, and burst in upon her. The sight of her—for her pregnancy was visible—added to the passions they were before enflamed with: they reproached, they reviled her in the most bitter terms; while poor Aristella, bound by the fatal oath she had taken, could say nothing in defence of her innocence, but what served to convince them more fully of her guilt. After having loaded her with opprobrious names, they left her with the same precipitation they had come, vowing never more to see or think of her as a sister.

Impossible it is for any one to conceive what the soul of Aristella suffered in this shocking stroke: conscious of innocence, yet labouring under all the appearance of guilt; scandalized, abused by those to whom she had been so dear, yet incapable either of defending her wronged virtue, or of blaming the severity she was treated with for her supposed fall; every passion that can agitate the human heart, at once assailed, and overwhelmed her with a variety of anguish; the force or which had such an effect upon her, as to cause an abortion that same night, and also to throw her into convulsions, which in a few hours rendered her life despaired of by all about her. In her intervals, between those fits which deprived her of all sense and motion, she cried out for Mutantius, asked where he was, and said she could not die without seeing him. Messengers were immediately dispatched to him; he came, seemed greatly affected at the condition he found her in, but was much more so, when he was informed what it was had thrown her into it. She was insensible on his entrance, but recovering soon after, and seeing him so near her, catched hold of his hand, and with agonies inexpressible, said to him—'Oh, Mutantius! you will 'now be rid of a tie you have been 'ashamed to own.'—'No, by Heaven!' cried he: 'Live, live, Aristella, and I 'will declare to all the world that you 'are my wife, my lawful married wife.'

Whether it were this sudden rush of joy, on hearing him speak these words,

T *.                              that

that was too powerful for her weakness to sustain, or that the lamp of life was wasted by the agonies she had before endured, is altogether uncertain; but she expired that moment, yielding up her last breath on the bosom of her too late repenting husband. Love, pity, and remorse, now engrossed all his faculties; he kept his promise, acknowledged her for his wife, had her intombed with great funeral pomp in his own family vault, and paid all imaginable honours to her memory. Whether he will ever relapse into his former vanities, time alone must shew; but at present, this once gay, thoughtless rover, either is, or affects to be, lost to the joys he lately was so fond of; behaves with the utmost indifference towards the fair sex; seldom goes to any publick place; sees but little company at home; and seems to be in every thing the very reverse of what he was.

As to the sisters of the unfortunate Aristella, they were seized with the most deep affliction, when they came to know the sad effects their rash resentment had occasioned—which may serve as a warning to all persons not to be over hasty in censuring actions, the true meaning of which they cannot immediately comprehend.

END OF THE FIFTH BOOK.

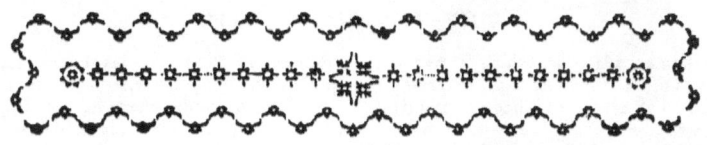

THE

# INVISIBLE SPY.

## BOOK VI.

### CHAP. I.

IS DEDICATED ENTIRELY TO THE
LADIES, AS IT RELATES AN AD-
VENTURE WHICH NEARLY CON-
CERNS THEM TO TAKE NOTICE OF.

AMONG all the numerous
modes which the wanton-
nefs of luxury has of late
years introduced into this
kingdom for deftroying of
time, I know of none more
fatal to the virtue and reputation of the
female fex than mafquerades; I mean,
as that amufement is at prefent conducted. Indeed, when a felect company of ladies and gentlemen agree
among themfelves, or are invited by
fome perfon of condition, to divert each
other in fuch difguifes as their feveral
fancies fhall make choice of, the cafe is
widely different; for there, after paffing
a few hours in mufick, dancing, and
pleafant raillery, according to the characters they affume, the mafks are all
thrown afide, and every one appears as
he is; fo that none will venture to talk
or act beneath a vizard, in fuch a manner as, when he ftands revealed, will
either reflect fhame on himfelf, or give
offence to thofe he has been entertain-

ing. Mafquerades, thus managed, I
cannot but allow to be not only innocent but laudable amufements, as they
ferve to whet the wit and exhilarate the
mind.
But here, forry am I to fay it, the mafquerade houfes may with propriety
enough be called fhops, where opportunities for immorality, prophanenefs,
obfcenity, and almoft every kind of vice,
are retailed to any one who will become
a cuftomer; and at the low rate of feven
and twenty fhillings, the moft abandoned
courtezan, the moft profligate rake, or
common fharper, purchafes the privilege of mingling with the firft peers and
peereffes of the realm, and not feldom
affronts both modefty and greatnefs
with impunity. I perceive, to my great
fatisfaction, there are fome ladies who,
touched with a juft fenfe of what is owing to their dignity, are determined not
to expofe themfelves any more in a place
where, if no worfe enfues, the moft licentious freedoms of fpeech, at leaft, are
often offered to the chafteft ears; and I
am not without hope, that the influence
of their example will prevail on many
others to do the fame. For the benefit,
however, of the unwary, and thofe who,
by their fmall acquaintance in town, are
ignorant of the cuftoms of thefe dangerous amufements, it will not be amifs to
relate

relate an adventure which I was witness of, and may serve as a warning to all who are truly innocent, and desire to remain so.

Alexis and Matilda were the son and daughter of two gentlemen who lived near Newcastle. They had loved each other even before either well knew what was meant by the passion; and, as their understanding ripened, their inclinations increased. Hope, for some time, gilded the prospect of their mutual wishes; but, when they least expected, a stop was put to the consummation by an unfortunate disagreement between their parents. Alexis was forbid to see Matilda, and Matilda ever to think on Alexis: but these commands had little authority over hearts so fondly enamoured as theirs; they formed the most romantick contrivances to keep alive the flame with which each had inspired the other; some of which succeeded so well, as to enable them to continue an intercourse by letters, and even to gain private interviews. It was the father of Alexis who of the two had been most refractory; and he dying a small time after, the young gentleman found means to reconcile matters so effectually with the parents of Matilda, that they at length consented to give her to him, and compleated the happiness of the equally loving and beloved pair.

Matilda, whose every care, hope, and joy, had all been centered in her dear Alexis, had nothing now to wish beyond what she was in possession of; and Alexis thought himself so blest, that he even defied the power of Fortune to give him any cause of disquiet. Fatal security! How little dependance for the future is there on the present good! They had not long enjoyed the sweets of this so-much-desired union, before Matilda, who had never been in London, expressed a curiosity to see it. Alexis, proud to embrace every opportunity of giving her pleasure, immediately took the hint, and told her he was ready to conduct her there as soon as she pleased. Accordingly they set out, and arrived in London about September. Alexis took ready-furnished lodgings, in a handsome house near St. James's, for six months; in which time he thought he should be able to shew Matilda every thing worth her seeing in town.

Alexis had received his first precepts at Westminster School; and having no

relations in London, his father requested me, by letters, to call sometimes at the house where he boarded, and have an eye over his behaviour. I did so; and the advice I gave him being delivered not in a magisterial but friendly manner, the lad conceived a very great affection for me from that time, and has preserved it ever since. He made me the compliment of a first visit on his coming to town, told me how happy he was, and begged I would be no stranger to the fair person who had made him so. I accepted the invitation, and went the next day. On his presenting Matilda to me, I was struck with admiration; for, besides every thing that could constitute a perfect beauty, there was a sweet simplicity, and a chearful, unaffected innocence, which shone through the whole, and brightened every grace.

As the sole excitement Matilda had to take a journey to London was to gratify her curiosity with the sight of it, there was no eminent structure, or place of note, to which she was not conducted by her Alexis. A new scene of diversions opened as the winter season came on; plays, operas, and masquerades, now began to attract attention: the two first of these amusements Matilda was not altogether a stranger to, having often seen somewhat like them acted by strolling companies in the country, but she had not the least notion of masquerades; and the little account Alexis was able to give her making her more impatient to know what sort of entertainment they afforded, it may be easily supposed that so indulgent an husband would not suffer her to continue long in suspence; it may be, too, that he had some curiosity of his own to gratify in this point, having, it seems, never been at a masquerade himself.

Tickets accordingly were purchased, and habits hired. I happened to make a morning visit the day they were to go, and found Matilda busy in ornamenting a little hat and crook. The moment I entered the room, she told me, with the greatest pleasure in her countenance, that she was to be at the masquerade that night, and was to assume the character of a shepherdess. I replied, she could not take upon her one more suitable to her youth and innocence.

I said nothing to them of my design; but, which evening came, I sculpped myself

myself with a domino, and hasted to that Babel of hurry and confusion; where it was no difficult matter to discover the persons I sought after, as I knew the dresses they were in. I soon distinguished the shepherdess, and the husband by the blue domino I had seen lying on a table in his dining-room, and perceived there were many eyes upon Matilda; for though her face was concealed, her shape and air had somewhat in them sufficiently attractive. But there was one who, above all the rest, seemed particularly attentive to her motions: he was in the habit of a huntsman; a character which I afterwards had reason to say to myself suited very well with the intentions he had in his head that night. Which way soever Matilda turned, he took care not to lose sight of her; but, as she kept close to Alexis, neither he nor any one else had an opportunity of speaking to her. I hovered as near them as I could without being taken notice of; and it gave me a good deal of diversion, to see the surprize this innocent country lady testified at hearing the freedoms with which some people, who seemed to be perfect strangers, accosted each other.

A gentleman crossing the room with his mask in his hand, was known to Alexis; who, on sight of him, cried out to Matilda—'Look yonder, my 'dear! there is Mr. Freeman! I never 'heard of his being in town. I will 'just step and tell him where we lodge: 'do you sit here till I come back.' He then seated her on a bench, and went hastily after his friend, who had passed into another room. I now doubted not but the huntsman would snatch his opportunity of entertaining Matilda; but I lost sight of him in an instant; he vanished, as it were, from the place, and I saw him no more. The fair shepherdess, however, was not to remain neglected. I found several advancing towards her; one of whom was the most grotesque, as well as disagreeable figure, I ever beheld: his stature was far from what could be called tall, but the circumference of his carcase exceeded that of any three men in the whole assembly; his legs looked like the pillars of a church-porch, and when he moved were at such a distance from each other, that a boar of a moderate size might easily pass between them without being incommoded. He had on the habit of a Turkish ba-

shaw; which was the worst, indeed, he could have chose; his huge ears, discovered by the shortness of his turban, hung upon his shoulders, as did the wallets under his chin upon his breast: in a word, he could have no deformity that the dress he was in did not shew to advantage.

This enormous creature had no sooner reached the place where Matilda sat, than he threw himself down by her on the bench, and accosted her with language which I should never forgive myself, nor expect to be forgiven by my reader, to repeat; but I was glad to find, by the whispers of some people behind me, that, instead of a gentleman, as I at first took him for, he was no other than a bully at a noted brothel in Covent Garden, and was known about town by the name of Lumper Hammock. I cannot pretend to say whether this fellow was encouraged by any other person to behave to Matilda in the manner he did merely to put her spirits into a hurry, or whether he was instigated to it only by his own impudence and brutality: but, whatever it might be, the situation of that poor lady was greatly to be pitied; she moved by little and little as far from him as the bench would give her leave; but he still followed, and would needs keep close to her, and persecute her with his ribaldry. Sometimes she got up, and looked round to see for her husband; then sat down again, not daring to leave the place for fear of missing him; but all the time shewed tokens of the utmost agitation of mind.

At length the blue domino appeared; on which she started from her seat, and running to him, cried—'Oh, my dear, 'I am glad you are come!' He only replied, in a low voice—'Aye, aye, let 'us be gone!' and, taking her by the hand, led her hastily away. I pleased myself with the thoughts of having seen Matilda safe under the protection of her husband, and was equally so that he had discovered little approbation of the masquerade, by his leaving it at a time when the diversion was at it's height, and more company coming in than going out.

But the satisfaction I enjoyed in both these points, vanished in a moment. Alexis returned; his mask was now off, and he passed directly to the place where he had left Matilda; then started back. Confusion and surprize overspread his
face;

face; he threw his eyes wildly round the room, then ran through every part of it; and, without considering how much he exposed himself to the ridicule of that giggling assembly, asked first of one, and then of another, if they had seen a shepherdess in green and silver, and if they knew what was become of her. This struck me with infinite concern, as it made me know Matilda had been deceived by the sight of the blue domino; and, in spite of my unwillingness to let him see I had come to a place where I had refused to accompany him, was just stepping forward to inform him of what had happened, when a lady, hearing his enquiries, said—' Sir, the lady I saw ' with you, in the dress you mention, ' went away a little while ago with a ' gentleman in a blue domino, much ' the same as your own.' On which he cried out—' Oh Heavens! what cursed ' mistake is this!'

In uttering this exclamation, he flew out of the room like lightning, without staying to thank the lady for her intelligence. I followed as fast as I could, and found him at the door of the house, encompassed with hackney-coachmen, chairmen, and link-boys; among whom he was vainly endeavouring to get some account of his lost shepherdess. One of them, it seems, had said he saw a lady, in the habit he described, go into a coach with a gentleman, but could tell nothing either of the figure of the coach, or where it was ordered to drive. Finding no information could be gained in the place where he was, he withdrew from the crowd, as I suppose to consider what method he should pursue; for he continued in a fixed posture for two or three minutes, leaning against some rails before an adjacent house. My heart bled for him; and if I had been capable of offering him either advice or consolation, would not have kept at the distance I did: but the accident that had happened was without a remedy; and I had often observed, that to preach up moderation in the first gusts of passion serve but to inflame it more.

· I thought there were no measures he could take that night; yet imagining he had something in his head, was desirous of seeing what event his cogitations would produce: I therefore laid hold of the opportunity I now had of stepping behind the cover of a hackney-coach in waiting, and girded on my Belt of Invisibility, which I always carried in my pocket, in case any thing should fall in my way to give me occasion to make use of it. The influence of my valuable gift had but just taken effect, by being warm upon my body, when Alexis rouzed himself out of his reverie. and walked very fast up the street. I kept pace with him till he came to the house where he lodged. The door being opened by his own footman, who sat up for him—' Is my wife come home?' cried he. The fellow answered in the negative; and seeming somewhat surprized at this question, he threw himself into the parlour, saying to himself—' How mad ' a hope did I entertain that she might ' have found some means to escape the ' hands of her ravisher. and been here ' before me!—No, no, 'tis impossible! ' the villain doubtless will secure his ' prey. Cursed, cursed masquerade! ' invented by the fiends for the de- ' struction of virtue!'

While he was thus speaking, he tore off his domino with agonies not to be expressed, and stamped it under his feet; then turning to his servant, went on thus—

*Alexis.* William, your mistress is run away with; stolen from me by some villain in a domino like my own: she is lost for ever unless immediately recovered. Fly, this minute, to every tavern and bagnio you can think of; describe her habit; enquire if such a one, with a person in a blue domino, entered there. Be gone this instant! while I run to a justice of peace, and get a warrant to search in all suspected places.

*William.* What part of the town, Sir, do you think it most likely I shall hear of her?

*Alexis.* Alas! I am as ignorant of that as you: but all parts must be searched. Fly, then, good William!—and, do you hear, ask every hackney-coachman you meet with if he set any such persons down, and where? Away, I say!—stay not to consider!—a moment may confirm her ruin and my dishonour!

The fellow obeyed without making any farther reply; but I perceived, by his countenance, was not very well contented with the errand he was sent upon: and Alexis went out of the house at the same time he did, in order to have recourse to a magistrate in this exigence, as he said he would. I had no inclination to follow either master or man on an expedi-

tion

tion which promised so little success; therefore made all the haste I could to my own apartment, very much fatigued in body, yet much more so in mind, at the unfortunate mistake poor Matilda had fallen into, and which I had all the reason in the world to fear would be attended with the most dreadful consequences.

## CHAP. II.

CONTAINS THE CONCLUSION OF A NARRATIVE, WHICH I AM CERTAIN THERE IS ONE PERSON IN THE WORLD WHO CANNOT READ WITHOUT BEING FILLED WITH THE MOST POIGNANT REMORSE, UNLESS HE IS AS DEAD TO ALL SENSE OF HUMANITY AS OF HONOUR.

MY impatience to know if Matilda was yet come home, or if the researches of Alexis had gained him any information concerning her, made me resolve to go to his lodgings in the morning; but whether I should make this visit in my Visible or Invisible capacity, I was for some time at a loss: at last, it seemed most eligible to appear in *propria persona*, as if I came only to ask some questions concerning the masquerade, and how they approved of that diversion, as it was the first time they partook of it; and also to take no notice of my being apprized of any thing that had happened there, unless he related it to me himself, which I did not much doubt of his doing. Accordingly I went; and, upon my entering into the dining-room, Alexis ran to me, and began the recital of his misfortune in this pathetick exclamation—' Oh, my friend, I am un-
' done and ruined for ever! The au-
' thor, giver, and partaker, of all my
' happiness, is lost! torn from me by
' some lascivious, some inhuman villain!
' and him whom yesterday you beheld
' the most blest of men, you now see
' the most accursed and most wretched
' of all created beings!'

He then proceeded to inform me, as well as the distraction of his thoughts would give him leave, of the method he had taken for the recovery of his lost treasure; how he had passed the whole night and that morning in search of her, and that all his enquiries had been fruitless.

I then advised him to put an advertisement in the papers, describing the shape and stature of Matilda, with all the particulars of her dress, and offering a handsome reward to any one who should give information of the place at which she alighted out of a hackney-coach, in company with a gentleman in a blue domino, between the hours of twelve and one. ' This you may do,' said I, ' without mentioning any name,
' except that of the person to whom
' such intelligence may be brought;
' and it is very likely either the coach-
' man who carried her, or some one
' who might be about the door where
' she was set down, or even the ser-
' vants of the house, will, for the sake
' of the gratuity, make that discovery
' which all your personal enquiries might
' not be able to obtain.'

I had no sooner ended, than a sudden dawn of chearfulness gleamed upon his languid face; and, to shew how much he approved of the thought, took pen and paper, and immediately wrote in almost the same terms I had expressed it; specifying, at the same time, a coffee-house where the reward should be paid, on the requested intelligence being brought. After this, Nature, who will not be denied her rites, whatever vexations may intervene to rob her of them, spread a certain drowsiness upon his eye-lids, which I perceiving, persuaded him to favour; and, on my promising to come again the same evening, he lay down on the bed, and left me at liberty to pursue my inclinations.

As I had now no engagement upon my hands, and had not been at White's for a considerable time, it was now my full design to go thither, imagining it might not be improbable but I might hear something of Matilda; but as I had some very good reasons not to appear in that place, I stepped into the first nook I found in my way, and put on my Belt of Invisibility. I was but just equipped, and passing on to my intended rout, when I saw a chair, with the curtains close drawn, stop at a few paces before me. I should have taken no notice of this, if one of the fellows had not lifted up the top, and told the person in it that he had forgot whether it were the Red or the Green Lamps. The

U                                    answer

anfwer was given in a voice which I prefently knew to be Matilda's; and, if I had not fo well remembered, as I did, the accents, I fhould have fufpected it was no other than herfelf, by her faying —' The Two Green Lamps.'

On finding it was fhe, the reader will eafily believe I had more curiofity to fee the interview between her and Alexis than any thing elfe I could have in my head. I followed the chair till it came to the houfe, and on the door being opened, flipped in with it. On her alighting, Mrs. Soberton, who was mif-trefs of the houfe, ran out of the parlour, and was beginning to teftify her joy at her return, though mingled with fome demonftrations of furprize, to fee her in the condition fhe was, which, indeed, was deplorable enough; her head with-out any other covering than a handker-chief carelefsly tied over her difhevelled hair, her garments torn, her eyes fwelled with tears, every feature diftorted, and all the tokens of diftraction and defpair about her. She made no anfwer to what the good gentlewoman faid; but, after throwing fome money to the chairmen, ran haftily up into the dining-room, where, flinging herfelf on a fettee, fhe cried out—' Where is Alexis!' To which Mrs. Soberton, who had followed as well as myfelf, replied—' Oh, Madam, ' you cannot imagine what trouble both ' he and all of us have had on your ac-' count!'

I know not whether that unhappy lady would have declared to Mrs. So-berton any part of what had befallen her or not; for Alexis, who either had not fallen afleep, or was eafily awaked, heard his wife's voice, and came flying out of the chamber that inftant. Mrs. Sober-ton, difcreetly judging that they might not chufe to have a third perfon witnefs of their difcourfe, went directly down ftairs; but the Invifible remained, and his wonderful Tablets received the im-preffion of the following dialogue be-tween them:

*Matilda.* Oh, Alexis, why did you leave me?

*Alexis.* Why did you leave the place where I defired you to wait for my re-turn?

*Matilda.* I ftirred not from it but to follow you, as I then thought.

*Alexis.* Confufion! How could you be fo miftaken?

*Matilda.* Alas, I had no apprehenfion

of the deception put upon me! His habit was exactly like yours; his ftature the fame; he fpoke in a low voice; but if he had not, my fpirits were in too much agitation at the impudence of a fellow who had but juft before accofted me, to have diftinguifhed the difference.

*Alexis.* Oh, my torn heart! But fay, Who is the villain that betrayed you! Where were you carried!

*Matilda.* Alas, the precautions he took have left me ignorant of both; and all I know is, that I am undone!

*Alexis.* Diftraction!—Undone, and not know by whom! nor even in what place! all means for my revenge barred up! Yet, perhaps, I may be able to dif-cover fomething—Tell me in an inftant all the particulars of the ftory!

*Matilda.* I will, though every word will ftab me to the foul, and inflict anew the fhocks I have undergone.

*Alexis.* No preparations; be quick, and anfwer my demand at once.

*Matilda.* Have patience, then; for while you look fo terrible I cannot fpeak.

*Alexis.* You cannot think I would hurt you; fpeak then, and break at once the heart of thy wretched nufband!

*Matilda.* Oh, which way fhall I be-gin?—how end?

*Alexis.* Keep me not on the rack!

*Matilda.* Soon as I faw the counter-feit Alexis approach, I rofe to meet him; and on his bidding me come, and ftretch-ing forth his hand, I gave him mine, glad to find myfelf conducted from that mingled crowd, which I had feen too much of to defire to continue any longer with. We went into a coach, where I began to tell him how I had been af-fronted by an ugly huge man in a Turkifh habit; but he made no anfwer either to that or any other idle prate I entertained him with, till the coach ftop-ped and he handed me into a houfe, the entry of which was full of men, who were running backwards and forwards with candles in their hands, and feemed very bufy. I afked where we were going; he ftill made no reply; but after a fhort whifper to one of the fellows, led me up ftairs.

*Alexis.* 'Sdeath! why did you go? Then was your time to have cried out for refcue!

*Matilda.* What, from my hufband! I could not as yet know him from any other than yourfelf. I was, indeed, a little furprized at this behaviour; but imagined

imagined it was owing to fome little whim you had taken into your head, on purpole to laugh at my fimplicity. Being warm with having my mask on fo long, I plucked it off as foon as we got into the room, but he clapped it on again, a man being then juft entering with a bottle and glaffes in his hand, which having fet down on a table, he immediately withdrew. My conductor then bolted the door, and running towards me, faid—' Now, my angel, I may feaft ' my eye with all that heaven of beauty, ' which, while beneath a cloud, attracted ' my admiration; and you behold the ' man who from this happy moment devotes himfelf entirely to your charms.' With thefe words, he took off both mine and his own vizard. I fhrieked, and furely had fainted with the fright, if an equal proportion of rage had not kept up my fpirits.

*Alexis.* What faid he then?

*Matilda.* A thoufand romantick lyes, fuch as I have read in plays and novels, which I anfwered only with revilings; till perceiving my juft fcorn had no effect upon him, I had recourfe to tears and entreaties; told him I was a married woman, that I had a hufband dearer to me than my foul, and by whom I was as much beloved, and conjured him not to detain me.

*Alexis.* Did not this move him?

*Matilda.* Oh no, not in the leaft, the audacious wretch but laughed at this remonftrance, faid that I was a fool, and knew not the true intereft of my fex, but that he would inftruct me better, and make me happy, though againft my will.

*Alexis.* Execrable dog! But go on.

*Matilda.* You may eafily believe, that he who could fpeak fuch words, would alfo accompany them with actions of the fame nature. I refifted all I could the indecent liberties he took, called heaven and earth to my affiftance, but in vain; I was at laft overpowered. In the midft of tears, reproaches, fwoonings, he effected his brutal purpofe, and made me the moft miferable of women!

*Alexis.* Moft miferable, indeed! After this, I fuppofe, he would have fuffered you to depart?

*Matilda.* Can you think me vile enough to continue one moment in the prefence of that detefted monfter, when I was at liberty to leave him? This, indeed, is cruel. Oh, Alexis! I hate myfelf for what I have been compelled to fuffer; do not you hate me too?

*Alexis.* Oh, 'tis too much for man to bear! Yet one thing more, Matilda; defcribe, as near as poffible, the features and complexion of this inhuman ravifher.

*Matilda.* Alas, the horror I was in from the firft moment I found myfelf in the power of a ftranger, hindered me from taking any great notice. All I can fay is, that he had dark eyes, a clear and ruddy fkin; and though his behaviour rendered him odious to me, with others, I believe, he may pafs for handfome.

*Alexis.* Young, I fuppofe?

*Matilda.* About five or fix and twenty, as far as I can judge.

*Alexis.* Had he the appearance of a man of rank and fortune?

*Matilda.* Every thing I faw about him, which properly belonged to himfelf, befpoke him fuch; but doubly difguifed. Did you not take notice of an huntfman at the mafquerade?

*Alexis.* Yes, and remember he always kept near us. Was he the ravifher?

*Matilda.* The fame. He told me he had his eye upon me from the firft moment I came in, and when he faw you left me, ran and procured him a domino as like yours as he could get, in hopes I might be, as, alas! I really was, deceived by that fatal habit.

*Alexis.* 'Tis well; I may perhaps hunt him.

The eyes of Alexis feemed to flafh fire while he uttered thefe words: after which he ftood mufing for fome time; then turning to his wife, who ftill fat weeping in the fame pofture fhe had thrown herfelf into at her entrance, fpoke thus to her—

*Alexis.* Rife, Matilda, retire to your chamber, and endeavour to compofe yourfelf to reft.

*Matilda.* What, fo early? 'Tis not yet fix o'clock.

*Alexis.* No matter, your condition requires it; you have wak'd too long, therefore pray go.

*Matilda.* Will you come too?

*Alexis.* Do not expect me, I have much to think upon, and muft be alone; there is a fermentation in my mind which muft have time to fettle; to-morrow I may be at more eafe, I pray you then to give me liberty this night.

With this, she took a candle and withdrew; but with a look and gesture so truly pity-moving, that if a painter had been to draw the picture of Despair, he could not have copied from an original more striking.

He then called for Mrs. Soherton, told her his wife had been very much frighted, and was indisposed; so begged she would assist her in any thing she might stand in need of. She made no reply, but went out of the room, I suppose, to do what he requested of her. I was about to follow her, but seeing Alexis put on his wig, which he had plucked off when he went to lie down, thought he was going on some expedition which it might be worth my taking the pains to explore. To this end I slipped down stairs while he was taking up his sword and hat, got out of the house before him, divested myself of my Belt, became visible, and met him some few paces distant. I told him I was returning to his lodgings according to my promise, and affected some surprize at seeing him abroad: he seemed pleased that he had not missed me, and repeated in a few words the sum of what I have been relating; adding, that he now flattered himself with being able to trace out the person who had injured him, by the description Matilda had given of him; and then intreated I would be so good as to accompany him in the search he was about to make; to which request I readily consented.

I found his scheme was, to enquire among those people who let out dresses for the masquerade, if any account could be given of a gentleman who the night before had hired, first the habit of a huntsman, and afterwards a blue domino. The thing, indeed, seemed feasible enough in itself, though it did not answer expectation. We went to several shops without receiving the least information; and all we could learn was, that a gentleman, habited like a huntsman, had come in a very great hurry for a blue domino, which had not been returned till about half an hour before our coming; but the name or quality of the person who hired it, the woman protested she knew nothing of. Alexis then demanded, somewhat hastily, who it was had brought it back: she smiled both at this interrogatory, and the manner in which it was made; and replied, that she was talking to customers at that time in the shop; but if she had been less engaged, she

should scarce have taken any notice—'For,' said she, 'provided we have our goods again, and are paid for the use of them, it is not our business to examine farther.'

Here ended the fruitless search of Alexis. He had now no shadow of hope for discovering the ravisher, but in the advertisement I had persuaded him to get inserted in the news-papers; and his despair became so outrageous, that it was with much difficulty I prevailed on him to go home. I went with him, fearing, if he was left alone in the street, he might be guilty of some extravagancy. It was one of the most fine frosty nights I had ever seen; and, while we were knocking at the door, he looked up towards the sky, and, with a voice denoting the extremest bitterness of heart, burst into this exclamation—'How many thousand twinkling stars are there, yet not one among them all a friend to me, or poor undone Matilda!'

I went home with him, but privately gave William a caution not to go to sleep, but keep near his master, and be attentive to all his motions, in order to prevent any fatal effect of the present distraction of his mind. I then went home, but with an anxiety for this truly worthy, though ill-fated pair, that made me quit my bed very early next morning, with a resolution to exert my utmost endeavours for the mitigation of their sorrows, and, if possible, to reconcile Alexis to a misfortune which was without a remedy; but, unluckily for my design, a person came to speak with me about some business which detained me till almost twelve o'clock.

On my arrival at the place where I so much wished to be, I found Alexis just come in before me. He appeared with a countenance much more composed than the night before, but very pensive and melancholy: he presently acquainted me, however, with the occasion of his having been abroad; it was this—He told me he had passed the whole night in considering how he should act in relation to Matilda; and finding it a thing inconsistent with his honour to suffer her to remain in town after what had happened, he resolved to send her immediately into the country, and was just returned from hiring a post-chaise for that purpose. The reason he gave for his proceeding in this manner, was as follows—'She cannot remain here, and be shut up, she

'must

'must appear sometimes; and who can tell but that in some unlucky minute she may be seen by the very villain who has ruined her, and who, either through curiosity, or the desire of renewing the gratification of his vicious flame, may discover whose wife she is, and wherever he sees me, point me to his lewd companions for the wretch he has made me!'

I had nothing to offer in opposition to what he said on this score, for indeed I thought it very proper they should both retire into the country; so replied, that I was glad I had called that morning, otherwise I should not have had the opportunity of wishing them a good journey: to which he hastily rejoined—' I shall not go.'—' How!' cried I, somewhat surprized, ' do you send away Matilda, and stay behind yourself!' A deep sigh was the first answer he gave; but the testimony of his discontent was presently succeeded by these words— ' Yes, my friend, she must go without me: two days ago, nothing was so precious to me as her presence; I lived, indeed, but in her sight; every glance, every look she gave me, shot pleasure to my heart; but now, alas! those happy moments are fled, and I can regard her as no other than the ruined reliques of the woman once so dear to me!'

It was in vain I represented to him, that as I doubted not but he was perfectly convinced of the purity of Matilda's mind, he ought not to love her less for the violence her person had sustained: he owned the justness of my reasons, but could not prevail on himself to be governed by them; and when I urged the cruelty of sending her so long a journey without any companion to alleviate her sorrows, he made me this reply —' She does not go alone; her waiting-maid, who, soon after our arrival in town, was obliged to be removed on account of the small-pox, is now quite recovered, and came home last night : this girl has attended Matilda for some years, and I know will be very careful of her.'

While we were discoursing, the chaise came to the door; on which Alexis called to have the luggage put in, and his wife to make herself ready. I asked him if he thought it proper I should take my leave of Matilda before her departure; he replied, that it was a ceremony which he believed she would gladly be

dispensed with from receiving, in her present unhappy situation ; but begged I would stay in the dining-room till he had dispatched this disagreeable affair. With these words he went out of the room, and I remained where I was. In less than half a quarter of an hour, looking through the window, I saw the disconsolate Matilda go out of the house, supported on one side by Alexis, and on the other by her attendant. I could not see her face; but her motions, and the distracted air with which she threw herself into the chaise, were enough to convince me of the extreme wretchedness of her condition.

Alexis returned to me in a situation little less pity-moving, yet could not my heart altogether absolve him for this last part of his behaviour to Matilda: it was now, however, a time to apply rather balms than corrosives to his bleeding and despairing mind ; I therefore said every thing in my power to administer consolation to him, but all my endeavours that way were unsuccessful; and though I staid with him the greatest part of the day, had the mortification to leave him as I found him.

Oh! had the dark unknown beheld the sad effects his wild inordinate desires produced, he surely could not have sustained the shock, but must have revenged upon himself the mischiefs he had brought upon two worthy persons, so lately blessed, so truly loving and beloved!

CHAP. III.

CONSISTS OF SOME FARTHER PARTICULARS RELATIVE TO THE PRECEDING ADVENTURE; WITH TWO LETTERS WROTE BY THAT UNFORTUNATE LADY TO HER HUSBAND IN HER EXILE.

I Am very much afraid that Alexis will stand but little justified in the opinion of my fair readers for his conduct towards Matilda; they will doubtless say, that the love he pretended to have for her had taken but a shallow root in his heart, when it could be shaken by a misfortune which she had no way contributed to bring upon herself. They will, perhaps, also add, that after she had with so much simplicity, some may think folly too, revealed to him the whole of what

what had befallen her, it was not only unkind, but highly ungenerous and cruel in him to abandon her to despair, at a time when she had so much need of the tenderest compassion and consolation.

I must confess, indeed, that these accusations have the strongest appearance of reason on their side; yet I must take upon me, notwithstanding, to aver, that how much a paradox soever it may seem to some, Love, when in excess, may, on more occasions than one, produce the same effects as hate. Certain it is, that it was chiefly owing to the too refined delicacy of the passion Alexis was possessed of for Matilda, that made them both so greatly wretched; the thoughts that another, though by force, had revelled in her charms, deprived those charms of all their relish, and sickened every wish. When we have been talking together on this head, often have I heard him, in the utmost bitterness of heart, express himself in these terms—

'I still adore her mind; I know it is all composed of sweetness, innocence, and truth; but, oh! the blemish cast upon her person cannot be washed off but with the villain's blood; and, unless fate allows me the means of doing her and myself that justice, can never look upon her but as the ghost of my once dear wife!'

Finding, that to prevail on him to live with Matilda as a wife, was utterly impracticable, at least till time had a little mellowed the asperity of his resentment, I forbore any farther speech on that head, believing, that if a change in Matilda's favour should ever happen, it must come wholly of himself, and not by the arguments of another.

It will be easy for the reader to judge of how little efficacy the persuasions of any friend could be to move him, when those of the tender, the endearing, the so lately adored Matilda, proved in vain; which abundantly appear by the many letters she sent to him after her retirement, two only of which I got an opportunity of transcribing: the first was wrote immediately on her arrival at their country seat.

'MY DEAR, DEAR ALEXIS!

'I Am a sufficient proof, that grief is 'not so fatal as some people would 'represent it, since I live to tell you I am 'safely arrived at ********. Yes, I

'am returned to that once blissful scene 'of soft delights, of pure and virtuous 'love. But, oh! that Heaven is fled, 'a sad reverse supplies it's place; and 'wheresoever I turn my eyes, horrors 'instead of joys rise to my distracted 'view! I remember, that when you 'turned me from you, your last words 'were—" Be comforted, Matilda." 'Alas! you well know, without Alexis 'there is no comfort for Matilda; your 'presence is the only balsam can assuage 'the tortures of my agonizing heart! 'If then, indeed, you wish me less the 'wretch I am, let me not linger long in 'a banishment more cruel than death! 'Quit that detested town, fly to my re- 'lief, and at least join with me in be- 'wailing what is past a remedy.

'But, oh! I have too much cause to 'fear you have withdrawn all your af- 'fection from me, and am doubly mi- 'serable in a confciousnefs of being 'rendered unworthy to retain it. Yet, 'had sickness, or any other accident, de- 'prived me of that little beauty nature 'has bestowed upon me, and made me 'become lame, or blind, or crooked, I 'flatter myfelf you would have loved 'me still; you would then have pitied 'and cherished me in your bosom; and 'sure, the misfortune that has befallen 'me, was as far removed from my secking, 'as any of those I have mentioned. I will 'not, however, anticipate the doom I 'so much dread; will not give way to 'apprehensions distracting to myself, and 'I hope injurious to you. I know you 'are generous and just, and will endea- 'vour to assure myfelf those noble prin- 'ciples, even without the aid of tender- 'nefs, will not permit you to hate me, 'to throw me off for ever, for my per- 'son having sustained a violence, to 'which I am persuaded you are con- 'vinced my mind was incapable of con- 'senting. I will believe that you feel 'all my woes, participate in my anguish, 'and that my pen ought rather to flow 'with words of confolation than re- 'proach. Yet, if it is ordained that 'we must both be wretched, let us be 'wretched together; let us mingle our 'tears, and interchangeably echo back 'each other's fighs; let us indulge de- 'spair; recal the memory of those blifs- 'ful hours we once enjoyed; compare 'the present with the past, and join in 'curfes on the base, the inhuman author 'of our woes!—But whither does my in- 'considerate

'considerate passion lead me! Does it
'become the love, the tenderness, the
'duty, of a wife, to wish you should
'partake my ruin? No; since I can
'no longer contribute to your happi-
'ness, rather forget, renounce, aban-
'don me for ever! Yet, oh! 'tis hard!
'—My brain grows wild on the re-
'flection—I can proceed no farther.
'Pity me, my most dear, my most adored
'Alexis! Pity, O pity, the undone,
'the lost,

'                                   MATILDA!

'P. S. If these distracting lines have
'  any power to move you, if any
'  remains of soft compassion to-
'  wards me still dwell within your
'  breast, write to me by the first
'  post. Fix, I beseech you, my
'  uncertain fate. Oh, that I should
'  live to stand in need of intreaties
'  to hear from you!'

When Alexis shewed me the above,
he seemed all dissolved in a flood of love
and tenderness; yet I believe the answer
he sent to it was dictated in terms not
altogether so satisfactory to Matilda
as the present disturbance of her mind
required. Here follows the second melancholy epistle of that unfortunate
lady.

'My for ever dear, tho' unkind ALEXIS,
'WITH what anxiety have I watched
'      the arrival of the post! how
'counted the tedious minutes as they
'glided on! how trembled between
'hope and fear on every knock given at
'the gate, while in expectation of a
'letter from you! At last it came;
'but, oh! I am not more at ease!
'Wherefore, Alexis, do you keep me
'in this cruel suspence? I asked no
'impossibilities of you, desired you not
'to love me still; I only begged the de-
'cision of my fate; and, sure, that is
'not a request too much for me to
'make, or you to grant!
'My father, uncles, all my kindred
'and acquaintance, nay, our very ser-
'vants, stand amazed to see me here
'without you; they perceive my altered
'looks; and, with officious love, en-
'quire into the cause. All the answer
'I can make is, that the air of London
'not agreeing with my constitution, I
'hurried back before some business you

had in town would permit you to return. These excuses may pass current
'for a time, but cannot do so long; I
'conjure you, therefore, by all you have
'to hope, or fear, or wish, not to ex-
'pose yourself and me to conjectures
'which cannot be to the advantage of
'either of our characters. Pronounce
'my doom; say that you will return,
'and live with me, in all appearance,
'as before, or scruple not to let me
'know you have resolved on an eternal
'separation; that I may retire, at once,
'to some dark corner of the world, and
'shut myself up from pity and con-
'tempt. I know this ought to have
'been thought upon before you obliged
'me to remove from London; but both
'of us were in too much confusion, at
'the time of parting, to give our cooler
'reason room to operate. We have
'since, however, had leisure to reflect on
'what was proper to be done in our un-
'happy circumstances; and I flatter
'myself you will not think me too pre-
'suming in being the first to mention it.
'O, Alexis! imagine not that, when
'I urge you to this eclaircissement, I
'am so vain as to soothe my fond heart
'with a belief, that since the dreadful
'accident you ever can love me as be-
'fore; no, I rather expect my sentence
'will be that of an everlasting banish-
'ment: perhaps it is already signed
'within your breast, and the compassion
'you have for me alone delays the exe-
'cution. If this should be the case,
'throw aside that cruel mercy which
'conceals it. Grief and despair have
'given me fortitude to bear the worst
'of ills, and sure there can be none
'half so dreadful to me as seeing you
'no more! So much the better for my
'eternal peace, as it will the sooner rid
'me of the burden of a hated life. But
'I will trouble you no more than to re-
'new my petition of knowing, in your
'next letter, what it is you have in ef-
'fect decreed for the innocently cri-
'minal

'                                   MATILDA.

'P. S. Your old acquaintance and
'  fellow collegian, Mr. L——,
'  has just now sent to enquire when
'  you are expected down. He de-
'  signs, it seems, to set up, at the next
'  general election, for the borough
'  of ******, and greatly depends
'  on the interest you have in that
'                               'place.

' place. I suppose you will shortly
' receive a letter from himself on
' the occasion. O may the calls
' of friendship give weight to those
' I have mentioned, and influence
' you to return!'

I happened to be with Alexis at the
time of his receiving this. He first read
it to himself, then communicated it to
me; and, when he had finished, cried
out, with an extraordinary emotion—
' Poor Matilda! unhappy, charming
' woman! with what enchanting elo-
' quence does she plead against herself!
' how sweetly labour to oppose what she
' most wishes to obtain!'

As I found the strongest reason in the
arguments urged in Matilda's letter, I
must confess that I was at a loss to comprehend what he meant by speaking in
this manner; therefore desired he would
explain himself, which he immediately
did, in these terms—' O friend! the
' more I discover of her merit, the less
' I am able to forget the violation of
' her honour! I must cease to love her
' as I do, must bring myself to look
' upon her with the same indifference
' that most husbands do upon their
' wives, before I can support, with
' any tolerable degree of patience, the
' thoughts that another has possessed
' her.' Thus did he always talk whenever we were alone; and had Matilda
known his sentiments, I believe it would
be a moot point whether she would not
rather have chose a separation than to
live with him, after he had reduced himself to such a state of insensibility.

He now, indeed, began to give great
indications that he had nothing more at
heart than to lose all remembrance, not
only of the injury done to Matilda, but
of herself also. By very swift degrees
he became the reverse of what he was
before his going to that fatal masquerade. The pleasures of the bottle, and
the conversation of the looser part of womankind, divide too much of his time
between them; and he seeks in riots
and debaucheries his relief from melancholy. I am told, however, that he is
at present preparing to set out for *****;
but what satisfaction can the virtuous
Matilda receive from his return, thus
transformed, thus debased in morals
and behaviour, from the man she had so
dearly loved, and who was once so
worthy her esteem?

How sad a reverse has a few weeks
made in the condition of this lately
happy pair! Surely the wretch—for so
I must call him, be he of what degree
or rank soever—who, for the sake of
gratifying the fleeting pleasure of a moment, has brought this ruin on them,
ought never to be forgiven in this world,
whatever a sincere contrition, if he is
capable of it, may entitle him to in the
next!

## CHAP. IV.

THE AUTHOR HAVING FOUND SOME-
THING IN HIS RAMBLES WHICH
HE SUPPOSES MAY BE OF VALUE
TO THE OWNER, CONDESCENDS
TO TAKE UPON HIM THE OFFICE
OF A TOWN-CRIER, BUT WAVES
THE CEREMONY OF THE GREAT
O YES.

HAPPENING one morning to
wake more early than ordinary, I
quitted my bed; and the weather being
fine, and my humour more inclined to seriousness than gaiety, I took a little walk
into Hyde Park, not with the least expectation of making any discovery of
other people's affairs, but merely to think
of my own with more liberty than I
could do at home. I met no living
creature in my way, except some birds
that perched upon the twigs of the leaf-
less trees, and in melodious notes
chanted forth praises to the approaching
spring. These rather indulging meditation, I passed slowly on by the side of
the Serpentine River; where my eyes
were attracted with the sight of a white
sattin pocket lying just before me. I
suppose it might have been dropped from
some lady's side the night before; for,
on my taking it up, I found it extremely
damp with dew. I looked upon this as
a lawful prize, and that I had a right to
keep it, at least till I could find somebody that had a better title; I therefore
tied it up in my handkerchief, and, after having finished my walk, took it
home with me, where my impatience
did not suffer me to continue long without examining it. I shall give a faithful inventory of all the particulars, re-
serving only one in petto, in order to
prevent being imposed upon by any fictitious claimant.

Money being the chief idol of mankind,

kind, I shall give that the preference, and begin with the purse, which had in it five gold ducats, a leaden French shilling, a bent half-crown, and a medal of the Duke of Cumberland in copper, very curious, but by some accident had been cracked, and the impression in several parts pretty much erased. The next thing that presented itself was a very small pocket-book; which I shall forbear to describe, as well as make any mention of the memorandums it contained, to any person in the world but to the lady who wrote and shall come to demand them. There was also a chrystal smelling-bottle half full of sal armoniac, a tortoise-shell snuff-box rimmed with gold, and a naked Venus painted on the inside.

But the most valuable part of this cargo, at least according to my opinion, was some papers; not Bank-bills, but letters, and other writings, more deserving the attention of the publick, and which I shall make no scruple to insert, as they gradually fell under my inspection; especially as all of them having been sent under covers, which were not in the packet, the name of the lady to whom they were directed can only be guessed at.

### LETTER I.

_MADAM_,

' I Now send you the catalogue you
' have so often requested; but in-
' treat you will be so good as not to let
' any one soul in the world know you
' had it from him who has the honour
' to be, with the greatest respect, &c.'

The name subscribed to this had been torn off, either by design or accident; but the paper which accompanied it was perfect and entire. Here follows a faithful transcript.

A CATALOGUE OF SOME VERY SCARCE AND CURIOUS PIECES, IN PROSE AND VERSE: ALL WROTE BY SOME OF THE MOST EMINENT HANDS.

1. THE Art of Pleasing in Conversation. An Heroick Poem. By the E— of C—.

2. An Essay on Power. Wrote originally in High Dutch, and now translated by a person of distinction into English. Bound in red Turkey, finely gilt and lettered.

3. The Virtues of Carmine, with a Recipe how to prepare it with success. _Probatum est._ By the C— of C—. Gilt back, and lettered.

4. Patient Grizel. A Poem in Six Cantos. By the real C— of C—. Bound in calf, very plain.

5. The Politician Defeated. A Novel. In Three Parts. By the E— of E—. Stitched in blue paper.

6. The Croaker. A Tragi-comical Farce of One Act. By L— R—.

7. Cookery Improved, after the Epicurean Stile. By a Club of Gentlemen. In sheets.

8. The Chaste Maid; or, A New Way to Amuse the Town. A Comedy of Three Acts, each sufficient for a Winter Night's Entertainment. By the facetious H— F—, Esq.

9. Rules to Chuse a Wife; shewing the Absurdity of all those generally observed. By Sir J— C—. In boards.

10. A Philosophical Definition of Card Craft, upwards of Forty Years compiling. By the very learned and most ingenious Professor Mr. H—e. Stitched in gilt paper.

11. Frugality. A Poem. In Nine Cantos. By the C— of B—. Bound in vellum.

12. A Collection of Jests and Merry Phrases, to keep Young People's Heads from Aching with more laborious Studies. By a Tutor in the Modish Sciences. Finely bound in blue Turkey, gilt back, and lettered.

13. Try before you Buy. A Poem after the Manner of Hudibras. By the E— of R—. In boards.

14. The Charms of Novelty. A Pindarick Essay. By Miss C—. In sheets.

15. The Pleasures of Matrimony; or, Who would not be a Husband? A Farce. By L— V—. Stitched, and very much sullied with often reading.

16. A Dissertation on Flies Eggs. By the President of a learned Society. In boards.

17. Laugh and Lie Down. A Ballad Opera of Three Acts. By L— P—. Stitched in blue paper.

18. An Essay to prove that True Honour is always concomitant with

X                    Good

Good Senſe. By the E—— of O——. Bound in plain blue Turkey.

19. Conjugal Love. A Paſtoral of One continued Scene. By the E—— of N——. Printed on a new Elzevir letter, and neatly bound, without tawdrineſs or affectation.

20. The Patriot. A Secret Hiſtory. By G—— D——, Eſq. Bound in clouded calf.

21. The Double Dealer; or, The Weſtminſter Diſappointment. A Farce of Two Acts. By Sir G—— V——. Stitched in cap paper.

22. An Eulogy on Apoſtacy. By L—— G——. Bound in calf, and gilt back.

23. Love in a Bottle. A Poem, in Three Cantos. By the E—— of M——. Stitched in blue paper.

24. Redivivus; or, Old Age and Gallantry Reconciled. A Humorous Farce, of One Act. By the E—— of H——. Stitched.

25. An Exhortation to Hoſpitality to Forcigners, even though it ſhould happen to be deſtructive to the Liberties of the Naʻives. By L—— T——, as he delivered it at the Haymarket. Bound in the French taſte.

26. Criticiſms on the Play of Rule a Wife and Have a Wife. By L—— P——. In boards.

27. The Fox Weary of Gooſe Hunting. A Fable. By the D—— of D——. Bound in parchment.

28. The Lover's Catechiſm. A New Ballad. By the celebrated Miſs A——.

29. An Infallible Remedy for Curing the Scotch Itch without Bleeding. By the D—— of A——.

30. The Beauties of Domeſtick Life, illuſtrated with Examples. A Paſtoral Eclogue. By the D—— of B——. Neatly bound.

31. Love Levels All; or, a Lucky Trip to Bath. An Epic Poem, without any Epiſodes. By C—— B——. Printed on a half worn-out letter, but very richly bound.

32. Inſtructions for a Supplement to Arthur Collins's Peerage of England. By L—— L——. Stitched in marble paper.

33. Verſes in Praiſe of Breeding. By Miſs W——.

34. True Magnificence. An Heroick Poem. By the D—— of M——. Finely bound.

35. Love in a Coach. A True Secret Hiſtory. By C—— V——. Stitched.

36. Second Thoughts Beſt. A Philoſophical Treatiſe, dedicated to a Brother of the Horn. By Mr. W——. Bound in ſheeps-ſkin.

37. The Triumvirate of Converts. Being a Series of Epiſtles on Moral and Religious Subjects, which paſſed between L—— T——, C—— G——, and Mrs. C——. In boards.

38. The Escape. A Satire. Inſcribed to L—— D—— M——, by a Well-wiſher to her Ladyſhip.

39. A Letter ſent with a Side of Veniſon to the celebrated Mrs. J—— D——, in the Piazza, Covent Garden. By L—— T——e.

40. A Short Treatiſe concerning Publick and Private Charities; proving to a Demonſtration, that the former are of much more Emolument to the Giver than the latter. By L—— E—— J——. Curiouſly bound, with a Regiſter.

41. The Humiliation. A Poem. Addreſſed to the Inexorables. By L—— G—— S——. Stitched.

42. A Prophecy that Votes for Members of Parliament will fall to no Price at the next Weſtminſter Election. By Sir W—— Y——.

Having folded and replaced this paper in the pocket whence I had taken it, I proceeded to the other.

## LETTER II.

' DEAR MADAM,

' IT muſt be confeſſed you are en-
' dowed with a courage and reſo-
' lution ſuperior to what moſt of your
' ſex can boaſt of; but you muſt give
' me leave to ſay, at the ſame time,
' that in theſe affairs we men run much
' the greateſt hazards: in caſe of a diſco-
' very, our perſons are liable to fall a ſa-
' crifice to the reſentment of an injured
' huſband, and our fortunes ſure to be
' ruined by way of reparation of his diſ-
' grace; whereas the worſt you have to
' fear is a divorce. The laws are fa-
' vourable to wives; the portion you
' brought with you is either returned,
' or an annuity equivalent: and as for
' the little ſhame you ſuſtain by ſuch a
' procedure, it is well atoned for by
' your

'your being freed from the loathsome
'caresses of the man you hate, and at
'full liberty to pursue your inclinations
'with him you love. Be assured, Ma-
'dam, I would venture much for the
'continuance of the blessing you permit
'me to enjoy; but I find the intercourse
'between us begins to be suspected, and
'you must therefore pardon me that I
'yield to necessity, and refrain any far-
'ther meetings with you, at least for
'the present. I was yesterday at court,
'and heard some whispers, that your
'jealous coxcomb would soon be sent
'abroad: if such a thing should happen,
'as I have some pretty good reasons to
'believe it will, I shall return with dou-
'ble transport to your embraces; till
'then, prudence obliges me to deny
'myself that happiness. But at how
'great a distance soever I keep my per-
'son, I beg you will do me the justice
'to believe my heart is always with
'you; and that I can never cease to be,
'with the greatest sincerity, &c.

'                              'PHILETES.'

'P. S. I would not have you har-
'bour any unjust suspicions either
'of me or your fair friend; for,
'upon my soul! I never had the
'least design upon her in the way
'you mean; and you will find,
'whenever it is convenient for me
'to renew my devoirs to you, that
'I like no woman better than your-
'self. Once more I bid you un-
'willingly adieu.'

### LETTER III.

'DEAR CREATURE,

'YOUR Damon, and my Strephon,
'     'as we call them, are both with
'me. They have found out the most
'charming place that ever was for us to
'scamper to, whenever we can delude
'the eyes of our impertinent gaolers.
'If you can find any excuse to get
'loose from yours, the rendezvous agreed
'upon is the banks of the Serpentine
'River, just after sun-set, whence we
'are to follow our leaders where they
'shall please to conduct us. Lady
'Fillup has a route to-night; you may
'tell your tyrant you are going there.
'But why should I put pretences into

'a head so much more fertile than my
'own? Fail not to come, however, if
'it be not a thing utterly impossible for
'human wit to accomplish: but let us
'know your resolution by the bearer.
'I am, &c.

'                              'CORINNA.

'P. S. While I was writing the
'above, Damon, to shew either
'his love or wit, or both, took up
'a pen, and employed it in the en-
'closed.'

"TO MY SOUL'S TREASURE.

"FLY, charmer, fly! leave homebred
"     cares behind;
"With thoughts of coming joys fill all
"     your mind:
"Let smiling pleasure wanton o'er your
"     face,
"And kindling transports brighten ev'ry
"     grace.
"Each vein of mine beats high with love's
"     alarms;
"Haste, then, and lull me gently in your
"     arms!"

"I know I am a bad poet, but you
"will find me a better lover, and that
"your charms are capable of inspiring
"me with more fire than all the ladies
"of Parnassus put together. I am, &c.

"                              "DAMON."

The letter of Philetes, and that of
Corinna and Damon, being dated on
the same day, discovered to me that the
lady who received them was not quite
inconsolable for the loss of one lover, as
she had another in store; and also that
she failed not to comply with the invitation of Damon, and that she had dropped her pocket at the rendezvous appointed by Corinna.

I make no question but that the inquisitive reader would be glad to know the
name and rank of this so much admired lady; but as I can do no more,
at most, than guess at either, I should
be loth to impose my bare and uncertain conjectures upon the publick, for
fear of a mistake, and being guilty of
the worst of wrongs, that of preju-
dicing the character of an innocent person. I wish every one would pay as
much regard as myself to what Shake-
speare says on this occasion—

'Good

' Good name, in man or woman,
' Is the immediate jewel of our fouls.
' Who fteals my purfe, fteals trafh; 'tis
   ' fomething, nothing;
' 'Twas mine, 'tis his, and has been flave
   ' to thoufands;
' But he that filches from me my good
   ' name,
' Robs me of that which not enriches him,
' And makes me poor indeed.'

Could I have formed even the moft diftant fuppofition to what place Strephon and Damon had conducted their ladies, I doubt not but my curiofity would have carried me thither, where my enquiries might perhaps have gained me the fatisfaction of knowing how much of the night thefe inamoratos had paffed together, and in what manner they had been entertained; but no mention being made of any thing farther than the place where they were to meet, I was obliged to content myfelf with what difcoveries I had made, and fo muft the reader alfo.

I cannot conclude this chapter without an obfervation which has conftantly occurred to me whenever any thing fell in my way of the kind I have been relating, which is this. As the wife has the honour of her hufband in keeping, it feems to me a moft ungenerous and cruel addition to the crime of wronging his bed, when by publick indifcretions fhe expofes him to that contempt and ridicule which the world, though without the leaft fhadow of reafon or juftice, is always fure to caft upon the hufband of a tranfgreffing wife.

I know very well people are apt to fay, that when a woman abandons herfelf to vice, fhe prefently becomes utterly incapable of paying any regard to her own reputation, much lefs to that of her hufband; and that it appears a much greater matter of furprize when they fee women, as it muft be confeffed many fuch there are, who, without being criminal in fact, behave in fuch a manner as to draw on themfelves the fevereft cenfures. Though I muft allow that this too frequently happens, yet I cannot agree in opinion with thofe who feem to wonder it fhould be fo, and look upon it as a kind of inconfiftency in nature; I rather imagine that guilt is more likely to infpire circumfpection. A woman who knows herfelf culpable, I fhould expect to be very careful not to

do any thing in publick that might caufe fufpicion of her being lefs referved in private; whereas a confcioufnefs of innocence, efpecially in a thoughtlefs difpofition, may eafily render a woman unguarded, and lefs obfervant of thofe decorums which, though not effential to virtue, are doubtlefs neceffary to reputation.

## CHAP. V.

TURNS CHIEFLY UPON THE SUBJECT OF EDUCATION, AND CONTAINS SOME THINGS WHICH THE AUTHOR IS APPREHENSIVE WILL NOT BE VERY AGREEABLE TO THE FEMALE PART OF HIS READERS.

THE good or the ill fortune of our whole lives chiefly depends on the firft bent given to our minds in youth. Impreffions made in our early years take a deep root within us, grow up with us to maturity, become part of ourfelves; fo that they may properly be called a fecond nature, and are feldom, if ever, totally eradicated. According to one of our Englifh poets—

' Children, like tender ofiers, take the bow;
' And, as they firft are fafhion'd, ftill will
   ' grow.'

For this reafon it is that parents, unlefs they are very remifs indeed, take fo much pride in the education of their children, beftowing on them every accomplifhment befitting their rank and circumftances, and oftentimes more than will well agree with either. Yet all this will not do; there are fome previous fteps to be taken, without which all the improvements we can make, from the leffons of the moft able mafters, will never render us worthy the efteem of others, or truly happy in ourfelves, for any length of time. Pride, and an impatience of controul, are the firft propenfities difcoverable in human nature: if thefe are humoured and indulged in their beginnings, which is indeed in our moft early years, they will foon become too headftrong and too turbulent to be afterwards reftrained and fubjected to the government of reafon by any methods whatever that can be taken for
that

that purpose; the firſt indications ſhould therefore be carefully watched, and checked in every inſtance.

I ſmile to think what objections are commonly made, by ſome over-fond parents, to ſuch a manner of proceeding. If I am not miſtaken, theſe two are the principal: that to curb children too much is apt to break their ſpirits; and that the world being ſo full of diſappointments, few people eſcape them when they come to maturity, it is pity the poor things ſhould know ſorrow before their time. To both which I take the liberty to make this reply—

Firſt, as to what they call the breaking of the ſpirit. That due decorum I would recommend, takes no more of the ſpirit from the young Maſter or Miſs than what is neceſſary to keep them from running into thoſe follies and exceſſes which, how excuſeable ſoever in childhood, render them contemptible in riper years; as the ſkilful gardener lops from his tender plant thoſe ſuperfluous branches which, if ſuffered to continue, would hinder it from growing to perfection. Then, as to the ſecond, every one knows the ſorrows their little hearts are capable of feeling make no laſting impreſſion on them; they will cry one moment, and laugh the next. The contradiction they meet with will only make them ſenſible that they neither can nor ought to expect they are to have their will in all things; and the trifling diſappointments given them, will enable them to ſuſtain with fortitude thoſe of more conſequence, which may hereafter poſſibly befal them. A boy is leſs liable to the danger of being ſpoiled by too much indulgence than a girl; becauſe he is no ſooner taken from the nurſery, than he is either put out to ſchool, or, if of a ſuperior rank, under the inſpection of a tutor.

I have the honour to be pretty nearly related, by marriage, to Lady Plyant; her late huſband being my firſt couſin. Decency obliges me to viſit the widow ſometimes: ſhe is a very affable, good-natured woman; and has, indeed, a greater ſhare of underſtanding than her too great compliance with the cuſtoms of the age will permit her to make ſhew of. She keeps a prodigious deal of company, for which reaſon I ſee her much leſs frequently than otherwiſe I ſhould do; but happening to paſs by her houſe one day when no coach or chair

was in waiting there, I ventured to knock at the door, and was glad to be told ſhe was alone. I had not, however, been with her above ten minutes, before two or three loud raps proclaimed the approach of ſome new gueſt, and preſently after a grave elderly lady was introduced. Lady Plyant received her with much politeneſs, and a great ſhew of friendſhip; and, after the firſt ſalutations were over, and we had re-ſeated ourſelves, ſaid to her—

Lady Plyant. Dear Mrs. Loyter, I have not ſeen you this age, and have been quite unhappy in the want of you.

Mrs. Loyter. Dear Lady Plyant, the loſs is wholly mine. But I have been ſo embarraſſed—my poor girl has been extremely indiſpoſed.

Lady Plyant. Bleſs me! Miſs not well, and I hear nothing of it! But I hope ſhe is better?

Mrs. Loyter. Perfectly recovered, Madam. She will have the honour of waiting on your ladyſhip this evening. She is gone to make a few viſits, but prayed heartily to find nobody at home, that ſhe might follow me here the ſooner.

Lady Plyant. How perfectly kind that was! Well, ſhe is a charming creature; you are the happieſt woman in the world in having ſuch a daughter. I proteſt, among all my acquaintance, I do not know any young lady that comes up to her; there is ſomething ſo ſweet, ſo engaging, in every thing ſhe does.

Mrs. Loyter. She is infinitely obliged to your ladyſhip. Indeed, I have taken a great deal of pains with her; for, as I have no other daughter, I ſhould never have forgiven myſelf if I had not uſed my utmoſt endeavours to form her mind ſo as to make her as agreeable as poſſible to her acquaintance.

Lady Plyant. Oh, Madam, the world muſt allow you have; Miſs is the darling of every body that knows her.

Mrs. Loyter. The girl has a great deal of good-nature, Madam, and does not want a genius and capacity to mingle in converſation on almoſt any ſubject becoming a young lady to be acquainted with.—

I had been upon the wing to take my flight almoſt from the moment Mrs. Loyter came in; but what was ſaid in relation to her daughter determined me to ſtay till Miſs arrived, in order to be convinced how far her perſon and behaviour correſponded with the high character

racter which had been given of her. At length Mifs Loyter appeared, and I ftretched my eyelids to their full extent, to take in all the charms I had heard fhe was poffeffed of. The girl, indeed, was well enough; but I could diicover nothing extraordinary about her, nor did her eyes or air give any indications of that capacity her mother feemed to boaft of; but as I thought it unfair to give a verdict on mere appearances, I fufpended my judgment on her underftanding till I had more fubftantial proofs.

The difcourfe at firft was only on where fhe had been, who fhe had feen, and how fuch and fuch a lady was dreffed. I found Mifs talked very learnedly on this fubject, and therefore was not without hope of hearing fomething from her equally lively on others of more importance; but none being ftarted, I was compelled to liften to the feveral animadverfions made by thefe three ladies on caps, flounces, and fuch like. At laft, Mifs happening to fay that fhe had met Mrs. O—— in one of the vifits fhe had been making, I prefently catched up the word, and faid to her—' Then, Madam, I ' doubt not but fome converfation paffed ' which you will do us the favour to re- ' peat, as the lady you mention is per- ' fectly acquainted with publick affairs, ' and indeed reafons on them very juftly.' To which fhe replied—' So they fay, Sir; ' but fhe was juft going out when I came ' in; and indeed I was heartily glad of ' it, for I hate to hear a deal of ftuff ' about things I know nothing of.' As I had a good fhare in the enfuing part of this converfation, I fhall, to avoid confufion, repeat my own words as if fpoke by another perfon.

*Author.* Then, Madam, you have no relifh for politicks?

*Mifs.* No truly, Sir. What bufinefs have I with the tranfactions of kings, and princes, and parliaments? It makes me fick to hear fo much of wars, and treaties, and conventions, and taxes, and grievances, and fuch nonfenfe.

*Author.* I muft confefs, Madam, the affairs of Europe are a little intricate at prefent, and may be puzzling to a lady's comprehenfion; but I fuppofe you are not unacquainted with the hiftories of former times.

*Mifs.* Lord, Sir, what have I to do with former times?

*Author.* Every one, Madam, has to do with the annals of the country they were born in.

*Mrs. Loyter.* Thefe things are quite out of my daughter's way; but for all that, I can affure you, Sir, fhe reads a great deal.

*Author.* It would be a pity, indeed, Madam, fo fine a young lady fhould be altogether ignorant of books. I imagine, therefore, that Mifs's genius foars to a higher pitch, the wonders of the creation; I make no queftion but fhe has read Le Spectacle de la Nature.

*Mrs. Loyter.* I believe not, Sir.—Have you, my dear?

*Mifs.* Not I, truly; but I have heard enough of it. They fay there are four volumes of it taken up with nothing but a defcription of trees, birds, beafts, fifhes, and nafty infects.

*Author.* What do you think, Madam, of Fontenelle's Plurality of Worlds?

*Mifs.* O hang it, I was never fo difappointed in my life; I thought by the beginning, when I found a gentleman and lady were taking their walk together by moon-light, fome pretty adventure would have enfued; but, good God! the author has made them talk of nothing but planets, and the things that happen in the fky.

*Author.* I fancy, then, Mifs, romances and novels are chiefly your tafte.

*Mifs.* I hate romances, they are too tedious; as for novels, I like fome of them well enough, particularly Mrs. Behn's: but I know not how it is, the authors now-a-days have got fuch a way of breaking off in the middle of their ftories, that one forgets one half before one comes to the other.

*Author.* Digreffions, Mifs, when they contain fine fentiments and judicious remarks, are certainly the moft valuable parts of that fort of writing.

*Mifs.* I cannot think fo; and I could wifh the authors would keep their fentiments and remarks to themfelves, or elfe have them printed in a different letter, that one might know when to begin and when to leave off.

*Author.* I prefume, Mifs, you are fond of poetry?

*Mifs.* Not very fond; I can't fay I ever read much of it.—

I thought I had now fufficiently founded the genius and capacity of this young lady; therefore ceafed to engrofs her any longer to myfelf, and foon after took

my

my leave, fecretly wondering at the ftrange partiality of Mrs. Loyter, in regard both of herfelf and daughter. A few hours, however, made me begin to judge fomewhat more favourably of thefe ladies. ' Though Mrs. Loyter,' faid I within myfelf, ' is miftaken in believing ' fhe has been able to make her daugh- ' ter pafs for a wit, her endeavours, not- ' withftanding, may have had better fuc- ' cefs in other accomplifhments more ' effential to her happinefs; fhe may have ' made her a good œconomift, and per- ' fectly acquainted with every thing re- ' quifite for the well managing a family.'

I had the more reafon to imagine that this young lady was trained up in frugality and good houfewifery, as I had been told, that Mr. Loyter lived to the height of his income ; that he faved no money ; had feveral fons, the eldeft of whom, after his deceafe, was to run away with the eftate ; fo that it could not be expected the daughter would have any fortune to entitle her to a hufband at all fuitable to the appearance fhe made. But, as I was always willing to be convinced whether my conjectures were right or wrong, I refolved to make an Invifible Vifit to this family. Juft as I came to the houfe, Mr. Loyter was going out, and the door being opened for him, I flipped in, and went up ftairs. The old lady was fitting in the dining-room window with her fpectacles on, very hard at work. Breakfaft was but juft over, as I found by the maid's removing the tea-equipage; and Mifs was gone up to drefs, it feems, for fhe came down prefently after in the fame form I had feen her at Lady Plyant's: fhe ran directly to the great glafs, in order to examine how her petticoats hung at the bottom; and then turned to her mother, and feeing what fhe was about, faid to her—

*Mifs.* Lord, mamma, have you not done mending my tippet yet !

*Mrs. Loyter.* Indeed, my dear, it is paft mending; you have torn the lace in twenty places, I believe, with thofe ugly pins in your ftomacher; I wifh you would take more care of your things.

*Mifs.* Indeed I can't be a flave to my cloaths.

*Mrs. Loyter.* I would not have you, my dear; but this vexes me, becaufe it is the only handfome tippet you have. You muft e'en try to coax your father to give you a couple of pieces to buy you another, the firft time you find him in a good hu-

mour; for I affure you I have not a fingle guinea in the world.

*Mifs.* Well, 'tis a fhameful thing one has not money enough without afking for, when one has a fancy to any thing. But, mamma, can nothing be done with this lace ?

*Mrs. Loyter.* It will never make up again in the fhape it is ; but I believe I may contrive to make a handfome tucker of it.

*Mifs.* Oh, I fhall like a tucker of it vaftly. Pray, mamma, do it as foon as you can.

*Mrs. Loyter.* Where are you going, my dear ?

*Mifs.* I am only going to the next ftreet to Lady Lovejoy's, to afk if Mifs will take a walk with me in the Park.

*Mrs. Loyter.* Do not ftay too long; your father brings company home to-day, and we are to have a great dinner. Mr. Bloffom, and his fon juft come from the univerfity, are to be here, fo I would not have you out of the way for the world ; who can tell what may happen ?

*Mifs.* Oh, why did not I know that fooner ? I would have had on my new gauze cap; but, 'tis no matter, I will come home time enough to change it.

With thefe words fhe fnatched up her little muff, and galloped down ftairs, leaving her poor mother poring over the breaches fhe had undertaken to rectify.

Methinks I hear how heartily the gay and witty part of my readers will laugh at the character of Mifs Loyter; they will certainly look upon her as a ftalking, ftaring, ftupid, notelefs creature; a moving piece of mere matter, uninformed by any foul or fpirit, wholly incapable of deferving praife, and equally infenfible of contempt. 'Tis true fhe appears fo, yet may it not be owing fo much to any deficiency of nature in her, as to the miftaken fondnefs of a mother, who, fearing to give her a moment's difcontent, neglected to rouze the native fluggifhnefs of her faculties by any exercife or employment.

What therefore can be expected from a young perfon bred in a fupine indolence, accuftomed to have her will in every thing, and fcarce taught the difference between good and evil; but that fhe fhould, all her life, act as chance, or as her own undiftinguifhing fancy fhall direct?— Blefs all fober and thinking men from a wife of this caft !

CHAP.

## CHAP. VI.

THE AUTHOR EXPECTS WILL MAKE
A FULL ATONEMENT TO THE
LADIES FOR TOO MUCH PLAIN
DEALING, AS SOME OF THEM MAY
THINK, OF THE PRECEDING
CHAPTER.

WOMEN and wedlock are the common topicks of ridicule among men who, without one fpark of genius or capacity, imagine themfelves wits, and fet up for fuch : but, whatever either they, or fome who even have a better way of thinking in other things, pretend to alledge againft the fex, it is very evident, and muft be confeffed, that Nature has endowed the minds of many women with as great and valuable talents as ever fhe beftowed on men.

Numberlefs are the examples which might be brought from the records, both of ancient and modern hiftory, to prove the truth of this affertion; but I fhall content myfelf with mentioning only a few, yet enough to make thofe unworthy maligners of a fex, to whom they know in their own hearts they are indebted for all the convenience and happinefs of their lives, take fhame to themfelves, and blufh for what they have faid. Who is fo ignorant, as not to have heard of the famed Cornelia of Rome; the mother of the Gracchi, and the wife of Brutus; the learned Hypatia of Greece; the Boadicea and the Cartifmuda of ancient Britain? But it is needlefs to look back into fuch diftant times; the wife of the late Peter the Great of Mufcovy; the imperial heroine of Germany; Signora Laura of Italy; and the prefent queens of Sweden and the Two Sicilies; are no lefs publick than fhining proofs of the capacity of a female mind. And even here, there are not wanting fome, I may fay many ladies, who in private, and almoft obfcure life, are poffeffed of qualifications that might add luftre to the higheft ftations. In fine, there is nothing more certain, than that if the women, generally fpeaking, are lefs knowing than the men, it is only becaufe they are denied the fame advantages of education, and the miftaken mother lavifhes her whole cares in embellifhing the pretty perfon of her daughter, and gives no attention to the cultivation of her underftanding.

I am happy in the acquaintance of a lady whom I fhall diftinguifh by the name of Amadea: fhe had been married very young to a gentleman whom fhe tenderly loved, and by whom fhe was no lefs beloved; but had the misfortune to lofe him at the age of twenty-five, and was at the fame time the mother of three daughters, the eldeft fcarce four years old. The land eftate, which was very confiderable, defcended to the next male heir of the family; and all the perfonals, with a jointure of four hundred per annum, to the fair widow, and each of her children five thoufand pounds.

The firft three years of her widowhood fhe lived the life of a recufe, feldom ftirring out of her own houfe, except to her devotions, or when the neceffity of her affairs obliged her. Nor did fhe, with her mourning, throw this referve entirely off: though it is now full thirteen years fince her dear hufband's death, fhe neither vifits nor receives vifits as formerly, but confines her converfation to thofe of her kindred, or very long and intimate acquaintance; never appears at any publick diverfion, and rejects even the firft mention of propofals for a fecond marriage, though feveral very advantageous ones have been attempted.

All her cares have been turned on the education of her children, and all her pleafures centered in obferving the improvements they made by the inftructions given to them. She had never fuffered their infancy to be frighted with idle ftories of fpirits and hobgohlins, nor amufed with fairy tales: from their moft early years fhe awakened reafon in them; and contrived it fo, that even the little fports fhe indulged them in, fhould fome way or other conduce to that great end.

As they grew bigger, fhe had matters to teach them mufick and dancing, the French and Italian languages, and as much of the Latin as was fufficient to make them fpeak and write Englifh properly: but thefe politer ftudies were not to take up all their time; the œconomy of domeftick life fhe looked upon as too neceffary a qualification not to be well attended to; fome hours in every day were fet apart for needle-work; and, whenever the table was to be furnifhed with any thing extraordinary, they were fure to be put under the tuition of the cook, and frequently affifted her in thofe parts of her bufinefs which were the moft delicate and leaft laborious.

Thus defirous of enriching their minds with

with every useful kind of knowledge, it cannot be supposed that books were out of the question; no, each of these young ladies takes upon her, in her turn, to read to the two others the whole time they are at work. But, above all other things, this discreet mother was studiously watchful to prevent the pride and little vanities, so incident to human nature, from taking too fast hold of their young hearts. Betimes she taught them, that nothing concerning themselves, except the embellishment of their minds, was worthy their attention; that all cares relating to dress or person, beyond what cleanliness and decency required, were superfluous and silly; and that every minute wasted at the toilet would rob them of some advantage they might otherwise receive. I am well aware, those of my fair readers who have been brought up in a different manner—which, by the way, I fear are much the greatest part—will be apt to cry out against the conduct of Amadea; they will perhaps say, they wonder the poor girls are not moped, and that they must certainly be dull, stupid creatures; but those who think thus need only have a sight of the young ladies to be convinced of their mistake: nothing can be more lively and spirituous than all the three sisters; smiles of innocence and joy dwell for ever on their faces, and denote an innate chearfulness and satisfaction, which all those hurrying pleasures, so eagerly pursued by others, have not the power of bestowing.

I made several Invisible Visits to them in their own apartment; and I know very few things capable of giving me a more sincere delight than I took in observing their behaviour, at times when they thought themselves entirely free from all inspection, and had no occasion to put restraint upon their words or actions. Never did I find them lolling out of a window, or consulting their looks or motions in the great glass; never heard them complaining they were not permitted to be first in every new fashion; never wishing to be in the Mall, or any other publick place; never wantonly giggling about love or lovers; never quarrelling with each other, or ridiculing the foibles of their acquaintance. Sometimes I caught them playing and singing to their instruments; at others, amusing themselves with practising some new dance, and not seldom busily employed in needle-work for the use of the family; and at the

same time, making such remarks as occurred to them on some passage or other in history: in fine, I could perceive nothing but what put me in mind of the three Graces, who, according to one of our poets, are actuated but by one soul, and that all harmony and sweet contentment.

The truth is, Amadea never makes use of any austerity; the precepts she gives are only enforced by her own example, and delivered in such a manner as to steal themselves upon the mind, and have no need of any compunction from authority: so that one may truly say—

‘ Wisdom in her appears so bright and gay,
‘ They hear with pleasure, and with pride
    ‘ obey.

Happy the children who have such a mother; happy the mother who has children such as these! I am persuaded, many examples of this kind might be found, if parents would be at the pains to pursue the same measures Amadea did, and instil into their offspring the principles of virtue and wisdom, before they knew what was meant by vice and folly.

## C H A P.  VII.

CONTAINS THE RECITAL OF AN ADVENTURE, WHICH, PERHAPS, WILL NOT BE FOUND LESS INTERESTING, FOR IT'S BEING NOT ALTOGETHER OF SO SINGULAR A NATURE AS SOME OTHERS IN THIS WORK MAY HAVE APPEARED.

I Was one morning taking my Invisible progression into those pleasant fields which lie behind Montague House, not with the least view of making any discoveries, for I could expect none in that retired place, but merely to enjoy the benefit of the fresh air. I had not walked many minutes, however, before I heard the tread of some persons close behind me. I stepped aside to let them pass, and saw that one of them was Narcissa, the only daughter of a gentleman who lived in that neighbourhood. The person who accompanied her was her maid, as I soon after found by the following dialogue between them—

*Narcissa.* Indeed, Betty, I think Captain Pike shews but little love to let us be here before him.

Y                                    *Betty.*

*Betty.* Oh, Madam, you fhould confider that gentlemen in his poft, are not
always mafters of their time: you know
he faid he came to town on affairs of the
regiment, and fomething, perhaps, may
have happened; but, whatever it is that
detains him, it cannot be for want of affection; I am fo certain of that, I would
pawn my life upon it.

*Narciffa.* You are very confident,
Betty, to offer fuch fecurity for a man
you have never feen but twice in your
life.

*Betty.* If I had never feen him but
once, Madam, I have feen enough to
make me know that he loves you to diftraction. Poor gentleman! if he fhould
not fucceed in his addreffes, I am fure
he has reafon to curfe me.

*Narciffa.* Curfe thee, Betty!—why
curfe thee?

*Betty.* He might never have feen you
if it had not been for me. Don't you remember, Madam, how I teazed you to
go into a fhop, and buy the laft new play?
He was fitting reading when we came in;
and I fhall never forget how he threw
down the pamphlet he had in his hand,
and ftared at you, and how he fighed.
Poor foul! he loft his heart from that very
moment. Then how he followed us into
the Park; and how he trembled when
he afked your leave to join us!

*Narciffa.* Pifh! that might be all affectation.

*Betty.* No, Madam, no fuch matter;
the tone may deceive one, but the eyes
cannot. And then, when you were fo
good to give him a meeting afterwards
in the walk by Rofamond's Pond, how
tenderly he expreffed himfelf! For my
part, my heart melted at every word he
faid.

*Narciffa.* He can talk moving enough,
that's certain; but yet, Betty, I ought not
to be too hafty in giving credit to a man
I know fo little of, or what defigns he
may have upon me.

*Betty.* Nay, Madam, I think you
know as much of him as you can do
without being married to him. Did not
he tell you his name was Pike, and that
he was a captain of Colonel ********'s
regiment? As to his defigns, you cannot doubt of their being honourable, as
he begged you would permit him to vifit
you, and afk your father's leave to make
his addreffes.

*Narciffa.* Ah, Betty, I wifh fuch a
thing could be, for he is a prodigious

pretty man; but it is impoffible! You
know my father hates a foldier, calls
them a pack of locufts; befides, he has
always defigned me for Mr. Oakly.

*Betty.* Aye, Madam, and will make
you have Mr. Oakly too, or lead apes in
hell, if you don't take care to prevent it.

*Narciffa.* Heigh ho!

*Betty.* Never figh, Madam, but refolve.

*Narciffa.* On what?

*Betty.* To run away from a forced
marriage; to exert the fpirit of a true-
born Englifhwoman, and be your own
provider.

*Narciffa.* How thou talkeft!

*Betty.* I talk nothing but reafon, Madam. But here comes one who I fancy
will be able to urge it more effectually.

The perfon whom fhe had been fo
ftrenuoufly pleading for, now appeared;
he was a tall, well-made man, and had a
good foldierly afpect; but yet I thought
I difcovered fomething about him that
fhewed he had not always been accuftomed to wear the rich cloaths he now
had on; there wanted that eafy freedom
in his air, which denotes the true-bred
gentleman; and I prefently fet him down
in my mind, either for an impoftor, or
one whom fome lucky chance had elevated far above his birth. He approached Narciffa with a low bow; and after
taking hold of one of her hands, and
kiffing it with the greateft fervency, addreffed her in thefe terms—

*Capt.* How miferable have I been,
my angel, in being kept thus long from
your divine prefence!

*Narciffa.* I do not doubt, Sir, but you
have been better engaged.

*Capt.* Cruel fuppofition! How can you
fo far wrong me, as to imagine that the
whole world has any thing in it I fhould
put in competition with the bleffing I
now enjoy? But the major of our regiment is in town, and unluckily fent
for me this morning: we fubalterns muft
obey our commanding officer; but I hope
in a few months to be colonel, and I
fhall then have leifure to lie eternally at
your feet.

*Betty.* Ah, Sir, I am afraid, before
that time, my lady will be obliged to
have fomebody elfe lie at her feet.

*Narciffa.* Hold your prating, huffy.
Who gave you the privilege of fpeaking?

*Betty.* Madam, the refpect I have for
you will not fuffer me to be filent.—I
tell

tell you nothing but the truth, Sir; my lady will be forced to marry a man to whom she has the greateſt averſion.

*Capt.* O Heaven! ſo near being torn from all my hopes! And can you, Madam, can a lady of your delicacy ſubmit——

*Narciſſa.* Sir, this fooliſh wench talks ſhe knows not what; I may live ſingle if I pleaſe.

*Capt.* Live ſingle! Heaven forbid! No, nature endowed you not with ſuch ſuperior charms, but to bleſs ſome man who, by his abundant love, might make him worthy of them. O that I were the happy he!

*Narciſſa.* Think not of it, Captain; my father would never give his conſent to any one but the perſon he has made choice of for me; much leſs would he endure to ſee me wedded to a gentleman in the army.

*Capt.* And have you, too, that implacable averſion to a ſaſh and croſlet?

*Narciſſa.* I will not pretend to ſay I have; I think the army our only ſecurity in time of war, and the greateſt ornament of our country in times of peace.

*Capt.* O, then, if I could flatter myſelf there was nothing in my perſon more diſagreeable to you than in my function, I ſhould have nothing left to fear.

*Narciſſa.* Yes, indeed, you would, Sir, a great deal; for I aſſure you, if I married you, my father would not give me a groat.

*Capt.* Let him keep his dirty traſh; I deſpiſe money; the commiſſion I enjoy at preſent will keep us above contempt, and I have money in the Bank ready to purchaſe the firſt vacant command of a regiment.

*Narciſſa.* Can you imagine I would give myſelf to a man who has but juſt begun to tell me that he loves me?

*Capt.* My whole life ſhall be but one continued ſcene of courtſhip; be aſſured I ſhall not be the leſs, but infinitely the more your adorer by being your huſband. O, then, be juſt to my ardent paſſion, generouſly put an end to my deſpair.

*Narciſſa.* Bleſs me, what would the world ſay of ſuch a thing?

*Capt.* The wiſe, Madam, deſpiſe all forms. Do not kings and princes marry thoſe they never ſaw before? Beſides, the late proceedings of the legiſlature lay you under a neceſſity of coming to a ſpeedy reſolution.

*Betty.* Aye, Madam, remember the act.

*Capt.* Aye, Madam, conſider how ſoon that fatal Monday will arrive, which takes from you the power of ſnatching from miſery the man who loves you more than life, and would ſacrifice every thing for you!

*Narciſſa.* I muſt confeſs, Captain, your offering to take me without a fortune demands ſome gratitude on my part; and if— But no more; I ſee a lady yonder whom I would not wiſh ſhould ſurprize us in this converſation: this evening you ſhall know my final reſolution. Where can I ſend to you?

*Capt.* I have an appointment with ſome young officers this afternoon at Will's Coffee-Houſe, Whitehall, and ſhall there wait my doom with the muſt ardent impatience; but before you paſs the ſentence of my fate, think, O think, my life or death depends upon it!

*Narciſſa.* Well, well, be eaſy; but go.

*Capt.* I muſt obey: may Love and all it's powers plead for me!

He ſaid no more, but turned away as his miſtreſs had commanded, and paſſed on to another part of the field, while ſhe advanced to meet the lady ſhe had mentioned. But Betty, who was heartily vexed at this accident, could not forbear crying out as they went along—' I won-' der what ſhould bring Marilla here!'

The words were either not heard, or not regarded by Narciſſa, who, I could perceive by her looks, was little leſs diſconcerted: ſhe met her friend, however, with a ſhew of gaiety and ſatisfaction; and as ſoon as they came near each other, ſaluted her in theſe terms—

*Narciſſa.* My dear Marilla! it is a wonder to ſee you in ſuch a place as this; you uſed to be an enemy to all ſolitary walks.

*Marilla.* So I am ſtill; but I have been at your houſe, and was told you were here, ſo came in mere good nature to hinder you from indulging melancholy; but I find I might have ſpared myſelf that trouble. Pray, who was that pretty fellow that left you juſt now?

*Narciſſa.* I know not, he only came up to us, ſeeing nobody elſe in the place, I ſuppoſe, to aſk which was the neareſt way to Great Ruſſel Street.

*Marilla.* Rather to aſk the way to a lady's heart, who lives not far from Great Ruſſel Street. Oh, Narciſſa, you cannot deceive me; I could eaſily perceive, at the diſtance I was, that he did not part from you with the air of a man who had no other buſineſs than to aſk ſuch an impertinent queſtion. Beſides, I muſt tell you that you are a very ill diſſembler; your bluſhes declare that he is a lover: I know well enough that you met him here by appointment. Pr'ythee, let me into the whole of the ſecret.

Narciſſa ſtill perſiſted in her firſt aſſertions; but the other ſeemed not to give credit on that ſcore, and aſſuming a more ſerious air, ſpoke thus—

*Marilla.* I perceive, my dear Narciſſa, I am not thought worthy of your confidence, though I am very certain you have not a friend in the world who wiſhes your happineſs with more ſincerity than I do.

*Narciſſa.* I believe it, my dear, and am much obliged to you; but you would not have me tell lyes to ſhew my gratitude?

*Marilla.* Well, well, I ſhall urge you no farther; and ſhould not have been ſo impertinent to take any notice of what I ſaw, but for the tranſport it gave me to imagine you might now have an opportunity of delivering yourſelf from the danger of being forced into a marriage with a man whom I have heard you declare ſo great an averſion for.

*Narciſſa.* And ſuppoſe the thing were really as you have taken it into your head to fancy, would you have me diſoblige my father by marrying without his conſent?

*Marilla.* Yes, when he will give his conſent to nobody but one with whom you muſt be miſerable; for, beſides the diſlike you have to the perſon of Oakly, his temper is ſuch as would break a woman's heart in two months. You know I am very intimate with his ſiſter, and cannot avoid ſeeing oddities in his behaviour as have made me tremble for you a thouſand times.

*Narciſſa.* I cannot think my father will ever go about to compel my inclinations.

*Marilla.* Oakly is of another opinion; for I can tell you, he makes no ſcruple to ſay, that if you do not marry him, you will marry nobody: therefore, without diving into the ſecrets of your heart, let me adviſe you, my dear creature, not to loſe the ſhort time allowed you, but if you have any offer leſs diſagreeable to you than Oakly, accept it at

once; three days hence it will be ont of your power.

*Narciſſa.* But, my dear, what man that is worth having will marry a woman without a fortune?

*Marilla.* If I were a man, I ſhould tell you that your perſon was a ſufficient fortune, and I do not doubt but that there are a great many who would think ſo. But you have two thouſand pounds left you by your grandmother, independent of your father; and I dare ſay, if you were once married, and the thing paſt recal, he would forgive it. Conſider, you are his only daughter, and both your brothers are provided for; the one by an eſtate, and the other by a good preferment in the church.

What anſwer Narciſſa would have made I know not: it began to rain very faſt, ſo that the ladies were obliged to mend their pace, and make all the haſte they could out of the field. Marilla took the firſt chair ſhe met with, ſaying it would be dinner time before ſhe ſhould be able to get dreſſed. Narciſſa and her maid ran home through the ſhower, and I followed; not only to take ſhelter, but alſo to hear the reſult of the young lady's determination on what had paſſed between her and Captain Pike. As ſoon as they had plucked off their wet hats and capuchins, and Narciſſa had a little re-ſettled herſelf, ſhe ſaid to her maid—

*Narciſſa.* Well, Betty, this has been an odd morning!

*Betty.* I hope it will prove a lucky one, Madam. But I am glad you did not tell Marilla any thing of the matter.

*Narciſſa.* She was ſo preſſing, that I had half a mind; but when I conſidered how great ſhe is with Oakly's ſiſter, I thought it was better to keep her in ignorance.

*Betty.* Much better, indeed, Madam. But, pray, what do you reſolve to do about the captain?

*Narciſſa.* Why, I muſt e'en have him, I think.

*Betty.* You made him a kind of promiſe to ſend to him.

*Narciſſa.* I did ſo, and will keep it. I will write to him this moment, before any company comes in to prevent me.

*Betty.* You are in the right, Madam: there is nothing like the time preſent,

TO

‘ TO CAPTAIN PIKE.

‘ SIR,

‘ I Should be guilty of an injuſtice
‘ both to myſelf and you, not to be
‘ ſenſible of the proof you offer of your
‘ ſincerity. I find in it, indeed, all that
‘ can be imagined, and much more than
‘ could be expected, of love, honour,
‘ and generoſity; and I hope I ſhall
‘ hereafter ſtand excuſed to my father
‘ and the world, for taking a ſtep ex-
‘ cited by gratitude, and approved of by
‘ my reaſon. Meet me, therefore, to-
‘ morrow morning, at eight preciſely,
‘ in the Piazza next King Street, Co-
‘ vent Garden; where I will put myſelf
‘ under your protection, and be con-
‘ ducted by you to whatever place you
‘ ſhall judge moſt proper for the ce-
‘ remony which muſt make me eternally
‘ yours.

‘ NARCISSA.’

Having ſealed this billet, ſhe gave it
to her maid, with a ſtrict charge to ſend
it by a truſty meſſenger. On which the
girl replied—‘ Yes, Madam, you may
‘ depend on the ſafe conveyance; for I
‘ will be the bearer of it myſelf.’
What farther chat paſſed between the
miſtreſs and maid was too inſignificant
to be repeated; nor, indeed, did I ſtay to
hear much of it, having already gained
all that was neceſſary for the preſent: ſo
ſhut up my Tablets, and retired on the
firſt opportunity I found for my leaving
the houſe.
As it was plain to me, however, that
Betty was deeply intereſted in the con-
ceſſion Narciſſa had made to the captain, and I had alſo ſome ſuſpicion that
he was not in reality the perſon he pretended to be, I reſolved to go in the
evening to the coffee-houſe, and be witneſs of his behaviour on receiving the
letter Betty was to bring. Accordingly
I went, and found him there; not, as he
ſaid, in company with young officers,
but ſitting alone, in a corner of the room,
with his hat very much flapped. A
few minutes after I came in, a waiter
called aloud to know if one Captain
Pike was there; on which he ſtarted up,
and anſwering to the name, was told a
gentlewoman at the door deſired to ſpeak
with him. He went haſtily out, and I
purſued his ſteps, not doubting but it

was the emiſſary of Narciſſa: as ſoon as
he ſaw it was ſhe, he cried out, in ſome
ſurprize—
Capt. What, ſiſter, are you come
yourſelf! You bring me no bad news,
I hope?
Betty. No, no; the beſt you can expect. But walk this way; it is not proper to ſtand here to talk. For Heaven’s ſake! why did you venture to appoint ſuch a publick place as this?
Capt. Nobody knows me here; my
captain never uſes this houſe. But tell
me, how goes our affair?
Betty. Rarely. She will have you;
here is her promiſe under her own hand.
By this time they were got about the
middle of Scotland Yard; where Betty
having given him the letter of Narciſſa,
he ſtopped to read it by the light of a
lamp at a gentleman’s door; and, as ſoon
as he had finiſhed, cried out—
Capt. This is brave, indeed! And
nothing, ſure, was ever ſo lucky as her
fixing to-morrow for our wedding; for
the captain went to Hampſtead this
morning, with a whore he picked up in
the Park the other night, and will not
be in town theſe two days; ſo I ſhall
have all that time to myſelf, and can
get at what cloaths and linen I want.
But, my dear ſiſter, what ſhall I do
with this girl when I have married her?
where muſt I carry her?
Betty. That is what I came to talk
about. You muſt take a fine lodging
for her, and order a handſome dinner to
be provided at ſome tavern or other.
Every thing muſt be done with a grand
air, that ſhe may ſuſpect nothing till after you have conſummated. Hah, brother!
Capt. But, Betty, I have no money: all will go wrong ſtill if you cannot help me out.
Betty. Nothing would go right, if
it were not for me: you may thank God
for having ſuch a ſiſter; you might have
been a foot-ſoldier elſe as long as you
lived. But there is no time to be loſt.
I have brought you four pieces, and I
believe that will be ſufficient for every
thing. Go and buy a ring, and ſecure
a lodging, immediately.
Capt. You may be ſure I ſhall not
fail. But harkye, Betty, take care ſhe
brings the writings of her two thouſand
pounds, and all her jewels.
Betty.

*Betty.* Aye, aye; she shall leave nothing of value behind her, I'll engage.

With these words they separated; and I went home, heartily glad that I had made this discovery, and determined to save Narcissa, if possible, from the misfortune she was so near falling into: to which end I sat down to my escritoire, and immediately wrote to her father in the following terms—

‘ TO JOHN ******, ESQ.

‘ SIR,

‘ THE shock I am now about to give
‘ you, can only be excused by
‘ it’s being done to prevent you from re-
‘ ceiving a much greater and more last-
‘ ing one. Sorry am I to tell you, yet
‘ so it is, your daughter Narcissa is on
‘ the point of utter destruction; she has
‘ premised, and is resolved to keep her
‘ word to join herself in marriage with
‘ a wretch who, though of the most ab-
‘ ject rank, in order to seduce her in-
‘ nocence, assumes the character of a
‘ gentleman, and calls himself Captain
‘ Pike. Betty, her waiting-maid, is
‘ sister to the impostor, and has been the
‘ conductress of he whole villainous de-
‘ sign. Every thing is prepared for the
‘ accomplishment, and to morrow is the
‘ day fixed, but I hope this intelligence
‘ will reach you time enough to pre-
‘ vent so irremediable an evil. I am,
‘ Sir, your unknown well-wisher and
‘ humble servant.’

Having sent this away, and fully discharged what my honour and conscience represented as a duty, I flattered myself with the expectation of seeing, the next day, treachery and deceit receive the mortification they justly merited.

## CHAP. VIII.

CONTAINS A BRIEF ACCOUNT OF
THE EFFECTS PRODUCED BY THE
GOOD INTENTIONS OF THE IN-
VISIBLE SPY, WITH SOME OTHER
SUBSEQUENT PARTICULARS.

THOUGH I had not the least room to doubt but that the information I had given the father of Narcissa would have all the success I wished, yet I could not avoid being extremely curious to see in what manner the persons concerned would behave on this occasion. Accordingly I went to the house the next morning about eleven, expecting to find that the maid had been turned out of doors, the mistress in tears for her disappointment, and the old gentleman rejoicing in the thoughts of having saved his beloved daughter from undoing herself. A servant happening to be at the door, receiving some shoes from a fellow who had been just cleaning them, I gained an easy access. Finding nobody in the lower floor, I went up stairs; but the same solitude reigned likewise there. I then proceeded a story higher, and there saw only a servant-maid sweeping out a room, which, by a toilette being set out, I judged was the chamber of Narcissa. I was very much surprized to find every thing so quiet in a place where I looked for nothing but confusion, and stopped on the stairs to consider what might be the occasion; when, on a sudden, I heard the ringing of a small bell, and presently after saw a footman running hastily up. I followed him where he went, which was into the chamber of Narcissa’s father, who was not yet up, but now called for his cloaths. As he was putting them on, he cast his eyes on the table, and seeing a letter lie there, asked his man when, and from whom, it came. To which he replied—‘ Sir, it was left for
‘ you last night by a porter; but as you
‘ came home so late, would not disturb
‘ you with it.’

I was astonished on finding that this was no other than the letter I had sent him; but more troubled that, by the delivery of it being delayed, poor Narcissa had fallen into the trap laid for her. But if I, a stranger, could be so much affected, what agony must rend the tender father’s heart! Scarce had he gone through the half of what I wrote, before he cried out, casting, at the same time, a look full of despair and rage upon his servant—

*Father.* Ill-fated wretch! what mischief, what ruin, has thy neglect brought upon me and my family! You imagined I was drunk last night, I suppose; but had I been so, here is enough in this letter to have brought me to my senses. But go, run up to my daughter’s chamber; see if she be there.

*Footman.*

*Footman.* Sir, she went out very early this morning with Mrs. Betty, and is not yet come back.

*Father.* Nor ever will, I fear. The intelligence this brings is too true, I find. Run to Mr. Oakly and my cousin Johnson's; bid them come this instant. Fly!—and, do you hear, bring a coach with you. If I can recover her before consummation, her ruin may be yet prevented.

The fellow went on his errand; and the old gentleman in the mean time stamping, biting his lips, and shewing all the marks of an inward distraction, made an end of putting on his cloaths, in order to go in search of his lost daughter, when the gentlemen he had sent for should arrive: but I staid not to hear what method would be pursued for that purpose, as thinking it of no moment, and that it would be better to return again in the evening, when I might probably hear what success had attended their endeavours. The time I chose for going was as late at night as I thought I might get an opportunity of entering, yet the disconsolate father was but just come home: his two friends were with him; they said all they could to alleviate his sorrows, but it availed no more than preaching to the winds. They had found out, it seems, where the marriage was performed: after which, they went to all the taverns, coffee-houses, and other publick places, which they heard were frequented by officers, to enquire concerning one who called himself Captain Pike, but could not receive the least information of any one who bore that name; and all the consolation the old gentleman had for the pains he had taken was, the cruel certainty that his dear daughter was inevitably undone.

Though I saw very little probability of my being able to learn any thing more at this house than I had already done, yet I could not forbear calling constantly there every day; and at last, by this dint of continued application, I became acquainted with the whole melancholy secret of Narcissa's fate almost as soon as the family knew it themselves. The pretended captain had managed every thing according to the direction of his sister. As soon as the ceremony was over, he had conducted his bride to very handsome lodgings, where an en-

tertainment suitable to the occasion was provided; and the poor deluded young lady, seeing nothing but what served to make her satisfied with what she had done, in return for his imaginary generosity, made him a present of her two thousand pounds, which was in India bonds.

Her contentment might, perhaps, have lasted some little time longer than it did, if she had not proposed waiting on her father, to implore his forgiveness and blessing; on which the impostor, having now got his ends, thinking it needless to continue the deception any longer, confessed that he was no more than a private man in the army; but told her that he was now treating with his captain for his discharge, and would purchase a commission with some part of the money she had given him; and added, that till these two points were accomplished, it would be altogether improper to appear before her father.

Narcissa fell into the utmost distraction on this eclaircissement, vowed not to live with a wretch who had put so base a trick upon her, but would go home to her father, who she doubted not would find means to punish such a flagrant piece of villainy. He only laughed at her reproaches, and said, that as she was his wife, she had it not in her choice to leave him. Betty, also, now threw off the character of a servant, and assuming the authority of a sister, pretended to rebuke her idle prating, as she insolently termed it.

She found an opportunity, however, of making her escape, and fled for refuge to the house of a near relation; who, on hearing her story, undertook to intercede with her father; which he did so successfully, that the old gentleman forgave, and took her again into favour. All possible measures were taken to set aside the marriage, and compel the impostor to refund the money Narcissa had so unwarily bestowed upon him; but as he knew the law was too much on his side, having not married her in a false name, though under a false character, he carried things with a very high hand; would part with nothing, not even the jewels she had left behind; but even threatened to commence a process against any one who detained her person. In fine, all that could be done was to get him to sign articles of separation. After which

Narcissa

Narciffa retired into the country, where I hear fhe refolves to wafte the whole remainder of her days in a melancholy contrition for the rafhnefs of her ungoverned conduct.

I muft not forget to let my readers know, that Marilla is fince married to Mr. Oakly; with whom, as I am credibly informed, fhe was long paffionately in love; and on that motive ufed the utmoft of her endeavours to ftrengthen the averfion her fair friend had for him.

END OF THE SIXTH BOOK.

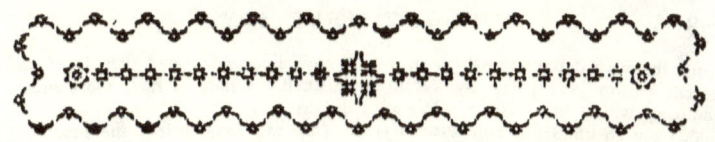

THE

# INVISIBLE SPY.

## BOOK VII.

### CHAP. I.

THE AUTHOR FLATTERS HIMSELF
WILL BE NO UNACCEPTABLE
PRESENT TO ALL THOSE OF THE
FAIR SEX, WHO ARE EITHER
TRULY INNOCENT, OR WOULD
PRESERVE THE REPUTATION OF
BEING SO.

HEN a young woman, of what rank or degree fo-ever, indulges herself in a too great freedom of con-verfation with one of a loofe and wanton behaviour, fhe cannot wonder that thofe who are wit-neffes of their intimacy fhould fufpeÉt her guilty of the fame inclinations; and that, though perfeÉtly innocent of the faults of her companion, is made an equal partaker of her fhame. Women, who are either born to, or reduced by accidents, to low and indigent circumftances, excufe themfelves by faying, that the neceffity of their af-fairs compels them to keep an acquaint-ance with perfons whom they find it their intereft to oblige. But if this be an in-fufficient pretence, as certainly it is, fince there is no intereft which ought to be put in competition with reputation, what can be alledged in behalf of ladies of for-

tune and quality, who have it in their power to chufe their company, and it cannot be fuppofed would converfe with any whofe manners they did not ap-prove?

In fine, there is no one error in con-duÉt, which, according to my opinion, the fex in general fhould be more upon their guard againft than this; for though fome, dazzled with the pomp of fhew and equipage, may be weak enough to ima-gine, that to appear in publick, or to be known to have an intimacy with a wo-man of a polluted fame, provided fhe be a perfon of condition, will bring no blemifh on their own charaÉters, nor be of any prejudice to their morals; yet that fuch an intimacy is extremely dangerous to both, may be very eafily demonftrated.

As to charaÉter. If the world fhould be more filent than it ever was, or ever will be on fuch occafions, it cannot be expeÉted that a woman, who has thrown off all regard for her own honour, fhould have any for that of the perfons fhe con-verfes with, or would even wifh they fhould be thought poffeffed of a virtue fhe is entirely deftitute of herfelf. No; on the contrary, fhe will rather have re-courfe to all the wicked artifices fhe may be miftrefs of, to caft a fhade over that brightnefs which would render her own deformity more confpicuous. But this

Z                                              is

is not the worſt danger to which an innocent peſſon is expoſed by keeping company with a bad woman. We are told, from an unqueſtionable authority, that it is hard to touch pitch without being defiled; and certainly there is nothing more evident, than that vice naturally loſes great part of it's horrors by becoming familiar to the ſight. The chaſte heart, which ſhudders at the bare repetition of indecent actions, by accuſtoming itſelf to be a witneſs of them, eeaſes firſt to wonder, and by degrees to deteſt them; and though I will not he ſo uncharitable as to ſay, that the mind is always corrupted by ſuch a communication, yet I will venture to affirm, that the manners will be ſo.

I know very well, that the timid modeſty I would recommend, as the ſureſt guardian of a virgin's honour, has for many years been exploded; and that ſince ſome foreign cuſtoms have unhappily been introduced among us, to be capable of bluſhing is looked upon, by thoſe who paſs for models of politeneſs, as an indication of the want both of wit and good-breeding. This audacity of behaviour being ſo much the mode, it is not a little difficult to diſtinguiſh between thoſe who really purſue the dictates of a licentious inclination, and thoſe who put on a ſhew of it, merely to comply with the example of others; and a perſon who judges of a woman by what he ſees of her in publick, runs a very great riſque of being miſtaken. Often has my opinion been led aſtray in this point, even in regard of ladies with whom I was moſt intimately acquainted, and ſaw every day; nor did I ever dare to give a character of any one of them, till my Belt of Inviſibility afforded me an opportunity of prying into the ſecrets of the alcove.

Coriſca and Emilia are two celebrated beauties. They are almoſt equally followed and admired by the men, but neither of them were ever jealous or envious of the praiſes given to the other; and there was once ſo exceſſive a fondneſs between them, that they were ſcarce ever ſeen aſunder. Coriſca has been married ſome years; Emilia has not yet been prevailed upon to part with her liberty: but though there is this difference in their circumſtances, there has been too much appearance upon exact ſimilitude in their humours and conſtitutions: I ſay in appearance, for

I have ſince diſcovered that light and darkneſs are not, in fact, more widely diſtant.

Coriſca, long before ſhe became a wife, was locked upon as what they call a female rake. Some there were, however, who imputed what ſhe did only to the too great vivacity of her humour, and would not believe her guilty of any real crime; but far the greater number were of a quite different opinion: and, indeed, the little regard ſhe takes of her family ſince her marriage, the publick contempt with which ſhe treats her huſband, and the frequent quarrels ſhe has with him in private, but too much juſtify the worſt character that can be given either of her œconomy or her chaſtity. Yet, notwithſtanding all this, there is a certain ſomething in her air, her wit, and manner of behaviour, ſo engaging to both ſexes, that ſhe has always been, and ſtill continues to be, conſtantly viſited by perſons not only of the beſt fortunes, but of the beſt reputations; who chuſe rather to ſeem blind to her faults, than deny themſelves the pleaſure of her converſation. It is, beyond all diſpute, a very great pity, that a woman ſo plenteouſly endowed by nature with every qualification to ſhew virtue in it's moſt amiable colours, ſhould, through a ſtrange depravity of principles and inclination, make uſe of all the fine talents ſhe is miſtreſs of only to varniſh over the foul face of vice, and give a pleaſing aſpect to the deformity of ſin and ſhame.

The beautiful perſon of Emilia, her ſprightly wit, her good humour and affability, rendered her the darling of all who knew her. They beheld, with an infinity of concern, her intimacy with Coriſca; and thoſe who, either by proximity of blood, or a long acquaintance with her, thought themſelves privileged to offer their advice, did it in the ſtrongeſt terms, and ſpared no remonſtrances that might prevail on her to break off ſo dangerous a communication; but ſhe was deaf to all that could be ſaid to her on this ſubject. It was her misfortune to become the miſtreſs of her own actions at too early an age; what fortune ſhe was poſſeſſed of was in her own hands; and as ſhe was entirely independent on her friends, would not ſubmit to be directed by them.

In juſtice to this young lady's character, however, I muſt ſay, and ſhall hereafter

hereafter prove, that there is a fund of honour and virtue in her foul fufficient to have made her look with contempt and deteſtation on the conduct of Corifca; and to have obliged her, if not to break off all converſation with her, at leaſt not to appear with her in publick, or make one in any party of pleaſure where ſhe was engaged. But, alas! the ſeeds of thoſe noble principles for a time lay dormant in her; choaked up with the natural levities of youth, and the modiſh exceſſes of the age, they had not power to ſhoot forth into action. Innocently wanton, and indolently gay, ſhe ſaw not the danger to which ſhe expoſed her perſon and reputation, becauſe ſhe thought not of it, nor gave herſelf the pains to examine what ſnares might poſſibly be ſpread for her; but ſuffering herſelf to be continually hurried from one amuſement to another, never conſidered or reflected on any thing farther than the preſent ſatisfaction.

I have been thus particular in deſcribing the character and humour of Emilia, becauſe in the courſe of my rambles I have found too many others of the ſame giddy bent, who, without the leaſt propenſity to ill, have heedleſsly run into actions which have involved their whole future lives in diſhonour. Theſe have reaſon to pardon this digreſſion, eſpecially as it has not been tedious; and I ſhall now return to the adventure which occaſioned it.

Among the many Inviſible Viſits which for a conſiderable time together I had made to the apartment of this celebrated Corifca, I happened to be there one morning when Favonius and Palamede were with her. The firſt of theſe gentlemen is of a very amorous inclination, and known to be what the world calls well with her; the other, though gay and lively as Mercury himſelf, has been reſtrained, either through want of inclination to her perſon, or his friendſhip to Favonius, from attempting to take any private liberties, and ſeldom viſits her but in his company. The diſcourſe they were engaged in, when I firſt broke in upon them, I found was on ſubjects of too trifling a nature for me to ſpread my Tablets for the reception of; ſo I ſhall make no repetition of any things which were ſaid till the entrance of Emilia, who came in ſoon after. The firſt ſalutations were

no ſooner over, than Corifca, taking her fondly by the hand, ſpoke thus—

*Corifca.* Dear creature, this is an exceſs of goodneſs in you to come thus early; I did not expect you till dinnertime.

*Emilia.* Indeed, my dear, I never waited on you with ſo ill a will, nor came on an errand ſo diſagreeable to my inclination; for I have but juſt time to tell you, that I am deprived of the pleaſure I propoſed of paſſing the whole day with you.

*Corifca.* On what occaſion?

*Emilia.* The moſt unlucky one that could have happened. An old aunt of mine has taken it into her head to quit her rookery and henhouſe in the country, and come to ſtare and be ſtared at in town. She arrived laſt night, and ſent me word ſhe muſt needs ſee me this morning: decency obliges me to go; ſhe is my godmother, and beſides is pretty rich.

*Corifca.* But cannot you make ſome excuſe to leave her as ſoon as you have paid your compliments? I ſhall have all the world here this afternoon, and would not have you abſent upon any ſcore.

*Emilia.* It cannot be avoided. She pretends to have a huge fondneſs for me, and I know will detain me, with a thouſand impertinent declarations of it, till bed-time: ſo, my dear, adieu for this whole tedious day; to-morrow, I hope, will atone for this vexation.— Gentlemen, your ſervant.

In ſpeaking theſe laſt words, ſhe turned upon her heel, and ran out of the room; but not ſo haſtily but that Palamede, with one ſtride, joined her at the door, and led her down ſtairs. In the mean time Corifca, looking on Favonius, ſaid to him—

*Corifca.* I pity poor Emilia. The impertinent fondneſs of an old relation is almoſt as great a mortification as the ſaucy indifference of a young fellow one likes.

*Favonius.* The beautiful Corifca, I am ſure, can never be in danger of experiencing the latter of theſe vexations. To prove the ſincerity of this aſſertion, he cloſed it with a ſtrenuous embrace, which Corifca returned. There was time for no more; Palamede came back; and Favonius, with a ſmile, ſpoke in this manner—

*Favonius.*

*Favonius.* By the fparkle in your eyes, Palamede, I fhould imagine the piece of gallantry you have fhewed to Emilia has been more than ordinarily well received.

*Palamede.* This, and all others I have yet had in my power to treat that lady with, have been too trifling to deferve much notice from her.

*Favonius.* Oh, every kind glance gives tranfport to a man in love!—You mult know, Madam, I have juft found out that Palamede is defperately in love with Emilia.

*Corifca.* Indeed!—And do you allow the charge, Palamede?

*Palamede.* Not altogether, Madam. I am not abfolutely in love; but confefs I think Emilia an extremely fine girl, and have had fome very odd dreams on her account.

*Corifca.* What hinders you, then, from making your addreffes to her?

*Palamede.* Why, faith, Madam, to confefs the truth, I was afraid of not fucceeding on the terms I wifh'd to do; and as for marriage, the circumftances of my eftate require I fhould make choice of a wife with a much larger fortune than Emilia is poffeffed of.

*Favonius.* You are perfectly in the right, Palamede. A good fortune with a wife is abfolutely neceffary for a man of pleafure, as it enables him to make handfome prefents and entertainments to thofe women he may happen to like better.

*Corifca.* So, Palamede, you durft not afk Emilia the queftion, for fear of meeting with a rebuff from her overfcrupulous virtue?

*Palamede.* That is indeed the cafe, Madam.

*Corifca.* Then you are a fool. Not but I believe Emilia is perfectly innocent as yet; but what is innocence, what is virtue, what is honour, when oppofed to love and inclination! Do you not know what Mrs. Behn, who muft be allowed to be a perfect judge of nature in our fex, fays upon this occafion?

' Oh, curfed Honour! thou who firft didft
    ' damn
' A woman to the fin of fhame!
' Honour! who taught her lovely eyes the art
' To wound, and not to cure the heart;
' With love t' invite, but to forbid with
    ' awe,
' And to themfelves prefcribe a cruel law.

' His chief attributes are pride and fuight,
' His pow'r is robbing lovers of delight.
' Honour! that puts our words, that fhould
    ' be free,
' Into a fet formality!
' Thou bafe debaucher of the gen'rous
    ' heart,
' That twacheft all our looks and actions
    ' art.
' What Love defign'd a facred gift,
' What Nature made to be poffefs'd,
' Miftaken Honour made a theft.
' Thou foe to Pleafure, Nature's worft dif-
    ' eafe!
' Thou tyrant over mighty kings,
' Be gone to princes palaces,
' But let the humble fwain go on,
' In the bleft paths of the firft race of man,
    ' That reareft were to gods allied,
' And, form'd for love, difdain'd all other
    ' pride.'

The emphatick accents and graceful manner with which Corifca pronounced thefe lines adding to the beauty of the poetry, ftruck fo much upon the hearts of the two gentlemen, that they could not forbear clapping their hands, and crying out—' Encore, encore, charming ' Corifca!' On which fhe laughed heartily, and replied—

*Corifca.* I want none of thefe theatrical teftimonies of approbation; I would only convince Palamede, from the unqueftionable authority of our Englifh Sappho, that when a woman loves, no confiderations are of force to reftrain her from acting up to the dictates of her paffion.

*Palamede.* Aye, Madam, if I could flatter myfelf with the hopes of being loved by Emilia, I fhould have nothing to apprehend.

*Corifca.* I will not pretend to tell you that fhe is fo much in love as not to be able to eat, drink, or fleep, for the thoughts of you; but I have heard her fay a thoufand times over, I believe, that you are, without exception, the prettieft fellow in the whole town; that you drefs the beft, and have fomething peculiarly agreeable in your air and manner of behaviour: and on the ftrength of this, and fome other indications I have obferved about her, I dare venture to affirm that you are far from being indifferent to her, and that fhe would be little lefs pleafed than yourfelf with an opportunity of being entertained by you in private.

*Palamede.* Dear Madam, you make me the moft tranfported man alive! But

by

by what means can fuch a thing be brought about? Some fcheme muft be laid for that purpofe.

*Corifca.* Nothing more eafy; I have it all in my head already; fhe will go any where with me; we fhall be together to-morrow; you two fhall come in as if by accident, and propofe going to take the air on the other fide of the waters there is a houfe the moft commodioufly fituated that can be; good gardens, good wine, good every thing.—Favonius is well acquainted with the place.

*Favonius.* I fuppofe you mean that kept by Mrs. *******?

*Corifca.* The fame. When we have been there fome time, and it begins to draw near the hour proper to think of going home, you fhall difcharge the coach, and pretend the fellow got drunk and went away without your knowledge. There will be no poffibility of procuring a vehicle to bring us to town, efpecially at night. Favonius muft be content to do penance with me in loitering about the gardens, or in fomething or other, till morning, while you make the moft of your time with Emilia.

*Palamede.* Excellent, my charming Machiavel! But how fhall we prevail on Emilia to be feparated from her dear Corifca?

*Corifca.* Leave that to my management; fhe fhall fufpect nothing of the matter, till fhe finds herfelf alone with you, and then it will be your bufinefs to make her fatisfied with being fo.

*Palamede.* Kind creature! where fhall I find words to thank this compaffion to a fuffering lover?

*Corifca.* Never trouble yourfelf about thanks; good actions, they fay, reward themfelves.

*Favonius.* As for my part, I fhall defer thofe acknowledgments which your excefs of goodnefs demands from me, both on my own fcore and that of my friend, till to-morrow night, when they fhall make part of that agreeable penance I am to perform.

This fpeech of Favonius paved the way for a converfation conformable enough to the characters of the perfons engaged in it; but I am certain would not be well relifhed by that part of my readers which I am moft ambitious of obliging: I fhall therefore clofe the fcene, as indeed I did foon after my Tablets, and quitted the apartments of this fair

libertine. in order to retire to my own, and contemplate at leifure on what I had feen and heard.

## CHAP. II.

PRESENTS THE READER WITH THE CATASTROPHE OF AN ADVEN-TURE VERY DIFFERENT FROM WHAT THE BEGINNING MAY HAVE GIVEN HIM REASON TO EXPECT.

THOUGH I had thought myfelf too well acquainted with the principles and inclination of Corifca, to be at all furprized at any act of licentiouf-nefs fhe could poffibly be guilty of, yet I could not defend my fenfes from being feized with the extremeft fhock, on finding fhe could be bafe enough to conde-fcend to become the inftrument of others pleafures, and betray the innocence of a young lady for whom fhe had as much friendfhip as is confiftent with a woman of her character—forgetting all this while what the good old poet, Mr. Philip Maffenger, tells us on an occafion fimilar to this of Corifca and Emilia—

‘ Virtue and Vice in one fole point agree,
‘ Each would be glad all like themfelves might
‘ be.

In ruminating very wifely, as I then imagined, on what Corifca had faid to Palamede, I muft confefs I entertained fufpicions not at all to the advantage of poor Emilia: I fancied that fhe had in reality confeffed a paffion to that gentleman; and Corifca, in forming this con-trivance to bring about a private inter-view between them, had done nothing but what fhe was convinced in her own mind would be highly fatisfactory to her fair friend. It was never my cuftom, however, to place an entire dependance on conjecture, whether my own or that of another perfon; fo refolved to be as convinced as my Invifible infpection could make me. Accordingly the next day, in the afternoon, I girded on my precious Belt, and went to the houfe of Corifca. Emilia was not yet come; but juft as I arrived I heard her give orders to refufe admittance to all of her own fex except that lady, and alfo to all thofe of the other except Favonius and Palamede.

A 3

As I doubted not but I should be able to fathom the whole truth of this affair, by the conversation that would pass between these two ladies while they believed themselves alone together, I was extremely impatient for the approach of Emilia, and equally rejoiced when I saw her enter. The first salutations they gave each other, were such as might be expected from persons who mutually professed so warm and tender a friendship. The subjects they afterwards talked upon were not of any consequence; not one word of Palemede nor the projected tour was mentioned; on which I absolved Emilia from all blame on this account, and was sorry I had ever wronged her. But the less room I had to condemn, the greater cause I had to pity her, and to detest the cruel plot contrived, and so near being put in execution against her virtue. But I had no time to indulge meditation; the gentlemen presently came in; the proposal, as agreed upon between them and Corisca, was immediately made; the ladies gave a ready assent; a hackney-coach was ordered to be called, and every one seemed equally on the wing to be gone.

The reader will now perhaps imagine, that it being easy to see into the end of this affair, there was no occasion for any farther enquiries in relation to it, and that curiosity had received it's utmost gratification; but I happened to be of a different way of thinking. I sincerely pitied Emilia, and could not help being desirous to see how she would resent the base artifice practised on her when she should discover it, and also how Corisca would conduct the plot she had contrived. It was no difficult matter for me to know the house they were going to, both by the description I had heard given of it the day before by Corisca, and also by what I had been told by other people concerning it's commodiousness for intrigue; so I no sooner found that a hackney-coach was ordered, than I hastily quitted the post I was in, made the best of my way to the place of rendezvous, got there before them, took up my stand at the entrance, saw them alight, and followed them into a well-furnished spacious room, to which they were ushered by a spruce waiter.

Wine and biscuits were immediately served up; and the company, after having refreshed themselves with this little regale, went to walk in the gardens,

which I found indeed very pleasant, well laid out into parterres and knots, and larger than I could have imagined. Favonius led Corisca, and Palamede had Emilia by the hand, who, during this promenade, took the opportunity of entertaining her with many tender speeches, but intermixed with nothing that the most chaste ear might not have listened to without calling a blush upon the face. I was sorry, however, to observe that she received what he said with a certain languishment in her eyes, which emboldened him to go on, and made me fear that he had indeed a secret ascendancy over her incautious, unsuspecting heart.

On their return into the house, a table was spread with every thing that could excite the appetite or exhilarate the spirits. The chearfulness and good humour of the guests gave a double relish to the repast; wit and sparkling Champagne crowned the board; and though the ladies allayed the too great potency of the one by the assistance of water, yet the other flowed with no less strength and vigour. After some hours had been passed in the height of gaiety, Corisca on a sudden looked upon her watch, and assuming a more serious air than she was accustomed to wear, told the company that it was near one o'clock, and they must think of departing for London. To which Favonius replied—

*Favonius.* Among all the ridiculous things mankind was ever guilty of, I know none more so than the having set their wits to work to invent a machine, and then submitting to be governed by it.

*Corisca.* There are many other laws, as well as this, by which the silly world have bound themselves to go contrary to the primitive rules of nature and inclination, indulging by stealth only those pleasures which they were born freely to enjoy: but, however, all these customs, disagreeable as they are to people of real wit and spirit, must in some measure be complied with, or the stupid vulgar would presently accuse us of irregularity and indecency.

*Palamede.* I look upon every one here, Madam, to be above the censures of the vulgar, yet I will not pretend to enter into any arguments on that head; and dare answer for Favonius, as well as for myself, that he would not presume to detain you a moment beyond the time you think proper to go.

*Emilia.*

*Emilia.* Indeed, gentlemen, I think, and I believe Corisca does so too, that to stay any longer at this time would rather diminish than add to the satisfaction we have hitherto enjoyed.

*Favonius.* After such a declaration, Madam, any farther pressures to the contrary on our part, might justly be looked upon as impertinent and troublesome; it is certainly your province to command, ours implicitly to obey.

In speaking these last words, he went out of the room with Palamede, as it might be supposed to discharge the reckoning of the house; but in a few minutes returned, and, with a seeming concern in their faces, said, that the coachman, either by having got drunk or mistaking his orders, had gone away soon after he had set them down: on which Corisca affected to be extremely surprized, and Emilia being really so, they both cried out at the same time—

*Corisca.* This is the oddest accident sure that ever happened!

*Emilia.* Bless me! which way shall we get home?

*Palamede.* As for going home, Madam, it is a thing quite out of the question: we have enquired, and there is no possibility of procuring either coach, chariot, post-chaise, or any sort of carriage whatever, till the morning breaks; so, ladies, you must content yourselves with being our guests for the remainder of the night.

*Corisca.* Well, since it is so, we must e'en make a virtue of necessity, and divert ourselves as well as we can.

*Palamede.* It would be an unpardonable vanity in us, Madam, to imagine that any thing in our conversation could compensate for the want of your repose; we will therefore order a bed to be got ready for you two ladies, while Favonius and myself watch the approach of day, in order to provide a vehicle for carrying us to town.

*Corisca.* No, no, by no means, we will all share the same fate; it would be strange indeed, if four people of taste and spirit could not find some way to amuse each other for the space of one night.

While she was speaking, a concert of flutes, a hautboy, a double curtal, and some other wind-musick, on a sudden saluted their ears; on which she cried out—

*Corisca.* Hark! musick! if it continues, it will very well atone for the loss of a few hours sleep.

*Emilia.* Nothing ever happened so fortunately for me; I love musick as I love my life, especially of this sort.

In speaking this, she ran hastily to the window and threw up the sash, in order to hear the several instruments more distinctly. Palamede followed, and they both seemed absorbed in a most profound attention; which Favonius and Corisca observing, took that opportunity of passing softly behind them, and slipped out of the room. Emilia turning her head presently after, with a design, as I suppose, to say something either to the one or the other, was surprized at seeing neither of them there, and cried out to Palamede—

*Emilia.* Bless me! what is become of Favonius and Corisca?

*Palamede.* I know not, Madam; perhaps they are gone down into the garden, to be nearer to the musick, which seems to proceed from the lower end of the walk.

*Emilia.* Very likely; they might have told us, however; but since it is so, we will follow them.

*Palamede.* With all my heart, Madam; but first permit me to reveal a secret to you which you ought to be told, and my breast has long laboured with an impatience of discovering.

*Emilia.* A secret! What secret can you have with me, that would be worth losing one note of this musick to listen to?

*Palamede.* I hope you will be of another opinion, Madam, when I shall tell you that the whole happiness of my future life, and even my soul's eternal peace, depends upon it.

*Emilia.* You may tell me what you will, but I shall believe nothing of the matter; so let us rejoin our friends.

It is not so much by what people say, as by the manner in which they deliver themselves, that the sincerity of their words may be guessed at; and I was heartily glad to find, both by the looks of Emilia and the tone of her voice, that she indeed had more inclination to do as she had proposed, than to stay and suffer herself to be entertained by Palamede in the way she might easily perceive he was about to do it. The discreet intentions of this young lady, however, could avail her but little in her present situation; Palamede got between her and the door as she was endeavouring to go out, and throwing himself upon his knees before her, and at the same time catching fast hold of both her hands, said to her—

*Palamede.*

*Palamede.* No, charming Emilia! I have not so long languished for an opportunity like this to let it now escape me! you must, you shall hear me. By Heaven I love you!—love you to the most raging height the passion can inspire! For many, many tedious weeks, you have been the only object of my nightly visions and waking thoughts; and——

He was going on, but Emilia interrupted him by replying in these terms, accompanied with an air full of resentment and confusion—

*Emilia.* Fye, Palamede, this raillery is impertinent and insipid, and what I could not have expected to be treated with by a person who has the character of good sense and breeding.

*Palamede.* Cruelly urged! Oh, could you see into my heart, you would find it all devoted to you! devoted to you with a tenderness so perfect as can be equalled by nothing but the charms that have subdued it. Frown not, adorable Emilia, nor struggle to get loose; for, by all my hopes, never will I quit the grasp I have taken of you nor rise from the posture I am in, till I have convinced you of the sincerity, as well as ardency, of the flame you have kindled in me!

*Emilia.* Sir, this nocturnal declaration is little consistent with that respect which is always the attendant of an honourable passion. If you had, indeed, any thoughts of me of the nature you pretend, I am no recluse, and you might have found a more proper season to acquaint me with them.

*Palamede.* The passion I am enflamed with, is not of a nature to submit to the dull forms observed by vulgar lovers. Besides, what season can be more fit for love than night, the friend of love? Turn your eyes towards the window, and behold the silver moon, with all the thousand twinkling stars! see how sweet, how mild they shine! with what benevolent aspects they dart their rays upon us! Listen to the melodious sounds you just now praised! Will not all these soften your soul, melt you into pity, and make you think such love as mine deserves some recompence?

*Emilia.* I'll hear no more; unhand me, Sir and give me liberty to seek our friends; or be assured my cries shall raise the house.

He then let go her hands, and rose from the posture he had been in; but still

kept his back close against the door, while with half a smile he replied to what she had said in this manner—

*Palamede.* Madam, you are obeyed in part; and if I acquiesce to every thing you demand, it is not to be imagined you would be one jot less in my power than now. Our friends are too deeply engaged with each other to suffer themselves to be interrupted; and as to the people of the house, they know their distance, and are always extremely deaf on these occasions.

On hearing him speak thus, she burst into a flood of tears, and throwing herself into a chair, cried out—

*Emilia.* O Heavens! is this possible! Can Corisca be so vile! Am I betrayed! basely given up by her to infamy and ruin!

On hearing her make this exclamation, he left the place where he had been standing, and seated himself near her; then taking one of her hands, and pressing it tenderly to his lips, spoke to this effect—

*Palamede.* Not so, my angel! By Heaven, the transactions of this night shall be for ever a sacred and inviolable secret! not even Favonius nor Corisca shall be acquainted with it if you desire the contrary: I know they will laugh at me; but no matter, I can bear all that, and much more, to comply with the least request made by my dear Emilia. O, then, be kind, and bless my longing wishes! let no reluctance damp the coming joys, but yield to share the happiness you give!

The consternation of Emilia, on finding she was exposed to the danger she now was in, by the very woman whom she most had loved, and most believed her friend, had thrown her into so profound a reverie, that I much question whether she heard any part of what Palamede had lately been speaking to her; till closing his protestations with a strenuous embrace, she started up, broke from him, and looking wildly round the room, she espied two swords, which Favonius and Palamede had plucked off on their entrance, and put in a window; she snatched up one of them, and drawing it out of the scabbard in an instant, held the point to her breast, saying at the same time—

*Emilia.* Here is at least a refuge from dishonour! That base woman, who thought to make me as vile as I now find she is herself, shall meet with a disappointment she perhaps does not expect.

If

If you offer to approach me, or advance one ſtep beyond the ſpot you ſtand upon, this goes into my heart.

The amazement, the ſhock, the confuſion Palamede was in at this aćtion, is altogether impoſſible to deſcribe: her words, her looks, her voice, convincing him ſhe was indeed in earneſt, he remained ſpeechleſs, without motion, his eyes fixed on her in a kind of ſtupid ſtare, and ſeemed like one transfixed with thunder; at length, recovering himſelf a little, he ſaid to her in a faultering voice—

*Palamede.* For Heaven's ſake, Madam, wound not thus my ſoul by the ſight of your deſpair! You have no cauſe. It is certain that I long have loved you, but never had a thought of ſeducing your innocence. The plot to bring you hither was not of my contriving. 'Tis true I came into it, as where is the man who would not? But be aſſured I am no raviſher, nor capable of owing my pleaſure to brutal violence: Oh, therefore, throw aſide that cruel weapon, or turn the point on me, and if I make the leaſt attempt to offend your modeſty, bury it to the hilt within my boſom.

*Emilia.* Sir, I once looked upon you as a man of honour, and ſhould rejoice to find you could redeem yourſelf in my opinion.

*Palamede.* By all that's ſacred, not the utmoſt gratification of my looſeſt wiſhes could have given me half the joy as now, to prove myſelf not wholly unworthy the eſteem of ſuch exalted virtue. Charming Emilia! perfećt in mind as well as form! in both angelic! behold me your convert! The love I had for you is now rarified into adoration! Your virtue, like chemiſts gold, turns all into itſelf, and leaves no groſſer particles behind! Forgive what is paſt, and never —never more will I preſume to entertain you with diſcourſes leſs chaſte and pure than your own virgin thoughts!

*Emilia.* May I believe this penitence ſincere?

*Palamede.* You may, by Heaven! and when I relapſe into my former crime, may infamy, diſeaſes, the contempt of the whole world, your eternal hatred, and every other curſe, fall on me!

*Emilia.* Then find ſome way, if poſſible, to take me immediately from this place, and condućt me ſafe to my own apartment.

*Palamede.* My readineſs to obey you,

Madam, I hope, will prove the integrity of my preſent intentions, and be ſome atonement for the paſt. It is my happineſs to have it in my power to do what you require with much more eaſe than you imagine; you ſhall no longer, beautiful Emilia! be impoſed upon: the coachman, whom we pretended had left us, has only put up at an inn not above forty yards diſtant from this houſe; I ſuppoſe he may be gone to bed by this time, as we told him we ſhould not return to London till the morning; but I will ſend and have him rouzed.

He had ſcarce made an end of ſpeaking theſe words, when he rang the bell, and a waiter coming preſently up, he gave him the neceſſary orders for fulfilling the promiſe he had juſt given to Emilia; on which that young lady, with the utmoſt ſatisfaćtion in her voice and eyes, cried out—' This is truly honourable indeed, ' and worthy of yourſelf.'

Something which that inſtant ſtarted into the mind of Palamede, hindered him from making any anſwer, or even, perhaps, from hearing what ſhe ſaid: he rang the bell a ſecond time with all his force, and called for pen, ink and paper; which being brought, he told Emilia that decency and good manners would not ſuffer him to depart without taking ſome notice of the occaſion to Favonius, with whom he had always lived in a perfećt good underſtanding, and therefore entreated her permiſſion to write a few lines to that gentleman. The requeſt was too reaſonable not to be complied with, and he ſat down and dićtated the following epiſtle—

' MY DEAR FRIEND,

' THINGS have happened very dif-
' ferently from what I was made to
' expećt in regard to Emilia: in fine,
' ſhe is not a woman, but an angel! As
' ſuch I ſhall always eſteem her, and
' think it my glory to obey every com-
' mand ſhe is pleaſed to lay upon me:
' the firſt ſhe has honoured me with, is
' to remove her hence, and condućt her
' to her own apartment, which I am juſt
' now about to do. I have no opportu-
' nity to diſcharge the muſick or the
' expences of the houſe, ſo beg you will
' take the whole upon you, and meet
' me to-morrow evening at Braund's,
' where we will ſup together, and ſettle
' that affair. Make what compliments

A a ' and

' and excufes you fhall think proper for
' me to Corifca; and believe me, yours,'
'&c.

'               PALAMEDE.'

While Palamede was thus employed,
it alfo came into Emilia's head to let Corifca know fome part of the refentment
fhe had conceived againft her: accordingly fhe took another pen out of the
ftandifh, and expreffed herfelf in thefe
terms—

'   MADAM,

' WHAT the united report of all
'    who know you could never have
' made me believe, your behaviour this
' night has not only convinced me of,
' but alfo that the tongue of malice can
' find nothing wherewith to aggravate
' your real guilt. Was it not enough,
' O moft ungenerous woman! to fink
' your own honour and reputation in
' eternal infamy, but you muft alfo en-
' deavour to drag others into perdition
' with you! Know, to your confu-
' fion, that I happily efcaped the fnare
' you had laid for me; and fhall reap
' this benefit by my late danger, as to
' avoid the company of a perfon whom
' to preferve an acquaintance with muft
' in the end have been the ruin of my
' character, if not of my virtue; for, be
' affured, I fhall henceforward be as
' careful to fhun your prefence, as ever
' I was eager to come into it. Here
' ceafes all farther intercourfe between
' us. May the difappointment of your
' bafe defigns on me, ferve as a warn-
' ing to you not to attempt the like on
' any other equally inadvertent and in-
' cautious as the much deceived

'                 EMILIA.'

They had juft finifhed, and made up
the above billets, when the waiter returned, and told Palamede that he had,
though not without fome difficulty, prevailed on the coachman to rife; and
that, before he left the inn, he had feen
him go into the ftable to bring out the
horfes. Palamede then gave him the
letter he had wrote to Favonius, faying
—' Be fure you deliver this to the gen-
' tleman who came with us as foon as he
' fhall be ftirring, and let him know I
' fhall fend the coach back in the morn-
' ing.' Emilia alfo put into his hands
her epiftle to Corifca, with thefe words—

' And let the lady know I left this for
' her.' The fellow replied, that they
might depend he would be punctual in
difcharging the commiffion they entrufted him with, and then withdrew.

Finding my Cryftalline Tablets were
now overcharged, I was obliged to fhut
them up; fo can relate no farther particulars of what converfation paffed between Palamede and Emilia during the
fmall time they waited for the coach to
carry them away; and can only fay in
general, that the greateft referve and diftance was obferved on both fides. Emilia, though now perfectly fatisfied with
the contrition of Palamede, thought it
would be imprudent to appear too gay;
and Palamede, fearful to renew her apprehenfions, behaved to her with all the
folemnity of a Chinefe mandarin.

On their going down, they were met
at the bottom of the ftairs by the woman
who kept this tavern, or rather brothel;
who ufhering in what fhe had to fay with
a low curtfey, told Emilia, that fhe
flattered herfelf with the expectation of
her fleeping there that night, and hoped
nothing difagreeable had happened to
occafion her departure at fo unfeafonable
an hour; adding, that fhe fhould never
forgive herfelf if any thing in her houfe
had difobliged fo fweet a young lady.
Emilia anfwered this fawning fpeech
only with a look of contempt; but Palamede told her fhe need be under no concern on that fcore; the lady had no objections to her houfe, but chofe never to
fleep out of her own apartment. No
more was faid; they went into the coach,
and I followed on foot; for I had not
curiofity enough to make me ftay the
remainder of the night in that place, for
no other purpofe than to fee how Favonius and Corifca would behave on
being told that Palamede and Emilia
were gone, and receiving the epiftles
that gentleman and lady had left for
them. I had a long walk home, but
my Invifibility fecured me from the danger of any infults; and the fatisfaction
that rofe in my mind, on the noble conqueft virtue had gained over vice, made
the way feem much lefs tedious.

A few days after I was informed, by
the report of the town, that Palamede
made his publick addreffes to Emilia.
Being willing to be better convinced of
the truth of this matter, I made feveral
vifits to Emilia's apartment, and found
that in fact the thing was as I had been
                                    told.

told. Palamede, who really loved Emilia much more than perhaps he was sensible of himself, before this proof she had given him of her virtue, got over that objection which the scantinefs of her fortune had before laid in his way; and Emilia, who had liked him as much as Corifca had faid she did, gave all the encouragement he could wish to his honourable paffion. I look upon the affair to be now in a manner concluded on, and that a very short time will confummate their mutual wishes; a cataftrophe which I doubt not but every generous reader will heartily rejoice at as well as myfelf.

Favonius, who is in reality a man of ftrict honour and good principles, though fomewhat too fanguine in his amours, ftill continues his intimacy with Palamede, and highly applauds his converfion in favour of the fair infpirer of his honourable flame. Corifca bites her lips whenever the name of Emilia is mentioned, and endeavours all she can to traduce that virtue which she had not the power to deftroy: but all she fays on that fcore ferves only to shew more plainly her own bad heart; and Emilia, by refraining all converfation with her, has entirely regained that efteem and good opinion which she had well nigh loft.

## CHAP. III.

CONTAINS THE REHEARSAL OF A CONVERSATION WHICH THE AUTHOR ACCIDENTALLY HAPPENED TO BE WITNESS OF, AND LOOKS UPON HIMSELF AS BOUND BY AN INDISPENSABLE OBLIGATION TO MAKE PUBLICK; THOUGH PERFECTLY CONSCIOUS, FROM HIS OBSERVATIONS OF MANKIND, THAT THERE ARE MANY OF HIS READERS WHO WILL LABOUR ALL THEY CAN TO BRING THESE PAGES INTO DISCREDIT.

ONE whom I shall always rank among the number of our beft Englifh authors, tells us, in a juftly efteemed poem, that—

‘ Wifdom is ftill to floth too great a flave;
‘ None are fo bufy as the fool and knave.’

How widely different are the pictures drawn of a perfon whofe prudence makes

him act and talk with circumfpection and referve! How various are the reprefentations made of him! He has almoft as many characters as there are fpeakers of him; by the abundance one hears of him the judgment is diftracted, and there is no forming a right idea of what he truly is. One can go into no company without hearing fome mention made of Lord Honorius, yet one shall feldom find any two people agree in their opinion concerning him, either as to his abilities or principles, whether in religious, moral, or political matters. He is no follower of the court, yet does not totally avoid going thither. He profeffes himfelf a member of the eftablifhed church, yet converfes freely with thofe of different perfuafions. He liftens attentively to the arguments urged by perfons of all parties and all fects, without offering any of his own, or giving his opinion which are wrong or which are right.

For this reafon all the zealots, both in religion and politicks, brand him with lukewarmnefs, and fay he is a man of an uncertain way of thinking, and has no fettled principle of acting. Some few there are who applaud his moderation, but many more who look upon it as a piece of low cunning, thereby to cover fome latent defigns he has within his bofom; but of what nature thefe are, I have heard many warm difputes about. Some will needs have him in the intereft of the Pretender, and others that he is fecretly a tool of the miniftry. Some have confidently averred, that they have feen a white rofe carried into his houfe on the tenth of June; and others, that he has worn a yellow waiftcoat on the birth-day of his prefent Majefty; as if an innocent flower, or the colour of a piece of filk, were fufficient tokens to shew the wifhes of the wearer's heart.

As to his œconomy in private life, he is not at all expenfive in drefs, equipage, or the furniture of his houfe; chufing rather to appear below his rank, than in any particular to exceed it. This is frequently attributed to his covetoufnefs, while more favourable judges fuppofe it to be owing to his contempt of the modifh fopperies of the age. He partakes of all the pleafures of the town, but never purfues them to an excefs, or with eagernefs. The graver fort of people afcribe this to his difcretion, and the more gay to want of fpirit and coldnefs of conftitution.

A a 2     Thus

Thus apt are we to form a vain judgment on things we know nothing of. The heart of man is incomprehenfible, unlefs difcovered by himfelf in fome glaring proof either of virtue or vice: he firft he may not have an opportunity to fet forth in any confpicuous light, and the latter he may have artifice and hypocrify enough to glofs over and conceal. How impoffible, then, is it to be certain to which of thefe he is in reality devoted!

Among the variety of defcriptions and reports in relation to Lord Honorius, I found, notwithftanding, that it was agreed on by all hands, that though he would not fuffer himfelf to be impofed upon by his tradefmen, yet he always took care their bills fhould be paid with the utmoft exactnefs and punctuality, and that he never dealt with foreigners. Thefe articles, however infignificant they may feem to fome of thofe who call themfelves the polite world, I confefs gave me fuch an idea both of his prudence and juftice, as made me immediately join with thofe who fpoke the greateft things in his praife in other refpects; but being defirous of penetrating more deeply into the reality of this nobleman's difpofition, I refolved to try how my Invifibilityfhip would ferve that end, and accordingly made a vifit one morning at his houfe.

I paffed through feveral neat rooms, the furniture of which was rich, and befitting the dignity and fortune of the owner, but had nothing of gaudinefs in it. At laft I found the perfon I went to feek; he was in a clofet within his dreffing-room, and had a book in his hand. I was curious to fee what was the fubject of his meditations; and, looking over his fhoulder, perceived it was the poems of our Englifh Pindar, the celebrated Mr. Cowley. The page he was employed in on my entrance contained, among others, thefe lines—

' O fountains ! when in you fhall I,
' Eas'd of unpeaceful thoughts, myfelf efpy !
' O fields ! O woods ! when fhall I be made
' The happy tenant of your fhade !
' Here's the fpring-head of pleafure's flood,
' Where all the riches lie,
' That fhe has coin'd and ftamp'd for good,
' To charm the mind as well as eye.
' Pride and ambition here,
' Only in far-fetch'd metaphors appear;
' Here's nought but winds can hurtful mur-
' murs fcatter,
' And nought but echo flatter.

' The gods, when they defcended hither
' From heaven, did always chufe their way ;
' And therefore we may boldly fay,
" That is the way, too, thither."

When he came to this part of the poem, he ftopped, and cried out with the greateft emphafis—' Charming, inimitable Cow-
' ley! how juft, how truly delicate, are
' all thy notions, and how widely dif-
' ferent from thofe of the age I have the
' misfortune to live in! If one may
' form a judgment, as fure one may, by
' the writings of feventy or eighty years
' ago, the genius of Britain was far un-
' like what it appears at prefent.'

He had fcarce finifhed this exclamation, when a fervant opened the door, and told him that Sir Whimfey Brainfick was come to wait upon him; on which he laid afide the book, and went into the next chamber to receive his gueft. After giving and returning the cuftomary falutations of the morning, and having feated themfelves, the following dialogue enfued between them—

*Honorius.* It is a wonder to fee you dreffed and abroad thus early, Sir Whimfey; I think you are commonly in your firft fleep after this time.

*Sir Whimfey.* Aye, my lord; but pleafure muft on fome occafions give way to bufinefs. I have vaft affairs upon my hands at prefent. I only fnatched a moment to take leave of your lordfhip, and two hours hence fhall fet out for the country.

*Honorius.* On your election, I fuppofe ?

*Sir Whimfey.* No, no; my Lord Triffli Traffli has fecured me a borough, without my taking the trouble of ever going near it. My bufinefs, at prefent, is down at ******, where I have a confiderable eftate, and, I believe, a pretty good intereft; and I have engaged myfelf to ftrain both, as far as they will go, in favour of Sir Crafty Shallowbuggen.

*Honorius.* Sir Crafty Shallowbuggen! What, then, has Mr. Worthy, the prefent member, declined ftanding?

*Sir Whimfey.* No, no, my lord, he has not declined; but we are refolved to have him out, at any rate.

*Honorius.* I would not have you deceive yourfelf, Sir Whimfey. Mr. Worthy is a gentleman who, I am told, is highly efteemed by his conftituents; and you may be at a great deal of expence to oppofe him, to no purpofe.

*Sir Whimfey.*

*Sir Whimfey.* As to the expence, I don't doubt but it will be made up to me fome way or other. I have my eye upon a place; and, I can tell you, am as good as promifed either that or a ribband.

*Honorius.* The chara&er I have heard of Mr. Worthy makes me forry fo powerful an oppofition fhould be fet on foot againft him.

*Sir Whimfey.* He has been ftubborn, my lord, very ftubborn; has voted againft the Jew and Clandeftine Marriage bills; and it is not fit the miniftry fhould be affronted. Your lordfhip, I fuppofe, is a friend to the miniftry?

*Honorius.* Sir, I never gave any man reafon to believe I was the contrary.

*Sir Whimfey.* No, no, your lordfhip is too wife. Thofe who are friends to the miniftry, are friends to them-.felves. For my own part, if it were not to oblige them, I would not give two-pence who had the election at ******, or any where elfe. But I muft beg your lordfhip's pardon; I have a thoufand things to difpatch, and would not be waited for by four or five gentlemen who accompany me on the fame expedition; fo your lordfhip's moft obedient.

*Honorius.* Yours, Sir Whimfey. I wifh you a good journey.

With thefe words they parted. Lord Honorius faw him to the top of the ftaircafe, and then turned back to his clofet, faying to himfelf as he went—' What ' a wild world is this! How do men ' toil to bring infamy on themfelves, ' and entail certain ruin on their pofte- ' rity!'

As I thought, by the little fample I had feen, that it was now in my power to.make a better judgment of the fentiments 'of this nobleman than by all I had heard from others, I was following Sir Whimfey down ftairs; but on hearing fome debate between a plain, honeft-looking countryman, and a fpruce footman, who, as I found afterwards, had been but lately taken into my lord's fervice, I ftopped fhort to liften to the occafion. I foon perceived that the countryman was defirous of fpeaking to his lordfhip; and the fellow, judging by appearances, thought it too great a prefumption, and would fain have turned him from the door; but the ruftick was not fo eafily repulfed as the other had

imagined. The firft words I could hear diftinctly were as follow—

*Footman.* I tell you, friend, I know not whether my lord is at home or not; or, if he is, whether he pleafes to be feen: but if you let me know what bufinefs you have with him, and from whom you came, I will take care his lordfhip fhall be informed, and you may have your anfwer to morrow.

*Countryman.* Goodlack, Mr. Skipjack, who are you? My lord is not ufed to have fuch malapert fellows about him. But if I muft not fee my lord, pray let me fpeak to Mr. Downright, the gentleman that dreffes and waits upon him; he knows me well enough, and will give me a better anfwer.

The footman then vouchfafed to call the'perfon he mentioned, and the countryman had the fatisfaction to find himfelf well received. Mr. Downright fhook him cordially by the.hand, told him he was glad to fee him in London, and afked him what bufinefs had brought him hither. To which the other replied—

*Countryman.* In good troth I did not come upon pleafure; I have bufinefs, very great bufinefs, with my lord, and would fain fpeak to him, if fo be I may have liberty to come into his prefence, as you know, Mr. Downright, I have done many a good time in the country; but that Mr. Finikin there, with his pigtail wig, ftands as it were like a mudwall to keep every body off the houfe.

*Mr. Downright.* Oh, he did not know you, Mr. Goodacre; and befides, he has lived in families where nobody without a coach or chair is admitted. But I will acquaint my lord you are here; he is alone, and I am fure will fee you.

*Countryman.* Thank you, Mr. Downright. It is well there are fome civil people in this fame town.

Mr. Downright then went on his meffage: the footman looked very fheepifh, and fneaked away; while the countryman ftrutted about the hall as great as an emperor, till the valet returned, and defired him to walk up. As I took Mr. Goodacre for one of my lord's tenants, and imagined he was only come on the fcore of renewing a leafe, or fome other country affairs relating to himfelf, which I had no manner of curiofity to pry into, I was in fome debate within myfelf whether I
fhould

should stay, or go directly out of the house; the door being then open; but a certain impulse, the meaning of which I cannot account for, swayed me to pursue my first thought, and I turned back and accompanied him into the presence of my lord, from whom he met with a reception not commonly given by persons of quality to a man of his plain appearance, except on particular occasions. His lordship made him sit down in a chair very near himself, and, with a smiling countenance, and the greatest affability in his voice and air, told him, he was glad to see him look so well and hearty; that he hoped his wife and family enjoyed the same share of good health; and then asked what business had brought him up to London. To the former part of these obliging speeches he only answered with several low bows, but to the latter replied in these terms—

*Goodacre.* Why, my lord, your lordship knows we are going to have a new parliament, and belike there will be a great bustle all over the king'om about elections; and no wonder if there be; every one makes us such fair promises when they come to ask us for our votes, that it is a hard matter to know which we can most depend upon. We have been served basely, very basely, by some of our representatives, and it behoves us to be very cautious for the future.

*Honorius.* Very true, Mr. Goodacre, it does so indeed; and I hope the nation will think so.

*Goodacre.* Now, as to our borough, no man could make finer speeches to us, or pretend he had our interest more at heart, than Squire Earnly, before he was chosen; yet he no sooner got into the House, than he shewed he did not care a straw for us, laughed at all our petitions and remonstrances, and, I am told, made a merit of it to the ministry.

*Honorius.* I am afraid there are too many who have done so. Does the same gentleman set up again?

*Goodacre.* No, my lord; he would have no chance for it if he did; we know him too well, he sees that well enough. But it is thought, however, that he will get in for some place or other.

*Honorius.* Nothing more likely. But do you hear who intends to offer himself in his stead?

*Goodacre.* Yes, my lord; great interest is already making for one Captain Sashbright. He is as fine a person, in-

deed, as the sun shines upon, but we know nothing of him. He is recommended by Sir Courtly Jobber, and has brought a power of money down with him. They went together in Sir Courtly's coach to ****** fair, bought a many things, and gave them to every body about them. Guineas and broad pieces fly about like hail; any one, almost, may have them for picking up.

*Honorius.* So then he may easily carry it, I suppose?

*Goodacre.* I cannot tell that, my lord. There was a numerous meeting at the Rose about a fortnight ago, and Squire Wellwood, of the Green, was put in nomination. His family has been settled for a long time at *******; he lives most part in the country, does a great deal of good among the poor, and is mainly beloved.

*Honorius.* I know him, Mr. Goodacre; he is certainly a very worthy gentleman.

*Goodacre.* Aye, my lord, he would have it all to nothing, if it was not for one consideration.

*Honorius.* What is that?

*Goodacre.* The captain has promised that, if he gets his election, he will procure an act of parliament for a new road to be cut, at the government's expence, from ***** to *****, which your lordship knows would be a great advantage to our market.

*Honorius.* A very great one, indeed.

*Goodacre.* Aye, my lord, if we were sure it would be done; but there lies the query. Some people will promise any thing to gain their point, and never think of it afterwards. We all know Squire Wellwood to be a noble gentleman, and so may Captain Sashbright too; he may, or he may not. Now we are strangely divided in our opinions, whether we ought to leave the certain good for the uncertain better, and have at length resolved to be decided by your lordship.

*Honorius.* By me!

*Goodacre.* Yes, my lord. We know your lordship to be a wise man, and a true lover of your country.

*Honorius.* I have always thought, Mr. Goodacre, that to meddle in these things would prove me deserving neither of the one nor the other of the epithets you give me. Every elector ought to give his vote according to the dictates of his conscience, and not suffer himself to

be

be fwayed by any intereft or motive whatever; and for a nobleman, or other perfon of diftinction, to attempt, either by menaces or cajolings, to make them act to the contrary, appears to me to be the moft grofs encroachment on liberty that can be offered.

*Goodacre.* But here the cafe is widely different, my lord.

*Honorius.* I grant it is. You defire my advice as a friend, not fubmit to be governed by me as a director; it would therefore be ungenerous, and even cruel, in me, to fuffer you to be deluded by falfe pretences, when it is fo eafily in my power to put you upon your guard againft them. In the firft place, you ought to confider that Caprain Sathbright, whatever his character may otherwife be, is an officer in the army; and, as fuch, it is his intereft to promote the continuance of a ftanding army, and confequently of thefe taxes which are neceffary for the fupport of it. In the fecond, Sir Courtly Jobber, who it feems is the perfon who recommends him, has for a long time, to my certain knowledge, been an agent for the miniftry, and is indebted for his title and the heft part of the eftate he is in poffeffion of, merely to the good fervices he has rendered them.

*Goodacre* Aye, marry, thefe things are worth thinking of indeed; fo I fuppofe, my lord, the money he fo plentifully throws about is none of his own?

*Honorius.* Not a doit; he will be reimburied with intereft.

*Goodacre.* And yet I know not, my lord, but there may be fome among us foolifh enough to be inveigled by this bait. Alackaday! we country people are ignorant of fuch practices; we little think what the great folks in town are doing; and a many there are that would not believe a word of it without good authority. Oh, I with your lordfhip were down at Egum Hall at this critical juncture!

*Honorius.* I will be there, Mr. Goodacre, in fpite of the averfion I have always had to appear at elections, or to diftinguifh myfelf on any occafion. My love to the place which gave me birth, and good-will to my countrymen, fhall overbalance all other confiderations. I will do all I can to ftrengthen the weak eyes which are in danger of being dazzled with Sir Courtly's gold, and fhew

them the falfe luftre of his fleeting promifes.

*Goodacre.* Heaven blefs your lordfhip!—A noble refolution!

*Honorius.* When do you return, Mr. Goodacre?

*Goodacre.* I fhall lie but this one night in town, my lord, and fet out betime tomorrow morning.

*Honorius.* I will not be two days behind you; in the mean time, you may tell them what I fay.

*Goodacre.* It will be joyful news to fome.

There paffed no farther converfation between them; the honeft countryman rofe up to take his leave, full of tranfport at the fuccefs of his negociation; but Lord Honorius would not permit him to depart, till he had rung the bell for Mr. Downright, and given orders that he fhould be made welcome to the beft entertainment the houfe afforded. I left him to accept the invitation, and returned to my apartment, well fatisfied in my mind that I was now enabled to form a right judgment of this nobleman's principles and difpofition.

## CHAP. IV.

PRESENTS THE READER WITH THE DETAIL OF A VERY REMARKABLE INCIDENT; WHICH, I BELIEVE, IF CONSIDERED WITH A DUE ATTENTION, THERE ARE BUT FEW PEOPLE, ESPECIALLY OF THE FAIR-SEX, WHO WILL NOT FIND THEMSELVES ENABLED TO BECOME BETTER MEMBERS OF SOCIETY BY HAVING PERUSED.

A Certain facred writer tell us, that the tongue is an unruly member, and preaches much concerning the government of it; but I dare not prefume to inflit too much on his authority, as he has been, with others of his cotemporaries, pretty much exploded; and I might be looked upon, by my polite readers, as a very old-fafhioned, filly fellow, to make any mention of him. But I may venture, without running the rifque of being read with a horfe-laugh, to quote the words of another very great and learned perfon of a more modern date, who fays, that the tongue is the moft moſt dangerous of all weapons; that it is capable of deſtroying all peace, all love, all harmony, in the world; of ſowing diſſenſions among families; of diſuniting the hearts of the deareſt friends and relations; of ruining the reputation and fortune of whomſoever it is levelled againſt; and that even murders and the worſt of miſchiefs may be occaſioned by it.

That the tongue, when it becomes the inſtrument of a malicious heart, carries a thouſand daggers in it, is a truth which the obſervation of every one evinces. But this is not all: publick abuſe or private ſcandal, defamation and detraction, are not the only vices of the tongue; an unguarded word is frequently productive of the moſt unhappy conſequences; it wounds, as it were, by chance-medley, and a perſon may be ſtabbed in the moſt tender part without any intention in the giver of the blow. A talkative diſpoſition, or, in other words, a paſſion for repeating every thing one ſees and hears, or even gueſſes at, is extremely dangerous to ſociety; and though it is a foible proceeding rather from levity than ill-nature, ſometimes produces the ſame effects. Thoſe guilty of it, perhaps, may mean no hurt; but, alas! they conſider not how far the perſon to whom they are ſpeaking may be intereſted in the report they make, and that what they imagine of no moment may ſtab him to the quick. Nothing is more common than for people to hurt thus at random; and, by their raſhneſs, to occaſion accidents, which, if they foreſaw, they would be moſt careful to prevent. As a late poet emphatically enough expreſſes it—

‘ Thinking to ſhoot my arrow o'er the
　‘ houſe,
‘ I have kill'd my brother.’

But this inadvertency, as great a weakneſs as it doubtleſs is, has in it ſomewhat yet more excuſable than to reveal a ſecret which we are conſcious muſt give the hearer pain. I confeſs that this is ſometimes done through good-will; but then it is a very miſtaken good-will in many caſes. If I know a perſon ſuſtains an injury, and has it in his power to redreſs the grievance, it is certainly my duty to acquaint him with it; but when the evil is without a remedy, it is infinitely more kind to ſuffer him to re

main in ignorance. To be well deceived, is almoſt equal to not being deceived at all: our happineſs conſiſts in the imagination of it; and if we firmly believe ourſelves poſſeſſed of what we wiſh, it is the ſame thing as being ſo in reality. How cruel is it, then, for any one to draw back the friendly curtain that hides ill-fortune from us, and compel us to behold our wretchedneſs! Every one who is thus unhappily undeceived, may cry out with Bellamira, in the play—

———————‘ Ah, cruel friend!
‘ Why didſt thou wake me from my dream
　‘ of bliſs!
‘ Why bring me from that ſcene of fancied
　‘ joy’,
‘ To one of real anguiſh, horror, and de
　‘ ſpair!’

Many unhappy inſtances of theſe well-meant ill offices have come to my knowledge ſince I was in poſſeſſion of the gift of Inviſibility; but I ſhall recite only one of them, which, as it is a very late tranſaction, and but few people know the real truth of, is at preſent a matter of much ſpeculation among thoſe who are any way acquainted with the parties concerned, or have even heard their names.

Meroveus and Deidamia were an extreme happy pair; the railers againſt marriage could find nothing in the conduct of either of them to countenance any ſarcaſms on that ſtate. The moſt tender affection had been the chief, if not the ſole motive of the union between them; and the ſecure and uninterrupted poſſeſſion of each other, inſtead of diminiſhing, ſeemed rather to increaſe their mutual ardour, and their firſt bridal fondneſs appeared in their behaviour after having ſerved a more than ſeven years apprenticeſhip to Hymen. Yet how, on a ſudden, have we ſeen all this ſweet ſerenity turned into ſtorms and tempeſts! Meroveus and Deidamia, who it was thought could not have lived a ſingle week out of each other's preſence, are now parted; according to all probability, parted to meet no more in love.

Beſides the many great accompliſhments which juſtified the affection they ſo long had towards each other, both of them were accounted perſons of an excellent underſtanding and ſolid ſenſe. Nothing, therefore, could have more amazed

amazed the world, than that they should come to this open rupture; even though some little cause of complaint had happened either on the one side or the other. An event so strange, so little dreamed of, put all conjecture to a stand; people pretended not even to guess what should be the occasion, much less to unravel so great a mystery; the accomplishment of that work was reserved by fate for the Invisible Spy alone. The manner in which I made this discovery, I shall relate as concisely as the conversation which let me into it will admit of.

As I was one day taking a solitary walk on Constitution Hill, I saw Deidamia leaning on the arm of Eutracia, a lady of birth and fortune, who had been bred up with her at the boarding-school, and ever since been her most intimate friend and companion. Just as they approached the place where I was, the following dialogue began between them—

*Deidamia.* Now for the secret you have to tell me; methinks I have a more than ordinary impatience to hear it, and we cannot be more retired: no living soul is near us, and there is no danger of any one coming to interrupt our discourse, as all the world are in the Mall.

*Eutracia.* I will not keep you long in suspence, my dear; but first you must answer two or three questions I have to ask you, and then resolve to arm yourself with all the fortitude you are mistress of, not to be too much shocked at what I shall relate.

*Deidamia.* I cannot conceive that there is any thing which either you or any one else can tell me capable of giving me a shock. But pray, what is it you would know from me?

*Eutracia.* The town looks upon you as one of the most happy women in it; is it true that you are really so?

*Deidamia.* Indeed, my dear, I think myself so; and if I would labour to be more blessed, know not how to form a single wish beyond what I possess.

*Eutracia.* There are many private causes of disquiet, which prudence obliges us to conceal. Are you thoroughly convinced of the affection of your husband?

*Deidamia.* I never had the least cause to doubt it; and the tenderness I have for him is so sincere and delicate, as I think would make me easily perceive a want of it in him. But wherefore do

you ask? you cannot have any reason to suspect him.

*Eutracia.* Ah, poor Deidamia!

*Deidamia.* Why do you sigh, and look so piteously upon me? Some wretch has certainly belied Meroveus to you.

*Eutracia.* No. But one more interrogatory, and I have done. Does he never absent himself without letting you know where he goes? never lie out of his own house?

*Deidamia.* Very seldom, and that but lately. An intimate friend of his makes his addresses to a young lady at Hammersmith. He frequently desires my husband's company with him, and they sometimes stay all night; when having supped there, it is dangerous to return to London, as the roads are now infested.

*Eutracia.* How easy is it to deceive the innocent!—Meroveus is a villain!

*Deidamia.* How, Eutracia! a villain! Had any other called him so, my resentment should have shewn how much I despised so base an accusation.

*Eutracia.* Alas! it is your own love and honour makes you so tenacious of his, but he is false in both; and I again repeat the name, he is a villain! and will put it in your power to prove him so, by the testimony of your own eyes and ears, provided you promise to give him no previous hints, that you have discovered, or even suspect his perfidy.

*Deidamia.* But how—how, Eutracia, is he a villain?

*Eutracia.* He keeps a mistress; some common wench, no doubt: but he adores, doats on her, pretends himself her husband; and those nights when you imagine him at Hammersmith, he passes with her.

The tender Deidamia was now so overcome at these words, that her spirits quite forsook her, and she must certainly have fallen on the earth, if they had not happened to be very near a bench, at the lower end of the walk, where Eutracia placed her. The keeper of the gate perceiving her condition, was so humane as to run and fetch some water, which being sprinkled on her face, soon brought her to herself. Eutracia, on seeing her fair friend thus agitated, seemed, and I believe really was, very much concerned at what she had done; for she could not refrain some tears from falling down her eyes, while she expressed herself in these terms—

B b                      ‘ My

'My deareſt Deidamia, if I had not thought you would have received this intelligence with more moderation, you ſhould have been for ever ignorant of it.' The afflicted lady made no reply to theſe words; but in a few minutes growing ſomewhat more compoſid, quitted the bench, and leaning on Eutracia, the converſation was renewed in this manner—

*Deidamia.* Oh, Eutracia! little are you capable of conceiving the agonies this poor, diſtracted, bleeding heart, ſuſtains! Yet I muſt know all. Tell me by what means you got information of this horrid ſecret, and how you are aſſured of it's veracity.

*Eutracia.* It was not my intention to conceal any part of it; but you muſt determine to liſten with calmneſs to me.

*Deidamia.* I will.

*Eutracia.* Well, then, I will tell you all. I believe you know Mrs. Flounceit, my mantua-maker.

*Deidamia.* I ſaw her once. You may remember I was with you when ſhe brought home your laſt new ſacque.

*Eutracia.* That woman, you muſt know, has an intereſt with ſome foreign merchants, and can frequently oblige her cuſtomers with ſome curious things which are prohibited to be ſold in publick. She came laſt Monday, and acquainted me that ſhe had ſeveral patterns of the moſt beautiful chintz that ever were ſeen. I went the next morning in order to ſee them, and was carried into a back-parlour, for the ſake of privacy. As I was looking over the goods, I heard a man call from the top of the ſtair-caſe, to know if the coach was come. I thought myſelf perfectly acquainted with the voice, though I could not juſt then recollect whoſe it was; but preſently after ſaw Meroveus lead a woman acroſs the garden, at the lower end of which there is a little door that opens into another ſtreet. A pebble, or ſome ſuch thing, happening to lie in the walk, ſhe ſtumbled in paſſing; on which he cried out, with the greateſt tenderneſs—'I hope you are not hurt, my love!'—'No,' replied ſhe, briſkly; 'not at all. I cannot receive any preļudice when my guardian angel is ſo near.' I was ſo aſtoniſhed at what I ſaw and heard, that I had not power to ſpeak; till Mrs. Flounceit, ſeeing me look earneſtly after them, told me they

were her lodgers; that they were lately married; but ſome reaſons obliging them to keep it private, they met each other there only once or twice a week. 'So,' ſaid ſhe, 'I have very little trouble with them, and they pay me a good rent.'—'But are you ſure,' cried I, 'that they are man and wife? It may be an intrigue.'—'No,' anſwered ſhe: 'they were recommended to me by a gentleman who formerly lodged with me himſelf, one Sir David Townly.'

*Deidamia.* Oh Heavens! Sir David Townly! Why he is the very perſon my huſband pretends he goes with to Hammerſmith.

*Eutracia.* It is very likely he may be his confidant in this amour.

*Deidamia.* Yet ſtill I know not how to think it real; one man may be like another. Are you certain it was Meroveus whom you ſaw?

*Eutracia.* As certain as that it is Deidamia to whom I am talking. Did he not lie abroad laſt Monday night?

*Deidamia.* He did.

*Eutracia.* And had he not on a dark brown velvet coat, and a black waiſtcoat trimmed with bugles?

*Deidamia.* He had. Oh, I can no longer ſhut my eyes againſt conviction! The dreadful truth is too glaring to be reſiſted, and I ſee myſelf the moſt miſerable of women!

*Eutracia.* Do not think ſo; rather exert the ſpirit of an injured wife, detect him in his guilt, ſhame him to repentance, and make him ſue for pardon.

*Deidamia.* Oh that ſuch love as ours has been ſhould come to this!

*Eutracia.* All may be yet retrieved; your juſt reproaches may make him lothe his paſt follies, and become more yours than if he never had tranſgreſſed. The next time he takes his pretended journey to Hammerſmith, let me know it.

*Deidamia.* He is gone thither now. Juſt before you came to call me to the Park, he told me Sir David had engaged his company, and he believed he ſhould not return till morning.

*Eutracia.* Well, then, he ſhall be met, my dear Deidamia; he ſhall be met by thoſe he leaſt expects, or deſires to ſee. I will take you in the morning to Mrs. Flounceit's, under pretence of bringing her a new cuſtomer; there you will have the ſame opportunity I had of diſcovering your huſband's guilt, and
may

may act as you shall judge proper on the occasion.

*Deidamia.* How shall I contain myself! Base, base man! cruel deceiver of my fond, my unsuspecting heart!—How bear the sight of that vile she! that infamous deluder of his honour! that curied she who has robbed me of the only treasure I valued upon earth, my husband's love!

Here she burst into the most vehement exclamations. But my Crystalline Remembrancer being already overcharged, I can only say that her behaviour verified the words of Mr. Nat. Lee; who, in his description he gives of the passions of womankind in general, has these lines—

‘ They shrink at thunder, dread the rust-
‘ ling wind,
‘ And glitt'ring swords the brightest eyes
‘ will blind;
‘ Yet when strong jealousy enflames the
‘ soul,
‘ The weak will rage, and calms to tem-
‘ pests roll.’

The ladies continued their walk, till Phœbus beginning to withdraw his beams, they both thought proper to retire from the approaching dews. Eutracia, justly apprehending the agitations of her friend would become more violent if left alone and at liberty to indulge them, offered to be her companion that night, which the other gladly accepted, and I saw them take coach together for Deidamia's house, after which I went home.

## CHAP. V.

WHICH, ACCORDING TO THE AU-
THOR'S OPINION, STANDS IN NO
NEED OF A PRELUDE, AS IT CON-
TAINS ONLY THE SEQUEL OF AN
ADVENTURE TOO INTERESTING
TO ALL DEGREES OF PEOPLE NOT
TO DEMAND THE ATTENTION OF
EVERY READER.

I Was truly concerned at the injustice which I perceived poor Deidamia sustained; and but little pleased with Eutracia, either for the information she had given her of it, or for advising her to detect Meroveus in the manner con-

certed between them: indeed, I feared that the consequences of such an interview would be only to make the husband become more hardened in his guilt, and her affliction increase by finding her resentment disregarded.

Few men can bear reproofs, much less reproaches. If ever they quit a darling folly, the reformation must come of themselves; it must proceed from a consciousness they have done amiss, and not from being told so by others. There is a pride in human nature which disdains admonition, and makes us persist in error, which, if not taken notice of, perhaps in time we might discover to be such, grow ashamed of, and amend. Besides, remonstrances from a person whom we look upon as any way our inferior, either in point of understanding or circumstances, will be so far from having any weight, that they will rather add to our contempt, and, it may be, raise in us an utter aversion to the giver. Custom has made the husband so much the head of the wife, that, tenacious of his authority, it is but seldom he submits to be influenced by her in matters of much less moment to him than his pleasures.

Indeed, when a woman is wronged in the manner Deidamia was, it must be confessed that the shock is greatly trying, and that she has the strongest reason for complaining; yet will she still find it most prudent to forbear. Love and gentleness are the only weapons by which that sex can hope to conquer; and she who attempts to have recourse to any other, only hurts herself. By seeming not to suspect her husband's vices, she will, at least, oblige him to keep them as private as he can, and also to treat her with all the respect due to her character, and the sacred union between them; whereas, by growing clamorous and impatient, she furnishes him with a pretence to use her ill, and turns the indifference he before had for her into hatred and detestation.

One of our best poets has an observation on this head, which I think is very well worthy of the serious attention of all who are either injured in reality, or imagine themselves to be so, yet find it their interest to preserve an amicable correspondence with the person guilty of the injury; as it is certain that no man, detected in the thing which he wishes to

concea

conceal, can ever love the perfon by whom he is detected. The words of the author I mentioned are thefe—

'Forgivenefs to the injur'd does belong;
'But they ne'er pardon who have done the
　'wrong.'

Thefe reflections, together with my impatience to fee how Deidamia would fupport the full conviction of her huf-band's falfhood, fo much took up my mind, that it was a confiderable time be-fore I remembered how great an impe-diment lay between me and the gratifi-cation of my curiofity. Mrs. Flounce-it's houfe was to be the fcene of action; and the ladies, during their whole con-verfation, had made no mention in what ftreet, nor even in what quarter of the town, that woman lived: however, as I fuppofed her to be a noted woman in her bufinefs, I hoped to get over this difficulty; and did fo, by fending an emiffary to enquire among the mercers, hoop-petticoat-makers, and other fuch people who are employed in the equip-ments of the ladies; and I went not to bed without receiving the direction I ftood in need of.

As I knew not the hour in which Me-roveus and the partner of his loofer plea-fures would be preparing to depart, nor that in which Deidamia would e con-ducted by Eutracia to behold this proof of her misfortune, I took care to go very early to Mrs. Flounceit's, and was obliged to wait a confiderable time be-fore the door happened to be opened to let any one pafs in or out: at laft, however, it was fo; I got an oppor-tunity to enter, went into the back par-lour, and pofted myfelf in that corner of it which I thought would be the fafeft and moft commodious. My patience was not here put to any long trial; the ladies ar-rived a few minutes after I came, ufhered into the room by Mrs. Flounceit, who placed them on a fet ee with a great deal of formal complaifance, and then made fome apologies, as many people do when they are dreffed as well as they can be, for being in fuch a difhabille, and not in the order fhe could wifh to re-ceive them.

It was eafy for me to perceive, by Deidamia's countenance. how ill fhe had paffed the night; Eutracia alfo feemed in fome agitation, though fhe diffembled it as well as fhe was able; and

after giving fome flight anfwer to Mrs. Flounceit's compliments, told her fhe had brought a friend to look over fome of her fine things; on which the man-tua-maker immediately opened a large prefs, and brought out feveral pieces of chintz, with fome French brocades, and rich Italian filks; thefe fhe fpread upon a table, accompanying that action with many praifes on the beauty and curiofity of each. But it was in vain fhe boafted, in vain fhe magnified; all fhe faid, as well as the real merit of the goods fhe exhibited to fale, was wholly loft on Deidamia; the mind of that afflicted lady was too much bent on thofe things which fhe expected to be witnefs of, to have any eyes or ears for thofe which were not prefent to her: fhe took up firft one piece, and then another, but with-out feeming to know what fhe did; and had fomething fo diftracted in her air and geftures, that Eutracia was obliged to keep Mrs. Flounceit in difcourfe, to prevent her taking any notice of it. Her behaviour, joined with my knowledge of the caufe, reminded me of Mr. Dry-den's words; which, if fhe had been in-clined to think of poetry, fhe might pretty juftly have applied to her own con-dition in this crifis—

'Love, juftice. nature, pity, and revenge,
'Have kindled a wildfire in my breaft;
'I am all a civil war within.
'And, like a veffel ftruggling in a ftorm,
'Require more hands than one to keep me
　'upright.'

But if fhe was fo little able to fup-port the bare idea of the fhock fhe came on purpofe to receive, what muft fhe en-dure when fufpenfe, and all the re-mains of hope, were fwallowed up in the cruel certainty of her misfortune, and conviction left no farther room for doubt? The maid of the houfe came into the room with a chocolate-pot in her hand, and told her miftrefs that the gentleman and lady above ftairs gave their compliments, and defired the fa-vour of her company to breakfaft with them. Mrs. Flounceit was about to make fome anfwer to this invitation, when Deidamia, not able to contain her-felf, flew out of the parlour, and di-rectly up ftairs, where fhe found Mero-veus and a young woman fitting on the fide of the bed they had but lately quit-ted.

Deidamia

R. Smirke del.                                                    Neagle sculp.

INVISIBLE SP.

Plate V.

Published as the Act directs, by Harrison & Cº Sepʳ₁,₁788.

Deidamia had scarce entered the chamber, when she surprized the guilty pair with these words—' I have a right, Sir, ' to think my company ought to be as ' acceptable to Meroveus as that of Mrs. ' Flounceit, or any other woman.'

Eutracia had followed Deidamia as fast as she could, in order, I suppose, to prevent any desperate effects of her present passion, and I was not far behind. But it will be more easy for the reader to conceive the surprize which appeared in the looks of Meroveus, than for me to express it; he started up, and, with a voice which the various emotions of his mind rendered almost unintelligible, said to her—

*Meroveus.* Confusion! Deidamia! —Madam, what brings you here?

*Deidamia.* That is a question which ought rather to be put to you. I came in pursuit of an ungrateful, too much beloved husband: you to indulge a lawless flame for an abandoned prostitute!

*Meroveus.* Madam, Madam, this does not become you!

*Deidamia.* Does it become you, Sir, to leave your honest home and wife, make pitiful excuses for your absence, and skulk in corners with a wretch like this—this abject hireling of licentious wishes!

*Mistress.* Madam, I would not have you think I am any such person: I did not know Meroveus was a married man.

*Deidamia.* 'Tis false, vile creature! You could not know Meroveus, without knowing he had a wife; a wife who, without boasting, is every way his equal. But get out of my sight, that I may have liberty to ask my perjured husband what he could see in that face of yours to be preferred to mine.

On this Meroveus was opening his mouth to speak, but was prevented by Mrs. Flounceit; who being astonished on the lady's running up stairs, and by the noise she immediately heard above, had hobbled up as fast as her fat would give her leave, and came into the room that moment, crying as she entered—

*Mrs. Flounceit.* Bless me! what is the matter here?

*Deidamia.* Perhaps, Madam, you are ignorant that your house is made a brothel?

*Mrs. Flounceit.* O, my stars!—A brothel! Heaven forbid!

*Eutracia.* My friend tells you true, indeed. She is the lawful wife of that

gentleman; they have been married above seven years; I was present at their wedding; and that woman, there, is no better than a prostitute.

*Mrs. Flounceit.* O the vile slut!—I wonder Sir David Townly should offer to bring me into this scrape; he knows very well I never countenance such doings.—Hussey, get out of my house this minute!

In speaking this, she advanced towards the mistress of Meroveus, and was about to push her out of the room; but that gentleman, perceiving her intent, stepped between; and with a visage all enflamed with wrath, said—' Hold, Madam, hold! This lady has put herself under my protection, and I will ' take care to defend her from all in-' sults whatsoever.' Then turning to Deidamia, went on thus—' As for you, ' Madam, you have only exposed me, ' and undone yourself. I will never ' see you more!' He then took his trembling mistress by the hand, to lead her down stairs: Deidamia, in the utmost agony of spirit, followed him; and catching him by the arm, cried out to him—' Oh stay, Meroveus! You will ' not, sure, add injury to injury! Stay, ' I conjure you, and let that woman ' go!' To which he replied—'' Stand ' off, Madam! Your touch is now ' more hateful to me than ever it was ' agreeable; so leave you to repent the ' cause.'

This cruel rebuff not making her let go the hold she had taken of him, he threw her off with the greatest contempt, and in an instant was out of the house with his dissolute companion; who was, doubtless, as hasty as himself to get from a place where she could expect nothing but affronts. Deidamia would have pursued her ungenerous husband, perhaps even into the street, had she not been withheld by Eutracia, who endeavoured to convince her how little it would avail to remonstrate any thing to him whilst he continued in this humour.

Rage had till now kept up the spirits of this unhappy lady; but the objects of it being removed, and the power of reflecting returned, she sunk into a grief no less immoderate; she wept, she wrung her hands, beat her lovely breast, she swooned several times, and in her intervals of sense could only cry out—' Cru-' el, barbarous Meroveus! Unfaithful, ' ungenerous

'ungenerous hufband! Good Heaven! t r what unknown trangreffion am I become thus mif·rable!' Neither Eutracia nor Mrs. Flounccit omitted any thing i. their power which they thought might ferve to give her confolation, but al they could do was infufficient; and it was fome hours before fhe was enough recovered even to be carried home. As foon as fhe was, Eutracia went with her in the coach; and I walked home, touched to the very foul at the fight of her dilrefs.

I have already given the reader my opinion concerning the extreme folly of reve iling unwelcome fecrets to our friends; fo fhall forbear adding any farther reflections on that head, and proceed, with as much brevity as the ftory will admit, to the cataftrophe of this unhappy adventure.

I went the next morning to the houfe of Meroveus, and was convinced, by what I heard the fervants fay among themfelves, that he had not been at home that night; which, indeed, I feared would be the cafe. On my going up ftairs, I found Deidamia lying on a couch, in a very dejected, melancholy pofture. Eutracia was fitting near her; that lady, it feems, having never quitted her fince the unfortunate vifit they made together at Mrs. Flounceit's. But as the difcourfe between them confifted only of complaints on the one fide, and perfuafions to moderation on the other, I think it not material enough to be inferted. I had not been in the room above a quarter of an hou, before a fervant prefented a letter to Deidamia; it was from her hufband, and contained thefe lines—

'MADAM,

'I Am determined to live eafy, which I am certain is utterly impracticable for me to do with you, after what paffed yefterday between us. What I then faid in heat of paffion, I now repeat in cool blood, and on the moft mature deliberation. In fine, an eternal difunion muft be the confequence of your behaviour, nor fhould the tongues of angels diffuade me from this refolution; you will do well to bear it with patience, as the misfortune, if it may be one, has happened entirely through your own fault.

'To leave you no juft reafon to complain, I fhall order the jointure, fettled on you by our marriage articles, to be regularly paid to you, as though I were no more; and fhall refign to you all the plate, linen, and houfhold furniture, excepting only my books, the India chelt and bureau in my dreffing-room.

'As to our children, the boy I fhall take under my care, the girl I leave to yours; and fhall alfo add one hundred pounds per annum to the abovementioned jointure, for her maintenance and education.

'Farewel for ever!—As we no more muft meet in love, it will be highly improper, and I think could not be very agreeable to either of us, to meet at all; I fhall therefore refrain, as much as poffible, going to any of thofe places you are accuftomed to frequent, and hope you will have prudence enough to take the fame precaution in avoiding me, efpecially when I tell you, that it is the only thing in which you can now oblige your ill-treated hufband,

'MEROVEUS.

'P. S. I fhall fend to-morrow for the things I mentioned.'

My fair readers will be the beft judges of what Deidamia felt on finding her hufband had taken a refolution which could not but give the moft mortal ftab both to her love and pride. She paufed a little after having read it, then gave it to Eutracia, crying out at the fame time, with the greateft emphafis—' See there, my dear Eutracia, this wicked hufband is the fole aggreffor, yet pretends to be the perfon who has reafon to refent!' That young lady, who was all fire and fpirit could not forbear loading Meroveus with reproaches at the end of every paragraph fhe read; and when fhe had finifhed, faid to Deidamia—

*Eutracia.* And how, my dear, do you intend to proceed with this bafe, this moft injurious man?

*Deidamia.* Indeed I know not.

*Eutracia.* If I were in your place, I would write him fuch an anfwer as fhould make his ears tingle.

*Deidamia.* Alas, you know not what it is to be a wife!—But I will write, however.

She then rung her bell for the footman, and afked whether the perfon who brought the letter waited for an anfwer.

*Footman.*

*Footman.* No, Madam, he only bid me deliver it into your own hands, and told me my master ordered me to come to him about two hours hence at George's Coffee-house, and bring some linen with me.

*Deidamia.* 'Tis very well. But do not go till I have spoke to you again; I have a message to send by you.

The fellow assured her he would not fail to obey her commands, and withdrew; after which she sat down to her escritoire, took pen and paper, and began to write in the following terms—

' Cruel and unjust, yet still dear Me-
' roveus!

' IF there needed any other proof than
' that shameful one I yesterday was
' witness of, that I am miserable in the
' total loss of your affection, the letter
' I have just now received would be a
' convincing one. What! after seven
' years conjugal tenderness, perfect and
' sincere on my side, and well dissembled
' on yours, can you entertain a thought
' of parting? of tearing a family to
' pieces which has hitherto lived so re-
' spectable in the world? Must I be
' doomed to mourn a husband's loss
' even while that husband lives? Must
' my son be bred an alien to his mother,
' and my daughter a stranger to her fa-
' ther? O think, Meroveus! and if no
' consideration of me has any weight,
' let that of your own reputation, and
' the interest of our children, prevail on
' you to alter this cruel resolution! We
' may at least live civilly together, if not
' with the same fondness as before this
' accident. Yet why should we not? I
' am willing to meet you more than half
' way in love. You cannot deny but
' you have wronged me in the most ten-
' der point. I confess I was too rash
' in the manner of detecting you. We
' both have been to blame. What is
' done cannot be recalled, but it may
' be repented of: let us exchange for-
' giveness, and endeavour to forget what
' is past.

' There was a time when every little
' ailment felt by your Deidamia gave
' equal pain to you; oh! can you then
' throw off at once all pity, all huma-
' nity, all remorse, for the agonies you
' cannot but be sensible my poor tor-
' mented heart now labours under!
' No, 'tis impossible! reason, honour,
' and good-nature, forbid it! You will

' return, accept the pardon I shall with
' joy bestow; and, in return, vouchsafe
' me yours. Let not my hopes deceive
' me; I am sure they will not, if you
' will suffer yourself to reflect seriously
' on the unhappy consequences that must
' infallibly attend a separation from her
' who ever has been, and desires to con-
' tinue, with the greatest sincerity, your
' most faithful, and most affectionate
' wife,

' DEIDAMIA.'

This she communicated to Eutracia, who approved of the former part of it, but highly condemned the latter, as thinking it too submissive. Deidamia, however, was of a different opinion; and the footman coming in soon after to know her commands, she sealed it up, and put it into his hands to deliver to his master; bidding him say withal, that she was very much indisposed.

After he was gone, the ladies began to enter into some dispute concerning the authority of a husband, and the duty that was expected from a wife; but as I could promise myself no farther infor-mation by their discourse on this sub-ject, and, besides, remembering that I had some business of my own to dispatch, I left the place that instant, not without an intention to return thither the next day. Accordingly I went in the morn-ing, and found poor Deidamia almost drowned in tears, and walking back-wards and forwards in one of her rooms in a distracted posture. The cause of these fresh agonies I easily perceived by a letter which lay open on the table; the contents whereof were as follow—

' MADAM,

' I Have been in some debate within
' my mind, whether to answer your
' epistle in the manner I now do, or not
' to answer it at all, would be the most
' effectual means to prevent your giv-
' ing me or yourself any future trouble.
' You find I have pursued the former of
' these methods, and hope you will
' have discretion enough not to involve
' me in a second dilemma on this score.
' Be assured, I did not resolve on a final
' separation without having well weighed
' the consequences attending it, and find
' them such as can no way come in com-
' petition with my peace of mind; with-
' out which life would be a curse, my
' bed a bed of thorns, my table a de-
' sart,

' fart, my houfe a hell, and every friend
' that came to vifit, a fury to torment
' me.

' See the reverfe your jealous folly
' has occafioned! tax me not, therefore,
' with ingratitude. A thoufand times
' you have confeffed you thought your-
' felf as happy as a woman could be,
' and it is certain you were truly fo.
' During the whole courfe of the years
' we lived together, you never had the
' leaft fhadow of a caufe to complain of
' my want either of refpect or tender-
' nefs. If I indulged any pleafures
' which I imagined would give you dif-
' quiet, I took care to be very private
' in them. Why, then, did you fuffer
' yourfelf to be led by an idle curiofity
' to pry into fecrets which the difcovery
' of muft give you pain, and poffibly
' prove the total deftruction of that love
' which once you called your greateft
' bleffing ?

' It is doubtlefs beft for both of us,
' as you rightly enough obferve, to for-
' get what is paft; but am far from
' thinking it can be done by the way
' you mean. No, to forget can only
' be accomplifhed by avoiding each
' other's prefence, and ceafing all kind
' of communication between us. I fhall
' therefore give orders to my fervant to
' charge himfelf with no letter or mef-
' fage you may think fit to fend; and
' defire you will affure yourfelf, that this
' is the very laft you ever fhall receive
' from me. Farewel. I wifh you all
' happinefs in any other fphere of life
' than that you lately lived in with

' MEROVEUS.'

After having examined this epiftle,
I liftened to what paffed between Eutracia and Deidamia: but though I ftaid
till my Tablets were crouded, I fhall forbear inferting the particulars of thefe ladies difcourfe, for reafons which will be
hereafter explained; and only fay in
general, that Eutracia would fain have
fpirited up her friend to refentment and
difdain againft a hufband whom fhe
thought fo unworthy of her; that Deidamia's love overcame her fex's pride;
and, in fine, that the one argued like a
virgin, and the other like an affectionate
wife. Whether Deidamia made any
further attempts to move her obdurate
hufband to a reconciliation, I cannot be
pofitive; but believe fhe did not, for

fhe retired foon after into the country,
whence fhe is but lately returned; and,
whatever her heart may endure, has
very much regained her ufual compofure of countenance and behaviour.

## CHAP. VI.

IS SOMEWHAT MORE CONCISE THAN
ORDINARY, BUT TO THE PUR-
POSE; AND WILL BE FOUND NOT
THE LEAST WORTHY OF ANY IN
THE BOOK OF BEING REGARDED
WITH ATTENTION.

AS during the courfe of thefe lucubrations I have been extremely
circumftantial in the reports I have
made, the reader has a right to be furprized that I omitted the difcourfe between Deidamia and Eutracia; I fhall,
therefore, according to my promife,
relate my motive for fo doing, and flatter myfelf it is fuch as will render me
perfectly excufable in this point. Much
about the time of the adventure related
in the two preceding chapters, I happened to be witnefs of a converfation
which, though between different perfons, and on a very different occafion,
was ftill on the fubject of marriage, the
authority of a hufband, and the fubmiffion expected from a wife; I left out the
former, and made choice of the latter,
as of the two the moft interefting.

Two fifters, whofe characters I prefent to the publick under the names of
Flavia and Celemena, have both of them
a tolerable fhare of beauty, but no other
qualification, either natural or acquired,
that could entitle them to the hope of
an elevated ftation; yet, by the benevolent afpect of their happy planets, are
they become the brides of Alcandor
and Thelamont, perfons diftinguifhed
in the world by their birth and fortune,
and ftill more fo by the greatnefs of their
merit. Thefe nuptials, fo aftonifhing
to the town, and which happened foon
after one another, gave me a curiofity to
difcover, by the help of my Invifibility,
in what fafhion the ladies would behave
themfelves in a fphere of life fo altogether new to them, and fo little expected,
even in their vaineft wifhes, ever to arrive at.

Flavia was the eldeft, and it was to
her I made my firft vifit. She was in
her dreffing-room, fitting at her toilet,
with

with her waiting-maid behind her, giving the finishing stroke to her head-tire. Thelamont was also there, and stood leaning his elbow on a bureau, with a good deal of diffatisfaction in his countenance; while she kept looking in the glafs, and, without turning her head towards him, faid—

*Flavia.* Pr'ythee, Thelamont, let us talk no more of this stuff; I am quite fick of it. I am certainly the best judge of thefe things, and it is in vain to perfuade me, for I will not be contradicted.

*Thelamont.* You will not, then, oblige me?

*Flavia.* Pofitively no; not when you intermeddle in thefe affairs.

*Thelamont.* Well, then, Madam, I shall fay no more; but muft tell you, that I thought I had a right to expect this proof of your complaifance.

With thefe words he flung out of the room, and she faid to herfelf—

*Flavia.* Pith! was there ever any thing fo teazing! Men are mighty foolifh fometimes.—Catharine, bring me my gauze handkerchief.

*Maid.* Oh, Ma'am, did not your ladyfhip fay you would wear your new tippet to-day?

*Flavia.* Hah!—Yes—no—it will shew too much of my neck.

*Maid.* Oh, Ma'am, your ladyfhip cannot shew too much of fo beautiful a part.

*Flavia.* That's true: but I fcratched one of my breafts with a pin this morning.

*Maid.* Oh the ugly pin! I wish I knew which it was, that I might crook it quite double, and throw it in the fire.

Juft as the maid had expreffed her refentment againft the weapon that had wounded her miftrefs, Celemena came into the room; and, after faluting her fifter with a freedom fuitable to the nearnefs of their blood and friendfhip, faid to her—

*Celemena.* What is the matter, my dear fifter? You do not look pleafed to-day.

*Flavia.* Umph! No, not very well pleafed; nor, indeed, much difpleafed.

*Celemena.* I met Thelamont going out as I came in. I thought he feemed more referved than ufual, and in a very ill humour.

*Flavia.* If he chufes to be fo, it would be a pity any one should attempt to put him out of it.

*Celemena.* I hope no mifunderftanding has happened between you?

*Flavia.* No, no, we underftand one another pretty well. I underftand that he would fain pretend to take upon him the government of my actions, and he underftands that I will not let him do it; fo we have exchanged a few words this morning, that's all.

*Celemena.* Have a care, fifter; quarrels in the beginning of marriage promife but little felicity in the continuance of that ftate.

*Flavia.* That's true: but it is very provoking when a man will needs interfere in things he has no manner of concern with.

*Celemena.* Pray, what is the fubject of your difpute, if it be not too great a fecret?

*Flavia.* Why, you muft know, he wants me to leave off putting any carmine upon my cheeks, calls it nafty daubing, and fays I should be a thoufand times handfomer without it.

*Celemena.* I can fee nothing extraordinary in all this. There are many men who have an utter averfion to a woman's ufing any art to her complexion.

*Flavia.* They may cry out againft it; but yet I am fure it is frequently owing to art that they fail fo much in love with us. A little red upon the cheeks gives a fparkle to the eyes, and a luftre to the features, which otherwife would appear flat and languid. But they are fo foolifh as not to confider this; they like us as they fee us altogether; and though they may be fenfible we are painted, never once imagine it is to that neceffary auxiliary to beauty that we are chiefly indebted for thofe charms which attract their admiration.

*Celemena.* Suppofe it as you fay, which, however, I am far from allowing to be always the cafe, Thelamont has now feen you fuch as Nature made you: the night wears off that borrowed luftre, and the morning shews you what you truly are; and if he approves of you in this light, I know of no other perfon whom you need be ftudious to pleafe.

*Flavia.* I am of a quite different opinion. O the joy of being gazed at and followed by a whole crouded Mall!

*Celemena.* Perhaps to laugh: but if fincere, a very empty joy, and what a married woman ought not to be too ambitious of.

*Flavia.* So, then, you would have

C c                                    me

me comply with my hufband's requeft?

. *Celemena.* Indeed I would advife you to it. I am fure, if Alcandor expreffed a defire that I fhould cut off my hair, and never let it grow again, though it is the gift of Nature, and beftowed upon us as the greateft ornament of our fex, I would not hefitate one moment to oblige him.

*Flavia.* Then you are a fool.

*Celemena.* In this point I do not think I am: for befides that duty which the law exacts from every wife to her hufband, there are other reafons which would oblige me to refufe nothing to Alcandor.

She accompanied thefe words with a very fignificant look; which Flavia obferving, ordered her maid, who had been all this time in the room, to withdraw; and, as foon as fhe was gone, replied to what her fifter had faid in thefe terms—

*Flavia.* I know not what you would fay; you would infer that, becaufe Alcandor and Thelamont married us without fortunes, we are therefore bound to be their flaves.

*Celemena.* Not fo: and I dare believe, that neither of them will ever require any fubmiffions from us but fuch as, if we had always been their equals, would very well become us to grant.

*Flavia.* Laird! what a buftle you make about equals! Whatever we were before, marriage has made us now their equals; and, for my own part, I fhall never fubmit to do any thing Thelamont requires of me, unlefs my own inclination happens to concur.

. *Celemena.* Oh, fifter, I am amazed to hear you talk in this manner! Have you been married but one month, and can already forget the unhappinefs of our fingle ftate; our fcanty and precarious dependance; the difficulties we found to fupply ourfelves with even the common neceffaries of life? We made, indeed, a kind of tawdry fhew when we appeared abroad; but how did we pinch for it at home! Is there no love, no gratitude, due from us to men who have raifed us to opulence, grandeur, and refpect!

*Flavia.* Pifh! they married us to pleafe themfelves, not out of pity to us. But let us have no more of this dull ftuff. You muft go with me to Mrs. Rakelove's route to-night; it is the firft fhe

has had, and I promifed her to bring all the company I could.

*Celemena.* Indeed you muft excufe me.

*Flavia.* For what reafon?

*Celemena.* Alcandor fups at home, and I cannot be abroad.

*Flavia.* Heavens! how ftrangely filly you are grown!—Alcandor fups at home! What then? he did not marry you to make you a cook! You do not drefs his victuals?

*Celemena.* No; but he married me to make me a companion at his victuals: and while he continues to defire my prefence, as I flatter myfelf he always will, I fhall never form any pretences to be abfent.

The face of Flavia grew more red than the carmine had made it, on finding in her fifter fentiments fo oppofite to her own; but was prevented from making any anfwer by the entrance of a fervant, who told her that fome ladies were come to vifit her; on which fhe went, accompanied by Celemena, into the dining-room, in order to receive them. Thus ended the converfation I mentioned; and I by it the reader may judge which of thefe two fifters had the greateft fhare of prudence, beft deferved her good fortune, and was moft likely to enjoy a long continuance of it.

## C H A P. VII.

PRESENTS THE ACCOUNT OF AN IN-
CIDENT WHICH CANNOT BUT BE
DEEPLY AFFECTING TO THE
YOUTH OF BOTH SEXES, AND NO
LESS REMARKABLE IN IT'S EVENT
THAN ANY THE AUTHOR'S INVI-
SIBILITYSHIP EVER ENABLED
HIM TO DISCOVER.

AMONG all the various deceptions which are carried on in this great world, I know of none more cruel, and more liable to be attended with the worft of confequences, than thofe practifed in the affairs of love; yet it is a crime which paffes with impunity, and is fcarce cenfured by any but the perfons injured by it, and their particular friends and confidants. Even the ladies, generally fpeaking, for they are no rule with all exceptions, are fcarce the friends of each other, that we know
and

find them taking up the quarrel of their fex in this point; on the contrary, they are apt to abfolve the vow-breaker, and let the whole blame fall on the believer. A man who has triumphed over the credulity of an hundred women, fees himfelf not lefs refpected; and fometimes the number of paft conquefts fhall ferve him as a recommendation, and be a means of his attaining new ones. Perjury is deemed but a venal tranfgreffion in this cafe; few think that oaths and imprecations, when dictated by the heart of an amorous inclination, though formed in the moft binding terms, and uttered in the moft folemn manner, are ever regiftered in heaven.

This vice, as I muft take the liberty to call it, is not, however, wholly confined to the male fex; I am forry to obferve, that thofe of the other, either through pride, vanity, or an inconftancy of nature, are fometimes found guilty of deluding their lovers with falacious expectations. I hope alfo to be forgiven by the more difcreet part of womankind, when I fay that a propenfity to fuch a behaviour is yet lefs excufable in them than in the men; as a perfect innocence, a fweetnefs of difpofition, and a fimplicity of manners, are, or ought to be, the diftinguifhing characterifticks of the fair-fex.

A young lady, to whom I fhall give the name of Syrenia, was endowed by nature with every requifite to command love and admiration; fhe had fine eyes, a regular fet of features, fine hair, and a moft delicate complexion; was tall, well-fhaped, and had fomewhat peculiarly attractive in her air. Fortune had not been altogether fo propitious to her; through the extravagances of her parents, fhe was left in poffeffion of a very moderate fortune: it was, however, entirely at her own difpofal, and fufficient, with the good œconomy fhe was miftrefs of, to fupport her in a very genteel, though not a grand way of life.

Propofals of marriage had often been made to her by feveral eminent and wealthy citizens; but fhe rejected them all, and defpifed the thoughts not only of a fhop, but alfo of all other callings and occupations whatever. Ambition was the predominant paffion of her foul; and fhe had vanity enough to think that her birth, her perfon, and accomplifhments, were fuch as might very well

compenfate for the fmallnefs of her fortune, and entitle her to higher expectations.

She had lived till the age of twenty-three without having any offer of the kind fhe hoped; but about the expiration of that æra, a young gentleman, named Roffano, happening to fee her at the houfe of a relation whom he vifited became violently in love with her; and foon after finding means to get himfelf introduced, made a declaration of his paffion; to which, knowing what and who he was, fhe gave all the encouragement he could wifh, or tha ,was befitting the character of a modeft woman. It would, indeed, have been much to be wondered at, if the addreffes of Roffano had not been acceptable to her: he is defcended from a very ancient and worthy family; has an eftate of eight hundred pounds per annum, entirely free from any incumbrance, either mortgage, dowry, or portions to be paid out of it; his perfon and behaviour are extremely agreeable; and, to add to all this, has defervedly the reputation of a man of ftrict honour, and more fobriety than could be expected from his years and the diffolutenefs of the prefent times.

The fincerity and warmth of his affection making him very ftrenuous in his preffures, and the advantages fhe found in a match with him rendering her complying, they were beginning to talk of ordering articles for their marriage to be drawn up; when an unexpected accident, relating to his eftate, obliged him to go immediately into the country. Though he propofed to ftay but a fhort time, yet he could not think of being deprived of the fight of his beloved Syrenia, even for a few weeks, without an infinity of grief. Sh teftified little lefs regret for this enforced feparation: their parting was extremely moving; each feemed to endeavour to outvie the other in expreffions of tendernefs; and the only confolation he had was, the repeated affurances fhe gave him, that wherever he went he carried her heart along with him.

It is highly probable, that the affection fhe profeffed for him was at that time perfectly fincere. and that fhe looked upon the accident which delayed the celebration of their nuptials as no inconfiderable misfortune to her; but whatever chagrin fhe might feel at firft on this account, it was very foon diffi-

pated,

ated, and gave way to ideas of a far different nature. The motive which brought about so sudden and so extraordinary a change in her sentiments, I shall relate, as I was afterwards fully informed of it by the several conversations I was present at by the help of my Invisibility.

She was one morning in the Park with a lady of her acquaintance called Delia, where they were met and joined by a young officer, brother to Delia, and a gentleman who was with him, and equally a stranger to both the ladies, but behaved towards them with the greatest respect and politeness. They walked two or three turns up and down the Mall; after which the gentlemen took their leave, and Syrenia and Delia went to their respective habitations, without thinking any more of what had passed. Little, indeed, could either of them apprehend the consequences of this adventure: but the next day, early in the forenoon, Syrenia was surprized with a visit from Delia; who came running into her apartment without any ceremony, crying out as she entred—

*Delia.* Joy to you, my dear! I come to wish you joy!

*Syrenia.* Of what? for I see no other subject of joy than what I always feel on seeing you.

*Delia.* Me! No, no; a thousand such as me are quite out of the question: but I have the pleasure to congratulate you on the greatest conquest your beauty ever made, or perhaps ever can make!

*Syrenia.* You are got into a vein of raillery this morning.

*Delia.* No, upon my honour I never was more serious. Do you not remember the fine gentleman that was with my brother yesterday in the Mall?

*Syrenia.* Yes; you know they joined company with us.

*Delia.* His name is Leontine; he is the eldest son of his father, and heir apparent to three thousand pounds a year. You saw his person; for my part, I think nothing can be more agreeable: and my brother tells me he is the most accomplished man he ever knew.

*Syrenia.* Well, and what is all this to me?

*Delia.* It is all to you. It seems he saw you last Sunday at Westminster Abbey, fell violently in love with you, and would have followed to have seen where you lived, but was prevented by

some gentlemen of his acquaintance, who that instant laid hold of him, and forced him along with them.

*Syrenia.* 'Tis possible such a one might be there; but I did not take notice of him.

*Delia.* That may be; but he took so much of you, as not to be able to sleep ever since.

*Syrenia.* Very romantick, truly! But, pray, how came you so well acquainted with the secrets of his heart, who yesterday seemed an utter stranger to his person?

*Delia.* I will tell you the whole affair, as my brother last night came and informed me of it. After they had left us, they went and dined together at a tavern. Leontine asked a thousand questions concerning your family, your fortune, and your character; all which, you may be sure, were answered not to your disadvantage. He then made my brother the confidant of the passion you had inspired him with, and intreated him to use his interest with me, as he found I was pretty intimate with you, to engage me to introduce him to you, which I have faithfully promised to do.

*Syrenia.* What! without my consent?

*Delia.* I hoped to be forgiven. Such an offer, my dear, is not to be rejected.

*Syrenia.* It is much beyond my expectations, I must confess; but the disparity between our fortunes is too great.

*Delia.* If he thinks your person an equivalent, it is not your business to make objections.

*Syrenia.* That is true: and if I could flatter myself he were really sincere—— But I will consider of it.

*Delia.* It will be time enough for you to consider, when you have heard what he has to say; for I have promised to bring you together this evening.

*Syrenia.* This evening! As how?

*Delia.* As thus: I invite you to sup with me to-night; my brother and Leontine shall come in, as if by accident. Neither your pride nor your modesty has any thing to scruple; for I assure you I will not let even my brother know that I have previously acquainted you with any thing of the matter.

*Syrenia.* Well, on that condition I will come.

*Delia.* Indeed, my dear, I should think you very much to blame to turn your back on a prospect so highly advantageous;

advantageous; for though you are well born, well-accomplished, are handsome, and have some fortune of your own, yet the three first of these as men now think of marriage, weigh but lightly against what they call the incumbrance of a wife; and as to the latter, you know it will not entitle you to a coach and six.

*Syrenia.* The justice of what you say cannot be denied; but I would do nothing that should occasion my character being called in question, nor would seem too forward, though to promote the highest expectations: therefore, my dear Delia, remember I depend on your prudence.

*Delia.* In this you safely may. I know too well what is owing to my sex, and the cruel aspersions men are apt to throw on our most innocent freedoms, not to be extremely cautious in avoiding giving the least room for censure.

*Syrenia.* Indeed, my dear, my observation on your own conduct ought to put to silence all my doubts on that score; and, whatever is the event of this affair, I shall always gratefully acknowledge your good wishes towards me.

*Delia.* If it succeeds, I shall be a sharer in your good fortune; as nothing gives me a more sensible satisfaction, than to have it in my power to contribute to the happiness of my friends. But I must leave you: I promised to let my brother know whether you could come or not, that he may apprize Leontine of it.

The good-natured Delia, who did not know how far Syrenia had gone with Rossano, went away in speaking these words: but I could easily perceive, by the glow on Syrenia's cheeks, how much she was transported with the purpose of her visit; and was yet more confirmed of her being so, by some disjointed soliloquies she uttered when she thought there was no witness of what she said. ' Three thousand pounds a year, ' and so fine a gentleman as Leontine ! ' so handsome, so polite, so every thing ' that is agreeable! If he is as sincere as ' Delia imagines him to be, I shall have ' cause to bless the hour I went to West- ' minster Abbey; or rather, that which ' carried me to the Park yesterday; with- ' out which, he might never have known ' who I was, or where to find me, and ' should have lost all the advantage ' my good stars seem to have decreed for ' me.'

Here she ceased to speak, other sort of emotions rising in her mind; to which she gave a loose in this exclamation— ' It was an unlucky thing I went so far ' with Rossano. The poor man loves ' me to distraction : he will certainly ' break his heart when he finds I have ' forsaken him; and, it may be, re- ' proach me as the occasion of his ' death.'

On this her countenance seemed a little disconcerted, but it soon wore off; and, after a short pause, she went on thus—' I am glad, however, that no ' contract has passed between us. The ' encouragement I gave his passion, and ' the verbal promises I made him, need ' be no impediment to my accepting a ' better offer. It will be prudence in ' me, however, not to throw him off, ' nor give him any room to suspect I ' have less affection for him than I had, ' till I am well assured that Leontine is ' in earnest.'

This was enough to shew me the principle and disposition of Syrenia; both which, indeed, were so little pleasing to me, that I had not patience to stay with her any longer, but quitted her apartment with a contempt which, could she have been sensible of, would no doubt have given her some mortification.

I made one of the company that night at Delia's, however; but as it could not be expected that in a meeting which was to pass for casual there should be any conversation except on general topicks, I reaped no other benefit by being present, than to be convinced that Leontine, by the glances he took every opportunity of casting at Syrenia, was indeed very much enamoured, and that she spared no pains to make him more so. The next day he went with the brother of Delia to visit her, and the succeeding one took the liberty of going thither alone, and made a declaration of his passion; which she, having well prepared herself with answers, received in such a manner, as neither to reject, nor with too much readiness encourage.

The ice once broke, he prosecuted his addresses with so much vigour and assiduity, that she thought it would be no breach of modesty to give him room to hope he was not altogether indifferent to her: by degrees, therefore, she became more kind on every visit he made; but did it with caution and reserve, neither by her looks or words forfeiting

that

that character of difcretion fhe fo much valued herfelf upon; dropping only fome hints, as if forced from her from a fund of tendernefs within, which fhe would fain endeavour to conceal, but had not the power of doing it. Thus artful in appearing artlefs, Leontine, though a man of very good fenfe and penetration, never once fufpected fhe was any other than fuch as fhe affected to be, plain, fimple, generous, and incapable of difguifing her fentiments.

It is certain, indeed, that her natural cunning was greatly affifted how to proceed on this occafion by the intelligence fhe daily received from Delia, to whofe brother Leontine made no fcruple of difburdening all that paffed in his heart in relation to his paffion for Syrenia. From this faithful friend fhe learned, that though it was not to be doubted but that Leontine was as much in love with her as man could be, yet the great refpect and reverence he had for his father would not permit him to think of venturing on a thing of fo much confequence as marriage, without having firft obtained his confent and approbation of the woman he made choice of for a wife; and that, to this end, he had already fent two letters to his father, who lived entirely in the country; but the anfwers he received not being quite fo fatisfactory as he wifhed, he had wrote a third, dictated in the moft paffionate and preffing terms.

She could not avoid being under fome very uneafy apprehenfions on the fcore of this old gentleman, and alfo feared that the paffion Leontine was infpired with might not of itfelf be ftrong enough to get the better of that obedience owing from him to a father's will; fhe therefore wifhed to intereft his good-nature and generofity in her favour, and judged that the fureft way to fecure his affection was to make him a confidant of her's. But the means of accomplifhing this was a difficulty fhe knew not prefently how to get over. To confefs by word of mouth fhe loved him, feemed too great a breach of modefty, efpecially as his courtfhip to her had not yet been of any long continuance; and to get him informed of it by Delia fhe thought would be the fame thing, as he would doubtlefs imagine it was not done without her privity and confent; befides, fhe knew not whether that lady would approve of fuch

a ftep. Being one day defired by him to favour him with a tune on her fpinnet, fhe entertained him with an air out of the opera of Arfinoe, the firft in the Italian tafte ever exhibited on the Englifh ftage, and, in my opinion, has been exceeded by none that have come after it. The words fhe fung to her inftrument were thefe—

‘ Wanton zephyrs, foftly blowing,
‘ Watching, catching, whifpering, going,
‘ Bear in fighs my foul away :
‘ Tell Ormondo what I feel,
‘ Tell him how his chains I wear,
‘ Tell him all my grief and care;
　　‘ Gently ftealing,
　　‘ And revealing,
‘ More of love than I can fay.’

But though Leontine extolled both the mufick and the voice which gave it utterance, yet he fhewed no indication of imagining fhe had any defign of flattering his paffion in the choice fhe made of this fong. This making her perceive fhe muft be more explicit, her fertile invention foon prefented her with a ftratagem, which pleafing her fancy at the fame time that it promifed the fuccefs fhe aimed at, fhe put into immediate execution. It was this—Having a natural talent for poetry, fhe fat down at her efcritoire, took pen, ink, and paper, and, without being at the pains of much ftudy, wrote the following lines—

‘ THE BREATHINGS OF A LOVE
　　‘ SICK HEART.

‘ Wit, manly beauty, every grace combine,
‘ To deck the youth I love with charms
　　‘ divine.
‘ But, ah! my too uncautious heart take
　　‘ heed,
‘ Nor with gay hopes the growing paffion
　　‘ feed.
‘ Wealth's the chief idol that mankind
　　‘ adore,
‘ The foveieign power they all fall down
　　‘ before;
‘ My niggard fortune does that charm deny,
‘ And love alone will not it's wants fupply:
‘ Let me then guard each av'nue to my
　　‘ breaft,
‘ And bar all entrance to this dangerous
　　‘ gueft;
‘ Left, by indulging the prefumptuous flame,
‘ I fall the victim of defpair and fhame:
‘ But, oh! 'tis vain!—the god of love con
　　‘ fpires

　　　　　　　　　　　　　　　　‘ To

‘ To aid my Leontine with all his fires;
‘ Speaks in his voice, and sparkles in his
    ‘ eyes;
‘ And what he sweetly forces, justifies.
‘ 'Tis sure determin'd in the book of fate;
‘ I must adore, ev'n though he proves un-
    ‘ grate.'

This paper, which she wanted him to
believe was a sincere confession of the
whole secret of her soul, she contrived
should fall into his hands in such a manner as should have too much the appearance of chance to be liable to any suspicion of design.  At his next visit, her
maid being well instructed by her how
to act, ran hastily into the room, and
told her that the man whom she had ordered to come for his money was below.
Syrenia affected not to understand what
she meant, and cried—
    *Syrenia.* What man? What mo-
ney?
    *Maid.* Mr. Shapely, Madam, your
staymaker.
    *Syrenia.* Oh, now I remember I did
bid him come for his money.  He takes
a strange unseasonable time.  People
should always come in a morning on these
affairs.  However, I'll see if I can find
his bill; and do you carry a pen and ink
into the parlour, that he may write me
a receipt on the back of it.
On this the maid withdrew, and Syrenia opened a little desk that stood in the
dining-room, and beginning to tumble
over some writings she had there, as in
search of the pretended bill, dexterously
slipped from among the rest the paper
which contained the above recited verses,
and let it fall to the ground without
seeming to observe that any thing was
dropped; then saying she had found what
she had looked for, shut up the desk in
a great hurry, begged Leontine would
excuse her absence for a few moments,
and went down stairs.  She was no
sooner gone, than Leontine, happening
to cast his eyes that way, saw the paper,
and took it up, as I suppose with no other
intention than to deliver it to Syrenia
when she should return; but it being pur-
posely folded in such a manner that part
of the writing appeared on the outside,
he must have been strangely incurious
indeed, if seeing it a poem, and wrote
in his mistress's hand, he had forbore
examining it.  Never was any transport
more visible than in the countenance of

Leontine while reading these delusive
stanzas: his look put me in mind of the
poet's words—

‘ Kindness has resistless charms,
‘ All things else but faintly warms;
‘ It gilds the lover's servile chain,
‘ And makes the slave grow pleas'd and
    ‘ vain.'

Though, by the particulars I have been
repeating, the reader will easily suppose I
was both an eye and an ear witness of
them, yet it is utterly impossible for
me to describe either the looks or attitude
of the one or the other, in the joyous
surprize of finding himself, as he imagined, thus extremely dear to the only
woman to whom he wished to be so.
She took care to stay so long below, as
to give him time to read over, more than
once, what she intended for his perusal.
It was still in his hands when she returned; but she seemed to take no notice
of it, and was beginning to apologize
for her absence, by laying the blame on
the impertinence of her staymaker; but
Leontine, with a gesture full of rapture,
interrupted her, saying—
    *Leontine.* O, Madam, you must al-
low me to become an advocate for this
honest tradesman, since by his fortunate
detaining you I am made the happiest of
mankind.
To this Syrenia, affecting not to comprehend the meaning of what he said,
replied with a smile—
    *Syrenia.* What riddle is this you are
about to pose me with?  I am the dul-
lest creature in the world at giving a so-
lution to these things.
    *Leontine.* This paper, Madam, wafted
to me by the god of love's own hand,
has given me the wished-for opportunity
of proving myself less unworthy of the
blessing I aspire to, than your doubts
suggest.  No, my charming Syrenia,
not all the treasures in the world could
add one ray of lustre to the graces of
your mind and person; 'tis those alone I
covet to enjoy, and in possessing them
shall be more rich than in possessing both
the Indies.
While he was thus speaking, Syrenia
cast her eyes upon the paper, and blushed
excessively; partly, perhaps, through
shame, but more through the pleasure
which diffused itself through all her veins
on perceiving, by the behaviour of Le-
                                        ontine,

ontine, how well the fuccefs of her plot had anfwered to the intention of it. The well-diffembled confufion fhe was in was an excufe for her not fpeaking; and Leontine went on to affure her, in the molt tender terms, that no confideration whatever fhould have the power to oblige him to withdraw that firm affection ne now vowed to her; and that he hoped a very little time would put a final period to all her apprehenfions on that fcore. What farther converfation paffed between them at this time I fhall forbear to repeat, as it may be eafily gueffed at; and proceed to the conduct of Syrenia in regard to her other lover, who the reader may think I have too long neglected.

The bufinefs which called Roffano into the country detained him there much longer than he had expected; and an unlucky fall from his horfe, the very day before he intended to fet out for London, occafioned a fecond delay to his journey. This abfence of his gave Syrenia a full opportunity of entertaining her new lover, though fhe received every poft a letter from the former, all which fhe did not fail to anfwer with that tendernefs which might be expected from a woman who had promifed to be his wife; ftill keeping clofe to her firft maxim, not to give any umbrage to the one, till fhe was perfectly fecure of the other. All impediments, however, being at laft removed, that gentleman arrived in town on the fame day that Syrenia and Leontine were engaged in the manner above recited. His impatience to fee his beloved miftrefs carried him immediately to her lodgings: he came while his rival was with her; but her maid, well knowing how improper it was that they fhould meet, told him her lady was abroad; on which he went away, faying he would return in the evening, as he knew fhe was not accuftomed to ftay late from home.

He was doubtlefs much difappointed, but not at all fufpicious of the caufe; till having croffed the ftreet, he happened to caft his eyes back upon the houfe, either by chance, or poffibly through fondnefs of the place which contained the idol of his wifhes. Syrenia was fitting in the window, and Leontine very near to her. Roffano had a full view of both; but Syrenia was too earneft in difcourfe to obferve him, though he ftood motionlefs on the fpot where he was for fome minutes. It feemed not

ftrange to him that a gentleman fhould be with her, though he could find no way to account why he fhould be denied accefs to her but one, which ftung him to the foul. He was more than once tempted by his jealoufy, as I afterwards difcovered, to return, and demand of the maid a reafon for his having been refufed admittance; but fecond thoughts prevailed, and he went home, to deliberate how it would beft become him to behave in fuch a circumftance.

Leontine ftaid fupper; and Syrenia ftepping out of the room to give fome neceffary orders to her maid, was informed by her that Roffano had been there, and the meffage he had left. This greatly difconcerted her; but, after a little paufe, fhe recovered herfelf enough to give thefe directions—'This is very unlucky! 'Leontine will probably ftay late: you 'you muft therefore tell Roffano that I 'am not yet come home, and that you 'believe I am gone to the play.' The maid punctually obeying thefe directions, Roffano only replied that, fince it had happened fo, he would do himfelf the honour to breakfaft with her lady the next morning; and then departed, feemingly well fatisfied. But though he forbore giving any indications of his jealoufy to this girl, he doubted not but that the fecond repulfe was owing to the fame motive the firft had been. Refolving, however, to be more fully convinced, he pofted his fervant, whom he had brought with him for that purpofe, under a lamp a few doors from the houfe where Syrenia lodged, charging him to obferve carefully who came in or out; and if he faw a gentleman in black velvet and a big wig. to follow him wherever he went, find out his name if poffible, and bring him an exact account.

Leontine was fo much charmed with the difcovery he had made of Syrenia's affection, that he quitted her apartment not till the night was far advanced. Roffano's fervant, however, kept clofe to his ftand, till a chair being called, he faw the gentleman his mafter had defcribed go into it. He followed; and as foon as Leontine had entered the houfe where he lodged, and the door was fhut, afked the chairmen if they knew the gentleman they had carried; but they anfwering in the negative, and he feeing no houfe open where he might enquire, could learn nothing farther that night; but early the next morning he went again,

again, and had the addrefs to find out all the particulars that could be expected from him.

Roffano was now affured not only that he had a rival, but alfo a rival highly favoured by his miftrefs. The diftraction he was in may eafily be conceived; but he diffembled it on his firft approach to Syrenia, whom he did not fail to vifit the next morning, as he had told her maid. Syrenia, before fhe was informed of it, knowing very well, that miffing feeing her that nigh', he would not let another day pafs over without coming, had the artifice to tell Leontine fhe was obliged to go fome few miles out of town to fee a relation who fhe heard was dangeroufly ill.

I am not a perfon who live without having fome bufinefs in the world, yet there are few things of confequence enough to me to have detained me from being a witnefs of what paffed in this interview between Roffano and Syrenia, and fhall prefent my readers with it as recorded in my faithful Tablets. Syrenia no fooner heard he was there, than fhe ran to the top of the ftair-cafe to receive him, and with the greateft fhew of tendernefs faluted him in thefe terms—

*Syrenia.* My dear Roffano, how grieved have I been for lofing the fight of you laft night, after having been fo long an age of time deprived of it!

*Roffano.* The misfortune, Madam, was wholly mine; for while I moaned your abfence, you doubtlefs found fomething to amufe and entertain you. I heard you were at the play.

*Syrenia.* I was fo: but what could I find there to compenfate for the fatisfaction I miffed by being fo unluckily from home!

*Roffano,* Were you at Covent Garden?

*Syrenia.* No, at Drury Lane. But why do you afk?

*Roffano.* Only for a foolifh fancy.

*Syrenia.* Nay, I may anfwer myfelf that queftion. I will lay my life you went in fearch of me. But I chofe to go in a difhabille, and fat on the back bench in Burton's box; fo it was impoffible for you to fee me

*Roffano.* Not fo impoffible as you imagine, Madam. But I had no need to go to either of the theatres; the object I fo much languifhed to behold prefented itfelf to me without my taking any pains.

Thefe words occafioned a vifible change in her countenance; fhe blufhed exceffively, caft her eyes upon the ground, and had not power to lift them up while fhe faid only—

*Syrenia.* What is it you mean?

*Roffano.* There needs no explanation: the diforder you in vain endeavour to conceal, fhews but too much how well you are acquainted with my meaning. Ah, Syrenia, Syrenia! how did I once flatter myfelf with an affurance that your heart was mine, inviolably mine; but now I find my abfence has been fatal to me!

*Syrenia.* Forbear to talk thus. Thefe fufpicions are unjuft to me, and cruel to yourfelf.

*Roffano.* Why, then, was I laft night turned from your door? Why twice repulfed, while my more happy rival was allowed the privilege of entertaining you till midnight?

*Syrenia.* Who tells you this?

*Roffano.* My own eyes, Madam, were my firft intelligencers. I faw you at that window; faw alfo your new favourite; and eafily judged, by both your attitudes, what was the fubject of your converfation. As to the reft, I was informed of it by means to which I afterwards had recourfe.

The falfe Syrenia was now abfolutely confounded. There was no giving the lye to ocular demonftration as to the firft part of Roffano's charge againft her; but fhe endeavoured to avoid the latter, by faying—

*Syrenia.* Well, Sir, I own I was at home, and had ordered myfelf to be denied; but expected not your coming, or knew you had been here till after you were gone. As for the gentleman you faw with me, 'tis your own jealous fancy alone that makes you regard him in the light of a lover.

*Roffano.* I grant you did not expect me; but as your fervant is no ftranger to the footing we are upon, fhe would certainly have looked on me as an exception to the general order you had given, if fhe had not known I was no proper perfon to join in the company you had above: befides, you cannot plead ignorance of my fecond vifit, yet I was again turned back.

*Syrenia.* You wrong me: I proteft I never heard of your being here till I was going to bed. Think no more, therefore, of fuch idle ftuff: this is not

difcourfe

difcourfe for two people who love, and have fo long been abfent from each other.

*Roffano.* Ah, Syrenia! I wifh the treatment I have received would allow me to entertain you with any other. There was a time when I could be as gay, perhaps, as he who now fupplants me in your efteem.

*Syrenia.* Still harping on the fame ftring? Remember what the poet fays—

‘ No figns of love in jealous men remains,
‘ But that which fick men have of life, their
‘ pains.’

She had juft done repeating thefe lines, when the tea-equipage was brought in for breakfaft; and Roffano, who I could perceive by his countenance was little pleafed with the trifling anfwers fhe had made to his reproaches, rofe up to take his leave; on which fhe fuddenly catched hold of his hand, and, with a well-counterfeited tendernefs in her voice and eyes, fa-d to him—

*Syrenia.* You will not go and leave me in this humour?

*Roffano.* Indeed I muft. I have this moment thought of a bufinefs that requires immediate difpatch.

*Syrenia.* Shall I then fee you in the afternoon?

*Roffano.* I cannot promife.

He was half way down ftairs while fpeaking thefe laft words; and though fhe followed him two or three fteps, and called to him to ftay, he turned not, nor even looked back upon her, but went haftily out of the houfe. I was refolved to fee what was his intent, and accompanied him to the houfe of that kinfwoman where he had firft feen Syrenia. He was beginning to tell her what caufe of complaint he had againft that lady, but fhe ftopped his mouth, by faying that fhe was already acquainted with every thing he had to relate; and then proceeded to inform him, that having a friend who lived oppofite to Syrenia, fhe had learned that fhe entertained a new lover, who vifited her almoft every day, and that the neighbourhood believed it would very fhortly be a match. Roffano went from this relation to his own lodgings; where, having vented fome part of his rage in exclamations on the levity and ingratitude of womankind, he fat down and wrote the following lines to Leontine—

‘ SIR,

‘ YOU have endeavoured to fupplant
‘ me in the affection of the wo-
‘ man I loved, and am engaged to
‘ marry; I need not tell you I mean
‘ Syrenia. I expect, therefore, you
‘ will either refign all pretenfions to her
‘ under your own hand, or give fuch fa-
‘ tisfaction as one gentleman has a right
‘ to demand from another in thefe cafes.
‘ I fhall attend you behind Montague
‘ Houfe at eight to-morrow morning;
‘ till when, yours,

‘ ROSSANO.’

This he fent immediately to Leontine; who having to be at home, returned an anfwer by the bearer in thefe terms—

‘ SIR,

‘ I Own myfelf a lover of Syrenia, but
‘ know nothing of your courtfhip
‘ to her, nor will believe fhe is under
‘ any engagement of the nature you
‘ mention, either to you or any other
‘ man; and fhall be fo far from refign-
‘ ing my pretenfions, that I will defend
‘ them to the laft moment of my life:
‘ you may therefore rely on my meeting
‘ you at the time and place appointed.
‘ Yours,

‘ LEONTINE.’

Roffano had fcarce finifhed reading this billet, when a porter brought him a letter from Syrenia, the contents where-of were thefe—

‘ MY VERY DEAR ROSSANO,

‘ YOUR behaviour this morning has
‘ thrown me into difquiets which
‘ might excite compaffion in a heart lefs
‘ devoted to me than I flattered myfelf
‘ yours was. I thought the love be-
‘ tween us was eftablifhed on a more fo-
‘ lid bafis, than to be fhook by every puff
‘ of jealous caprice; I doubt not but to
‘ convince you that yours is no other.
‘ If this is fo lucky as to find you at
‘ home, or you receive it time enough, I
‘ beg to fee you this evening; for I can-
‘ not bear you fhould pafs another night
‘ in fuch cruel fufpicions of your faith-
‘ fully affectionate

‘ SYRENIA.’

I perceived he was in fome dilemma on reading this billet; he paufed awhile, then faid—‘ My compliments to the la-
‘ dy, and——’ Then paufed again; at
laft

laft cried—' Tell her I am engaged
' this day, but will wait on her to-
' morrow.'

Various reflections feemed now rolling
in the mind of this much-abufed lover;
but I left him in them, and contented
myfelf with going the next morning to
the field of battle, in order to fee how
the combatants would behave. They
were both fo punctual to the time, that
it is hard to fay which of them was firft
within the lifts. Roffano, however,
having fome idea of Leontine, as he had
feen him through Syrenia's window,
advanced towards him, and faid—

*Roffano.* I guefs, Sir, you are the
gentleman I invited hither.

*Leontine.* You are not deceived, Sir,
if your name be Roffano.

*Roffano.* The fame, Sir.

*Leontine.* Mine, then, is Leontine;
and you find me ready to maintain my
pretenfions to the fair Syrenia.

*Roffano.* And I to affert that right
which a long feries of encouraged courtfhip and mutual vows has given me.

*Leontine.* This, then, is the way we
muft difpute the prize.

Both their fwords were already drawn;
and Roffano, either through fuperior
fkill or better fortune, gave his antago-
nift a flight wound in the fide on the firft
pafs, and on the fecond a much deeper
on the right-arm; which occafioning a
great effufion of blood, he was obliged
to drop his fword; on which the other,
imagining the mifchief to be greater than
it really proved, ftepped haftily towards
him, with thefe words—' Sir, though I
' might expect the juftice of my caufe
' would give me fome advantage over
' you, I fhould be extremely forry to
' find it attended with any bad effects; I
' beg, therefore, as there are fcarce any
' chairs abroad fo early, you will give
' me leave to fupport you to my lodg-
' ings, which are very near, and where
' you may have immediate affiftance.'

Leontine accepted the offer. A fur-
geon was immediately called, and his
cloaths ftripped off in order to have his
wounds examined: that on his fide was
not at all deep; and that on his arm
happening not to be near any tendon,
required little more than a tight bandage
for it's cure. He was advifed, however,
to drink fome mulled wine, and then
endeavour to compofe himfelf to fleep
for a few hours. Roffano, with a great
deal of humanity and politenefs, took

care to fee this injunction performed;
and, on Leontine's requefting it, fent to
his lodging for frefh cloaths and linen
for him to put on when he fhould awake.

As Roffano was retiring, to leave his
gueft to that repofe which was thought
needful for him, he faw a paper lying
on the floor, which he took up, not
knowing but it was fomething belonging to himfelf; but how great was his
amazement when he found what it contained, this being the very verfes Syrenia had wrote on Leontine, and had
fortuitoufly been fhook out of that
gentleman's pocket as his cloaths were
haftily thrown to the other fide of the
room. Till now, the love he had bore
Syrenia kept him from entertaining
any worfe opinion of her conduct, than
that it was the vanity incident to her
fex, which alone had made her encourage the addreffes of Leontine; but this
plain proof of her inconftancy gave a
fudden turn to his fentiments, and
changed at once all the tendernefs he ever
had for her into contempt and hatred.
Leontine alfo had fome uneafy thoughts
on the fcore of Syrenia; Roffano feemed
to him to be a man of too much honour to affert a falfhood; and began
to fear that himfelf had been deceived
in his opinion of that lady's fincerity.
Being lefs inclined to fleep than to be
fatisfied in this point, he rung a bell
which hung by the bedfide; on which
Roffano, who was no farther than the
next room, went in, and afked how he
did; to which he replied—

*Leontine.* So well, that I think I
need lie here no longer than till my
man brings me fome clean apparel,
that I may rife with decency. In the
mean time, Sir, fhould take it as a favour you would let me know how far I
have been guilty of injuftice to you in
regard of Syrenia. In your billet to me,
you mention an engagement: if it be fo,
I was perfectly ignorant of it, and, at
that time, imagined I had ftrong reafons
for difbelieving it; otherwife, I do affure
you, Sir, not all my paffion for that lady
fhould have made me attempt to difunite
your loves.

*Roffano.* Though it may feem ungenerous to boaft a lady's favours, as I
have no other way to juftify my rafh
proceedings towards you, be pleafed to
read that letter.

In fpeaking this, he prefented to Leontine the letter he had received from Sy-

renia the day before; which that gentleman had no sooner looked over, than he cried out, with the greatest surprize—

*Leontine.* Good Heaven! Why this was dated but yesterday!

*Rossano.* Yes, Sir; and wrote on account of my testifying some jealousy on your being with her the evening before. But I have now done with that idle passion, and can now resign my claim with as much calmness as I would lately have maintained it with eagerness.

*Leontine.* Is it possible you can be in earnest!

*Rossano.* Were Syrenia more beautiful than she is, the enjoyment of her person, without her heart, could give me no happiness; and had this paper, which accidentally fell from your pocket in the hurry this morning, happened sooner into my hands, I should not have proceeded as I have done.

In speaking this, he gave Leontine the paper he had taken up: the other immediately saw what it was; and, receiving it with a smile, made this reply—' I thank you, Sir; but I assure ' you I am not at all vain of these ' verses, as they serve only to prove that ' the lady was willing to be double ' armed; and in case one lover should ' fail, to be provided with another.'

After this they began to enter into a very free discussion on the conduct of Syrenia towards them both; and there now appeared so much deceit, mean artifice, ingratitude, and perfidy, as well to the one as the other, that it is hard to say which of them entertained the most despicable notions of her: in fine, they agreed to resent the impositions she had practised on them in such a manner as some of my fair readers, how greatly soever they may condemn Syrenia, will not, perhaps, easily absolve them for.

The servant of Leontine being arrived with the things his master had ordered to be brought, that gentleman rose, and got himself dressed; and Rossano in the mean time employed himself in gathering up all the letters he had received from Syrenia, and made them up in a large packet, and wrote on the cover—

' Amorous billets from a lady of a very ' extraordinary character.'

They went in two chairs to the house

where Syrenia lodged; and the door being opened, rushed up stairs without any ceremony, and even into the dining-room where she was sitting. Leontine was the first that entered: she rose to receive him; but seeing his arm in a scarf, cried out—

*Syrenia.* Oh, Sir! what accident has befallen you?

*Leontine.* No unlucky one, Madam. I have indeed received two slight wounds on your account; but I bless the hand that gave them, since they have been the means of curing one of a more dangerous nature in my heart.

She had no time to ask what he meant by these words; Rossano was now in the room, and rejoined to what the other had said in this manner—

*Rossano.* My heart is also in a pretty good condition too; for though I have lost a mistress, I have gained a friend, from whom I have reason to hope more sincerity. You see, Madam, two persons together, whom doubtless you wished to keep separate, while we had separate interests: but we have now agreed; and as we lately joined to persecute you with our addresses, now join in the resolution of troubling you no more.

*Leontine.* I have nothing to add, Madam, to what my friend has delivered, but to restore this paper; which can be of no use to me, and may be of some to you; as, change but the name, the picture may suit some happier man.

*Rossano.* And I return those letters you have from time to time favoured me with.

He then laid down the packet, at the same time Leontine did the verses, upon a table. Syrenia was all this while immoveable as a statue: she had found, from their first entrance, that they had compared notes; that she was exposed, her arts laid open, and her hopes irrecoverably lost with both. Fain would she have spoke, but had not power; and all she could utter at last was—

*Syrenia.* Mighty well!—So, then, I am to be insulted?

*Rossano.* No, Madam, your birth and beauty are your protection; and had your mind been equal to either, neither of us, I believe, would have broke his chain, or even wished to regain that liberty

INVISIBLE SPY

Plate IV                    Publish'd as the Act directs by Harrison & C? Oct. 1 1788

liberty we now have so much cause to triumph in.

*Leontine.* Come, Sir, you see the lady is disconcerted : let us leave her to meditate on this adventure; it may be of service in some future one.

*Roffano.* With all my heart.—A good husband to you, Madam.

*Leontine.* I join in the same wish.—Your servant, Madam.

They departed with these words, and I staid not long after them; the sight of Syrenia's despair, how justly soever she had brought it on herself, giving more pain than satisfaction.


END OF THE SEVENTH BOOK.

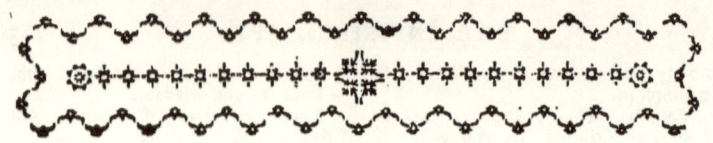

THE

# INVISIBLE SPY.

## BOOK VIII.

### CHAP. I.

CONTAINS A VERY BRIEF DETAIL
OF SUCH OCCURRENCES AS PRE-
SENTED THEMSELVES TO THE
AUTHOR'S OBSERVATION IN AN
EVENING'S INVISIBLE RAMBLE
THROUGH SEVERAL PARTS OF
THIS METROPOLIS.

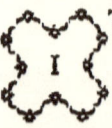T has often been a matter of
very great concern to me,
and I believe must be the
same to every thinking
mind, to see how some people are continually hurried
and busied about mere trifles, of no
manner of consequence to themselves,
or scarce to any body else; while all the
duties of religion, all the regard for the
welfare of their most particular friends, all
love of country, and even the dearest interests of their own families, are totally
neglected. What judgment can we
form of a person of such, but that he
has a vacuum in his head ready to be
filled up with the first toy that presents
itself; and not being endowed with a
strength of reason sufficient to direct his
choice, suffers himself to be engrossed
by such things as he finds make most
noise in the world, not such as have

most relation to his own affairs, either as
to fortune or reputation?

Can there be a sight more farcical
than for a man who, without any petition to prefer, or suit to solicit; in fine,
without any call or business whatsoever,
is continually cringing at the levee of a
minister of state; and, when the compliments are paid, and the circle is dif-
miffed, runs through the whole round of
his acquaintance. reporting where he
has been and what he has seen, saga-
ciously remarking on every nod, wink,
or smile, of the great man, and finding
mystery even in the tye of his wig, or the
loose or strait buttoning his coat?

Another, whose affairs at home perhaps are involved in the utmost perplexities, shall pass the best part of his
time among the jobbers in 'Change Alley, go from coffee-house to coffee-
house, enquire of every broker he meets
with the price of stocks, in which he
has no share, or money to purchase any;
and be more solicitous in finding out the
uses to which the Sinking-fund is ap-
propriated, than for the means of extri-
cating himself out of his present difficulties.

A third values himself much upon being a great connoisseur in politicks, re-
gisters all the publick papers from year
to year, pretends to reconcile all the con-
tradictions

traditions they contain, and to difcover fome latent meaning in every paragraph; and takes more pains to unriddle their imaginary ænigmas, than a poor fervitor at the univerfity does to tranflate Perfeus for a rich ftudent who pays, and fathers the labour of his brain.

Others have a tafte for building, are extremely curious in ornamenting the ftructures they caufe to be erected with carvings, paintings, and fuch like fuperficial beauties; but never once examine how the foundation is laid, or whether the pompous outworks may not be liable to fink very foon into a heap of rubbifh. Some employ their whole cares on the breeding and well managing their horfes, hounds, and game-cocks, leaving the education of their fons entirely unregarded.

Impoffible is it to enumerate the various trifles with which too many, even among the higheft clafs of life, fuffer themfelves not only to be amufed, but wholly taken up; but I think, without any danger of being accufed of too much feverity, one may juftly fay, with Shakefpeare, of fuch men, that—

' The earth has bubbles, as the water
' hath,
' And thefe are fome of them.'

In a word, ' Much Ado about Nothing,' is a play fo univerfally acted in this town, that one can go to very few places without being witnefs of fome fcenes of it. As infignificant, however, as thefe people may feem by the defcription I have given of them, and as in effect they really are, they are yet of more confequence to the publick than is generally believed, or than they themfelves, with all the ftock of vanity they are ufually poffeffed of, are capable of imagining. This, though it may be thought a paradox, will be eafy for me to make appear; as thus—Thefe unjudging creatures, for I have already proved them to be fuch, are frequently made the tools by which evil and defigning men fafhion out their ends. When thofe in power have any thing on foot from which they find it neceffary to divert the attention of the nation, it is but throwing out fome whifper, though of ever fo abfurd and ridiculous a nature, among the people I am fpeaking of, and they will immediately ring it in the ears of the populace till it becomes the cry, and every argument that truth and reafon can alledge is deafened with the noife.

An experience of many years, joined with a diligent obfervation of the world, has convinced me, beyond all doubt, that thefe inconfiderates, without being fenfible of the mifchief they do, have been, and daily are, the inftruments of propagating the moft infamous fcandals, grofs falfities, and bafe afperfions, on the great and good; as alfo the moft ridiculous and idle ftories, invented and calculated by men of more thinking heads, to amufe and divert the attention of the publick from what moft demands it's regard. A glaring inftance of this latter kind now takes up the town; all mouths are full of it, all ears open to it: but it appears to me that there are few eyes clear enough to difcern the fecret ground-work of this mountain of abfurdities, and on what motive it was erected. I think it not my province, however, nor fhall prefume to inform the judgment of any one in this point; but fhall only relate a paffage I happened to be witnefs of, which every one is at liberty to defcant upon as he fhall think proper.

Being one day on the other fide of the Royal Exchange, where fome bufinefs I had there being difpatched fooner than I expected, it came into my head to call in at a certain celebrated coffee-houfe, which I had been told was frequented by a great number of the moft eminent and wealthy citizens; but as I had no acquaintance with them, and fome other more fubftantial reafons for not appearing in *propria perfona*, I chofe to go in my Invifible capacity. Purfuant to this refolution, I ftepped into the firft obfcure alley I could find, and there girded on my precious Belt; which, as well as my Tablets, I feldom went out without taking with me, and then haftened to the place I mentioned.

I found the room very full of company, moft of whom were of that fect of diffenters from the eftablifhed church which are under the denomination of Prefbyterians. I would not here be underftood to mean any thing in ridicule of thofe gentlemen; for I love and revere every man of real virtue and good fenfe, be he of what perfuafion foever. How far the perfons I have juft now occafion to fpeak of anfwer to either of thefe characters I will not pretend to fay; let their own words teftify. I fhall, according
to

to the phrafe of the infpired writer, fet a guard upon my mouth, that I offend not with my lips. But to proceed—

Three or four, who I afterwards perceived were leading men among them, were engaged in a very warm difpute with a gentleman, who endeavoured, with a great deal of fpirit, to expofe the grofs abfurdities and falfhood of a caufe they took upon them to maintain, and with a kind of magifterial air attempted to enforce the belief of in others. The odds appeared to me at firft, I confefs, a little ungenerous; but I was the more ftrengthened in this opinion, when I heard the manner in which they delivered their arguments, and that were urged in favour of one of the moft prepofterous and ridiculous complaints that ever engaged the attention of any men of common fenfe. After faying this, I think it is needlefs to add, it was the affair of Squires and Canning. As I am utterly unacquainted with the names either of thofe who defended the caufe of the latter, or of him who treated it with contempt, I fhall diftinguifh the one by that of Affertors, and the other by that of Opponent. The converfation which paffed on both fides, after I had got a convenient place to poft myfelf, and had fpread my Tablets, I fhall give the publick a faithful tranfcript of, as taken from thofe unerring teftimonies, and was as the reader will find underwritten.

*Firft Affertor.* I am furprized, Sir, you fhould rack your brain for arguments againft the caufe of helplefs innocence and virtue in diftrefs.

*Second Affertor.* 'Tis barbarous! 'tis cruel! Where fhall we find an object of compaffion, if Betty Canning is not one? We know her, Sir.

*Third Affertor.* Aye, fhe is of our congregation; has always been a diligent frequenter of the meeting-houfe, and fervent in her devotions.

*Opponent.* So, becaufe fhe is of your congregation, it naturally follows fhe muft be chafte; the lambs of your flock never go aftray. But I forbear to make any reflection on this fcore, and fhall only fay, I never fhall give credit to a ftory fo full of inconfiftencies and improbabilities as this which has been forged by her and her accomplices.

*Firft Affertor.* Sir, there is no reafoning againft fact. She has fworn to the truth of it before a magiftrate, and that magiftrate has teftified his belief of it.

*Opponent.* Yes, the ftory fhe told was romantick; it fuited his tafte; he thought it might be a proper fubject to work up into a farce or puppet-fhew; to was willing to promote the credibility of it.

*Firft Affertor.* Mere fpite and fcandal.

*Opponent.* Not at all: and I doubt not but the impofition will be fully laid open by another magiftrate, fuperior in every degree to h m who takes her part.

*Firft Affertor.* Sir, it is profane and impious in him, or you, or any man, to efpoufe the caufe of a wicked old hag, a vagabond, a gipfey, fuch as Mary Squires; and a known inftrument of libidinous pleafures, fuch as Mother Wells.

*Opponent.* Gentlemen, I have nothing to alledge in defence of thefe creatures, but that, however guilty they may have been, or continue to be, in other refpects, they are entirely innocent in this they are accufed of.

*Firft Affertor.* No, no; 'tis impoffible.

*Opponent.* Saying a thing does not prove it to be fo. But give me leave only to offer a few queries, in relation to fome of the many inconfiftencies in the tale told by that idle wench Betty Canning.

*Second Affertor.* Do fo; we fhall know how to anfwer them.

*Opponent.* Firft, then, fuppofing her to have been robbed, in the manner fhe pretends, by two ruffians, what could induce fellows who live upon the fpoil, after having taken from her all they found worth taking, to quit the purfuit of other booty, and lofe their time in dragging her into the country, only to throw her into the houfe, and then leave her there; for fhe does not accufe them of making any attempt upon her chaftity ?

*Firft Affertor.* As to that, it is highly probable they might be feed by Mother Wells to bring the firft young woman they could meet with to her houfe, in order to be made a facrifice to her mercenary views, and the luft of fome vile fellow.

*Opponent.* Then they would certainly have chofen an object of a more tempting afpect, or would have deferved little for their pains: but let that pafs. If it were as you imagine, would any woman, who it is faid has long been in practice in the feducing trade, have behaved

haved towards the prey brought into her clutches in the fashion she did to Betty Canning? Would she not rather have soothed the frighted maid, revived her drooping spirits with good eating and drinking, promised her fine cloaths, and then introduced some man to her, who might have allured her to the sin she aimed to make her guilty of? Surely the way to tempt her to be a prostitute was not to lock her up alone in a wild, desolate room, without a bed to lie upon, or any other refreshment than a little bread and water; such usage, one must think, was intended to mortify, not excite a carnal inclination.

*First Assertor.* Sir, I am grieved, greatly grieved in spirit, to find you so ignorant of the force of virtue. I tell you, Sir, that the courage and resolution of this virgin struck such an awe into the minds of those profligate wretches she was placed among, that they had not the power of putting their wicked designs in execution: Heaven, indeed, for a trial of her patience, permitted them to distress her helpless innocence, but not to destroy it.

*Opponent.* Very extraordinary, truly! But pray, Sir, why did this suffering saint remain so long under the roof of such abandoned creatures, since all accounts agree, that in three days, nay, in three hours, after her confinement, she had the same opportunity of making her escape as at the time she pretends to effect it?

*Second Assertor.* Her eyes were not open to the means of her deliverance till that blessed moment: it was ordained she should undergo the persecution she did, in order to make her virtue more triumphant over sin and shame.

*Opponent.* Oh, gentlemen, these arguments will never be swallowed any where but in a conventicle.

*Third Assertor.* Sir, they will always have their due weight with every one but a reprobate.

*Opponent.* How, Sir!

The Opponent was so much incensed at these words, that he started from his seat, and was about to reply with his fist; but some of the more moderate part of the company interposed, and prevented the mischief that might otherwise have ensued. By their persuasions he sat down again; and the dispute would doubtless have been renewed, it may be

with greater vehemence than before, if a drawer from a neighbouring tavern had not luckily come, and told him that two gentlemen, whose names he mentioned, desired to speak with him: on which he went away, perhaps to the great satisfaction of the assertors of Betty Canning's cause; who, if he had staid and continued his queries, might probably have been a little puzzled to find answers to them.

During the debate I have been repeating, every one in the room kept a profound silence; but afterwards the conversation became general; several other subjects were started by particular persons, but they were not listened to: the majority seemed to have their heads so full of Betty Canning, that they could scarce think or speak of any thing beside. It is true, indeed, they did not all give credit to her story; yet the positiveness with which they heard it affirmed, made the least credulous divided in their thoughts, and afraid to pass a judgment either on the one or the other side of the question. The reader will doubtless naturally suppose, that it was impossible for me to live in the world, and have any acquaintance in it, without having heard, long before I came to this place, much talk of Elizabeth Canning, her pitiful distress, miraculous preservation and escape, and all the other prodigies of that amazing story.

It is true, indeed, I was a stranger to no part of it; but then my conversation being chiefly among the gay part of the town, I was not much surprized that people who can find very little to employ their thoughts should be fond of a tale which had so much of the marvellous in it; as children, before they arrive at years capable of being instructed in more solid matters, listen with pleasure to their nurses stories of giants, fairies, and enchanted castles: as such I regarded all they said, and thought no farther of it. But when I heard grave citizens, men of business, of a sedate deportment, and good understanding in other things, argue with serious countenances on such a heap of wild absurdities, I cannot say whether my astonishment or indignation had most dominion over my faculties; but this I know, that both together destroyed all the little stock of patience I am master of, and would not suffer me to stay any longer to listen to thofe infignificant debates which I found were likely to continue among this company.

## CHAP. II.

RELATES SOME FARTHER INCIDENTS OF A PRETTY PARTICULAR NATURE, WHICH FELL UNDER THE AUTHOR'S OBSERVATION IN THE SAME EVENING'S INVISIBLE PROGRESSION.

THOSE turbulent emotions which the fcene I had juft come from being witnefs of had raifed in me, being fomewhat quieted by air and walking, I had the curiofity to call in at another great coffee-houfe, hoping I fhould find there fomething to give a turn to the prefent difpofition of my mind; but I found that the remains of my ill-humour were not to be fo foon diffipated as I had imagined. Here was indeed a vaft deal of company; clerks in publick offices, lawyers, phyficians, tradefmen, and fome few divines, compofed the promifcuous affembly: but all were engaged on the fame dirty, draggle-tail fubject, as one of our news-writers juftly terms it; the names of Betty Canning, the Gipfey, and Mother Wells, refounded from each quarter of the crouded room, and the caufe then depending between thefe creatures made the whole converfation at every table.

Here I would not be at the trouble of opening my Tablets, eafily perceiving that nothing worthy of being recorded in them, or of communicating to the publick, was likely to enfue; and alfo that the fmalleft part of time I fhould wafte in this company, would be paying too dear for any difcourfes I fhould hear from them. Accordingly I left the houfe after having ftaid there about feven minutes; but had not reached the next ftreet, before a confufed noife behind obliged me to ftand up in the porch of a door till the hubbub was paffed by. The occafion of this uproar prefently appeared. It was a poor fellow carried on a bier, with very little figns of life in him; his face covered with blood, which iffued from his nofe and mouth; his cloaths torn, that the naked flefh appeared in many places, but fo deformed with bruifes, that it could fcarce be known, for what it was; a mixed rabble of men, women, and children, followed, fhouting, hallooing, and crying, it was good enough for him, and that they were glad he had got his reward.

I was ftartled at fo much inhumanity, for I thought nothing could excufe fuch cruel treatment, though I doubted not but the fellow had been guilty of fome attrocious crime: but I was foon undeceived in this point, and let into the whole affair; which was no other than a quarrel this fellow had entered into on account of Canning.

I had now no defign in my head, no particular courfe to fteer; but as I was entirely free from any engagement that evening, and thought it too foon to go home, I rambled from one ftreet to another for a confiderable time, yet without meeting any one thing fufficient to tempt my curiofity to make a farther enquiry into. Any obferving reader may reafonably imagine, that the little fatisfaction I had been able to reap in the vifits I had made at the two coffeehoufes I had been already in, would have hindered me from going into another, and indeed I was of that opinion myfelf: but I foon found I was miftaken, and fo will he; I really ventured into a third; but the motive which excited me to do fo was this—

As I was paffing by, I perceived through the windows—for then the candles within were lighted up—feveral gentlemen with newfpapers before them, on which feemed to be difcomfing with each other with a great deal of ferioufnefs and gravity. As I have naturally an extreme paffion for knowing the affairs of the world, thofe of Europe efpecially, I thought it highly eligible in me to hear what was faid upon them by perfons who had the appearance of fome underftanding in them. At the firft table I came to were fix or feven gentlemen, moft of whom were fome way or other concerned in the Britifh herringfifhery: but though they talked very learnedly on the fubject, it fuited not my tafte; fo ftaid not long with them, but adjourned to the next company. Thefe were merchants; who I found were greatly difconcerted at an article they had been juft reading in relation to the ftrict engagements the French had entered into with the Indians, and the daily incurfions thofe mifcalled friends and allies made on the Englifh colonies: but as I cannot pretend to any fkill in commerce,

commerce, I did not spread my Tablets to receive the impression of their discourse; so can only say, in general, that they made very heavy complaints, and cried out, that if speedy care were not taken to put a stop to those proceedings, trade must be ruined, and our settlements in that part of the world utterly destroyed.

The third table was filled with persons who seemed to be of no avocation, nor at all interested in any branch of business or publick affairs, but talked of every thing they had been reading merely as things which afforded matter for conversation. On my joining them, the magnanimity of the Prussian monarch was the topick; they extolled his wisdom, his bravery, his temperance, his elemency, the encouragement he gave to merit wheresoever he found it; and all unanimously agreed that he was the father of his people, a blessing to the land he governed, and a pattern to his fellow-rulers of the earth. The just admiration I ever had of this truly great and most amiable prince, exclusive of that regard due to him as so near a relation to our gracious sovereign, would certainly have kept me at that table as long as the company had continued speaking on so agreeable a subject, if I had not been hurried from it by a propensity, I believe more or less natural to all mankind, that of being most eager to explore what is hid from us with most care.

I observed at a little table, which was placed at one corner of the room, a good distance from the others, two elderly persons, who seemed very earnest in discourse on some important and secret affair. By the winks, nods, and other significant gestures, I doubted not but that they were profound politicians, and were discussing some extraordinary transaction of the cabinet. Their heads were pretty close together, and they spoke in so low a voice as to render it impossible to be heard by any one except each other: but this precaution had no efficacy when once my wonderful Tablets were displayed; which had this excellent property, of receiving the impression of whatever was said within the distance of nine yards, though uttered in the most soft whispers. On my drawing near to them, they seemed a little impatient for the coming of a person who they expected, and who presently

after appeared. As soon as he had seated himself, the following dialogue ensued—

*First Man.* Oh, Mr. Slycraft, I am glad you are come! We were beginning to think you long.

*Slycraft.* I am somewhat beyond my hour, indeed; but I assure you nothing could have made me so but the good of the cause.

*Second Man.* Your zeal and diligence are not to be doubted. But let us hear what success your endeavours have met with.

*Slycraft.* Truly not so much as I hoped. I do not think there is a more difficult thing in the world than getting people to subscribe: I have been half the town over, and have been able to procure no more than three.

*First Man.* Then I hope they are fat ones?

*Slycraft.* Pretty well, as times go. Credulous Woodcock, Esq. has set his name for twenty guineas.

*First Man.* Very handsome! Five or six hundred such as he would do the business.

*Slycraft.* Aye; but where shall we find them?

*Second Man.* Well, but who are the others?

*Slycraft.* Then there is Mr. Simon Goosly, the haberdasher, ten guineas; but has promised to prevail on some friends of his to set their names very generously.

*Second Man.* I dare say he will do all he can. But have you seen Mrs. Waver?

*Slycraft.* Yes; but she still desires a little more time to consider; says she will enquire farther into the affair, and hear what her friends think of it: and all I could get from her was an assurance, that if she found it proper to subscribe at all, she would not set her name for less than a hundred pieces.

*First Man.* Then we may be pretty certain of her; for I know she will be directed by Mr. Cantwell, the Nonconformist preacher, who labours all he can to promote the cause in question.

*Second Man.* Have you yet found an opportunity of talking with the orator?

*Slycraft.* I was with him above an hour; and when I had once convinced him that he should find his account in it, he gave me his word and honour that he

E e 2 would

would rant and roar till his chapel echoes in favour of the party.

*First Man.* That is well. All engines must be set to work, or the town will grow cool on this business, and begin to renew their clamour against the Jew bill, &c. The spirit of the people will have vent on something or another, and you know it behoves us to keep them silent on those scores: nothing ever did it more effectually than this we are upon. But it must be kept up for a time. I could wish, methinks, we had the Wesleys on our side.

*Second Man.* 'Tis a vain attempt. They are now grown too rich to accept of a small gratuity; and I much question whether their exhortations would answer the expence.

*Slycraft.* I am of your opinion. Besides, you know there is a person who can influence their congregations as much as any thing they can hear from the pulpit. But I will tell you what I have done to-day; I have engaged a clergyman of the established church to write a pamphlet in behalf of the cause we have in hand.

*First Man.* A clergyman of the established church employ his pen in behalf of such a cause! Pr'ythee, Slycraft, how did'st thou work upon him? It must certainly be by some very extraordinary method.

*Slycraft.* The promise of a small present at first wrought upon his necessities; but on my telling him who and who were concerned in this business, and the motives which induced them to be so, the hopes of having a good fat living made him wholly ours.

*First Man.* Admirable!

*Second Man.* But may we depend upon his secresy?

*Slycraft.* Never doubt that, as his own interest is concerned.

*First Man.* Hitherto things go pretty swimmingly on our side. But let me see the subscription-book: I have received five guineas to-day from Mr. Prim. and must insert his name.

Till now I was at the greatest loss, as it is probable the reader will also be, to know what all this meant, or in whose favour, or on what account, the subscription they talked of was raised; but on Mr. Slycraft's delivering the book to his friend, I looked over the shoulder of the latter as he opened it, and saw, in

the first leaf, by way of title-page, these words, wrote in a very fair hand—

'A List of those worthy Persons who
' have subscribed to the Relief of
' Elizabeth Canning.'

The names underwritten were too numerous to be inserted; I shall therefore only say, that the sum of what was raised by their subscription amounted to little less than a thousand pounds. Monstrous abuse of charity! preposterous benevolence! which will hereafter reflect more shame than honour on the bestowers. 'Good God!' said I to myself, 'in an age when numberless, nameless miseries, abound; when all our prisons labour with the weight of wretches confined within their walls, many for small debts which their necessities obliged them to contract, and some by unjust and malicious prosecutions; while every parish, nay almost every street, affords objects of real distress; while a girl sprung from the lowest dregs of the people, bred up to toil, a drudge, one of the very meanest class of servants, receives donations which she as little knows how to make a proper use of as to deserve!—a girl who, if she had really suffered all she pretends to have done, would indeed have had a claim to justice against those who had wronged her, but none to the bounties so lavishly bestowed upon her.'

These kind of meditations would doubtless have accompanied me to my own door, if they had not been interrupted, as well as my course towards home, by an unexpected accident, which the reader will find faithfully related in the succeeding chapter.

## CHAP. III.

PRESENTS THE READER WITH AN ADVENTURE OF MUCH MORE IMPORTANCE TO THE PUBLICK THAN ANY CONTAINED IN THE TWO LAST FOREGOING CHAPTERS.

THE human heart is liable to many bad propensities, which, if not timely corrected by reason, shoot forth into practice, and become vices. But of these there are two sorts; the one born with

with us, and part of our nature; the other imbibed by the fatal prevalence of example, and rooted in us by custom, which is a second nature. Those born with us, as the indulging them is attended with some pleasure, urge in their defence the unconquerable desire of gratifying the senses: the lustful man pleads the warmth of his constitution, and the strong allurements of beauty; the soul of the ambitious triumphs and exults on every degree of power he gains over his fellow-creatures; the miser thinks himself happy in counting over his bags, and being master of a thing that will purchase all things else; and the epicure feels no care, no sorrow, while he is emptying the full-charged goblet, and palating the delicious viand. But what has the blasphemer, the profane swearer, or the gamester, to alledge in his vindication? These are crimes in which nature has no part, nor are the senses any way concerned in them, as they neither excite nor feel any satisfaction in them. One might therefore be apt to imagine, that men thus guilty sinned merely for the sake of sinning. But I will not allow myself to think that there are many so impudently daring; a few distinguished persons will serve to bring up a mode, and every one knows that at present an indiscriminate imitation is the reigning folly of the English nation.

These were reflections which occurred to me after I came home, as I was about to transcribe the remaining part of my evening's progress out of my precious Tablets. I had some farther thoughts on the occasion, but as they might seem more proper for the pulpit than a work of this nature, I shall add no more, but proceed to the narrative of that adventure which gave rise to them.

As I was passing, in my way home, through a street of no very good repute, two persons, from a little narrow alley, bolted hastily upon me, to the no small danger of my Invisibilityship, if an agility not very common with me had not that instant enabled me to give a sudden spring, by which I avoided the rush I must otherwise have received. They went on before me. The night was extremely dark; neither moon nor stars to assist the visual ray: but, by the help of some candles burning in a shop not yet shut up, I distinguished that the one was very richly dressed, and had much the appearance of a man of fashion; and that

the other was a fellow I had often seen on many occasions, and whose character I was perfectly acquainted with.

Scarce is there a greater villain to be found in low life: I say in low life, because should any persons in authority, or dignified with titles—which Heaven forbid!—ever appear in this nation, to deserve such black denominations, their crimes would, like their ranks, be distinguished; and, though placed in an orb too high to be reached by the just vengeance of their oppressed fellow-creatures, would doubtless incur what Mr. Addison makes Cato prophetically say in relation to Julius Cæsar, on his endeavouring to subvert the old Roman constitution, and become absolute and perpetual dictator—

‘ Sure there are bolts in the right-hand of
‘ Jove,
‘ Red with uncommon wrath, to blast the
‘ man
‘ Who owes his greatness to his country's
‘ ruin.’

But to return to my little knave. The wretch is now called Mr. Makeplea; he was formerly servant to a lawyer whom I employed in several affairs I had the misfortune to be engaged in. Living with that gentleman a considerable time, he picked up some scraps of law, and all the terms and phrases of that abstruse science, by rote; knew how to take out a writ, set an officer to work, fill up a bail-bond, and procure evidences in a dubious cause. With this fund he had the impudence, after his master's death, to pretend he had been his clerk; got himself entered as an attorney, and has ever since practised as such. His sole business, however, as may he easily supposed, has always been among the very meanest sort of people; fomenting litigious quarrels, and then making them up, after having drained the purses on both sides. I could not, therefore, avoid being amazed at seeing him in the company I now did; but my wonder soon ceased on hearing, as I was close at their heels, the following discourse between them—

*Makeplea.* It is very lucky, Mr. Coaxum, that I happened to be at home when you came. There are some of the profession who would have scrupled to undertake this business; but, for my part, I am always ready to venture every thing to serve my friends.

*Coaxum.*

*Coaxum.* My dear Makeplea, you never loſt any thing, nor ever ſhall, by our fraternity. I know there are ſome who will ſneak their heads out of the collar, and leave their lawyer in the lurch.

*Makeplea.* Aye, faith, I narrowly eſcaped the pillory once. A vile dog who, after I had procured him three evidences, pretended a panick in his conſcience, threw up his cauſe, and ſuffered himſelf to be nonſuited.

*Coaxum.* You know we ſcorn ſuch doings. And I can tell you, this will be a pretty good job to you. We drained the fool's pocket of above an hundred pieces before we plaid upon credit; ſo that there is enough in bank to make you a handſome preſent for your trouble.

*Makeplea.* Well, but concerning this reverſion. I hope he has loſt enough to give an air of juſtice—that is, a *quantum ſufficit*, for the making over his eſtate after the deceaſe of his father?

*Coaxum.* Upwards of a thouſand pounds; beſides a gold watch and a diamond-ring, which he ſeems to ſet a high value upon. The two laſt Count Cogdy has agreed to ſell him again at a great price; ſo that, all together, the ſum will amount to a ſufficient purchaſe of the reverſion of an eſtate of four hundred a year; eſpecially as the preſent poſſeſſor is not above fifty, and may live a long time. Beſides, we hear the young fellow is going to be married to a woman of fortune; ſo that the deeds may be made redeemable. We do not regard his dirty acres, the ready rhino is what we want; and he may pay the money out of his wife's fortune, and be clear of us again.

*Makeplea.* Oh, then it will be a mortgage, rather than a ſale. Who are with him?

*Coaxum.* Only Count Cogdy, Jack Hazard, and Tom Wheedle.

*Makeplea.* They cannot be witneſſes, as I ſuppoſe they are parties concerned.

*Coaxum.* We are equal ſharers in the booty; but the money was loſt wholly to the count. However, there will be no want of witneſſes; the landlord of the houſe and his ſon will ſet their hands.

Theſe words brought them to a door, which being opened at the firſt knock by one of the moſt ill-looked fellows that ever diſgraced human nature, they went through a long, dark, narrow paſſage,

into a back-parlour; where I accompanied them, and was witneſs of a ſcene ſomewhat like what I remember to have ſeen ſome years ago in a play of Mrs. Centlivre's, called the Gameſter. Count Cogdy, as he was called, ſat leaning his arm upon a table, in a careleſs poſture; Jack Hazard was walking backwards and forwards in the room humming an old tune; a gentleman, whoſe name I had not yet heard, had thrown himſelf acroſs two chairs, with all the tokens of deſpair about him; Tom Wheedle ſtood near him, and, as we came in, was endeavouring to give him ſome conſolation, in theſe terms—' Pr'ythee, dear Clerimont, do not be thus diſconcerted; I ' have loſt as much as you twenty times ' over, and as often recovered it again: ' theſe things will happen to gentlemen ' that play. Fortune, indeed, has been ' againſt you to-night, but may not always be ſo; one lucky hit at another ' time may bring all back.'

Clerimont made no anſwer, nor ſeemed to regard what he ſaid, till hearing the name of Makeplea, and Count Cogdy beginning to inſtruct him in the buſineſs he was to do, that unfortunate gentleman ſtarted up at once, and ſtaring ſomewhat wildly in the face of Makeplea, cried to him—.

*Clerimont.* Are you the fiend who is to convey my ſoul, that is, my eſtate, into the regions of eternal darkneſs, whence it can never, never more return?

*Makeplea.* What do you mean, Sir?

*Cogdy.* The gentleman is only a little out of humour.—Faith, Mr. Clerimont you do not do well to behave in this faſhion. You have loſt ſome money indeed, but you have loſt it fairly. I never take an advantage of any man, and ſhall be ready to give you your revenge at any time.

*Hazard.* Aye, I will ſay that for the count; he ſcorns a mean thing.

*Cogdy.* I believe there is not a more unlucky fellow at play in the world than myſelf, though I have happened to win to-night: yet, as I ſaid before, I am ready to give Mr. Clerimont an opportunity of retrieving all he has loſt whenever he pleaſes. For my part, I would ſtake all I am worth againſt a pair of ſhoe-buckles, rather than any gentleman ſhould think I impoſed upon him.

*Coaxum.* No, no, you are above any ſuch thing,

*Hazard.*

*Hazard.* We all know that.

*Makeplea.* Come, come, gentlemen, this is doing nothing; all lofs of time, and every moment of mine is precious. There are two noblemen now waiting for me at the Garter tavern. Pray proceed to the bufinefs: let me know how the deeds I have brought with me are to be filled up.

*Cogdy.* I will tell you immediately; but firft I muft do juftice to this gentleman.—Here, Sir, aré the watch and ring you ftaked; the value of which, you know, is added to the other fums.

Clerimont put the one in his pocket, and the other on his finger, with a deep figh; and the count went on repeating to Makeplea the fubftance of what he was to write. The latter, at the end of every article, demanded of Clerimont whether he agreed to it; to which he fullenly replied—' I do; I fee no other remedy.' The lawyer having difpatched his part, Clerimont was defired to fign and feal; he did both; but with fuch a trembling hand, and vifible diftraction of mind, that my heart bled for him. In delivering the writings to the count, he faid—

*Clerimont.* There, Sir—I fuppofe this is all that is required of me, and I may now depart?

*Cogdy.* No, no, we muft have a bottle and a bird together, to fhew we are all ftill good friends.

*Hazard.* Aye, and each of us a wench, too. I know where there is a covey of as young, pretty, plump, partridges, as any in Covent Garden.

*Clerimont.* Rot your bottle, and your bird, and your wenches! I have done with them, and you, and the world, for ever!

In fpeaking thefe words he fnatched up his fword and hat, and ran directly out of the houfe. As for me, I had as little inclination as himfelf to ftay in the company of fuch blood-fuckers; but having never feen him before, I was curious to know fomewhat more of him, and alfo how he would behave when alone, and at liberty to ruminate on the misfortune he had plunged himfelf into; fo followed his fteps with all the fpeed I could. It was not difficult to keep pace with him; for though he gain ed groun of me at firft, he foon halted, and gave me an opportunity of coming up with him. Never did man traverfe the ftreets with more difordered motions; croffing the way an hundred times, I believe, within

the fpace of half a quarter of a mile, without having the leaft occafion to do fo. Sometimes he woul! run as if in purfuit of fomebody, and fometimes ftand quite ftill. And it was well the darknefs of the night befriended him, otherwife whoever had met him would doubtlefs have taken him to be mad.

In this fafhion he went part of the Strand, and turned down one of thofe ftreets leading to the water-fide. He ftopped about the middle of it at a door, and had his hand upon the knocker; but a fudden thought coming that inftant into his head, he left it, without making the fignal for admittance, and walked flowly to the end of the ftreet; where leaning on a little wall that overlooks the river, he remained for fome minutes in the moft thoughtful and contemplative attitude; then faid to himfelf—

' How profound, how folemn, is the
' filent fcene! inviting to a certain reft
' from mifery and fhame! Here, with-
' in the bofom of this friendly element,
' may all my follies and misfortunes be
' hid for ever from the talking world!'

I feared nothing lefs would enfue, than that I fhould fee him prefently attempt to do as his words had hinted; I therefore drew as near to him as I could, in order to prevent fo bad an effect of his defpair. Here I cannot help remarking, that if the thing had happened as I expected, and Clerimont had found himfelf fnatched from his fate by an Invifible hand, he would doubtlefs have imagined his prefervation owing to the interpofition of fome Supernatural Being, and reported it as a miracle.

But how he would have acted on fuch an odd occafion, is uncertain; for, after a paufe, and difburthening himfelf of fome few fighs, he ftarted from the pofture he had been in, and cried—

' No, it muft not be; I have fome bufi-
' nefs ftill for life—revenge on the curft
' cheat, the villain, that has undone
' me! Love, too, demands fomething
' from me; but by what means I fhall
' repay that mighty debt, I know not.
' Oh, Charlotte! Charlotte! on how
' loft a wretch haft thou beftowed thy
' heart!'

Thefe words were uttered with a groan which feemed to cleave his breaft, and were the laft I heard from him at that time. He turned back, and went haftily to the houfe where he had firft ftopped: the door was opened on his knocking;

and

and too fuddenly fhut again for me to have entered with him if I had intended it; but the variety of accidents prefented to me in this evening's ramble, had already fufficiently filled my head, and made me glad to retire to my repofe.

## CHAP. IV.

RELATES SOME PASSAGES WHICH MAY PROBABLY DRAW SIGHS FROM MANY A TENDER HEART. OF BOTH SEXES.

THE next morning, running over in my mind the detail of the tranfactions of the evening before, the vexation I had received on the fcore of Betty Canning very much fubfided, and I looked upon the whole thing as below a ferious confideration. I could not help, indeed, retaining fome concern that the people of England fhould be fo infatuated as to fuffer their thoughts to be led aftray and alienated from affairs of the greateft confequence by fuch an idle ftory; but as I doubted not but that the impofition fhe had been guilty of would be detected, though her abettors might perhaps find means to fcreen her perfon from the punifhment, I became more eafy, and refolved to banifh, as much as poffible, all remembrance of it.

But my ideas were widely different in regard to poor Clerimont. As much a ftranger as he was to me, I was convinced, by what I had feen and heard, that as he had no ftock of ready money to prevent the mortgage he had made of his reverfion, fo I was equally affured, by his defpair, that he had no vifible means of raifing a fum fufficient to redeem it. His calling on the name of Charlotte with fo much vehemence, made me alfo not doubt but that he had fome tender attachment, which he feared would be broke through by what he had done.

Though I know no vice for which I have a more real contempt than the love of gaming, yet the age of this gentleman, which could not exceed three and twenty, feemed to me a very moving plea in his behalf; and the graces of his mien and afpect fo much interefted me in his favour, that I lefs blamed his inadvertency than compaffionated the misfortune it had brought him into. In fine, his perfon and his fufferings had made a very ftrong impreffion on me; he was the firft object of my waking thoughts; and my impatience to be better acquainted with his circumftances, obliged me to leave my bed fome hours before the time in which I was accuftomed to do fo. I rofe in a hurry, tranfcribed what I have been relating, and got the dialogues expunged from my Tablets by the pure fingers of my little virgin; then haftened to the houfe where I had feen Clerimont enter the night before, and which, by the help of fome lamps in the ftreet, I had taken fufficient notice of to be able to know again. The door was luckily open when I came to it. A fervant-maid, who feemed to have more inclination to hold a goffip's tale than to do the bufinefs fhe was hired for, ftood leaning with both her hands upon her mop, very earneft in difcourfe with one of her own occupation in the neighbourhood. A few words ferved to convince me that thefe wenches were defcanting on the affairs of the families they lived in; which, as I was not at prefent in a humour to pry into, I ftaid not to hear what was faid, but went directly into the houfe, and up ftairs, fuppofing Clerimont might be lodged in the firft floor. I was not deceived; I found him writing at his bureau in the dining-room. A letter lay by him directed to Count Cogdy: this was folded, and ready for fealing, fo it was not in my power to examine the contents; but his pen, on my entrance, was employed on another; which, looking over his fhoulder, I faw was dictated in the following terms—

'  My only dear, and forever dear CHAR-
'          LOTTE!

'A Thoufand heart-rending fighs, a
'          thoufand pangs more terrible
' than any death can inflict, accompany
' every fyllable of this diftracted epiftle!
' I forefee the anguifh it will give you,
' and feel all the weight of yours added to my own. Oh, Charlotte! I
' muft fee you no more! That love, fo
' long cemented by the utmoft proofs
' of mutual tendernefs, and fo near being fulfilled in a happy union, muft be
' now broke off at once—diffolved for
' ever! I have renounced all claim to
' every future good, and juftly incurred
' the fate that now attends me. A few
'                                      hours

' hours will inform you, that I either
' do not exist at all, or exist only to
' be a vagrant! a wretched exile from
' father, country, friends, and you,
' more dear than all! In fine, my
' Charlotte, such is the sad necessity to
' which I have reduced myself, as com-
' pels me to do a thing which nature
' most abhors; I go this morning either
' to kill or be killed: which of these two
' shall happen, is in the hand of Heaven;
' each equally tears me from every
' earthly comfort. I chose to acquaint
' you previously with this accident, to
' the end you may be the less surprized
' when you shall hear it from the mouth
' of others. I can say no more. Fare-
' wel, thou loveliest, best, and dearest
' of thy sex! Hate not the memory of
' the undone

' CLERIMONT.

' P. S. As I have rendered myself
' unworthy of preserving any marks
' of your affection, I return the
' ring with which you blessed my
' finger in our happier days. Ac-
' cept once more my last adieu!
' May endless blessings await you,
' superior, if possible, to my woes!'

This unhappy gentleman diff mbled
not in the lines he wrote; his heart now
laboured with agonies greater than could
be expressed with words, and shewed
themselves in every look and gesture.
After having carefully inclosed the ring,
and put both that and the letter under a cover, he ordered a chairman to be called;
and delivering to him both these dis-
patches, and telling him where they were
to be carried, he proceeded to give some
farther instructions—' This, to Miss
' Charlotte, you are to leave with her
' servant, with orders to give it to her
' lady when she is stirring; this, to Count
' Cogdy, requires an immediate answer,
' which you must wait for.' The fellow, having assured him that he wou'd
be punctual in obeying his commands,
went on his errand; and Clerimont con
tinued walking backwards and forwards
in the room, with a motion extremely
discomposed; then threw himself down on
a settee, and presently seemed buried, as
it were, in a profound reverie.

I am pretty certain it was a full half
hour before he exchanged this fixed and
death-like position for one in a quite
contrary extreme; his looks and gestures now, methought, had somewhat
like frantick in them; he beat his head
against the wainscot, stamped, and ever
and anon burst into the most vehement
exclamations; some of which are these—
' How unhappy a creature is man! The
' very reason we are so proud of makes
' us miserable! The brutes, equally
' void of passions as of sorrow, neither
' feel torments here, nor dread a future
' hell! What will poor Charlotte say
' on reading of my letter! How wil
' my father support the story of my fate,
' when it shall reach his ears! Wretch,
' wretch, that I am! born to be a curse
' to all who love me!'

The return of the chairman brought
him a little to his senses, and he demanded hastily whether he had got an
answer from Count Cogdy; to which the
man replied—

Chairman. No, Sir. I went there
first, but the people of the house told me
he was not stirring, nor they believed
would be for a great while; so I went on
to Madam Charlotte's, and left the letter
with her maid, as your honour bid me:
but I had not got above half the street,
before her footboy ran after me, and said
his lady would speak to me; on which
I went back with him.

Clerimont. Charlotte already up! that's
strange.—What did she say to you?

Chairman. Sir, she only asked where
the gentleman was that sent the letter by
me, and whether you were alone. I
told her you were at home, and that
there was nobody with you that I saw.
She said it was very well, and I came
away; went again to the count's, and
waited there till his own man told me
that his master had not been in bed above
two hours, and he was sure would not
rise till twelve or one o'clock at soonest;
said I might leave the letter, and come
about that time for an answer. Now
as I did not know whether that would
be proper, I thought it best to bring it
back.

Clerimont. You did well. I shall see
him myself.

On this the chairman laid down the
letter on the table; and finding Clerimont had no farther commands for him,
withdrew. Clerimont then fell into a
second pause, but it lasted not long, and
he cried out—' Yes, I will go. And
' perhaps 'tis better that he did not see
' my billet; he might have found some
' way to evade the challenge that I sent

F f ' him

' him; but I shall now surprize and
' force him to accept it.'

While he was speaking, he stepped
to the closet, and brought out a pair of
pocket pistols, with some ammunition to
load them with: he was just beginning
to perform that work, when the maid of
the house came up, and told him a lady
desired to speak with him. Clerimont
turned hastily about; but before he had
time to speak, his fair guest was in the
room. Charlotte, (for it was she herself,
but extremely disordered both in her dress
and looks) on finding how Clerimont
was employed, thus accosted him—

*Charlotte.* Oh, Clerimont! Clerimont! what means that cruel letter you
just now sent me? Wherefore these
dreadful preparations? Tell me, this
instant tell me, or I shall die with apprehension!

*Clerimont.* Ah, Charlotte! never till
now unwelcome to my sight, why, in
this fatal moment, 'oft thou set before
me that angelick form, which serves but
to remind me more of the heaven I have
lost!

*Charlotte.* Shock not my soul with
this despair, yet cruelly conceal from me
the cause! I have a right to be made
the partner of your griefs as well as
joys. Speak, then, I conjure you; let
me know all.

*Clerimont.* I cannot.

*Charlotte.* You love me not, if you
hide aught from me. The worst of evils
could not give me half the pain as this
uncertainty. Clear, then, the tempest on
your brow; compose your mind; remove those murderous instruments from
my sight, and——Ha! what's here!

In pointing towards the pistols, she
saw the letter directed to Count Cogdy;
which she hastily snatched up, and went
on, saying—

*Charlotte.* A letter to that infamous
villain!—Ah! then I guess what has
happened; some cursed gaming quarrel!
—Clerimont, I must read this letter.

*Clerimont.* You may: it will in part
reveal what my tongue has not the power
to utter.

Ever since my coming into the room,
I had been extremely impatient to see
the contents of this billet; so while the
lady, with a trembling hand, was breaking open the seal, I slipped behind her,
and read, at the same time she did, these
lines—

' SIR,

' I Remember that, in the midst of my
' confusion last night, you offered
' to give me my revenge whenever I
' should demand it; which I now do,
' and expect you will meet me within
' an hour in the long field behind the
' bason in Mary le Bon, armed with
' sword and pistol; for it is not with
' cards or dice we now must try our
' skill. You have left me nothing but
' my life to lose, and I am impatient
' till I stake it against yours. Come
' without a second; for I know no gen-
' tleman whom I would demean so far
' as to engage him with any of your in-
' famous associates. If you refuse to
' comply with this summons, which
' does you too much honour, you may
' depend that, the first time I see you,
' in what place soever it be, I shall make
' you an example to all scoundrels,
' cheats, and cowards. So no more
' at present from

' CLERIMONT.

' P. S. Send your answer by the
' bearer.'


*Charlotte.* Then you would fight!
would hazard a life so precious to me,
only in revenge for being defrauded of
a paltry sum! Pray how much have
you lost?

*Clerimont.* My all.

*Charlotte.* Be more explicit.

He then related to her all the particulars of his misfortune; which, as the
reader is already acquainted with, would
be needless to repeat. When he had
given over speaking, Charlotte, with
the greatest serenity and sweetness, said
to him—

*Charlotte.* And is this all that has
disconcerted you in so terrible a manner?

*Clerimont.* What means my Charlotte? Am I not a beggar! irrecoverably a beggar!

*Charlotte.* How can that be, when you
say the writings will be returned to you
on payment of a thousand pounds? and
am not I in possession of eight times that
sum, which, with myself, you are shortly
to be master of?

*Clerimont.* Plunder my Charlotte!
No, forbid it honour, justice, love!
First let me perish!

*Charlotte.*

*Charlotte.* Be not so rash. You must, you shall accept it.

*Clerimont.* Oh, Charlotte! could I abuse such goodness, I were a villain, meaner, viler far than he that has undone me!

*Charlotte.* Indeed I will not be denied: and if you persist in this obstinacy, will go myself in person, pay the money, and redeem the obligation.

*Clerimont.* Oh, speak not, think not, of such a thing, unless you wish to see me turn against myself one of those weapons I intended for my adversary!

*Charlotte.* Hold, Clerimont! Forbear to fright me thus!—Just as you spoke, a sudden thought started into my head, as if there were a way to rid you of this incumbrance without any expence either to yourself or me.

*Clerimont.* How! By what miracle!

*Charlotte.* The project is not yet quite fashioned in my brain. But you must come with me to my lodgings, for I dare not trust you with yourself. As we go, perhaps I may be able to bring my scheme to more perfection.

*Clerimont.* Oh, Charlotte, thy softness quite unmans me!

*Charlotte.* No, it is your own despair unmans you. Let me prevail on you to give only some respite to these horrible ideas.

*Clerimont.* Well, you must be obeyed. I will defer the execution of my intentions till another day.

Charlotte seemed transported at having won thus far upon him; and a coach being called, they both went into it. I listened to the directions given where to drive; and, eager to know what turn this affair would take, followed on foot as fast as I was able.

## CHAP. V.

MAY POSSIBLY BECOME THE SUBJECT OF SOME FUTURE COMEDY, AS THERE IS NOTHING IN THE STORY THAT CAN BE OBJECTED TO AT THE LICENCE-OFFICE.

AMONG all the indefatigable enquiries I had so long been making after things intended to be kept secret, never had my curiosity met with a greater disappointment than it did at the time I am speaking of. I arrived at the house where Charlotte lodged the very moment that the coach which brought that lady and her lover thither was discharged and driving off; and had the mortification to see the door shut when I was not at the distance of above ten paces from it. Every present minute, however, flattering me with the hopes that the succeeding ones would be more successful, I waited, though I cannot say with much patience about two hours; no one having any occasion, I suppose, either to go in or out. At last a friendly baker knocked at the door; which being opened, I took the opportunity to slip in while he delivered a loaf of bread to the servant of the house.

I went up stairs, and found the persons I sought for in the dining-room. But here, alas! I was a second time disappointed; the grand consultation between them was over before my entrance, and what I heard after I came in could not make me able to form any judgment of the subject they had been upon. I could only know that something of great moment had been concluded, as the reader will easily perceive by the following short dialogue—

*Charlotte.* You cannot imagine how much you have obliged me by this confession; but I will not detain you, lest the villain should be gone out. Remember to fix the appointment at seven, or between seven and eight, this evening.

*Clerimont.* Yes, yes.

*Charlotte.* By that time I shall be able to get every thing in order; and you will see I shall play my part as well as the best actress of them all. Do you take care that no unguarded look or word gives the count any room to suspect you are less in go d-humour than you pretend to be.

*Clerimont.* Fear not; I shall be cautious n t to spoil so good a plot by my ill performance.

*Charlotte.* If it succeeds, as I have not the least doubt it will, the story will be a subject of mirth for us as lasting as our lives.

*Clerimont.* And as lasting a subject for my admiration of the wit and contrivance of my dear, dear Charlotte.

*Charlotte.* Well, well, defer your encomiums till a more seasonable opportunity. I long, methinks, to have this

F f 2 business

bufinefs over; and it is high time for you to begin to fet the firft wheel of our machine in motion.

*Clerimont.* I am going. Adieu, my love.

He accompanied thefe words with a very tender and paffionate falute, then left the room. Though I eafily perceived that Charlotte had fomewhat of great importance to tranfact in this affair, yet, as I could not be in two places at once, I chofe to follow Clerimont. He went directly to Cogdy's lodgings; and, on afking if he were at home, was fhewed into a handfome parlour; where, after waiting about a minute, the count's fervant came to him, and faid his mafter had not been long out of bed, and was not quite dreffed, but defired he would walk up; which he did, with his Invifible attendant clofe behind him. The count no fooner faw him enter, than he ran to embrace him with a French complaifance, faying at the fame time—

*Cogdy.* Dear Clerimont, I am glad to fee you.

*Clerimont.* My dear count, a lucky morning to you. I behaved fomewhat oddly laft night, and could not be eafy till I came and afked your pardon.

*Cogdy.* Oh, Sir, you have it, you have it; I thought no more of it. I know it is natural for a gentleman to be a little out of humour at firft lofing his money.

*Clerimont.* But I was lefs excufable than you imagine; for, to confefs the truth, I had, in Bank bills, upwards of two thoufand pounds lying in my bureau at home; fo was under no neceffity either of playing upon tick, or of troubling a lawyer to mortgage the reverfion of my eftate.

*Cogdy.* Is it poffible! Are you in earneft?

*Clerimont.* To convince you I am fo, you fhall have the teftimony of your own eyes. See here, count—and here.

In fpeaking this, he took out of his pocket-book feveral bills to the amount of the fum he had mentioned. The count ftretched his eyes broad open; looked at the bills, feemed much furprized, and faid—

*Cogdy.* Thefe are Bank-bills, indeed!

*Clerimont.* Aye, I can turn them into ready fpecie at any banker's in town.

*Cogdy.* Well, I cannot help wondering how a man who had two thoufand

pounds by him could fuffer himfelf to be difconcerted at the lofs of one.

*Clerimont.* Hang it, it was not the lofs of the money that vexed me; but I had the hyppo, and that damned hyp makes one affront one's beft friends.

*Cogdy.* So, then, I fuppofe you will redeem your mortgage?

*Clerimont.* Time enough for that. But, now I think on it, you offered me my revenge, and I'll e'en try my chance once more.

*Cogdy.* As how?

*Clerimont.* Why, ftake one of thefe thoufands againft my mortgage, fo either win the horfe or lofe the faddle.

*Cogdy.* With all my heart: whenever you pleafe.

*Clerimont.* Let it be to-night, then.

*Cogdy.* Agreed. Will you ftay and dine with me?

*Clerimont.* I am engaged with a young fellow juft come to town, and to the poffeffion of a great eftate; but I will meet you at night, and perhaps bring him with me.

*Cogdy.* Do; I fhall be glad of his acquaintance.

*Clerimont.* We knew one another in the country: he will go any where with me.—But, harkye, count, I don't like that houf we were in laft night; every thing in it, methinks, has the face of poverty and ill-luck. My young fpark is vaftly nice, and will be apt to turn up his nofe at it. Can't you think of a more agreeable place?

*Cogdy.* I know of feveral. The only reafon that makes me chufe to go thither fo often is, becaufe I think it the moft fafe. This curfed act of parliament has laid fuch reftriction on us who love play, that it is not every where we dare venture to indulge ourfelves in that diverfion.

*Clerimont.* What objection have you to Mixum's, in ***** Street?

*Cogdy.* 'Tis a good houfe, and excellent accommodation. But don't you know that it was fearched three or four nights ago by a whole poffe of conftables?

*Clerimont.* Yes, but they found nothing of what they came to look for; therefore the moft fecure at prefent, as they will fcarce come again in hafte.

*Cogdy.* Well, then, we will meet there, if you pleafe. At what hour?

*Clerimont.* **Seven**, or a little after, if it fuits you.

*Cogdy.*

*Cogdy.* Extremely well, then we fhall have the whole evening before us.

He was about to take his leave, and had rofe up for that purpofe, when Wheedle, Hazard, and Coaxum, came all together into the room; they feemed a little furprized at feeing him there, but faluted him with their ufual familiarity.

*Hazard.* Hah! dear Clerimont, good morning to you.

*Wheedle.* Now you look like your-felf again; you were quite another man laft night.

*Coaxum.* Aye, faith, you muft ex-pect to be well roafted.

*Clerimont.* I know I deferve it. But you muft defer your farcafms till night, for I am in great hafte at prefent; fo, gentlemen, your fervant.

He was going out of the room with thefe words; but, juft as he came to the door, he turned back, and faid to Count Cogdy—

*Clerimont.* Be fure, count, not to forget to bring the writings with you.

*Cogdy.* No, no; they have never been out of my pocket fince you delivered them to me laft night.

There paffed no more between them: Clerimont went haftily down ftairs, and I gladly would have followed him; but Hazard and Wheedle happened to ftand between the door and the corner where I had unluckily pofted myfelf, fo that it was impoffible for me to remove my quar-ters without running a very great rifque of being felt either by the one or the other. During the fhort time I was compelled to ftay, I heard the following converfation, which I would not trouble my readers with the repetition of, but to fhew what monfters of mankind thefe degenerate wretches are who get their livelihood by gaming.

*Coaxum.* What does he mean by writings? Sure he is not going to re-deem his mortgage!

*Cogdy.* No; but he is going to find a thoufand, or, it is likely, two thou-fand pounds after it. We have made an appointment to play again to night.

*Hazard.* What, upon tick?

*Wheedle.* Phoo! that is doing of no-thing; the fool has no more eftates in re-verfion to make over.

*Cogdy.* You cannot imagine me fo weak as to lofe my time with a fellow that has no money nor effects; no, no,

I always go upon good grounds. I tell you he has two thoufand pounds in Bank-bills; he fhewed them to me.

*Hazard.* How did he come by them?

*Cogdy.* 'Tis no matter to us how he came by them; we are fure of making them ours before we fleep.

*Wheedle.* They muft certainly be bills his father has intrufted him with to buy ftock either for himfelf or fome of his friends in the country. The young fellow will hang himfelf to-morrow, when he reflects on what he has done.

*Hazard.* Let him hang himfelf, when we have got all he has to lofe.

*Cogdy.* Aye, aye. But I can tell you better news than this: he brings a rich young heir with him; one that knows nothing of the world; a mere fap, a greenhorn. There will be fleec-ing, my boys!

Juft as the count had done fpeaking, fome little noife in the ftreet made them all run to the windows; by which means I got the fo much wifhed-for oppor-tunity of efcaping from my confine-ment. When I found myfelf at liber-ty, I began to confider not only on what I had feen and heard, but alfo on what I had not feen nor heard. I was ftill as much in the dark as ever as to Char-lotte's contrivance, and could not keep myfelf from fretting at the many difap-pointments I had met with on that ac-count; I was doomed, however, to re-ceive yet one more.

Though I doubted not but when the gamefters met the whole would be laid open to me, yet the time feemed too te-dious for my impatience. I wanted to know the bufinefs of the plot before I faw it acted, and fet myfelf to think on the moft probable means to accomplifh my defigns. Accordingly I went to the lodgings of Charlotte, hoping to find Clerimont there, and difcover fome-thing farther by the difcourfe they would have together; but, to my great morti-fication, perceived the rooms quite empty, excepting a little lap dog lying on a cufhion before the fire. I had now no other refource than to go home to dinner, which I did; and after having got my Tablets made ready to receive a new impreffion, diverted myfelf in the beft manner I could till the hour arrived which enabled me to explore what at prefent appeared fo myfterious to me.

CHAP.

# CHAP. VI.

AS precious a thing as time is, and as much as I always knew the real value of it, the hours, methought, moved slowly on till the clock struck seven, and told me that I might now hope for the full eclaircissement of an adventure I had already taken so much fruitless pains to explore. Pretty secure, however, that I should not lose my labour any more on this occasion, I went with great glee and jollity of mind to the house of Mr. Mixum. Count Cogdy and his three associates came presently after, and were shewn into the best room, where I accompanied them. On their calling for wine, Mixum came up with it himself, to pay his compliments, as not having seen them for a considerable time; and there ensued some discourse concerning the search-warrant that had been granted against the house, the manner in which those persons who were there had made their escape from the officers, and such like affairs; which not being at all material to my purpose, I regarded not, nor spread my Tablets to receive.

Within about half an hour Clerimont and his young friend appeared. The first sight of the latter extremely struck me; I thought I had somewhere seen that face, but when, or where, or on what occasion, I could not presently recollect, and it was some minutes before I knew this seeming beau for a real belle; in fine, it was no other than Charlotte herself. She was, indeed, so artfully disguised in all points, that a person much better acquainted with her features might have been deceived; her cheeks, which had naturally no more red in them than was necessary to preserve her complexion from the character of a dead paleness, were now, by the help of carmine or Portugal paste, of a high ruddy colour; her eye-brows, which were of a fine light brown, were now black as jet; and that sweet and modest air so becoming in the amiable Charlotte, converted into one all bold and rakish.

Clerimont, with a well-dissembled gaiety in his voice and countenance, presented her to the company, telling them he had taken the liberty to introduce a friend, whose conversation he doubted not would be agreeable to them. They received her with the greatest politeness and good-breeding: for I must here observe, that though these men, either through the calamities of the times, or their own mismanagement and ill-conduct, were reduced to the wretched course they now took for subsistence, they had all of them been endowed with a liberal education, and knew how to behave like persons of real honour and fashion whenever they found it suitable to their interest to do so. The glass went round two or three times, while they talked only on ordinary matters; but our fair Amazon being impatient, I suppose, to put the finishing stroke to the stratagem she had formed, started up on a sudden, and said—

*Charlotte.* Well, but, gentlemen, how are we to pass the evening? I hope in something more agreeable than mere chit-chat? Clerimont talked of play, and I see you have implements ready.

*Cogdy.* Sir, we amuse ourselves that way sometimes; and, if you chuse it, shall be ready to oblige you.

*Charlotte.* Oh, by all means. I love play extravagantly: the musick of a dice-box is to me beyond all Handel's operas and oratorios; here is more real harmony than in the spheres themselves, and I could dance eternally to the sound. Come, gentlemen, which of you will engage me? I have some loose pieces in my pocket, which I am ready to throw away, if chance should so determine.

*Hazard.* Then, Sir, I am your man, if you think fit; for I know the count has made an agreement to play with Clerimont on a very particular occasion.

*Charlotte.* Then, Sir, I will content myself a while with being a by-stander.

*Hazard.* You need not, Sir; you see here are more tables than one.

*Charlotte.* Aye; but I chuse to bet on my friend's side.

*Hazard.* Nay, as you please for that; we shall any of us be ready to take you up.

The count and Clerimont being now in an attitude to play, and the writings laid down on the one side, and a thousand pound

pound Bank-bill on the other, Charlotte cried out—

*Charlotte.* What! paper against parchment! These are the oddest stakes I ever saw. Yours, Clerimont, I think, is a thousand pounds?

*Cogdy.* I assure you, Sir, that mine is the full equivalent.

*Charlotte.* I believe so. But, before you begin, you must give me leave to speak a word or two.

*Cogdy.* As many as you please, Sir.

*Charlotte.* It is only this—You must lose, count.

*Cogdy.* Must lose, Sir!

*Charlotte.* Aye, Sir, must lose.

*Cogdy.* That, Sir, will happen, as Fortune shall decree.

*Charlotte.* Sir, I stand in the place of Fortune, and tell you that you must lose those writings to Clerimont.

*Hazard.* What means all this!

*Cogdy.* I do not understand you, Sir.

*Charlotte.* I will speak plainer. Your false dice will be of no service to you at this time. You must willingly return to Clerimont that deed of reversion which you drew him in to sign as a security for money you had basely cheated him of: I say willingly; for, if you do not, I am come prepared with means to force you to it.

*Cogdy.* Sir, I scorn both your words and threats. I never cheated any man; nor will part with what chance has bestowed upon me.

*Hazard.* 'Sdeath! shall we be bullied by such a prig!

*Charlotte.* None of your big words; I have that will silence you. See here, the copy of a warrant from Justice Ferrit, to apprehend and bring before him the bodies of George Van Helmock, alias Count Cogdy, John Hazard, Thomas Wheedle, and William Coaxum. The original of this is in the hands of persons who, on the least stamp of my foot, will come up and put it in execution.

The gamesters now looked on each other with all the marks of consternation; but, before they had time to make any reply to what Charlotte had said, Mixum, all pale and trembling, came running into the room, and said—

*Mixum.* Oh, gentlemen, we are all undone! Three or four constables are at the door; one of my drawers saw them as he went out to carry a pint of wine to a neighbour's house: and there

is a young man below, too, who I dare say is a spy; for he does not stay in the room, but walks backwards and forwards in the entry, and looks at every body as they pass by; so that there is no escaping, either one way or the other.

*Charlotte.* He tells you truth; the person he speaks of is planted there by me, and, on my giving the signal, will call in his myrmidons; so that you have nothing for it but to deliver the writings quietly to Clerimont: if you do this, I will instantly go down, and send away the officers, under pretence that the information was wrong, and that no gamesters are here.

*Cogdy.* Confusion! What is to be done!

*Hazard.* 'Sdeath, count, do not part with the writings! We'll fight our way through them!

*Charlotte.* Nay, then, I give the signal.

She advanced towards the door with these words; but Mixum threw himself between, and, with the most pity-moving gesture, said—

*Mixum.* Hold, Sir, I beseech you! Consider, I never offended you! Do not ruin me and my house for ever!

*Clerimont.* Oh, you will be provided with lodgings in Bridewell, and fare no worse than these worthy gentlemen here, your customers.

*Cogdy.* Well, I did not think Mr. Clerimont would have turned informer.

*Clerimont.* Nor did I think I had associated myself with common sharpers, cheats, and villains, till last night convinced me of it.

*Charlotte.* These altercations are only loss of time; the officers will be impatient. Speak, count, resolve at once; shall I dismiss, or call them to the exercise of their function?

*Cogdy.* Hell and the devil!—What say you, gentlemen?

*Wheedle.* E'en give up the writings, and the devil go with them!

*Coaxum.* Aye, aye, give them up.

*Hazard.* Since there is no remedy, I give my vote.

*Cogdy.* Nothing vexes me so much as to be thus outwitted, gulled, tricked. —There, Mr. Clerimont, take back your mortgage. But I must tell you, Sir, that you have not acted like a gentleman.

*Clerimont.* I threw off the gentleman when I condescended to play in such

fuch company. A gameſter is the low-
eſt and moſt infamous of all characters;
nay, the moſt dangerous, too; worſe
even than a highway robber: he takes
but part; you plunder, without remorfe,
the whole fortune of him whom you de-
coy into your ſnares. Nor can there be
any excufe from your neceſſities, while
we have fo numerous a fleet and ſtand-
ing army, which are continually wanting recruits, and refuſe none who have
health and vigour.

*Cogdy.* Sir, you have got what you
wanted; fo pray keep your remonſtrances
to yourſelf.

*Charlotte.* Aye, aye, advice is loſt
on fuch hardened profligates. Come,
let us go.

*Clerimont.* I attend you.

Neither Clerimont nor his fair cham-
pion faid any more, but went directly
out of the room: a volley of curfes from
the mouths of all thefe miſcreants purfued their ſteps. I had no inclination to
ſtay where I was; but, juſt as I paſſed
the door, I heard Jack Hazard, who was
the moſt violent of the four, fay to his
companions—' It is that faucy, pert,
' young coxcomb, that has ſpirited up
' Clerimont to do all this: but if ever I
' meet him in a convenient place, I'll
' pink him—I'll make a loop-hole in his
' fleſh big enough to let out twenty fuch
' puny fouls.'

I could not forbear laughing within
myſelf at this menace; which, though
it ſhewed the villainous difpofition of the
wretch who ſpoke it, I knew it was impoſſible ever to reach the perfon it was
levelled againſt. The amiable and witty
Charlotte kept her promiſe; and, on her
coming down ſtairs, gave orders to the
young man who waited her commands
to ſend away the conſtables; after which
ſhe took coach with her lover, attended
with as many bleſſings and good-wiſhes
from Mixum, as ſhe had been loaded
with curfes from thofe above.

As I could expect no more from this
adventure than the retributions of Clerimont to his beloved Charlotte, for the
happy deliverance ſhe had given him
from deſtruction, and which I could
eafily conceive without hearing, I returned to my own apartment, in order
to get my Tablets made ready for the
acquiſition of fome new difcovery. I
muſt not, however, take leave of thefe
lovers, without letting the publick know
that a marriage between them, which

had fome time before been agreed upon,
is now confummated; and that Clerimont, fincerely touched with the danger
he has efcaped, has made a firm refolution never to play but for ſmall fums,
and for thofe only with perfons whofe
honour and integrity he is well aſſured
of. As for the gameſters, they ſtill continue to infeſt this great town, like Sa-
tan, watching to devour all the prey
they can get into their clutches. If this
little narrative may warn any perfon to
avoid the ſnare, the pains I have taken
to explain it will be well rewarded.

## CHAP. VII.

CONTAINS SOMETHING WHICH PER-
HAPS THERE ARE MORE LADIES
THAN ONE WILL NOT THINK
THEMSELVES OBLIGED TO THE
AUTHOR FOR REVEALING.

THERE is no refentment fo implacable and laſting as that which is
occafioned by love converted into hatred
by ill treatment; and by the more flow
degree this paſſion rifes in our minds,
the more virulent it becomes after having once gained poſſeſſion.

Cleanthes, a gentleman of good family, great worth, and opulent eſtate,
loved to the moſt romantick excefs a
young woman who, excepting a tolerable ſhare of beauty, had no one real
charm to recommend her to a perfon of
his character. She was meanly born,
more meanly educated; ſhe was filly,
vain, capricious, and of a reputation not
quite unblemiſhed. Yet did he no
fooner become acquainted with her, than
he broke off the addreſſes he had long
made to a lady of great merit and fortune; and, in a ſhort time, contrary to
all the remonſtrances and diſſuafions of
his friends, publickly married her.

Being a huſband made him not leſs a
lover. His obfequioufnefs is not to be
paralleled; his whole ſtudy was to pleafe
her; every fucceeding day brought with
it an addition of his dotage of her; he
was always happy in her prefence, never
eafy in her abfence; and, to ufe Shakefpeare's expreſſion—

' Appetite increas'd by what it fed on.'

Auglara, for fo ſhe is called, had
fo little fenfe of the happinefs ſhe enjoyed,

joyed, or affection or gratitude for the man who bestowed it on her, that she presently gave the greatest loose to her too amorous inclinations; thought of nothing but engaging new admirers; and, to that end, made advances, which it would be shocking to repeat, to every pretty fellow she came in company with, even before the face of her much-injured husband; who, blinded by his passion, for a long time looked on all that she did as proceeding only from the too great vivacity of her temper. Had she observed the least degree of circumspection in her amours, he would scarce ever have believed there was a possibility of her being guilty; but she took no pains to deceive him; and though she knew he lived but in her sight, was scarce ever at home; and, through the want either of artifice or complaisance, gave herself not the pains of making any excuses for her continual rambles.

This made him at last fall into a deep melancholy; yet still he loved her, and could not for a great while prevail on himself to lay any restrictions on her conduct. All who had any knowledge of the manner in which they lived together, while they highly condemned her treatment of him, were ready to despise his lenity and forbearance. At length, however, the tables were entirely turned; from having been at first the most fond, and afterwards the passive husband, he became, all at once, the most cruel and tyrannick: he took from her all the jewels and other ornaments he had bestowed upon her; locked her into a garret; suffered no one to come near her, except a servant, who carried food to her of the coarsest kind, and no more than would just suffice to keep her from perishing.

It cannot be supposed but that so strange an alteration in the behaviour of the late fond, and indeed madly doating Cleanthes, must become the subject of much conversation in town. A lady of my acquaintance, who is reckoned to have some taste for poetry, shewed me a few lines she had wrote on the occasion, which I think may not be disagreeable to my readers. They are as follow—

ON THE PRESENT CRUELTY OF CLE-ANTHES, TO A WIFE WHOM HE ONCE LOVED TO AS GREAT AN EX-CESS.

' AS tapers languish at th' approach of
'     day,
' And, by degrees, melt slow their shine
'     away,
' Awhile they glimmer with contracted
'     fires,
' Trembling, unable to relax their spires;
' But, when the sun's broad eye is open'd
'     wide,
' And beams, thick flashing, shoot on every
'     side,
' No more their emulative force they try,
' But, struck with radiance, sink at once,
'     and die:
'   So in his heart love long maintain'd it's
'     place,
' Till full conviction glar'd him in the face,
' And forc'd th' unwilling softness to give
'     way
' To hate, and rage, and fierce resentment's
'     sway.
' Unhappy man!
' What wild extremes hurry thy head-
'     strong will!
' What boist'rous passions thy vex'd bo-
'     som fill!
' To reason's sacred rules a truant still,
' Whoe'er be the golden mean foregoes,
' Exchanges hop'd-for joys for certain woes.'

By all the discourses I heard wherever I went concerning this affair, I found, that though scarce any one pitied Aglaura, yet almost every one condemned Cleanthes; no less for his present ill-usage of her, than they had formerly done for the extravagance of his love.

' It is beneath the dignity of a man ' of sense or honour,' said one, ' to treat ' thus inhumanly a woman, how un-' worthy soever she may be, who is yet ' his wife.'

' If she is really guilty of having ' wronged his bed,' cried another, ' as ' indeed there is not the least room to ' doubt, why, on the discovery of her ' crime, did he not turn her out of doors? ' Why did he not sue for a divorce?'

It is certain that his way of proceeding with her appeared so odd, that many people were apt to think that her present sufferings were owing rather to a change in his own humour, than to any detection he had made of her falshood:

G g                    others,

others, on the contrary, imagined he still loved her; and that, after he had punished her a while, he would forgive all that was past, and again take her to his bosom. Various and widely different conjectures were formed in relation both to the husband and the wife; at all which I laughed in my sleeve, believing, I dare say with a good deal of reason, that no one person in the whole world, except the Invisible Spy, was at the bottom of this secret. The means by which I became master of it I shall now acquaint my readers with.

I supped one night at the house of an intimate friend at Kensington; and happening to stay there more late than it was judged safe for me to go home alone, was very much pressed by him to take a servant with me; but knowing I had a better security about me than any servant could be, rejected his offer; and when I was got a little way from the house, girded on my Belt of Invisibility, and walked on at my leisure, equally free from danger as from fear.

Many minutes had not elapsed in this employment, before I was disturbed from it by the murmurs of some human voices which I heard at a small distance. My natural curiosity making me draw nearer to the place whence the sound proceeded, I easily distinguished a man of good appearance holding by the arm a genteel well dressed woman, whom he seemed rather to drag than lead. As these persons were no other than Cleanthes and Aglaura, I shall insert what was said by each of them under their respective names.

*Cleanthes.* Shameless wretch!—Can you call it an innocent frolick to come to the door of a publick coffee-house, and send in for your gallant? Had I not happened to be there, had not these eyes and ears been witness's of your guilt, you might, and doubtless would, have denied, forsworn it.

*Aglaura.* I meant no harm: I only wanted to raise him a little about something I had heard concerning him.

*Cleanthes.* Infamous, abandoned prostitute! Have I not an hundred times insisted on your never speaking to that fellow more, nor to that other coxcomb, Le Brune? yet, had you not the front to run arm in arm this morning with the one into the vineyard, in the face of the whole Mall, and at night

came in pursuit of the other!—But this is no time for expostulation; I am now convinced of the injury you have done me.

I kept pretty near to them, till they went into a coach, and drove away; and I went home so much astonished at what I had heard, that I had not power to make any reflections on it for some time.

My mind, however, grew more settled by a night's repose; and, impatient to know how they would behave to each other after what had passed, I went directly to their house. Cleanthes was up, alone, and at breakfast. Soon after my entrance, a servant-maid came in, and said to him—

*Maid.* Sir, my lady has called for a dish of chocolate, but I would not presume to carry any up without your permission, as your orders last night were so positive that she should be fed with nothing but water-gruel and dry bread.

*Cleanthes.* Why, then, do you trouble me now? Do you think I gave orders at night to retract them in the morning? Be gone, and let me hear no more of it.

The maid withdrew, and I followed her to the room where Aglaura was now lodged, which was indeed a wretched garret. She was in bed, weeping; but, on the maid's repeating the commands of Cleanthes, her tears flowed faster: she wrung her hands, she beat her breast. But it is more easy for the reader to conceive her despair, than for me to express it; so I shall only say the spectacle was too moving, I could not bear it, but left the house immediately, and returned not thither till eight or ten days; in which time the town was apprized of the suffering of Aglaura, and spoke of the strange change of Cleanthes in the manner I have already related.

On my next visit, Cleanthes had with him an elderly lady, who I afterwards understood was his aunt. She came, it seems, to persuade him to treat his transgressing wife with less severity. The discourse between them was as follows—

*Lady.* I am as sensible as you can be of the faults of Aglaura, and the dishonour she has brought upon you; yet, my dear nephew, you demean yourself by using in this fashion a woman who, though unworthy, is still your wife.

*Cleanthes.* Madam, I can no longer think

think of her as a wife, nor even as a woman; but as a dog that had bit me, or a serpent that had stung me.

*Lady.* Put her, then, out of your house.

*Cleanthes.* That would be giving her an opportunity of disgracing me more by her prostitutions. No, since I have not proofs for a divorce, I will confine her here till I can send her for ever from my sight. I have already wrote to a tenant of mine in Yorkshire; he will be in town next week, and take her with him to his house.

The good lady took her leave, after having heard and approved this resolution; which, as I have been since informed, he put in execution as he had said.

### THE CONCLUSION.

HERE, O reader! a total stop is put to my endeavours to oblige thee. Nature has baffled all my vain precautions to preserve my little virgin in her native purity. The woman whom I appointed to attend her accidentally dropped from her pocket the picture of a very lovely youth; the girl, unfortunately for me, as well as for thee, took it up, and was charmed with it: sleep renewed the pleasing image in her mind, and added life and motion to it; she dreamed that it was her bedfellow; that it kissed, embraced, and lay within her arms; so that, in spite of all my cares, and without ever having seen the substance of a man, she has received an idea of the difference of sexes.

Her pretty fingers no longer have the power to cleanse my Tablets; the dialogue last repeated remains still unexpunged, and leaves no room for any future impression. How grievous a disappointment to me! how terrible a mortification!—But we must all submit to destiny, which compels me now to bid thee eternally adieu! adieu! adieu!

F I N I S.

www.ingramcontent.com/pod-product-compliance
Lightning Source LLC
Chambersburg PA
CBHW030809020726
47499CB00006B/1834